SHORT FICTION

A Critical Collection

Jack London   William Faulkner   Isaac Babel   Anton Chekhov   Ring Lardner   Henry James   Flannery O'Connor Isaac Bashevis Singer   D. H. Lawrence   Heinrich Böll   Sarah Orne Jewett   Liam O'Flaherty   Guy de Maupassant   Nathaniel Hawthorne   Edward Loomis   J. F. Powers   Donald Barthelme   Frank O'Connor   Malcolm Lowry   Hugo von Hofmannsthal Italo Svevo   Sean O'Faolain   Gustave Flaubert   Yehuda Amichai   Jorge Luis Borges   James Joyce   Eudora Welty   Ernest Hemingway   Franz Kafka   Thomas Mann

SHORT FICTION
A Critical Collection

℘ SECOND EDITION

Edited by

James R. Frakes
Department of English
Lehigh University

Isadore Traschen
Department of Language and Literature
Rensselaer Polytechnic Institute

PRENTICE-HALL, INC., *Englewood Cliffs, N.J.*

Prentice-Hall English Literature Series
MAYNARD MACK, EDITOR

© 1969 by Prentice-Hall, Inc., Englewood Cliffs, N.J.

Library of Congress Catalog Card Number: 69–11382

Printed in the United States of America

Current printing (last number):

10   9   8   7

PRENTICE-HALL INTERNATIONAL, INC., *London*
PRENTICE-HALL OF AUSTRALIA, PTY. LTD., *Sydney*
PRENTICE-HALL OF CANADA, LTD., *Toronto*
PRENTICE-HALL OF INDIA PRIVATE LTD., *New Delhi*
PRENTICE-HALL OF JAPAN, INC., *Tokyo*

ABOUT THIS BOOK

Students often object to "tearing a story apart." Why, they ask, can't we just enjoy it? There is plenty of sense in the question. Even the sophisticated reader should approach a story innocently, open himself to it, allow it to penetrate. He should not let his critical apparatus get in the way of the story. The innocent response is one kind of enjoyment, and it is primary. It would be regrettable to lose it while learning to read analytically.

But serious readers go back to a story a second, third, fourth, a tenth time. Their pleasures are unknown to the casual reader, the pleasures of saturation and continued discovery. It is the pleasure of discovery that we hope to introduce to the student; and it is this, we believe, that justifies the analyses in the first part of this book. As a matter of fact, every student knows that talking about a story heightens his interest and reveals things he had not noticed. The personal encounter, the trade in ideas, are stimulating—in the classroom as well as in the dormitory. Indeed, students sometimes need to be cautioned that analysis is the beginning, not the end of wisdom. At best analysis can only begin to articulate the complications and nuances of short fiction, and this is all we claim for our analyses here: they are a beginning whose goal is discovery.

Our plan is evident from the table of contents. The elements of action, character, point of view, irony, and symbolism are discussed in separate introductions, and each is illustrated in two stories analyzed to suggest its range and modifications. Two groups of questions accompany each of the analyzed stories. The first inquires further into the particular element under consideration; the second introduces other considerations such as style, setting, atmosphere. Twenty stories follow, arranged roughly in order of difficulty. After five stories we have appended sets of critical comments by other writers. These have several uses. Representing a variety of styles and approaches (sociological, psychological, biographical, impressionistic, moralistic, etc.), they provide the student with criticism different from our own. (An unfortunate characteristic of most critical anthologies is that the editors' commentary is the only one the student sees.) Moreover, since the critical comments often contradict one another, it becomes clear to the student that there is no interpretation that cannot be at some point challenged and improved on—certainly none that is exhaustive and "correct." He is thus encouraged—so we hope—to grope toward his own response. Sixteen stories receive no analysis and have no critical appendices. We feel that about half the stories in a collection should be left untouched, for this too is an invitation to the reader to throw away his crutch and put on critical maturity.

Our stories were selected for many reasons. Except in the case of "The White Silence," we have chosen stories we believe to be good. In certain instances, to represent an author fairly, we have chosen a familiar story simply because it is his best. Especially, we have sought teachable stories containing a variety of techniques and a range of subject matter that make possible useful comparisons. Our selection concludes with "Death in Venice," an introduction to the novelette, the bridge between the short story and the novel. A masterpiece of our time, its style, density, irony, allusiveness, symbolism, and cultural scope provide the teacher with a crowning opportunity to unite all the elements of fiction.

The selections in this revised edition extend from the American Hawthorne (1835) to the Israeli Amichai (1967). They include some newer experimental fiction, as in the stories by Svevo, Borges, Loomis, Lowry, Barthelme, and Amichai; they also include some additional older stories, such as those by James and von Hofmannsthal, which offer their own innovations. All of the introductions and most of the analyses have been revised and expanded; two have been replaced with new ones—those of "The Tree of Knowledge" and "The Blind Man."

Again we wish to thank our wives and families for their invaluable patience and encouragement, our students for their questions and insights, and our colleagues for their candid suggestions. In addition to those who helped us so graciously with the first edition of *Short Fiction* (Bernard Wolpert and Professors Mark Goldman and James Westbrook), we wish to acknowledge a debt to John Ross Baker of Lehigh University for assistance in the preparation of this revised edition.

J.R.F.
I.T.

TABLE OF CONTENTS

Stories

CHRONOLOGY OF STORIES

1835	Young Goodman Brown	Nathaniel Hawthorne (1804–1864)
1877	The Legend of St. Julian the Hospitaller	Gustave Flaubert (1821–1880)
1881	Madame Tellier's Excursion	Guy de Maupassant (1850–1893)
1890	Gusev	Anton Chekhov (1860–1904)
1890	The Town Poor	Sarah Orne Jewett (1849–1909)
1899	The White Silence	Jack London (1876–1916)
1900	The Tree of Knowledge	Henry James (1843–1916)
1911	Twilight and Nocturnal Storm	Hugo von Hofmannsthal (1874–1929)
1912	Death in Venice	Thomas Mann (1875–1955)
1912	The Judgment	Franz Kafka (1883–1924)
1914	Grace	James Joyce (1882–1941)
1922	The Blind Man	D. H. Lawrence (1885–1930)
1922	The Golden Honeymoon	Ring Lardner (1885–1933)
1923	How It Was Done in Odessa	Isaac Babel (1894–1940)
1927	The Fairy Goose	Liam O'Flaherty (1897–)
1928	In My Indolence	Italo Svevo (1861–1928)
1930	Red Leaves	William Faulkner (1897–1962)
1933	A Clean, Well-Lighted Place	Ernest Hemingway (1898–1961)
1941	Powerhouse	Eudora Welty (1909–)
1947	The Silence of the Valley	Sean O'Faolain (1900–)
1953	Gimpel the Fool	Isaac Bashevis Singer (1904–)
1953	Strange Comfort Afforded by the Profession	Malcolm Lowry (1909–1957)
1954	Eternal Triangle	Frank O'Connor (1903–1966)
1956	Dawn	J. F. Powers (1917–)
1956	The Artificial Nigger	Flannery O'Connor (1925–1964)
1956	The Library of Babel	Jorge Luis Borges (1899–)
1957	Christmas Every Day	Heinrich Böll (1917–)
1960	Wounds	Edward Loomis (1924–)
1964	Margins	Donald Barthelme (1931–)
1967	Nina of Ashkelon	Yehuda Amichai (1924–)

SHORT FICTION

A Critical Collection

READING THE SHORT STORY

The short story is one of the most demanding—and rewarding—of literary forms. From the writer it demands careful selectivity, economy of means, and an instinct for the revealing detail. To the trained reader it offers intensity, the satisfaction that comes from compact unity. Since a short story can usually be read at one sitting, one might assume that its value and staying power are restricted and of slight consequence. One purpose of this collection is to demonstrate the inaccuracy of this assumption. Because of its density, subtlety, and concentration, the good short story repays a close reading.

Can the short story be defined? One critic, Mark Schorer, says we cannot distinguish among the forms of fiction—short story, novelette, and novel—by length alone. But he makes a helpful distinction: "The short story is an art of moral revelation, the novel an art of moral evolution. . . ." The implication is that the short story presents a sudden vision whereas the novel offers a much wider, sustained view by supplying all causes and all effects, setting forth detailed background material and the resolution of the change vital to all fiction. As Schorer further points out, "in both story and novel there is change, but the first is change in view that we are briefly shown, the other a change in conduct that more leisurely we trace." [1] That is to say, the scope of a short story is narrower than that of a novel; it does not attempt so much, nor does it elaborate so fully. We almost never follow a character from birth to death, as we often do in a novel, but rather see him during a typical or critical moment—a moment chosen because it is representative or because it is the end result of his life's activities or because it is a turning point after which he will never be the same. Furthermore, although a novelist may handle many themes, plots, subplots, and characters in a single work, a short-story writer *usually* restricts himself to a single theme, a single plot, and a limited number of characters.

The short novel, sometimes called the novelette or *novella,* is a sort of compromise between the short story and the novel. Retaining the thematic unity of the short story and its few characters, the short novel permits a more gradual unfolding of events and emotions and more space for ramifications. Had Thomas Mann written his outstanding short novel "Death in Venice" as a novel, he would probably have spread be-

[1] From *The Story: A Critical Anthology,* second edition, by Mark Schorer, pp. 330–331, copyright 1967, by Prentice-Hall, Inc., Englewood Cliffs, N.J.

1

fore us Aschenbach's entire life, with sections devoted to his childhood, education, friendships, marriage, family life, growth as an artist, and travels. Having chosen the short novel form, Mann introduces Aschenbach as an elderly man, a famous and respected artist past the age of violent passions; he confines the action to a little over a month, and the setting almost exclusively to a single city. The only other important characters are Tadzio and the recurring "stranger" figures, seen only from Aschenbach's point of view. So far, "Death in Venice" might have been written as a short story. But consider what the short-novel form allows Mann to do: he devotes paragraphs of exposition to Aschenbach's ancestry and career so that we can see the heights from which he falls; he describes Venice at length so that the unhealthy and mysterious atmosphere can play an important role as complementary background for Aschenbach's decline; he shows us the psychological steps in that decline; and in passages of philosophical and esthetic meditation he presents the forces that reduce Aschenbach spiritually. Written as a short story, "Death in Venice" would have lacked the cumulative power and majesty it has.

A short story, then, can best be defined by reference not to word-count but to its concentrated tension, its highly selective choice of details and incidents, and its unity. These earmarks of the modern short story owe much to three writers: Poe, Chekhov, and Joyce.

Edgar Allan Poe's definition of the short story is famous:

> A skilful literary artist has constructed a tale. If wise, he has not fashioned his thoughts to accommodate his incidents; but having conceived, with deliberate care, a certain unique or single *effect* to be wrought out, he then invents such incidents—he then combines such events as may best aid him in establishing this preconceived effect. If his very initial sentence tend not to the outbringing of this effect, then he has failed in his first step. In the whole composition there should be no word written, of which the tendency, direct or indirect, is not to the one pre-established design.[2]

This theory of the "single effect" dominates Poe's stories as well as most of Hawthorne's (see "Young Goodman Brown" in this collection). And although it has been modified somewhat by more recent writers (notice the mixture of effects in "Christmas Every Day," "Gusev," and "Dawn"), its controlling principles of unity and functionalism are generally recognized as vital to a well-made story.

Anton Chekhov complemented Poe's definition by warning that if a gun hangs on the wall in the first part of a story, it must be discharged before the story ends. In other words, *every* detail must contribute something to the action, atmosphere, or characterization. The theory of the active detail demands that nothing be simply decorative, that nothing lie passive or inert. Note the use Hawthorne makes of the pink cap-

---

[2] Edgar Allan Poe, review of Hawthorne's *Twice-Told Tales, Graham's Magazine,* May 1842.

ribbon in "Young Goodman Brown"; for other examples see the shadow of the single tree in "A Clean, Well-Lighted Place," the North Cemetery at the beginning of "Death in Venice," and Nelson's oversized gray hat in "The Artificial Nigger."

It has become fashionable to credit James Joyce with the development of the fictional device called the "epiphany" (literally, a "showing forth"), the point in the story when the veil is raised, the shadowy brought to light, the hidden meaning grasped by the reader if not by the protagonist. Scholars, however, have established that Joyce used the term only for certain fragments of prose recorded early in his career, some of which he later worked into his stories and novels; these "epiphanies" were notebook jottings, raw material rather than artistically finished work. Nevertheless, the term is still a handy—if humorously pretentious because of its connotation of the viewing of Christ by the Magi—designation for the moment of revelation frequent in modern short fiction. A word or phrase, a shrug of the shoulders, a curl of the lip, a red necktie, a falling leaf—any of these apparently trivial objects or events can be a manifestation, illuminating all that went before in the story. In Joyce's "Grace," for instance, Father Purdon's worldly sermon, especially the metaphor "spiritual accountant," is the act of revelation; the light that this scene throws on the cheapness and compromise in Dublin's religious life, although indirect, is brilliant. And Flannery O'Connor's use of the plaster figure of a Negro in "The Artificial Nigger" does approach an actual religious manifestation.

The single effect, the active detail, the epiphany—these suggest better than any formal definition what sets the short story apart as a literary form.

II

Another distinguishing feature of modern fiction—of both the novel and the short story—is the emphasis on *dramatization*. In the early story "The Town Poor" (1890), the reader will notice that Miss Jewett often merely *asserts* rather than dramatizes a feeling, as in this passage: "She was most warm-hearted and generous, and in her limited way played the part of Lady Bountiful in the town of Hampden." The warm-heartedness and generosity have not yet been shown through action, nor have the limitations been demonstrated; rather, we are expected to take the author's word for these qualities of Mrs. Trimble. And when a quality or feeling is merely asserted, the effect is less vivid and convincing. More recent writers, influenced particularly by James, Chekhov, and Joyce, prefer to dramatize their material, feeling under artistic obligation to let the event give rise to the emotion. This obligation makes their task more difficult, as Hemingway testifies. In his early efforts he found that the greatest difficulty was to set down "what really happened in action; what the actual things were which produced the emotion that you experienced . . . the real thing, the sequence of motion and fact which made the emotion." [3] For many writers dramatization rules out authorial interpretation—such abstract assertions of the meaning of the story as are found in "Young Goodman Brown": "Be it so if you will; but, alas! it was a dream of evil omen for young Goodman Brown. A stern, a sad, a darkly meditative, a distrustful, if not a desperate man did he become from the night of that fearful dream." Instead, the dramatized action has to do full duty in conveying the meaning.

In fulfilling this self-imposed obligation, writers like Hemingway often limit the range of the story by presenting little more than scenes in dialogue form—a kind of play with an absolute minimum of comment by the author, as in "A Clean, Well-Lighted Place." Therefore, though this form is more immediate in its effect, for greater flexibility writers like Faulkner and Mann favor the narrated scene. Departing even further from the play-like scene, they use what we might call narrative reflection—philosophical, psychological, and political: "But it seems that a noble and active mind blunts itself against nothing so quickly as the sharp and bitter irritant of knowledge" ("Death in Venice"); ". . . he had watched the rat, civilized, by association with man reft of its inherent cunning of limb and eye" ("Red Leaves").

Each of these methods of presenting a subject has its own particular effects. All we need keep in mind is that, whatever the method, the modern tendency is to render the subject dramatically and thus to allow the reader to deduce the effect. One of the more striking consequences of the emphasis on dramatization over assertion is the change of the reader from a relatively passive observer to an active collaborator with the author.

III

Understanding a story involves two kinds of meaning, *abstract* and *concrete*. Frank O'Connor once defined the abstract meaning, or *theme,* as "something that is worth something to everybody." [4] That is, it is a statement with a general, abstract significance. For example, we might say that in *Macbeth* the theme is that excessive ambition proves its own undoing, or (less satisfactorily) that woman has an evil effect on man. A work may have many meanings, but each must be borne out by the total data.

But that a work have general, universal meanings is less important than that it be a special, unique expression, a concrete, individual action. The genesis of William Faulkner's *The Sound and the Fury* is instruc-

---

[3] From *Death in the Afternoon,* by Ernest Hemingway, p. 2, copyright 1932 by Charles Scribner's Sons, reprinted by permission of Charles Scribner's Sons, New York.

[4] From *Writers at Work: The Paris Review Interviews,* edited by Malcolm Cowley, p. 8, copyright 1958 by The Viking Press, Inc., reprinted by permission of The Viking Press, Inc., New York.

tive: Faulkner once remarked that it began with a mental picture of "the muddy seat of a little girl's drawers in a pear tree, where she could see through a window where her grandmother's funeral was taking place and report what was happening to her brothers on the ground below." [5] His original interest was in a particular character in action, and our first interest is in the same thing: in the concrete event. It is the image of the little girl with muddy drawers, of Goodman Brown's cheek sprinkled with dew from a hanging twig, of Aschenbach eating overripe strawberries that we remember longest. A literary work, then, has the power of the concrete and the stamp of the unique, as well as the relevance of the universal. Since the universality of a theme makes it more or less commonplace, we may say that literature reinvigorates ideas, renewing them in the flesh, blood, and bone of the historical moment, of contemporary feeling.

From the example of Faulkner we are in a position to understand the relation between theme and story. For Faulkner, as for most writers, some seminal image such as that of the little girl in the pear tree is the germ of the story. But Faulkner went on to say that, in the course of setting down the image, he "realized the symbolism of the soiled pants," their *meaning*. "Theme alone," as Robert Frost said, "can steady us down." [6] The writer selects and arranges his material with respect to the theme, the meaning he sees in it. This is the *form* the unfolding story takes.

Some readers stop with the abstract formulation of the story in the belief that they have now "got" it. But how would they differentiate between *Macbeth* and a play in which, say, an ambitious executive, goaded by his wife, murders the corporation president to usurp an industrial kingdom? The differences are manifold, but, put simply, they lie in the *total* sense each work has for us. That is, we respond to the full impact of the story, to elements like character in action, atmosphere, setting, tone, diction, sentence rhythms, structural patterns, imagery, and symbolism. We shall call this full sense the *total concrete meaning*, which is nothing less than the work itself. The point of the distinction is this: the total concrete meaning of a story is dense and complex, requiring every word in the story for its expression; an abstract formulation violates that density and complexity. Although *Macbeth* and our hypothetical play have the same abstract theme, their total concrete meanings are *absolutely* different because they are expressed differently.

The difference between abstract meaning and total concrete meaning has further implications. What, for instance, is the fundamental objection to abridgements of fiction, such as those appearing in the *Reader's Digest* or those done with esthetic indecorum by W. Somerset Maugham? No words are changed; parts are merely left out, and the editing is usu-

---

[5] From *Writers at Work: The Paris Review Interviews*, edited by Malcolm Cowley, p. 130, copyright 1958 by The Viking Press, Inc., reprinted by permission of The Viking Press, Inc., New York.

[6] From *Complete Poems of Robert Frost*, p. vi, copyright 1930, 1949 by Henry Holt and Company, reprinted by permission of Henry Holt and Company, New York.

ally done shrewdly enough for the theme to come through. The objection is that the remaining parts no longer have their full meaning, which involved their relation to the parts taken out. The full meaning is lost both for the story as a whole and for the parts retained. And if a "faithful" abridgement distorts the full meaning of a work, then paraphrase or synopsis is even more inadequate. In fact, these last two reductions lack everything: the *particular* expression of the original. Now we are often rightly passionate about abstract themes, but the reader should be aware that when he compares similar themes or uses them as points of departure for excursions into philosophy, psychology, economics, or sociology, he is not talking about the work as *literature*. The ideal reader responds not only to ideas but also to their literary treatment. Accordingly, he is responsive to any ideas that are presented well, not just to those he agrees with. Thus a Catholic may be affected favorably by *Paradise Lost* or "Madame Tellier's Excursion," a Jew by *The Divine Comedy* or "Dawn," a teenager by "The Golden Honeymoon" or "In My Indolence," and a white supremacist by "Powerhouse" or "Red Leaves." Indeed, a reader who finds even a pet idea of his treated sympathetically but crudely will very likely resent the work.

The way a story is presented determines the quality of our experience of it; in fact, all that we have said leads to the principle that a story should be approached as an experience. There is all the difference in the world between our experience of the older waiter's mock prayer in "A Clean, Well-Lighted Place" ("Our nada who art in nada, nada be thy name . . .") and our *idea* of it as a tragic parody of faith. To experience the work is to know it as it is; to experience its ideas is to know it only abstractly. Ideas take on passionate life through literature; the literary work is a *felt* idea given artistic form.

We may further illustrate what we mean by the "experience" of a work by distinguishing between our approach to a story and to a report giving information about a new development in physics. We go *through* the report for the ideas in it, but we *stop*, we *live* with the story. The report is the means to an end; the story is the end. The experience of a story is like that of Jacob wrestling with the angel: as Jacob was wounded, so may we be—never again to be the same. More than an acquisition of ideas, reading a story is an act of communion. The ideas we derive are significant, but they form only one part of our experience of the work. The total experience as it sinks into us is what endures.

IV

The valuation of experience over ideas reflects the distrust of reason that marks one tendency of the romantic revolution. This distrust has been polarized in many different terms. For example, the irrational has been posed against the rational, body against mind, the unconscious against the conscious, nature against civilization, intuition against logic.

Examples of these polarities are evident in "Red Leaves," "Gusev," "The Fairy Goose," "Madame Tellier's Excursion," "The Blind Man," and "Death in Venice." These polarities give rise to the familiar theme of the self against society, with the self represented by the sensitive young man, sometimes the artist. This questioning of the reasoned structures of society results in a sense of alienation, of estrangement, and with this a crisis in identity. These themes are also evident in much of the fiction collected here.

But writers have not been nihilistic in their response to the break-down of the old order. On the contrary, they represent one of the sources of vitality in our culture. To replace what they consider our sterile culture they very often pose such revitalizing forces as those noted above: the body, the unconscious, nature, intuition—in short, the single person grounded in his natural and existential self. This distrust of reasoned structures is reflected technically in various ways: for example, in the break with older forms of rhetoric (see our comments on "Gusev"), of character (see the introduction to the section "Character"), and of plot.

The latter break needs clarification at this point. Although we have been loosely using the term *story* to designate the artistic selection and arrangement of events, the term *plot* is more exact. E. M. Forster's distinction between these two terms is helpful:

> We have defined a story as a narrative of events arranged in their time-sequence. A plot is also a narrative of events, the emphasis falling on causality. "The king died and then the queen died" is a story. "The king died and then the queen died of grief" is a plot. The time-sequence is preserved, but the sense of causality overshadows it. Or again: "The queen died, no one knew why, until it was discovered that it was through grief at the death of the king." This is a plot with a mystery in it, a form capable of high development. It suspends the time-sequence, it moves as far away from the story as its limitations will allow. Consider the death of the queen. If it is in a story we say "and then?" If it is in a plot we ask "why?" [7]

Although Forster speaks elsewhere of inexplicable, non-logical causes for human action, the emphasis in the simplified examples above is certainly on causes that can be explained in rational terms. In the traditional plotted story each effect has its cause, each conflict its resolution. This logical structure is grounded in the *rationalism* of the bourgeois epoch; Conan Doyle's Sherlock Holmes stories are extreme instances. Such a structure fulfills our need for order, inevitability, and clarity. In this collection, rational plots support "Madame Tellier's Excursion," "Dawn," "The Town Poor," "The White Silence," and "Red Leaves"— although many of these stories develop an *irrationalist* thesis.

The rational plot, however, does not reflect our contemporary sense of things. Events now seem to be fragmentary, haphazard, unrelated.

[7] From *Aspects of the Novel*, by E. M. Forster, p. 86, copyright 1927 by Harcourt, Brace & World, Inc., renewed 1954 by E. M. Forster, reprinted by permission of Harcourt, Brace & World, Inc., New York.

Hence stories like those in this anthology by Hemingway, Kafka, Chekhov, Borges, Barthelme, and Amichai tend to be episodic, without clear sequences and neat, unambiguous resolutions. But of course there is an esthetic logic: the logic of symbols, of archetypal patterns, of feelings. We may call this the logic of the irrational. Thus, though episodes seem to be random, they are nonetheless shaped and given meaning. The formless is given esthetic form; and the unplotted or plotless story is really "plotted," but not in a rational sequence of cause and effect. So it is that in a modern story the action tends to flatten out, to avoid, as in "The Silence of the Valley," the strong, definitive climax. Such a climax is unpersuasive not only because it seems exaggerated and rhetorical but also because it implies a meaningful sequence. When a definitive climax appears, it is likely to be muted, as in "The Town Poor." Even strong climaxes, rising out of deep convictions, as in "The Artificial Nigger" and "Death in Venice," are modulated by what follows. Ordinarily the strong climax occurs in the story of *action*—a "threshold" element of fiction to which we now turn.

Elements of Fiction

ACTION

The most popular kind of story emphasizes simple action with elemental suspense: the fight, the chase, the hunt, the race, the duel, the showdown, the contest. It satisfies a need: how often have you heard people say they like a story in which "something happens"? And, conversely, they may dismiss a story as dull or meaningless because "nothing happens in it." Of course, by "happening" they usually mean an overt action rather than an inward one—mental, emotional, or spiritual. An account of the decline of Irish pastoralism, as in "The Silence of the Valley," or of the failure and reawakening of New England charity, as in "The Town Poor," or of the philosophical paradoxes of infinity, as in "The Library of Babel," may have no appeal to the reader who prefers a tale of physical conflict.

No matter how exciting an overt action may be, however, a literal transcription artlessly following a chronological pattern is likely to be dull. We are not concerned with the "truth" of the experience but rather with the excitement stirred up in the telling, the shaping of the raw material of experience—the fear, thrills, danger, suspense. Rough edges are smoothed; irrelevant or distracting details are deleted; time is compressed or stretched; incidents are invented for the sake of color, symmetry, contrast, or further illustration. For example, a straight report of a fifteen-round boxing match, if given round by round, minute by minute, blow by blow, will almost certainly be less readable—even less meaningful—than a selective version of the same fight. The artful writer may provide the background of the boxers, supply motivation and undercurrents of emotion, ignore the lulls, and concentrate, say, on rounds one, three, nine, and fifteen—rounds in which knockdowns occurred or in which one boxer intentionally fouled the other or in which the decision was determined. Briefly, what the artist does with his raw material is to eliminate dead spots and heighten key episodes. In Forster's terminology, he transforms a "story" into a "plot."

Fictional *form* is classically described as a pattern of rising action, climax, denouement, and, at times, falling action. The rising action, or complication, includes everything that leads to the climax: establishment of setting, characters, character relationships, and motivations, all of which is handled assertively or dramatically (see the second section of the introduction, "Reading the Short Story"). The climax is the turning point, the crucial moment when the hero faces the villain or when the champion fighter is being counted out. What follows the climax is called

11

the denouement (literally, the untying of the knot), which resolves the complication: the hero disarms the villain; the champion rises at the count of nine and smashes the challenger to the floor of the ring. The falling action is the aftermath: the hero turns the villain over to the authorities; the victorious champion regains his self-respect and decides to retire undefeated.

Usually these elements appear more subtly than in the above examples. The denouement in "Red Leaves," for instance, is hardly breathtaking because the reader has little doubt that the Negro will eventually be captured by the Indians. In this story the falling action—the Negro's return to the plantation and his facing death—is much more important. On the other hand, Jack London, in "The White Silence," dispenses altogether with falling action. Malemute Kid shoots Mason (denouement) and, London says without much flourish, "lashed the dogs into a wild gallop as he fled across the snow." The story is over, and the implications of the remaining two-hundred-mile trek across the Alaskan waste are ignored.

Both stories deal with overt action, but the authors charge the action with universalizing implications that carry the narrative beyond the moment. Both use exotic settings—frontier swamps of Mississippi in the early 19th century and the frozen Alaskan wilderness; and both use fairly primitive characters. But, as our analyses demonstrate, important differences exist between the stories.

The White Silence

Jack London

"Carmen won't last more than a couple of days." Mason spat out a chunk of ice and surveyed the poor animal ruefully, then put her foot in his mouth and proceeded to bite out the ice which clustered cruelly between the toes.

"I never saw a dog with a highfalutin' name that ever was worth a rap," he said, as he concluded his task and shoved her aside. "They just fade away and die under the responsibility. Did ye ever see one go wrong with a sensible name like Cassiar, Siwash, or Husky? No, sir! Take a look at Shookum here; he's—"

Snap! The lean brute flashed up, the white teeth just missing Mason's throat.

"Ye will, will ye?" A shrewd clout behind the ear with the butt of the dogwhip stretched the animal in the snow, quivering softly, a yellow slaver dripping from its fangs.

"As I was saying, just look at Shookum, here—he's got the spirit. Bet ye he eats Carmen before the week's out."

"I'll bank another proposition against that," replied Malemute Kid, reversing the frozen bread placed before the fire to thaw. "We'll eat Shookum before the trip is over. What d' ye say, Ruth?"

The Indian woman settled the coffee with a piece of ice, glanced from Malemute Kid to her husband, then at the dogs, but vouchsafed no reply. It was such a palpable truism that none was necessary. Two hundred miles of unbroken trail in prospect, with a scant six days' grub for themselves and none for the dogs, could admit no other alternative. The two men and the woman grouped about the fire and began their meagre meal. The dogs lay in their harnesses, for it was a midday halt, and watched each mouthful enviously.

"No more lunches after to-day," said Malemute Kid. "And we've got to keep a close eye on the dogs,—they're getting vicious. They'd just as soon pull a fellow down as not, if they get a chance."

"And I was president of an Epworth once, and taught in the Sunday-school." Having irrelevantly delivered himself of this, Mason fell into a dreamy contemplation of his steaming moccasins, but was aroused by Ruth filling his cup. "Thank God, we've got slathers of tea! I've seen it growing, down in Tennessee. What wouldn't I give for a hot corn-pone just now! Never mind, Ruth; you won't starve much longer, nor wear moccasins either."

From The Son of the Wolf, *copyright 1900 by Jack London, published by Houghton Mifflin Company, Boston.*

The woman threw off her gloom at this, and in her eyes welled up a great love for her white lord,—the first white man she had ever seen,—the first man she had known to treat a woman as something better than a mere animal or beast of burden.

"Yes, Ruth," continued her husband, having recourse to the macaronic jargon in which it was alone possible for them to understand each other; "wait till we clean up and pull for the Outside. We'll take the White Man's canoe and go to the Salt Water. Yes, bad water, rough water,—great mountains dance up and down all the time. And so big, so far, so far away,—you travel ten sleep, twenty sleep, forty sleep" (he graphically enumerated the days on his fingers), "all the time water, bad water. Then you come to great village, plenty people, just the same mosquitoes next summer. Wigwams oh, so high,—ten, twenty pines. Hi-yu skookum!"

He paused impotently, cast an appealing glance at Malemute Kid, then laboriously placed the twenty pines, end on end, by sign language. Malemute Kid smiled with cheery cynicism; but Ruth's eyes were wide with wonder, and with pleasure; for she half believed he was joking, and such condescension pleased her poor woman's heart.

"And then you step into a—a box, and pouf! up you go." He tossed his empty cup in the air by way of illustration, and as he deftly caught it, cried: "And biff! down you come. Oh, great medicine-men! You go Fort Yukon, I go Arctic City,—twenty-five sleep,—big string, all the time,—I catch him string,—I say, 'Hello, Ruth! How are ye?'—and you say, 'Is that my good husband?'—and I say, 'Yes,'—and you say, 'No can bake good bread, no more soda,'—then I say, 'Look in cache, under flour; good-by.' You look and catch plenty soda. All the time you Fort Yukon, me Arctic City. Hi-yu medicine-man!"

Ruth smiled so ingenuously at the fairy story that both men burst into laughter. A row among the dogs cut short the wonders of the Outside, and by the time the snarling combatants were separated, she had lashed the sleds and all was ready for the trail.

"Mush! Baldy! Hi! Mush on!" Mason worked his whip smartly, and as the dogs whined low in the traces, broke out the sled with the gee-pole. Ruth followed with the second team, leaving Malemute Kid, who had helped her start, to bring up the rear. Strong man, brute that he was, capable of felling an ox at a blow, he could not bear to beat the poor animals, but humored them as a dog-driver rarely does,—nay, almost wept with them in their misery.

"Come, mush on there, you poor sore-footed brutes!" he murmured, after several ineffectual attempts to start the load. But his patience was at last rewarded, and though whimpering with pain, they hastened to join their fellows.

No more conversation; the toil of the trail will not permit such extravagance. And of all deadening labors, that of the Northland trail is the worst. Happy is the man who can weather a day's travel at the price of silence, and that on a beaten track.

And of all heart-breaking labors, that of breaking trail is the worst. At every step the great webbed shoe sinks till the snow is level with the knee. Then up, straight up, the deviation of a fraction of an inch being a certain precursor of disaster, the snowshoe must be lifted till the surface is cleared; then forward, down, and the other foot is raised perpendicularly for the matter of half a yard. He who tries this for the first time, if haply he avoids bringing his shoes in dangerous propinquity and measures not his length on the treacherous footing, will give up exhausted at the end of a hundred yards; he who can keep out of the way of the dogs for a whole day may well crawl into his sleeping-bag with a clear conscience and a pride which passeth all understanding; and he who travels twenty sleeps on the Long Trail is a man whom the gods may envy.

The afternoon wore on, and with the awe, born of the White Silence, the voiceless travellers bent to their work. Nature has many tricks wherewith she convinces man of his finity,—the ceaseless flow of the tides, the fury of the storm, the shock of the earthquake, the long roll of heaven's artillery,—but the most tremendous, the most stupefying of all, is the passive phase of the White Silence. All movement ceases, the sky clears, the heavens are as brass; the slightest whisper seems sacrilege, and man becomes timid, affrighted at the sound of his own voice. Sole speck of life journeying across the ghostly wastes of a dead world, he trembles at his audacity, realizes that his is a maggot's life, nothing more. Strange thoughts arise unsummoned, and the mystery of all things strives for utterance. And the fear of death, of God, of the universe, comes over him,—the hope of the Resurrection and the Life, the yearning for immortality, the vain striving of the imprisoned essence,—it is then, if ever, man walks alone with God.

So wore the day away. The river took a great bend, and Mason headed his team for the cut-off across the narrow neck of land. But the dogs balked at the high bank. Again and again, though Ruth and Malemute Kid were shoving on the sled, they slipped back. Then came the concerted effort. The miserable creatures, weak from hunger, exerted their last strength. Up—up—the sled poised on the top of the bank; but the leader swung the string of dogs behind him to the right, fouling Mason's snowshoes. The result was grievous. Mason was whipped off his feet; one of the dogs fell in the traces; and the sled toppled back, dragging everything to the bottom again.

Slash! the whip fell among the dogs savagely, especially upon the one which had fallen.

"Don't, Mason," entreated Malemute Kid; "the poor devil's on its last legs. Wait and we'll put my team on."

Mason deliberately withheld the whip till the last word had fallen, then out flashed the long lash, completely curling about the offending creature's body. Carmen—for it was Carmen—cowered in the snow, cried piteously, then rolled over on her side.

It was a tragic moment, a pitiful incident of the trail,—a dying dog, two comrades in anger. Ruth glanced solicitously from man to man. But Malemute Kid restrained himself, though there was a world of reproach in his eyes, and bending over the dog, cut the traces. No word was spoken. The teams were double-spanned and the difficulty overcome; the sleds were under way again, the dying dog dragging herself along in the rear. As long as an animal can travel, it is not shot, and this last chance is accorded it,—the crawling into camp, if it can, in the hope of a moose being killed.

Already penitent for his angry action, but too stubborn to make amends, Mason toiled on at the head of the cavalcade, little dreaming that danger hovered in the air. The timber clustered thick in the sheltered bottom, and through this they threaded their way. Fifty feet or more from the trail towered a lofty pine. For generations it had stood there, and for generations destiny had had this one end in view,—perhaps the same had been decreed of Mason.

He stooped to fasten the loosened thong of his moccasin. The sleds came to a halt and the dogs lay down in the snow without a whimper. The stillness was weird; not a breath rustled the frost-encrusted forest; the cold and silence of outer space had chilled the heart and smote the trembling lips of nature. A sigh pulsed through the air,—they did not seem to actually hear it, but rather felt it, like the premonition of movement in a motionless void. Then the great tree, burdened with its weight of years and snow, played its last part in the tragedy of life. He heard the warning crash and attempted to spring up, but, almost erect, caught the blow squarely on the shoulder.

The sudden danger, the quick death,—how often had Malemute Kid faced it! The pine-needles were still quivering as he gave his commands and sprang into action. Nor did the Indian girl faint or raise her voice in idle wailing, as might many of her white sisters. At his order, she threw her weight on the end of a quickly extemporized handspike, easing the pressure and listening to her husband's groans, while Malemute Kid attacked the tree with his axe. The steel rang merrily as it bit into the frozen trunk, each stroke being accompanied by a forced, audible respiration, the "Huh! Huh!" of the woodsman.

At last the Kid laid the pitiable thing that was once a man in the snow. But worse than his comrade's pain was the dumb anguish in the woman's face, the blended look of hopeful, hopeless query. Little was said; those of the Northland are early taught the futility of words and the inestimable value of deeds. With the temperature at sixty-five below zero, a man cannot lie many minutes in the snow and live. So the sled-lashings were cut, and the sufferer, rolled in furs, laid on a couch of boughs. Before him roared a fire, built of the very wood which wrought the mishap. Behind and partially over him was stretched the primitive fly,—a piece of canvas, which caught the radiating heat and threw it back and down upon him,—a trick which men may know who study physics at the fount.

And men who have shared their bed with death know when the call is sounded. Mason was terribly crushed. The most cursory examination revealed it. His right arm, leg, and back were broken; his limbs were paralyzed from the hips; and the likelihood of internal injuries was large. An occasional moan was his only sign of life.

No hope; nothing to be done. The pitiless night crept slowly by,— Ruth's portion, the despairing stoicism of her race, and Malemute Kid adding new lines to his face of bronze. In fact, Mason suffered least of all, for he spent his time in Eastern Tennessee, in the Great Smoky Mountains, living over the scenes of his childhood. And most pathetic was the melody of his long-forgotten Southern vernacular, as he raved of swimming-holes, and coon-hunts and watermelon raids. It was as Greek to Ruth, but the Kid understood and felt,—felt as only one can feel who has been shut out for years from all that civilization means.

Morning brought consciousness to the stricken man, and Malemute Kid bent closer to catch his whispers.

"You remember when we foregathered on the Tanana, four years come next ice-run? I didn't care so much for her then. It was more like she was pretty, and there was a smack of excitement about it, I think. But d' ye know, I've come to think a heap of her. She's been a good wife to me, always at my shoulder in the pinch. And when it comes to trading, you know there isn't her equal. D' ye recollect the time she shot the Moose-horn Rapids to pull you and me off that rock, the bullets whipping the water like hailstones?—and the time of the famine at Nuklukyeto?—or when she raced the ice-run to bring the news? Yes, she's been a good wife to me, better 'n that other one. Didn't know I'd been there? Never told you, eh? Well, I tried it once, down in the States. That's why I'm here. Been raised together, too. I came away to give her a chance for divorce. She got it.

"But that's got nothing to do with Ruth. I had thought of cleaning up and pulling for the Outside next year,—her and I,—but it's too late. Don't send her back to her people, Kid. It's beastly hard for a woman to go back. Think of it!—nearly four years on our bacon and beans and flour and dried fruit, and then to go back to her fish and cariboo. It's not good for her to have tried our ways, to come to know they're better 'n her people's, and then return to them. Take care of her, Kid,—why don't you, —but no, you always fought shy of them,—and you never told me why you came to this country. Be kind to her, and send her back to the States as soon as you can. But fix it so as she can come back,—liable to get homesick, you know.

"And the youngster—it's drawn us closer, Kid. I only hope it is a boy. Think of it!—flesh of my flesh, Kid. He mustn't stop in this country. And if it's a girl, why she can't. Sell my furs; they'll fetch at least five thousand, and I've got as much more with the company. And handle my interests with yours. I think that bench claim will show up. See that he gets a good schooling; and Kid, above all, don't let him come back. This country was not made for white men.

"I'm a gone man, Kid. Three or four sleeps at the best. You've got to go on. You must go on! Remember, it's my wife, it's my boy,—O God!

I hope it's a boy! You can't stay by me,—and I charge you, a dying man, to pull on."

"Give me three days," pleaded Malemute Kid. "You may change for the better; something may turn up."

"No."

"Just three days."

"You must pull on."

"Two days."

"It's my wife and my boy, Kid. You would not ask it."

"One day."

"No, no! I charge—"

"Only one day. We can shave it through on the grub, and I might knock over a moose."

"No,—all right; one day, but not a minute more. And Kid, don't—don't leave me to face it alone. Just a shot, one pull on the trigger. You understand. Think of it! Think of it! Flesh of my flesh, and I'll never live to see him!

"Send Ruth here. I want to say good-by and tell her that she must think of the boy and not wait till I'm dead. She might refuse to go with you if I didn't. Good-by, old man; good-by.

"Kid! I say—a—sink a hole above the pup, next to the slide. I panned out forty cents on my shovel there.

"And Kid!" he stooped lower to catch the last faint words, the dying man's surrender of his pride. "I'm sorry—for—you know—Carmen."

Leaving the girl crying softly over her man, Malemute Kid slipped into his *parka* and snowshoes, tucked his rifle under his arm, and crept away into the forest. He was no tyro in the stern sorrows of the Northland, but never had he faced so stiff a problem as this. In the abstract, it was a plain, mathematical proposition,—three possible lives as against one doomed one. But now he hesitated. For five years, shoulder to shoulder, on the rivers and trails, in the camps and mines, facing death by field and flood and famine, had they knitted the bonds of their comradeship. So close was the tie, that he had often been conscious of a vague jealousy of Ruth from the first time she had come between. And now it must be severed by his own hand.

Though he prayed for a moose, just one moose, all game seemed to have deserted the land, and nightfall found the exhausted man crawling into camp, light-handed, heavy-hearted. An uproar from the dogs and shrill cries from Ruth hastened him.

Bursting into the camp, he saw the girl in the midst of the snarling pack, laying about her with an axe. The dogs had broken the iron rule of their masters and were rushing the grub. He joined the issue with his rifle reversed, and the hoary game of natural selection was played out with all the ruthlessness of its primeval environment. Rifle and axe went up and down, hit or missed with monotonous regularity; lithe bodies flashed, with wild eyes and dripping fangs; and man and beast fought for supremacy to the bitterest conclusion. Then the beaten brutes crept to the edge of the firelight, licking their wounds, voicing their misery to the stars.

The whole stock of dried salmon had been devoured, and perhaps five pounds of flour remained to tide them over two hundred miles of wilderness. Ruth returned to her husband, while Malemute Kid cut up the warm body of one of the dogs, the skull of which had been crushed by the axe. Every portion was carefully put away, save the hide and offal, which were cast to his fellows of the moment before.

Morning brought fresh trouble. The animals were turning on each other. Carmen, who still clung to her slender thread of life, was downed by the pack. The lash fell among them unheeded. They cringed and cried under the blows, but refused to scatter till the last wretched bit had disappeared,—bones, hide, hair, everything.

Malemute Kid went about his work, listening to Mason, who was back in Tennessee, delivering tangled discourses and wild exhortations to his brethren of other days.

Taking advantage of neighboring pines, he worked rapidly, and Ruth watched him make a cache similar to those sometimes used by hunters to preserve their meat from the wolverines and dogs. One after the other, he bent the tops of two small pines toward each other and nearly to the ground, making them fast with thongs of moosehide. Then he beat the dogs into submission and harnessed them to two of the sleds, loading the same with everything but the furs which enveloped Mason. These he wrapped and lashed tightly about him, fastening either end of the robes to the bent pines. A single stroke of his hunting-knife would release them and send the body high in the air.

Ruth had received her husband's last wishes and made no struggle. Poor girl, she had learned the lesson of obedience well. From a child, she had bowed, and seen all women bow, to the lords of creation, and it did not seem in the nature of things for woman to resist. The Kid permitted her one outburst of grief, as she kissed her husband,—her own people had no such custom,—then led her to the foremost sled and helped her into her snowshoes. Blindly, instinctively, she took the gee-pole and whip, and "mushed" the dogs out on the trail. Then he returned to Mason, who had fallen into a coma; and long after she was out of sight, crouched by the fire, waiting, hoping, praying for his comrade to die.

It is not pleasant to be alone with painful thoughts in the White Silence. The silence of gloom is merciful, shrouding one as with protection and breathing a thousand intangible sympathies; but the bright White Silence, clear and cold, under steely skies, is pitiless.

An hour passed,—two hours,—but the man would not die. At high noon, the sun, without raising its rim above the southern horizon, threw a suggestion of fire athwart the heavens, then quickly drew it back. Malemute Kid roused and dragged himself to his comrade's side. He cast one glance about him. The White Silence seemed to sneer, and a great fear came upon him. There was a sharp report; Mason swung into his aerial sepulchre; and Malemute Kid lashed the dogs into a wild gallop as he fled across the snow.

COMMENT

From its provocative opening sentence to its melodramatic long-shot movie ending, this story appears to be pure narrative. Stripped of its pseudo-Darwinian philosophizing, its "literary" language, and its flashbacks, "The White Silence" might serve as an example of the oldest form of story-telling: an account of a hunt, a chase, a physical struggle. The romanticized picture of cavemen crouching around the fire, gesturing and grunting about the day's tree-felling or last week's mastodon-killing, is only hypothetical. But something like this must have been the origin of narrative.

As he gives form to the raw data, the point of view of the story-teller affects the interpretation of events: Jack London, as the all-knowing observer, tells us the past history of the characters ("For five years, shoulder to shoulder, . . . had they knitted the bonds of their comradeship"); describes their unexpressed feelings ("Already penitent for his angry action, but too stubborn to make amends . . ."); establishes a context for the action ("Two hundred miles of unbroken trail in prospect, with a scant six days' grub for themselves and none for the dogs"); and makes generalized comments ("It was a tragic moment, a pitiful incident of the trail"; "And men who have shared their bed with death know when the call is sounded"; "Poor girl, she had learned the lesson of obedience well"). He also creates suspense by setting traps for his characters, teasing the reader by predicting the consequences of some acts, and underlining risks and temptations. He says that the food is likely to run out; he describes the terrors of trail-breaking; and before the tree falls he explains that the destinies of this "lofty pine" and of Mason are about to intersect.

An action story has another necessary ingredient of fiction, conflict and complication of conflict. In "The White Silence" two conflicts stand out: man against animal and, more inclusively, man against a pitiless, indifferent Nature. These are timeless, universal conflicts, part of the fairly limited list used by all story-tellers: man against man, man against society, man against nature, man against himself. The latter conflict is the mainstay of many contemporary writers—in this book, Hemingway, Mann, Svevo, and Lowry, among others. But even London's rather simple action story contains an internal conflict, for Malemute Kid must decide whether to abandon Mason or to remain with him and risk the lives of Ruth, of whom he has been vaguely jealous, and her unborn child.

Since the London story is primarily one of suspense, the theme is subordinated and the characters are simple, almost stereotyped. Consider Malemute Kid: the noble white hunter, anonymous except for his animal-nickname, both ruthless and honorable, taciturn, invincible, kind to dogs and children, he appears in many of London's stories surrounded by legend. In "The Son of the Wolf," for instance, he is described as "a mighty man, straight as a willow-shoot, and tall; strong as the bald-faced grizzly, with a heart like the full summer moon." He is, then, an almost mythical figure—a superman of the frozen North ("capable of felling an ox at a blow"), a Paul Bunyan in a parka—larger than life and practically without human weaknesses and foibles. Mythical figures are, in fact, often simply conceived, hence the plentiful supply from radio, movies, television, and comic books: the Lone Ranger, Tarzan of the Apes, the Cisco Kid, and James Bond. But they can be very complex, as in "Powerhouse" and "Death in Venice."

As for theme, despite the fact that London indulges in speculations about "the hoary game of natural selection," the survival of the fittest, the debilitating effects of civilization (compare Faulkner's rich, dramatic treatment of this subject), and in some misty musings about man walking alone with God in the great White Silence, the reader is left with little besides an impression of solid heroism against merciless odds. And after he has reached the outcome of the struggle—Mason in his "aerial sepulchre" and Malemute Kid "mushing" the dogs out on the trail after Ruth—nothing pulls the reader back to the story because nothing is left to engage the mind or the heart, nothing to repay a closer reading. Fate has played its little trick on Mason, and Malemute Kid—after perhaps a few cursory arrangements about Mason's widow and child—will soon be off to further adventures.

We do not wish to imply that London does not strive for anything more complex than a naked tale of action and death. There is some structural subtlety in the analogy between the deaths of Carmen and Mason, suggesting the correspondence of man and beast in the struggle for survival. But much material is extraneous: for example, London introduces a reference to miscegenation—a white man married to an Indian woman—but neither develops it fully nor treats it originally. Also, the levels of language indicate a rather pathetic attempt to be "literary," that is, to raise the tone of the story by a fancy, usually Latinate, incongruous vocabulary: Mason did not look at the dog, he "surveyed the poor animal ruefully"; Ruth "vouchsafed no reply" to Malemute Kid's question because it was "such a palpable truism"; Mason "graphically enumerated the days"; a trailbreaker must avoid bringing his shoes "in dangerous propinquity"; a handspike is "quickly extemporized." Used ironically, this diction would reduce the story to college-humor level; used seriously in "The White Silence," it turns drama into melodrama, dilutes the experience, and makes much of the tale unwittingly ludicrous.

It would be too easy to dismiss the simple action story as not worth serious consideration. Such a story is often carefully constructed, precisely trimmed, and gripping on at least the first reading. Told without pretense or apology for not being something more ambitious, it may well be a minor work of art. And when an exciting action is given shape by a serious theme, the result is "The Open Boat," by Stephen Crane, *Moby-Dick, Huckleberry Finn, The Old Man and the Sea,* "The Bear," or the next story, William Faulkner's "Red Leaves."

QUESTIONS ON ACTION

1. The above analysis lists some of the most common fictional conflicts. Note that although "man" is a member of each conflict, London himself has written a number of stories about animals in conflict with other animals. In what sense might we say that these stories still deal with human conflict?

2. We have described Malemute Kid as a superhuman, almost mythical figure. In what ways can the reader nevertheless identify himself with him?

3. Can you defend the inclusion in an action story of the paragraph London devotes to "the White Silence"? Notice that London does not dramatize the effects of this silence but simply describes them. How could the same material have been rendered dramatically? In "Red Leaves," how does Faulkner dramatize the silence and emptiness of the slave quarters, the suffocating terror of the swamp?

OTHER CONSIDERATIONS

1. Is there any point in London's making Mason a former Sunday-school teacher? president of an Epworth League? a Southerner?

2. Are Mason and Ruth blatantly stereotyped characters or do they have human, unpredictable qualities?

3. One of the tenets of literary naturalism is that environment determines character. Does London appear to subscribe to this tenet in "The White Silence"? Compare the way Sarah Orne Jewett's characters in "The Town Poor" manage to transcend their environment.

4. Compare the relatively abstract, generalized descriptions of nature in "The White Silence" with the more specific descriptions in such stories as "Red Leaves," "The Town Poor," and "Nina of Ashkelon."

Red Leaves

William Faulkner ❦

The two Indians crossed the plantation toward the slave quarters. Neat with whitewash, of baked soft brick, the two rows of houses in which lived the slaves belonging to the clan, faced one another across the mild shade of the lane marked and scored with naked feet and with a few homemade toys mute in the dust. There was no sign of life.

"I know what we will find," the first Indian said.

"What we will not find," the second said. Although it was noon, the lane was vacant, the doors of the cabins empty and quiet; no cooking smoke rose from any of the chinked and plastered chimneys.

"Yes. It happened like this when the father of him who is now the Man died."

"You mean, of him who was the Man."

"Yao."

The first Indian's name was Three Basket. He was perhaps sixty. They were both squat men, a little solid, burgherlike; paunchy, with big heads, big, broad, dust-colored faces of a certain blurred serenity like carved heads on a ruined wall in Siam or Sumatra, looming out of a mist. The sun had done it, the violent sun, the violent shade. Their hair looked like sedge grass on burnt-over land. Clamped through one ear Three Basket wore an enameled snuffbox.

"I have said all the time that this is not the good way. In the old days there were no quarters, no Negroes. A man's time was his own then. He had time. Now he must spend most of it finding work for them who prefer sweating to do."

"They are like horses and dogs."

"They are like nothing in this sensible world. Nothing contents them save sweat. They are worse than the white people."

"It is not as though the Man himself had to find work for them to do."

"You said it. I do not like slavery. It is not the good way. In the old days, there was the good way. But not now."

"You do not remember the old way either."

"I have listened to them who do. And I have tried this way. Man was not made to sweat."

"That's so. See what it has done to their flesh."

"Yes. Black. It has a bitter taste, too."

"You have eaten of it?"

"Once. I was young then, and more hardy in the appetite than now. Now it is different with me."

"Yes. They are too valuable to eat now."

"There is a bitter taste to the flesh which I do not like."

"They are too valuable to eat, anyway, when the white men will give horses for them."

They entered the lane. The mute, meager toys—the fetish-shaped objects made of wood and rags and feathers—lay in the dust about the patinaed doorsteps, among bones and broken gourd dishes. But there was no sound from any cabin, no face in any door; had not been since yesterday, when Issetibbeha died. But they already knew what they would find.

It was in the central cabin, a house a little larger than the others, where at certain phases of the moon the Negroes would gather to begin their ceremonies before removing after nightfall to the creek bottom, where they kept the drums. In this room they kept the minor accessories, the cryptic ornaments, the ceremonial records which consisted of sticks daubed with red clay in symbols. It had a hearth in the center of the floor, beneath a hole in the roof, with a few cold wood ashes and a suspended iron pot. The window shutters were closed; when the two Indians entered, after the abashless sunlight they could distinguish nothing with the eyes save a movement, shadow, out of which eyeballs rolled, so that the place appeared to be full of Negroes. The two Indians stood in the door.

"Yao," Basket said. "I said this is not the good way."

"I don't think I want to be here," the second said.

"That is black man's fear which you smell. It does not smell as ours does."

"I don't think I want to be here."

"Your fear has an odor too."

"Maybe it is Issetibbeha which we smell."

"Yao. He knows. He knows what we will find here. He knew when he died what we should find here today." Out of the rank twilight of the room the eyes, the smell, of Negroes rolled about them. "I am Three Basket, whom you know," Basket said into the room. "We are come from the Man. He whom we seek is gone?" The Negroes said nothing. The smell of them, of their bodies, seemed to ebb and flux in the still hot air. They seemed to be musing as one upon something remote, inscrutable. They were like a single octopus. They were like the roots of a huge tree uncovered, the earth broken momentarily upon the writhen, thick, fetid tangle of its lightless and outraged life. "Come," Basket said. "You know our errand. Is he whom we seek gone?"

"They are thinking something," the second said. "I do not want to be here."

"They are knowing something," Basket said.

"They are hiding him, you think?"

"No. He is gone. He has been gone since last night. It happened like this before, when the grandfather of him who is now the Man died. It took us three days to catch him. For three days Doom lay above the ground, saying, 'I see my horse and my dog. But I do not see my slave.

What have you done with him that you will not permit me to lie quiet?' "

"They do not like to die."

"Yao. They cling. It makes trouble for us, always. A people without honor and without decorum. Always a trouble."

"I do not like it here."

"Nor do I. But then, they are savages; they cannot be expected to regard usage. That is why I say that this way is a bad way."

"Yao. They cling. They would even rather work in the sun than to enter the earth with a chief. But he is gone."

The Negroes had said nothing, made no sound. The white eyeballs rolled, wild, subdued; the smell was rank, violent. "Yes, they fear," the second said. "What shall we do now?"

"Let us go and talk with the Man."

"Will Moketubbe listen?"

"What can he do? He will not like to. But he is the Man now."

"Yao. He is the Man. He can wear the shoes with the red heels all the time now." They turned and went out. There was no door in the door frame. There were no doors in any of the cabins.

"He did that anyway," Basket said.

"Behind Issetibbeha's back. But now they are his shoes, since he is the Man."

"Yao. Issetibbeha did not like it. I have heard. I know that he said to Moketubbe: 'When you are the Man, the shoes will be yours. But until then, they are my shoes.' But now Moketubbe is the Man; he can wear them."

"Yao," the second said. "He is the Man now. He used to wear the shoes behind Issetibbeha's back, and it was not known if Issetibbeha knew this or not. And then Issetibbeha became dead, who was not old, and the shoes are Moketubbe's, since he is the Man now. What do you think of that?"

"I don't think about it," Basket said. "Do you?"

"No," the second said.

"Good," Basket said. "You are wise."

II

The house sat on a knoll, surrounded by oak trees. The front of it was one story in height, composed of the deck house of a steamboat which had gone ashore and which Doom, Issetibbeha's father, had dismantled with his slaves and hauled on cypress rollers twelve miles home overland. It took them five months. His house consisted at the time of one brick wall. He set the steamboat broadside on to the wall, where now the chipped and flaked gilding of the rococo cornices arched in faint splendor above the gilt lettering of the stateroom names above the jalousied doors.

Doom had been born merely a subchief, a Mingo, one of three children on the mother's side of the family. He made a journey—he was a young man then and New Orleans was a European city—from north Mississippi to New Orleans by keel boat, where he met the Chevalier Sœur Blonde de Vitry, a man whose social position, on its face, was as equivocal as Doom's own. In New Orleans, among the gamblers and cutthroats of the river front, Doom, under the tutelage of his patron, passed as the chief, the Man, the hereditary owner of that land which belonged to the male side of the family; it was the Chevalier de Vitry who called him *du homme,* and hence Doom.

They were seen everywhere together—the Indian, the squat man with a bold, inscrutable, underbred face, and the Parisian, the expatriate, the friend, it was said, of Carondelet and the intimate of General Wilkinson. Then they disappeared, the two of them, vanishing from their old equivocal haunts and leaving behind them the legend of the sums which Doom was believed to have won, and some tale about a young woman, daughter of a fairly well-to-do West Indian family, the son and brother of whom sought Doom with a pistol about his old haunts for some time after his disappearance.

Six months later the young woman herself disappeared, boarding the Saint Louis packet, which put in one night at a wood landing on the north Mississippi side, where the woman, accompanied by a Negro maid, got off. Four Indians met her with a horse and wagon, and they traveled for three days, slowly, since she was already big with child, to the plantation, where she found that Doom was now chief. He never told her how he accomplished it, save that his uncle and his cousin had died suddenly. Before that time the house had consisted of a brick wall built by shiftless slaves, against which was propped a thatched lean-to divided into rooms and littered with bones and refuse, set in the center of ten thousand acres of matchless parklike forest where deer grazed like domestic cattle. Doom and the woman were married there a short time before Issetibbeha was born, by a combination itinerant minister and slave trader who arrived on a mule, to the saddle of which was lashed a cotton umbrella and a three-gallon demijohn of whiskey. After that, Doom began to acquire more slaves and to cultivate some of his land, as the white people did. But he never had enough for them to do. In utter idleness the majority of them led lives transplanted whole out of African jungles, save on the occasions when, entertaining guests, Doom coursed them with dogs.

When Doom died, Issetibbeha, his son, was nineteen. He became proprietor of the land and of the quintupled herd of blacks for which he had no use at all. Though the title of Man rested with him, there was a hierarchy of cousins and uncles who ruled the clan and who finally gathered in squatting conclave over the Negro question, squatting profoundly beneath the golden names above the doors of the steamboat.

"We cannot eat them," one said.

"Why not?"

"There are too many of them."

"That's true," a third said. "Once we started, we should have to eat them all. And that much flesh diet is not good for man."

"Perhaps they will be like deer flesh. That cannot hurt you."

"We might kill a few of them and not eat them," Issetibbeha said.

They looked at him for a while. "What for?" one said.

"That is true," a second said. "We cannot do that. They are too valuable; remember all the bother they have caused us, finding things for them to do. We must do as the white men do."

"How is that?" Issetibbeha said.

"Raise more Negroes by clearing more land to make corn to feed them, then sell them. We will clear the land and plant it with food and raise Negroes and sell them to the white men for money."

"But what will we do with this money?" a third said.

They thought for a while.

"We will see," the first said. They squatted, profound, grave.

"It means work," the third said.

"Let the Negroes do it," the first said.

"Yao. Let them. To sweat is bad. It is damp. It opens the pores."

"And then the night air enters."

"Yao. Let the Negroes do it. They appear to like sweating."

So they cleared the land with the Negroes and planted it in grain. Up to that time the slaves had lived in a huge pen with a lean-to roof over one corner, like a pen for pigs. But now they began to build quarters, cabins, putting the young Negroes in the cabins in pairs to mate; five years later Issetibbeha sold forty head to a Memphis trader, and he took the money and went abroad upon it, his maternal uncle from New Orleans conducting the trip. At that time the Chevalier Sœur Blonde de Vitry was an old man in Paris, in a toupee and a corset and a careful, toothless old face fixed in a grimace quizzical and profoundly tragic. He borrowed three hundred dollars from Issetibbeha and in return he introduced him into certain circles; a year later Issetibbeha returned home with a gilt bed, a pair of girandoles by whose light it was said that Pompadour arranged her hair while Louis smirked at his mirrored face across her powdered shoulder, and a pair of slippers with red heels. They were too small for him, since he had not worn shoes at all until he reached New Orleans on his way abroad.

He brought the slippers home in tissue paper and kept them in the remaining pocket of a pair of saddlebags filled with cedar shavings, save when he took them out on occasion for his son, Moketubbe, to·play with. At three years of age Moketubbe had a broad, flat, Mongolian face that appeared to exist in a complete and unfathomable lethargy, until confronted by the slippers.

Moketubbe's mother was a comely girl whom Issetibbeha had seen one day working in her shift in a melon patch. He stopped and watched her for a while—the broad, solid thighs, the sound back, the serene face. He was on his way to the creek to fish that day, but he didn't go any farther; perhaps while he stood there watching the unaware girl he may have remembered his own mother, the city woman, the fugitive with her fans and laces and her Negro blood, and all the tawdry shabbiness of that sorry affair. Within the year Moketubbe was born; even at three he could not get his feet into the slippers. Watching him in the still, hot afternoon as he struggled with the slippers with a certain monstrous repudiation of fact,

Issetibbeha laughed, quietly to himself. He laughed at Moketubbe's antics with the shoes for several years, because Moketubbe did not give up trying to put them on until he was sixteen. Then he quit. Or Issetibbeha thought he had. But he had merely quit trying in Issetibbeha's presence. Issetibbeha's newest wife told him that Moketubbe had stolen and hidden the shoes. Issetibbeha quit laughing then, and he sent the woman away, so that he was alone. "Yao," he said, "I too like being alive, it seems." He sent for Moketubbe. "I give them to you," he said.

Moketubbe was twenty-five then, unmarried. Issetibbeha was not tall, but he was taller by six inches than his son and almost a hundred pounds lighter. Moketubbe was already diseased with flesh, with a pale, broad, inert face and dropsical hands and feet. "They are yours now," Issetibbeha said, watching him. Moketubbe had looked at him once when he entered, a glance brief, discreet, veiled.

"Thanks," he said.

Issetibbeha looked at him. He could never tell if Moketubbe saw anything, looked at anything. "Why will it not be the same if I give the slippers to you?"

"Thanks," Moketubbe said. Issetibbeha was using snuff at the time; a white man had shown him how to put the powder into his lip and scour it against his teeth with a twig of gum or of alphea.

"Well," he said, "a man cannot live forever." He looked at his son, then his gaze went blank in turn unseeing, and he mused for an instant. You could not tell what he was thinking, save that he said half aloud: "Yao. But Doom's uncle had no shoes with red heels." He looked at his son again, fat, inert. "Beneath all that, a man might think of doing anything and it not be known until too late." He sat in a splint chair hammocked with deer thongs. "He cannot even get them on; he and I are both frustrated by the same gross meat which he wears. He cannot even get them on. But is that my fault?"

He lived for five years longer, then he died. He was sick one night, and though the doctor came in a skunk-skin vest and burned sticks, Issetibbeha died before noon.

That was yesterday; the grave was dug, and for twelve hours now the People had been coming in wagons and carriages and on horseback and afoot, to eat the baked dog and the succotash and the yams cooked in ashes and to attend the funeral.

III

"It will be three days," Basket said, as he and the other Indian returned to the house. "It will be three days and the food will not be enough; I have seen it before."

The second Indian's name was Louis Berry. "He will smell too, in this weather."

"Yao. They are nothing but a trouble and a care."

"Maybe it will not take three days."

"They run far. Yao. We will smell this Man before he enters the earth. You watch and see if I am not right."

They approached the house.

"He can wear the shoes now," Berry said. "He can wear them now in man's sight."

"He cannot wear them for a while yet," Basket said. Berry looked at him. "He will lead the hunt."

"Moketubbe?" Berry said. "Do you think he will? A man to whom even talking is travail?"

"What else can he do? It is his own father who will soon begin to smell."

"That is true," Berry said. "There is even yet a price he must pay for the shoes. Yao. He has truly bought them. What do you think?"

"What do you think?"

"What do you think?"

"I think nothing."

"Nor do I. Issetibbeha will not need the shoes now. Let Moketubbe have them; Issetibbeha will not care."

"Yao. Man must die."

"Yao. Let him; there is still the Man."

The bark roof of the porch was supported by peeled cypress poles, high above the texas of the steamboat, shading an unfloored banquette where on the trodden earth mules and horses were tethered in bad weather. On the forward end of the steamboat's deck sat an old man and two women. One of the women was dressing a fowl, the other was shelling corn. The old man was talking. He was barefoot, in a long linen frock coat and a beaver hat.

"This world is going to the dogs," he said. "It is being ruined by white men. We got along fine for years and years, before the white men foisted their Negroes upon us. In the old days the old men sat in the shade and ate stewed deer's flesh and corn and smoked tobacco and talked of honor and grave affairs; now what do we do? Even the old wear themselves into the grave taking care of them that like sweating." When Basket and Berry crossed the deck he ceased and looked up at them. His eyes were querulous, bleared; his face was myriad with tiny wrinkles. "He is fled also," he said.

"Yes," Berry said, "he is gone."

"I knew it. I told them so. It will take three weeks, like when Doom died. You watch and see."

"It was three days, not three weeks," Berry said.

"Were you there?"

"No," Berry said. "But I have heard."

"Well, I was there," the old man said. "For three whole weeks, through the swamps and the briers—" They went on and left him talking.

What had been the saloon of the steamboat was now a shell, rotting slowly; the polished mahogany, the carving glinting momentarily and fading through the mold in figures cabalistic and profound; the gutted windows were like cataracted eyes. It contained a few sacks of seed or grain, and the fore part of the running gear of a barouche, to the axle of which two C-springs rusted in graceful curves, supporting nothing. In one corner a fox cub ran steadily and soundlessly up and down a willow cage; three scrawny gamecocks moved in the dust, and the place was pocked and marked with their dried droppings.

They passed through the brick wall and entered a big room of chinked logs. It contained the hinder part of the barouche, and the dismantled body lying on its side, the window slatted over with willow withes, through which protruded the heads, the still, beady, outraged eyes and frayed combs of still more game chickens. It was floored with packed clay; in one corner leaned a crude plow and two hand-hewn boat paddles. From the ceiling, suspended by four deer thongs, hung the gilt bed which Issetibbeha had fetched from Paris. It had neither mattress nor springs, the frame criss-crossed now by a neat hammocking of thongs.

Issetibbeha had tried to have his newest wife, the young one, sleep in the bed. He was congenitally short of breath himself, and he passed the nights half reclining in his splint chair. He would see her to bed and, later, wakeful, sleeping as he did but three or four hours a night, he would sit in the darkness and simulate slumber and listen to her sneak infinitesimally from the gilt and ribboned bed, to lie on a quilt pallet on the floor until just before daylight. Then she would enter the bed quietly again and in turn simulate slumber, while in the darkness beside her Issetibbeha quietly laughed and laughed.

The girandoles were lashed by thongs to two sticks propped in a corner where a ten-gallon whiskey keg lay also. There was a clay hearth; facing it, in the splint chair, Moketubbe sat. He was maybe an inch better than five feet tall, and he weighed two hundred and fifty pounds. He wore a broadcloth coat and no shirt, his round, smooth copper balloon of belly swelling above the bottom piece of a suit of linen underwear. On his feet were the slippers with the red heels. Behind his chair stood a stripling with a punkah-like fan made of fringed paper. Moketubbe sat motionless, with his broad, yellow face with its closed eyes and flat nostrils, his flipper-like arms extended. On his face was an expression profound, tragic, and inert. He did not open his eyes when Basket and Berry came in.

"He has worn them since daylight?" Basket said.

"Since daylight," the stripling said. The fan did not cease. "You can see."

"Yao," Basket said. "We can see." Moketubbe did not move. He looked like an effigy, like a Malay god in frock coat, drawers, naked chest, the trivial scarlet-heeled shoes.

"I wouldn't disturb him, if I were you," the stripling said.

"Not if I were you," Basket said. He and Berry squatted. The stripling moved the fan steadily. "O Man," Basket said, "listen." Moketubbe did not move. "He is gone," Basket said.

"I told you so," the stripling said. "I knew he would flee. I told you."

"Yao," Basket said. "You are not the first to tell us afterward what we should have known before. Why is it that some of you wise men took no steps yesterday to prevent this?"

"He does not wish to die," Berry said.

"Why should he not wish it?" Basket said.

"Because he must die some day is no reason," the stripling said. "That would not convince me either, old man."

"Hold your tongue," Berry said.

"For twenty years," Basket said, "while others of his race sweat in the fields, he served the Man in the shade. Why should he not wish to die, since he did not wish to sweat?"

"And it will be quick," Berry said. "It will not take long."

"Catch him and tell him that," the stripling said.

"Hush," Berry said. They squatted, watching Moketubbe's face. He might have been dead himself. It was as though he were cased so in flesh that even breathing took place too deep within him to show.

"Listen, O Man," Basket said. "Issetibbeha is dead. He waits. His dog and his horse we have. But his slave has fled. The one who held the pot for him, who ate of his food, from his dish, is fled. Issetibbeha waits."

"Yao," Berry said.

"This is not the first time," Basket said. "This happened when Doom, thy grandfather, lay waiting at the door of the earth. He lay waiting three days, saying, 'Where is my Negro?' And Issetibbeha, thy father, answered, 'I will find him. Rest; I will bring him to you so that you may begin the journey.' "

"Yao," Berry said.

Moketubbe had not moved, had not opened his eyes.

"For three days Issetibbeha hunted in the bottom," Basket said. "He did not even return home for food, until the Negro was with him; then he said to Doom, his father, 'Here is thy dog, thy horse, thy Negro; rest.' Issetibbeha, who is dead since yesterday, said it. And now Issetibbeha's Negro is fled. His horse and his dog wait with him, but his Negro is fled."

"Yao," Berry said.

Moketubbe had not moved. His eyes were closed; upon his supine monstrous shape there was a colossal inertia, something profoundly immobile, beyond and impervious to flesh. They watched his face, squatting.

"When thy father was newly the Man, this happened," Basket said. "And it was Issetibbeha who brought back the slave to where his father waited to enter the earth." Moketubbe's face had not moved, his eyes had not moved. After a while Basket said, "Remove the shoes."

The stripling removed the shoes. Moketubbe began to pant, his bare chest moving deep, as though he were rising from beyond his unfathomed flesh back into life, like up from the water, the sea. But his eyes had not opened yet.

Berry said, "He will lead the hunt."

"Yao," Basket said. "He is the Man. He will lead the hunt."

IV

All that day the Negro, Issetibbeha's body servant, hidden in the barn, watched Issetibbeha's dying. He was forty, a Guinea man. He had a flat nose, a close, small head; the inside corners of his eyes showed red a little, and his prominent gums were a pale bluish red above his square, broad teeth. He had been taken at fourteen by a trader off Kamerun, before his teeth had been filed. He had been Issetibbeha's body servant for twenty-three years.

On the day before, the day on which Issetibbeha lay sick, he returned to the quarters at dusk. In that unhurried hour the smoke of the cooking fires blew slowly across the street from door to door, carrying into the opposite one the smell of the identical meat and bread. The women tended them; the men were gathered at the head of the lane, watching him as he came down the slope from the house, putting his naked feet down carefully in a strange dusk. To the waiting men his eyeballs were a little luminous.

"Issetibbeha is not dead yet," the headman said.

"Not dead," the body servant said. "Who not dead?"

In the dusk they had faces like his, the different ages, the thoughts sealed inscrutable behind faces like the death masks of apes. The smell of the fires, the cooking, blew sharp and slow across the strange dusk, as from another world, above the lane and the pickaninnies naked in the dust.

"If he lives past sundown, he will live until daybreak," one said.

"Who says?"

"Talk says."

"Yao. Talk says. We know but one thing." They looked at the body servant as he stood among them, his eyeballs a little luminous. He was breathing slow and deep. His chest was bare; he was sweating a little. "He knows. He knows it."

"Yao. Let the drums tell it."

The drums began after dark. They kept them hidden in the creek bottom. They were made of hollowed cypress knees, and the Negroes kept them hidden; why, none knew. They were buried in the mud on the bank of a slough; a lad of fourteen guarded them. He was undersized, and a mute; he squatted in the mud there all day, clouded over with mosquitoes, naked save for the mud with which he coated himself against the mosquitoes, and about his neck a fiber bag containing a pig's rib to which black shreds of flesh still adhered, and two scaly barks on a wire. He slobbered onto his clutched knees, drooling; now and then Indians came noiselessly out of the bushes behind him and stood there and contemplated him for a while and went away, and he never knew it.

From the loft of the stable where he lay hidden until dark and after, the Negro could hear the drums. They were three miles away, but he could hear them as though they were in the barn itself below him, thudding and thudding. It was as though he could see the fire too, and the black limbs turning into and out of the flames in copper gleams. Only there would be no fire. There would be no more light there than where he lay in the dusty loft, with the whispering arpeggios of rat feet along the warm and immemorial ax-squared rafters. The only fire there would be the smudge against mosquitoes where the women with nursing children crouched, their heavy, sluggish breasts nippled full and smooth into the mouths of men children; contemplative, oblivious of the drumming, since a fire would signify life.

There was a fire in the steamboat, where Issetibbeha lay dying among his wives, beneath the lashed girandoles and the suspended bed. He could see the smoke, and just before sunset he saw the doctor come out, in a waistcoat made of skunk skins, and set fire to two clay-daubed sticks at the bows of the boat deck. "So he is not dead yet," the Negro said into the whispering gloom of the loft, answering himself; he could hear the two voices, himself and himself:

"Who not dead?"

"You are dead."

"Yao, I am dead," he said quietly. He wished to be where the drums were. He imagined himself springing out of the bushes, leaping among the drums on his bare, lean, greasy, invisible limbs. But he could not do that, because man leaped past life, into where death was; he dashed into death and did not die because when death took a man, it took him just this side of the end of living. It was when death overran him from behind, still in life. The thin whisper of rat feet died in fainting gusts along the rafters. Once he had eaten rat. He was a boy then, but just come to America. They had lived ninety days in a three-foot-high 'tween deck in tropic latitudes, hearing from topside the drunken New England captain intoning aloud from a book which he did not recognize for ten years afterward to be the Bible. Squatting in the stable so, he had watched the rat, civilized, by association with man reft of its inherent cunning of limb and eye; he had caught it without difficulty, with scarce a movement of his hand, and he ate it slowly, wondering how any of the rats had escaped so long. At that time he was still wearing the single white garment which the trader, a deacon in the Unitarian church, had given him, and he spoke then only his native tongue.

He was naked now, save for a pair of dungaree pants bought by Indians from white men, and an amulet slung on a thong about his hips. The amulet consisted of one half of a mother-of-pearl lorgnon which Issetibbeha had brought back from Paris, and the skull of a cottonmouth moccasin. He had killed the snake himself and eaten it, save the poison head. He lay in the loft, watching the house, the steamboat, listening to the drums, thinking of himself among the drums.

He lay there all night. The next morning he saw the doctor come out, in his skunk vest, and get on his mule and ride away, and he became quite still and watched the final dust from beneath the mule's delicate feet die away, and then he found that he was still breathing and it seemed strange

to him that he still breathed air, still needed air. Then he lay and watched
quietly, waiting to move, his eyeballs a little luminous, but with a quiet
light, and his breathing light and regular, and saw Louis Berry come out
and look at the sky. It was good light then, and already five Indians
squatted in their Sunday clothes along the steamboat deck; by noon there
were twenty-five there. That afternoon they dug the trench in which the
meat would be baked, and the yams; by that time there were almost a
hundred guests—decorous, quiet, patient in their stiff European finery—
and he watched Berry lead Issetibbeha's mare from the stable and tie her
to a tree, and then he watched Berry emerge from the house with the old
hound which lay beside Issetibbeha's chair. He tied the hound to the tree
too, and it sat there, looking gravely about at the faces. Then it began
to howl. It was still howling at sundown, when the Negro climbed down
the back wall of the barn and entered the spring branch, where it was already dusk. He began to run then. He could hear the hound howling behind him, and near the spring, already running, he passed another Negro.
The two men, the one motionless and the other running, looked for an
instant at each other as though across an actual boundary between two
different worlds. He ran on into full darkness, mouth closed, fists
doubled, his broad nostrils bellowing steadily.

He ran on in the darkness. He knew the country well, because he had
hunted it often with Issetibbeha, following on his mule the course of the
fox or the cat beside Issetibbeha's mare; he knew it as well as did the men
who would pursue him. He saw them for the first time shortly before sunset of the second day. He had run thirty miles then, up the creek bottom,
before doubling back; lying in a pawpaw thicket he saw the pursuit for
the first time. There were two of them, in shirts and straw hats, carrying
their neatly rolled trousers under their arms, and they had no weapons.
They were middle-aged, paunchy, and they could not have moved very
fast anyway; it would be twelve hours before they could return to where
he lay watching them. "So I will have until midnight to rest," he said. He
was near enough to the plantation to smell the cooking fires, and he
thought how he ought to be hungry, since he had not eaten in thirty
hours. "But it is more important to rest," he told himself. He continued
to tell himself that, lying in the pawpaw thicket, because the effort of
resting, the need and the haste to rest, made his heart thud the same as
the running had done. It was as though he had forgot how to rest, as
though the six hours were not long enough to do it in, to remember again
how to do it.

As soon as dark came he moved again. He had thought to keep going
steadily and quietly through the night, since there was nowhere for him
to go, but as soon as he moved he began to run at top speed, breasting his
panting chest, his broad-flaring nostrils through the choked and whipping
darkness. He ran for an hour, lost by then, without direction, when suddenly he stopped, and after a time his thudding heart unraveled from the
sound of the drums. By the sound they were not two miles away; he followed the sound until he could smell the smudge fire and taste the acrid

smoke. When he stood among them the drums did not cease; only the headman came to him where he stood in the drifting smudge, panting, his nostrils flaring and pulsing, the hushed glare of his ceaseless eyeballs in his mud-daubed face as though they were worked from lungs.

"We have expected thee," the headman said. "Go, now."

"Go?"

"Eat, and go. The dead may not consort with the living; thou knowest that."

"Yao. I know that." They did not look at one another. The drums had not ceased.

"Wilt thou eat?" the headman said.

"I am not hungry. I caught a rabbit this afternoon, and ate while I lay hidden."

"Take some cooked meat with thee, then."

He accepted the cooked meat, wrapped in leaves, and entered the creek bottom again; after a while the sound of the drums ceased. He walked steadily until daybreak. "I have twelve hours," he said. "Maybe more, since the trail was followed by night." He squatted and ate the meat and wiped his hands on his thighs. Then he rose and removed the dungaree pants and squatted again beside a slough and coated himself with mud—face, arms, body and legs—and squatted again, clasping his knees, his head bowed. When it was light enough to see, he moved back into the swamp and squatted again and went to sleep so. He did not dream at all. It was well that he moved, for, waking suddenly in broad daylight and the high sun, he saw the two Indians. They still carried their neatly rolled trousers; they stood opposite the place where he lay hidden, paunchy, thick, soft-looking, a little ludicrous in their straw hats and shirt tails.

"This is wearying work," one said.

"I'd rather be at home in the shade myself," the other said. "But there is the Man waiting at the door to the earth."

"Yao." They looked quietly about; stooping, one of them removed from his shirt tail a clot of cockleburs. "Damn that Negro," he said.

"Yao. When have they ever been anything but a trial and care to us?"

In the early afternoon, from the top of a tree, the Negro looked down into the plantation. He could see Issetibbeha's body in a hammock between the two trees where the horse and the dog were tethered, and the concourse about the steamboat was filled with wagons and horses and mules, with carts and saddlehorses, while in bright clumps the women and the smaller children and the old men squatted about the long trench where the smoke from the barbecuing meat blew slow and thick. The men and the big boys would all be down there in the creek bottom behind him, on the trail, their Sunday clothes rolled carefully up and wedged into tree crotches. There was a clump of men near the door to the house, to the saloon of the steamboat, though, and he watched them, and after a while he saw them bring Moketubbe out in a litter made of buckskin and persimmon poles; high hidden in his leafed nook the Negro, the quarry, looked quietly down upon his irrevocable doom with an expression as profound as Moketubbe's own. "Yao," he said quietly. "He will go then. That man whose body has been dead for fifteen years, he will go also."

In the middle of the afternoon he came face to face with an Indian. They were both on a footlog across a slough—the Negro gaunt, lean, hard, tireless and desperate; the Indian thick, soft-looking, the apparent embodiment of the ultimate and the supreme reluctance and inertia. The Indian made no move, no sound; he stood on the log and watched the Negro plunge into the slough and swim ashore and crash away into the undergrowth.

Just before sunset he lay behind a down log. Up the log in slow procession moved a line of ants. He caught them and ate them slowly, with a kind of detachment, like that of a dinner guest eating salted nuts from a dish. They too had a salt taste, engendering a salivary reaction out of all proportion. He ate them slowly, watching the unbroken line move up the log and into oblivious doom with a steady and terrific undeviation. He had eaten nothing else all day; in his caked mud mask his eyes rolled in reddened rims. At sunset, creeping along the creek bank toward where he had spotted a frog, a cottonmouth moccasin slashed him suddenly across the forearm with a thick, sluggish blow. It struck clumsily, leaving two long slashes across his arm like two razor slashes, and half sprawled with its own momentum and rage, it appeared for the moment utterly helpless with its own awkwardness and choleric anger. "Olé, Grandfather," the Negro said. He touched its head and watched it slash him again across his arm, and again, with thick, raking, awkward blows. "It's that I do not wish to die," he said. Then he said it again—"It's that I do not wish to die"—in a quiet tone, of slow and low amaze, as though it were something that, until the words had said themselves, he found that he had not known, or had not known the depth and extent of his desire.

V

Moketubbe took the slippers with him. He could not wear them very long while in motion, not even in the litter where he was slung reclining, so they rested upon a square of fawnskin upon his lap—the cracked, frail slippers a little shapeless now, with their scaled patent-leather surface and buckleless tongues and scarlet heels, lying upon the supine, obese shape just barely alive, carried through swamp and brier by swinging relays of men who bore steadily all day long the crime and its object, on the business of the slain. To Moketubbe it must have been as though, himself immortal, he were being carried rapidly through hell by doomed spirits which, alive, had contemplated his disaster, and, dead, were oblivious partners to his damnation.

After resting for a while, the litter propped in the center of the squatting circle and Moketubbe motionless in it, with closed eyes and his face at once peaceful for the instant and filled with inescapable foreknowledge, he could wear the slippers for a while. The stripling put them on him, forcing his big, tender, dropsical feet into them; whereupon into his face came again that expression, tragic, passive, and profoundly attentive, which dyspeptics wear. Then they went on. He made no move, no sound, inert in the rhythmic litter out of some reserve of inertia, or maybe of some kingly virtue such as courage or fortitude. After a time they set the litter down and looked at him, at the yellow face like that of an idol, beaded over with sweat. Then Three Basket or Louis Berry would say: "Take them off. Honor has been served." They would remove the shoes. Moketubbe's face would not alter, but only then would his breathing become perceptible, going in and out of his pale lips with a faint ah-ah-ah sound, and they would squat again while the couriers and the runners came up.

"Not yet?"

"Not yet. He is going east. By sunset he will reach Mouth of Tippah. Then he will turn back. We may take him tomorrow."

"Let us hope so. It will not be too soon."

"Yao. It has been three days now."

"When Doom died, it took only three days."

"But that was an old man. This one is young."

"Yao. A good race. If he is taken tomorrow, I will win a horse."

"May you win it."

"Yao. This work is not pleasant."

That was the day on which the food gave out at the plantation. The guests returned home and came back the next day with more food, enough for a week longer. On that day Issetibbeha began to smell; they could smell him for a long way up and down the bottom when it got hot toward noon and the wind blew. But they didn't capture the Negro on that day, nor on the next. It was about dusk on the sixth day when the couriers came up to the litter; they had found blood. "He has injured himself."

"Not bad, I hope," Basket said. "We cannot send with Issetibbeha one who will be of no service to him."

"Nor whom Issetibbeha himself will have to nurse and care for," Berry said.

"We do not know," the courier said. "He has hidden himself. He has crept back into the swamp. We have left pickets."

They trotted with the litter now. The place where the Negro had crept into the swamp was an hour away. In the hurry and excitement they had forgotten that Moketubbe still wore the slippers; when they reached the place Moketubbe had fainted. They removed the slippers and brought him to.

With dark, they formed a circle about the swamp. They squatted, clouded over with gnats and mosquitoes; the evening star burned low and close down the west, and the constellations began to wheel overhead. "We will give him time," they said. "Tomorrow is just another name for today."

"Yao. Let him have time." Then they ceased, and gazed as one into the darkness where the swamp lay. After a while the noise ceased, and soon the courier came out of the darkness.

"He tried to break out."

"But you turned him back?"

"He turned back. We feared for a moment, the three of us. We could smell him creeping in the darkness, and we could smell something else, which we did not know. That was why we feared, until he told us. He said to slay him there, since it would be dark and he would not have to see the face when it came. But it was not that which we smelled; he told us what it was. A snake had struck him. That was two days ago. The arm swelled, and it smelled bad. But it was not that which we smelled then, because the swelling had gone down and his arm was no larger than that of a child. He showed us. We felt the arm, all of us did; it was no larger than that of a child. He said to give him a hatchet so he could chop the arm off. But tomorrow is today also."

"Yao. Tomorrow is today."

"We feared for a while. Then he went back into the swamp."

"That is good."

"Yao. We feared. Shall I tell the Man?"

"I will see," Basket said. He went away. The courier squatted, telling again about the Negro. Basket returned. "The Man says that it is good. Return to your post."

The courier crept away. They squatted about the litter; now and then they slept. Sometime after midnight the Negro waked them. He began to shout and talk to himself, his voice coming sharp and sudden out of the darkness, then he fell silent. Dawn came; a white crane flapped slowly across the jonquil sky. Basket was awake. "Let us go now," he said. "It is today."

Two Indians entered the swamp, their movements noisy. Before they reached the Negro they stopped, because he began to sing. They could see him, naked and mud-caked, sitting on a log, singing. They squatted silently a short distance away, until he finished. He was chanting something in his own language, his face lifted to the rising sun. His voice was clear, full, with a quality wild and sad. "Let him have time," the Indians said, squatting, patient, waiting. He ceased and they approached. He looked back and up at them through the cracked mud mask. His eyes were bloodshot, his lips cracked upon his square short teeth. The mask of mud appeared to be loose on his face, as if he might have lost flesh since he put it there; he held his left arm close to his breast. From the elbow down it was caked and shapeless with black mud. They could smell him, a rank smell. He watched them quietly until one touched him on the arm. "Come," the Indian said. "You ran well. Do not be ashamed."

VI

As they neared the plantation in the tainted bright morning, the Negro's eyes began to roll a little, like those of a horse. The smoke from the cooking pit blew low along the earth and upon the squatting and waiting guests about the yard and upon the steamboat deck, in their bright, stiff, harsh finery; the women, the children, the old men. They had sent couriers along the bottom, and another on ahead, and Issetibbeha's body had already been removed to where the grave waited, along with the horse and the dog, though they could still smell him in death about the house where he had lived in life. The guests were beginning to move toward the grave when the bearers of Moketubbe's litter mounted the slope.

The Negro was the tallest there, his high, close, mud-caked head looming above them all. He was breathing hard, as though the desperate effort of the six suspended and desperate days had capitulated upon him at once; although they walked slowly, his naked scarred chest rose and fell above the close-clutched left arm. He looked this way and that continuously, as if he were not seeing, as though sight never quite caught up with the looking. His mouth was open a little upon his big white teeth; he began to pant. The already moving guests halted, pausing, looking back, some with pieces of meat in their hands, as the Negro looked about at their faces with his wild, restrained, unceasing eyes.

"Will you eat first?" Basket said. He had to say it twice.

"Yes," the Negro said. "That's it. I want to eat."

The throng had begun to press back toward the center; the word passed to the outermost: "He will eat first."

They reached the steamboat. "Sit down," Basket said. The Negro sat on the edge of the deck. He was still panting, his chest rising and falling, his head ceaseless with its white eyeballs, turning from side to side. It was as if the inability to see came from within, from hopelessness, not from absence of vision. They brought food and watched quietly as he tried to eat it. He put the food into his mouth and chewed it, but chewing, the half-masticated matter began to emerge from the corners of his mouth and to drool down his chin, onto his chest, and after a while he stopped chewing and sat there, naked, covered with dried mud, the plate on his knees, and his mouth filled with a mass of chewed food, open, his eyes wide and unceasing, panting and panting. They watched him, patient, implacable, waiting.

"Come," Basket said at last.

"It's water I want," the Negro said. "I want water."

The well was a little way down the slope toward the quarters. The slope lay dappled with the shadows of noon, of that peaceful hour when, Issetibbeha napping in his chair and waiting for the noon meal and the long afternoon to sleep in, the Negro, the body servant, would be free. He would sit in the kitchen door then, talking with the women that prepared the food. Beyond the kitchen the lane between the quarters would be quiet, peaceful, with the women talking to one another across the lane and the smoke of the dinner fires blowing upon the pickaninnies like ebony toys in the dust.

"Come," Basket said.

The Negro walked among them, taller than any. The guests were moving on toward where Issetibbeha and the horse and the dog waited. The Negro walked with his high ceaseless head, his panting chest. "Come," Basket said. "You wanted water."

"Yes," the Negro said. "Yes." He looked back at the house, then down to the quarters, where today no fire burned, no face showed in any door, no pickaninny in the dust, panting. "It struck me here, raking me across this arm; once, twice, three times. I said, 'Olé, Grandfather.'"

"Come now," Basket said. The Negro was still going through the motion of walking, his knee action high, his head high, as though he were on a treadmill. His eyeballs had a wild, restrained glare, like those of a horse. "You wanted water," Basket said. "Here it is."

There was a gourd in the well. They dipped it full and gave it to the Negro, and they watched him try to drink. His eyes had not ceased rolling as he tilted the gourd slowly against his caked face. They could watch his throat working and the bright water cascading from either side of the gourd, down his chin and breast. Then the water stopped. "Come," Basket said.

"Wait," the Negro said. He dipped the gourd again and tilted it against his face, beneath his ceaseless eyes. Again they watched his throat working and the unswallowed water sheathing broken and myriad down his chin, channeling his caked chest. They waited, patient, grave, decorous, implacable; clansman and guest and kin. Then the water ceased, though still the empty gourd tilted higher and higher, and still his black throat aped the vain motion of his frustrated swallowing. A piece of water-loosened mud carried away from his chest and broke at his muddy feet, and in the empty gourd they could hear his breath: ah-ah-ah.

"Come," Basket said, taking the gourd from the Negro and hanging it back in the well.

COMMENT

Like London, Faulkner constructs his story around the elemental conflict of man against man (and also man against nature, including at least one animal), but unlike London he makes his story more than a simple action. The reader is interested in more than the question: Will the Negro escape or will the Indians capture him? Are we really ever in doubt about this question in "Red Leaves"? Fatality, emphasized by the recurrence of the word "doom," pervades the atmosphere, and we soon feel certain of the inevitable end of the hunt. Certainly the hunt holds our interest, but the elements in conflict are not balanced evenly enough to arouse real doubt and to tempt the reader to sneak a glance at the last page.

Faulkner builds his story so that interest focuses not on the outcome of the chase but on the Negro's actions and reactions, on the values and limitations of unquestioning adherence to tradition, and on the unusual treatment of familiar abstractions such as pride and honor. Consider, for instance, the honor sought by Moketubbe, who painfully forces his "big, tender, dropsical feet" into the red-heeled slippers, and the honor achieved by the Negro, who when he walks among the Indians is "taller than any." The one is comic, the other heroic and yet realistic, since the Negro does not face death stoically, romantically, but in dumbstruck, hypnotized terror. What heroism he has is accorded him by his captors: "You ran well. Do not be ashamed."

Another important theme is the contrast between past and present, the traditional and the modern. The central action is an attempt to fulfill an ancient tradition, the burial of a dead king's servants and animals with his body; the conflict arises because the Negro resists. The past-present theme concerns the decadence of the old order, tainted by modern softness and corruption: the steamboat, the girandoles, and the gilt bed have encroached on the tribal land; the trip to Paris and the red-heeled slippers have introduced artificial concepts and dangerously alluring symbols into the lives of these "noble savages"; even the rat has been "reft of its inherent cunning of limb and eye" by civilization. The old, innocent Adamic world in which "man was not made to sweat" and "where deer grazed like domestic cattle" has been ruined since white men "foisted their Negroes" upon the Indians. The Negroes are "savages," "without honor and without decorum," and they "cannot be expected to regard usage." Slavery and sweat have destroyed Eden. The Indians' attempts to maintain some semblance of tradition and established usage are constantly thwarted by the Negroes, who try to avoid playing their assigned part in the burial ritual. But at least the formula for royal descent (the King is dead; long live the King) is still intact:

> "Yao. Man must die."
> "Yao. Let him; there is still the Man."

"Red Leaves" is packed with implications pointed up by irony, often humorous, as in the treatment of cannibalism, racial supremacy, the economic and moral complexities of slavery, the "Negro question," segregation, and disengagement (Basket and Berry refusing to "think about" what may have happened to Issetibbeha).

Finally, every chase story, by the very fact that the hunted man or animal tries to escape capture and death, implies something about the value of life, of simply staying alive. But Faulkner reaffirms this truism by making the quarry one of a group of slaves, "like horses and dogs . . . like nothing in this sensible world." And this Negro slave, uprooted from his racial past and staring into a blank future, acting by animal instinct, trying to explain to himself his futile running, says, " 'It's that I do not wish to die'— in a quiet tone, of slow and low amaze, as though it were something that, until the words had said themselves, he found that he had not known, or had not known the depth and extent of his desire." "Red Leaves" is an action story of tragic transcendence; there is no sentimental pathos as in "The White Silence" when Mason moans about "flesh of my flesh." Further, the ritual basis of the action draws form and meaning from a pattern central to human experience, the myth celebrated from antiquity of the death and rebirth of the god-king. It is an instance of how a pattern from myth is used in modern literature to give form and meaning to material; so Joyce's *Ulysses* and, in this collection, "Powerhouse" and "Death in Venice."

QUESTIONS ON ACTION

1. Is Faulkner's language at odds with his subject matter, as, we have noted, Jack London's is? Is it the language of the "ideal" objective story-teller? Does he interpret events for the reader? How inharmonious with the tone of the story are figures of speech like "the whispering arpeggios of rat feet," "the gutted windows . . . like cataracted eyes," and the comparison of the Negro eating ants to "a dinner guest eating salted nuts from a dish"?

2. Why does Faulkner supply so much historical background in Section II? Is it superfluous; does it slow down the action without sufficient reason? Does it establish atmosphere? enlarge theme? Could a "pure" action story afford to include so much exposition?

3. If the lack of an ordinary name ("Malemute Kid") is often the case with the mythical hero, does the lack of more specific identification raise "the Negro" to the mythical level?

4. The thematic material in "The White Silence" seems irrelevant philosophical padding intended to disguise the bare bones of action. Does the thematic material in "Red Leaves" similarly break the back of the narrative or is it integral to the story?

OTHER CONSIDERATIONS

1. The tension between descriptive language and its subject can add a new dimension of satire, parody, or irony. What effect does Faulkner achieve by describing the expression on Moketubbe's face as "tragic, passive, and profoundly attentive" when the expression is actually one of near-unconsciousness caused by the Indian's fat feet being squeezed into a pair of tiny slippers? Notice that the narrator *seems* to offer us a choice of interpretations of Moketubbe's uncomplaining silence: "some reserve of inertia, or maybe of some kingly virtue such as courage or fortitude."

2. Faulkner often depicts man's closeness to nature as an ideal state and his separation or estrangement from nature as a loss of primal virtues. How can this concept be applied to the scene in which the Negro, slashed by the snake, greets it with "Olé, Grandfather"? Is this a scene of identification with the snake? of reconciliation with nature? Does this act set the Negro apart from the Indians or link him more closely to them?

3. This story contains many religious allusions and Biblical echoes: "He whom we seek is gone?"; "He has hidden himself"; "He showed us. We felt the arm, all of us did"; "It's water I want. . . . I want water." Do these echoes deliberately stir up the Christian myth, and, if so, to what effect? Are there other consistent parallels in the story?

4. Account for Faulkner's inclusion of the following details:

(a) Three Basket's admission that he had "eaten of" Negro flesh when he was young.

(b) The fan-wielding stripling's cynical attitude.

(c) The Negro's detailed memory of the slave-ship.

(d) The enameled snuffbox clamped through Basket's ear.

(e) The Indians' courteous treatment of the slave in Section VI.

(f) The contents of the fiber bag about the neck of the fourteen-year-old drum-guardian and of the amulet about the hips of the hunted Negro.

5. When asked about the title of this story, Faulkner once said that it "referred to the Indian. It was the deciduation of Nature which no one could stop that had suffocated, smothered, destroyed the Negro." Does this seem to you an adequate answer? Do you detect other relationships between the title and the story itself?

6. Compare the handling of myth in "Red Leaves" with that in "Death in Venice," "Grace," "Powerhouse," and "The Silence of the Valley."

CHARACTER

Up to this point we have distinguished between two kinds of action stories. The first appealed to the reader who wanted a narrative that would engross him with little regard for meaning; the second appealed to the reader who also wanted an engrossing narrative, but with something more, some meaning. Trivial stories are demoralizing after a while. The rest of this anthology is in one sense designed to satisfy some of the other interests of the mature reader.

Character is the element with the largest interest for most of us. This is in good measure owing to the particularly modern preoccupation with the self, reflected historically in the Renaissance and the Reformation, in romanticism, and, more recently, in explorations like depth psychology and existentialism. The reader will see that many stories, such as "The Artificial Nigger," "Dawn," and "Death in Venice," dramatize the discovery of the self. But we are naturally and immediately interested in all kinds of people: neurotic, wholesome; cruel, kind; Yankees, Southerners, Russian peasants, Negro slaves, blonde waitresses, fur-trappers, and gangsters. Although these are general categories, they help us to know people by establishing their contexts. We are all included in any number of types or categories. A character might be an engineering student, a Baptist, a Chicagoan, a folk-rock fan, an extrovert, and an only child of a middle-class Republican family. These categories establish a context by which the reader knows something about the character in advance. The temptation is to present a stereotype: the mean aunt, the kindly uncle, the crusty old teacher, the demagogic senator. Jack London, having described Ruth as an Indian woman in Alaska, gives her the predictable stereotyped qualities of passivity, patience, fortitude, "a great love for her white lord," childlike wonder, manlike strength and courage, and an inability to comprehend anything but "macaronic jargon" and sign language. F. Scott Fitzgerald's dictum is sound: "Begin with an individual, and before you know it you find that you have created a type; begin with a type, and you find that you have created—nothing." [1] Fitzgerald was himself notable for creating individuals who yet were types of their age.

An individual character may be presented, first, by *exposition*, a straightforward account through which we are given necessary informa-

[1] From "The Rich Boy," in *All the Sad Young Men*, by F. Scott Fitzgerald, copyright 1926 by Charles Scribner's Sons, reprinted by permission of Charles Scribner's Sons, New York.

tion. Mere assertion is often ineffective, as when London declares that Malemute Kid was "no tyro in the stern sorrows of the Northland." Expository matter, avoiding a mere report of data, should bear on meaning and set the tone. For example, in "Madame Tellier's Excursion" de Maupassant says of Madame Tellier's social background, "Madame, who came of a respectable family of peasant proprietors in the department of the Eure, had taken up her profession, just as she would have become a milliner or dressmaker." De Maupassant establishes an ironic tone by juxtaposing a traditionally respectable social background with the novel respectability of Madame Tellier's present profession. By placing the background in the subordinate clause, he casually understates the humor.

Contemporary writers usually present expository matter dramatically through the action, as in "Red Leaves." Although for instructional purposes we have distinguished between stories of action and of character, we do not at all mean that character is different from action. On the contrary: it is a truism that character is action and action, character. Action includes not only overt events but also a person's dreams, daydreams, gestures, manner of walking and breathing, and particularly his thoughts and speech, with their special idiom and rhythm. The trick, of course, is to make each action register vividly as a quality of the man. "Red Leaves" makes vivid how the Negro breathes and sweats, how he walks among the Indians, his reaction to the snake's bite, and his last efforts to chew and drink. Action is also desirable for revealing character because it is concrete as well as dramatic. The concrete event affects us more than abstract analysis can, for it is an enduring image. After all the analysis, it remains a mystery, as profound as the mystery of the concrete universe. And as action is the principal way of revealing character, so *contrasts* and *similarities* are the principal ways of defining it; for example, we know Malemute Kid better through his differences from Mason. This method of defining character is shown in considerable detail in our analysis of "Gusev."

The foregoing discussion assumes a stability in character that has of late years become difficult to accept. D. H. Lawrence argued that the concept of the "old, stable ego" was no longer valid; before him Dostoyevsky, Nietzsche, and others had demonstrated the contradictory nature of the self; and Freud had shown the conflicts between the rational, social self and the unconscious self. It is true that man has always been aware of his contradictions; still, our awareness today seems more radical, rooted as it is in the general breakdown of those traditional religious, economic, political, and social structures that once integrated a person in his culture despite his self-doubts.

The present breakdown has led to what is commonly known as a crisis in identity. Although the old hero may still be found in Westerns, the typical modern hero—more accurately, perhaps, the un-hero or anti-hero —does not know with the old certainty who he is, what he should be, how he should act. He has become problematic, alienated, and increasingly estranged from the rest of the world. We continue to identify ourselves as, for example, Protestant, middle-class, suburban, student, but these labels do not seem as meaningful, hence as forceful, as they once did. Everything seems transient: the face of a city changes in a generation; social classes are fluid; and their once clearly distinct ways or manners are less obvious. At the mercy of movies, television, and advertising, manners have largely dissolved into an undefined middle that changes regularly with each new fad in speech, clothing, or dance. Rich and poor speak pretty much alike, drive the same cars, dress alike, practice the same diluted and socially-oriented religion. In "Grace" we have a parody of Catholicism, a witness to the absence of religion as a force in the formation of character. Furthermore, we have no relation to nature, to our own bodies, as in the case of Bertie in "The Blind Man" (see our comments). In "Red Leaves" the character of the Indian, rooted in nature, is corrupted by the incursions of civilization; the story is also an analogue of what has happened to the white man.

The breakdown of traditional structures and values has led to various attempts to redefine and reaffirm the self, of which existentialism is the most familiar. In "The Blind Man" the self is maintained through a reaffirmation of nature over civilization. An extreme instance of the problem of the self appears in "A Clean, Well-Lighted Place," where no structures and values exist, not even as forces to resist. There is only an old man, without a name, confronting nothingness. "It was all a nothing and a man was nothing too." Yet he is at least *conscious* of his nothingness, unlike the equally old middle-class couple in "The Golden Honeymoon," who *are* nothing because they are not really conscious. But the old waiter's consciousness is all he has. He desperately wants some kind of structure, but all he can ask for with any integrity is freedom from abstract illusions of order. He turns to what is *there,* the minimal order of a clean, well-lighted place. In this story the self has shifted from the social preoccupations of "The Golden Honeymoon" and "Grace" to the existential preoccupations of a person in his loneliness. In "The Legend of St. Julian the Hospitaller" and "The Judgment" the same preoccupation is present, but in terms of the relation of man to God.

But a story is not a mere character sketch; it presents an action that generally results in a revelation or a transformation of character or both. The revelation may be of the character's innocence, as in "The Tree of Knowledge" (see our comments), where Peter Brench learns he has been protecting himself from a critical fact. In stories of revelation the character tends to be diminished; in stories of transformation, enlarged. The moment of transformation is often dramatized by a heightened style, as in "The Artificial Nigger" (see our comments) and "How It Was Done in Odessa" (see our comments), or by a symbolic image, as in "The Town Poor" and "Gusev" (see our comments).

The two stories that follow illustrate the relationship of character to different kinds of action: in "How It Was Done in Odessa" character is developed largely by outward action; in "Gusev," by inward action such as meditation, dreams, fantasy, and memory.

How It Was Done
in Odessa

Isaac Babel

It was I that began.

"Reb* Arye-Leib," I said to the old man, "let us talk of Benya Krik. Let us talk of his thunderclap beginning and his terrible end. Three black shadows block up the path of my imagination. Here is the one-eyed Ephraim Rook. The russet steel of his actions, can it really not bear comparison with the strength of the King? Here is Nick Pakovsky. The simple-minded fury of that man held all that was necessary for him to wield power. And did not Haim Drong know how to distinguish the brilliance of the rising star? Why then did Benya Krik alone climb to the top of the rope ladder, while all the rest hung swaying on the lower rungs?"

Reb Arye-Leib was silent, sitting on the cemetery wall. Before us stretched the green stillness of the graves. A man who thirsts for an answer must stock himself with patience. A man possessing knowledge is suited by dignity. For this reason Reb Arye-Leib was silent, sitting on the cemetery wall. Finally he said:

"Why he? Why not they, you wish to know? Then see here, forget for a while that you have spectacles on your nose and autumn in your heart. Cease playing the rowdy at your desk and stammering while others are about. Imagine for a moment that you play the rowdy in public places and stammer on paper. You are a tiger, you are a lion, you are a cat. You can spend the night with a Russian woman, and satisfy her. You are twenty-five. If rings were fastened to heaven and earth, you would grasp them and draw heaven and earth together. And your father is Mendel Krik the drayman. What does such a father think about? He thinks about drinking a good glass of vodka, of smashing somebody in the face, of his horses—and nothing more. You want to live, and he makes you die twenty times a day. What would you have done in Benya Krik's place? You would have done nothing. But *he* did something. That's why he's the King, while you thumb your nose in the privy."

He—Benya Krik—went to see Ephraim Rook, who, already in those days looking at the world out of only one eye, was already then what he is now. He said to Ephraim:

"Take me on. I want to moor to your bollard. The bollard I moor to will be the winning one."

*Mister.

Rook asked him:

"Who are you, where do you come from, and what do you use for breath?"

"Give me a try, Ephraim," replied Benya, "and let us stop smearing gruel over a clean table."

"Let us stop smearing gruel," assented Rook. "I'll give you a try."

And the gangsters went into conference to consider the matter of Benya Krik. I wasn't at that conference, but they say that a conference was held. Chairman at that time was Lyovka Bullock.

"What goes on under his hat, under little Benya's hat?" asked the late Bullock.

And the one-eyed Rook gave his opinion:

"Benya says little, but what he says is tasty. He says little, and one would like him to say more."

"If so," exclaimed the late Bullock, "then let's try him on Tartakovsky."

"Let's try him on Tartakovsky," resolved the conference, and all in whom conscience still had lodgings blushed when they heard this decision. Why did they blush? You will learn this if you come where I shall lead you.

We used to call Tartakovsky "Jew-and-a-Half" or "Nine Holdups." "Jew-and-a-Half" he was called because no single Jew could have had so much dash and so much cash as Tartakovsky. He was taller than the tallest cop in Odessa, and weighed more than the fattest of Jewesses. And "Nine Holdups" he was called because the firm of Lyovka Bullock and Co. had made on his office not eight nor yet ten raids, but nine precisely. To the lot of Benya Krik, who was not yet the King, fell the honor of carrying out the tenth raid on Jew-and-a-Half. When Ephraim informed him accordingly, he said "O.K." and went out, banging the door. Why bang the door? You will learn this if you come where I shall lead you.

Tartakovsky has the soul of a murderer, but he is one of us. He originated with us. He is our blood. He is our flesh, as though one momma had born us. Half Odessa serves in his shops. And it was through his own Moldavanka lads that he suffered. Twice they held him for ransom, and once during a pogrom they buried him with a choir. The Sloboda thugs were then beating up the Jews on Bolshaya Arnautskaya. Tartakovsky escaped from them, and on Sofiyskaya met a funeral procession with a choir. He asked:

"Who's that they're burying with a choir?"

The passers-by replied that it was Tartakovsky they were burying. The procession got to the Sloboda Cemetery. Then our chaps produced a machine gun from the coffin and started plastering the Sloboda thugs. But Jew-and-a-Half had not foreseen this. Jew-and-a-Half was scared to death. And what boss would not have been scared in his place?

The tenth raid on a man who has already once been buried was a coarse action. Benya, who was not then the King, understood this better than anyone. But he said "O.K." to Rook, and that day wrote Tartakovsky a letter similar to all letters of this sort:

"Highly respected Ruvim son of Joseph! Be kind enough to place, on Saturday, under the rain barrel, etc. If you refuse, as last time you refused, know that a great disappointment awaits you in your private life. Respects from the Bentzion Krik you know of."

Tartakovsky did not play the sluggard, and replied without delay:

"Benya! If you were a half-wit I should write to you as to a half-wit. But I do not know you as such, and God forfend I ever shall! You, it is evident, want to play the child. Do you really mean you don't know that this year there is such a crop in the Argentine that there's enough to drown in, and we sitting with all our wheat and no customers? And I will tell you, hand on heart, that in my old age I am finding it tedious to swallow so bitter a piece of bread and to experience these unpleasantnesses, having worked all my life as hard as the least of draymen. And what have I from all this endless convict-labor? Ulcers, sores, troubles, and insomnia. Give up this nonsense, Benya. Your friend (much more than you suppose) Ruvim Tartakovsky."

Jew-and-a-Half had done what he could. He had written a letter. But the letter wasn't delivered to the right address. Receiving no reply, Benya waxed wroth. Next day he turned up with four pals at Tartakovsky's office. Four youths in masks and with revolvers bowled into the office.

"Hands up!" they cried, and started waving their pistols about.

"A little more *Sang-frwa*, Solomon," observed Benya to one who was shouting louder than the rest. "Don't make a habit of being nervous on the job." And turning to the clerk, who was white as death and yellow as clay, he asked him:

"Is Jew-and-a-Half on the premises?"

"No, sir," replied the clerk, one Muginstein by name. His first name was Joseph, and he was the bachelor son of Aunt Pesya the poultry-dealer on Seredinskaya Square.

"Well then, who's in charge in the old man's absence?" they started third-degreeing the wretched Muginstein.

"I am," said the clerk, green as green grass.

"Then with God's help open up the safe!" Benya ordered, and the curtain rose on a three-act opera.

The nervous Solomon was packing cash, securities, watches, and monograms in a suitcase; the late Joseph stood before him with his hands in the air, and at that moment Benya was telling anecdotes about Jews.

"Since he's forever playing the Rothschild," Benya was saying of Tartakovsky, "let him burn on a slow fire. Explain this to me, Muginstein, as to a friend: if he receives, as he has, a businesslike letter from me, why shouldn't he take a five-copeck streetcar-ride and come over and see me at my place and drink a glass of vodka with my family and take potluck? What prevented him from opening his heart to me? 'Benya,' he might have said, 'so on and so forth, here's my balance-sheet, gimme a coupla days to draw breath and see how things stand.' What should I have replied? Pig does not see eye to eye with pig, but man with man does. Muginstein, do you catch my drift?"

"I d-do," stuttered Muginstein, but he lied, for he hadn't the remotest idea why Jew-and-a-Half the wealthy and respected should want to take a streetcar-ride to eat a snack with the family of Mendel Krik the drayman.

And meantime misfortune lurked beneath the window like a pauper at daybreak. Misfortune broke noisily into the office. And though on this occasion it bore the shape of the Jew Savka Butsis, this misfortune was as drunk as a water-carrier.

"Ho-hoo-ho," cried the Jew Savka, "forgive me, Benya, I'm late." And he started stamping his feet and waving his arms about. Then he fired, and the bullet landed in Muginstein's belly.

Are words necessary? A man was, and is no more. A harmless bachelor was living his life like a bird on a bough, and had to meet a nonsensical end. There came a Jew looking like a sailor and took a potshot not at some clay pipe or dolly but at a live man. Are words necessary?

"Let's scram," cried Benya, and ran out last. But as he departed he managed to say to Butsis:

"I swear by my mother's grave, Savka, that you will lie next to him . . ."

Now tell me, young master, you who snip coupons on other people's shares, how would you have acted in Benya's place? You don't know how you would have acted. But he knew. That's why he's the King, while you and I are sitting on the wall of the Second Jewish Cemetery and keeping the sun off with our palms.

Aunt Pesya's unfortunate son did not die straightaway. An hour after they had got him to the hospital, Benya appeared there. He asked for the doctor in charge and the nurse to be sent out to him, and said to them, not taking his hands out of his cream pants:

"It is in my interest," he said, "that the patient Joseph Muginstein should recover. Let me introduce myself, just in case: Bentzion Krik. Camphor, air-cushions, a private ward—supply them with liberal hands. Otherwise every Tom, Dick, and Harry of a doctor, even if he's a doctor of philosophy, will get no more than six feet of earth."

But Muginstein died that night. And only then did Jew-and-a-Half raise a stink through all Odessa.

"Where do the police begin," he wailed, "and where does Benya end?"

"The police end where Benya begins," replied sensible folk, but Tartakovsky refused to take the hint, and he lived to see the day when a red automobile with a music box for horn played its first march from the opera *Pagliacci* on Seredinskaya Square. In broad daylight the car flew up to the little house in which Aunt Pesya dwelt.

The automobile cast thunderbolts with its wheels, spat fumes, shone brassily, stank of gasoline, and performed arias on its horn. From the car someone sprang out and passed into the kitchen where little Aunt Pesya was throwing hysterics on the earthen floor. Jew-and-a-Half was sitting in a chair waving his hands about.

"You hooligan!" he cried, perceiving the visitor, "you bandit, may the earth cast you forth! A fine trick you've thought up, killing live people."

"Monsieur Tartakovsky," Benya Krik replied quietly, "it's forty-eight hours now that I've been weeping for the dear departed as for my own brother. But I know that you don't give a damn for my youthful tears. Shame, Monsieur Tartakovsky. In what sort of safe have you locked up your sense of shame? You had the gall to send the mother of our deceased Joseph a hundred paltry roubles. My brains shivered along with my hair when I heard this."

Here Benya paused. He was wearing a chocolate jacket, cream pants, and raspberry boots.

"Ten thousand down," he roared, "ten thousand down and a pension till she dies, and may she live to a hundred and twenty. Otherwise we will depart from this residence, Monsieur Tartakovsky, and we will sit in my limousine."

Then they used bad language at one another hammer and tongs, Jew-and-a-Half and Benya. I wasn't present at this quarrel, but those who were remember it. They compromised on five thousand in cash and fifty roubles a month.

"Aunt Pesya," Benya said to the disheveled old woman who was rolling on the floor, "if you need my life you may have it, but all make mistakes, God included. A terrible mistake has been made, Aunt Pesya. But wasn't it a mistake on the part of God to settle Jews in Russia, for them to be tormented worse than in Hell? How would it hurt if the Jews lived in Switzerland, where they would be surrounded by first-class lakes, mountain air, and nothing but Frenchies? All make mistakes, God not excepted. Listen to me with all your ears, Aunt Pesya. You'll have five thousand down and fifty roubles a month till you croak. Live to a hundred and twenty if you like. Joseph shall have a Number One funeral: six horses like six lions, two carriages with flowers, the choir from the Brody Synagogue. Minkovsky in person will sing at your deceased son's funeral."

And the funeral was performed next morning. Ask the cemetery beggars about that funeral. Ask the shamessim * from the synagogue of the dealers in kosher poultry about it, or the old women from the Second Almshouse. Odessa had never before seen such a funeral, the world will never see such a funeral. On that day the cops wore cotton gloves. In the synagogues, decked with greenstuff and wide open, the electric lights were burning. Black plumes swayed on the white horses harnessed to the hearse. A choir of sixty headed the cortege: a choir of boys, but they sang with the voice of women. The elders of the synagogue of the dealers in kosher poultry helped Aunt Pesya along. Behind the elders walked mem-

*Sextons.

bers of the Association of Jewish Shop Assistants, and behind the Jewish
Shop Assistants walked the lawyers, doctors of medicine, and certified
midwives. On one side of Aunt Pesya were the women who trade in
poultry on the Old Market, and on the other side, draped in orange
shawls, were the honorary dairymaids from Bugayevka. They stamped
their feet like gendarmes parading on a holiday. From their wide hips
wafted the odors of the sea and of milk. And behind them all plodded
Ruvim Tartakovsky's employees. There were a hundred of them, or two
hundred, or two thousand. They wore black frock coats with silk lapels
and new shoes that squeaked like sacked sucking-pigs.

And now I will speak as the Lord God spoke on Mount Sinai from the
Burning Bush. Put my words in your ears. All I saw, I saw with my own
eyes, sitting here on the wall of the Second Cemetery next to Little Lisping Mose and Samson from the undertaker's. I, Arye-Leib, saw this—I,
a proud Jew dwelling by the dead.

The hearse drove up to the cemetery synagogue. The coffin was placed
on the steps. Aunt Pesya was trembling like a little bird. The cantor
crawled out of the carriage and began the service. Sixty singers seconded
him. And at this moment a red automobile flew around the turning. It
played "Laugh, clown" and drew up. People were as silent as the dead.
Silent were the trees, the choir, the beggars. Four men climbed out of the
red car and at a slow pace bore to the hearse a wreath of roses such as was
never seen before. And when the service ended the four men inserted
their steel shoulders beneath the coffin and with burning eyes and swelling
breasts walked side by side with the members of the Association of Jewish
Shop Assistants.

In front walked Benya Krik, whom no one as yet called the King. He
was the first to approach the grave. He climbed the mound of earth and
spread out his arms.

"What have you in mind, young man?" cried Kofman of the Burial
Brotherhood, running over to him.

"I have it in mind to make a funeral oration," replied Benya Krik.

And a funeral oration he made. All who wished listened to it. I listened to it; I, Arye-Leib, and Little Lisping Mose, who was sitting on the
wall beside me.

"Ladies and gentlemen, and dames," said Benya Krik. "Ladies and
gentlemen, and dames," said he, and the sun rose above his head like an
armed sentry. "You have come to pay your last respects to a worthy
laborer who perished for the sake of a copper penny. In my name, and in
the name of all those not here present, I thank you. Ladies and gentlemen! What did our dear Joseph get out of life? Nothing worth mentioning. How did he spend his time? Counting other people's cash. What did
he perish for? He perished for the whole of the working class. There are
people already condemned to death, and there are people who have not
yet begun to live. And lo and behold a bullet flying into a condemned
breast pierces our Joseph, who in his whole life had seen nothing worth
mentioning, and comes out on the other side. There are people who

know how to drink vodka, and there are people who don't know how to drink vodka but drink it all the same. And the first lot, you see, get satisfaction from joy and from sorrow, and the second lot suffer for all those who drink vodka without knowing how to. And so, ladies and gentlemen, and dames, after we have said a prayer for our poor Joseph I will ask you to accompany to his last resting-place one unknown to you but already deceased, one Savka Butsis."

And having finished his oration Benya Krik descended from the mound. No sound came from the people, the trees, or the cemetery beggars. Two gravediggers bore an unpainted coffin to the next grave. The cantor, stammering, finished his prayers. Benya threw in the first spadeful of soil and crossed over to Savka's grave. After him like sheep went all the lawyers, all the ladies with brooches. He made the cantor sing the full funeral service over Savka, and the sixty choirboys seconded the cantor. Savka had never dreamed of having such a funeral—take it from Arye-Leib, an old man who has seen many things.

They say that on that day Jew-and-a-Half decided to shut up shop. I wasn't present. But that neither the cantor, nor the choir, nor the Funeral Brotherhood charged anything for the funeral, this I saw with the eyes of Arye-Leib. Arye-Leib, that's what they call me. And more than that I couldn't see, for the people, creeping quietly at first from Savka's grave, then started running as from a house on fire. They flew off in carriages, in carts, and on foot. And only the four who had driven up in the red automobile also drove off in it. The music box played its march, the car shuddered and was gone.

"A King," said Little Lisping Mose, looking after the car—Little Mose who does me out of the best seats on the wall.

"Now you know all. You know who first uttered the word 'King.' It was Little Mose. You know why he didn't give that name to One-Eyed Rook, or to Crazy Nick. You know all. But what's the use, if you still have spectacles on your nose and autumn in your heart?"

COMMENT

In this story what obviously attracted Babel was Benya Krik, modelled after a real Odessa gangster, because he was a man of action, one who could "play the rowdy in public places." The action is magnificent. It begins with an initiation rite, moves through the complication of the murder and the extraction of the proper compensation for Aunt Pesya, and concludes with the climax of the gaudy funeral and the equally gaudy oration. But the action—his career from initiate to king—is there primarily to reveal Benya's character.

Yet Babel uses other means besides surface action to give density and significance to his characterization. There is, for example, the *perspective* from which the story is told, the recollections of an old man, Reb Arye-Leib. As old people like to do, he sits down one quiet afternoon to talk about Benya with the same awe and admiration that old men in our West once talked about outlaws like Jesse James. Benya is transformed by the folklorist of the Moldavanka from a gangster into a folk hero. Telling the tale through the old man establishes a time perspective. Seen in retrospect, at a distance from the actual event, Benya is naturally magnified in the minds of both teller and audience.

Benya stands out among the other gangsters, even among his superiors. A more important contrast is that between Benya and the first-person narrator, a writer to whom the story is told. It would seem as though the only reason for having a writer as the audience is to indicate how the story was heard and happened to be set down. This indeed gives the subject an air of reality, but this strategy is one of many artifices an author uses to *create,* not reproduce reality. (It is an artifice even when, as in Babel's case, the author heard or witnessed the events he writes about.) A more important reason lies in the writer's relation to Benya. He is an artist, a man of too much thought and imagination and too little action, as we are made to understand when the old man beautifully chides him to "forget for a while that you have spectacles on your nose and autumn in your heart [a passage important enough to be repeated as the closing line]. Cease playing the rowdy at your desk and stammering while others are about." The relation is significant because the artist is another kind of hero, a culture hero (using "culture" in the narrow sense) like Goethe or T. S. Eliot. In the dramatic contrast of two kinds of heroes, one of the folk and one of the cultural elite, one the man of action and the other the man of thought, the man of thought does not come out very well. As Reb Arye-Leib declares, where Benya Krik "did something" about his brutal father, the writer would probably only "thumb [his] nose in the privy." The writer serves as a foil for Benya; the shortcomings of the culture hero magnify the folk hero.

The perspective of the old man, telling the tale in retrospect, and the contrast with the writer are both realized through the narrative frame. From this we can see that the author's narrative strategy, the frame, is not a technical "gimmick," but integral to the meaning of the story. It is one of the ways the total meaning is expressed.

Although the story is told by the old folklorist, it is not a spontaneous, naive folk tale, the kind passed down orally from generation to generation, familiar in the legends of Paul Bunyan and Davy Crockett. It is instead a sophisticated story, a literary folk tale, as Babel's strategies on the contrast in heroes and the narrative frame show. Further, though the story is made up of audacious, fabulous actions, it does not stop with a simple attitude towards the folk hero. Babel admires Benya, but he cannot help smiling at him too. The comic—incongruous, absurd, or excessively different from the normal—is inherent in the fabulous, in the difference between our normal ways and those of the hero. Babel works these differences thoroughly, as in Benya's absurd car and clothes, and his sensitivity to justice, honor, and death—he weeps forty-eight hours for "the dear departed." And through this complication of attitude—a combination of admiration and affectionate, comic irony—Babel gives further density to his character.

The phrase "the dear departed" leads directly to the question of Benya's style. The dictum that style is the man is clearly illustrated not only in the sure flourish of Benya's actions, unquestionably those of a leader, but also in his rampant language. It is here, in the handling of the delicate instrument of language, that a writer encounters one of his most severe artistic tests, and it is precisely here that Babel manages his most brilliant delineation of Benya's comic-fabulous character. "The dear departed," a stilted and euphemistic phrase, is comic since the gangster Benya thinks it elegant. It is also comic as funeral cant, as is, in the Communist milieu, the claim, "He perished for the whole of the working class," comic too in its irrelevance. But Benya's magnificence transforms the banal. His literary bravura, comic yet marvelous in its sense and nonsense, exhibits a range of styles, formal and colloquial; a range of diction, Latinate and Anglo-Saxon in Morison's translation; and the equipment of the public speaker: parallelisms, inversions of syntax, rhetorical questions, banal appeals to sentiment, philosophy, and the like. It is a rhetorical traffic jam, a grand, kingly indifference to relevance or logic. Benya's verbal style is another reflection of both his fabulous and comic aspects, another way of realizing his character. Babel's achievement is this: he renders the fabulous in complex as well as simple terms.

QUESTIONS ON CHARACTER

1. How extensive is the evidence of Benya's comic side? Consider, for example, the style of his letter to Tartakovsky and his business methods.

2. How do Babel's many metaphors for Benya affect our sense of him? Should they be taken ambiguously, that is, somewhat humorously?

3. In what other ways does Babel reveal character? Are there any mythological allusions?

4. Before we see Benya in action we have a strong impression of him through exposition. Is the exposition abstract or concrete? Is it dramatized or merely stated?

5. The story is of a test of character in the tradition of archetypal rites of passage, the initiation of a young man into adult society. The other gangsters "try" Benya on Tartakovsky. Compare "Gimpel the Fool," "Young Goodman Brown," "Wounds," and "Twilight and Nocturnal Storm" as stories of initiation.

OTHER CONSIDERATIONS

1. To test and expand our definition of the comic, apply it to stories usually not considered comic like "The Judgment" and "Red Leaves."

2. If you haven't already, compare the handling of glamor, sex, and violence in Babel's myth of a gangster and that in Hollywood and cheap fiction. Newspapers, magazines, and textbooks stress psychological and sociological factors. Do these play a role in Babel?

3. Since both Babel and Hollywood make heroes of gangsters, are they immoral? Consider the question of artistic morality, of fidelity to one's conception.

4. What is the effect of the narrator's setting?

5. Compare Benya's confidence about the uses of language with the old man's attitude in "A Clean, Well-Lighted Place." Compare it also with Chekhov's attitude towards Pavel's rhetoric in "Gusev" (see our comments).

6. Underlying the story is another archetypal pattern, that of death and rebirth (see our introduction to the section "Symbolism"): Lyovka Bullock was Chairman; Benya becomes the new King. Consider the variants on this pattern in "Red Leaves" (see our comments) and "Powerhouse." Is the pattern fulfilled in "Powerhouse"?

Gusev

Anton Chekhov ℰ

It is already dark, it will soon be night.

Gusev, a discharged private, half rises in his bunk and says in a low voice:

"Do you hear me, Pavel Ivanych? A soldier in Suchan was telling me: while they were sailing, their ship bumped into a big fish and smashed a hole in its bottom."

The individual of uncertain social status whom he is addressing, and whom everyone in the ship infirmary calls Pavel Ivanych, is silent as though he hasn't heard.

And again all is still. The wind is flirting with the rigging, the screw is throbbing, the waves are lashing, the bunks creak, but the ear has long since become used to these sounds, and everything around seems to slumber in silence. It is dull. The three invalids—two soldiers and a sailor—who were playing cards all day are dozing and talking deliriously.

The ship is apparently beginning to roll. The bunk slowly rises and falls under Gusev as though it were breathing, and this occurs once, twice, three times . . . Something hits the floor with a clang: a jug must have dropped.

"The wind has broken loose from its chain," says Gusev, straining his ears.

This time Pavel Ivanych coughs and says irritably:

"One minute a vessel bumps into a fish, the next the wind breaks loose from its chain . . . Is the wind a beast that it breaks loose from its chain?"

"That's what Christian folks say."

"They are as ignorant as you . . . They say all sorts of things. One must have one's head on one's shoulders and reason it out. You have no sense."

Pavel Ivanych is subject to seasickness. When the sea is rough he is usually out of sorts, and the merest trifle irritates him. In Gusev's opinion there is absolutely nothing to be irritated about. What is there that is strange or out of the way about that fish, for instance, or about the wind breaking loose from its chain? Suppose the fish were as big as the mountain and its back as hard as a sturgeon's, and supposing, too, that over yonder at the end of the world stood great stone walls and the fierce winds were chained up to the walls. If they haven't broken loose, why then do they rush all over the sea like madmen and strain like hounds tugging at their leash? If they are not chained up what becomes of them when it is calm?

Gusev ponders for a long time about fishes as big as a mountain and about stout, rusty chains. Then he begins to feel bored and falls to thinking about his home, to which he is returning after five years' service in the Far East. He pictures an immense pond covered with drifts. On one side of the pond is the brick-colored building of the pottery with a tall chimney and clouds of black smoke; on the other side is a village. His brother Alexey drives out of the fifth yard from the end in a sleigh; behind him sits his little son Vanka in big felt boots, and his little girl Akulka also wearing felt boots. Alexey has had a drop, Vanka is laughing, Akulka's face cannot be seen, she is muffled up.

"If he doesn't look out, he will have the children frostbitten," Gusev reflects. "Lord send them sense that they may honor their parents and not be any wiser than their father and mother."

"They need new soles," a delirious sailor says in a bass voice. "Yes, yes!"

Gusev's thoughts abruptly break off and suddenly without rhyme or reason the pond is replaced by a huge bull's head without eyes, and the horse and sleigh are no longer going straight ahead but are whirling round and round, wrapped in black smoke. But still he is glad he has had a glimpse of his people. In fact, he is breathless with joy, and his whole body, down to his fingertips, tingles with it. "Thanks be to God we have seen each other again," he mutters deliriously, but at once opens his eyes and looks for water in the dark.

He drinks and lies down, and again the sleigh is gliding along, then again there is the bull's head without eyes, smoke, clouds . . . And so it goes till daybreak.

II

A blue circle is the first thing to become visible in the darkness—it is the porthole; then, little by little, Gusev makes out the man in the next bunk, Pavel Ivanych. The man sleeps sitting up, as he cannot breathe lying down. His face is gray, his nose long and sharp, his eyes look huge because he is terribly emaciated, his temples are sunken, his beard skimpy, his hair long. His face does not reveal his social status: you cannot tell whether he is a gentleman, a merchant, or a peasant. Judging from his expression and his long hair, he may be an assiduous churchgoer or a lay brother, but his manner of speaking does not seem to be that of a monk. He is utterly worn out by his cough, by the stifling heat, his illness, and he breathes with difficulty, moving his parched lips. Noticing that Gusev is looking at him he turns his face toward him and says:

"I begin to guess . . . Yes, I understand it all perfectly now."

"What do you understand, Pavel Ivanych?"

"Here's how it is . . . It has always seemed strange to me that terribly ill as you fellows are, you should be on a steamer where the stifling air, the heavy seas, in fact everything, threatens you with death; but now it is all clear to me . . . Yes . . . The doctors put you on the steamer to get rid of you. They got tired of bothering with you, cattle . . . You don't pay them any money, you are a nuisance, and you spoil their statistics with your deaths . . . So, of course, you are just cattle. And it's not hard to get rid of you . . . All that's necessary is, in the first place, to have no conscience or humanity, and, secondly, to deceive the ship authorities. The first requirement need hardly be given a thought—in that respect we are virtuosos, and as for the second condition, it can always be fulfilled with a little practice. In a crowd of four hundred healthy soldiers and sailors, five sick ones are not conspicuous; well, they got you all onto the steamer, mixed you with the healthy ones, hurriedly counted you over, and in the confusion nothing untoward was noticed, and when the steamer was on the way, people discovered that there were paralytics and consumptives on their last legs lying about the deck . . ."

Gusev does not understand Pavel Ivanych; thinking that he is being reprimanded, he says in self-justification:

"I lay on the deck because I was so sick; when we were being unloaded from the barge onto the steamer, I caught a bad chill."

"It's revolting," Pavel Ivanych continues. "The main thing is, they know perfectly well that you can't stand the long journey and yet they put you here. Suppose you last as far as the Indian Ocean, and then what? It's horrible to think of . . . And that's the gratitude for your faithful, irreproachable service!"

Pavel Ivanych's eyes flash with anger. He frowns fastidiously and says, gasping for breath, "Those are the people who ought to be given a drubbing in the newspapers till the feathers fly in all directions."

The two sick soldiers and the sailor have waked up and are already playing cards. The sailor is half reclining in his bunk, the soldiers are sitting near by on the floor in most uncomfortable positions. One of the soldiers has his right arm bandaged and his wrist is heavily swathed in wrappings that look like a cap, so that he holds his cards under his right arm or in the crook of his elbow while he plays with his left. The ship is rolling heavily. It is impossible to stand up, or have tea, or take medicine.

"Were you an orderly?" Pavel Ivanych asks Gusev.

"Yes, sir, an orderly."

"My God, my God!" says Pavel Ivanych and shakes his head sadly. "To tear a man from his home, drag him a distance of ten thousand miles, then wear him out till he gets consumption and . . . and what is it all for, one asks? To turn him into an orderly for some Captain Kopeykin or Midshipman Dyrka! How reasonable!"

"It's not hard work, Pavel Ivanych. You get up in the morning and polish the boots, start the samovars going, tidy the rooms, and then you have nothing more to do. The lieutenant drafts plans all day, and if you like, you can say your prayers, or read a book or go out on the street. God grant everyone such a life."

"Yes, very good! The lieutenant drafts plans all day long, and you sit in the kitchen and long for home . . . Plans, indeed! . . . It's not plans that matter but human life. You have only one life to live and it mustn't be wronged."

"Of course, Pavel Ivanych, a bad man gets no break anywhere, either at home or in the service, but if you live as you ought and obey orders, who will want to wrong you? The officers are educated gentlemen, they understand . . . In five years I have never once been in the guard house, and I was struck, if I remember right, only once."

"What for?"

"For fighting. I have a heavy hand, Pavel Ivanych. Four Chinks came into our yard; they were bringing firewood or something, I forget. Well, I was bored and I knocked them about a bit, the nose of one of them, damn him, began bleeding . . . The lieutenant saw it all through the window, got angry, and boxed me on the ear."

"You are a poor, foolish fellow . . ." whispers Pavel Ivanych. "You don't understand anything."

He is utterly exhausted by the rolling of the ship and shuts his eyes; now his head drops back, now it sinks forward on his chest. Several times he tries to lie down but nothing comes of it: he finds it difficult to breathe.

"And what did you beat up the four Chinks for?" he asks after a while.

"Oh, just like that. They came into the yard and I hit them."

There is silence . . . The card-players play for two hours, eagerly, swearing sometimes, but the rolling and pitching of the ship overcomes them, too; they throw aside the cards and lie down. Again Gusev has a vision: the big pond, the pottery, the village . . . Once more the sleigh is gliding along, once more Vanka is laughing and Akulka, the silly thing, throws open her fur coat and thrusts out her feet, as much as to say: "Look, good people, my felt boots are not like Vanka's, they're new ones."

"Going on six, and she has no sense yet," Gusev mutters in his delirium. "Instead of showing off your boots you had better come and get your soldier uncle a drink. I'll give you a present."

And here is Andron with a flintlock on his shoulder, carrying a hare he has killed, and behind him is the decrepit old Jew Isaychik, who offers him a piece of soap in exchange for the hare; and here is the black calf in the entry, and Domna sewing a shirt and crying about something, and then again the bull's head without eyes, black smoke . . .

Someone shouts overhead, several sailors run by; it seems that something bulky is being dragged over the deck, something falls with a crash. Again some people run by . . . Has there been an accident? Gusev raises his head, listens, and sees that the two soldiers and the sailor are playing cards again; Pavel Ivanych is sitting up and moving his lips. It is stifling, you haven't the strength to breathe, you are thirsty, the water is warm, disgusting. The ship is still rolling and pitching.

Suddenly something strange happens to one of the soldiers playing cards. He calls hearts diamonds, gets muddled over his score, and drops his cards, then with a frightened, foolish smile looks round at all of them.

"I shan't be a minute, fellows . . ." he says, and lies down on the floor. Everybody is nonplussed. They call to him, he does not answer.

"Stepan, maybe you are feeling bad, eh?" the soldier with the bandaged arm asks him. "Perhaps we had better call the priest, eh?"

"Have a drink of water, Stepan . . ." says the sailor. "Here, brother, drink."

"Why are you knocking the jug against his teeth?" says Gusev angrily. "Don't you see, you cabbage-head?"

"What?"

"What?" Gusev mimicks him. "There is no breath in him, he's dead! That's what! Such stupid people, Lord God!"

III

The ship has stopped rolling and Pavel Ivanych is cheerful. He is no longer cross. His face wears a boastful, challenging, mocking expression. It is as though he wants to say: "Yes, right away I'll tell you something that will make you burst with laughter." The round porthole is open and a soft breeze is blowing on Pavel Ivanych. There is a sound of voices, the splash of oars in the water . . . Just under the porthole someone is droning in a thin, disgusting voice; must be a Chinaman singing.

"Here we are in the harbor," says Pavel Ivanych with a mocking smile. "Only another month or so and we shall be in Russia. M'yes, messieurs of the armed forces! I'll arrive in Odessa and from there go straight to Kharkov. In Kharkov I have a friend, a man of letters. I'll go to him and say, 'Come, brother, put aside your vile subjects, women's amours and the beauties of Nature, and show up the two-legged vermin . . . There's a subject for you.' "

For a while he reflects, then says:

"Gusev, do you know how I tricked them?"

"Tricked who, Pavel Ivanych?"

"Why, these people . . . You understand, on this steamer there is only a first class and a third class, and they only allow peasants, that is, the common herd, to go in the third. If you have got a jacket on and even at a distance look like a gentleman or a bourgeois, you have to go first class, if you please. You must fork out five hundred rubles if it kills you. 'Why do you have such a regulation?' I ask them. 'Do you mean to raise the prestige of the Russian intelligentsia thereby?' 'Not a bit of it. We don't let you simply because a decent person can't go third class; it is too horrible and disgusting there.' 'Yes, sir? Thank you for being so solicitous about decent people's welfare. But in any case, whether it's nasty there or nice, I haven't got five hundred rubles. I didn't loot the Treasury, I didn't exploit the natives, I didn't traffic in contraband, I flogged nobody to

death, so judge for yourselves if I have the right to occupy a first class
cabin and even to reckon myself among the Russian intelligentsia.' But
logic means nothing to them. So I had to resort to fraud. I put on a peasant coat and high boots, I pulled a face so that I looked like a common
drunk, and went to the agents: 'Give us a little ticket, your Excellency,'
said I—"

"You're not of the gentry, are you?" asked the sailor.

"I come of a clerical family. My father was a priest, and an honest
one; he always told the high and mighty the truth to their faces and, as a
result, he suffered a great deal."

Pavel Ivanych is exhausted from talking and gasps for breath, but still
continues:

"Yes, I always tell people the truth to their faces. I'm not afraid of anyone or anything. In this respect, there is a great difference between me
and all of you, men. You are dark people, blind, crushed; you see nothing
and what you do see, you don't understand . . . You are told that the
wind breaks loose from its chain, that you are beasts, savages, and you
believe it; someone gives it to you in the neck—you kiss his hand; some
animal in a racoon coat robs you and then tosses you a fifteen-kopeck tip
and you say: 'Let me kiss your hand, sir.' You are outcasts, pitiful
wretches. I am different, my mind is clear. I see it all plainly like a hawk
or an eagle when it hovers over the earth, and I understand everything.
I am protest personified. I see tyranny—I protest. I see a hypocrite—I protest. I see a triumphant swine—I protest. And I cannot be put down, no
Spanish Inquisition can silence me. No. Cut out my tongue and I will
protest with gestures. Wall me up in a cellar—I will shout so that you will
hear me half a mile away, or will starve myself to death, so that they may
have another weight on their black consciences. Kill me and I will haunt
them. All my acquaintances say to me: 'You are a most insufferable person, Pavel Ivanych.' I am proud of such a reputation. I served three
years in the Far East and I shall be remembered there a hundred years.
I had rows there with everybody. My friends wrote to me from Russia:
'Don't come back,' but here I am going back to spite them . . . Yes . . .
That's life as I understand it. That's what one can call life."

Gusev is not listening; he is looking at the porthole. A junk, flooded
with dazzling hot sunshine, is swaying on the transparent turquoise
water. In it stand naked Chinamen, holding up cages with canaries in
them and calling out: "It sings, it sings!"

Another boat knocks against it; a steam cutter glides past. Then there
is another boat: a fat Chinaman sits in it, eating rice with chopsticks.
The water sways lazily, white sea gulls languidly hover over it.

"Would be fine to give that fat fellow one in the neck," reflects Gusev,
looking at the stout Chinaman and yawning.

He dozes off and it seems to him that all nature is dozing too. Time
flies swiftly by. Imperceptibly the day passes. Imperceptibly darkness
descends . . . The steamer is no longer standing still but is on the move
again.

IV

Two days pass. Pavel Ivanych no longer sits up but is lying down. His eyes are closed, his nose seems to have grown sharper.

"Pavel Ivanych," Gusev calls to him. "Hey, Pavel Ivanych."

Pavel Ivanych opens his eyes and moves his lips.

"Are you feeling bad?"

"No . . . It's nothing . . ." answers Pavel Ivanych gasping for breath. "Nothing, on the contrary . . . I am better . . . You see, I can lie down now . . . I have improved . . ."

"Well, thank God for that, Pavel Ivanych."

"When I compare myself to you, I am sorry for you, poor fellows. My lungs are healthy, mine is a stomach cough . . . I can stand hell, let alone the Red Sea. Besides, I take a critical attitude toward my illness and the medicines. While you— Your minds are dark . . . It's hard on you, very, very hard!"

The ship is not rolling, it is quiet, but as hot and stifling as a Turkish bath; it is hard, not only to speak, but even to listen. Gusev hugs his knees, lays his head on them and thinks of his home. God, in this stifling heat, what a relief it is to think of snow and cold! You're driving in a sleigh; all of a sudden, the horses take fright at something and bolt. Careless of the road, the ditches, the gullies, they tear like mad things right through the village, across the pond, past the pottery, across the open fields. "Hold them!" the pottery hands and the peasants they meet shout at the top of their voices. "Hold them!" But why hold them? Let the keen cold wind beat in your face and bite your hands; let the lumps of snow, kicked up by the horses, slide down your collar, your neck, your chest; let the runners sing, and the traces and the whippletrees break, the devil take them. And what delight when the sleigh upsets and you go flying full tilt into a drift, face right in the snow, and then you get up, white all over with icicles on your mustache, no cap, no gloves, your belt undone . . . People laugh, dogs bark . . .

Pavel Ivanych half opens one eye, fixes Gusev with it and asks softly: "Gusev, did your commanding officer steal?"

"Who can tell, Pavel Ivanych? We can't say, we didn't hear about it."

And after that, a long time passes in silence. Gusev broods, his mind wanders, and he keeps drinking water: it is hard for him to talk and hard for him to listen, and he is afraid of being talked to. An hour passes, a second, a third; evening comes, then night, but he doesn't notice it; he sits up and keeps dreaming of the frost.

There is a sound as though someone were coming into the infirmary, voices are heard, but five minutes pass and all is quiet again.

"The kingdom of Heaven be his and eternal peace," says the soldier with a bandaged arm. "He was an uneasy chap."

"What?" asks Gusev. "Who?"

"He died, they have just carried him up."

"Oh, well," mutters Gusev, yawning, "the kingdom of Heaven be his."

"What do you think, Gusev?" the soldier with the bandaged arm says after a while. "Will he be in the kingdom of Heaven or not?"

"Who do you mean?"

"Pavel Ivanych."

"He will . . . He suffered so long. Then again, he belonged to the clergy and priests have a lot of relatives. Their prayers will get him there."

The soldier with the bandage sits down on Gusev's bunk and says in an undertone:

"You too, Gusev, aren't long for this world. You will never get to Russia."

"Did the doctor or the nurse say so?" asks Gusev.

"It isn't that they said so, but one can see it. It's plain when a man will die soon. You don't eat, you don't drink, you've got so thin it's dreadful to look at you. It's consumption, in a word. I say it not to worry you, but because maybe you would like to receive the sacrament and extreme unction. And if you have any money, you had better turn it over to the senior officer."

"I haven't written home," Gusev sighs. "I shall die and they won't know."

"They will," the sick sailor says in a bass voice. "When you die, they will put it down in the ship's log, in Odessa they will send a copy of the entry to the army authorities, and they will notify your district board or somebody like that."

Such a conversation makes Gusev uneasy and a vague craving begins to torment him. He takes a drink—it isn't that; he drags himself to the porthole and breathes the hot, moist air—it isn't that; he tries to think of home, of the frost—it isn't that . . . At last it seems to him that if he stays in the infirmary another minute, he will certainly choke to death.

"It's stifling, brother," he says. "I'll go on deck. Take me there, for Christ's sake."

"All right," the soldier with the bandage agrees. "You can't walk, I'll carry you. Hold on to my neck."

Gusev puts his arm around the soldier's neck, the latter places his uninjured arm round him and carries him up. On the deck, discharged soldiers and sailors are lying asleep side by side; there are so many of them it is difficult to pass.

"Get down on the floor," the soldier with the bandage says softly. "Follow me quietly, hold on to my shirt."

It is dark, there are no lights on deck or on the masts or anywhere on the sea around. On the prow the seaman on watch stands perfectly still like a statue, and it looks as though he, too, were asleep. The steamer seems to be left to its own devices and to be going where it pleases.

"Now they'll throw Pavel Ivanych into the sea," says the soldier with the bandage, "in a sack and then into the water."

"Yes, that's the regulation."

"At home, it's better to lie in the earth. Anyway, your mother will come to the grave and shed a tear."

"Sure."

There is a smell of dung and hay. With drooping heads, steers stand at the ship's rail. One, two, three—eight of them! And there's a pony. Gusev puts out his hand to stroke it, but it shakes its head, shows its teeth, and tries to bite his sleeve.

"Damn brute!" says Gusev crossly.

The two of them thread their way to the prow, then stand at the rail, peering. Overhead there is deep sky, bright stars, peace and quiet, exactly as at home in the village. But below there is darkness and disorder. Tall waves are making an uproar for no reason. Each one of them as you look at it is trying to rise higher than all the rest and to chase and crush its neighbor; it is thunderously attacked by a third wave that has a gleaming white mane and is just as ferocious and ugly.

The sea has neither sense nor pity. If the steamer had been smaller, not made of thick iron plates, the waves would have crushed it without the slightest remorse, and would have devoured all the people in it without distinguishing between saints and sinners. The steamer's expression was equally senseless and cruel. This beaked monster presses forward, cutting millions of waves in its path; it fears neither darkness nor the wind, nor space, nor solitude—it's all child's play for it, and if the ocean had its population, this monster would crush it, too, without distinguishing between saints and sinners.

"Where are we now?" asks Gusev.

"I don't know. Must be the ocean."

"You can't see land . . ."

"No chance of it! They say we'll see it only in seven days."

The two men stare silently at the white phosphorescent foam and brood. Gusev is first to break the silence.

"There is nothing frightening here," he says. "Only you feel queer as if you were in a dark forest; but if, let's say, they lowered the boat this minute and an officer ordered me to go fifty miles across the sea to catch fish, I'll go. Or, let's say, if a Christian were to fall into the water right now, I'd jump in after him. A German or a Chink I wouldn't try to save, but I'd go in after a Christian."

"And are you afraid to die?"

"I am. I am sorry about the farm. My brother at home, you know, isn't steady; he drinks, he beats his wife for no reason, he doesn't honor his father and mother. Without me everything will go to rack and ruin, and before long it's my fear that my father and old mother will be begging their bread. But my legs won't hold me up, brother, and it's stifling here. Let's go to sleep."

V

Gusev goes back to the infirmary and gets into his bunk. He is again tormented by a vague desire and he can't make out what it is that he wants. There is a weight on his chest, a throbbing in his head, his mouth is so dry that it is difficult for him to move his tongue. He dozes and talks in his sleep and, worn out with nightmares, with coughing and the stifling heat, towards morning he falls into a heavy sleep. He dreams that they have just taken the bread out of the oven in the barracks and that he has climbed into the oven and is having a steam bath there, lashing himself with a besom of birch twigs. He sleeps for two days and on the third at noon two sailors come down and carry him out of the infirmary. He is sewn up in sailcloth and to make him heavier, they put two gridirons in with him. Sewn up in sailcloth, he looks like a carrot or a radish: broad at the head and narrow at the feet. Before sunset, they carry him on deck and put him on a plank. One end of the plank lies on the ship's rail, the other on a box placed on a stool. Round him stand the discharged soldiers and the crew with heads bared.

"Blessed is our God," the priest begins, "now, and ever, and unto ages of ages."

"Amen," three sailors chant.

The discharged men and the crew cross themselves and look off at the waves. It is strange that a man should be sewn up in sailcloth and should soon be flying into the sea. Is it possible that such a thing can happen to anyone?

The priest strews earth upon Gusev and makes obeisance to him. The men sing "Memory Eternal."

The seaman on watch duty raises the end of the plank, Gusev slides off it slowly and then flying, head foremost, turns over in the air and— plop! Foam covers him, and for a moment, he seems to be wrapped in lace, but the instant passes and he disappears in the waves.

He plunges rapidly downward. Will he reach the bottom? At this spot the ocean is said to be three miles deep. After sinking sixty or seventy feet, he begins to descend more and more slowly, swaying rhythmically as though in hesitation, and, carried along by the current, moves faster laterally than vertically.

And now he runs into a school of fish called pilot fish. Seeing the dark body, the little fish stop as though petrified and suddenly all turn round together and disappear. In less than a minute they rush back at Gusev, swift as arrows and begin zigzagging round him in the water. Then another dark body appears. It is a shark. With dignity and reluctance, seeming not to notice Gusev, as it were, it swims under him; then while he, moving downward, sinks upon its back, the shark turns, belly upward, basks in the warm transparent water and languidly opens its jaws with two rows of teeth. The pilot fish are in ecstasy; they stop to see what will happen next. After playing a little with the body, the shark nonchalantly puts his jaws under it, cautiously touches it with his teeth and the sailcloth is ripped from the full length of the body, from head to foot; one of the gridirons falls out, frightens the pilot fish and striking the shark on the flank, sinks rapidly to the bottom.

Meanwhile, up above, in that part of the sky where the sun is about to set, clouds are massing, one resembling a triumphal arch, another a lion, a third a pair of scissors. A broad shaft of green light issues from the clouds and reaches to the middle of the sky; a while later, a violet beam appears alongside of it and then a golden one and a pink one . . . The heavens turn a soft lilac tint. Looking at this magnificent enchanting sky, the ocean frowns at first, but soon it, too, takes on tender, joyous, passionate colors for which it is hard to find a name in the language of man.

COMMENT

"Gusev" is a classic example of the modern short story in which apparently very little happens. Character is revealed principally through inward action (meditation, recollection, and fantasy), with conversation supplying most of the surface action. The action of a story is determined by the nature of the characters. In "How It Was Done in Odessa" Benya Krik is a young man making his way to the throne and so is naturally given to large, public actions; Gusev, on the other hand, a dying peasant not much given to talk, is more naturally revealed through his long silences. Chekhov's technique is a counterpoint of silence and speech, reflection and dialogue. And if the way a story is told is determined by the character, then the way also reveals character.

The story is built on the contrast between Gusev and his companion Pavel. Gusev's modesty, conversational brevity, and general acquiescence are reinforced by the strong contrast with Pavel, whose raging protests are more often speeches rather than conversation. This surface difference reflects a more profound one, the degree of community each has with things. Gusev is at home in the army or on shipboard; Pavel is alienated from the army and is seasick. Gusev is rooted in tradition and a faith in authority (he hopes that the children "may honor their parents and not be any wiser than their father and mother"); Pavel has no use for either tradition or authority. Pavel is one kind of modern intellectual, the abstract man divorced from the past, from present institutions, and from nature; Gusev, the "natural man," is habituated to the hardships of nature, taking them and all other hardships as a matter of course. He has learned to accept the conditions of life—a tragic view; Pavel only protests against them—a modern, ameliorative view. The consequence of *only* protesting would seem to be the alienation of a man from everything, including himself.

Does Chekhov present stereotypes of the simple, likeable peasant and the complicated, unlikeable intellectual, or romanticize the man of nature at the expense of the man of thought? Not really, for Chekhov is critical of Gusev too—of his narrow nationalism, superstition, and blind acceptance of all things as they are. Rightly, however, Chekhov's criticism takes the tone of the gentlest possible irony, for Gusev is not willfully bad: his deplorable attitudes are rooted in the social order of his world.

Pavel serves as a *foil* to Gusev; a closer look at him will lead us, by contrast, to a further understanding of Gusev. Certain differences are apparently in Pavel's favor: Gusev is a superstitious peasant, Pavel a member of the enlightened intelligentsia; Gusev is filled with national and racial prejudices, Pavel has none; Gusev worries only about his family, Pavel about mankind, protesting violently against all sorts of tyranny. From our modern point of view, the liberal Pavel should attract us and Gusev should repel us; yet this is not what we feel. There is no necessary connection between a man's public virtues and his attractiveness. As a matter of fact, Pavel is an absurd person, not truly a liberal, but a parody of one: "I am protest personified. I see tyranny—I protest. I see a hypocrite—I protest. I see a triumphant swine—I protest. And I cannot be put down, no Spanish Inquisition can silence me. No. Cut out my tongue and I will protest with gestures. Wall me up in a cellar—I will shout so that you will hear me half a mile away. . . ." Is Chekhov unfair? Some readers may think so; but others will see this parody as an illuminating, if exaggerated, portrait of a liberal. (Any attitude, even Gusev's, can be parodied.) Pavel's protests about the lot of mankind degenerate into mere complaint about his own lot; his liberal altruism becomes illiberal egoism. But Gusev never complains. He worries not about mankind in the abstract, but only about particular persons—Vanka, Akulka, Alexey. But Chekhov is not making an unqualified indictment of the liberal Pavel. He takes only the mildest tone, and, in fact, we sympathize with Pavel despite his absurdity, for he genuinely suffers.

This tone is perhaps the crown of Chekhov's art. It is, as many have pointed out, much more than a matter of objectivity and neutrality. Alone, such qualities could make Chekhov lifeless. But he is fully alive, filled with tenderness, sympathy, *and* irony. His tone brightens the drab and miserable. Unobtrusive, gentle, yet firmly critical, it renders the fine shadings of attitude which make for a candid yet compassionate treatment.

But is the story then merely a sketch in contrasts, with no resolution? Even the deaths of Gusev and Pavel seem, at first, to be treated as just another moment in the chronology of their last days. But directly after Pavel is dropped overboard, the sea is all "darkness and disorder," the waves are "ferocious and ugly." In death poor Pavel is still out of tune with nature, with existence. The manner of his dying is continuous with the manner of his living. And so with Gusev. But after Gusev's death the clouds resemble a triumphal arch, a lion, and a pair of scissors: the heavens are symbolically declaring the glory (the arch) and the majesty (the lion) of Gusev's humble life and his mortality (the scissors of Atropos, one of the three Greek Fates). And from these clouds issue shafts of light. Finally, even the frowning ocean responds, taking on "tender, joyous, passionate colors for which it is hard to find a name in the language of man." In this remarkable climax and harmonious resolution suggesting death and transfiguration, Chekhov is saying that by living tenderly, joyously, and passionately man may transform nature, which includes man and the fact of his mortality; that is, man may transcend death.

QUESTIONS ON CHARACTER

1. Events should be believable and probable, and the last paragraph might seem neither—after all, clouds do not usually take the shape of an arch, a lion, and a pair of scissors. With the dictum in mind that an impossible probability is preferable to an improbable possibility, can the arrangement of clouds be justified? What about the personification of the ocean?

2. Is the last paragraph a romantic glorification of Gusev? In answering, consider its relation to the preceding paragraph with the shark.

3. How do the other characters contribute to an understanding of Gusev and Pavel?

4. Are the last words Pavel and Gusev speak characteristic?

5. Consider the contrast or similarity of characters in "Eternal Triangle," "A Clean, Well-Lighted Place," and "The Blind Man."

OTHER CONSIDERATIONS

1. What is the general effect of Chekhov's understatement in, for example, the paragraph of the shark? Is the style of the last paragraph typical? If not, is the change justifiable? effective?

2. How does Chekhov convey atmosphere and tone?

3. How does the setting contribute to the story? Is the setting only the ship? In "Nina of Ashkelon," especially in the description of the ancient town site, Yehuda Amichai uses setting not only to reveal character but also to actively forward the narrative.

4. The story has been interpreted as a drama of nature's indifference to man's concerns. A satisfactory interpretation must account for all the facts in a story. Does this one account for the differences between Pavel and Gusev? If you do not agree with this alternative interpretation, how do you explain the paragraph beginning, "The sea has neither sense nor pity"? A consideration of the last two paragraphs will be helpful.

5. How many different points of view does Chekhov present? Does this frequent shifting create what Henry James called a "fluid pudding"? How is the sense of unity conveyed? Would a story necessarily be unified if only one point of view were taken?

6. How does the first line foreshadow the entire story? What other instances of foreshadowing are there?

7. Ideas expressed by the author or by a character should be considered as dramatic elements in a story. "Death in Venice" is filled with such ideas from the barest abstract statement to the very dramatic imaginary dialogues of Socrates. Illustrate this dramatic function of ideas with some of Pavel's statements.

POINT OF VIEW

In our discussions of action and character, we have only briefly touched on the importance of the writer's choice of point of view, and its advantages and disadvantages. It must first be made clear that in itself point of view is a literary *convention*, a tacit agreement by the reader to accept whatever liberties the author takes. Among these liberties are the illusion of reality provided by a first-person narrator and the wide-ranging knowledge and insight of a third-person omniscient narrator.

If a writer chooses a *first-person* point of view, he must decide whether the "I" is to be a main character, a relatively uninvolved minor character, or somebody repeating the narrative at second or third hand. Whatever his choice, any first-person narrative is totally dramatized. What would otherwise be asserted material is a revelation of the narrator's interests, attitudes, vocabulary, manner of speaking—in short, a dramatic rendition of "character." See "The Golden Honeymoon," "Eternal Triangle," "In My Indolence," and "Gimpel the Fool."

If the "I" is a main character, a deeply involved narrator with whom we "identify" and in whose fortunes we are most interested, we must consider the narrator's prejudices, his emotional and intellectual limitations and biases, his purpose in telling the story, and his degree of candor, before we can arrive at an accurate idea of what is taking place. In "The Golden Honeymoon," for example, we must remember that the "unreliable narrator" is an old man of limited intellect who is jealous of his wife's former suitor and something less than frank about his own weaknesses. And in the light of this knowledge we must reinterpret his versions of cultural activities in St. Petersburg, his accounts of the card games and the checkers and horseshoe matches, and his appraisal of the Hartsells.

If the "I" is a minor character whose primary function is to observe, he is likely to have a greater objectivity, a clearer sense of the actual situation, and a more oblique and ironic approach. But we are limited to what this narrator can see, hear, and perceive; he may not be in a position to describe the climactic confrontation of principals or other potentially dramatic scenes. But certain values replace these losses, such as the effect of understatement in reporting the scene at second hand. Much also depends on the degree of objectivity or reliability of the narrator: Is he a relative or friend of the principals, as in "Christmas Every Day"? Does he observe everything at first hand or does he rely on rumors

71

and gossip for some information, as in "Nina of Ashkelon"? Is he affected at all by the conflict?

The function of the detached second- or third-hand narrator approaches that of the third-person narrator insofar as he is uninvolved in the conflict and free to interpret the action objectively. Only his authority is in question: Who told him this story? How keen is his memory? What are his qualifications for interpreting the action? Quite often, as in much of W. Somerset Maugham, the device of the detached narrator serves simply to frame the story and to give an air of reality; for an interesting variation, see the last sentence of Flaubert's "The Legend of St. Julian the Hospitaller." In stories by Joseph Conrad, Henry James, and Isaac Babel, this device is often vital to the total effect as contrast, complement, or ironic commentary on the enclosed tale—as shown in our analysis of "How It Was Done in Odessa." Too much has been made of this question of the "reality" of the first-person story. It may be true that an eyewitness account gives a stronger illusion of the actual event than does a third-person account, but surely no one believes that the use of an "I" narrator automatically insures the "truth" of what is being told. People do not read fiction for literal truth.

The *third-person* point of view can be that of one character, either central or peripheral, as in "Dawn"; that of several characters in alternation, as in "The Blind Man"; or that of the omniscient narrator, as in "The Silence of the Valley."

When a writer chooses the first alternative, the restricted third-person point of view, as in "Gusev," he presents the inner workings of only one character and tells only what this character is capable of observing. Through a perceptive character, as in "Dawn" and "Strange Comfort Afforded by the Profession," we gain more than ordinary insight without a sacrifice of credibility. But with a simple character like Gusev, the author's job is harder, since he must convey subtleties through the responses of a man unlikely to notice nuances. Chekhov, evidently restless under the restriction to a single character's viewpoint, does not adhere strictly to Gusev's consciousness; and in Part V, after Gusev's death, the point of view suddenly becomes omniscient.

The second alternative, the point of view that shifts among characters, escapes this restriction, though it seldom appears in its unalloyed form; most often, it merges with the omniscient viewpoint and is used more frequently in the novel than in the short story.

The omniscient viewpoint, the traditional storyteller's technique (as in "The White Silence," "Red Leaves," "Madame Tellier's Excursion," "The Fairy Goose"), gives the least illusion of reality. This convention implies a control and understanding of existence that seem incompatible with reality. The author becomes a kind of god, capable of being in many places at the same time, of knowing the past and the future, of penetrating into every character's mind and heart and hence of labeling each motive and thought with the infallibility of his superior vantage point. "Red Leaves" illustrates the extreme flexibility of this technique:

Faulkner shifts back and forth between the Indians' point of view and the single consciousness of the fleeing Negro, ending the story with a coldly detached description of the return to the Indian camp—a description forceful in its lack of comment and its reduction to what is physically observable.

Shadings and modifications of these alternatives are, of course, possible. An author may extend a character's powers of perception and interpretation until what we really have are the author's superimposed comments. In "Red Leaves" we readily accept the Negro's observation that the ants moved slowly up the log and that they had a salt taste, but when the Negro is next described as "watching the unbroken line move up the log and into oblivious doom with a steady and terrific undeviation," we know we have left the Negro far behind and are now observing through the eyes of William Faulkner. An author may also alternate between the restricted third-person and the omniscient point of view, as in "Gusev," "The Tree of Knowledge," "The Artificial Nigger," and "Death in Venice." Or he may maintain his omniscience throughout but deny himself the privilege of penetrating beneath surface appearances, confining his account to sounds, sights, and smells, with an absolute minimum of interpretation or comment. Hemingway is noted for his use of this technique, and his "A Clean, Well-Lighted Place" demonstrates its effectiveness.

Consistent point of view establishes one kind of unity in a story; that is, the reader always knows through whose eyes he is seeing the action and by whose authority he is given insights into the characters' thoughts and emotions. But a story may still be loose and rambling despite a single point of view because even a single consciousness may ramble. True unity involves meaning, as in any novel or play where the central character is not always present. Nevertheless, a short-story writer usually finds it more practical—because of the form's narrower range—to maintain a consistent point of view.

One helpful way for a reader to test the appropriateness of a given point of view is to ask the following questions:

1. Does this point of view seem the inevitable choice?
2. What would happen to the story if it were told from another point of view?
3. Do the limitations of this point of view contribute irony, humor, or suspense to the story's final effect or do they create discords?

Apply these questions to "The Golden Honeymoon," which is told by the principal character, and to "The Tree of Knowledge," which is told from a provocatively mixed point of view.

The Golden Honeymoon

✌ *Ring Lardner*

Mother says that when I start talking I never know when to stop. But I tell her the only time I get a chance is when she ain't around, so I have to make the most of it. I guess the fact is neither one of us would be welcome in a Quaker meeting, but as I tell Mother, what did God give us tongues for if He didn't want we should use them? Only she says He didn't give them to us to say the same thing over and over again, like I do, and repeat myself. But I say:

"Well, Mother," I say, "when people is like you and I and been married fifty years, do you expect everything I say will be something you ain't heard me say before? But it may be new to others, as they ain't nobody else lived with me as long as you have."

So she says:

"You can bet they ain't, as they couldn't nobody else stand you that long."

"Well," I tell her, "you look pretty healthy."

"Maybe I do," she will say, "but I looked even healthier before I married you."

You can't get ahead of Mother.

Yes, sir, we was married just fifty years ago the seventeenth day of last December and my daughter and son-in-law was over from Trenton to help us celebrate the Golden Wedding. My son-in-law is John H. Kramer, the real estate man. He made $12,000 one year and is pretty well thought of around Trenton; a good, steady, hard worker. The Rotarians was after him a long time to join, but he kept telling them his home was his club. But Edie finally made him join. That's my daughter.

Well, anyway, they come over to help us celebrate the Golden Wedding and it was pretty crimpy weather and the furnace don't seem to heat up no more like it used to and Mother made the remark that she hoped this winter wouldn't be as cold as the last, referring to the winter previous. So Edie said if she was us, and nothing to keep us home, she certainly wouldn't spend no more winters up here and why didn't we just shut off the water and close up the house and go down to Tampa, Florida? You know we was there four winters ago and staid five weeks, but it cost us over three hundred and fifty dollars for hotel bill alone. So Mother said we wasn't going no place to be robbed. So my son-in-law spoke up and said that Tampa wasn't the only place in the South, and besides we didn't have to stop at no high price hotel but could rent us a couple of rooms and board out somewheres, and he had heard that St.

From How to Write Short Stories, *by Ring Lardner, copyright 1922, 1950 by Ellis A. Lardner, reprinted by permission of Charles Scribner's Sons, New York.*

Petersburg, Florida, was *the* spot and if we said the word he would write down there and make inquiries.

Well, to make a long story short, we decided to do it and Edie said it would be our Golden Honeymoon and for a present my son-in-law paid the difference between a section and a compartment so we could have a compartment and have more privacy. In a compartment you have an upper and lower berth just like the regular sleeper, but it is a shut in room by itself and got a wash bowl. The car we went in was all compartments and no regular berths at all. It was all compartments.

We went to Trenton the night before and staid at my daughter and son-in-law and we left Trenton the next afternoon at 3.23 p.m.

This was the twelfth day of January. Mother set facing the front of the train, as it makes her giddy to ride backwards. I set facing her, which does not affect me. We reached North Philadelphia at 4.03 p.m. and we reached West Philadelphia at 4.14, but did not go into Broad Street. We reached Baltimore at 6.30 and Washington, D.C., at 7.25. Our train laid over in Washington two hours till another train come along to pick us up and I got out and strolled up the platform and into the Union Station. When I come back, our car had been switched on to another track, but I remembered the name of it, the La Belle, as I had once visited my aunt out in Oconomowoc, Wisconsin, where there was a lake of that name, so I had no difficulty in getting located. But Mother had nearly fretted herself sick for fear I would be left.

"Well," I said, "I would of followed you on the next train."

"You couldn't of," said Mother, and she pointed out that she had the money.

"Well," I said, "we are in Washington and I could of borrowed from the United States Treasury. I would of pretended I was an Englishman."

Mother caught the point and laughed heartily.

Our train pulled out of Washington at 9.40 p.m. and Mother and I turned in early, I taking the upper. During the night we passed through the green fields of old Virginia, though it was too dark to tell if they was green or what color. When we got up in the morning, we was at Fayetteville, North Carolina. We had breakfast in the dining car and after breakfast I got in conversation with the man in the next compartment to ours. He was from Lebanon, New Hampshire, and a man about eighty years of age. His wife was with him, and two unmarried daughters and I made the remark that I should think the four of them would be crowded in one compartment, but he said they had made the trip every winter for fifteen years and knowed how to keep out of each other's way. He said they was bound for Tarpon Springs.

We reached Charleston, South Carolina, at 12.50 p.m. and arrived at Savannah, Georgia, at 4.20. We reached Jacksonville, Florida, at 8.45 p.m. and had an hour and a quarter to lay over there, but Mother made a fuss about me getting off the train, so we had the darky make up our berths and retired before we left Jacksonville. I didn't sleep good as the train done a lot of hemming and hawing, and Mother never sleeps good on a train as she says she is always worrying that I will fall out. She says she would rather have the upper herself, as then she would not have to worry about me, but I tell her I can't take the risk of having it get out that I allowed my wife to sleep in an upper berth. It would make talk.

We was up in the morning in time to see our friends from New Hampshire get off at Tarpon Springs, which we reached at 6.53 a.m.

Several of our fellow passengers got off at Clearwater and some at Belleair, where the train backs right up to the door of the mammoth hotel. Belleair is the winter headquarters for the golf dudes and everybody that got off there had their bag of sticks, as many as ten and twelve in a bag. Women and all. When I was a young man we called it shinny and only needed one club to play with and about one game of it would of been a-plenty for some of these dudes, the way we played it.

The train pulled into St. Petersburg at 8.20 and when we got off the train you would think they was a riot, what with all the darkies barking for the different hotels.

I said to Mother, I said:

"It is a good thing we have got a place picked out to go to and don't have to choose a hotel, as it would be hard to choose amongst them if everyone of them is the best."

She laughed.

We found a jitney and I give him the address of the room my son-in-law had got for us and soon we was there and introduced ourselves to the lady that owns the house, a young widow about forty-eight years of age. She showed us our room, which was light and airy with a comfortable bed and bureau and washstand. It was twelve dollars a week, but the location was good, only three blocks from Williams Park.

St. Pete is what folks calls the town, though they also call it the Sunshine City, as they claim they's no other place in the country where they's fewer days when Old Sol don't smile down on Mother Earth, and one of the newspapers gives away all their copies free every day when the sun don't shine. They claim to of only give them away some sixty-odd times in the last eleven years. Another nickname they have got for the town is "the Poor Man's Palm Beach," but I guess they's men that comes there that could borrow as much from the bank as some of the Willie boys over to the other Palm Beach.

During our stay we paid a visit to the Lewis Tent City, which is the headquarters for the Tin-Can Tourists. But maybe you ain't heard about them. Well, they are an organization that takes their vacation trips by auto and carries everything with them. That is, they bring along their tents to sleep in and cook in and they don't patronize no hotels or cafeterias, but they have got to be bona fide auto campers or they can't belong to the organization.

They tell me they's over 200,000 members to it and they call themselves the Tin-Canners on account of most of their food being put up in tin cans. One couple we seen in the Tent City was a couple from Brady, Texas, named Mr. and Mrs. Pence, which the old man is over eighty years of age and they had come in their auto all the way from home, a distance of 1,641 miles. They took five weeks for the trip, Mr. Pence driving the entire distance.

The Tin-Canners hails from every State in the Union and in the summer time they visit places like New England and the Great Lakes region, but in the winter the most of them comes to Florida and scatters all over the State. While we was down there, they was a national convention of them at Gainesville, Florida, and they elected a Fredonia, New York, man as their president. His title is Royal Tin-Can Opener of the World. They have got a song wrote up which everybody has got to learn it before they are a member:

> "The tin can forever! Hurrah, boys! Hurrah!
> Up with the tin can! Down with the foe!
> We will rally round the campfire, we'll rally once again,
> Shouting, 'We auto camp forever!' "

That is something like it. And the members has also got to have a tin can fastened on to the front of their machine.

I asked Mother how she would like to travel around that way and she said:

"Fine, but not with an old rattle brain like you driving."

"Well," I said, "I am eight years younger than this Mr. Pence who drove here from Texas."

"Yes," she said, "but he is old enough to not be skittish."

You can't get ahead of Mother.

Well, one of the first things we done in St. Petersburg was to go to the Chamber of Commerce and register our names and where we was from as they's great rivalry amongst the different States in regards to the number of their citizens visiting in town and of course our little State don't stand much of a show, but still every little bit helps, as the fella says. All and all, the man told us, they was eleven thousand names registered, Ohio leading with some fifteen hundred-odd and New York State next with twelve hundred. Then come Michigan, Pennsylvania and so on down, with one man each from Cuba and Nevada.

The first night we was there, they was a meeting of the New York-New Jersey Society at the Congregational Church and a man from Ogdensburg, New York, made the talk. His subject was Rainbow Chasing. He is a Rotarian and a very convincing speaker, though I forget his name.

Our first business, of course, was to find a place to eat and after trying several places we run on a cafeteria on to Central Avenue that suited us up and down. We eat pretty near all our meals there and it averaged about two dollars per day for the two of us, but the food was well cooked and everything nice and clean. A man don't mind paying the price if things is clean and well cooked.

On the third day of February, which is Mother's birthday, we spread ourselves and eat supper at the Poinsettia Hotel and they charged us seventy-five cents for a sirloin steak that wasn't hardly big enough for one.

I said to Mother: "Well," I said, "I guess it's a good thing every day ain't your birthday or we would be in the poorhouse."

"No," says Mother, "because if every day was my birthday, I would be old enough by this time to of been in my grave long ago."

You can't get ahead of Mother.

In the hotel they had a card room where they was several men and ladies playing five hundred and this new fangled whist bridge. We also seen a place where they was dancing, so I asked Mother would she like to trip the light fantastic toe and she said no, she was too old to squirm like you have got to do now days. We watched some of the young folk at it awhile till Mother got disgusted and said we would have to see a good movie to take the taste out of our mouth. Mother is a great movie heroyne and we go twice a week here at home.

But I want to tell you about the Park. The second day we was there we visited the Park, which is a good deal like the one in Tampa, only bigger, and they's more fun goes on here every day than you could shake a stick at. In the middle they's a big bandstand and chairs for the folks to set and listen to the concerts, which they give you music for all tastes, from "Dixie" up to classical pieces like "Hearts and Flowers."

Then all around they's places marked off for different sports and games—chess and checkers and dominoes for folks that enjoys those kind of games, and roque and horse-shoes for the nimbler ones. I used to pitch a pretty fair shoe myself, but ain't done much of it in the last twenty years.

Well, anyway, we bought a membership ticket in the club which costs one dollar for the season, and they tell me that up to a couple of years ago it was fifty cents, but they had to raise it to keep out the riffraff.

Well, Mother and I put in a great day watching the pitchers and she wanted I should get in the game, but I told her I was all out of practice and would make a fool of myself, though I seen several men pitching who I guess I could take their measure without no practice. However, they was some good pitchers, too, and one boy from Akron, Ohio, who could certainly throw a pretty shoe. They told me it looked like he would win the championship of the United States in the February tournament. We come away a few days before they held that and I never did hear if he win. I forget his name, but he was a clean cut young fella and he has got a brother in Cleveland that's a Rotarian.

Well, we just stood around and watched the different games for two or three days and finally I set down in a checker game with a man named Weaver from Danville, Illinois. He was a pretty fair checker player, but he wasn't no match for me, and I hope that don't sound like bragging. But I always could hold my own on a checkerboard and the folks around here will tell you the same thing. I played with this Weaver pretty near all morning for two or three mornings and he beat me one game and the only other time it looked like he had a chance, the noon whistle blowed and we had to quit and go to dinner.

While I was playing checkers, Mother would set and listen to the band, as she loves music, classical or no matter what kind, but anyway she was setting there one day and between selections the woman next to her opened up a conversation. She was a woman about Mother's own age, seventy or seventy-one, and finally she asked Mother's name and Mother told her her name and where she was from and Mother asked her the same question, and who do you think the woman was?

Well, sir, it was the wife of Frank M. Hartsell, the man who was engaged to Mother till I stepped in and cut him out, fifty years ago!

Yes, sir!

You can imagine Mother's surprise! And Mrs. Hartsell was surprised, too, when Mother told her she had once been friends with her husband, though Mother didn't say how close friends they had been, or that Mother and I was the cause of Hartsell going out West. But that's what we was. Hartsell left his town a month after the engagement was broke off and ain't never been back since. He had went out to Michigan and become a veterinary, and that is where he had settled down, in Hillsdale, Michigan, and finally married his wife.

Well, Mother screwed up her courage to ask if Frank was still living and Mrs. Hartsell took her over to where they was pitching horse-shoes and there was old Frank, waiting his turn. And he knowed Mother as soon as he seen her, though it was over fifty years. He said he knowed her by her eyes.

"Why, it's Lucy Frost!" he says, and he throwed down his shoes and quit the game.

Then they come over and hunted me up and I will confess I wouldn't of knowed him. Him and I is the same age to the month, but he seems to show it more, some way. He is balder for one thing. And his beard is all white, where mine has still got a streak of brown in it. The very first thing I said to him, I said:

"Well, Frank, that beard of yours makes me feel like I was back north. It looks like a regular blizzard."

"Well," he said, "I guess yourn would be just as white if you had it dry cleaned."

But Mother wouldn't stand that.

"Is that so!" she said to Frank. "Well, Charley ain't had no tobacco in his mouth for over ten years!"

And I ain't!

Well, I excused myself from the checker game and it was pretty close to noon, so we decided to all have dinner together and they was nothing for it only we must try their cafeteria on Third Avenue. It was a little more expensive than ours and not near as good, I thought. I and Mother had about the same dinner we had been having every day and our bill was $1.10. Frank's check was $1.20 for he and his wife. The same meal wouldn't of cost them more than a dollar at our place.

After dinner we made them come up to our house and we all set in the parlor, which the young woman had give us the use of to entertain company. We begun talking over old times and Mother said she was a-scared Mrs. Hartsell would find it tiresome listening to we three talk over old times, but as it turned out they wasn't much chance for nobody else to talk with Mrs. Hartsell in the company. I have heard lots of women that could go it, but Hartsell's wife takes the cake of all the women I ever seen. She told us the family history of everybody in the State of Michigan and bragged for a half hour about her son, who she said is in the drug business in Grand Rapids, and a Rotarian.

When I and Hartsell could get a word in edgeways we joked one another back and forth and I chafed him about being a horse doctor.

"Well, Frank," I said, "you look pretty prosperous, so I suppose they's been plenty of glanders around Hillsdale."

"Well," he said, "I've managed to make more than a fair living. But I've worked pretty hard."

"Yes," I said, "and I suppose you get called out all hours of the night to attend births and so on."

Mother made me shut up.

Well, I thought they would never go home and I and Mother was in misery trying to keep awake, as the both of us generally always takes a nap after dinner. Finally they went, after we had made an engagement to meet them in the Park the next morning, and Mrs. Hartsell also invited us to come to their place the next night and play five hundred. But she had forgot that they was a meeting of the Michigan Society that evening, so it was not till two evenings later that we had our first card game.

Hartsell and his wife lived in a house on Third Avenue North and had a private setting room besides their bedroom. Mrs. Hartsell couldn't quit talking about their private setting room like it was something wonderful. We played cards with them, with Mother and Hartsell partners against his wife and I. Mrs. Hartsell is a miserable card player and we certainly got the worst of it.

After the game she brought out a dish of oranges and we had to pretend it was just what we wanted, though oranges down there is like a young man's whiskers; you enjoy them at first, but they get to be a pesky nuisance.

We played cards again the next night at our place with the same partners and I and Mrs. Hartsell was beat again. Mother and Hartsell was full of compliments for each other on what a good team they made, but the both of them knowed well enough where the secret of their success laid. I guess all and all we must of played ten different evenings and they was only one night when Mrs. Hartsell and I come out ahead. And that one night wasn't no fault of hern.

When we had been down there about two weeks, we spent one evening as their guest in the Congregational Church, at a social give by the Michigan Society. A talk was made by a man named Bitting of Detroit, Michigan, on How I was Cured of Story Telling. He is a big man in the Rotarians and give a witty talk.

A woman named Mrs. Oxford rendered some selections which Mrs. Hartsell said was grand opera music, but whatever they was my daughter Edie could of give her cards and spades and not made such a hullaballoo about it neither.

Then they was a ventriloquist from Grand Rapids and a young woman about forty-five years of age that mimicked different kinds of birds. I whispered to Mother that they all sounded like a chicken, but she nudged me to shut up.

After the show we stopped in a drugstore and I set up the refreshments and it was pretty close to ten o'clock before we finally turned in. Mother and I would of preferred tending the movies, but Mother said we mustn't offend Mrs. Hartsell, though I asked her had we came to Florida to enjoy ourselves or to just not offend an old chatter-box from Michigan.

I felt sorry for Hartsell one morning. The women folks both had an engagement down to the chiropodist's and I run across Hartsell in the Park and he foolishly offered to play me checkers.

It was him that suggested it, not me, and I guess he repented himself before we had played one game. But he was too stubborn to give up and set there while I beat him game after game and the worst part of it was that a crowd of folks had got in the habit of watching me play and there they all was, looking on, and finally they seen what a fool Frank was making of himself, and they began to chafe him and pass remarks. Like one of them said:

"Who ever told you you was a checker player!"

And:

"You might maybe be good for tiddle-de-winks, but not checkers!"

I almost felt like letting him beat me a couple games. But the crowd would of knowed it was a put up job.

Well, the women folks joined us in the Park and I wasn't going to mention our little game, but Hartsell told about it himself and admitted he wasn't no match for me.

"Well," said Mrs. Hartsell, "checkers ain't much of a game anyway, is it?" She said: "It's more of a children's game, ain't it? At least, I know my boy's children used to play it a good deal."

"Yes, ma'am," I said. "It's a children's game the way your husband plays it, too."

Mother wanted to smooth things over, so she said:

"Maybe they's other games where Frank can beat you."

"Yes," said Mrs. Hartsell, "and I bet he could beat you pitching horseshoes."

"Well," I said, "I would give him a chance to try, only I ain't pitched a shoe in over sixteen years."

"Well," said Hartsell, "I ain't played checkers in twenty years."

"You ain't never played it," I said.

"Anyway," says Frank, "Lucy and I is your master at five hundred."

Well, I could of told him why that was, but had decency enough to hold my tongue.

It had got so now that he wanted to play cards every night and when I or Mother wanted to go to a movie, any one of us would have to pretend we had a headache and then trust to goodness that they wouldn't see us sneak into the theater. I don't mind playing cards when my partner keeps their mind on the game, but you take a woman like Hartsell's wife and how can they play cards when they have got to stop every couple seconds and brag about their son in Grand Rapids?

Well, the New York-New Jersey Society announced that they was going to give a social evening too and I said to Mother, I said:

"Well, that is one evening when we will have an excuse not to play five hundred."

"Yes," she said, "but we will have to ask Frank and his wife to go to the social with us as they asked us to go to the Michigan social."

"Well," I said, "I had rather stay home than drag that chatter-box everywheres we go."

So Mother said:

"You are getting too cranky. Maybe she does talk a little too much but she is good hearted. And Frank is always good company."

So I said:

"I suppose if he is such good company you wished you had of married him."

Mother laughed and said I sounded like I was jealous. Jealous of a cow doctor!

Anyway we had to drag them along to the social and I will say that we give them a much better entertainment than they had given us.

Judge Lane of Paterson made a fine talk on business conditions and a Mrs. Newell of Westfield imitated birds, only you could really tell what they was the way she done it. Two young women from Red Bank sung a choral selection and we clapped them back and they gave us "Home to Our Mountains" and Mother and Mrs. Hartsell both had tears in their eyes. And Hartsell, too.

Well, some way or another the chairman got wind that I was there and asked me to make a talk and I wasn't even going to get up, but Mother made me, so I got up and said:

"Ladies and gentlemen," I said. "I didn't expect to be called on for a speech on an occasion like this or no other occasion as I do not set myself up as a speech maker, so will have to do the best I can, which I often say is the best anybody can do."

Then I told them the story about Pat and the motorcycle, using the brogue, and it seemed to tickle them and I told them one or two other stories, but altogether I wasn't on my feet more than twenty or twenty-five minutes and you ought to of heard the clapping and hollering when I set down. Even Mrs. Hartsell admitted that I am quite a speechifier and said if I ever went to Grand Rapids, Michigan, her son would make me talk to the Rotarians.

When it was over, Hartsell wanted we should go to their house and play cards, but his wife reminded him that it was after 9.30 p.m., rather a late hour to start a card game, but he had went crazy on the subject of cards, probably because he didn't have to play partners with his wife. Anyway, we got rid of them and went home to bed.

It was the next morning, when we met over to the Park, that Mrs. Hartsell made the remark that she wasn't getting no exercise so I suggested that why didn't she take part in the roque game.

She said she had not played a game of roque in twenty years, but if Mother would play she would play. Well, at first Mother wouldn't hear of it, but finally consented, more to please Mrs. Hartsell than anything else.

Well, they had a game with a Mrs. Ryan from Eagle, Nebraska, and a young Mrs. Morse from Rutland, Vermont, who Mother had met down to the chiropodist's. Well, Mother couldn't hit a flea and they all laughed at her and I couldn't help from laughing at her myself and finally she quit and said her back was too lame to stoop over. So they got another lady and kept on playing and soon Mrs. Hartsell was the one everyone was laughing at, as she had a long shot to hit the black ball, and as she made the effort her teeth fell out on to the court. I never seen a woman so flustered in my life. And I never heard so much laughing, only Mrs. Hartsell didn't join in and she was madder than a hornet and wouldn't play no more, so the game broke up.

Mrs. Hartsell went home without speaking to nobody, but Hartsell stayed around and finally he said to me, he said:

"Well, I played you checkers the other day and you beat me bad and now what do you say if you and me play a game of horse-shoes?"

I told him I hadn't pitched a shoe in sixteen years, but Mother said:

"Go ahead and play. You used to be good at it and maybe it will come back to you."

Well, to make a long story short, I give in. I oughtn't to of never tried it, as I hadn't pitched a shoe in sixteen years, and I only done it to humor Hartsell.

Before we started, Mother patted me on the back and told me to do my best, so we started in and I seen right off that I was in for it, as I hadn't pitched a shoe in sixteen years and didn't have my distance. And besides, the plating had wore off the shoes so that they was points right where they stuck into my thumb and I hadn't throwed more than two or three times when my thumb was raw and it pretty near killed me to hang on to the shoe, let alone pitch it.

Well, Hartsell throws the awkwardest shoe I ever seen pitched and to see him pitch you wouldn't think he would ever come nowheres near, but he is also the luckiest pitcher I ever seen and he made some pitches where the shoe lit five and six feet short and then schoonered up and was a ringer. They's no use trying to beat that kind of luck.

They was a pretty fair size crowd watching us and four or five other ladies besides Mother, and it seems like, when Hartsell pitches, he has got to chew and it kept the ladies on the anxious seat as he don't seem to care which way he is facing when he leaves go.

You would think a man as old as him would of learnt more manners.

Well, to make a long story short, I was just beginning to get my distance when I had to give up on account of my thumb, which I showed to Hartsell and he seen I couldn't go on, as it was raw and bleeding. Even if I could of stood it to go on myself, Mother wouldn't of allowed it after she seen my thumb. So anyway I quit and Hartsell said the score was nineteen to six, but I don't know what it was. Or don't care, neither.

Well, Mother and I went home and I said I hoped we was through with the Hartsells as I was sick and tired of them, but it seemed like she had promised we would go over to their house that evening for another game of their everlasting cards.

Well, my thumb was giving me considerable pain and I felt kind of out of sorts and I guess maybe I forgot myself, but anyway, when we was about through playing Hartsell made the remark that he wouldn't never lose a game of cards if he could always have Mother for a partner.

So I said:

"Well, you had a chance fifty years ago to always have her for a partner, but you wasn't man enough to keep her."

I was sorry the minute I had said it and Hartsell didn't know what to say and for once his wife couldn't say nothing. Mother tried to smooth things over by making the remark that I must of had something stronger than tea or I wouldn't talk so silly. But Mrs. Hartsell had froze up like an iceberg and hardly said good night to us and I bet her and Frank put in a pleasant hour after we was gone.

As we was leaving, Mother said to him: "Never mind Charley's nonsense, Frank. He is just mad because you beat him all hollow pitching horse-shoes and playing cards."

She said that to make up for my slip, but at the same time she certainly riled me. I tried to keep ahold of myself, but as soon as we was out of the house she had to open up the subject and began to scold me for the break I had made.

Well, I wasn't in no mood to be scolded. So I said:

"I guess he is such a wonderful pitcher and card player that you wished you had married him."

"Well," she said, "at least he ain't a baby to give up pitching because his thumb has got a few scratches."

"And how about you," I said, "making a fool of yourself on the roque court and then pretending your back is lame and you can't play no more!"

"Yes," she said, "but when you hurt your thumb I didn't laugh at you, and why did you laugh at me when I sprained my back?"

"Who could help from laughing!" I said.

"Well," she said, "Frank Hartsell didn't laugh."

"Well," I said, "why didn't you marry him?"

"Well," said Mother, "I almost wished I had!"

"And I wished so, too!" I said.

"I'll remember that!" said Mother, and that's the last word she said to me for two days.

We seen the Hartsells the next day in the Park and I was willing to apologize, but they just nodded to us. And a couple of days later we heard they had left for Orlando, where they have got relatives.

I wished they had went there in the first place.

Mother and I made it up setting on a bench.

"Listen, Charley," she said. "This is our Golden Honeymoon and we don't want the whole thing spoilt with a silly old quarrel."

"Well," I said, "did you mean that about wishing you had married Hartsell?"

"Of course not," she said, "that is, if you didn't mean that you wished I had, too."

So I said:

"I was just tired and all wrought up. I thank God you chose me instead of him as they's no other woman in the world who I could of lived with all these years."

"How about Mrs. Hartsell?" says Mother.

"Good gracious!" I said. "Imagine being married to a woman that plays five hundred like she does and drops her teeth on the roque court!"

"Well," said Mother, "it wouldn't be no worse than being married to a man that expectorates towards ladies and is such a fool in a checker game."

So I put my arm around her shoulder and she stroked my hand and I guess we got kind of spoony.

They was two days left of our stay in St. Petersburg and the next to the last day Mother introduced me to a Mrs. Kendall from Kingston, Rhode Island, who she had met at the chiropodist's.

Mrs. Kendall made us acquainted with her husband, who is in the grocery business. They have got two sons and five grandchildren and one great-grandchild. One of their sons lives in Providence and is way up in the Elks as well as a Rotarian.

We found them very congenial people and we played cards with them the last two nights we was there. They was both experts and I only wished we had met them sooner instead of running into the Hartsells. But the Kendalls will be there again next winter and we will see more of them, that is, if we decide to make the trip again.

We left the Sunshine City on the eleventh day of February, at 11 a.m. This gave us a day trip through Florida and we seen all the country we had passed through at night on the way down.

We reached Jacksonville at 7 p.m. and pulled out of there at 8.10 p.m. We reached Fayetteville, North Carolina, at nine o'clock the following morning, and reached Washington, D.C., at 6.30 p.m., laying over there half an hour.

We reached Trenton at 11.01 p.m. and had wired ahead to my daughter and son-in-law and they met us at the train and we went to their house and they put us up for the night. John would of made us stay up all night, telling about our trip, but Edie said we must be tired and made us go to bed. That's my daughter.

The next day we took our train for home and arrived safe and sound, having been gone just one month and a day.

Here comes Mother, so I guess I better shut up.

Before reading the editors' analysis of "The Golden Honeymoon," note the following critical comments on this story.

CRITICAL COMMENTS

Clifton Fadiman:

Lardner's subtlest story . . . When this was first published, most readers thought it very touching, even a trifle sentimental—this account of an old couple's wedding-anniversary trip to Florida, their little quarrels, their small-town complacencies, their petty satisfactions. Actually it is one of the most smashing indictments of a "happy marriage" ever written, composed with a fury so gelid as to hide completely the bitter passion seething beneath every line. Under the level of homey sentiment lies a terrific contempt for this quarrelsome, vain, literal old couple who for fifty years have disliked life and each other without ever having had the courage or the imagination to face the reality of their own meanness.[1]

Vernon Loggins:

Fifty years of suffering for two married couples because no one of the four persons concerned had sense enough to bring about the sensible coupling.[2]

H. L. Mencken:

Has any other living [in 1925] American ever written a better story than "The Golden Honeymoon"? There is more of sheer reality in such a story . . . than in the whole canon of Henry James, and there is also, I believe, more expert craftsmanship.[3]

[1] From "Ring Lardner and the Triangle of Hate," by Clifton Fadiman, *The Nation,* CXXXVI (March 22, 1933), 316, reprinted by permission of *The Nation.*
[2] From *I Hear America* . . . , by Vernon Loggins, 1927, p. 299, reprinted by permission of Thomas Y. Crowell Company, New York.
[3] From "Hiring a Hall," by H. L. Mencken, *New York World,* May 31, 1925, reprinted by permission of Jackson, Nash, Brophy, Barringer & Brooks, authorized on behalf of the publisher.

Burton Rascoe:

> . . . that tender, pathetic comedy of futility . . . a masterpiece of implication.[4]

William Bolitho:

> . . . one of the deepest manifestations of sheer world despair since "The City of Dreadful Night." [5]

Donald Elder:

> Such people as the old man and Mother must remain blissfully unaware of what they have contributed to the pessimism of mankind, because, whatever gelid fury and bitter passion Ring concealed so successfully, the old folks have quite a good time at horseshoes, watching the timetable, haggling over prices at restaurants, and enjoying a resurgence of youthful jealousy that has survived half a century of marital drabness. Their complacency is harmless, their irritability only standard human equipment, their sentimentality is normal for their age, there is no sign that they have disliked life or each other at all, and they have the kind of "happy marriage" which smashing indictments don't smash. If Ring had meant anything other than this, he would have contrived to get it into the story. By this time he knew pretty well what he was doing. The old couple are rather amiable bores; compared to other married couples in Ring's stories, they are utterly blessed.[6]

COMMENT

The primary problem for the reader intent on a close analysis of this story is one of attitude. A writer using an omniscient point of view can easily and clearly reveal his attitude, as London does in "The White Silence"; but the use of a first-person narrator places the reader at two removes from the material and thus demands of us a double job of interpretation: "What is the narrator's attitude?" and "What is the writer's attitude towards the narrator?" If the narrator is presented as sufficiently intelligent, candid, perceptive, and unprejudiced, then we might assume that he speaks for the author and that we need not go beyond his reactions. If, however, he is slow-witted, evasive, unaware, or involved so deeply in his own version of events that he cannot possibly be objective,

---

4 From *A Bookman's Daybook,* by Burton Rascoe, p. 251, copyright renewed 1956 by Mrs. Hazel L. Rascoe, reprinted by permission of Liveright Publishing Corporation.

5 From "Ring Lardner," by William Bolitho, *New York World,* March 27, 1930, reprinted by permission of Jackson, Nash, Brophy, Barringer & Brooks, authorized on behalf of the publisher.

6 From *Ring Lardner,* by Donald Elder, p. 211, copyright 1956 by Donald Elder, reprinted by permission of Doubleday & Company, Inc., New York.

then we must be skeptical of his authority. Indeed, quite often the importance of such a story lies in what the telling ironically reveals about the narrator rather than in the plot; the *way* of telling the story overshadows *what* is told.

As in many stories told from the first-person point of view, irony accrues here. The reader's knowledge is limited to the insights of the narrator, a rather insensitive old man who has a terrible need to preserve his pride and to demonstrate his mastery of all situations. But the reader sees through the narrator's needs and comprehends more than the old man intends to reveal.

Next we must determine Lardner's attitude towards this narrator. Is the old man foolish? despicable? pitiable? Is he simply a normal, harmless, garrulous figure approaching senility? Is he a purely comic character, or is there also something pathetic about him? Before coming to any final conclusions, consider the various interpretations immediately following the story.

The accuracy of Lardner's ear for the American vernacular has been cited as the one quality of his work that is unassailable. And in his reproduction of the narrator's grammatical and syntactical mayhem, he reveals the imprecision, shallowness, and unawareness of the old man. Lardner caught not only the illiterate pronunciations, the subtle slips of grammar, the malapropisms, and the deadly repetitions of phrase and cliché, but, as Gilbert Seldes pointed out, he understood the "habits of mind which make our speech, and his ear actually 'heard' the authentic rhythm of common speech, so that if the words were corrected the language would still be the language of the illiterate because of the cadence in which the words fell." [1] Lardner seems to have placed this feature of his style above his satire. "Where do they get that stuff about me being a satirist?" he once asked an interviewer. "I ain't no satirist. I just listen."

In addition to the revealing language, notice what Charley talks about. His favorite pastime seems to be delivering long monologues and memorizing train schedules. His account of the train trip from Trenton to St. Petersburg, his appreciative descriptions of the entertainment provided by the State societies, his relish of his own feeble repartee—all these reinforce the close relationship between style and meaning. By letting this old man talk and talk, Lardner allows us to see the emptiness of his life, of these four lives isolated from each other, having nothing to say.

"The Golden Honeymoon" deals with old age, one of the sacred cows of American culture. Lardner here demonstrates that age does not automatically produce wisdom, patience, tolerance, kindness, understanding, or mellowness. Like every other Lardner couple,

---

[1] From "American Humor," by Gilbert Seldes, in *America As Americans See It*, edited by Fred J. Ringel (New York: Harcourt, Brace & World, Inc., 1932), p. 352, reprinted by permission of Harcourt, Brace & World, Inc.

this pair have learned nothing in their long life together. They have managed to remain together probably because it no longer makes any difference: any other pairing would have had similar results, as the Hartsells demonstrate.

Application of the questions at the end of our introduction to the section "Point of View" makes clear that Lardner did choose the inevitable point of view, since this is a story not of action (which might have justified the omniscient narrator) or of the sadness of old age (which a sensitive restricted third-person observer might best have captured) but of comically unaware self-revelation. The author does not have to tell us that the old man is boring and literal-minded; instead, he lets the old man explain that the distance between Brady, Texas, and St. Petersburg, Florida, is 1,641 miles, and that Mother "hoped this winter wouldn't be as cold as the last, referring to the winter previous." Everything is immediate; and the language of the narrator (most of which would be lost if the point of view were changed), in all its flatness and redundancy, conveys with unwitting humor the unimaginativeness and drabness that form the substance of his life.

QUESTIONS ON POINT OF VIEW

1. How does Lardner allow Charley to reveal the weaknesses in his own character and still remain credible? What are these weaknesses? Are any strengths evident? Is it plausible that he should repeat those dialogues in which Mother gets the better of him?

2. Who is the superior member of this couple? How would the story be changed if Lucy were the narrator?

3. Does Lardner ever violate the consistency of the first-person point of view by intruding his own observations? Are any of Charley's observations out of keeping with his personality?

OTHER CONSIDERATIONS

1. Do you agree with Vernon Loggins' statement of the theme in the Critical Comments? Would the marriage of Lucy Frost and Frank Hartsell have been any more sensible or happy than the choice she did make?

2. Clifton Fadiman claims that most readers missed the sub-surface hatred and bitterness of this story and thought it touching and sentimental. How could such a misreading occur? Or is it not a misreading? See Donald Elder's rebuttal of Fadiman.

3. Most stories about elderly persons have a difficult time avoiding sentimentality; that is, the writers usually rely on the reader's stock responses of sympathy, solicitude, compassion, tender respect. In his attempt to avoid sentimentality, does Lardner "load" his study

of old age unfairly? How much does Lardner exaggerate? In "The Town Poor" Sarah Orne Jewett deals with old women in what is potentially a very sentimental situation. Can she be accused of sentimentality? If not, how does she avoid it? For a discussion of sentimentality, see our introduction to the section "Irony."

4. Consider the similarities and differences, particularly in attitude and self-awareness, between Lardner's narrator and the aging narrator of Italo Svevo's "In My Indolence."

5. Account for Lardner's inclusion of the following details:

(a) The old New Hampshire couple with two unmarried daughters, all of whom have made the trip annually in a single compartment for the past fifteen years.

(b) Mr. and Mrs. Pence, the Tin-Canners from Texas.

(c) The disastrous game of roque.

6. This story resembles a dramatic monologue, in which the speaker addresses a silent audience. To whom does Charley appear to be talking?

7. In what way is the title ironic?

The Tree of Knowledge

Henry James ❦

I

It was one of the secret opinions, such as we all have, of Peter Brench that his main success in life would have consisted in his never having committed himself about the work, as it was called, of his friend, Morgan Mallow. This was a subject on which it was, to the best of his belief, impossible, with veracity, to quote him, and it was nowhere on record that he had, in the connection, on any occasion and in any embarrassment, either lied or spoken the truth. Such a triumph had its honour even for a man of other triumphs—a man who had reached fifty, who had escaped marriage, who had lived within his means, who had been in love with Mrs. Mallow for years without breathing it, and who, last but not least, had judged himself once for all. He had so judged himself in fact that he felt an extreme and general humility to be his proper portion; yet there was nothing that made him think so well of his parts as the course he had steered so often through the shallows just mentioned. It became thus a real wonder that the friends in whom he had most confidence were just those with whom he had most reserves. He couldn't tell Mrs. Mallow—or at least he supposed, excellent man, he couldn't—that she was the one beautiful reason he had never married; any more than he could tell her husband that the sight of the multiplied marbles in that gentleman's studio was an affliction of which even time had never blunted the edge. His victory, however, as I have intimated, in regard to these productions, was not simply in his not having let it out that he deplored them; it was, remarkably, in his not having kept it in by anything else.

The whole situation, among these good people, was verily a marvel, and there was probably not such another for a long way from the spot that engages us—the point at which the soft declivity of Hampstead began at that time to confess in broken accents to St. John's Wood. He despised Mallow's statues and adored Mallow's wife, and yet was distinctly fond of Mallow, to whom, in turn, he was equally dear. Mrs. Mallow rejoiced in the statues—though she preferred, when pressed, the busts; and if she was visibly attached to Peter Brench it was because of his affection for Morgan. Each loved the other, moreover, for the love borne in each case to Lancelot, whom the Mallows respectively cherished as their only child and whom the friend of their fireside identified as the third—but decidedly the handsomest—of his godsons. Already in the old

From The Soft Side, *by Henry James, published by* The Macmillan Company, New York, 1900.

years it had come to that—that no one, for such a relation, could possibly have occurred to any of them, even to the baby itself, but Peter. There was luckily a certain independence, of the pecuniary sort, all round: the Master could never otherwise have spent his solemn *Wanderjahre* in Florence and Rome and continued, by the Thames as well as by the Arno and the Tiber, to add unpurchased group to group and model, for what was too apt to prove in the event mere love, fancy-heads of celebrities either too busy or too buried—too much of the age or too little of it— to sit. Neither could Peter, lounging in almost daily, have found time to keep the whole complicated tradition so alive by his presence. He was massive, but mild, the depositary of these mysteries—large and loose and ruddy and curly, with deep tones, deep eyes, deep pockets, to say nothing of the habit of long pipes, soft hats, and brownish, greyish, weather-faded clothes, apparently always the same.

He had "written," it was known, but had never spoken—never spoken, in particular, of that; and he had the air (since, as was believed, he continued to write) of keeping it up in order to have something more—as if he had not, at the worst, enough—to be silent about. Whatever his air, at any rate, Peter's occasional unmentioned prose and verse were quite truly the result of an impulse to maintain the purity of his taste by establishing still more firmly the right relation of fame to feebleness. The little green door of his domain was in a garden-wall on which the stucco was cracked and stained, and in the small detached villa behind it everything was old, the furniture, the servants, the books, the prints, the habits, and the new improvements. The Mallows, at Carrara Lodge, were within ten minutes, and the studio there was on their little land, to which they had added, in their happy faith, to build it. This was the good fortune, if it was not the ill, of her having brought him, in marriage, a portion that put them in a manner at their ease and enabled them thus, on their side, to keep it up. And they did keep it up—they always had—the infatuated sculptor and his wife, for whom nature had refined on the impossible by relieving them of the sense of the difficult. Morgan had, at all events, everything of the sculptor but the spirit of Phidias—the brown velvet, the becoming *beretto,* the "plastic" presence, the fine fingers, the beautiful accent in Italian, and the old Italian factotum. He seemed to make up for everything when he addressed Egidio with the "tu" and waved him to turn one of the rotary pedestals of which the place was full. They were tremendous Italians at Carrara Lodge, and the secret of the part played by this fact in Peter's life was, in a large degree, that it gave him, sturdy Briton that he was, just the amount of "going abroad" he could bear. The Mallows were all his Italy, but it was in a measure for Italy he liked them. His one worry was that Lance— to which they had shortened his godson—was, in spite of a public school, perhaps a shade too Italian. Morgan, meanwhile, looked like somebody's flattering idea of somebody's own person as expressed in the great room provided at the Uffizzi museum for Portraits of Artists by Themselves. The Master's sole regret that he had not been born rather to the brush than to the chisel sprang from his wish that he might have contributed to that collection.

It appeared, with time, at any rate, to be to the brush that Lance had been born; for Mrs. Mallow, one day when the boy was turning twenty, broke it to their friend, who shared, to the last delicate morsel, their problems and pains, that it seemed as if nothing would really do but that he should embrace the career. It had been impossible longer to remain blind to the fact that he gained no glory at Cambridge, where Brench's own college had, for a year, tempered its tone to him as for Brench's own sake. Therefore why renew the vain form of preparing him for the impossible? The impossible—it had become clear—was that he should be anything but an artist.

"Oh dear, dear!" said poor Peter.

"Don't you believe in it?" asked Mrs. Mallow, who still, at more than forty, had her violet velvet eyes, her creamy satin skin, and her silken chestnut hair.

"Believe in what?"

"Why, in Lance's passion."

"I don't know what you mean by 'believing in it.' I've never been unaware, certainly, of his disposition, from his earliest time, to daub and draw; but I confess I've hoped it would burn out."

"But why should it," she sweetly smiled, "with his wonderful heredity? Passion is passion—though of course, indeed, you, dear Peter, know nothing of that. Has the Master's ever burned out?"

Peter looked off a little and, in his familiar, formless way, kept up for a moment a sound between a smothered whistle and a subdued hum. "Do you think he's going to be another Master?"

She seemed scarce prepared to go that length, yet she had, on the whole, a most marvellous trust. "I know what you mean by that. Will it be a career to incur the jealousies and provoke the machinations that have been at times almost too much for his father? Well—say it may be, since nothing but clap-trap, in these dreadful days, *can*, it would seem, make its way, and since, with the curse of refinement and distinction, one may easily find one's self begging one's bread. Put it at the worst—say he *has* the misfortune to wing his flight further than the vulgar taste of his stupid countrymen can follow. Think, all the same, of the happiness—the same that the Master has had. He'll *know*."

Peter looked rueful. "Ah, but *what* will he know?"

"Quiet joy!" cried Mrs. Mallow, quite impatient and turning away.

II

He had of course, before long, to meet the boy himself on it and to hear that, practically, everything was settled. Lance was not to go up again, but to go instead to Paris, where, since the die was cast, he would find the best advantages. Peter had always felt that he must be taken as he was, but had never perhaps found him so much as he was as on this occasion. "You chuck Cambridge then altogether? Doesn't that seem rather a pity?"

Lance would have been like his father, to his friend's sense, had he had less humour, and like his mother had he had more beauty. Yet it was a good middle way, for Peter, that, in the modern manner, he was, to the eye, rather the young stockbroker than the young artist. The youth reasoned that it was a question of time—there was such a mill to go through, such an awful lot to learn. He had talked with fellows and had judged. "One has got, to-day," he said, "don't you see? to know."

His interlocutor, at this, gave a groan. "Oh, hang it, *don't* know!"

Lance wondered. " 'Don't'? Then what's the use—?"

"The use of what?"

"Why, of anything. Don't you think I've talent?"

Peter smoked away, for a little, in silence; then went on: "It isn't knowledge, it's ignorance that—as we've been beautifully told—is bliss."

"Don't you think I've talent?" Lance repeated.

Peter, with his trick of queer, kind demonstrations, passed his arm round his godson and held him a moment. "How do I know?"

"Oh," said the boy, "if it's your own ignorance you're defending—!"

Again, for a pause, on the sofa, his godfather smoked. "It isn't. I've the misfortune to be omniscient."

"Oh, well," Lance laughed again, "if you know *too* much—!"

"That's what I do, and why I'm so wretched."

Lance's gaiety grew. "Wretched? Come, I say!"

"But I forgot," his companion went on—"you're not to know about that. It would indeed, for you too, make the too much. Only I'll tell you what I'll do." And Peter got up from the sofa. "If you'll go up again, I'll pay your way at Cambridge."

Lance stared, a little rueful in spite of being still more amused. "Oh, Peter! You disapprove so of Paris?"

"Well, I'm afraid of it."

"Ah, I see."

"No, you don't see—yet. But you will—that is, you would. And you mustn't."

The young man thought more gravely. "But one's innocence, already—"

"Is considerably damaged? Ah, that won't matter," Peter persisted—"we'll patch it up here."

"Here? Then you want me to stay at home?"

Peter almost confessed to it. "Well, we're so right—we four together—just as we are. We're so safe. Come, don't spoil it."

The boy, who had turned to gravity, turned from this, on the real pressure in his friend's tone, to consternation. "Then what's a fellow to be?"

"My particular care. Come, old man"—and Peter now fairly pleaded—"*I'll* look out for you."

Lance, who had remained on the sofa with his legs out and his hands in his pockets, watched him with eyes that showed suspicion. Then he got up. "You think there's something the matter with me—that I can't make a success?"

"Well, what do you call a success?"

Lance thought again. "Why, the best sort, I suppose, is to please one's self. Isn't that the sort that, in spite of cabals and things, is—in his own peculiar line—the Master's?"

There were so much too many things in this question to be answered at once that they practically checked the discussion, which became particularly difficult in the light of such renewed proof that, though the young man's innocence might, in the course of his studies, as he contended, somewhat have shrunken, the finer essence of it still remained. That was indeed exactly what Peter had assumed and what, above all, he desired; yet, perversely enough, it gave him a chill. The boy believed in the cabals and things, believed in the peculiar line, believed, in short, in the Master. What happened a month or two later was not that he went up again at the expense of his godfather, but that a fortnight after he had got settled in Paris this personage sent him fifty pounds.

He had meanwhile, at home, this personage, made up his mind to the worst; and what it might be had never yet grown quite so vivid to him as when, on his presenting himself on Sunday night, as he never failed to do, for supper, the mistress of Carrara Lodge met him with an appeal as to—of all things in the world—the wealth of the Canadians. She was earnest, she was even excited. "Are many of them *really* rich?"

He had to confess that he knew nothing about them, but he often thought afterwards of that evening. The room in which they sat was adorned with sundry specimens of the Master's genius, which had the merit of being, as Mrs. Mallow herself frequently suggested, of an unusually convenient size. They were indeed of dimensions not customary in the products of the chisel and had the singularity that, if the objects and features intended to be small looked too large, the objects and features intended to be large looked too small. The Master's intention, whether in respect to this matter or to any other, had, in almost any case, even after years, remained undiscoverable to Peter Brench. The creations that so failed to reveal it stood about on pedestals and brackets, on tables and shelves, a little staring white population, heroic, idyllic, allegoric, mythic, symbolic, in which "scale" had so strayed and lost itself that the public square and the chimney-piece seemed to have changed places, the monumental being all diminutive and the diminutive all monumental; branches, at any rate, markedly, of a family in which stature was rather oddly irrespective of function, age, and sex. They formed, like the Mallows themselves, poor Brench's own family—having at least, to such a degree, a note of familiarity. The occasion was one of those he had long ago learnt to know and to name—short flickers of the faint flame, soft gusts of a kinder air. Twice a year, regularly, the Master believed in his fortune, in addition to believing all the year round in his genius. This time it was to be made by a bereaved couple from Toronto, who had given him the handsomest order for a tomb to three lost children, each of whom they desired to be, in the composition, emblematically and characteristically represented.

Such was naturally the moral of Mrs. Mallow's question: if their wealth was to be assumed, it was clear, from the nature of their admiration, as well as from mysterious hints thrown out (they were a little odd!) as to other possibilities of the same mortuary sort, that their further patronage might be; and not less evident that, should the Master become at all known in those climes, nothing would be more inevitable than a run of Canadian custom. Peter had been present before at runs of custom, colonial and domestic—present at each of those of which the aggregation had left so few gaps in the marble company round him; but it was his habit never, at these junctures, to prick the bubble in advance. The fond illusion, while it lasted, eased the wound of elections never won, the long ache of medals and diplomas carried off, on every chance, by every one but the Master; it lighted the lamp, moreover, that would glimmer through the next eclipse. They lived, however, after all—as it was always beautiful to see—at a height scarce susceptible of ups and downs. They strained a point, at times, charmingly, to admit that the public was, here and there, not too bad to buy; but they would have been nowhere without their attitude that the Master was always too good to sell. They were, at all events, deliciously formed, Peter often said to himself, for their fate; the Master had a vanity, his wife had a loyalty, of which success, depriving these things of innocence, would have diminished the merit and the grace. Any one could be charming under a charm, and, as he looked about him at a world of prosperity more void of proportion even than the Master's museum, he wondered if he knew another pair that so completely escaped vulgarity.

"What a pity Lance isn't with us to rejoice!" Mrs. Mallow on this occasion sighed at supper.

"We'll drink to the health of the absent," her husband replied, filling his friend's glass and his own and giving a drop to their companion; "but we must hope that he's preparing himself for a happiness much less like this of ours this evening—excusable as I grant it to be!—than like the comfort we have always—whatever has happened or has not happened—been able to trust ourselves to enjoy. The comfort," the Master explained, leaning back in the pleasant lamplight and firelight, holding up his glass and looking round at his marble family, quartered more or less, a monstrous brood, in every room—"the comfort of art in itself!"

Peter looked a little shyly at his wine. "Well—I don't care what you may call it when a fellow doesn't—but Lance must learn to *sell*, you know. I drink to his acquisition of the secret of a base popularity!"

"Oh yes, *he* must sell," the boy's mother, who was still more, however, this seemed to give out, the Master's wife, rather artlessly conceded.

"Oh," the sculptor, after a moment, confidently pronounced, "Lance *will*. Don't be afraid. He will have learnt."

"Which is exactly what Peter," Mrs. Mallow gaily returned—"why in the world were you so perverse, Peter?—wouldn't, when he told him, hear of."

Peter, when this lady looked at him with accusatory affection—a grace, on her part, not infrequent—could never find a word; but the Master, who was always all amenity and tact, helped him out now as he had often helped him before. "That's his old idea, you know—on which we've so often differed: his theory that the artist should be all impulse and instinct. *I* go in, of course, for a certain amount of school. Not too much—but a due proportion. There's where his protest came in," he continued to explain to his wife, "as against what *might,* don't you see? be in question for Lance."

"Ah, well,"—and Mrs. Mallow turned the violet eyes across the table at the subject of this discourse,—"he's sure to have meant, of course, nothing but good; but that wouldn't have prevented him, if Lance *had* taken his advice, from being, in effect, horribly cruel."

They had a sociable way of talking of him to his face as if he had been in the clay or—at most—in the plaster, and the Master was unfailingly generous. He might have been waving Egidio to make him revolve. "Ah, but poor Peter was not so wrong as to what it may, after all, come to that he *will* learn."

"Oh, but nothing artistically bad," she urged—still, for poor Peter, arch and dewy.

"Why, just the little French tricks," said the Master: on which their friend had to pretend to admit, when pressed by Mrs. Mallow, that these æsthetic vices had been the objects of his dread.

III

"I know now," Lance said to him the next year, "why you were so much against it." He had come back, supposedly for a mere interval, and was looking about him at Carrara Lodge, where indeed he had already, on two or three occasions, since his expatriation, briefly appeared. This had the air of a longer holiday. "Something rather awful has happened to me. It *isn't* so very good to know."

"I'm bound to say high spirits don't show in your face," Peter was rather ruefully forced to confess. "Still, are you very sure you do know?"

"Well, I at least know about as much as I can bear." These remarks were exchanged in Peter's den, and the young man, smoking cigarettes, stood before the fire with his back against the mantel. Something of his bloom seemed really to have left him.

Poor Peter wondered. "You're clear then as to what in particular I wanted you not to go for?"

"In particular?" Lance thought. "It seems to me that, in particular, there can have been but one thing."

They stood for a little sounding each other. "Are you quite sure?"

"Quite sure I'm a beastly duffer? Quite—by this time."

"Oh!"—and Peter turned away as if almost with relief.

"It's *that* that isn't pleasant to find out."

"Oh, I don't care for 'that,' " said Peter, presently coming round again. "I mean I personally don't."

"Yet I hope you can understand a little that I myself should!"

"Well, what do you mean by it?" Peter sceptically asked.

And on this Lance had to explain—how the upshot of his studies in Paris had inexorably proved a mere deep doubt of his means. These studies had waked him up, and a new light was in his eyes; but what the new light did was really to show him too much. "Do you know what's the matter with me? I'm too horribly intelligent. Paris was really the last place for me. I've learnt what I can't do."

Poor Peter stared—it was a staggerer; but even after they had had, on the subject, a longish talk in which the boy brought out to the full the hard truth of his lesson, his friend betrayed less pleasure than usually breaks into a face to the happy tune of "I told you so!" Poor Peter himself made now indeed so little a point of having told him so that Lance broke ground in a different place a day or two after. "What was it then that—before I went—you were afraid I should find out?" This, however, Peter refused to tell him—on the ground that if he hadn't yet guessed perhaps he never would, and that nothing at all, for either of them, in any case, was to be gained by giving the thing a name. Lance eyed him, on this, an instant, with the bold curiosity of youth—with the air indeed of having in his mind two or three names, of which one or other would be right. Peter, nevertheless, turning his back again, offered no encouragement, and when they parted afresh it was with some show of impatience on the side of the boy. Accordingly, at their next encounter, Peter saw at a glance that he had now, in the interval, divined and that, to sound his note, he was only waiting till they should find themselves alone. This he had soon arranged, and he then broke straight out. "Do you know your conundrum has been keeping me awake? But in the watches of the night the answer came over me—so that, upon my honour, I quite laughed out. Had you been supposing I had to go to Paris to learn *that?*" Even now, to see him still so sublimely on his guard, Peter's young friend had to laugh afresh. "You won't give a sign till you're sure? Beautiful old Peter!" But Lance at last produced it. "Why, hang it, the truth about the Master."

It made between them, for some minutes, a lively passage, full of wonder, for each, at the wonder of the other. "Then how long have you understood—"

"The true value of his work? I understood it," Lance recalled, "as soon as I began to understand anything. But I didn't begin fully to do that, I admit, till I got *là-bas*."

"Dear, dear!"—Peter gasped with retrospective dread.

"But for what have you taken me? I'm a hopeless muff—that I *had* to have rubbed in. But I'm not such a muff as the Master!" Lance declared.

"Then why did you never tell me—?"

"That I hadn't, after all"—the boy took him up—"remained such an idiot? Just because I never dreamed *you* knew. But I beg your pardon. I only wanted to spare you. And what I don't now understand is how the deuce then, for so long, you've managed to keep bottled."

Peter produced his explanation, but only after some delay and with a gravity not void of embarrassment. "It was for your mother."

"Oh!" said Lance.

"And that's the great thing now—since the murder *is* out. I want a promise from you. I mean"—and Peter almost feverishly followed it up —"a vow from you, solemn and such as you owe me, here on the spot, that you'll sacrifice anything rather than let her ever guess—"

"That *I've* guessed?"—Lance took it in. "I see." He evidently, after a moment, had taken in much. "But what is it you have in mind that I may have a chance to sacrifice?"

"Oh, one has always something."

Lance looked at him hard. "Do you mean that *you've* had—?" The look he received back, however, so put the question by that he found soon enough another. "Are you really sure my mother doesn't know?"

Peter, after renewed reflection, was really sure. "If she does, she's too wonderful."

"But aren't we all too wonderful?"

"Yes," Peter granted—"but in different ways. The thing's so desperately important because your father's little public consists only, as you know then," Peter developed—"well, of how many?"

"First of all," the Master's son risked, "of himself. And last of all too. I don't quite see of whom else."

Peter had an approach to impatience. "Of your mother, I say—*always.*"

Lance cast it all up. "You absolutely feel that?"

"Absolutely."

"Well then, with yourself, that makes three."

"Oh, *me!*"—and Peter, with a wag of his kind old head, modestly excused himself. "The number is, at any rate, small enough for any individual dropping out to be too dreadfully missed. Therefore, to put it in a nutshell, take care, my boy—that's all—that *you're* not!"

"I've got to keep on humbugging?" Lance sighed.

"It's just to warn you of the danger of your failing of that that I've seized this opportunity."

"And what do you regard in particular," the young man asked, "as the danger?"

"Why, this certainty: that the moment your mother, who feels so strongly, should suspect your secret—well," said Peter desperately, "the fat would be on the fire."

Lance, for a moment, seemed to stare at the blaze. "She'd throw me over?"

"She'd throw *him* over."

"And come round to us?"

Peter, before he answered, turned away. "Come round to *you*." But he had said enough to indicate—and, as he evidently trusted, to avert—the horrid contingency.

IV

Within six months again, however, his fear was, on more occasions than one, all before him. Lance had returned to Paris, to another trial; then had reappeared at home and had had, with his father, for the first time in his life, one of the scenes that strike sparks. He described it with much expression to Peter, as to whom—since they had never done so before—it was a sign of a new reserve on the part of the pair at Carrara Lodge that they at present failed, on a matter of intimate interest, to open themselves—if not in joy, then in sorrow—to their good friend. This produced perhaps, practically, between the parties, a shade of alienation and a slight intermission of commerce—marked mainly indeed by the fact that, to talk at his ease with his old playmate, Lance had, in general, to come to see him. The closest, if not quite the gayest, relation they had yet known together was thus ushered in. The difficulty for poor Lance was a tension at home, begotten by the fact that his father wished him to be, at least, the sort of success he himself had been. He hadn't "chucked" Paris—though nothing appeared more vivid to him than that Paris had chucked him; he would go back again because of the fascination in trying, in seeing, in sounding the depths—in learning one's lesson, in fine, even if the lesson were simply that of one's impotence in the presence of one's larger vision. But what did the Master, all aloft in his senseless fluency, know of impotence, and what vision—to be called such—had he, in all his blind life, ever had? Lance, heated and indignant, frankly appealed to his godparent on this score.

His father, it appeared, had come down on him for having, after so long, nothing to show, and hoped that, on his next return, this deficiency would be repaired. *The* thing, the Master complacently set forth, was—for any artist, however inferior to himself—at least to "do" something. "What can you do? That's all I ask!" *He* had certainly done enough, and there was no mistake about what he had to show. Lance had tears in his eyes when it came thus to letting his old friend know how great the strain might be on the "sacrifice" asked of him. It wasn't so easy to continue humbugging—as from son to parent—after feeling one's self despised for not grovelling in mediocrity. Yet a noble duplicity was what, as they intimately faced the situation, Peter went on requiring; and it was still, for a time, what his young friend, bitter and sore, managed loyally to comfort him with. Fifty pounds, more than once again, it was true, rewarded, both in London and in Paris, the young friend's loyalty; none the less sensibly, doubtless, at the moment, that the money was a direct advance on a decent sum for which Peter had long since privately prearranged an ultimate function. Whether by these arts or others, at all events, Lance's just resentment was kept for a season—but only for a season—at bay. The day arrived when he warned his companion that he could hold out—or hold in—no longer. Carrara Lodge had had to listen to another lecture delivered from a great height—an infliction really heavier, at last, than, without striking back or in some way letting the Master have the truth, flesh and blood could bear.

"And what I don't see is," Lance observed with a certain irritated eye for what was, after all, if it came to that, due to himself too—"What I don't see is, upon my honour, how *you,* as things are going, can keep the game up."

"Oh, the game for me is only to hold my tongue," said placid Peter. "And I have my reason."

"Still my mother?"

Peter showed, as he had often shown it before—that is, by turning it straight away—a queer face. "What will you have? I haven't ceased to like her."

"She's beautiful—she's a dear, of course," Lance granted; "but what is she to you, after all, and what is it to you that, as to anything whatever, she should or she shouldn't?"

Peter, who had turned red, hung fire a little. "Well—it's all, simply, what I make of it."

There was now, however, in his young friend, a strange, an adopted, insistence. "What are you, after all, to *her?*"

"Oh, nothing. But that's another matter."

"She cares only for my father," said Lance the Parisian.

"Naturally—and that's just why."

"Why you've wished to spare her?"

"Because she cares so tremendously much."

Lance took a turn about the room, but with his eyes still on his host. "How awfully—always—you must have liked her!"

"Awfully. Always," said Peter Brench.

The young man continued for a moment to muse—then stopped again in front of him. "Do you know how much she cares?" Their eyes met on it, but Peter, as if his own found something new in Lance's, appeared to hesitate, for the first time for so long, to say he did know. *"I've* only just found out," said Lance. "She came to my room last night, after being present, in silence and only with her eyes on me, at what I had had to take from him; she came—and she was with me an extraordinary hour."

He had paused again, and they had again for a while sounded each other. Then something—and it made him suddenly turn pale—came to Peter. "She *does* know?"

"She does know. She let it all out to me—so as to demand of me no more than that, as she said, of which she herself had been capable. She has always, always known," said Lance without pity.

Peter was silent a long time; during which his companion might have heard him gently breathe and, on touching him, might have felt within him the vibration of a long, low sound suppressed. By the time he spoke, at last, he had taken everything in. "Then I do see how tremendously much."

"Isn't it wonderful?" Lance asked.

"Wonderful," Peter mused.

"So that if your original effort to keep me from Paris was to keep me from knowledge—!" Lance exclaimed as if with a sufficient indication of this futility.

It might have been at the futility that Peter appeared for a little to gaze. "I think it must have been—without my quite at the time knowing it—to keep *me!*" he replied at last as he turned away.

COMMENT

In his preface to the volume of stories entitled *The Author of Beltraffio,* Henry James records the anecdote—"the grain of suggestion, the tiny air-blown particle"—from which "The Tree of Knowledge" eventually grew. The original anecdote is of the discovery by an artist-son that his artist-father lacked talent. Though in its raw form this anecdote lacked focus, it would acquire one by necessity as it turned into a piece of fiction. Feeling compelled, as always, to "dramatize" this grain of suggestion, James had to decide how and by whom the events were to be viewed. Instead of having the son describe his loss of belief in his father, James introduces a friend of the family, Peter Brench, who has devoted much of his life to protecting the artist's wife and son from the knowledge of the "Master's" ineptitude. Having long been in love with the Master's wife, Peter thinks of his silence as an act of self-sacrifice. Whereas the anecdote was about the son's discovery, the story is about Peter's discovery. Peter painfully learns that the son has understood for years what a "muff" his father is, that the son has been sparing *him,* and—most ravaging disclosure of all—that the wife has "always, always known." Thus James's choice of point of view seems to have determined plot, character, and theme.

Presented through the consciousness of the family friend, the story becomes not that of a son's disillusionment but that of the friend's discovery of how little he really *knows* about the Mallows. Emerging from this reshaping of a father-son relationship into a comic version of the familiar love-triangle, the theme is, patently, a cliché, the essential truth of which is exhibited with affectionate irony. The cliché is put into words by Peter, who is aware of its triteness but unaware that it applies to him: "It isn't knowledge, it's ignorance that—as we've been beautifully told—is bliss." Ignorance is bliss. And if the opposite of ignorance is knowledge, we are led back to the title and its source in *Genesis:*

> And the Lord God commanded the man, saying, Of every tree of
> the garden thou mayest freely eat:
> But of the tree of the knowledge of good and evil, thou shalt not
> eat of it: for in the day that thou eatest thereof thou shalt surely die.
>
> . . .
>
> And the serpent said unto the woman, Ye shall not surely die:
> For God doth know that in the day ye eat thereof, then your eyes
> shall be opened, and ye shall be as gods, knowing good and evil.

Like the author of *Genesis,* James also plays with the ambiguities
of the word *knowledge,* showing its relation to man's unhappiness.
Variations on the word as noun, verb, and verbal appear on almost
every page, sometimes casually, as when Mrs. Mallow tells Peter,
"Passion is passion—though of course, indeed, you . . . know nothing of that," and sometimes most pointedly, as in the concluding
exchange between Lance and Peter:

> "So that if your original effort to keep me from Paris was to keep
> me from knowledge—" . . .
> . . . "I think it must have been—without my quite at the time
> knowing it—to keep *me!*"

And again we return to the connection between theme and point
of view: for Peter's essential ignorance (another term in this story
for innocence) lies in his belief that knowledge would turn Mrs.
Mallow against her husband; in this ignorance, indeed, is his bliss.

Although James frequently uses the first-person "unreliable narrator" (see our introduction to the section "Point of View") in his
short stories, he could not work up much enthusiasm for what he
called "the romantic privilege of the 'first person.'" According to
him, this "double privilege" of being both subject and object—
"the terrible fluidity of self-revelation"—is simply too easy a technique. In "The Tree of Knowledge" there is the voice of a first-
person narrator, but not the voice of Peter Brench nor that of the
author, exactly; it is rather that of a disembodied story-teller—"the
friend of the reader," James once labeled it. But this voice, a minimal carry-over from the older convention of the omniscient narrator, lacks a personality of its own to color the story and is surely
peripheral to the unifying device of the central intelligence of the
restricted third-person point of view. This intelligence or consciousness (obviously neither so intelligent nor so keenly conscious as it
believes itself to be) belongs to Peter Brench. Consequently, this
story, like many others of James's, is concerned less with action,
with what happens, than with reaction, with what the central intelligence feels about what happens; the major ironic point depends
on the contrast between what Peter feels has happened and what
actually is happening in the minds of Lance and his mother.

The point of view, the central intelligence, then, shapes the
story, forcing the writer to make choices and sacrifices. For instance,

in Section IV Lance refers to "an extraordinary hour" he has spent
in conversation with his mother. This apparently vital scene is
omitted because the point of view demands that Peter be present
at all of the dramatized scenes and because its main importance
lies in its effect on Peter, which must be dramatized in the final
scene. It may be argued that this effect could likewise have been
achieved if the story were told by Peter himself. But James chose
not to take advantage of this "fluidity" but rather—though limiting
the point of view largely to Peter—to maintain an air of dramatic
detachment about a character so self-effacing that even his best
friends talk "around" him as though he were a chunk of statuary.
This detachment is emphasized by the physical description of Peter
at the end of the second paragraph; by the narrator's arm's-length
comments about Peter's "occasional unmentioned prose and verse"
and his "trick of queer, kind demonstrations"; and by the epithets
for Peter: "excellent man," "the depositary of these mysteries,"
"sturdy Briton that he was," and the significantly repeated "poor
Peter."

From the first sentence, point of view and characterization are
closely related as we learn that Peter considers his self-effacement
(specifically his refusal to commit himself on the artistic quality of
Mallow's sculpture) as "his main success in life." And his list of
"other triumphs" as a man of fifty is consistent: "a man . . . who
had escaped marriage, who had lived within his means, who had
been in love with Mrs. Mallow for years without breathing it, and
who, last not least, had judged himself once for all." All of these
triumphs are negative except the last, and even this judgment has
led to a passive virtue, "an extreme and general humility." The
movement of the story is towards the destruction of this complacency and towards the revelation that his vaunted humility is
in reality the subtlest and most insidious kind of pride.

For Peter is convinced that if he were to disabuse Mrs. Mallow of
her "illusion" that her husband is a great but unappreciated artist
—if she *knew* the truth—she would turn to him, if not in love, at
least on the rebound from the phony to "the real thing." (Remember that Peter, also an "artist," has never spoken about his work,
and thus in his silence has maintained "the purity of his taste."
The suggestion is that Peter has a great deal to be humble and
silent about.) This compulsive belief and his "noble," lifelong self-
denial seem to be the very core of his existence. Therefore Peter
is desolated in the final confrontation with Lance, which is his first
confrontation with himself: he is at last brought face to face with
the truth—the *knowledge*—that Mrs. Mallow is more perceptive
than he dared suspect and that her awareness of the Master's ineptitude not only has failed to wheel her into Peter's waiting arms but
has actually strengthened her love for her husband by calling on
her maternal protectiveness as well as her wifely affection.

Because the point of view is restricted almost entirely to the consciousness of Peter, the reader must draw certain inferences about how much of Peter's long silence was motivated consciously and how much unconsciously. Consciously, Peter likes to think that he has kept the secret out of friendship for the Mallows and out of chivalrous self-sacrifice; unconsciously, he has kept the "secret"—which is a secret only to Mr. Mallow—to prevent himself from ever knowing how deeply in love with her husband Mrs. Mallow really is. To paraphrase *Genesis:* "And his eyes were opened, and he knew that he was naked."

QUESTIONS ON POINT OF VIEW

1. Other than those mentioned in the above analysis, what examples of intrusive commentary are there in "The Tree of Knowledge"? Does the author ever penetrate into the consciousness of any character other than Peter Brench? If so, what effect does he gain?

2. In Section IV, Peter learns at second hand about two "scenes" between father and son and one "scene" between mother and son. Could these scenes have been "dramatized" through a description by Lance to Peter without straining the reader's credulity? Would it have been believable, in other words, for Lance to repeat for Peter the actual verbal exchanges, the gestures, and so forth, that occurred?

3. Describe as precisely as possible the author's attitude towards Peter Brench: contemptuous? derisive? patronizing? pitying? Remember that we have witnessed only a part of Peter's life-span, a turning point, a "crisis situation," after which nothing will be quite the same for him. Is it justifiable to conjecture what is to become of what James would call the rest of Peter's "unlived life"?

4. Compare the use of the restricted third-person central intelligence in this story with the much stricter confinement to a single consciousness in "Dawn" and "Strange Comfort Afforded by the Profession."

OTHER CONSIDERATIONS

1. Henry James once described "The Tree of Knowledge" as a novel "intensely compressed" by means of "successful duplicity." Does the story contain—or imply—enough material for a novel? What "duplicity" did James use in condensing it?

2. The events of this story cover a long period of time. How does the author bridge the time-gaps? Other than chronological order, what principles of selection has he used in choosing the seven scenes to dramatize? How is each scene crucial to Peter's final self-awareness?

3. Is there plausible motivation for what Peter considers the Mallows' "sign of a new reserve" in not telling "their good friend" about the first quarrel between Lance and the Master, described at the beginning of Section IV?

4. Examine James's rich allusive language and imagery, particularly all variations on *knowing* and *learning* and the metaphorical references to *vision* and *eating*.

5. What effects does James gain by making Morgan Mallow a sculptor rather than, say, a painter or poet? One suggestion: just as Mallow's most distinctive stylistic trait is lack of proper or natural "scale" in his figures, so may this story be read as a study in proportions—or disproportions.

6. Is there a serpent in James's allegory of Eden?

IRONY

There are two primary ways of realizing irony in literature: (1) through the *passage of time* and (2) at any *single moment*. In the context of the passage of time, irony is the sense that all human enterprises necessarily turn out different from what was hoped for. We say necessarily because a person changes, and therefore what he hopes for changes too. To an eighteen-year-old, a millionaire may seem altogether enviable; to a forty-year-old, the complications of the intervening years as well as the mere process of aging give a very different value to being a millionaire. Irony through the passage of time is realized in the structure—this we may call *irony of structure.* In the context of a single moment, irony is the sense that each moment is characterized by ambiguities, by discrepancies, by contradictions, by contrary attitudes. The underlying or real meaning is different from the surface or apparent meaning. In fiction the irony of any single moment is realized in the *situation* at each moment—this we can call *irony of situation.*

Irony of structure develops in time through an unexpected *reversal* in the action. This reversal is sometimes called the *peripety,* a term introduced by Aristotle; he added that the reversal is most powerful when it is accompanied by a *recognition,* that is, when the hero is conscious of the reversal, when he discovers, for example, he is not what he thought he was. The classic instance occurs in the play *Oedipus Rex,* when King Oedipus discovers that he is himself the murderer he has been looking for. In "Death in Venice" the honored writer Gustave von Aschenbach, a culture hero, recognizes that his interest in the beautiful boy Tadzio is not esthetic but erotic; at this point his passion drives him to reverse the direction of his life and he abandons culture and civilization for the boy. The reversal exposes the underlying irony in the action and leads directly to the meaning of the action. In these two works, where events take a downturn, the reversal drives in the direction of tragedy; in "Gimpel the Fool" and "Powerhouse," where events take an upturn, the reversal drives in the direction of comedy—that is, things turn out well.

Irony of structure is relatively easy to perceive; we can readily see the irony in a hero of culture becoming an enemy of culture. But readers sometimes have difficulty seeing irony of situation, the irony in a particular moment. How can we tell when the author is presenting his matter unequivocally and when with irony? Most helpful, probably, is to know the values of the author. Are his values in agreement with those of his characters? If there is a difference, there is an irony at work. In "The Golden Honeymoon" the narrator announces that one year his son-in-law made $12,000 in real estate and that he is a Rotarian and is "pretty well thought of around Trenton." Because we can be sure that these criteria of money and middle-class status are different from those of Lardner or of any serious modern writer, we can say the facts are presented ironically. The value of status is also the source of much irony in "Grace," as when Mr. McCoy vulgarizes religion with his remark about the Jesuits that "they're the boyos have influence." The irony of Pavel's rhetoric in "Gusev" is more complicated: "I am protest personified. I see tyranny—I protest. I see a hypocrite—I protest." The complexity is first in the discrepancy between Pavel's morality, with which we presumably are happy, and his rhetoric, with which we are unhappy. To perceive the irony, the reader must have enough sophistication about language to recognize the cheapness of Pavel's lofty rhetoric, which betrays the morality behind it. The irony is further complicated, for Chekhov is fond of as well as ironic about Pavel. To convey their ironic attitudes writers have their own rhetoric, which takes many forms: paradox ("The heart has its reasons which reason knows nothing of"); understatement ("Last week I saw a woman flayed, and you will hardly believe how much it altered her person for the worse"); exaggeration ("His appointment as postmaster at Laramie, Wyoming, is one of the epochs in the nation's onward march toward political purity and perfection"); anticlimax ("I have lost my heroism and my hair"; "into his face came again that expression, tragic, passive, and profoundly attentive, which dyspeptics wear")—and many tones: wry, sardonic, sarcastic, bitter, humorous.

Another frequent ironic situation develops out of differences in intelligence and taste, as in "The Golden Honeymoon," where Charley's crude mind and tastes are clearly different from Lardner's. A writer is not, of course, always ironic about people who are not developed intellectually or who do not have sophisticated tastes. Chekhov admires Gusev's simplicity, which, unlike Charley's in Lardner's story, is unaffected and inoffensive even when it reflects his prejudices. In fact, since the romantic period readers have tended to overvalue the simple, the natural, the primitive, and to be ironic about the sophisticated intellectual, as we indicate in our comments on "The Blind Man."

To recognize irony, the reader should have at least a moderately sophisticated sense of the times, and, in particular, a sense of the ideas and values of writers, although, of course, these vary. Sex, for example, can be redemptive for D. H. Lawrence, as in *Lady Chatterley's Lover;* for Faulkner it is generally a curse, an occasion for disintegrating lust, as in *The Sound and the Fury.* On the whole, the values of writers do not correspond to the generally accepted values of society; in our time serious writers are usually—though not always—ironic about middle-class values. But they can be ironic also about their own values. In "The Blind Man" (see our comments) Bertie Reid's literary cultivation is part of the civilized armor which hinders his full development as a person.

What is the relation between irony of structure and irony of situation? In a well-integrated story in which the structure turns on a meaningful irony, the irony of each moment or successive situation builds to the peripety, the moment that reverses the direction of the action and makes for irony of structure. So *Oedipus Rex,* and so, in our collection, "Death in Venice," "Grace," and "The Artificial Nigger." It is otherwise in "The White Silence." It can be said that the pine tree which falls on Mason gives the story an ironic turn, but it is not a meaningful irony for it does not grow out of the story. The falling tree is gratuitous, an example of cheap, sensational irony. For an irony to be valid, it must be integral to the story.

The ironic attitude reveals an ability to hold contradictory ideas at the same time. And whereas the ironic attitude is thus content only with complexity, the sentimental attitude is content only with simplicity. Sentimentality (not to be confused with sentiment) is the opposite of irony, and we need to understand both to fully understand either. Good writers abhor sentimentality, for although it is feeling, it is feeling mostly about oneself. When a lover moons over his lady or when a patriot sobs at the sight of the flag, both certainly have feelings about these objects, but more important to them—*without their being aware of it*—is the enjoyment of their own feelings, something quite different from a passion for someone or something else. Flaubert remarks about Emma Bovary, "She had to gain some personal profit from things, and she rejected as useless whatever did not contribute to the immediate satisfaction of her heart's desires—being of a temperament more sentimental than artistic, looking for emotions, not landscapes." Luxuriating in his feelings, the sentimentalist takes an uncritical, oversimplified view of the object. He abdicates his mind, the seat of irony. Irony is a function of mind at its critical best; sentimentality is a function of feeling at its self-indulgent worst. Sentimental, and therefore immature, literature is often melodrama. Sentimental characters are all good or evil—not, as people are, a mixture of these. We weep without qualification over the poor widow, the neglected mother, the jilted country girl, and the tortured political prisoner, and we hiss at the villain. The pity of it is that our tears express not our personal, but our conventional, stock response to a stock situation. Our feelings have been manipulated, not moved. It should be added that we are all sentimental to some extent, more perhaps than we realize. Hugo von Hofmannsthal observed that "each epoch has its own sentimentality, its specific way of overemphasizing strata of emotion." Examples in our time are notions like the human condition, the "little man," art, one world, and brotherhood. These examples indicate that the best intellectuals and artists can be sentimental as well as those who are generally less aware and so less critical of things.

Irony reflects the problematic, ambiguous character of modern life which has followed the breakdown of values. But it is an attitude that has undoubtedly always existed (the word originated with the Greeks) because a discrepancy between the ideals of a culture and actuality is inevitable. With this in mind we may possibly clear up a popular misconception. Even so wise a philosopher as Alfred North Whitehead deplores irony, saying that it "signifies the state of mind of people of an age which has lost faith. They conceal their loss, or even flaunt it by laughter. You seldom get irony except from people who have been somehow more or less cleaned out." [1] This, the popular charge, is certainly fair in some instances, but it does not account for the feeling in the bitterly ironic remarks of Hamlet or of the fool in *King Lear,* or in the ironic laughter of Homer. Shakespeare and Homer, unlike logical philosophers, find irony compatible with reverence and passion; they have a passionate belief in life while also feeling dismay, bitterness, horror, or amusement at its shortcomings. And, far from the triviality often associated with it, the ironic sensibility is particularly conscious of the supreme irony, death—that contradiction of all our aspirations. This consciousness leads to a tragic sense of life, ironic in that it is stubbornly affirmative. As F. Scott Fitzgerald once defined it, the tragic sense is a feeling "that life is essentially a cheat and its conditions are those of defeat, and that the redeeming things are not 'happiness and pleasure' but the deeper satisfactions that come out of struggle." [2] In this collection the tragic sense is variously realized—on a lesser scale, certainly, than that of Shakespeare—especially in the stories of Mann, Hemingway, and Kafka; and the irony of the comic sense is realized in the stories of Böll, Frank O'Connor, Singer, and de Maupassant.

Although in our comments we examine irony of structure in "The Artificial Nigger" and irony of situation in "Gimpel the Fool," note that each story has both kinds.

[1] From *Dialogues of Alfred North Whitehead,* by Lucien Price, copyright 1954 by Little, Brown & Company, reprinted by permission of Little, Brown & Company, Boston.

[2] From *The Crack-Up,* edited by Edmund Wilson, p. 306, copyright 1945 by New Directions, reprinted by permission of New Directions, New York.

The Artificial Nigger

Flannery O'Connor

Mr. Head awakened to discover that the room was full of moonlight. He sat up and stared at the floor boards—the color of silver—and then at the ticking on his pillow, which might have been brocade, and after a second, he saw half of the moon five feet away in his shaving mirror, paused as if it were waiting for his permission to enter. It rolled forward and cast a dignifying light on everything. The straight chair against the wall looked stiff and attentive as if it were waiting an order and Mr. Head's trousers, hanging to the back of it, had an almost noble air, like the garment some great man had just flung to his servant; but the face on the moon was a grave one. It gazed across the room and out the window where it floated over the horse stall and appeared to contemplate itself with the look of a young man who sees his old age before him.

Mr. Head could have said to it that age was a choice blessing and that only with years does a man enter into that calm understanding of life that makes him a suitable guide for the young. This, at least, had been his own experience.

He sat up and grasped the iron posts at the foot of his bed and raised himself until he could see the face on the alarm clock which sat on an overturned bucket beside the chair. The hour was two in the morning. The alarm on the clock did not work but he was not dependent on any mechanical means to awaken him. Sixty years had not dulled his responses; his physical reactions, like his moral ones, were guided by his will and strong character, and these could be seen plainly in his features. He had a long tube-like face with a long rounded open jaw and a long depressed nose. His eyes were alert but quiet, and in the miraculous moonlight they had a look of composure and of ancient wisdom as if they belonged to one of the great guides of men. He might have been Vergil summoned in the middle of the night to go to Dante, or better, Raphael, awakened by a blast of God's light to fly to the side of Tobias. The only dark spot in the room was Nelson's pallet, underneath the shadow of the window.

Nelson was hunched over on his side, his knees under his chin and his heels under his bottom. His new suit and hat were in the boxes that they had been sent in and these were on the floor at the foot of the pallet where he could get his hands on them as soon as he woke up. The slop jar, out of the shadow and made snow-white in the moonlight, appeared to stand guard over him like a small personal angel. Mr. Head lay back down, feeling entirely confident that he could carry out the moral mission of the coming day. He meant to be up before Nelson and to have the breakfast cooking by the time he awakened. The boy was always irked when Mr. Head was the first up. They would have to leave the house at four to get to the railroad junction by five-thirty. The train was to stop for them at five forty-five and they had to be there on time for this train was stopping merely to accommodate them.

This would be the boy's first trip to the city though he claimed it would be his second because he had been born there. Mr. Head had tried to point out to him that when he was born he didn't have the intelligence to determine his whereabouts but this had made no impression on the child at all and he continued to insist that this was to be his second trip. It would be Mr. Head's third trip. Nelson had said, "I will've already been there twict and I ain't but ten."

Mr. Head had contradicted him.

"If you ain't been there in fifteen years, how you know you'll be able to find your way about?" Nelson had asked. "How you know it hasn't changed some?"

"Have you ever," Mr. Head had asked, "seen me lost?"

Nelson certainly had not but he was a child who was never satisfied until he had given an impudent answer and he replied, "It's nowhere around here to get lost at."

"The day is going to come," Mr. Head prophesied, "when you'll find you ain't as smart as you think you are." He had been thinking about this trip for several months but it was for the most part in moral terms that he conceived it. It was to be a lesson that the boy would never forget. He was to find out from it that he had no cause for pride merely because he had been born in a city. He was to find out that the city is not a great place. Mr. Head meant him to see everything there is to see in a city so that he would be content to stay at home for the rest of his life. He fell asleep thinking how the boy would at last find out that he was not as smart as he thought he was.

He was awakened at three-thirty by the smell of fatback frying and he leaped off his cot. The pallet was empty and the clothes boxes had been thrown open. He put on his trousers and ran into the other room. The boy had a corn pone on cooking and had fried the meat. He was sitting in the half-dark at the table, drinking cold coffee out of a can. He had on his new suit and his new gray hat pulled low over his eyes. It was too big for him but they had ordered it a size larger because they expected his head to grow. He didn't say anything but his entire figure suggested satisfaction at having arisen before Mr. Head.

Mr. Head went to the stove and brought the meat to the table in the skillet. "It's no hurry," he said. "You'll get there soon enough and it's no guarantee you'll like it when you do neither," and he sat down across from the boy whose hat teetered back slowly to reveal a fiercely expressionless face, very much the same shape as the old man's. They were grandfather and grandson but they looked enough alike to be brothers and brothers not too far apart in age, for Mr. Head had a youthful expression by daylight, while the boy's look was ancient, as if he knew everything already and would be pleased to forget it.

Mr. Head had once had a wife and daughter and when the wife died, the daughter ran away and returned after an interval with Nelson. Then one morning, without getting out of bed, she died and left Mr. Head with sole care of the year-old child. He had made the mistake of telling Nelson that he had been born in Atlanta. If he hadn't told him that, Nelson couldn't have insisted that this was going to be his second trip.

"You may not like it a bit," Mr. Head continued. "It'll be full of niggers."

The boy made a face as if he could handle a nigger.

"All right," Mr. Head said. "You ain't ever seen a nigger."

"You wasn't up very early," Nelson said.

"You ain't ever seen a nigger," Mr. Head repeated. "There hasn't been a nigger in this county since we run that one out twelve years ago and that was before you were born." He looked at the boy as if he were daring him to say he had ever seen a Negro.

"How you know I never saw a nigger when I lived there before?" Nelson asked. "I probably saw a lot of niggers."

"If you seen one you didn't know what he was," Mr. Head said, completely exasperated. "A six-month-old child don't know a nigger from anybody else."

"I reckon I'll know a nigger if I see one," the boy said and got up and straightened his slick sharply creased gray hat and went outside to the privy.

They reached the junction some time before the train was due to arrive and stood about two feet from the first set of tracks. Mr. Head carried a paper sack with some biscuits and a can of sardines in it for their lunch. A coarse-looking orange-colored sun coming up behind the east range of mountains was making the sky a dull red behind them, but in front of them it was still gray and they faced a gray transparent moon, hardly stronger than a thumbprint and completely without light. A small tin switch box and a black fuel tank were all there was to mark the place as a junction; the tracks were double and did not converge again until they were hidden behind the bends at either end of the clearing. Trains passing appeared to emerge from a tunnel of trees and, hit for a second by the cold sky, vanish terrified into the woods again. Mr. Head had had to make special arrangements with the ticket agent to have this train stop and he was secretly afraid it would not, in which case, he knew Nelson would say, "I never thought no train was going to stop for you." Under the useless morning moon the tracks looked white and fragile. Both the old man and the child stared ahead as if they were awaiting an apparition.

Then suddenly, before Mr. Head could make up his mind to turn back, there was a deep warning bleat and the train appeared, gliding very slowly, almost silently around the bend of trees about two hundred yards down the track, with one yellow front light shining. Mr. Head was still not certain it would stop and he felt it would make an even bigger idiot of him if it went by slowly. But he and Nelson, however, were prepared to ignore the train if it passed them.

The engine charged by, filling their noses with the smell of hot metal and then the second coach came to a stop exactly where they were standing. A conductor with the face of an ancient bloated bulldog was on the step as if he expected them, though he did not look as if it mattered one way or the other to him if they got on or not. "To the right," he said.

Their entry took only a fraction of a second and the train was already speeding on as they entered the quiet car. Most of the travelers were still sleeping, some with their heads hanging off the chair arms, some stretched across two seats, and some sprawled out with the feet in the aisle. Mr. Head saw two unoccupied seats and pushed Nelson toward them. "Get in there by the winder," he said in his normal voice which was very loud at this hour of the morning. "Nobody cares if you set there because it's nobody in it. Sit right there."

"I heard you," the boy muttered. "It's no use in you yelling," and he sat down and turned his head to the glass. There he saw a pale ghost-like face scowling at him beneath the brim of a pale ghost-like hat. His grandfather, looking quickly too, saw a different ghost, pale but grinning, under a black hat.

Mr. Head sat down and settled himself and took out his ticket and started reading aloud everything that was printed on it. People began to stir. Several woke up and stared at him. "Take off your hat," he said to Nelson and took off his own and put it on his knee. He had a small amount of white hair that had turned tobacco-colored over the years and this lay flat across the back of his head. The front of his head was bald and creased. Nelson took off his hat and put it on his knee and they waited for the conductor to come ask for their tickets.

The man across the aisle from them was spread out over two seats, his feet propped on the window and his head jutting into the aisle. He had on a light blue suit and a yellow shirt unbuttoned at the neck. His eyes had just opened and Mr. Head was ready to introduce himself when the conductor came up from behind and growled, "Tickets."

When the conductor had gone, Mr. Head gave Nelson the return half of his ticket and said, "Now put that in your pocket and don't lose it or you'll have to stay in the city."

"Maybe I will," Nelson said as if this were a reasonable suggestion.

Mr. Head ignored him. "First time this boy has ever been on a train," he explained to the man across the aisle, who was sitting up now on the edge of his seat with both feet on the floor.

Nelson jerked his hat on again and turned angrily to the window.

"He's never seen anything before," Mr. Head continued. "Ignorant as the day he was born, but I mean for him to get his fill once and for all."

The boy leaned forward, across his grandfather and toward the stranger. "I was born in the city," he said. "I was born there. This is my second trip." He said it in a high positive voice but the man across the aisle didn't look as if he understood. There were heavy purple circles under his eyes.

Mr. Head reached across the aisle and tapped him on the arm. "The thing to do with a boy," he said sagely, "is to show him all it is to show. Don't hold nothing back."

"Yeah," the man said. He gazed down at his swollen feet and lifted the left one about ten inches from the floor. After a minute he put it down and lifted the other. All through the car people began to get up and move about and yawn and stretch. Separate voices could be heard here and there and then a general hum. Suddenly Mr. Head's serene expression changed. His mouth almost closed and a light, fierce and cautious both, came into his eyes. He was looking down the length of the car. Without turning, he caught Nelson by the arm and pulled him forward. "Look," he said.

A huge coffee-colored man was coming slowly forward. He had on a light suit and a yellow satin tie with a ruby pin on it. One of his hands rested on his stomach which rode majestically under his buttoned coat, and in the other he held the head of a black walking stick that he picked up and set down with a deliberate outward motion each time he took a step. He was proceeding very slowly, his large brown eyes gazing over the heads of the passengers. He had a small white mustache and white crinkly hair. Behind him there were two young women, both coffee-colored, one in a yellow dress and one in a green. Their progress was kept at the rate of his and they chatted in low throaty voices as they followed him.

Mr. Head's grip was tightening insistently on Nelson's arm. As the procession passed them, the light from a sapphire ring on the brown hand that picked up the cane reflected in Mr. Head's eye, but he did not look up nor did the tremendous man look at him. The group proceeded up the rest of the aisle and out of the car. Mr. Head's grip on Nelson's arm loosened. "What was that?" he asked.

"A man," the boy said and gave him an indignant look as if he were tired of having his intelligence insulted.

"What kind of a man?" Mr. Head persisted, his voice expressionless.

"A fat man," Nelson said. He was beginning to feel that he had better be cautious.

"You don't know what kind?" Mr. Head said in a final tone.

"An old man," the boy said and had a sudden foreboding that he was not going to enjoy the day.

'That was a nigger," Mr. Head said and sat back.

Nelson jumped up on the seat and stood looking backward to the end of the car but the Negro had gone.

"I'd of thought you'd know a nigger since you seen so many when you was in the city on your first visit," Mr. Head continued. "That's his first nigger," he said to the man across the aisle.

The boy slid down into the seat. "You said they were black," he said in an angry voice. "You never said they were tan. How do you expect me to know anything when you don't tell me right?"

"You're just ignorant is all," Mr. Head said and he got up and moved over in the vacant seat by the man across the aisle.

Nelson turned backward again and looked where the Negro had disappeared. He felt that the Negro had deliberately walked down the aisle in order to make a fool of him and he hated him with a fierce raw fresh hate; and also, he understood now why his grandfather disliked them. He looked toward the window and the face there seemed to suggest that he might be inadequate to the day's exactions. He wondered if he would even recognize the city when they came to it.

After he had told several stories, Mr. Head realized that the man he was talking to was asleep and he got up and suggested to Nelson that they walk over the train and see the parts of it. He particularly wanted the boy to see the toilet so they went first to the men's room and examined the plumbing. Mr. Head demonstrated the ice-water cooler as if he had invented it and showed Nelson the bowl with the single spigot where the travelers brushed their teeth. They went through several cars and came to the diner.

This was the most elegant car in the train. It was painted a rich egg-yellow and had a wine-colored carpet on the floor. There were wide windows over the tables and great spaces of the rolling view were caught in miniature in the sides of the coffee pots and in the glasses. Three very black Negroes in white suits and aprons were running up and down the aisle, swinging trays and bowing and bending over the travelers eating breakfast. One of them rushed up to Mr. Head and Nelson and said, holding up two fingers, "Space for two!" but Mr. Head replied in a loud voice, "We eaten before we left!"

The waiter wore large brown spectacles that increased the size of his eye whites. "Stan' aside then please," he said with an airy wave of the arm as if he were brushing aside flies.

Neither Nelson nor Mr. Head moved a fraction of an inch. "Look," Mr. Head said.

The near corner of the diner, containing two tables, was set off from the rest by a saffron-colored curtain. One table was set but empty but at the other, facing them, his back to the drape, sat the tremendous Negro. He was speaking in a soft voice to the two women while he buttered a muffin. He had a heavy sad face and his neck bulged over his white collar on either side. "They rope them off," Mr. Head explained. Then he said, "Let's go see the kitchen," and they walked the length of the diner but the black waiter was coming fast behind them.

"Passengers are not allowed in the kitchen!" he said in a haughty voice. "Passengers are NOT allowed in the kitchen!"

Mr. Head stopped where he was and turned. "And there's good reason for that," he shouted into the Negro's chest, "because the cockroaches would run the passengers out!"

All the travelers laughed and Mr. Head and Nelson walked out, grinning. Mr. Head was known at home for his quick wit and Nelson felt a sudden keen pride in him. He realized the old man would be his only support in the strange place they were approaching. He would be entirely alone in the world if he were ever lost from his grandfather. A terrible excitement shook him and he wanted to take hold of Mr. Head's coat and hold on like a child.

As they went back to their seats they could see through the passing windows that the countryside was becoming speckled with small houses and shacks and that a highway ran alongside the train. Cars sped by on it, very small and fast. Nelson felt that there was less breath in the air than there had been thirty minutes ago. The man across the aisle had left and there was no one near for Mr. Head to hold a conversation with so he looked out the window, through his own reflection, and read aloud the names of the buildings they were passing. "The Dixie Chemical Corp!" he announced. "Southern Maid Flour! Dixie Doors! Southern Belle Cotton Products! Patty's Peanut Butter! Southern Mammy Cane Syrup!"

"Hush up!" Nelson hissed.

All over the car people were beginning to get up and take their luggage off the overhead racks. Women were putting on their coats and hats. The conductor stuck his head in the car and snarled, "Firstoppppppmry," and Nelson lunged out of his sitting position, trembling. Mr. Head pushed him down by the shoulder.

"Keep your seat," he said in dignified tones. "The first stop is on the edge of town. The second stop is at the main railroad station." He had come by this knowledge on his first trip when he had got off at the first stop and had had to pay a man fifteen cents to take him into the heart of town. Nelson sat back down, very pale. For the first time in his life, he understood that his grandfather was indispensable to him.

The train stopped and let off a few passengers and glided on as if it had never ceased moving. Outside, behind rows of brown rickety houses, a line of blue buildings stood up, and beyond them a pale rose-gray sky faded away to nothing. The train moved into the railroad yard. Looking down, Nelson saw lines and lines of silver tracks multiplying and crisscrossing. Then before he could start counting them, the face in the window stared out at him, gray but distinct, and he looked the other way. The train was in the station. Both he and Mr. Head jumped up and ran to the door. Neither noticed that they had left the paper sack with the lunch in it on the seat.

They walked stiffly through the small station and came out of a heavy door into the squall of traffic. Crowds were hurrying to work. Nelson didn't know where to look. Mr. Head leaned against the side of the building and glared in front of him.

Finally Nelson said, "Well, how do you see what all it is to see?"

Mr. Head didn't answer. Then as if the sight of people passing had given him the clue, he said, "You walk," and started off down the street.

Nelson followed, steadying his hat. So many sights and sounds were flooding in on him that for the first block he hardly knew what he was seeing. At the second corner, Mr. Head turned and looked behind him at the station they had left, a putty-colored terminal with a concrete dome on top. He thought that if he could keep the dome always in sight, he would be able to get back in the afternoon to catch the train again.

As they walked along, Nelson began to distinguish details and take note of the store windows, jammed with every kind of equipment—hardware, drygoods, chicken feed, liquor. They passed one that Mr. Head called his particular attention to where you walked in and sat on a chair with your feet upon two rests and let a Negro polish your shoes. They walked slowly and stopped and stood at the entrances so he could see what went on in each place but they did not go into any of them. Mr. Head was determined not to go into any city store because on his first trip here, he had got lost in a large one and had found his way out only after many people had insulted him.

They came in the middle of the next block to a store that had a weighing machine in front of it and they both in turn stepped up on it and put in a penny and received a ticket. Mr. Head's ticket said, "You weigh 120 pounds. You are upright and brave and all your friends admire you." He put the ticket in his pocket, surprised that the machine should have got his character correct but his weight wrong, for he had weighed on a grain scale not long before and knew he weighed 110. Nelson's ticket said, 'You weigh 98 pounds. You have a great destiny ahead of you but beware of dark women." Nelson did not know any women and he weighed only 68 pounds but Mr. Head pointed out that the machine had probably printed the number upsidedown, meaning the 9 for a 6.

They walked on and at the end of five blocks the dome of the terminal sank out of sight and Mr. Head turned to the left. Nelson could have stood in front of every store window for an hour if there had not been another more interesting one next to it. Suddenly he said, "I was born here!" Mr. Head turned and looked at him with horror. There was a sweaty brightness about his face. "This is where I come from!" he said.

Mr. Head was appalled. He saw the moment had come for drastic action. "Lemme show you one thing you ain't seen yet," he said and took him to the corner where there was a sewer entrance. "Squat down," he said, "and stick your head in there," and he held the back of the boy's coat while he got down and put his head in the sewer. He drew it back quickly, hearing a gurgling in the depths under the sidewalk. Then Mr. Head explained the sewer system, how the entire city was underlined with it, how it contained all the drainage and was full of rats and how a man could slide into it and be sucked along down endless pitchblack tunnels. At any minute any man in the city might be sucked into the sewer and never heard from again. He described it so well that Nelson was for some seconds shaken. He connected the sewer passages with the entrance to hell and understood for the first time how the world was put together in its lower parts. He drew away from the curb.

Then he said, "Yes, but you can stay away from the holes," and his face took on that stubborn look that was so exasperating to his grandfather. "This is where I come from!" he said.

Mr. Head was dismayed but he only muttered, "You'll get your fill," and they walked on. At the end of two more blocks he turned to the left, feeling that he was circling the dome; and he was correct for in a half-hour they passed in front of the railroad station again. At first Nelson did not notice that he was seeing the same stores twice but when they passed the one where you put your feet on the rests while the Negro polished your shoes, he perceived that they were walking in a circle.

"We done been here!" he shouted. "I don't believe you know where you're at!"

"The direction just slipped my mind for a minute," Mr. Head said and they turned down a different street. He still did not intend to let the dome get too far away and after two blocks in their new direction, he turned to the left. This street contained two- and three-story wooden dwellings. Anyone passing on the sidewalk could see into the rooms and Mr. Head, glancing through one window, saw a woman lying on an iron bed, looking out, with a sheet pulled over her. Her knowing expression shook him. A fierce-looking boy on a bicycle came driving down out of nowhere and he had to jump to the side to keep from being hit. "It's nothing to them if they knock you down," he said. "You better keep closer to me."

They walked on for some time on streets like this before he remembered to turn again. The houses they were passing now were all unpainted and the wood in them looked rotten; the street between was narrower. Nelson saw a colored man. Then another. Then another. "Niggers live in these houses," he observed.

"Well come on and we'll go somewhere else," Mr. Head said. "We didn't come to look at niggers," and they turned down another street but they continued to see Negroes everywhere. Nelson's skin began to prickle and they stepped along at a faster pace in order to leave the neighborhood as soon as possible. There were colored men in their undershirts standing in the doors and colored women rocking on the sagging porches. Colored children played in the gutters and stopped what they were doing to look at them. Before long they began to pass rows of stores with colored customers in them but they didn't pause at the entrances of these. Black eyes in black faces were watching them from every direction. "Yes," Mr. Head said, "this is where you were born—right here with all these niggers."

Nelson scowled. "I think you done got us lost," he said.

Mr. Head swung around sharply and looked for the dome. It was nowhere in sight. "I ain't got us lost either," he said. "You're just tired of walking."

"I ain't tired, I'm hungry," Nelson said. "Give me a biscuit."

They discovered then that they had lost the lunch.

"You were the one holding the sack," Nelson said. "I would have kepaholt of it."

"If you want to direct this trip, I'll go on by myself and leave you right here," Mr. Head said and was pleased to see the boy turn white. However, he realized they were lost and drifting farther every minute from the station. He was hungry himself and beginning to be thirsty and since they had been in the colored neighborhood, they had both begun to sweat. Nelson had on his shoes and he was unaccustomed to them. The concrete sidewalks were very hard. They both wanted to find a place to sit down but this was impossible and they kept on walking, the boy muttering under his breath, "First you lost the sack and then you lost the way," and Mr. Head growling from time to time, "Anybody wants to be from this nigger heaven can be from it!"

By now the sun was well forward in the sky. The odor of dinners cooking drifted out to them. The Negroes were all at their doors to see them pass. "Whyn't you ast one of these niggers the way?" Nelson said. "You got us lost."

"This is where you were born," Mr. Head said. "You can ast one yourself if you want to."

Nelson was afraid of the colored men and he didn't want to be laughed at by the colored children. Up ahead he saw a large colored woman lean-ing in a doorway that opened onto the sidewalk. Her hair stood straight out from her head for about four inches all around and she was resting on bare brown feet that turned pink at the sides. She had on a pink dress that showed her exact shape. As they came abreast of her, she lazily lifted one hand to her head and her fingers disappeared into her hair.

Nelson stopped. He felt his breath drawn up by the woman's dark eyes. "How do you get back to town?" he said in a voice that did not sound like his own.

After a minute she said, "You in town now," in a rich low tone that made Nelson feel as if a cool spray had been turned on him.

"How do you get back to the train?" he said in the same reed-like voice.

"You can catch you a car," she said.

He understood she was making fun of him but he was too paralyzed even to scowl. He stood drinking in every detail of her. His eyes traveled up from her great knees to her forehead and then made a triangular path from the glistening sweat on her neck down and across her tre-mendous bosom and over her bare arm back to where her fingers lay hidden in her hair. He suddenly wanted her to reach down and pick him up and draw him against her and then he wanted to feel her breath on his face. He wanted to look down and down into her eyes while she held him tighter and tighter. He had never had such a feeling before. He felt as if he were reeling down through a pitchblack tunnel.

"You can go a block down yonder and catch you a car take you to the railroad station, Sugarpie," she said.

Nelson would have collapsed at her feet if Mr. Head had not pulled him roughly away. "You act like you don't have any sense!" the old man growled.

They hurried down the street and Nelson did not look back at the woman. He pushed his hat sharply forward over his face which was already burning with shame. The sneering ghost he had seen in the train window and all the foreboding feelings he had on the way returned to him and he remembered that his ticket from the scale had said to beware of dark women and that his grandfather's had said he was upright and brave. He took hold of the old man's hand, a sign of dependence that he seldom showed.

They headed down the street toward the car tracks where a long yellow rattling trolley was coming. Mr. Head had never boarded a streetcar and he let that one pass. Nelson was silent. From time to time his mouth trembled slightly but his grandfather, occupied with his own problems, paid him no attention. They stood on the corner and neither looked at the Negroes who were passing, going about their business just as if they had been white, except that most of them stopped and eyed Mr. Head and Nelson. It occurred to Mr. Head that since the streetcar ran on tracks, they could simply follow the tracks. He gave Nelson a slight push and explained that they would follow the tracks on into the railroad station, walking, and they set off.

Presently to their great relief they began to see white people again and Nelson sat down on the sidewalk against the wall of a building. "I got to rest myself some," he said. "You lost the sack and the direction. You can just wait on me to rest myself."

"There's the tracks in front of us," Mr. Head said. "All we got to do is keep them in sight and you could have remembered the sack as good as me. This is where you were born. This is your old home town. This is your second trip. You ought to know how to do," and he squatted down and continued in this vein but the boy, easing his burning feet out of his shoes, did not answer.

"And standing there grinning like a chim-pan-zee while a nigger woman gives you directions. Great Gawd!" Mr. Head said.

"I never said I was nothing but born here," the boy said in a shaky voice. "I never said I would or wouldn't like it. I never said I wanted to come. I only said I was born here and I never had nothing to do with that. I want to go home. I never wanted to come in the first place. It was all your big idea. How you know you ain't following the tracks in the wrong direction?"

This last had occurred to Mr. Head too. "All these people are white," he said.

"We ain't passed here before," Nelson said. This was a neighborhood of brick buildings that might have been lived in or might not. A few empty automobiles were parked along the curb and there was an occasional passerby. The heat of the pavement came up through Nelson's thin suit. His eyelids began to droop, and after a few minutes his head tilted forward. His shoulders twitched once or twice and then he fell over on his side and lay sprawled in an exhausted fit of sleep.

Mr. Head watched him silently. He was very tired himself but they could not both sleep at the same time and he could not have slept anyway because he did not know where he was. In a few minutes Nelson would wake up, refreshed by his sleep and very cocky, and would begin complaining that he had lost the sack and the way. You'd have a mighty sorry time if I wasn't here, Mr. Head thought; and then another idea occurred to him. He looked at the sprawled figure for several minutes; presently he stood up. He justified what he was going to do on the grounds that it is sometimes necessary to teach a child a lesson he won't forget, particularly when the child is always reasserting his position with some new impudence. He walked without a sound to the corner about twenty feet away and sat down on a covered garbage can in the alley where he could look out and watch Nelson wake up alone.

The boy was dozing fitfully, half conscious of vague noises and black forms moving up from some dark part of him into the light. His face worked in his sleep and he had pulled his knees up under his chin. The sun shed a dull light on the narrow street; everything looked like exactly what it was. After a while Mr. Head, hunched like an old monkey on the garbage can lid, decided that if Nelson didn't wake up soon, he would make a loud noise by bamming his foot against the can. He looked at his watch and discovered that it was two o'clock. Their train left at six and the possibility of missing it was too awful for him to think of. He kicked hs foot backwards on the can and a hollow boom reverberated in the alley.

Nelson shot up onto his feet with a shout. He looked where his grandfather should have been and stared. He seemed to whirl several times and then, picking up his feet and throwing his head back, he dashed down the street like a wild maddened pony. Mr. Head jumped off the can and galloped after but the child was almost out of sight. He saw a streak of gray disappearing diagonally a block ahead. He ran as fast as he could, looking both ways down every intersection, but without sight of him again. Then as he passed the third intersection completely winded, he saw about half a block down the street a scene that stopped him altogether. He crouched behind a trash box to watch and get his bearings.

Nelson was sitting with both legs spread out and by his side lay an elderly woman, screaming. Groceries were scattered about the sidewalk. A crowd of women had already gathered to see justice done and Mr. Head distinctly heard the old woman on the pavement shout, "You've broken my ankle and your daddy'll pay for it! Every nickel! Police! Police!" Several of the women were plucking at Nelson's shoulder but the boy seemed too dazed to get up.

Something forced Mr. Head from behind the trash box and forward, but only at a creeping pace. He had never in his life been accosted by a policeman. The women were milling around Nelson as if they might suddenly all dive on him at once and tear him to pieces, and the old woman continued to scream that her ankle was broken and to call for an officer. Mr. Head came on so slowly that he could have been taking a backward step after each forward one, but when he was about ten feet away, Nelson saw him and sprang. The child caught him around the hips and clung panting against him.

The women all turned on Mr. Head. The injured one sat up and shouted, "You sir! You'll pay every penny of my doctor's bill that your boy has caused. He's a juvenile delinquent! Where is an officer? Somebody take this man's name and address!"

Mr. Head was trying to detach Nelson's fingers from the flesh in the back of his legs. The old man's head had lowered itself into his collar like a turtle; his eyes were glazed with fear and caution.

"Your boy has broken my ankle!" the old woman shouted. "Police!"

Mr. Head sensed the approach of the policeman from behind. He stared straight ahead at the women who were massed in their fury like a solid wall to block his escape. "This is not my boy," he said. "I never seen him before."

He felt Nelson's fingers fall out of his flesh.

The women dropped back, staring at him with horror, as if they were so repulsed by a man who would deny his own image and likeness that they could not bear to lay hands on him. Mr. Head walked on, through a space they silently cleared, and left Nelson behind. Ahead of him he saw nothing but a hollow tunnel that had once been the street.

The boy remained standing where he was, his neck craned forward and his hands hanging by his sides. His hat was jammed on his head so that there were no longer any creases in it. The injured woman got up and shook her fist at him and the others gave him pitying looks, but he didn't notice any of them. There was no policeman in sight.

In a minute he began to move mechanically, making no effort to catch up with his grandfather but merely following at about twenty paces. They walked on for five blocks in this way. Mr. Head's shoulders were sagging and his neck hung forward at such an angle that it was not visible from behind. He was afraid to turn his head. Finally he cut a short hopeful glance over his shoulder. Twenty feet behind him, he saw two small eyes piercing into his back like pitchfork prongs.

The boy was not of a forgiving nature but this was the first time he had ever had anything to forgive. Mr. Head had never disgraced himself before. After two more blocks, he turned and called over his shoulder in a high desperately gay voice, "Let's us go get us a Co' Cola somewheres!"

Nelson, with a dignity he had never shown before, turned and stood with his back to his grandfather.

Mr. Head began to feel the depth of his denial. His face as they walked on became all hollows and bare ridges. He saw nothing they were passing but he perceived that they had lost the car tracks. There was no dome to be seen anywhere and the afternoon was advancing. He knew that if dark overtook them in the city, they would be beaten and robbed. The speed of God's justice was only what he expected for himself, but he could not stand to think that his sins would be visited upon Nelson and that even now, he was leading the boy to his doom.

They continued to walk on block after block through an endless section of small brick houses until Mr. Head almost fell over a water spigot sticking up about six inches off the edge of a grass plot. He had not had a drink of water since early morning but he felt he did not deserve it now. Then he thought that Nelson would be thirsty and they would both drink and be brought together. He squatted down and put his mouth to the nozzle and turned a cold stream of water into his throat. Then he called out in the high desperate voice, "Come on and getcher some water!"

This time the child stared through him for nearly sixty seconds. Mr. Head got up and walked on as if he had drunk poison. Nelson, though he had not had water since some he had drunk out of a paper cup on the train, passed by the spigot, disdaining to drink where his grandfather had. When Mr. Head realized this, he lost all hope. His face in the waning afternoon light looked ravaged and abandoned. He could feel the boy's steady hate, traveling at an even pace behind him and he knew that (if by some miracle they escaped being murdered in the city) it would continue just that way for the rest of his life. He knew that now he was wandering into a black strange place where nothing was like it had ever been before, a long old age without respect and an end that would be welcome because it would be the end.

As for Nelson, his mind had frozen around his grandfather's treachery as if he were trying to preserve it intact to present at the final judgment. He walked without looking to one side or the other, but every now and then his mouth would twitch and this was when he felt, from some remote place inside himself, a black mysterious form reach up as if it would melt his frozen vision in one hot grasp.

The sun dropped down behind a row of houses and hardly noticing, they passed into an elegant suburban section where mansions were set back from the road by lawns with birdbaths on them. Here everything was entirely deserted. For blocks they didn't pass even a dog. The big white houses were like partially submerged icebergs in the distance. There were no sidewalks, only drives and these wound around and around in endless ridiculous circles. Nelson made no move to come nearer to Mr. Head. The old man felt that if he saw a sewer entrance he would drop down into it and let himself be carried away; and he could imagine the boy standing by, watching with only a slight interest, while he disappeared.

A loud bark jarred him to attention and he looked up to see a fat man approaching with two bulldogs. He waved both arms like someone shipwrecked on a desert island. "I'm lost!" he called. "I'm lost and can't find my way and me and this boy have got to catch this train and I can't find the station. Oh Gawd I'm lost! Oh help me Gawd I'm lost!"

The man, who was bald-headed and had on golf knickers, asked him what train he was trying to catch and Mr. Head began to get out his tickets, trembling so violently he could hardly hold them. Nelson had come up to within fifteen feet and stood watching.

"Well," the fat man said, giving him back the tickets, "you won't have time to get back to town to make this but you can catch it at the suburb stop. That's three blocks from here," and he began explaining how to get there.

Mr. Head stared as if he were slowly returning from the dead and when the man had finished and gone off with the dogs jumping at his heels, he turned to Nelson and said breathlessly, "We're going to get home!"

The child was standing about ten feet away, his face bloodless under the gray hat. His eyes were triumphantly cold. There was no light in them, no feeling, no interest. He was merely there, a small figure, waiting. Home was nothing to him.

Mr. Head turned slowly. He felt he knew now what time would be like without seasons and what heat would be like without light and what man would be like without salvation. He didn't care if he never made the train and if it had not been for what suddenly caught his attention, like a cry out of the gathering dusk, he might have forgotten there was a station to go to.

He had not walked five hundred yards down the road when he saw, within reach of him, the plaster figure of a Negro sitting bent over on a low yellow brick fence that curved around a wide lawn. The Negro was about Nelson's size and he was pitched forward at an unsteady angle because the putty that held him to the wall had cracked. One of his eyes was entirely white and he held a piece of brown watermelon.

Mr. Head stood looking at him silently until Nelson stopped at a little distance. Then as the two of them stood there, Mr. Head breathed, "An artificial nigger!"

It was not possible to tell if the artificial Negro were meant to be young or old; he looked too miserable to be either. He was meant to look happy because his mouth was stretched up at the corners but the chipped eye and the angle he was cocked at gave him a wild look of misery instead.

"An artificial nigger!" Nelson repeated in Mr. Head's exact tone.

The two of them stood there with their necks forward at almost the same angle and their shoulders curved in almost exactly the same way and their hands trembling identically in their pockets. Mr. Head looked like an ancient child and Nelson like a miniature old man. They stood gazing at the artificial Negro as if they were faced with some great mystery, some monument to another's victory that brought them together in their common defeat. They could both feel it dissolving their differences like an action of mercy. Mr. Head had never known before what mercy felt like because he had been too good to deserve any, but he felt he knew now. He looked at Nelson and understood that he must say something to the child to show that he was still wise and in the look the boy returned he saw a hungry need for that assurance. Nelson's eyes seemed to implore him to explain once and for all the mystery of existence.

Mr. Head opened his lips to make a lofty statement and heard himself say, "They ain't got enough real ones here. They got to have an artificial one."

After a second, the boy nodded with a strange shivering about his mouth, and said, "Let's go home before we get ourselves lost again."

Their train glided into the suburb stop just as they reached the station and they boarded it together, and ten minutes before it was due to arrive at the junction, they went to the door and stood ready to jump off if it did not stop; but it did, just as the moon, restored to its full splendor, sprang from a cloud and flooded the clearing with light. As they stepped off, the sage grass was shivering gently in shades of silver and the clinkers under their feet glittered with a fresh black light. The treetops, fencing the junction like the protecting walls of a garden, were darker than the sky which was hung with gigantic white clouds illuminated like lanterns.

Mr. Head stood very still and felt the action of mercy touch him again but this time he knew that there were no words in the world that could name it. He understood that it grew out of agony, which is not denied to any man and which is given in strange ways to children. He understood it was all a man could carry into death to give his Maker and he suddenly burned with shame that he had so little of it to take with him. He stood appalled, judging himself with the thoroughness of God, while the action of mercy covered his pride like a flame and consumed it. He had never thought himself a great sinner before but he saw now that his true depravity had been hidden from him lest it cause him despair. He realized that he was forgiven for sins from the beginning of time, when he had conceived in his own heart the sin of Adam, until the present, when he had denied poor Nelson. He saw that no sin was too monstrous for him to claim as his own, and since God loved in proportion as He forgave, he felt ready at that instant to enter Paradise.

Nelson, composing his expression under the shadow of his hat brim, watched him with a mixture of fatigue and suspicion, but as the train glided past them and disappeared like a frightened serpent into the woods, even his face lightened and he muttered, "I'm glad I've went once, but I'll never go back again!"

COMMENT

This story is at bottom a theological drama of the sin of pride, and of redemption through grace. The drama is played out on three levels of conflict: personal, interpersonal, and social. There is conflict within the self, generated within Mr. Head and Nelson by their pride. At the same time there is conflict between them, the familiar Oedipal conflict between father (in this case, grand-father) and son (in this case, grandson). And there is conflict be-tween the two whites and the Negro. These conflicts are resolved in the passage of Mr. Head and Nelson from innocence to knowl-edge, a classic theme which for Nelson takes the form of the initi-ation of a young boy into the adult world. He unwittingly sets out on a road of trials, a journey into the unknown. His trial is the Negro, whom he has never seen before and whom he now en-counters continually, on the train and in the city. The strange and the unknown create in Nelson a crisis in identity. Thus the social conflict between Negro and white ironically reveals Nelson's con-flict within himself, caused in part by his pride as a white. And the confrontation of the artificial Negro crystallizes the theo-logical drama, the meaning of which is evident only to Mr. Head, for Nelson is only a boy. Mr. Head comes to know himself, his depravity; and, God being infinitely forgiving, he also comes to know the promise of redemption.

The central irony of the story is revealed through the plot. Mr. Head is a man who is very sure of himself, who believes that "age was a choice blessing and that only with years does a man enter into that calm understanding of life that makes him a suitable guide for the young"; he is confident that he can "carry out the moral mission of the coming day." But in the course of events Mr. Head learns how profoundly unsuitable a guide he is, not only geo-graphically but also morally and spiritually. This is irony of structure: things turn out differently from what Mr. Head ex-pected.

The plot develops along the lines of what is called dramatic or tragic irony: in *Oedipus Rex* Oedipus learns he is the murderer he has been seeking; similarly, Mr. Head, who at first considers himself moral and upright, learns that he is actually a man whose "true depravity had been hidden from him lest it cause him de-spair." The trip "was to be a lesson that the boy would never for-get," but it proves to be a lesson for him too. One distinction between modern and earlier tragedy lies in the magnitude of the hero; it was formerly argued that there can be no proper tragedy without an imposing figure like a king or a prince. Yet ordinary people may take on magnitude at times—at least this is Miss O'Connor's belief, as we see, for example, in the description of Mr. Head's clothes, which have "an almost noble air, like the garment [of] some great man," and at the end in his intense, apoca-lyptic vision. It is his *conscious* confrontation of his fate that makes Mr. Head a proper, and indeed a considerable, tragic figure. His tragedy, nevertheless, is only potential; it is actually converted into a special kind of comedy.

Mr. Head's denial of Nelson leads to his recognition of his moral depravity and his consequent spiritual forlornness; this is the first reversal in the story, its first irony. "He felt he knew now what time would be like without seasons and what heat would be like without light and what man would be like without salvation." This is a vision of hell. Miss O'Connor, however, is concerned not only with Mr. Head's fall but also with his salvation. And it was here that Miss O'Connor faced her perhaps most difficult problem: What would be an experience altogether realistic yet powerful enough to convince the reader that Mr. Head had experienced salvation? Precisely a confrontation with a Negro, the prime occasion of his pride. It is an ironic means of salvation for a Southerner, perhaps the only one for all whites, and the particular means is marvelously comic since the Negro is not real. Mr. Head and Nelson are confronted by the plaster figure of a Negro boy, which to them is "some great mystery, some monument to another's victory that brought them together in their common defeat." Ironies abound here for they believe that a Negro has had a statue erected to him, thus "their common defeat." That the figure is a symbol of social oppression and degradation is a counter irony which escapes them. Their defeat humbles them and draws them together. Pride separates them; humility unites them. Their differences are dissolved "like an action of mercy." And so Mr. Head learns that mercy grows "out of agony, which is not denied to any man and which is given in strange ways to children"; it grows in particular out of the agony of children like Nelson and the artificial Negro, who represents all Negroes. As the crucified Christ forgave mankind, so the "crucified" Negro—an analogue of Christ—forgives the white man. The plot, which up to this point develops along the lines of classical tragic irony, now takes another ironic turn, that of the Christian paradox that you must lose your life in order to find it, that you must die to be reborn. This is the archetypal pattern (see our introduction to the section "Symbolism") of Mr. Head's experience. Returned home, "he saw that no sin was too monstrous for him to claim as his own, and since God loved in proportion as He forgave, he felt ready at that instant to enter Paradise." Mr. Head's tragedy becomes, in Dante's sense, a divine comedy: subdued, muted, characteristically modern. He first suffers the irony of his tragic fall; he then is blessed with the irony of his redemption. This double ironic reversal is the pattern which stories of fall and redemption take, as the reader will see again in "Gimpel the Fool."

Irony may be crude or cheap, as in O. Henry's stories. The irony of a man's fall and redemption is sentimentalized in Sunday pulpits, popular fiction, and movies—for example, in technicolor renovations of the heavens at the moment of redemption, with the redeemed all starry-eyed, all pure. What distinguishes Miss O'Connor's handling is her complex tough-mindedness, as in the bewilderment and general ambiguity which mark Mr. Head and Nelson after their redemption or in Nelson's refusal to forgive Mr. Head after Mr. Head has betrayed him.

Miss O'Connor's sense of irony is given its severest test in the relationship between the Negro and the white man. She does not lapse into the easy sentimentality of most Northern newspapers and popular magazines, in which melodramas of white evil and black virtue regularly appear—or did appear until the black-power movement endowed the Negro with the ambiguities of power previously reserved for the white man. Miss O'Connor's total conception of the Negro is shaded with ironies. Consider that the fat, sad Negro on the train is prosperous and that his upper-class bearing indicates that he practices his own kind of discrimination. Recall also that the Negro waiter is as proud and haughty as Mr. Head is. The prostitute, who easily manages Nelson, is undoubtedly oppressed in a social sense, but as a particular person she gives every evidence of well-being. And in her views of the white man Miss O'Connor avoids as well the misleading simplifications of the popular, melodramatic version of our greatest national problem. Although Mr. Head is guilty of the usual faults (he would keep the Negro in his place and he boasts about having run one out of the county), he is nonetheless a man of good will, bent on giving moral and spiritual instruction. This subtle defining of the relation between the Negro and the white man suggests one distinction between "pure" art and propagandistic art. In the latter, people and events are represented without the ironies that make up a real situation. Miss O'Connor indicts the white man but makes demands of the Negro too. The white man must humble himself and admit his sin, but the Negro must learn to forgive him—perhaps a harder task. This is mercy, the ironic force which resolves the three principal conflicts we noted at the beginning of our comments. The theological drama resolves the conflicts within the self, between one self and another, and between the white self and a society in part Negro.

QUESTIONS ON IRONY

1. Humor is a form of irony. Thus the fat, bald-headed suburbanite wearing golf knickers, grotesquely humorous in the context of Mr. Head's despair, functions ironically as a momentary guide when he directs Mr. Head to the station. What other instances of humorous irony are there?

2. How does Miss O'Connor keep the humility of Mr. Head and Nelson unsentimental? Note Mr. Head's explanation of the statue.

3. "The Artificial Nigger" and "Grace" have grace as their subjects. Irony is a central force in both, but with what different attitudes and consequences?

4. Analyze the ironic structure of Nelson's initiation.

5. Keeping in mind that the ironic structure reveals meaning, analyze the ironic structure of "Gusev," "Red Leaves," and "Death in Venice."

6. Though at odds with each other, Mr. Head and Nelson are identical in several ways; for example, in the shape of the face. What does this irony signify? How does it prepare us for the resolution?

OTHER CONSIDERATIONS

1. With the theme of the fall and redemption of man in mind, we may take the analogy at the end between Mr. Head and Adam to be allegorical. Mr. Head is Adam, the *head* man, the first man, not merely Nelson's grandfather but the *grand* father of us all. How does Miss O'Connor give body to this allegory of Adam? Consider the allusions to the Garden of Eden at the end, the image of the departing train, and the changes in the moon from the opening to the close. Of course, the success of the story is dependent not on this muted allegory—although it does increase the story's density—but on the dramatic, natural surface.

2. Although Miss O'Connor's style is rich in imagery, its syntax is simple, its diction plain, and its tone flat. Is the change in the next-to-last paragraph simply fancy, elegant writing? Is the change dramatically effective? Consider also the effect of such stylistic changes in the conclusions of "Grace" and "A Clean, Well-Lighted Place" and in many places in "Death in Venice."

3. Does the idea in the next-to-last paragraph function dramatically as one element in the total meaning or is it merely tacked on as a kind of preachy moral?

4. Nelson is unnerved because the Negroes are strange to him. The advent of the strange—a stranger, a strange place, or a strange situation—marks the beginning of a crisis in identity. Consider similar moments in "Death in Venice," "Nina of Ashkelon," "Young Goodman Brown," and "The Blind Man."

5. Consider the handling of the theme of the passage from innocence to knowledge in "Wounds," "Gimpel the Fool" (see our comments), "Christmas Every Day" (see our comments), "Death in Venice," and "In My Indolence."

6. What images give concrete force to the theological abstraction that to sin is to be in hell?

7. The Negro is a redemptive force in "Powerhouse" also, primarily in relation to other Negroes but in relation to whites too. What is the difference in this redemptive force? Is it similar to the force in "The Blind Man," "The Fairy Goose," and "The Silence of the Valley"?

Gimpel the Fool

Isaac Bashevis Singer ❧

I

I am Gimpel the Fool. I don't think myself a fool. On the contrary. But that's what folks call me. They gave me the name while I was still in school. I had seven names in all: imbecile, donkey, flax-head, dope, glump, ninny, and fool. The last name stuck. What did my foolishness consist of? I was easy to take in. They said, "Gimpel, you know the rabbi's wife has been brought to childbed?" So I skipped school. Well, it turned out to be a lie. How was I supposed to know? She hadn't had a big belly. But I never looked at her belly. Was that really so foolish? The gang laughed and hee-hawed, stomped and danced and chanted a good-night prayer. And instead of the raisins they give when a woman's lying in, they stuffed my hand full of goat turds. I was no weakling. If I slapped someone he'd see all the way to Cracow. But I'm really not a slugger by nature. I think to myself: Let it pass. So they take advantage of me.

I was coming home from school and heard a dog barking. I'm not afraid of dogs, but of course I never want to start up with them. One of them may be mad, and if he bites there's not a Tartar in the world who can help you. So I made tracks. Then I looked around and saw the whole market place wild with laughter. It was no dog at all but Wolf-Leib the Thief. How was I supposed to know it was he? It sounded like a howling bitch.

When the pranksters and leg-pullers found that I was easy to fool, every one of them tried his luck with me. "Gimpel, the Czar is coming to Frampol; Gimpel, the moon fell down in Turbeen; Gimpel, little Hodel Furpiece found a treasure behind the bathhouse." And I like a golem * believed everyone. In the first place, everything is possible, as it is written in the Wisdom of the Fathers, I've forgotten just how. Second, I had to believe when the whole town came down on me! If I ever dared to say, "Ah, you're kidding!" there was trouble. People got angry. "What do you mean! You want to call everyone a liar?" What was I to do? I believed them, and I hope at least that did them some good.

I was an orphan. My grandfather who brought me up was already bent toward the grave. So they turned me over to a baker, and what a time they gave me there! Every woman or girl who came to bake a batch of noodles had to fool me at least once. "Gimpel, there's a fair in heaven; Gimpel, the rabbi gave birth to a calf in the seventh month;

Translated from the Yiddish by Saul Bellow, from A Treasury of Yiddish Stories, *edited by Irving Howe and Eliezer Greenberg, copyright 1953, 1954 by The Viking Press, Inc., reprinted by permission of The Viking Press, Inc., New York.*
*golem: a blockhead.

Gimpel, a cow flew over the roof and laid brass eggs." A student from
the yeshiva* came once to buy a roll, and he said, "You, Gimpel, while
you stand here scraping with your baker's shovel the Messiah has come.
The dead have arisen." "What do you mean?" I said. "I heard no one
blowing the ram's horn!" He said, "Are you deaf?" And all began to
cry, "We heard it, we heard!" Then in came Rietze the Candle-dipper
and called out in her hoarse voice, "Gimpel, your father and mother
have stood up from the grave. They're looking for you."

To tell the truth, I knew very well that nothing of the sort had happened, but all the same, as folks were talking, I threw on my wool vest
and went out. Maybe something had happened. What did I stand to lose
by looking? Well, what a cat music went up! And then I took a vow to
believe nothing more. But that was no go either. They confused me so
that I didn't know the big end from the small.

I went to the rabbi to get some advice. He said, "It is written, better
to be a fool all your days than for one hour to be evil. You are not a
fool. They are the fools. For he who causes his neighbor to feel shame
loses Paradise himself." Nevertheless the rabbi's daughter took me in.
As I left the rabbinical court she said, "Have you kissed the wall yet?"
I said, "No; what for?" She answered, "It's the law; you've got to do it
after every visit." Well, there didn't seem to be any harm in it. And she
burst out laughing. It was a fine trick. She put one over on me, all right.

I wanted to go off to another town, but then everyone got busy match-
making, and they were after me so they nearly tore my coat tails off.
They talked at me and talked until I got water on the ear. She was no
chaste maiden, but they told me she was virgin pure. She had a limp,
and they said it was deliberate, from coyness. She had a bastard, and
they told me the child was her little brother. I cried, "You're wasting
your time. I'll never marry that whore." But they said indignantly, "What
a way to talk! Aren't you ashamed of yourself? We can take you to the
rabbi and have you fined for giving her a bad name." I saw then that
I wouldn't escape them so easily and I thought: They're set on making
me their butt. But when you're married the husband's the master, and
if that's all right with her it's agreeable to me too. Besides, you can't
pass through life unscathed, nor expect to.

I went to her clay house, which was built on the sand, and the whole
gang, hollering and chorusing, came after me. They acted like bear-
baiters. When we came to the well they stopped all the same. They
were afraid to start anything with Elka. Her mouth would open as if it
were on a hinge, and she had a fierce tongue. I entered the house. Lines
were strung from wall to wall and clothes were drying. Barefoot she
stood by the tub, doing the wash. She was dressed in a worn hand-me-
down gown of plush. She had her hair put up in braids and pinned
across her head. It took my breath away, almost, the reek of it all.

Evidently she knew who I was. She took a look at me and said,
"Look who's here! He's come, the drip. Grab a seat."

*yeshiva: an orthodox Jewish rabbinical seminary.

I told her all; I denied nothing. "Tell me the truth," I said, "are you really a virgin, and is that mischievous Yechiel actually your little brother? Don't be deceitful with me, for I'm an orphan."

"I'm an orphan myself," she answered, "and whoever tries to twist you up, may the end of his nose take a twist. But don't let them think they can take advantage of me. I want a dowry of fifty guilders, and let them take up a collection besides. Otherwise they can kiss my you-know-what." She was very plainspoken. I said, "It's the bride and not the groom who gives a dowry." Then she said, "Don't bargain with me. Either a flat 'yes' or a flat 'no'—Go back where you came from."

I thought: No bread will ever be baked from *this* dough. But ours is not a poor town. They consented to everything and proceeded with the wedding. It so happened that there was a dysentery epidemic at the time. The ceremony was held at the cemetery gates, near the little corpse-washing hut. The fellows got drunk. While the marriage contract was being drawn up I heard the most pious high rabbi ask, "Is the bride a widow or a divorced woman?" And the sexton's wife answered for her, "Both a widow and divorced." It was a black moment for me. But what was I to do, run away from under the marriage canopy?

There was singing and dancing. An old granny danced opposite me, hugging a braided white *chalah*.* The master of revels made a "God'a mercy" in memory of the bride's parents. The schoolboys threw burrs, as on Tishe b'Av † fast day. There were a lot of gifts after the sermon: a noodle board, a kneading trough, a bucket, brooms, ladles, household articles galore. Then I took a look and saw two strapping young men carrying a crib. "What do we need this for?" I asked. So they said, "Don't rack your brains about it. It's all right, it'll come in handy." I realized I was going to be rooked. Take it another way though, what did I stand to lose? I reflected: I'll see what comes of it. A whole town can't go altogether crazy.

II

At night I came where my wife lay, but she wouldn't let me in. "Say, look here, is this what they married us for?" I said. And she said, "My monthly has come." "But yesterday they took you to the ritual bath, and that's afterward, isn't it supposed to be?" "Today isn't yesterday," said she, "and yesterday's not today. You can beat it if you don't like it." In short, I waited.

Not four months later she was in childbed. The townsfolk hid their laughter with their knuckles. But what could I do? She suffered intolerable pains and clawed at the walls. "Gimpel," she cried, "I'm going. Forgive me!" The house filled with women. They were boiling pans of water. The screams rose to the welkin.

* chalah: the Sabbath bread.
†Tishe b'Av: holiday commemorating the destruction of the Second Temple in 70 A.D. by the Romans.

The thing to do was to go to the House of Prayer to repeat Psalms, and that was what I did.

The townsfolk liked that, all right. I stood in a corner saying Psalms and prayers, and they shook their heads at me, "Pray, pray!" they told me. "Prayer never made any woman pregnant." One of the congregation put a straw to my mouth and said, "Hay for the cows." There was something to that too, by God!

She gave birth to a boy. Friday at the synagogue the sexton stood up before the Ark, pounded on the reading table, and announced, "The wealthy Reb Gimpel invites the congregation to a feast in honor of the birth of a son." The whole House of Prayer rang with laughter. My face was flaming. But there was nothing I could do. After all, I *was* the one responsible for the circumcision honors and rituals.

Half the town came running. You couldn't wedge another soul in. Women brought peppered chick-peas, and there was a keg of beer from the tavern. I ate and drank as much as anyone, and they all congratulated me. Then there was a circumcision, and I named the boy after my father, may he rest in peace. When all were gone and I was left with my wife alone, she thrust her head through the bed-curtain and called me to her.

"Gimpel," said she, "why are you silent? Has your ship gone and sunk?"

"What shall I say?" I answered. "A fine thing you've done to me! If my mother had known of it she'd have died a second time."

She said, "Are you crazy, or what?"

"How can you make such a fool," I said, "of one who should be the lord and master?"

"What's the matter with you?" she said. "What have you taken into your head to imagine?"

I saw that I must speak bluntly and openly. "Do you think this is the way to use an orphan?" I said. "You have borne a bastard."

She answered, "Drive this foolishness out of your head. The child is yours."

"How can he be mine?" I argued. "He was born seventeen weeks after the wedding."

She told me then that he was premature. I said, "Isn't he a little too premature?" She said, she had had a grandmother who carried just as short a time and she resembled this grandmother of hers as one drop of water does another. She swore to it with such oaths that you would have believed a peasant at the fair if he had used them. To tell the plain truth, I didn't believe her; but when I talked it over next day with the schoolmaster he told me the very same thing had happened to Adam and Eve. Two they went up to bed, and four they descended.

"There isn't a woman in the world who is not the granddaughter of Eve," he said.

That was how it was; they argued me dumb. But then, who really knows how such things are?

I began to forget my sorrow. I loved the child madly, and he loved me too. As soon as he saw me he'd wave his little hands and want me to pick him up, and when he was colicky I was the only one who could pacify him. I bought him a little bone teething ring and a little gilded cap. He was forever catching the evil eye from someone, and then I had to run to get one of those abracadabras for him that would get him out of it. I worked like an ox. You know how expenses go up when there's an infant in the house. I don't want to lie about it; I didn't dislike Elka either, for that matter. She swore at me and cursed, and I couldn't get enough of her. What strength she had! One of her looks could rob you of the power of speech. And her orations! Pitch and sulphur, that's what they were full of, and yet somehow also full of charm. I adored her every word. She gave me bloody wounds though.

In the evening I brought her a white loaf as well as a dark one, and also poppyseed rolls I baked myself. I thieved because of her and swiped everything I could lay hands on: macaroons, raisins, almonds, cakes. I hope I may be forgiven for stealing from the Saturday pots the women left to warm in the baker's oven. I would take out scraps of meat, a chunk of pudding, a chicken leg or head, a piece of tripe, whatever I could nip quickly. She ate and became fat and handsome.

I had to sleep away from home all during the week, at the bakery. On Friday nights when I got home she always made an excuse of some sort. Either she had heartburn, or a stitch in the side, or hiccups, or headaches. You know what women's excuses are. I had a bitter time of it. It was rough. To add to it, this little brother of hers, the bastard, was growing bigger. He'd put lumps on me, and when I wanted to hit back she'd open her mouth and curse so powerfully I saw a green haze floating before my eyes. Ten times a day she threatened to divorce me. Another man in my place would have taken French leave and disappeared. But I'm the type that bears it and says nothing. What's one to do? Shoulders are from God, and burdens too.

One night there was a calamity in the bakery; the oven burst, and we almost had a fire. There was nothing to do but go home, so I went home. Let me, I thought, also taste the joy of sleeping in bed in midweek. I didn't want to wake the sleeping mite and tiptoed into the house. Coming in, it seemed to me that I heard not the snoring of one but, as it were, a double snore, one a thin enough snore and the other like the snoring of a slaughtered ox. Oh, I didn't like that! I didn't like it at all. I went up to the bed, and things suddenly turned black. Next to Elka lay a man's form. Another in my place would have made an uproar, and enough noise to rouse the whole town, but the thought occurred to me that I might wake the child. A little thing like that— why frighten a little swallow, I thought. All right then, I went back to the bakery and stretched out on a sack of flour and till morning I never shut an eye. I shivered as if I had had malaria. "Enough of being a donkey," I said to myself. "Gimpel isn't going to be a sucker all his life. There's a limit even to the foolishness of a fool like Gimpel."

In the morning I went to the rabbi to get advice, and it made a great commotion in the town. They sent the beadle for Elka right away. She came, carrying the child. And what do you think she did? She denied it, denied everything, bone and stone! "He's out of his head," she said. "I know nothing of dreams or divinations." They yelled at her, warned her, hammered on the table, but she stuck to her guns: it was a false accusation, she said.

The butchers and the horse-traders took her part. One of the lads from the slaughterhouse came by and said to me, "We've got our eye on you, you're a marked man." Meanwhile the child started to bear down and soiled itself. In the rabbinical court there was an Ark of the Covenant, and they couldn't allow that, so they sent Elka away.

I said to the rabbi, "What shall I do?"

"You must divorce her at once," said he.

"And what if she refuses?" I asked.

He said, "You must serve the divorce. That's all you'll have to do."

I said, "Well, all right, Rabbi. Let me think about it."

"There's nothing to think about," said he. "You mustn't remain under the same roof with her."

"And if I want to see the child?" I asked.

"Let her go, the harlot," said he, "and her brood of bastards with her."

The verdict he gave was that I mustn't even cross her threshold—never again, as long as I should live.

During the day it didn't bother me so much. I thought: It was bound to happen, the abscess had to burst. But at night when I stretched out upon the sacks I felt it all very bitterly. A longing took me, for her and for the child. I wanted to be angry, but that's my misfortune exactly, I don't have it in me to be really angry. In the first place—this was how my thoughts went—there's bound to be a slip sometimes. You can't live without errors. Probably that lad who was with her led her on and gave her presents and what not, and women are often long on hair and short on sense, and so he got around her. And then since she denies it so, maybe I was only seeing things? Hallucinations do happen. You see a figure or a mannikin or something, but when you come up closer it's nothing, there's not a thing there. And if that's so, I'm doing her an injustice. And when I got so far in my thoughts I started to weep. I sobbed so that I wet the flour where I lay. In the morning I went to the rabbi and told him that I had made a mistake. The rabbi wrote on with his quill, and he said that if that were so he would have to reconsider the whole case. Until he had finished I wasn't to go near my wife, but I might send her bread and money by messenger.

III

Nine months passed before all the rabbis could come to an agreement. Letters went back and forth. I hadn't realized that there could be so much erudition about a matter like this.

Meanwhile Elka gave birth to still another child, a girl this time. On the Sabbath I went to the synagogue and invoked a blessing on her. They called me up to the Torah,* and I named the child for my mother-in-law—may she rest in peace. The louts and loudmouths of the town who came into the bakery gave me a going over. All Frampol refreshed its spirits because of my trouble and grief. However, I resolved that I would always believe what I was told. What's the good of *not* believing? Today it's your wife you don't believe; tomorrow it's God Himself you won't take stock in.

By an apprentice who was her neighbor I sent her daily a corn or a wheat loaf, or a piece of pastry, rolls or bagels, or, when I got the chance, a slab of pudding, a slice of honeycake, or wedding strudel—whatever came my way. The apprentice was a goodhearted lad, and more than once he added something on his own. He had formerly annoyed me a lot, plucking my nose and digging me in the ribs, but when he started to be a visitor to my house he came kind and friendly. "Hey, you, Gimpel," he said to me, "you have a very decent little wife and two fine kids. You don't deserve them."

"But the things people say about her," I said.

"Well, they have long tongues," he said, "and nothing to do with them but babble. Ignore it as you ignore the cold of last winter."

One day the rabbi sent for me and said, "Are you certain, Gimpel, that you were wrong about your wife?"

I said, "I'm certain."

"Why, but look here! You yourself saw it."

"It must have been a shadow," I said.

"The shadow of what?"

"Just of one of the beams, I think."

"You can go home then. You owe thanks to the Yanover rabbi. He found an obscure reference in Maimonides † that favored you."

I seized the rabbi's hand and kissed it.

I wanted to run home immediately. It's no small thing to be separated for so long a time from wife and child. Then I reflected: I'd better go back to work now, and go home in the evening. I said nothing to anyone, although as far as my heart was concerned it was like one of the Holy Days. The women teased and twitted me as they did every day, but my thought was: Go on, with your loose talk. The truth is out, like the oil upon the water. Maimonides says it's right, and therefore it is right!

At night, when I had covered the dough to let it rise, I took my share of bread and a little sack of flour and started homeward. The moon was full and the stars were glistening, something to terrify the soul. I hurried onward, and before me darted a long shadow. It was winter, and a fresh snow had fallen. I had a mind to sing, but it was growing late and I didn't want to wake the householders. Then I felt like whistling, but I remem-

---

*One is called up to the altar to witness the reading of a passage from the Pentateuch, also called the Torah.

†A Spanish-Jewish philosopher and scholar, 1135–1204.

bered that you don't whistle at night because it brings the demons out. So I was silent and walked as fast as I could.

Dogs in the Christian yards barked at me when I passed, but I thought: Bark your teeth out! What are you but mere dogs? Whereas I am a man, the husband of a fine wife, the father of promising children.

As I approached the house my heart started to pound as though it were the heart of a criminal. I felt no fear, but my heart went thump! thump! Well, no drawing back. I quietly lifted the latch and went in. Elka was asleep. I looked at the infant's cradle. The shutter was closed, but the moon forced its way through the cracks. I saw the newborn child's face and loved it as soon as I saw it—immediately—each tiny bone.

Then I came nearer to the bed. And what did I see but the apprentice lying there beside Elka. The moon went out all at once. It was utterly black, and I trembled. My teeth chattered. The bread fell from my hands, and my wife waked and said, "Who is that, ah?"

I muttered, "It's me."

"Gimpel?" she asked. "How come you're here? I thought it was forbidden."

"The rabbi said," I answered and shook as with a fever.

"Listen to me, Gimpel," she said, "go out to the shed and see if the goat's all right. It seems she's been sick." I have forgotten to say that we had a goat. When I heard she was unwell I went into the yard. The nanny-goat was a good little creature. I had a nearly human feeling for her.

With hesitant steps I went up to the shed and opened the door. The goat stood there on her four feet. I felt her everywhere, drew her by the horns, examined her udders, and found nothing wrong. She had probably eaten too much bark. "Good night, little goat," I said. "Keep well." And the little beast answered with a "Maa" as though to thank me for the good will.

I went back. The apprentice had vanished.

"Where," I asked, "is the lad?"

"What lad?" my wife answered.

"What do you mean?" I said. "The apprentice. You were sleeping with him."

"The things I have dreamed this night and the night before," she said, "may they come true and lay you low, body and soul! An evil spirit has taken root in you and dazzles your sight." She screamed out, "You hateful creature! You moon calf! You spook! You uncouth man! Get out, or I'll scream all Frampol out of bed!"

Before I could move, her brother sprang out from behind the oven and struck me a blow on the back of the head. I thought he had broken my neck. I felt that something about me was deeply wrong, and I said, "Don't make a scandal. All that's needed now is that people should accuse me of raising spooks and *dybbuks*." * For that was what she had meant. "No one will touch bread of my baking."

*dybbuks: condemned souls that, to escape the torments of evil spirits, often sought refuge in the bodies of pious persons.

In short, I somehow calmed her.

"Well," she said, "that's enough. Lie down, and be shattered by wheels."

Next morning I called the apprentice aside. "Listen here, brother!" I said. And so on and so forth. "What do you say?" He stared at me as though I had dropped from the roof or something.

"I swear," he said, "you'd better go to an herb doctor or some healer. I'm afraid you have a screw loose, but I'll hush it up for you." And that's how the thing stood.

To make a long story short, I lived twenty years with my wife. She bore me six children, four daughters and two sons. All kinds of things happened, but I neither saw nor heard. I believed, and that's all. The rabbi recently said to me, "Belief in itself is beneficial. It is written that a good man lives by his faith."

Suddenly my wife took sick. It began with a trifle, a little growth upon the breast. But she evidently was not destined to live long; she had no years. I spent a fortune on her. I have forgotten to say that by this time I had a bakery of my own and in Frampol was considered to be something of a rich man. Daily the healer came, and every witch doctor in the neighborhood was brought. They decided to use leeches, and after that to try cupping. They even called a doctor from Lublin, but it was too late. Before she died she called me to her bed and said, "Forgive me, Gimpel."

I said, "What is there to forgive? You have been a good and faithful wife."

"Woe, Gimpel!" she said. "It was ugly how I deceived you all these years. I want to go clean to my Maker, and so I have to tell you that the children are not yours."

If I had been clouted on the head with a piece of wood it couldn't have bewildered me more.

"Whose are they?" I asked.

"I don't know," she said. "There were a lot . . . but they're not yours." And as she spoke she tossed her head to the side, her eyes turned glassy, and it was all up with Elka. On her whitened lips there remained a smile.

I imagined that, dead as she was, she was saying, "I deceived Gimpel. That was the meaning of my brief life."

IV

One night, when the period of mourning was done, as I lay dreaming on the flour sacks, there came the Spirit of Evil himself and said to me, "Gimpel, why do you sleep?"

I said, "What should I be doing? Eating *kreplach*?" *

"The whole world deceives you," he said, "and you ought to deceive the world in your turn."

"How can I deceive all the world?" I asked him.

He answered, "You might accumulate a bucket of urine every day

*kreplach: a small patty of dough filled with chopped meat.

and at night pour it into the dough. Let the sages of Frampol eat filth."

"What about the judgment in the world to come?" I said.

"There is no world to come," he said. "They've sold you a bill of goods and talked you into believing you carried a cat in your belly. What nonsense!"

"Well then," I said, "and is there a God?"

He answered, "There is no God either."

"What," I said, "*is* there, then?"

"A thick mire."

He stood before my eyes with a goatish beard and horn, long-toothed, and with a tail. Hearing such words, I wanted to snatch him by the tail, but I tumbled from the flour sacks and nearly broke a rib. Then it happened that I had to answer the call of nature, and, passing, I saw the risen dough, which seemed to say to me, "Do it!" In brief, I let myself be persuaded.

At dawn the apprentice came. We kneaded the bread, scattered caraway seeds on it, and set it to bake. Then the apprentice went away, and I was left sitting in the little trench by the oven, on a pile of rags. Well, Gimpel, I thought, you've revenged yourself on them for all the shame they've put on you. Outside the frost glittered, but it was warm beside the oven. The flames heated my face. I bent my head and fell into a doze.

I saw in a dream, at once, Elka in her shroud. She called to me, "What have you done, Gimpel?"

I said to her, "It's all your fault," and started to cry.

"You fool!" she said. "You fool! Because I was false is everything false too? I never deceived anyone but myself. I'm paying for it all, Gimpel. They spare you nothing here."

I looked at her face. It was black; I was startled and waked, and remained sitting dumb. I sensed that everything hung in the balance. A false step now and I'd lose Eternal Life. But God gave me His help. I seized the long shovel and took out the loaves, carried them into the yard, and started to dig a hole in the frozen earth.

My apprentice came back as I was doing it. "What are you doing, boss?" he said, and grew pale as a corpse.

"I know what I'm doing," I said, and I buried it all before his very eyes.

Then I went home, took my hoard from its hiding place, and divided it among the children. "I saw your mother tonight," I said. "She's turning black, poor thing."

They were so astounded they couldn't speak a word.

"Be well," I said, "and forget that such a one as Gimpel ever existed." I put on my short coat, a pair of boots, took the bag that held my prayer shawl in one hand, my stock in the other, and kissed the *mezzuzah*.* When people saw me in the street they were greatly surprised.

"Where are you going?" they said.

---

*mezzuzah: a small parchment inscribed with passages from Deut. VI. 4–9 and XI. 13–21 inserted in a case and nailed in a slanting position to the right-hand doorpost as a talisman against evil.

I answered, "Into the world." And so I departed from Frampol.

I wandered over the land; and good people did not neglect me. After many years I became old and white; I heard a great deal, many lies and falsehoods, but the longer I lived the more I understood that there were really no lies. Whatever doesn't really happen is dreamed at night. It happens to one if it doesn't happen to another, tomorrow if not today, or a century hence if not next year. What difference can it make? Often I heard tales of which I said, "Now this is a thing that cannot happen." But before a year had elapsed I heard that it actually had come to pass somewhere.

Going from place to place, eating at strange tables, it often happens that I spin yarns—improbable things that could never have happened—about devils, magicians, windmills, and the like. The children run after me, calling, "Grandfather, tell us a story." Sometimes they ask for particular stories, and I try to please them. A fat young boy once said to me, "Grandfather, it's the same story you told us before." The little rogue, he was right.

So it is with dreams too. It is many years since I left Frampol, but as soon as I shut my eyes I am there again. And whom do you think I see? Elka. She is standing by the washtub, as at our first encounter, but her face is shining and her eyes are as radiant as the eyes of a saint, and she speaks outlandish words to me, strange things. When I wake I have forgotten it all. But while the dream lasts I am comforted. She answers all my queries, and what comes out is that all is right. I weep and implore, "Let me be with you." And she consoles me and tells me to be patient. The time is nearer than it is far. Sometimes she strokes and kisses me and weeps upon my face. When I awaken I feel her lips and taste the salt of her tears.

No doubt the world is entirely an imaginary world, but it is only once removed from the true world. At the door of the hovel where I lie, there stands the plank on which the dead are taken away. The gravedigger Jew has his spade ready. The grave waits and the worms are hungry; the shrouds are prepared—I carry them in my beggar's sack. Another *schnorrer* * is waiting to inherit my bed of straw. When the time comes I will go joyfully. Whatever may be there, it will be real, without complication, without ridicule, without deception. God be praised: there even Gimpel cannot be deceived.

COMMENT

"Gimpel the Fool" is in the tradition that fools and idiots are touched with holiness—"foolish to the point of holy innocence," as Turgenev put it—as are Parsifal and Dostoyevsky's holy "idiot,"

*schnorrer: a shameless beggar, here used affectionately.

Prince Myshkin. The irony of the situation lies in Gimpel's innocent belief in what everyone else sees as an obvious deception. The villagers report that the moon fell down in Turbeen and Gimpel believes it; Elka argues that no one has been in bed with her and he believes that too. Put another way, the irony stems from the difference between Gimpel's foolishness and everyone else's common sense—everyone's, that is, but the Rabbi's. He is Gimpel's counterpart in holy foolishness, in the weighty scholasticism he brings to bear on Gimpel's absurd questions. The irony is humorous, as is foolishness from the point of view of common sense. But the irony of Gimpel's foolishness is complicated by the fact that he only half-believes what the others tell him. When the villagers report that his parents "have stood up from the grave," he says to himself, "To tell the truth, I knew very well that nothing of the sort had happened. . . ." Nor does he accept Elka's explanation of her child's "premature" birth. But he reflects, "who really knows how such things are?" This is the intuition of a man ready for miracles, and it prepares us for the conclusion. A double irony defines Gimpel's situations. There is, first, the irony of his foolishness from the point of view of common sense, and, second, the irony that he is only half-credulous, hence, half-ironic about what he is told. But he is not ironic about the others; he does not think for a moment he is fooling them, nor does he gain satisfaction at their expense by ironically going along with them. He would not be Gimpel if he did. He is ironic only about his own role as a fool, for as he declares at the beginning, "I don't think myself a fool."

The irony of Gimpel's innocence vis-à-vis the common sense of the villagers is itself double-edged. The irony is ultimately at the expense of the villagers, for what is folly to them is faith to Gimpel. If you don't believe others, he explains, then "tomorrow it's God Himself you won't take stock in." Life as an act of faith is set against the villagers' common sense. What is at issue is a fatal incapacity of common sense: it cannot grasp the holy, sacramental character of life.

In consigning Elka to hell, is Singer being excessively moral? Should anyone be punished, and so severely, for making a fool of a man who lets himself be continually fooled? The comic spirit has always laughed at follies, and the moral spirit has never gotten along with it. In his treatment of Elka, Singer shifts from the amoral comic to a moral point of view, from laughter at Gimpel's folly to punishment of those who laugh at him. He has changed the rules of the game, and esthetically this is disruptive.

But the story is not therefore a sentimental account of the virtue of innocence. Singer's ironic sense of Gimpel's folly is a counterforce that toughens his conception of Gimpel's innocence. Singer is affectionate towards Gimpel but nonetheless firm in presenting his comic side. Further, he shows the simple-minded inadequacy of innocence before the temptations of the Devil. It requires the experience of a sinner, Elka, to save the innocent. The story treats realistically the weakness of innocence in the everyday world.

To judge this treatment rightly, we must know when to leave our practical sense behind for the transcendental. At least Gimpel knows when to do so, when, that is, to turn to God to resolve an earthly impasse. "God gave me His help," he says, and he buries the contaminated loaves. God's aid and Elka's warning from the grave make for a *reversal* in the direction of the story from half-consciousness to full consciousness. Gimpel's concern shifts from the things of this world to the things of the next. Gimpel's aim now is to become not less but more simple, and he formulates his absolute simplicity in the observation that "the longer I lived the more I understood that there were really no lies." He transcends his own critical intelligence, which has told him that the others were lying even while he chose to accept them on faith. He reaffirms his old faith in folly on a saintly basis. He becomes a true holy fool for whom only so-called foolish things, things not of this world, are worth talking about. So he wanders from town to town telling improbable stories about devils, magicians, and the like. The improbable—folly raised to the supernatural—is now his only serious preoccupation. At the end, then, Singer abandons his irony towards Gimpel and reserves it only for the villagers. In his last, transcendent phase Gimpel is reconciled to everyone, and his holy affirmation lets him see Elka's eyes "as radiant as the eyes of a saint." Holiness transforms; Gimpel moves to an ideal reality impossible on earth except to saints but nonetheless there. "Whatever may be there, it will be real, without complication, without ridicule, without deception," and, we might add, without irony. Though we can also add, ironically, that saintliness derives from the paradox (a form of irony) that folly is holy wisdom: irony can be constructive, even transcendental.

QUESTIONS ON IRONY

1. What is the connection between irony of situation and irony of structure in this story?

2. "Gimpel the Fool" and "The Artificial Nigger" have in common at least the theme of the fall and redemption of a man. Are their structural ironies similar?

3. Trace the ironic development of Elka's life, including Gimpel's visions of her after death, and compare it with Gimpel's development.

4. Consider the use of paradox, understatement, and other rhetorical forms and attitudes noted in our introduction to "Irony" as means of realizing irony of situation.

5. Consider irony of situation in "Grace," "Dawn," "Madame Tellier's Excursion," and "Eternal Triangle."

OTHER CONSIDERATIONS

1. Is the affirmation at the end of "Gimpel the Fool" a conventional gesture or an esthetic fulfillment? Consider also the affirmations near the end of "The Town Poor," "The Legend of St. Julian the Hospitaller," and "The Artificial Nigger." What is the effect of the last paragraph in each case?

2. One of the merits of "Gimpel the Fool" is its gaiety. Is it therefore not serious? Are wit and seriousness mutually exclusive? Consider also "The Artificial Nigger," "Red Leaves," "How It was Done in Odessa," and "Margins."

3. In "Reading the Short Story" we have said that to know the meaning of a story abstractly is inadequate, that a full sense of the meaning requires a grasp of how it is presented. "The Artificial Nigger" and "Gimpel the Fool" have some themes in common and yet they differ vastly because of the way they are presented. Analyze such distinguishing factors as style (particularly in the narrow sense of language), setting, imagery, and Miss O'Connor's apparent allegorical intention.

4. What would be lost if the story were told in the third person rather than the first?

5. Is "Gimpel the Fool," which is in general a narrative rather than scenic story (see "Reading the Short Story"), less effective than the primarily scenic stories of Babel and Chekhov? What is gained and what is lost with each method? Consider, in the light of these two methods, "Nina of Ashkelon," "Wounds," and "The Library of Babel."

6. "The Artificial Nigger" and "Gimpel the Fool" are stories of initiation in which the trials are resolved through a transcendence by faith. Consider the nature of the resolutions in secular stories (not necessarily of initiation) like "The Town Poor," "Wounds," and "Strange Comfort Afforded by the Profession."

SYMBOLISM

A symbol is that which stands for something else. There is a critical difference, however, between a mathematical symbol, standing for an exact and objective quantity, and a literary symbol, standing for a moral and spiritual quality. The mathematical symbol is neutral; the literary symbol is charged with values. Further, the mathematical symbol *reduces* the objective world to an equation or formula; the literary symbol *enlarges* our subjective, transcendent world.

As its root meaning, "a throwing together," indicates, a symbol is a concentration. Like the concentration of energy in the atom, the energy in the symbol is power too. Its power lies in its transcendence of prosaic reality. It speaks in the manner of revelation rather than reason. Men are willing to die for a flag, cross, star of David, or crescent. Thus, apart from all that it represents, the symbol rides on its own power: so the artificial Negro in Miss O'Connor's story and the transfigured sky in "Gusev."

There is a danger of devaluing or ignoring actual things and persons. A symbol may lift but it may also dehumanize, as in the case of political and religious crusades. In literature it can lead to an absence of the unique particulars of the surface. Although the bizarre tale "The Library of Babel" is rich in particulars, the human being is barely evident. This is one limitation of allegory. Allegory is symbolism that has become over-rationalized; that is, the symbol has been reduced to a single meaning. There is a one-to-one relation between the event or person in the story and its equivalent outside the story, as in the historical parallels in *Gulliver's Travels* and *Animal Farm;* or as in the morality play *Everyman,* where the characters' names indicate their reduction to a single quality: Good Deeds, Knowledge, Fellowship, Beauty, Strength, and so forth.

The impulse to symbolize probably satisfies our need for myth, our need to give a meaning to things and events. The symbol in literature is a concentration of *felt* meanings. It is, further, a concrete representation of those meanings. For the abstract name "United States" we have the concrete flag; for the abstract archetypal pattern of sin and redemption we have the concrete events of Mr. Head's day.

Modern symbolism developed out of a sense of the limitations of realism and its offshoot, naturalism. The case for realistic fiction does not have to be argued; it is one of the great achievements of literature, as the works of Richardson, Balzac, Stendhal, and others testify. But no art form repeats itself: we do not want Picasso to paint like Rembrandt. Symbolist fiction, or something else, would have appeared simply as a consequence of the inevitable changes in any art form. In *Madame Bovary*, Gustave Flaubert simultaneously introduced a rigorous naturalism and the "art novel," largely symbolist in conception. Absorbing the rich particularity of realism into a symbolic structure, he set the example for the main direction of symbolist fiction. Later, naturalists like the Goncourts, Zola, and Dreiser ignored Flaubert's symbolism and tried to imitate science by accumulating a mass of allegedly objective data that was intended to explain and determine the course of a character's life. The philosophy was objectionable because it denied free will, as in "The White Silence." And the method was objectionable, for art gives life form not through mere accumulation but through the selection and organization of material. As they approximated life, they to that extent removed the work from art. Of course, like all writers they did select and organize their material, though less economically. And like all writers they used the artifices of fiction that are the means of selection and organization: literary conventions like point of view, plot, character, motifs, and themes.

In general, writers became dissatisfied with the realistic preoccupation with the social surface, the naturalistic denial of free will, and the overestimation of reason and objectivity. Psychoanalysts, for example, pointed to another kind of reality, figured by the unconscious, which they argued was the real source of our motivations. The unconscious did not yield to reason; it thrived beneath the surface in the domain of the irrational. It found its expression in dreams, fairy tales, and myths. The myth, a symbol in narrative form, has been understood to be an expression of the world view of a people. Anthropology and psychoanalysis have shown myth to be also expressive of the unconscious life of a person or a race. Myth has its own language, that of symbols, and its own forms, those of archetypal patterns: death and rebirth; the hero's departure, trials, and return; the initiation into manhood; and so forth. We have discussed instances of the initiation archetype in "The Artificial Nigger" and "Gimpel the Fool." For the even more prevalent archetype of death and rebirth see especially "The Artificial Nigger," "The Legend of St. Julian the Hospitaller," "Gusev," "Wounds," and "Death in Venice." Sometimes a pattern will be used ironically, as in "Eternal Triangle" and "Death in Venice"; sometimes parodistically, as in "Grace."

Archetypal patterns, and the myths that symbolically embody them, reveal what lies beneath the surface. And, grounded in the experience of the race, they provide meaning and coherence to the fragmented character of modern life. Legendary, usually supernatural myths have been shown to have a naturalist basis, and so have been turned to humanistic use. The "myths" of Christianity are frequent in modern literature, but pagan myths and tales are behind the stories of Mann, Welty, Faulkner, O'Flaherty, and others in this collection.

Though symbolists were dissatisfied with a merely literal, realistic presentation, the surface of their stories is generally fairly familiar and realistic, even in extreme instances like those of Böll and Kafka in this collection. Borges' "The Library of Babel" provides a more bizarre symbolism in one sense, a world totally invented, and yet it relies on our familiarity with large libraries. Most symbolists would probably feel they had failed if their stories were of interest only symbolically. The surface, the moment-to-moment life, must have its own primary interest. Generally symbolists did not reject the data of the surface; they simply gave the data their underlying significance as well as surface value.

In the largest sense all fiction is symbolic. Even faithful reproductions of life like those of Zola, Dreiser, and Farrell, or like those in "The Golden Honeymoon" and "The Town Poor"—even these represent more than what the literal surface reveals. This may be true of the detail as well as of the underlying archetypal pattern. A word, phrase, or image that recurs frequently assumes a significance larger than itself. It forms a constellation of meaning; it becomes a symbolic *presence*, as our comments on "The Blind Man" indicate.

In realistic fiction the symbols are a recognizable part of the scene, like Lardner's St. Petersburg, a symbol of middle-class senility in America. We may call such symbols *natural*, meaning familiar. For the most part they are the kind of symbols found in symbolic fiction too. In "The Artificial Nigger," for example, the symbols are natural: one is likely to get lost in a big city, and one might see just such a Negro statue. Yet the conception of the story makes the symbolism clear.

Less common are two other kinds of symbol, the *supernatural* and the *non-natural*. The witch-meeting in "Young Goodman Brown" and the gods in "Death in Venice" are supernatural symbols; the celebration of Christmas throughout the year in "Christmas Every Day" (see our comments) and the succession of strangers who resemble each other in "Death in Venice" are non-natural symbols. Realistic fiction sometimes uses metaphoric non-natural symbols to express transcendence, as in the image of the halo in the largely naturalistic "The Town Poor." Here naturalism is itself transcended by the capacity for dignity under the most oppressive circumstances. But non-natural symbols are usually found only in strictly symbolic fiction. This suggests another significant difference between realistic and symbolic fiction. In realistic fiction the writer's vision gradually emerges from a selected but recognizable, *unaltered* segment of reality; in symbolic fiction his vision is imposed on reality. The symbolic writer does not submit to everyday reality; his vision determines, *alters* the way he looks at it. For example, Christ alters the way a Christian sees his everyday life.

In realistic fiction the detail is cumulative, for it builds towards meaning; in symbolic fiction, since the detail is altered or selected for its symbolic meaning, it reverberates from the beginning with its meaning. But though the symbolic story is denser with significance and though it has the compressed power of symbolist poetry, it is not necessarily more effective than the realistic story.

In our comments on the moderate symbolism of "The Blind Man" we pay particular attention to detail, to show the significance, for example, of matter that might seem to be used only for setting and atmosphere. In our comments on the fairly extreme symbolism of "Christmas Every Day" we consider only the large, controlling symbols.

The Blind Man

D. H. Lawrence ❧

Isabel Pervin was listening for two sounds—for the sound of wheels on the drive outside and for the noise of her husband's footsteps in the hall. Her dearest and oldest friend, a man who seemed almost indispensable to her living, would drive up in the rainy dusk of the closing November day. The trap had gone to fetch him from the station. And her husband, who had been blinded in Flanders, and who had a disfiguring mark on his brow, would be coming in from the outhouses.

He had been home for a year now. He was totally blind. Yet they had been very happy. The Grange was Maurice's own place. The back was a farmstead, and the Wernhams, who occupied the rear premises, acted as farmers. Isabel lived with her husband in the handsome rooms in front. She and he had been almost entirely alone together since he was wounded. They talked and sang and read together in a wonderful and unspeakable intimacy. Then she reviewed books for a Scottish newspaper, carrying on her old interest, and he occupied himself a good deal with the farm. Sightless, he could still discuss everything with Wernham, and he could also do a good deal of work about the place—menial work, it is true, but it gave him satisfaction. He milked the cows, carried in the pails, turned the separator, attended to the pigs and horses. Life was still very full and strangely serene for the blind man, peaceful with the almost incomprehensible peace of immediate contact in darkness. With his wife he had a whole world, rich and real and invisible.

They were newly and remotely happy. He did not even regret the loss of his sight in these times of dark, palpable joy. A certain exultance swelled his soul.

But as time wore on, sometimes the rich glamour would leave them. Sometimes, after months of this intensity, a sense of burden overcame Isabel, a weariness, a terrible ennui, in that silent house approached between a colonnade of tall-shafted pines. Then she felt she would go mad, for she could not bear it. And sometimes he had devastating fits of depression, which seemed to lay waste his whole being. It was worse than depression—a black misery, when his own life was a torture to him, and when his presence was unbearable to his wife. The dread went down to the roots of her soul as these black days recurred. In a kind of panic she tried to wrap herself up still further in her husband. She forced the old spontaneous cheerfulness and joy to continue. But the effort it cost her was almost too much. She knew she could not keep it up. She felt she would scream with the strain, and would give anything, anything, to escape. She longed to possess her husband utterly; it gave her inordinate joy to have him entirely to herself. And yet, when again he was gone in a black and massive misery, she could not bear him, she could not bear herself; she wished she could be snatched away off the earth altogether, anything rather than live at this cost.

Dazed, she schemed for a way out. She invited friends, she tried to give him some further connection with the outer world. But it was no good. After all their joy and suffering, their dark, great year of blindness and solitude and unspeakable nearness, other people seemed to them both shallow, rattling, rather impertinent. Shallow prattle seemed presumptuous. He became impatient and irritated, she was wearied. And so they lapsed into their solitude again. For they preferred it.

But now, in a few weeks' time, her second baby would be born. The first had died, an infant, when her husband first went out to France. She looked with joy and relief to the coming of the second. It would be her salvation. But also she felt some anxiety. She was thirty years old, her husband was a year younger. They both wanted the child very much. Yet she could not help feeling afraid. She had her husband on her hands, a terrible joy to her, and a terrifying burden. The child would occupy her love and attention. And then, what of Maurice? What would he do? If only she could feel that he, too, would be at peace and happy when the child came! She did so want to luxuriate in a rich, physical satisfaction of maternity. But the man, what would he do? How could she provide for him, how avert those shattering black moods of his, which destroyed them both?

She sighed with fear. But at this time Bertie Reid wrote to Isabel. He was her old friend, a second or third cousin, a Scotchman, as she was a Scotchwoman. They had been brought up near to one another, and all her life he had been her friend, like a brother, but better than her own brothers. She loved him—though not in the marrying sense. There was a sort of kinship between them, an affinity. They understood one another instinctively. But Isabel would never have thought of marrying Bertie. It would have seemed like marrying in her own family.

Bertie was a barrister and a man of letters, a Scotchman of the intellectual type, quick, ironical, sentimental, and on his knees before the woman he adored but did not want to marry. Maurice Pervin was different. He came of a good old country family—the Grange was not a very great distance from Oxford. He was passionate, sensitive, perhaps oversensitive, wincing—a big fellow with heavy limbs and a forehead that flushed painfully. For his mind was slow, as if drugged by the strong provincial blood that beat in his veins. He was very sensitive to his own mental slowness, his feelings being quick and acute. So that he was just the opposite to Bertie, whose mind was much quicker than his emotions, which were not so very fine.

From the first the two men did not like each other. Isabel felt that they ought to get on together. But they did not. She felt that if only each could have the clue to the other there would be such a rare understanding between them. It did not come off, however. Bertie adopted a slightly ironical attitude, very offensive to Maurice, who returned the Scotch irony with English resentment, a resentment which deepened sometimes into stupid hatred.

This was a little puzzling to Isabel. However, she accepted it in the course of things. Men were made freakish and unreasonable. Therefore, when Maurice was going out to France for the second time, she felt that, for her husband's sake, she must discontinue her friendship with Bertie. She wrote to the barrister to this effect. Bertram Reid simply replied that in this, as in all other matters, he must obey her wishes, if these were indeed her wishes.

For nearly two years nothing had passed between the two friends. Isabel rather gloried in the fact; she had no compunction. She had one great article of faith, which was, that husband and wife should be so important to one another, that the rest of the world simply did not count. She and Maurice were husband and wife. They loved one another. They would have children. Then let everybody and everything else fade into insignificance outside this connubial felicity. She professed herself quite happy and ready to receive Maurice's friends. She was happy and ready: the happy wife, the ready woman in possession. Without knowing why, the friends retired abashed, and came no more. Maurice, of course, took as much satisfaction in this connubial absorption as Isabel did.

He shared in Isabel's literary activities, she cultivated a real interest in agriculture and cattle-raising. For she, being at heart perhaps an emotional enthusiast, always cultivated the practical side of life and prided herself on her mastery of practical affairs. Thus the husband and wife had spent the five years of their married life. The last had been one of blindness and unspeakable intimacy. And now Isabel felt a great indifference coming over her, a sort of lethargy. She wanted to be allowed to bear her child in peace, to nod by the fire and drift vaguely, physically, from day to day. Maurice was like an ominous thunder-cloud. She had to keep waking up to remember him.

When a little note came from Bertie, asking if he were to put up a tombstone to their dead friendship, and speaking of the real pain he felt on account of her husband's loss of sight, she felt a pang, a fluttering agitation of reawakening. And she read the letter to Maurice.

"Ask him to come down," he said.

"Ask Bertie to come here!" she re-echoed.

"Yes—if he wants to."

Isabel paused for a few moments.

"I know he wants to—he'd only be too glad," she replied. "But what about you, Maurice? How should you like it?"

"I should like it."

"Well—in that case— But I thought you didn't care for him—"

"Oh, I don't know. I might think differently of him now," the blind man replied. It was rather abstruse to Isabel.

"Well, dear," she said, "if you're quite sure—"

"I'm sure enough. Let him come," said Maurice.

So Bertie was coming, coming this evening, in the November rain and darkness. Isabel was agitated, racked with her old restlessness and indecision. She had always suffered from this pain of doubt, just an agonizing sense of uncertainty. It had begun to pass off, in the lethargy of maternity. Now it returned, and she resented it. She struggled as usual to maintain her calm, composed, friendly bearing, a sort of mask she wore over all her body.

A woman had lighted a tall lamp beside the table and spread the cloth. The long dining-room was dim, with its elegant but rather severe pieces of old furniture. Only the round table glowed softly under the light. It had a rich, beautiful effect. The white cloth glistened and dropped its heavy, pointed lace corners almost to the carpet, the china was old and handsome, creamy-yellow, with a blotched pattern of harsh red and deep blue, the cups large and bell-shaped, the teapot gallant. Isabel looked at it with superficial appreciation.

Her nerves were hurting her. She looked automatically again at the high, uncurtained windows. In the last dusk she could just perceive outside a huge fir-tree swaying its boughs: it was as if she thought it rather than saw it. The rain came flying on the window panes. Ah, why had she no peace? These two men, why did they tear at her? Why did they not come—why was there this suspense?

She sat in a lassitude that was really suspense and irritation. Maurice, at least, might come in—there was nothing to keep him out. She rose to her feet. Catching sight of her reflection in a mirror, she glanced at herself with a slight smile of recognition, as if she were an old friend to herself. Her face was oval and calm, her nose a little arched. Her neck made a beautiful line down to her shoulder. With hair knotted loosely behind, she had something of a warm, maternal look. Thinking this of herself, she arched her eyebrows and her rather heavy eyelids, with a little flicker of a smile, and for a moment her grey eyes looked amused and wicked, a little sardonic, out of her transfigured Madonna face.

Then, resuming her air of womanly patience—she was really fatally self-determined—she went with a little jerk towards the door. Her eyes were slightly reddened.

She passed down the wide hall and through a door at the end. Then she was in the farm premises. The scent of dairy, and of farm-kitchen, and of farm-yard and of leather almost overcame her: but particularly the scent of dairy. They had been scalding out the pans. The flagged passage in front of her was dark, puddled, and wet. Light came out from the open kitchen door. She went forward and stood in the doorway. The farm-people were at tea, seated at a little distance from her, round a long, narrow table, in the centre of which stood a white lamp. Ruddy faces, ruddy hands holding food, red mouths working, heads bent over the tea-cups: men, land-girls, boys: it was tea-time, feeding-time. Some faces caught sight of her. Mrs. Wernham, going round behind the chairs with a large black teapot, halting slightly in her walk, was not aware of her for a moment. Then she turned suddenly.

"Oh, is it Madam!" she exclaimed. "Come in, then, come in! We're at tea." And she dragged forward a chair.

"No, I won't come in," said Isabel. "I'm afraid I interrupt your meal."

"No—no—not likely, Madam, not likely."

"Hasn't Mr. Pervin come in, do you know?"

"I'm sure I couldn't say! Missed him, have you, Madam?"

"No, I only wanted him to come in," laughed Isabel, as if shyly.

"Wanted him, did ye? Get up, boy—get up, now—"

Mrs. Wernham knocked one of the boys on the shoulder. He began to scrape to his feet, chewing largely.

"I believe he's in top stable," said another face from the table.

"Ah! No, don't get up. I'm going myself," said Isabel.

"Don't you go out on a dirty night like this. Let the lad go. Get along wi' ye, boy," said Mrs. Wernham.

"No, no," said Isabel, with a decision that was always obeyed. "Go on with your tea, Tom. I'd like to go across to the stable, Mrs. Wernham."

"Did ever you hear tell!" exclaimed the woman.

"Isn't the trap late?" asked Isabel.

"Why, no," said Mrs. Wernham, peering into the distance at the tall, dim clock. "No, Madam—we can give it another quarter or twenty minutes yet, good—yes, every bit of a quarter."

"Ah! It seems late when darkness falls so early," said Isabel.

"It do, that it do. Bother the days, that they draw in so," answered Mrs. Wernham. "Proper miserable!"

"They are," said Isabel, withdrawing.

She pulled on her overshoes, wrapped a large tartan shawl around her, put on a man's felt hat, and ventured out along the causeways of the first yard. It was very dark. The wind was roaring in the great elms behind the outhouses. When she came to the second yard the darkness seemed deeper. She was unsure of her footing. She wished she had brought a lantern. Rain blew against her. Half she liked it, half she felt unwilling to battle.

She reached at last the just visible door of the stable. There was no sign of a light anywhere. Opening the upper half, she looked in: into a simple well of darkness. The smell of horses and ammonia, and of warmth was startling to her, in that full night. She listened with all her ears but could hear nothing save the night, and the stirring of a horse.

"Maurice!" she called, softly and musically, though she was afraid. "Maurice—are you there?"

Nothing came from the darkness. She knew the rain and wind blew in upon the horses, the hot animal life. Feeling it wrong, she entered the stable and drew the lower half of the door shut, holding the upper part close. She did not stir, because she was aware of the presence of the dark hind-quarters of the horses, though she could not see them, and she was afraid. Something wild stirred in her heart.

She listened intensely. Then she heard a small noise in the distance— far away, it seemed—the chink of a pan, and a man's voice speaking a brief word. It would be Maurice, in the other part of the stable. She stood motionless, waiting for him to come through the partition door. The horses were so terrifyingly near to her, in the invisible.

The loud jarring of the inner door-latch made her start; the door was opened. She could hear and feel her husband entering and invisibly passing among the horses near to her, in darkness as they were, actively intermingled. The rather low sound of his voice as he spoke to the horses came velvety to her nerves. How near he was, and how invisible! The darkness seemed to be in a strange swirl of violent life, just upon her. She turned giddy.

Her presence of mind made her call quietly and musically:

"Maurice! Maurice—dear-ar!"

"Yes," he answered. "Isabel?"

She saw nothing, and the sound of his voice seemed to touch her.

"Hello!" she answered cheerfully, straining her eyes to see him. He was still busy, attending to the horses near her, but she saw only darkness. It made her almost desperate.

"Won't you come in, dear?" she said.

"Yes, I'm coming. Just half a minute. Stand over—now! Trap's not come, has it?"

"Not yet," said Isabel.

His voice was pleasant and ordinary, but it had a slight suggestion of the stable to her. She wished he would come away. Whilst he was so utterly invisible, she was afraid of him.

"How's the time?" he asked.

"Not yet six," she replied. She disliked to answer into the dark. Presently he came very near to her, and she retreated out of doors.

"The weather blows in here," he said, coming steadily forward, feeling for the doors. She shrank away. At last she could dimly see him.

"Bertie won't have much of a drive," he said, as he closed the doors.

"He won't indeed!" said Isabel calmly, watching the dark shape at the door.

"Give me your arm, dear," she said.

She pressed his arm close to her, as she went. But she longed to see him, to look at him. She was nervous. He walked erect, with face rather lifted, but with a curious tentative movement of his powerful, muscular legs. She could feel the clever, careful, strong contact of his feet with the earth, as she balanced against him. For a moment he was a tower of darkness to her, as if he rose out of the earth.

In the house-passage he wavered and went cautiously, with a curious look of silence about him as he felt for the bench. Then he sat down heavily. He was a man with rather sloping shoulders, but with heavy limbs, powerful legs that seemed to know the earth. His head was small, usually carried high and light. As he bent down to unfasten his gaiters and boots he did not look blind. His hair was brown and crisp, his hands were large, reddish, intelligent, the veins stood out in the wrists; and his thighs and knees seemed massive. When he stood up his face and neck were surcharged with blood, the veins stood out on his temples. She did not look at his blindness.

Isabel was always glad when they had passed through the dividing door into their own regions of repose and beauty. She was a little afraid of him, out there in the animal grossness of the back. His bearings also changed, as he smelt the familiar indefinable odour that pervaded his wife's surroundings, a delicate, refined scent, very faintly spicy. Perhaps it came from the potpourri bowls.

He stood at the foot of the stairs, arrested, listening. She watched him, and her heart sickened. He seemed to be listening to fate.

"He's not here yet," he said. "I'll go up and change."

"Maurice," she said, "you're not wishing he wouldn't come, are you?"

"I couldn't quite say," he answered. "I feel myself rather on the qui vive."

"I can see you are," she answered. And she reached up and kissed his cheek. She saw his mouth relax into a slow smile.

"What are you laughing at?" she said roguishly.

"You consoling me," he answered.

"Nay," she answered. "Why should I console you? You know we love each other—you know how married we are! What does anything else matter?"

"Nothing at all, my dear."

He felt for her face and touched it, smiling.

"You're all right, aren't you?" he asked anxiously.

"I'm wonderfully all right, love," she answered. "It's you I am a little troubled about, at times."

"Why me?" he said, touching her cheeks delicately with the tips of his fingers. The touch had an almost hypnotizing effect on her.

He went away upstairs. She saw him mount into the darkness, unseeing and unchanging. He did not know that the lamps on the upper corridor were unlighted. He went on into the darkness with unchanging step. She heard him in the bath-room.

Pervin moved about almost unconsciously in his familiar surroundings, dark though everything was. He seemed to know the presence of objects before he touched them. It was a pleasure to him to rock thus through a world of things, carried on the flood in a sort of blood-prescience. He did not think much or trouble much. So long as he kept this sheer immediacy of blood-contact with the substantial world he was happy, he wanted no intervention of visual consciousness. In this state there was a certain rich positivity, bordering sometimes on rapture. Life seemed to move in him like a tide lapping, lapping, and advancing, enveloping all things darkly. It was a pleasure to stretch forth the hand and meet the unseen object, clasp it, and possess it in pure contact. He did not try to remember, to visualize. He did not want to. The new way of consciousness substituted itself in him.

The rich suffusion of this state generally kept him happy, reaching its culmination in the consuming passion for his wife. But at times the flow would seem to be checked and thrown back. Then it would beat inside him like a tangled sea, and he was tortured in the shattered chaos of his own blood. He grew to dread this arrest, this throw-back, this chaos inside himself, when he seemed merely at the mercy of his own powerful and conflicting elements. How to get some measure of control or surety, this was the question. And when the question rose maddening in him, he would clench his fists as if he would compel the whole universe to submit to him. But it was in vain. He could not even compel himself.

Tonight, however, he was still serene, though little tremors of unreasonable exasperation ran through him. He had to handle the razor very carefully, as he shaved, for it was not at one with him, he was afraid of it. His hearing also was too much sharpened. He heard the woman lighting the lamps on the corridor, and attending to the fire in the visitors' room. And then, as he went to his room, he heard the trap arrive. Then came Isabel's voice, lifted and calling, like a bell ringing:

"Is it you, Bertie? Have you come?"

And a man's voice answered out of the wind:

"Hello, Isabel! There you are."

"Have you had a miserable drive? I'm so sorry we couldn't send a closed carriage. I can't see you at all, you know."

"I'm coming. No, I liked the drive—it was like Perthshire. Well, how are you? You're looking fit as ever, as far as I can see."

"Oh, yes," said Isabel. "I'm wonderfully well. How are you? Rather thin, I think—"

"Worked to death—everybody's old cry. But I'm all right, Ciss. How's Pervin?—isn't he here?"

"Oh, yes, he's upstairs changing. Yes, he's awfully well. Take off your wet things; I'll send them to be dried."

"And how are you both, in spirits? He doesn't fret?"

"No—no, not at all. No, on the contrary, really. We've been wonderfully happy, incredibly. It's more than I can understand—so wonderful: the nearness, and the peace—"

"Ah! Well, that's awfully good news—"

They moved away. Pervin heard no more. But a childish sense of desolation had come over him, as he heard their brisk voices. He seemed shut out—like a child that is left out. He was aimless and excluded, he did not know what to do with himself. The helpless desolation came over him. He fumbled nervously as he dressed himself, in a state almost of childishness. He disliked the Scotch accent in Bertie's speech, and the slight response it found on Isabel's tongue. He disliked the slight purr of complacency in the Scottish speech. He disliked intensely the glib way in which Isabel spoke of their happiness and nearness. It made him recoil.

He was fretful and beside himself like a child, he had almost a childish nostalgia to be included in the life circle. And at the same time he was a man, dark and powerful and infuriated by his own weakness. By some fatal flaw, he could not be by himself, he had to depend on the support of another. And this very dependence enraged him. He hated Bertie Reid, and at the same time he knew the hatred was nonsense, he knew it was the outcome of his own weakness.

He went downstairs. Isabel was alone in the dining-room. She watched him enter, head erect, his feet tentative. He looked so strong-blooded and healthy and, at the same time, cancelled. Cancelled—that was the word that flew across her mind. Perhaps it was his scar suggested it.

"You heard Bertie come, Maurice?" she said.

"Yes—isn't he here?"

"He's in his room. He looks very thin and worn."

"I suppose he works himself to death."

A woman came in with a tray—and after a few minutes Bertie came down. He was a little dark man, with a very big forehead, thin, wispy hair, and sad, large eyes. His expression was inordinately sad—almost funny. He had odd, short legs.

Isabel watched him hesitate under the door, and glance nervously at her husband. Pervin heard him and turned.

"Here you are," said Isabel. "Come, let us eat."

Bertie went across to Maurice.

"How are you, Pervin?" he said, as he advanced.

The blind man stuck his hand out into space, and Bertie took it.

"Very fit. Glad you've come," said Maurice.

Isabel glanced at them, and glanced away, as if she could not bear to see them.

"Come," she said. "Come to table. Aren't you both awfully hungry? I am, tremendously."

"I'm afraid you waited for me," said Bertie, as they sat down.

Maurice had a curious monolithic way of sitting in a chair, erect and distant. Isabel's heart always beat when she caught sight of him thus.

"No," she replied to Bertie. "We're very little later than usual. We're having a sort of high tea, not dinner. Do you mind? It gives us such a nice long evening, uninterrupted."

"I like it," said Bertie.

Maurice was feeling, with curious little movements, almost like a cat kneading her bed, for his plate, his knife and fork, his napkin. He was getting the whole geography of his cover into his consciousness. He sat erect and inscrutable, remote-seeming. Bertie watched the static figure of the blind man, the delicate tactile discernment of the large, ruddy hands, and the curious mindless silence of the brow, above the scar. With difficulty he looked away, and without knowing what he did, picked up a little crystal bowl of violets from the table, and held them to his nose.

"They are sweet-scented," he said. "Where do they come from?"

"From the garden—under the windows," said Isabel.

"So late in the year—and so fragrant! Do you remember the violets under Aunt Bell's south wall?"

The two friends looked at each other and exchanged a smile, Isabel's eyes lighting up.

"Don't I?" she replied. "Wasn't she queer!"

"A curious old girl," laughed Bertie. "There's a streak of freakishness in the family, Isabel."

"Ah—but not in you and me, Bertie," said Isabel. "Give them to Maurice, will you?" she added, as Bertie was putting down the flowers. "Have you smelled the violets, dear? Do!—they are so scented."

Maurice held out his hand, and Bertie placed the tiny bowl against his large, warm-looking fingers. Maurice's hand closed over the thin white fingers of the barrister. Bertie carefully extricated himself. Then the two watched the blind man smelling the violets. He bent his head and seemed to be thinking. Isabel waited.

"Aren't they sweet, Maurice?" she said at last, anxiously.

"Very," he said. And he held out the bowl. Bertie took it. Both he and Isabel were a little afraid, and deeply disturbed.

The meal continued. Isabel and Bertie chatted spasmodically. The blind man was silent. He touched his food repeatedly, with quick, delicate touches of his knife-point, then cut irregular bits. He could not bear to be helped. Both Isabel and Bertie suffered: Isabel wondered why. She did not suffer when she was alone with Maurice. Bertie made her conscious of a strangeness.

After the meal the three drew their chairs to the fire, and sat down to talk. The decanters were put on a table near at hand. Isabel knocked the logs on the fire, and clouds of brilliant sparks went up the chimney. Bertie noticed a slight weariness in her bearing.

"You will be glad when your child comes now, Isabel?" he said.

She looked up to him with a quick wan smile.

"Yes, I shall be glad," she answered. "It begins to seem long. Yes, I shall be very glad. So will you, Maurice, won't you?" she added.

"Yes, I shall," replied her husband.

"We are both looking forward so much to having it," she said.

"Yes, of course," said Bertie.

He was a bachelor, three or four years older than Isabel. He lived in beautiful rooms overlooking the river, guarded by a faithful Scottish manservant. And he had his friends among the fair sex—not lovers, friends. So long as he could avoid any danger of courtship or marriage, he adored a few good women with constant and unfailing homage, and he was chivalrously fond of quite a number. But if they seemed to encroach on him, he withdrew and detested them.

Isabel knew him very well, knew his beautiful constancy, and kindness, also his incurable weakness, which made him unable ever to enter into close contact of any sort. He was ashamed of himself because he could not marry, could not approach women physically. He wanted to do so. But he could not. At the centre of him he was afraid, helplessly and even brutally afraid. He had given up hope, had ceased to expect any more that he could escape his own weakness. Hence he was a brilliant and successful barrister, also a litterateur of high repute, a rich man, and a great social success. At the centre he felt himself neuter, nothing.

Isabel knew him well. She despised him even while she admired him. She looked at his sad face, his little short legs, and felt contempt of him. She looked at his dark grey eyes, with their uncanny, almost childlike, intuition, and she loved him. He understood amazingly—but she had no fear of his understanding. As a man she patronized him.

And she turned to the impassive, silent figure of her husband. He sat leaning back, with folded arms, and face a little uptilted. His knees were straight and massive. She sighed, picked up the poker, and again began to prod the fire, to rouse the clouds of soft brilliant sparks.

"Isabel tells me," Bertie began suddenly, "that you have not suffered unbearably from the loss of sight."

Maurice straightened himself to attend but kept his arms folded.

"No," he said, "not unbearably. Now and again one struggles against it, you know. But there are compensations."

"They say it is much worse to be stone deaf," said Isabel.

"I believe it is," said Bertie. "Are there compensations?" he added to Maurice.

"Yes. You cease to bother about a great many things." Again Maurice stretched his figure, stretched the strong muscles of his back, and leaned backwards, with uplifted face.

"And that is a relief," said Bertie. "But what is there in place of the bothering? What replaces the activity?"

There was a pause. At length the blind man replied, as out of a negligent, unattentive thinking:

"Oh, I don't know. There's a good deal when you're not active."

"Is there?" said Bertie. "What exactly? It always seems to me that when there is no thought and no action, there is nothing."

Again Maurice was slow in replying.

"There is something," he replied. "I couldn't tell you what it is."

And the talk lapsed once more, Isabel and Bertie chatting gossip and reminiscence, the blind man silent.

At length Maurice rose restlessly, a big obtrusive figure. He felt tight and hampered. He wanted to go away.

"Do you mind," he said, "if I go and speak to Wernham?"

"No—go along, dear," said Isabel.

And he went out. A silence came over the two friends. At length Bertie said:

"Nevertheless, it is a great deprivation, Cissie."

"It is, Bertie. I know it is."

"Something lacking all the time," said Bertie.

"Yes, I know. And yet—and yet—Maurice is right. There is something else, something there, which you never knew was there, and which you can't express."

"What is there?" asked Bertie.

"I don't know—it's awfully hard to define it—but something strong and immediate. There's something strange in Maurice's presence—indefinable—but I couldn't do without it. I agree that it seems to put one's mind to sleep. But when we're alone I miss nothing; it seems awfully rich, almost splendid, you know."

"I'm afraid I don't follow," said Bertie.

They talked desultorily. The wind blew loudly outside, rain chattered on the window-panes, making a sharp drum-sound because of the closed, mellow-golden shutters inside. The logs burned slowly, with hot, almost invisible small flames. Bertie seemed uneasy, there were dark circles round his eyes. Isabel, rich with her approaching maternity, leaned looking into the fire. Her hair curled in odd, loose strands, very pleasing to the man. But she had a curious feeling of old woe in her heart, old timeless night-woe.

"I suppose we're all deficient somewhere," said Bertie.

"I suppose so," said Isabel wearily.

"Damned, sooner or later."

"I don't know," she said, rousing herself. "I feel quite all right, you know. The child coming seems to make me indifferent to everything, just placid. I can't feel that there's anything to trouble about, you know."

"A good thing, I should say," he replied slowly.

"Well, there it is. I suppose it's just Nature. If only I felt I needn't trouble about Maurice, I should be perfectly content—"

"But you feel you must trouble about him?"

"Well—I don't know—" She even resented this much effort.

The night passed slowly. Isabel looked at the clock. "I say," she said. "It's nearly ten o'clock. Where can Maurice be? I'm sure they're all in bed at the back. Excuse me a moment."

She went out, returning almost immediately.

"It's all shut up and in darkness," she said. "I wonder where he is. He must have gone out to the farm—"

Bertie looked at her.

"I suppose he'll come in," he said.

"I suppose so," she said. "But it's unusual for him to be out now."

"Would you like me to go out and see?"

"Well—if you wouldn't mind. I'd go, but—" She did not want to make the physical effort.

Bertie put on an old overcoat and took a lantern. He went out from the side door. He shrank from the wet and roaring night. Such weather had a nervous effect on him: too much moisture everywhere made him feel almost imbecile. Unwilling, he went through it all. A dog barked violently at him. He peered in all the buildings. At last, as he opened the upper door of a sort of intermediate barn, he heard a grinding noise, and looking in, holding up his lantern, saw Maurice, in his shirtsleeves, standing listening, holding the handle of a turnip-pulper. He had been pulping sweet roots, a pile of which lay dimly heaped in a corner behind him.

"That you, Wernham?" said Maurice, listening.

"No, it's me," said Bertie.

A large, half-wild grey cat was rubbing at Maurice's leg. The blind man stooped to rub its sides. Bertie watched the scene, then unconsciously entered and shut the door behind him. He was in a high sort of barn-place, from which, right and left, ran off the corridors in front of the stalled cattle. He watched the slow, stooping motion of the other man, as he caressed the great cat.

Maurice straightened himself.

"You came to look for me?" he said.

"Isabel was a little uneasy," said Bertie.

"I'll come in. I like messing about doing these jobs."

The cat had reared her sinister, feline length against his leg, clawing at his thigh affectionately. He lifted her claws out of his flesh.

"I hope I'm not in your way at all at the Grange here," said Bertie, rather shy and stiff.

"My way? No, not a bit. I'm glad Isabel has somebody to talk to. I'm afraid it's I who am in the way. I know I'm not very lively company. Isabel's all right, don't you think? She's not unhappy, is she?"

"I don't think so."

"What does she say?"

"She says she's very content—only a little troubled about you."

"Why me?"

"Perhaps afraid that you might brood," said Bertie, cautiously.

"She needn't be afraid of that." He continued to caress the flattened grey head of the cat with his fingers. "What I am a bit afraid of," he resumed, "is that she'll find me a dead weight, always alone with me down here."

"I don't think you need think that," said Bertie, though this was what he feared himself.

"I don't know," said Maurice. "Sometimes I feel it isn't fair that she's saddled with me." Then he dropped his voice curiously. "I say," he asked, secretly struggling, "is my face much disfigured? Do you mind telling me?"

"There is the scar," said Bertie, wondering. "Yes, it is a disfigurement. But more pitiable than shocking."

"A pretty bad scar, though," said Maurice.

"Oh, yes."

There was a pause.

"Sometimes I feel I am horrible," said Maurice, in a low voice, talking as if to himself. And Bertie actually felt a quiver of horror.

"That's nonsense," he said.

Maurice again straightened himself, leaving the cat.

"There's no telling," he said. Then again, in an odd tone, he added: "I don't really know you, do I?"

"Probably not," said Bertie.

"Do you mind if I touch you?"

The lawyer shrank away instinctively. And yet, out of very philanthropy, he said, in a small voice: "Not at all."

But he suffered as the blind man stretched out a strong, naked hand to him. Maurice accidentally knocked off Bertie's hat.

"I thought you were taller," he said, starting. Then he laid his hand on Bertie Reid's head, closing the dome of the skull in a soft, firm grasp, gathering it, as it were; then, shifting his grasp and softly closing again, with a fine, close pressure, till he had covered the skull and the face of the smaller man, tracing the brows, and touching the full, closed eyes, touching the small nose and the nostrils, the rough, short moustache, the mouth, the rather strong chin. The hand of the blind man grasped the shoulder, the arm, the hand of the other man. He seemed to take him, in the soft, travelling grasp.

"You seem young," he said quietly, at last.

The lawyer stood almost annihilated, unable to answer.

"Your head seems tender, as if you were young," Maurice repeated. "So do your hands. Touch my eyes, will you?—touch my scar."

Now Bertie quivered with revulsion. Yet he was under the power of the blind man, as if hypnotized. He lifted his hand, and laid the fingers on the scar, on the scarred eyes. Maurice suddenly covered them with his own hand, pressed the fingers of the other man upon his disfigured eye-sockets, trembling in every fibre, and rocking slightly, slowly, from side to side. He remained thus for a minute or more, whilst Bertie stood as if in a swoon, unconscious, imprisoned.

Then suddenly Maurice removed the hand of the other man from his brow, and stood holding it in his own.

"Oh, my God," he said, "we shall know each other now, shan't we? We shall know each other now."

Bertie could not answer. He gazed mute and terrorstruck, overcome by his own weakness. He knew he could not answer. He had an unreasonable fear lest the other man should suddenly destroy him. Whereas Maurice was actually filled with hot, poignant love, the passion of friendship. Perhaps it was this very passion of friendship which Bertie shrank from most.

"We're all right together now, aren't we?" said Maurice. "It's all right now, as long as we live, so far as we're concerned?"

"Yes," said Bertie, trying by any means to escape.

Maurice stood with head lifted, as if listening. The new delicate fulfilment of mortal friendship had come as a revelation and surprise to him, something exquisite and unhoped-for. He seemed to be listening to hear if it were real.

Then he turned for his coat.

"Come," he said, "we'll go to Isabel."

Bertie took the lantern and opened the door. The cat disappeared. The two men went in silence along the causeways. Isabel, as they came, thought their footsteps sounded strange. She looked up pathetically and anxiously for their entrance. There seemed a curious elation about Maurice. Bertie was haggard, with sunken eyes.

"What is it?" she asked.

"We've become friends," said Maurice, standing with his feet apart, like a strange colossus.

"Friends!" re-echoed Isabel. And she looked again at Bertie. He met her eyes with a furtive, haggard look; his eyes were as if glazed with misery.

"I'm so glad," she said, in sheer perplexity.

"Yes," said Maurice.

He was indeed so glad. Isabel took his hand with both hers, and held it fast.

"You'll be happier now, dear," she said.

But she was watching Bertie. She knew that he had one desire—to escape from this intimacy, this friendship, which had been thrust upon him. He could not bear it that he had been touched by the blind man, his insane reserve broken in. He was like a mollusc whose shell is broken.

COMMENT

This is a story of how we know and do not know each other. The theme is dramatically realized in two confrontations: one between Isabel and Maurice, and one between Bertie and Maurice. These confrontations provide the surface structure of the story, the structure of the action, but as usual in the modern short story the overt action is minimal. We must look at the *texture* to uncover the meaning of the confrontations, for the meaning is present in the symbolic detail as well as in the more obviously dramatic moments. The story has its dramatic event, certainly, but the gravity of the story is everywhere, in every moment. We might put it this way: Lawrence is first of all presenting states of being, the way people are when they are doing nothing.

Darkness is the controlling symbol. The story begins in the darkness of rain, of evening, of November, and ends in the wet and roaring night; and the confrontations take place in the darkness. Darkness is the blind man's natural element; where he *is*. Joy is "dark" to him. But Isabel is afraid as she goes out to meet him in the first confrontation. He appears like a "tower of darkness" to her, "as if he rose out of the earth." She is afraid, too, of the "animal grossness" of the *back* part of the house. Her civilized, social self is in a crisis at this confrontation with the unknown and primitive, and she is therefore glad when she passes "through the dividing door into their own regions of repose and beauty." At this point her relation with Maurice remains unresolved: half she is drawn to him, half she is afraid. And so her invitation to Bertie, the civilized man.

The darkness symbolizes the primitive as a hostile force to Isabel, but it is the source of Maurice's well-being:

> Pervin moved about almost unconsciously in his familiar surroundings, dark though everything was. He seemed to know the presence of objects before he touched them. It was a pleasure to him to rock thus through a world of things, carried on the flood in a sort of blood-prescience. He did not think much or trouble much. So long as he kept this sheer immediacy of blood-contact with the substantial world he was happy, he wanted no intervention of visual consciousness. In this state there was a certain rich positivity, bordering sometimes on rapture. Life seemed to move in him like a tide lapping, lapping, and advancing, enveloping all things darkly. It was a pleasure to stretch forth the hand and meet the unseen object, clasp it, and possess it in pure contact. He did not try to remember, to visualize. He did not want to. The new way of consciousness substituted itself in him.

Darkness endows Maurice with the immediacy of all the senses except sight, linking him naturally to "blood-prescience" and "blood-contact." By "blood-prescience" the blind man knows through his instincts. Lawrence explained in a letter to Bertrand Russell, "One lives, knows and has one's being in the blood, without any reference to nerves and brain. This is one half of life belonging to the darkness." Darkness is synonymous with the blood, the ground of knowing another person. In the same letter Lawrence says, "When I take a woman, then the blood percept is supreme. My blood knowing is overwhelming. We should realize that we have a blood being, a blood consciousness, a blood soul complete and apart from a mental and nerve consciousness." Lawrence means that feeling and passion, which are rooted in the blood, are ways of knowing at least as valid as those of thought and reason. Note that "knowing" has a specifically sexual as well as general meaning, as in Elizabethan usage.

Just as darkness is linked to blood-consciousness, so is touch, as the term "blood-contact" indicates. To know someone is to contact him, to touch him. Maurice has "tactile discernment": it is a pleasure for him to "stretch forth the hand and meet the unseen object, clasp it, and possess it in pure contact." Touch, blood, darkness—for Maurice these are identical ways of knowing a person.

Bertie Reid, on the other hand, at home with concepts, categories, books, the abstractions of the law, shrinks from darkness, bodily contact, and sex. He gets "on his knees before the woman he adored"; he idealizes woman, elevates her above nature, and so removes the possibility of knowing her sexually. His framework of abstractions—social, legal, philosophical—serve as an armor to shield him from knowing another personally. When, unarmored, he is forced to meet a person as a person, he collapses. Maurice is free because he is blind and thus not so readily available to the abstract structures of society and the state. In this sense Lawrence's blind man is artificial, an experiment in the possibilities of freedom, of living on one's natural resources. It is significant that Maurice grasps Bertie's skull, the seat of the mind which creates the abstractions structuring a civilization. In the widest symbolic sense, the collapse of Bertie, a successful civilized type, is the collapse of our civilization. This collapse is a persistent Lawrentian theme, present in *Lady Chatterley's Lover,* for example, in the figure of the sexually paralyzed industrialist, Lord Chatterley. Characteristically, in that novel a gamekeeper, a man at home in nature, symbolizes the force for rebirth, for renewal.

Up to this point Isabel Pervin oscillates between Bertie and Maurice. She is linked to Bertie by their lifelong friendship. She has loved him, "though not in the marrying sense." They also have a common interest in literature, which included the abstractions of literary criticism, for Isabel reviews books. In contrast to their abstract and nonsexual.relation, Isabel is linked to Maurice by marriage, that is, through sex, the blood. Isabel's conflict is resolved in the climax, the confrontation between Maurice and Bertie.

The confrontation is a test of their capacity to know another person. The testing ground is darkness; the test is touching each other. The outcome is foreshadowed in the incident with the bowl of violets. As Bertie places the bowl against Maurice's "large, warm-looking fingers," Maurice's hand closes over Bertie's "thin white fingers." The difference in their capacity for relating is indicated by the difference in their fingers. Bertie "carefully extricated himself" from Maurice's hand. He cannot stand to be touched bodily and therefore, for Lawrence, feelingly. Maurice can. In the climax Maurice touches and so destroys Bertie. Maurice appears to Isabel like a "strange colossus"; Bertie seems like a "mollusc whose shell is broken." The shell is Bertie's social armor that keeps him from being in *touch* with another person. The climax is realized through the conjunction of two primary symbols: darkness and touch. Maurice's resolution is suggested in the transcendent image of the colossus. Isabel, however, has still to act on her own. She is perplexed by what she sees, but what she sees turns her to Maurice. For she now understands that Bertie cannot bear intimacy, that his reserve is "insane." She breaks through her own armor by taking Maurice's hand with both hers and holding it fast. Her resolution is probably only potential.

We said that "The Blind Man" was a story about two ways of knowing. The ways are those of the structured social self, which knows through abstractions and conventions, and of the unstructured natural self, which knows through the darkness of the blood.

This is a familiar contemporary idea, which Lawrence gives concrete dramatic form. His particular achievement is the symbolic rendering of the *sensations* of his ideas about blood, darkness, and touch—and smell and sound. Lawrence, who was a painter too, applies the tactile values of painting to fiction. It is this symbolic texture of sensations that carries the meaning that blood, darkness, touch, smell, and sound are a way of being.

Lawrence honors the everyday for itself, but he transforms it symbolically too. To understand how he evokes the profound in the everyday, one would have to know the secret of artistic creativity. We can say, at least, that his vision penetrates everything and transforms the familiar. This penetration creates the Lawrentian universe, as it does the universe of Joyce, Mann, and Kafka. It is probably the definitive sign of artistic commitment.

QUESTIONS ON SYMBOLISM

1. What is the significance of the fact that Maurice is blinded in Flanders, that is, in a world war?

2. One paradox, as in *Oedipus Rex,* is that the blind have special powers: in Maurice's case, his sensuous way of knowing a person. Is there an implied limitation to this way of knowing? How well, for example, does he understand Bertie? or Isabel? Consider Lawrence's letter to Russell in this connection.

3. What do you make of the physical differences between Maurice and Bertie? Compare the two with the Wernhams. Is the difference in color related to the primary symbols?

4. Just before the climax Maurice knocks off Bertie's hat by accident. How does this prepare us for the climax?

5. Consider the clusters of imagery of smell and sound. What is their general significance and the significance of smell and sound to each of the three main characters?

6. Is there any ambiguity in the symbol of darkness?

OTHER CONSIDERATIONS

1. "The Blind Man" presents the relationship among three people familiarly known as the love triangle, a subject that is naturally appealing, as is evident from its relentless exploitation in popular fiction. Does Lawrence exploit it for its sensational interest? If not, how does he lift it above the level of the stock situation? For range of treatment of this subject, see the stories in this collection by Lardner, James, Amichai, and Frank O'Connor.

2. The short story usually concentrates on a single effect. Is this effect diluted by the break in the unity of time in the first few

pages? by the shifts in the center of consciousness? by the fact that the story has the two developments, for Maurice and for Isabel?

3. Does Lawrence underestimate the role of the mind in a sentimentally romantic way?

4. Maurice's feelings are "quick and acute"; Bertie's "mind [is] much quicker than his emotions, which [are] not so very fine." This is a classic romantic polarization, reversing the usual high valuation of the mind and, by implication, the abstract structures of the mind. What evidence of this polarization is there in such stories as "Madame Tellier's Excursion," "The Silence of the Valley," "The Fairy Goose," and "Nina of Ashkelon"?

5. Does the story contain a revaluation of the idea of character (see our introduction to the section "Character")?

6. Lawrence wrote to Katherine Mansfield that the end of "The Blind Man" is "queer and ironical." What is the content of the irony and at whom is it directed? At everyone, perhaps?

Christmas Every Day

ಆ *Heinrich Böll*

Symptoms of decline have become evident in our family. For a time we were at pains to disregard them, but now we have resolved to face the danger. I dare not, as yet, use the word breakdown, but disturbing facts are piling up at such a rate as to constitute a menace and to compel me to report things that will sound disagreeable to my contemporaries; no one, however, can dispute their reality. The minute fungi of destruction have found lodgement beneath the hard, thick crust of respectability; colonies of deadly parasites that proclaim the end of a whole tribe's irreproachable correctness. Today we must deplore our disregard of Cousin Franz, who began long ago to warn us of the dreadful consequences that would result from an event that was harmless enough in itself. So insignificant indeed was the event that the disproportion of the consequences now terrifies us. Franz warned us betimes. Unfortunately he had too little standing. He had chosen a calling that no member of the family had ever followed before, and none ever should have: he was a boxer. Melancholy even in youth and possessed by a devoutness that was always described as "pious fiddle-faddle," he early adopted ways that worried my Uncle Franz, that good, kind man. He was wont to neglect his schoolwork to a quite abnormal degree. He used to meet disreputable companions in the thickets and deserted parks of the suburbs, and there practice the rough discipline of the prize fight, with no thought for his neglected humanistic heritage. These youngsters early revealed the vices of their generation, which, as has since become abundantly evident, is really worthless. The exciting spiritual combats of earlier centuries simply did not interest them; they were far too concerned with the dubious excitements of their own. At first I thought Franz's piety in contradiction to his systematic exercises in passive and active brutality. But today I begin to suspect a connection. This is a subject I shall have to return to.

And so it was Franz who warned us in good time, who refused above all to have anything to do with certain celebrations, calling the whole thing a folly and a disgrace, and later on declined to participate in those measures that proved necessary for the continuance of what he considered evil. But, as I have said, he had too little standing to get a hearing in the family circle.

Now, to be sure, things have gone so far that we stand helpless, not knowing how to call a halt.

Franz has long since become a famous boxer, but today he rejects the

Translated from the German by Denver Lindley, copyright © 1957 by Heinrich Böll, reprinted by permission of the author.

praises that the family lavishes on him with the same indifference he once showed toward their criticism.

His brother, however—my Cousin Johannes, a man for whom I would at any time have walked through fire, the successful lawyer and favorite son of my uncle—Johannes is said to have struck up relations with the Communist Party, a rumor I stubbornly refuse to believe. My Cousin Lucie, hitherto a normal woman, is said to frequent disreputable night clubs, accompanied by her helpless husband, and to engage in dances that I can only describe as existential. Even Uncle Franz, that good, kind man, is reported to have remarked that he is weary of life, he whom the whole family considered a paragon of vitality and the very model of what we were taught to call a Christian businessman.

Doctors' bills are piling up, psychiatrists and analysts are being called in. Only my Aunt Milla, who must be considered the cause of it all, enjoys the best of health, smiling, well and cheerful, as she has been almost all her life. Her liveliness and cheerfulness are slowly beginning to get on our nerves after our very serious concern about the state of her health. For there was a crisis in her life that threatened to be serious. It is just this that I must explain.

II

In retrospect it is easy enough to determine the source of a disquieting series of events, but only now, when I regard the matter dispassionately, do the things that have been taking place in our family for almost two years appear out of the ordinary.

We might have surmised earlier that something was not quite right. Something in fact was not, and if things ever were quite right—which I doubt—events are now taking place that fill me with consternation.

For a long time Aunt Milla has been famous in our family for her delight in decorating the Christmas tree, a harmless though particularized weakness which is fairly widespread in our country. This weakness of hers was indulgently smiled at by one and all, and the resistance that Franz showed from his earliest days to this "nonsense" was treated with indignation, especially since Franz was in other respects a disturbing young man. He refused to take part in the decoration of the tree. Up to a certain point all this was taken in stride. My aunt had become accustomed to Franz's staying away from the preparations at Advent and also from the celebration itself and only putting in an appearance for the meal. It was not even mentioned.

At the risk of making myself unpopular, I must here mention a fact in defense of which I can only say that it really is a fact. In the years 1939 to 1945 we were at war. In war there is singing, shooting, oratory, fighting, starvation and death—and bombs are dropped. These are thoroughly disagreeable subjects, and I have no desire to bore my contemporaries by dwelling on them. I must only mention them because the war had an influence on the story I am about to tell. For the war registered on my aunt simply as a force that, as early as Christmas 1939, began to threaten her Christmas tree. To be sure, this tree of hers was peculiarly sensitive.

As its principal attraction my Aunt Milla's Christmas tree was furnished with glass gnomes that held cork hammers in their upraised hands. At their feet were bell-shaped anvils, and under their feet candles were fastened. When the heat rose to a certain degree, a hidden mechanism went into operation, imparting a hectic movement to the gnomes' arms; a dozen in number, they beat like mad on the bell-shaped anvils with their cork hammers, thus producing a concerted, high-pitched, elfin tinkling. And at the top of the tree stood a red-cheeked angel, dressed in silver, who at certain intervals opened his lips and whispered "Peace, peace." The mechanical secret of the angel was strictly guarded, and I only learned about it later, when as it happened I had the opportunity of admiring it almost weekly. Naturally in addition to this my aunt's Christmas tree was decorated with sugar rings, cookies, angel hair, marzipan figures and, not to be forgotten, strands of tinsel. I still remember that the proper preparation of these varied decorations cost a good deal of trouble, demanding the help of all, and the whole family on Christmas Eve was too nervous to be hungry. The mood, as people say, was simply terrible, and the one exception was my Cousin Franz, who of course had taken no part in the preparations and was the only one to enjoy the roasts, asparagus, creams and ices. If after that we came for a call on the day after Christmas and ventured the bold conjecture that the secret of the speaking angel resided in the same sort of mechanism that makes certain dolls say "Mama" or "Papa," we were simply greeted by derisive laughter.

Now it is easy to understand that in the neighborhood of falling bombs such a sensitive tree would be in great danger. There were terrible times when the gnomes pitched down from the tree, and once even the angel fell. My aunt was inconsolable. She went to endless pains to restore the tree completely after each air raid so as to preserve it at least through the Christmas holidays. But by 1940 it was out of the question. Once more at the risk of making myself unpopular I must briefly mention here that the number of air raids on our city was considerable, to say nothing of their severity. In any case my aunt's Christmas tree fell victim to the modern art of war (regulations forbid me to say anything about other victims); foreign ballistics experts temporarily extinguished it.

We all sympathized with our aunt, who was an amiable and charming woman, and pretty into the bargain. It pained us that she was compelled, after bitter struggles, endless disputes, scenes and tears, to agree to forego her tree for the duration.

Fortunately—or should I say unfortunately?—this was almost the only aspect of the war that was brought home to my aunt. The bunker my uncle built was really bombproof; in addition a car was always ready to whisk my Aunt Milla away to places where nothing was to be seen of the immediate effects of war. Everything was done to spare her the sight of the horrible ruins. My two cousins had the good fortune not to see military service in its harshest form. Johannes at once entered my uncle's firm, which played an essential part in the wholesale grocery business of our city. Besides, he suffered from gall bladder trouble. Franz on the other hand became a soldier, but he was only engaged in guarding prisoners, a post which he exploited to the extent of making himself unpopular with his military superiors by treating Russians and Poles like human beings. My Cousin Lucie was not yet married at that time and helped with the business. One afternoon a week she did voluntary war work, embroidering swastikas. But this is not the place to recite the political sins of my relations.

On the whole, then, there was no lack of money or food or reasonable safety, and my aunt's only sorrow was the absence of her tree. My Uncle Franz, that good, kind man, had for almost fifty years rendered invaluable service by purchasing oranges and lemons in tropical and subtropical countries and selling them at an appropriate profit. During the war he extended his business to less valuable fruits and to vegetables. After the war, however, the principal objects of his interest became popular once more under the name of citrus fruits and caused sharp competition in business circles. Here Uncle Franz succeeded once more in playing a decisive role by introducing the populace to a taste for vitamins and himself to a sizable fortune. He was almost seventy by that time, however, and wanted to retire and leave the business to his son-in-law. It was then that the event took place which made us smile at the time but which we now recognize as the cause of the whole affair.

My Aunt Milla began again with her Christmas tree. That was harmless in itself; even the tenacity with which she insisted that everything should be "as it used to be" only caused us to smile. At first there was really no reason to take the matter too seriously. To be sure, the war had caused much havoc which it was our duty to put right, but why—so we asked ourselves—deprive a charming old lady of this small joy?

Everyone knows how hard it was at that time to get butter and bacon. And even for my Uncle Franz, who had the best connections, it was impossible in the year 1945 to procure marzipan figures and chocolate rings. It was not until 1946 that everything could be made ready. Fortunately a complete set of gnomes and anvils as well as an angel had been preserved.

I still clearly remember the day on which we were invited. It was in January '47 and it was cold outside. But at my uncle's it was warm and there was no lack of delicacies. When the lights were turned out and the candles lighted, when the gnomes began to hammer and the angel whispered "Peace, peace," I had a vivid feeling of being restored to a time that I had assumed was gone forever.

This experience, however, though surprising was not extraordinary. The extraordinary thing was what happened three months later. My mother—it was now the middle of March—sent me over to find out whether "there was anything doing" with Uncle Franz. She needed fruit.

I wandered into the neighboring quarter—the air was mild and it was twilight. Unsuspecting, I walked past the overgrown piles of ruins and the untended parks, turned in at the gate to my uncle's garden and suddenly stopped in amazement. In the evening quiet I could distinctly hear someone singing in my uncle's living room. Singing is a good old German custom, and there are lots of spring songs—but here I clearly heard:

> *Unto us a child is born!*
> *The King of all creation . . .*

I must admit I was confused. Slowly I approached and waited for the end of the song. The curtains were drawn and so I bent down to the keyhole. At that moment the tinkling of the gnomes' bells reached my ear, and I distinctly heard the angel whispering.

I did not have the courage to intrude, and walked slowly home. My report caused general merriment in the family, and it was not until Franz turned up and told us the details that we discovered what had happened.

In our region Christmas trees are dismantled at Candlemas and are then thrown on the rubbish heap where good-for-nothing children pick them up, drag them through ashes and other debris and play all sorts of games with them. This was the time when the dreadful thing happened. On Candlemas Eve after the tree had been lighted for the last time, and Cousin Johannes began to unfasten the gnomes from their clamps, my aunt who had hitherto been so gentle set up a dreadful screaming, so loud and sudden that my cousin was startled, lost control of the swaying tree, and in an instant it was all over; there was a tinkling and ringing; gnomes and bells, anvils and angel, everything pitched down; and my aunt screamed.

She screamed for almost a week. Neurologists were summoned by telegram, psychiatrists came rushing up in taxicabs—but all of them, even the specialists, left with a shrug of the shoulders and a faint expression of dread.

No one could put an end to this shrill and maddening concert. Only the strongest drugs provided a few hours' rest, and the dose of Luminal that one can daily prescribe for a woman in her sixties without endangering her life is, alas, slight. But it is anguish to have a woman in the house screaming with all her might: on the second day the family was completely disorganized. Even the consolation of the priest, who was accustomed to attend the celebration on Holy Eve, remained unavailing: my aunt screamed.

Franz made himself particularly unpopular by advising that a regular exorcism be performed. The minister rebuked him, the family was alarmed by his medieval views, and his reputation for brutality eclipsed for several weeks his reputation as a boxer.

Meanwhile everything was tried to cure my aunt's ailment. She refused nourishment, did not speak, did not sleep; cold water was tried, hot water, foot baths, alternate cold and hot baths; the doctors searched the lexicons for the name of this complex but could not find it. And my aunt screamed. She screamed until my Uncle Franz—that really kind, good man—hit on the idea of putting up a new Christmas tree.

III

The idea was excellent, but to carry it out proved extremely hard. It was now almost the middle of February, and to find a presentable fir tree in the market at that time is naturally difficult. The whole business world has long since turned with happy alacrity to other things. Carnival time is near: masks, pistols, cowboy hats and fanciful gypsy headgear fill the shop windows where angels and angel hair, candles and mangers, were formerly on view. In the candy stores Christmas items have long since gone back to the storeroom, while fireworks now adorn the windows. Nowhere in the regular market is a fir tree to be found.

Finally an expedition of rapacious grandchildren was fitted out with pocket money and a sharp hatchet. They rode to the state forest and came back toward evening, obviously in the best of spirits, with a silver fir. But meanwhile it was discovered that four gnomes, six bell-shaped anvils and the crowning angel had been completely destroyed. The marzipan figures and the cookies had fallen victim to the rapacious grandchildren. This coming generation, too, is worthless, and if any generation was ever of any worth—which I doubt—I am slowly coming to the belief that it was the generation of our fathers.

Although there was no lack of cash or the necessary connections, it took four days more before the decorations were complete. Meanwhile my aunt screamed uninterruptedly. Messages to the German centers of the toy business, which were just then resuming operations, were dispatched by wireless, hurried telephone conversations were carried on, packages were delivered in the night by heated young postal employees, an import license from Czechoslovakia was obtained, by bribery, without delay.

These days will stand out in the chronicle of my uncle's family by reason of the extraordinary consumption of coffee, cigarettes and nervous energy. Meanwhile my aunt fell into a decline: her round face became harsh and angular, her expression of kindliness changed to one of unalterable severity, she did not eat, she did not drink, she screamed constantly, she was attended by two nurses, and the dose of Luminal had to be increased daily.

Franz told us that the whole family was in the grip of a morbid tension when finally, on the twelfth of February, the decoration of the Christmas tree was at last completed. The candles were lighted, the curtains were drawn, my aunt was brought out from her sickroom, and in the family circle there was only the sound of sobs and giggles. My aunt's expression relaxed at the sight of the candles, and when the heat had reached the proper point and the glass gnomes began to pound like mad and finally the angel, too, whispered "Peace, peace," a beautiful smile illuminated her face. Shortly thereafter everyone began to sing "O Tannenbaum." To complete the picture, they had invited the minister, whose custom it was to spend Christmas Eve at my Uncle Franz's; he, too, smiled, he too was relieved and joined in the singing.

What no test, no psychological opinion, no expert search for hidden traumas had succeeded in doing, my uncle's sympathetic heart had accomplished. This good, kind man's Christmas-tree therapy had saved the situation.

My aunt was reassured and almost—so they hoped at the time—cured. After more songs had been sung and several plates of cookies had been emptied, everyone was tired and went to bed. And, imagine, my aunt slept without sedatives. The two nurses were dismissed, the doctors shrugged their shoulders, and everything seemed in order. My aunt ate again, drank again, was once more kind and amiable.

But the following evening at twilight, when my uncle was reading his newspaper beside his wife under the tree, she suddenly touched him gently on the arm and said: "Now we will call the children for the celebration. I think it's time." My uncle admitted to us later that he was startled, but he got up and hastily summoned his children and grandchildren and dispatched a messenger for the minister. The latter appeared, somewhat distraught and amazed; the candles were lighted, the gnomes hammered away, the angel whispered, there was singing and eating—and everything seemed in order.

Now all vegetation is subject to certain biological laws, and fir trees torn from the soil have a well-known tendency to wilt and lose their needles, especially if they are kept in a warm room, and in my uncle's house it was warm. The life of the silver fir is somewhat longer than that of the common variety, as the well-known work *Abies Vulgaris and Abies Nobilis* by Doctor Hergenring has shown. But even the life of the silver fir is not unlimited. As Carnival approached it became clear that my aunt would have to be prepared for a new sorrow: the tree was rapidly losing its needles, and at the evening singing a slight frown appeared on her forehead. On the advice of a really outstanding psychologist an attempt was made in light, casual conversation to warn her of the possible end of the Christmas season, especially as the trees outside were now covered with leaves, which is generally taken as a sign of approaching spring whereas in our latitudes the word Christmas connotes wintry scenes. My resourceful uncle proposed one evening that the songs "All the birds are now assembled" and "Come, lovely May" should be sung, but at the first verse of the former such a scowl appeared on my aunt's face that the singers quickly broke off and intoned "O Tannenbaum." Three days later my Cousin Johannes was instructed to undertake a quiet dismantling operation, but as soon as he stretched out his hand and took the cork hammer from one of the gnomes my aunt broke into such violent screaming that the gnome was immediately given back his implement, the candles were lighted and somewhat hastily but very loudly everyone began to sing "Silent Night."

But the nights were no longer silent; groups of singing, youthful revelers streamed through the city with trumpets and drums, everything was covered with streamers and confetti, masked children crowded the streets, fired guns, screamed, some sang as well, and a private investigation showed that there were at least sixty thousand cowboys and forty thousand gypsy princesses in our city: in short it was Carnival, a holiday that is celebrated in our neighborhood with as much enthusiasm as Christmas or even more. But my aunt seemed blind and deaf: she deplored the carnival costumes that inevitably appeared at this time in the wardrobes of our household; in a sad voice she lamented the decline of morals that caused people even at Christmas to indulge in such disgraceful practices, and when she discovered a toy balloon in Lucie's bedroom, a balloon that had, to be sure, collapsed but nevertheless clearly showed a white fool's cap painted on it, she broke into tears and besought my uncle to put an end to these unholy activities.

They were forced to realize with horror that my aunt actually believed it was still Christmas Eve. My uncle called a family council, requested consideration for his wife in view of her extraordinary state of mind, and at once got together an expedition to insure that at least the evening celebration would be peacefully maintained.

While my aunt slept the decorations were taken down from the old tree and placed on a new one, and her state of health continued to be satisfactory.

Carnival, too, went by, spring came for fair; instead of "Come, Lovely May" one might properly have sung "Lovely May, Thou Art Here." June arrived. Four Christmas trees had already been discarded and none of the newly summoned doctors could hold out hope of improvement. My aunt remained firm. Even that internationally famous authority, Doctor Bless, had returned to his study, shrugging his shoulders, after having pocketed an honorarium in the sum of 1365 marks, thereby demonstrating once more his complete unworldliness. A few tentative attempts to put an end to the celebration or to intermit it were greeted with such outcries from my aunt that these sacrileges had to be abandoned once and for all.

The dreadful thing was that my aunt insisted that all those closest to her must be present. Among these were the minister and the grandchildren. Even the members of the family could only be compelled by extreme severity to appear punctually; with the minister it was even more difficult. For some weeks he kept it up without protest, out of consideration for his aged pensioner, but then he attempted, clearing his throat in embarrassment, to make it clear to my uncle that this could not go on. The actual celebration was short—it lasted only about thirty-eight minutes—but even this brief ceremonial, the minister maintained, could not be kept up indefinitely. He had other obligations, evening conferences with his confratres, duties connected with his cure of souls, not to mention his regular Saturday confessional. He agreed, however, to some weeks' continuance; but toward the end of May, he began energetic attempts to escape. Franz stormed about, seeking accomplices in the family for his plan to have his mother put in an institution. Everyone turned him down.

And yet difficulties continued. One evening the minister was missing and could not be located either telephonically or by messenger, and it became evident that he had simply skipped out. My uncle swore horribly and took the occasion to describe the servants of the Church in words I must decline to repeat. In this extremity one of the chaplains, a man of humble origin, was requested to help out. He did so, but behaved so abominably that it almost resulted in a catastrophe. However, one must bear in mind that it was June and therefore hot; nevertheless the curtains were drawn to give at least an illusion of wintry twilight and in addition the candles had been lighted. Then the celebration began. The chaplain had, to be sure, heard of this extraordinary event but had no proper idea of it. There was general apprehension when he was presented to my aunt as the minister's substitute. Unexpectedly she accepted this change in the program. Well then, the gnomes hammered, the angel whispered, "O Tannenbaum" was sung, then there was the eating of cookies, more singing, and suddenly the chaplain was overcome by a paroxysm of laughter. Later he admitted that it was the line ". . . in winter, too, when snow is falling" that had been too much for him to endure without laughing. He burst out with clerical tactlessness, left the room and was seen no more. All looked at my aunt apprehensively, but she only murmured resignedly something about "proletarians in priest's robes" and put a piece of marzipan in her mouth. We too deplored this event at the time—but today I am inclined to regard it as an outbreak of quite natural hilarity.

Here I must remark, if I am to be true to the facts, that my uncle exploited his connection with the highest Church authorities to lodge a complaint against both the minister and the chaplain. The matter was taken up with utmost correctness, proceedings were instituted on the grounds of neglect of pastoral duty, and in the first instance the two clergymen were exonerated. Further proceedings are in preparation.

Fortunately a pensioned prelate was found in the neighborhood. This charming old gentleman agreed, with amiable matter-of-factness, to hold himself in readiness daily for the evening celebration. But I am anticipating. My Uncle Franz, who was sensible enough to realize that no medical aid would be of avail and who stubbornly refused to try exorcism, was also a good enough businessman to plan economies for the long haul. First of all, by mid-June, the grandchildren's expeditions were stopped because they proved too expensive. My resourceful Cousin Johannes, who was on good terms with all branches of the business world, discovered that Söderbaum and Company were in a position to provide fresh fir trees. For almost two years now this firm has done noble service in sparing my relations' nerves. At the end of six months Söderbaum and Company substantially reduced their charges and agreed to have the period of delivery determined most precisely by their conifer specialist Doctor Alfast, so that three days before the old tree became unpresentable a new one would be delivered and could be decorated at leisure. As an additional precaution two dozen gnomes and three crowning angels were kept constantly in reserve.

To this day the candies remain a sore point. They show a disturbing tendency to melt and drip down from the tree more quickly and completely than wax, at any rate in the summer months. Every effort to preserve them by carefully concealed refrigeration has thus far come to grief, as has a series of attempts to substitute artificial decorations. The family remains, however, gratefully receptive toward any proposal that might result in reducing the costs of this continuing festival.

IV

Meanwhile the daily celebrations in my uncle's house have taken on an almost professional regularity. People assemble under the tree or around the tree. My aunt comes in, the candles are lighted, the gnomes begin to hammer and the angel whispers "Peace, peace," songs are sung, cookies are nibbled, there is a little conversation and then everyone retires, yawning and murmuring "Merry Christmas to you, too." The young people turn to the forms of diversion dictated by the season, while my good, kind Uncle Franz goes to bed when Aunt Milla does. The smoke of the candles lingers in the room, there is the mild aroma of heated fir needles and the smell of spices. The gnomes, slightly phosphorescent, remain motionless in the darkness, their arms raised threateningly, and the angel can be seen in his silvery robes which are obviously phosphorescent too.

Perhaps it is superfluous to state that in our whole family circle the enjoyment of the real Christmas Eve has suffered a considerable diminution: we can, if we like, admire a classical Christmas tree at our uncle's at any time—and it often happens when we are sitting on the veranda in summertime after the toil and trouble of the day, pouring my uncle's mild orange punch down our throats, that the soft tinkling of glass bells comes to us and we can see in the twilight the gnomes hammering away like spry little devils while the angel whispers "Peace, peace." And it is still disconcerting to hear my uncle in mid-summer suddenly whisper to his children: "Please light the tree, Mother will be right out." Then, usually on the dot, the prelate enters, a kindly old gentleman whom we have all taken to our hearts because he plays his role so admirably, if indeed he knows that he is playing one. But no matter: he plays it, white-haired, smiling, with the violet band beneath his collar giving his appearance the final touch of distinction. And it gives one an extraordinary feeling on a mild summer evening to hear the excited cry: "The snuffer, quick, where is the snuffer?" It has even happened during severe thunderstorms that the gnomes have been suddenly impelled to lift their arms without the agency of heat and swing them wildly as though giving a special performance—a phenomenon that people have tried, rather unimaginatively, to explain by the prosaic word "electricity."

A by no means inessential aspect of this arrangement is the financial one. Even though in general our family suffers no lack of cash, such extraordinary expenses upset all calculations. For naturally, despite precautions, the breakage of gnomes, anvils, and hammers is enormous, and the delicate mechanism that causes the angel to speak requires constant care and attention and must now and again be replaced. I have, incidentally, discovered its secret: the angel is connected by a cable with a microphone in the adjoining room, in front of whose metal snout there is a constantly rotating phonograph record which, at proper intervals, whispers "Peace, peace." All these things are the more costly because they are designed for use on only a few occasions during the year, whereas with us they are subjected to daily wear and tear. I was astounded when my uncle told me one day that the gnomes actually had to be replaced every three months, and that a complete set of them cost no less than 128 marks. He said he had requested an engineering friend of his to try strengthening them by a rubber covering without spoiling the beauty of the tone. This experiment was unsuccessful. The consumption of candles, butter-and-almond cookies, marzipan, the regular payments for the trees, doctors' bills and the quarterly honorarium that has to be given to the prelate, altogether, said my uncle, come to an average daily expense of 11 marks, not to mention the nervous wear and tear and other disturbances of health that began to appear in the fall of the first year. These upsets were generally ascribed, at the time, to that autumnal sensibility that is always noticeable.

The real Christmas celebration went off quite normally. Something like a sigh of relief ran through my uncle's family when other families could be seen gathered under Christmas trees, others too had to sing and eat butter-and-almond cookies. But the relief lasted only as long as the Christmas holidays. By the middle of January my Cousin Lucie began to suffer from a strange ailment: at the sight of Christmas trees lying on the streets and on rubbish heaps she broke into hysterical sobs. Then she had a real attack of insanity which the family tried to discount as a nervous breakdown. At a coffee party in a friend's house she struck a dish out of her hostess' hand as the latter was smilingly offering her butter-and-almond cookies. My cousin is, to be sure, what is called a temperamental woman: and so she struck the dish from her friend's hand, went up to the Christmas tree, tore it from its stand and trampled on the glass balls, the artificial mushrooms, the candles and the stars, the while emitting a continuous roar. The assembled ladies fled, including the hostess. They let Lucie rage, and stood waiting for the doctor in the vestibule, forced to give ear to the sound of crashing china within. Painful though it is for me, I must report that Lucie was taken away in a straitjacket.

Sustained hypnotic treatment checked her illness, but the actual cure proceeded very slowly. Above all, release from the evening celebration, which the doctor demanded, seemed to do her visible good; after a few days she began to brighten. At the end of ten days the doctor could risk at least talking to her about butter-and-almond cookies, although she stubbornly persisted in refusing to eat them. The doctor then struck on the inspired idea of feeding her some sour pickles and offering her salads and nourishing meat dishes. That was poor Lucie's real salvation. She laughed once more and began to interject ironic observations into the endless therapeutic interviews she had with her doctor.

To be sure, the vacancy caused by her absence from the evening cele-bration was painful to my aunt, but it was explained to her by a circum-stance that is an adequate excuse in any woman's eyes—pregnancy.

But Lucie had created what is called a precedent: she had proved that although my aunt suffered when someone was absent, she did not immedi-ately begin to scream, and now my Cousin Johannes and his brother-in-law Carl attempted to infringe on the severe regulations, giving sickness as excuse or business appointments or some other quite transparent pre-text. But here my uncle remained astonishingly inflexible: with iron severity he decreed that only in exceptional cases upon presentation of acceptable evidence could very short leaves of absence be permitted. For my aunt noticed every further dereliction at once and broke into silent but continuing tears, which gave rise to the most serious apprehensions.

At the end of four weeks Lucie, too, returned and said she was ready to take part once more in the daily ceremony, but her doctor had insisted that a jar of pickles and a platter of nourishing sandwiches should be held in readiness, since her butter-and-almond trauma had proved incurable. Thus for a time, through my uncle's unexpected severity, all breaches of discipline were suppressed.

Shortly after the first anniversary of the daily Christmas celebration, disquieting rumors began to circulate: my Cousin Johannes was said to have consulted a doctor friend of his about my aunt's life expectancy, a truly sinister rumor which throws a disturbing light on a peaceful family's evening gatherings. The doctor's opinion is said to have been crushing for Johannes. All my aunt's vital organs, which had always been sound, were in perfect condition; her father's age at the time of his death had been seventy-eight, and her mother's eighty-six. My aunt herself is sixty-two, and so there is no reason to prophesy an early passing. Still less reason, I consider, to wish for one. After this when my aunt fell ill in midsummer—the poor woman suffered from vomiting and diarrhea—it was hinted that she had been poisoned, but I expressly declare here and now that this rumor was simply the invention of evil-minded relations. The trouble was clearly shown to have been caused by an infection brought into the house by one of the grandchildren. Moreover, analyses that were made of my aunt's stools showed not the slightest traces of poison.

That same summer Johannes gave the first evidences of anti-social in-clinations: he resigned from the singing circle and gave notice in writing that he planned to take no further part in the cultivation of the German song. It is only fair for me to add, however, that, despite the academic distinctions he had won, he was always an uncultivated man. For the "Virhymnia" the loss of his bass voice was a serious matter.

My brother-in-law Carl began secretly to consult travel agencies. The land of his dreams had to have unusual characteristics: no fir trees must grow there and their importation must be forbidden or rendered unfeasible by a high tariff; besides—on his wife's account—the secret of preparing butter-and-almond cookies must be unknown and the singing of German Christmas songs forbidden by law. Carl declared himself ready to undertake hard physical labor.

Since then he has been able to dispense with secrecy because of a complete and very sudden change which has taken place in my uncle. This happened at such a disagreeable level that we have really had cause to be disconcerted. The sober citizen, of whom it could be said that he was as stubborn as he was good and kind, was observed performing actions that are neither more nor less than immoral and will remain so as long as the world endures. Things became known about him, testified to by witnesses, that can only be described by the word adultery. And the most dreadful thing is that he no longer denies them, but claims for himself the right to live in circumstances and in relationships that make special legislation seem justifiable. Awkwardly enough, this sudden change became evident just at the time when the second hearing of the two parish priests was called. My Uncle Franz seems to have made such a deplorable impression as a witness, as disguised plaintiff indeed, that it must be ascribed to him alone that the second hearing turned out favorably for the two priests. But in the meantime all this had become a matter of indifference to Uncle Franz: his downfall is complete, already accomplished.

He too was the first to hit upon the shocking idea of having himself represented by an actor at the evening celebration. He had found an unemployed *bon vivant,* who for two weeks imitated him so admirably that not even his wife noticed the impersonation. Nor did his children notice it either. It was one of the grandchildren who, during a pause in the singing, suddenly shouted: "Grandpapa has on socks with rings," and triumphantly raised the *bon vivant's* trouser leg. This scene must have been terrifying for the poor artist; the family, too, was upset and to avoid disaster struck up a song, as they had done so often before in critical situations. After my aunt had gone to bed, the identity of the artist was quickly established. It was the signal for almost complete collapse.

However one must bear in mind that a year and a half is a long time, and it was mid-summer again, the time when participation in the play is hardest on my relations. Listless in the heat, they nibble at sand tarts and ginger cookies, smile vacantly while they crack dried-out nuts, listen to the indefatigable hammering of the gnomes and wince when the rosy-cheeked angel above their heads whispers "Peace, peace." But they carry on while, despite their summer clothing, sweat streams down their cheeks and necks and soaks their shirts. Or rather: they have carried on so far.

For the moment money plays no part—almost the reverse. People are beginning to whisper that Uncle Franz has adopted business methods, too, which can hardly be described as those of a "Christian businessman." He is determined not to allow any material lessening of the family fortune, a resolution that both calms and alarms us.

The unmasking of the *bon vivant* led to a regular mutiny, as a result of which a compromise was reached: Uncle Franz agreed to pay the expenses of a small theatrical troupe which would replace him, Johannes, my brother-in-law Carl, and Lucie, and it was further understood that one of the four would always take part in person in the evening celebration in order to keep the children in check. Up till now the prelate has not noticed this deception, which can hardly be described as pious. Aside from my aunt and the children, he is the only original figure still in the play.

An exact schedule has been worked out which, in the family circle, is known as the operational program, and thanks to the provision that one of them is always present in person, the actors too are allowed certain vacations. Meanwhile it was observed that the latter were not averse to the celebration and were glad to earn some additional money; thus it was possible to reduce their wages, since fortunately there is no lack of unemployed actors. Carl tells me that there is reason to hope that these "salaries" can be reduced still more, especially as the actors are given a meal and it is well known that art becomes cheaper when food is involved.

I have already briefly mentioned Lucie's unhappy history: now she spends almost all her time in night spots and, on those days when she is compelled to take part in the household celebration, she is beside herself. She wears corduroy britches, colored pullovers, runs around in sandals and she has cut off her splendid hair in order to wear unbecoming bangs and a coiffure that I only recently discovered was once considered modern —it is known as a pony-tail. Although I have so far been unable to observe any overt immorality on her part, but only a kind of exultation, which she herself describes as existentialism, nevertheless I cannot regard this development as desirable; I prefer quiet women, who move decorously to the rhythm of the waltz, know how to recite agreeable verses and whose nourishment is not exclusively sour pickles and goulash seasoned with paprika. My brother-in-law Carl's plans to emigrate seem on the point of becoming a reality: he has found a country, not far from the equator, which seems to answer his requirements, and Lucie is full of enthusiasm; in this country people wear clothes not unlike hers, they love sharp spices and they dance to those rhythms without which she maintains life is no longer possible for her. It is a little shocking that these two do not plan to obey the command "Abide in the land I have given you," but on the other hand I can understand their desire to flee.

Things are worse with Johannes. Unfortunately the evil rumor has proved true: he has become a Communist. He has broken off all relations with the family, pays no attention to anything and takes part in the evening celebration only in the person of his double. His eyes have taken on a fanatical expression, he makes public appearances behaving like a dervish at party meetings, neglects his practice and writes furious articles in the appropriate journals. Strangely enough he now sees more of Franz, who is vainly trying to convert him—and vice versa. Despite all their spiritual estrangement, they seem personally to have grown somewhat closer.

Franz I have not seen in a long time, but I have had news of him. He is said to have fallen into a profound depression, to spend his time in dim churches, and I believe that his piety can be fairly described as exaggerated. After the family misfortunes began he started to neglect his calling, and recently I saw on the wall of a ruined house a faded poster saying: "Last Battle of our Veteran Lenz against Lecoq. Lenz is Hanging up the Gloves." The date on the poster was March, and now we are well into August. Franz is said to have fallen on bad times. I believe he finds himself in a situation which has never before occurred in our family: he is poor. Fortunately he has remained single, and so the social consequences of his irresponsible piety harm only him. He has tried with amazing perseverance to have a guardian appointed for Lucie's children because he considers they are endangered by the daily celebration. But his efforts have remained fruitless; thank God, the children of wealthy people are not exposed to the interference of social institutions.

The one least removed from the rest of the family circle is, for all his deplorable actions, Uncle Franz. To be sure, despite his advanced years, he has a mistress. And his business practices, too, are of a sort that we admire, to be sure, but cannot at all approve. Recently he has appointed an unemployed stage manager to supervise the evening celebration and see that everything runs like clockwork. Everything does in fact run like clockwork.

V

Almost two years have now gone by—a long time. And I could not resist the temptation, during one of my evening strolls, to stop in at my uncle's house, where no true hospitality is any longer possible, since strange actors wander about every evening and the members of the family have devoted themselves to reprehensible pleasures. It was a mild summer evening, and as I turned into the avenue of chestnut trees I heard the verse:

The wintry woods are clad in snow . . .

A passing truck made the rest inaudible. Slowly and softly I approached the house and looked through a crack in the curtains. The similarity of the actors who were present to those of my relations whom they represented was so startling that for an instant I could not recognize which one this evening was the superintendent, as they called him. I could not see the gnomes but I could hear them. Their chirping tinkle has a wave length that can penetrate any wall. The whispering of the angel was inaudible. My aunt seemed to be really happy: she was chatting with the prelate, and it was only later that I recognized my brother-in-law as the one real person present—if that is the right word. I recognized him by the way he rounded and pointed his lips as he blew out a match. Apparently there are unchangeable individual traits. This led me to reflect that the actors, too, were obviously treated to cigars, cigarettes and wine—in addition there was asparagus every evening. If their appetites were shameless—and what artist's is not?—this meant a considerable additional expense for my uncle. The children were playing with dolls and wooden wagons in a corner of the room. They looked pale and tired. Perhaps one really ought to have some consideration for them. I was struck by the idea that they might perhaps be replaced by wax dolls of the kind one sees in the windows of drugstores as advertisements for powdered milk and skin lotions. It seems to me those look quite natural.

As a matter of fact I intend to call the family's attention to the possible effect on the children's temperament of this unnatural daily excitement. Although a certain amount of discipline does no harm, it seems to me that they are being subjected to excessive demands.

I left my observation post when the people inside began to sing: "Silent Night." I simply could not bear the song. The air was so mild—and for an instant I had the feeling that I was watching an assembly of ghosts. Suddenly I had a craving for sour pickles and this gave me some inkling of how very much Lucie must have suffered.

I have now succeeded in having the children replaced by wax dolls. Their procurement was costly—Uncle Franz hesitated for some time— but one really could not go on irresponsibly feeding the children on marzipan every day and making them sing songs which in the long run might cause them psychic injury. The procurement of the dolls proved to be useful because Carl and Lucie really emigrated and Johannes also withdrew his children from his father's household. I bade farewell to Carl and Lucie and the children as they stood amid large traveling trunks. They seemed happy, if a little worried. Johannes, too, has left our town. Somewhere or other he is engaged in reorganizing a Communist cell.

Uncle Franz is weary of life. Recently he complained to me that people are always forgetting to dust off the dolls. His servants in particular cause him difficulties, and the actors seem inclined to be undisciplined. They drink more than they ought, and some of them have been caught filling their pockets with cigars and cigarettes. I advised my uncle to provide them with colored water and cardboard cigars.

The only reliable ones are my aunt and the prelate. They chat together about the good old times, giggle and seem to enjoy themselves, interrupting their conversation only when a song is struck up.

In any event, the celebration goes on.

My Cousin Franz has taken an amazing step. He has been accepted as a lay brother in a nearby monastery. When I saw him for the first time in a cowl I was startled: that large figure, with broken nose, thickened lips and melancholy expression, reminded me more of a prisoner than a monk. He seemed almost to have read my thoughts. "Life is a prison sentence," he said softly. I followed him into the interview room. We conversed haltingly, and he was obviously relieved when the bell summoned him to the chapel for prayers. I remained behind, thoughtful, as he departed: he went in a great hurry, and his haste seemed genuine.

COMMENT

In the opening sentence the narrator observes, "Symptoms of decline have become evident in our family." In this way Böll abruptly announces a major theme of the story, the breakdown of the family. The opening is dramatic but not sensational, muted as it is by the formal diction and tone. Since the family is the central institution of the middle class, a second theme is the breakdown of that class. Further, everyone but Cousin Franz goes through his own personal crisis; thus the breakdown extends to the individual too.

In this story the context of the breakdowns has more than usual significance. The place is Germany, the time the catastrophic period from the Nazi dictatorship in the 1930's, through the Second World War, to the immediate postwar period. By the time of the postwar period, as the narrator remarks, "The minute fungi of destruction have found lodgement beneath the hard, thick crust of respectability; colonies of deadly parasites that proclaim the end of a whole tribe's irreproachable correctness." To the breakdown of the individual, family, and the middle class we must add that of the state, in particular the Nazi state.

The Nazi state moved from success to success until the Second World War destroyed it. This sequence is much like that of Aunt Milla's Christmas celebrations. *Milla* derives from the Latin *mille,* meaning thousand; Hitler had projected a thousand-year Reich. There is, then, the suggestion of an identity between the fates of Aunt Milla and the Nazi state. The story may be seen as an allegory of the Nazi period, the inevitable subject of much postwar German literature. It is only a partial allegory, certainly, but it gives otherwise insignificant details symbolic meaning. For example, Uncle Franz builds a bomb-proof bunker for Aunt Milla; Hitler had one too. Uncle Franz whisks her to the country so she need not witness the war ruins; Hitler had a country retreat at Berchtesgaden. The gnomes on the Christmas tree lift their arms and swing them wildly; the gnome-like Goebbels, the Nazi propagandist, had such a style.

Symbolically, then, Aunt Milla stands for the middle class; allegorically she and her Christmas celebrations have a reasonably specific, one-to-one relation to the Nazi state. The allegorical interpretation clarifies the passage in the opening paragraph, "colonies of deadly parasites . . . proclaim the end of a whole tribe's irreproachable correctness." The Germans prided themselves on their correctness, but their moral disintegration under the parasitic Nazis revealed it to be a mere form (another German example will be found in "Death in Venice"). The term *tribe* points to the Nazis' romantic patriotic appeal to Germany's tribal Teutonic origins.

All this also clarifies the principal action, the daily celebration —a non-natural symbol brilliantly merged into the realistic surface. By distorting the natural order, the yearly celebration of Christmas, it symbolizes the breakdown of the yearly ritual. Further, it dramatizes Aunt Milla's psychotic inability to deal with reality, allegorically pointing to the equally psychotic character of the Nazis and those others who wanted to restore "the good old times" of the Nazi order that Aunt Milla and the senile prelate compulsively return to in their talk.

Besides the breakdown of the individual, the family, the middle class, and the state, the breakdown of the yearly celebration also symbolizes the breakdown of religion. The empty mechanical character of contemporary practice of the ritual celebration is heightened by its daily recurrence, and the added expense underlines the commercialism of the season. By the device of the daily celebration, the criticism is given the dimension of caricature, humorous exaggeration. The religious breakdown has its allegorical counterpart in the historical failure of the churches to resist the fundamentally pagan and anti-Christian Nazi state. But if the churches generally found it expedient to submit, there was nonetheless some heroic clerical opposition. In Böll's story this is symbolized by Cousin Franz, especially by his entry into the monastery as a lay brother. By this action he rejects the secular world, particularly comfortable, expedient, middle-class Christianity. For him "life is a prison sentence," a trial of the spirit. Johannes and Lucie also reject middle-class Christianity, in their cases for the secular faiths of Communism and existentialism. But these turns are presented as ironic and humorous counterpoints because they are largely therapeutic reactions.

The marvelous humor that leavens the story is one instance of Böll's skill in presenting his allegory. The allegory is subtly worked in, unlabored, without straining, done with consummate artistic tact. It is civilized by the humor, which is itself remarkable when we consider the barbaric subject. And though there is caricature, it has none of the crudeness frequent in such presentations of the contemporary practice of religion. Finally, though the richer for it, the story stands up very well without the allegory.

QUESTIONS ON SYMBOLISM

1. What is the significance of the many items that make up a cluster of pagan symbols, for example, the mistletoe, Carnival time, the tribal allusion, the gnomes, and the swastika (a crooked cross)? For information on their origins, the reader might consult Sir James Frazer's *The Golden Bough* and other anthropological studies.

2. The full meaning of a symbol is developed by what happens to it. What changes take place in the celebration, in the trees, and in the family?

3. Why do the members of the family at first object and then withdraw their objections to Cousin Franz as a boxer? What is the connection between his boxing and his "pious fiddle-faddle"?

4. Consider the role of the recurrent images of class, business, the state, and religion in the development of the story's texture.

5. Consider the archetypal patterns and the myths that embody them in the highly symbolic stories "Death in Venice," "Grace," "Powerhouse," "Young Goodman Brown," "The Library of Babel," and "The Judgment."

6. Consider in connection with the Nazi allegory the pagan symbols, the references to German nationalism, and the several revelations and crises.

OTHER CONSIDERATIONS

1. How do Böll's simple style and matter-of-fact tone work with the unusual subject matter? Consider also the stories in this collection by Kafka, Borges, Hemingway, and Barthelme.

2. The principal ironic device is the use of the first-person narrator. What is gained by his innocence? How does his point of view, that of a solid citizen, make for irony? Does his formal, Latinate diction function ironically?

3. What are some of the structural ironies in this story? Consider the changes especially in Uncle Franz. Does the narrator change his attitude?

4. The story is in one respect a drama of bourgeois character. Consider the treatment of the virtues of honesty, hard work, sexual fidelity, and religious piety. Is there an identity crisis here? In what other stories is an identity crisis present?

5. What is the effect of the story's beginning near the chronological end of the action? Is suspense sacrificed or heightened?

Stories

The Town Poor

Sarah Orne Jewett ❦

Mrs. William Trimble and Miss Rebecca Wright were driving along Hampden east road, one afternoon in early spring. Their progress was slow. Mrs. Trimble's sorrel horse was old and stiff, and the wheels were clogged by clay mud. The frost was not yet out of the ground, although the snow was nearly gone, except in a few places on the north side of the woods, or where it had drifted all winter against a length of fence.

"There must be a good deal o' snow to the nor'ard of us yet," said weather-wise Mrs. Trimble. "I feel it in the air; 't is more than the ground-damp. We ain't goin' to have real nice weather till the upcountry snow's all gone."

"I heard say yesterday that there was good sleddin' yet, all up through Parsley," responded Miss Wright. "I shouldn't like to live in them northern places. My cousin Ellen's husband was a Parsley man, an' he was obliged, as you may have heard, to go up north to his father's second wife's funeral; got back day before yesterday. 'T was about twenty-one miles, an' they started on wheels; but when they'd gone nine or ten miles, they found 't was no sort o' use, an' left their wagon an' took a sleigh. The man that owned it charged 'em four an' six, too. I shouldn't have thought he would; they told him they was goin' to a funeral; an' they had their own buffaloes an' everything."

"Well, I expect it's a good deal harder scratchin', up that way; they have to git money where they can; the farms is very poor as you go north," suggested Mrs. Trimble kindly. "'T ain't none too rich a country where we be, but I've always been grateful I wa'n't born up to Parsley."

The old horse plodded along, and the sun, coming out from the heavy spring clouds, sent a sudden shine of light along the muddy road. Sister Wright drew her large veil forward over the high brim of her bonnet. She was not used to driving, or to being much in the open air; but Mrs. Trimble was an active business woman, and looked after her own affairs herself, in all weathers. The late Mr. Trimble had left her a good farm, but not much ready money, and it was often said that she was better off in the end than if he had lived. She regretted his loss deeply, however; it was impossible for her to speak of him, even to intimate friends, without emotion, and nobody had ever hinted that this emotion was insincere. She was most warm-hearted and generous, and in her limited way played the part of Lady Bountiful in the town of Hampden.

"Why, there's where the Bray girls lives, ain't it?" she exclaimed, as,

"The Town Poor," by Sarah Orne Jewett, published by Houghton Mifflin Company, Boston.

beyond a thicket of witch-hazel and scrub-oak, they came in sight of a weather-beaten, solitary farmhouse. The barn was too far away for thrift or comfort, and they could see long lines of light between the shrunken boards as they came nearer. The fields looked both stony and sodden. Somehow, even Parsley itself could be hardly more forlorn.

"Yes'm," said Miss Wright, "that's where they live now, poor things. I know the place, though I ain't been up here for years. You don't suppose, Mis' Trimble—I ain't seen the girls out to meetin' all winter. I've re'lly been covetin'—"

"Why, yes, Rebecca, of course we could stop," answered Mrs. Trimble heartily. "The exercises was over earlier 'n I expected, an' you're goin' to remain over night long o' me, you know. There won't be no tea till we git there, so we can't be late. I'm in the habit o' sendin' a basket to the Bray girls when any o' our folks is comin' this way, but I ain't been to see 'em since they moved up here. Why, it must be a good deal over a year ago. I know 't was in the late winter they had to make the move. 'T was cruel hard, I must say, an' if I hadn't been down with my pleurisy fever I'd have stirred round an' done somethin' about it. There was a good deal o' sickness at the time, an'—well, 't was kind o' rushed through, breakin' of 'em up, an' lots o' folks blamed the selec'*men;* but when 't was done, 't was done, an' nobody took holt to undo it. Ann an' Mandy looked same 's ever when they come to meetin', 'long in the summer,—kind o' wishful, perhaps. They've always sent me word they was gittin' on pretty comfortable."

"That would be their way," said Rebecca Wright. "They never was any hand to complain, though Mandy's less cheerful than Ann. If Mandy'd been spared such poor eyesight, an' Ann hadn't got her lame wrist that wa'n't set right, they'd kep' off the town fast enough. They both shed tears when they talked to me about havin' to break up, when I went to see 'em before I went over to brother Asa's. You see we was brought up neighbors, an' we went to school together, the Brays an' me. 'T was a special Providence brought us home this road, I've been so covetin' a chance to git to see 'em. My lameness hampers me."

"I'm glad we come this way, myself," said Mrs. Trimble.

"I'd like to see just how they fare," Miss Rebecca Wright continued. "They give their consent to goin' on the town because they knew they'd got to be dependent, an' so they felt 't would come easier for all than for a few to help 'em. They acted real dignified an' right-minded, contrary to what most do in such cases, but they was dreadful anxious to see who would bid 'em off, town-meetin' day; they did so hope 't would be somebody right in the village. I just sat down an' cried good when I found Abel Janes's folks had got hold of 'em. They always had the name of bein' slack an' poor-spirited, an' they did it just for what they got out o' the town. The selectmen this last year ain't what we have had. I hope they've been considerate about the Bray girls."

"I should have be'n more considerate about fetchin' of you over," apologized Mrs. Trimble. "I've got my horse, an' you're lame-footed; it is too far for you to come. But time does slip away with busy folks, an' I forgit a good deal I ought to remember."

"There's nobody more considerate than you be," protested Miss Rebecca Wright.

Mrs. Trimble made no answer, but took out her whip and gently touched the sorrel horse, who walked considerably faster, but did not think it worth while to trot. It was a long, round-about way to the house, farther down the road and up a lane.

"I never had any opinion of the Bray girls' father, leavin' 'em as he did," said Mrs. Trimble.

"He was much praised in his time, though there was always some said his early life hadn't been up to the mark," explained her companion. "He was a great favorite of our then preacher, the Reverend Daniel Longbrother. They did a good deal for the parish, but they did it their own way. Deacon Bray was one that did his part in the repairs without urging. You know 't was in his time the first repairs was made, when they got out the old soundin'-board an' them handsome square pews. It cost an awful sight o' money, too. They hadn't done payin' up that debt when they set to alter it again an' git the walls frescoed. My grandmother was one that always spoke her mind right out, an' she was dreadful opposed to breakin' up the square pews where she'd always set. They was countin' up what 't would cost in parish meetin', an' she riz right up an' said 't wouldn't cost nothin' to let 'em stay, an' there wa'n't a house carpenter left in the parish that could do such nice work, an' time would come when the great-grandchildren would give their eye-teeth to have the old meetin'-house look just as it did then. But haul the inside to pieces they would an' did."

"There come to be a real fight over it, didn't there?" agreed Mrs. Trimble soothingly. "Well, 't wa'n't good taste. I remember the old house well. I come here as a child to visit a cousin o' mother's, an' Mr. Trimble's folks was neighbors, an' we was drawed to each other then, young 's we was. Mr. Trimble spoke of it many's the time,—that first time he ever see me, in a leghorn hat with a feather; 't was one that mother had, an' pressed over."

"When I think of them old sermons that used to be preached in that old meetin'-house of all, I'm glad it's altered over, so's not to remind folks," said Miss Rebecca Wright, after a suitable pause. "Them old brimstone discourses, you know, Mis' Trimble. Preachers is far more reasonable, nowadays. Why, I set an' thought, last Sabbath, as I listened, that if old Mr. Longbrother an' Deacon Bray could hear the difference they'd crack the ground over 'em like pole beans, an' come right up 'long side their headstones."

Mrs. Trimble laughed heartily, and shook the reins three or four times by way of emphasis. "There's no gittin' round you," she said, much pleased. "I should think Deacon Bray would want to rise, any way, if 't was so he could, an' knew how his poor girls was farin'. A man ought to provide for his folks he's got to leave behind him, specially if they're women. To be sure, they had their little home; but we've seen how, with all their industrious ways, they hadn't means to keep it. I s'pose he thought he'd got time enough to lay by, when he give so generous in collections; but he didn't lay by, an' there they be. He might have took lessons from the squirrels: even them little wild creatur's makes them their winter hoards, an' menfolks ought to know enough if squirrels does. 'Be just before you are generous': that's what was always set for the B's in the copy-books, when I was to school, and it often runs through my mind."

" 'As for man, his days are as grass,'—that was for A; the two go well together," added Miss Rebecca Wright soberly. "My good gracious, ain't this a starved-lookin' place? It makes me ache to think them nice Bray girls has to brook it here."

The sorrel horse, though somewhat puzzled by an unexpected deviation from his homeward way, willingly came to a stand by the gnawed corner of the door-yard fence, which evidently served as hitching-place. Two or three ragged old hens were picking about the yard, and at last a face appeared at the kitchen window, tied up in a handkerchief, as if it were a case of toothache. By the time our friends reached the side door next this window, Mrs. Janes came disconsolately to open it for them, shutting it again as soon as possible, though the air felt more chilly inside the house.

"Take seats," said Mrs. Janes briefly. "You'll have to see me just as I be. I have been suffering these four days with the ague, and everything to do. Mr. Janes is to court, on the jury. 'T was inconvenient to spare him. I should be pleased to have you lay off your things."

Comfortable Mrs. Trimble looked about the cheerless kitchen, and could not think of anything to say; so she smiled blandly and shook her head in answer to the invitation. "We'll just set a few minutes with you, to pass the time o' day, an' then we must go in an' have a word with the Miss Brays, bein' old acquaintance. It ain't been so we could git to call on 'em before. I don't know 's you're acquainted with Miss R'becca Wright. She's been out of town a good deal."

"I heard she was stopping over to Plainfields with her brother's folks," replied Mrs. Janes, rocking herself with irregular motion, as she sat close to the stove. "Got back some time in the fall, I believe?"

"Yes'm," said Miss Rebecca, with an undue sense of guilt and conviction. "We've been to the installation over to the East Parish, an' thought we'd stop in; we took this road home to see if 't was any better. How is the Miss Brays gettin' on?"

"They're well's common," answered Mrs. Janes grudgingly. "I was put out with Mr. Janes for fetchin' of 'em here, with all I've got to do, an' I own I was kind o' surly to 'em 'long to the first of it. He gets the money from the town, an' it helps him out but he bid 'em off for five dollars a month, an' we can't do much for 'em at no such price as that. I went an' dealt with the selec'men, an' made 'em promise to find their firewood an' some other things extra. They was glad to get rid o' the matter the fourth time I went, an' would ha' promised 'most anything. But Mr. Janes don't keep me half the time in oven-wood, he's off so much, an' we was cramped o' room, any way. I have to store things up garrit a good deal, an' that keeps me trampin' right through their room. I do the best for 'em I can, Mis' Trimble, but 't ain't so easy for me as 't is for you, with all your means to do with."

The poor woman looked pinched and miserable herself, though it was evident that she had no gift at house or home keeping. Mrs. Trimble's heart was wrung with pain, as she thought of the unwelcome inmates of such a place but she held her peace bravely, while Miss Rebecca again gave some brief information in regard to the installation.

"You go right up them back stairs," the hostess directed at last. "I'm glad some o' you church folks has seen fit to come an' visit 'em. There ain't been nobody here this long spell, an' they've aged a sight since they come. They always send down a taste out of your baskets, Mis' Trimble, an' I relish it, I tell you. I'll shut the door after you, if you don't object. I feel every draught o' cold air."

"I've always heard she was a great hand to make a poor mouth. Wa'n't she from somewheres up Parsley way?" whispered Miss Rebecca, as they stumbled in the half-light.

"Poor meechin' body, wherever she come from," replied Mrs. Trimble, as she knocked at the door.

There was silence for a moment after this unusual sound; then one of the Bray sisters opened the door. The eager guests stared into a small, low room, brown with age, and gray, too, as if former dust and cobwebs could not be made wholly to disappear. The two elderly women who stood there looked like captives. Their withered faces wore a look of apprehension, and the room itself was more bare and plain than was fitting to their evident refinement of character and self-respect. There was an uncovered small table in the middle of the floor, with some crackers on a plate; and, for some reason or other, this added a great deal to the general desolation.

But Miss Ann Bray, the elder sister, who carried her right arm in a sling, with piteously drooping fingers, gazed at the visitors with radiant joy. She had not seen them arrive.

The one window gave only the view at the back of the house, across the fields, and their coming was indeed a surprise. The next minute she was laughing, and crying together. "Oh, sister!" she said, "if here ain't our dear Mis' Trimble!—an' my heart o' goodness, 't is 'Becca Wright, too! What dear good creatur's you be! I've felt all day as if something good was goin' to happen, an' was just sayin' to myself 't was most sundown now, but I wouldn't let on to Mandany I'd give up hope quite yet. You see, the scissors stuck in the floor this very mornin' an' it's always a reliable sign. There, I've got to kiss ye both again!"

"I don't know where we can all set," lamented sister Mandana. "There ain't but the one chair an' the bed; t' other chair's too rickety; an' we've been promised another these ten days; but first they've forgot it, an' next Mis' Janes can't spare it,—one excuse an' another. I am goin' to git a

stump o' wood an' nail a board on to it, when I can git outdoor again,"
said Mandana, in a plaintive voice. "There, I ain't goin' to complain o'
nothin', now you've come," she added; and the guests sat down, Mrs.
Trimble, as was proper, in the one chair.

"We've sat on the bed many's the time with you, 'Becca, an' talked
over our girl nonsense, ain't we? You know where 't was—in the little
back bedroom we had when we was girls, an' used to peek out at our
beaux through the strings o' mornin'-glories," laughed Ann Bray delightedly, her thin face shining more and more with joy. "I brought
some o' them mornin'-glory seeds along when we come away, we'd raised
'em so many years; an' we got 'em started all right, but the hens found 'em
out. I declare I chased them poor hens, foolish as 't was; but the mornin'-
glories I'd counted on a sight to remind me o' home. You see, our debts
was so large, after my long sickness an' all, that we didn't feel 't was right
to keep back anything we could help from the auction."

It was impossible for any one to speak for a moment or two; the sisters
felt their own uprooted condition afresh, and their guests for the first
time really comprehended the piteous contrast between that neat little
village house, which now seemed a palace of comfort, and this cold, unpainted upper room in the remote Janes farmhouse. It was an unwelcome
thought to Mrs. Trimble that the well-to-do town of Hampden could
provide no better for its poor than this, and her round face flushed with
resentment and the shame of personal responsibility. "The girls shall be
well settled in the village before another winter, if I pay their board myself," she made an inward resolution, and took another almost tearful
look at the broken stove, the miserable bed, and the sisters' one hair-
covered trunk, on which Mandana was sitting. But the poor place was
filled with a golden spirit of hospitality.

Rebecca was again discoursing eloquently of the installation; it was
so much easier to speak of general subjects, and the sisters had evidently
been longing to hear some news. Since the late summer they had not been
to church, and presently Mrs. Trimble asked the reason.

"Now, don't you go to pouring out our woes, Mandy!" begged little
old Ann, looking shy and almost girlish, and as if she insisted upon playing that life was still all before them and all pleasure. "Don't you go to
spoilin' their visit with our complaints! They know well's we do that
changes must come, an' we'd been so wonted to our home things that this
come hard at first; but then they felt for us, I know just as well's can be.
'T will soon be summer again, an' 't is real pleasant right out in the fields
here, when there ain't too hot a spell. I've got to know a sight o' singin'
birds since we come."

"Give me the folks I've always known," sighed the younger sister, who
looked older than Miss Ann, and less even-tempered. "You may have
your birds, if you want 'em. I do re'lly long to go to meetin' and see folks
go by up the aisle. Now, I will speak of it, Ann, whatever you say. We
need, each of us, a pair o' good stout shoes an' rubbers,—ours are all wore
out; an' we've asked an' asked, an' they never think to bring 'em, an'—"

Poor old Mandana, on the trunk, covered her face with her arms and sobbed aloud. The elder sister stood over her, and patted her on the thin shoulder like a child, and tried to comfort her. It crossed Mrs. Trimble's mind that it was not the first time one had wept and the other had comforted. The sad scene must have been repeated many times in that long, drear winter. She would see them forever after in her mind as fixed as a picture, and her own tears fell fast.

"You didn't see Mis' Janes's cunning little boy, the next one to the baby, did you?" asked Ann Bray, turning round quickly at last, and going cheerfully on with the conversation. "Now, hush, Mandy, dear; they'll think you're childish! He's a dear, friendly little creatur', an' likes to stay with us a good deal, though we feel 's if it was too cold for him, now we are waitin' to get us more wood."

"When I think of the acres o' woodland in this town!" groaned Rebecca Wright. "I believe I'm goin' to preach next Sunday, 'stead o' the minister, an' I'll make the sparks fly. I've always heard the saying, 'What's everybody's business is nobody's business,' an' I've come to believe it."

"Now, don't you, 'Becca. You've happened on a kind of a poor time with us, but we've got more belongings than you see here, an' a good large cluset, where we can store those things there ain't room to have about. You an' Mis' Trimble have happened on a kind of poor day, you know. Soon's I git me some stout shoes an' rubbers, as Mandy says, I can fetch home plenty o' little dry boughs o' pine; you remember I was always a great hand to roam in the woods? If we could only have a front room, so 't we could look out on the road an' see passin', an' was shod for meetin', I don' know's we should complain. Now we're just goin' to give you what we've got, an' make out with a good welcome. We make more tea 'n we want in the mornin', an' then let the fire go down, since 't has been so mild. We've got a *good* cluset" (disappearing as she spoke), "an' I know this to be good tea, 'cause it's some o' yourn, Mis' Trimble. An' here's our sprigged chiny cups that R'becca knows by sight, if Mis' Trimble don't. We kep' out four of 'em, an' put the even half dozen with the rest of the auction stuff. I've often wondered who'd got 'em, but I never asked, for fear 't would be somebody that would distress us. They was mother's, you know."

The four cups were poured, and the little table pushed to the bed, where Rebecca Wright still sat, and Mandana, wiping her eyes, came and joined her. Mrs. Trimble sat in her chair at the end, and Ann trotted about the room in pleased content for a while, and in and out of the closet, as if she still had much to do; then she came and stood opposite Mrs. Trimble. She was very short and small, and there was no painful sense of her being obliged to stand. The four cups were not quite full of cold tea, but there was a clean old tablecloth folded double, and a plate with three pairs of crackers neatly piled, and a small—it must be owned, a very small—piece of hard white cheese. Then, for a treat, in a glass dish, there was a little preserved peach, the last—Miss Rebecca knew it instinctively—of the household stores brought from their old home. It was very sugary, this bit of peach; and as she helped her guests and sister Mandy, Miss Ann Bray said, half unconsciously, as she often had said with less reason in the old days, "Our preserves ain't so good as usual this year; this is beginning to candy." Both the guests protested, while Rebecca added that the taste of it carried her back, and made her feel young again. The Brays had always managed to keep one or two peach-trees alive in their corner of a garden. "I've been keeping this preserve for a treat," said her friend. "I'm glad to have you eat some, 'Becca. Last summer I often wished you was home an' could come an' see us, 'stead o' being away off to Plainfields."

The crackers did not taste too dry. Miss Ann took the last of the peach on her own cracker; there could not have been quite a small spoonful, after the others were helped, but she asked them first if they would not have some more. Then there was a silence, and in the silence a wave of tender feeling rose high in the hearts of the four elderly women. At this moment the setting sun flooded the poor plain room with light; the unpainted wood was all of a golden-brown, and Ann Bray, with her gray hair and aged face, stood at the head of the table in a kind of aureole. Mrs. Trimble's face was all aquiver as she looked at her; she thought of the text about two or three being gathered together, and was half afraid.

"I believe we ought to 've asked Mis' Janes if she wouldn't come up," said Ann. "She's real good feelin', but she's had it very hard, an' gits discouraged. I can't find that she's ever had anything real pleasant to look back to, as we have. There, next time we'll make a good heartenin' time for her too."

The sorrel horse had taken a long nap by the gnawed fence-rail, and the cool air after sundown made him impatient to be gone. The two friends jolted homeward in the gathering darkness, through the stiffening mud, and neither Mrs. Trimble nor Rebecca Wright said a word until they were out of sight as well as out of sound of the Janes house. Time must elapse before they could reach a more familiar part of the road and resume conversation on its natural level.

"I consider myself to blame," insisted Mrs. Trimble at last. "I haven't no words of accusation for nobody else, an' I ain't one to take comfort in calling names to the board o' selec'*men*. I make no reproaches, an' I take it all on my own shoulders; but I'm goin' to stir about me, I tell you! I shall begin early to-morrow. They're goin' back to their own house, —it's been standin' empty all winter,—an' the town's goin' to give 'em the rent an' what firewood they need; it won't come to more than the board's payin' out now. An' you an' me'll take this same horse an' wagon, an' ride an' go afoot by turns, an' git means enough together to buy back their furniture an' whatever was sold at that plaguey auction; an' then we'll put it all back, an' tell 'em they've got to move to a new place, an' just carry 'em right back again where they come from. An' don't you never tell, R'becca, but here I be a widow woman, layin' up what I make from my farm for nobody knows who, an' I'm goin' to do for them Bray girls all I'm a mind to. I should be sca't to wake up in heaven, an' hear any-body there ask how the Bray girls was. Don't talk to me about the town o' Hampden, an' don't ever let me hear the name o' town poor! I'm ashamed to go home an' see what's set out for supper. I wish I'd brought 'em right along."

"I was goin' to ask if we couldn't git the new doctor to go up an' do somethin' for poor Ann's arm," said Miss Rebecca. "They say he's very smart. If she could get so's to braid straw or hook rugs again, she'd soon be earnin' a little somethin'. An' may be he could do somethin' for Mandy's eyes. They did use to live so neat an' ladylike. Somehow I couldn't speak to tell 'em there that 't was I bought them six best cups an' saucers, time of the auction; they went very low, as everything else did, an' I thought I could save it some other way. They shall have 'em back an' welcome. You're real whole-hearted, Mis' Trimble. I expect Ann'll be sayin' that her father's child'n wa'n't goin' to be left desolate, an' that all the bread he cast on the water's comin' back through you."

"I don't care what she says, dear creatur'!" exclaimed Mrs. Trimble. "I'm full o' regrets I took time for that installation, an' set there seepin' in a lot o' talk this whole day long, except for its kind of bringin' us to the Bray girls. I wish to my heart 't was to-morrow mornin' a'ready, an' I a'startin' for the selec'*men.*"

The Fairy Goose

❦ Liam O'Flaherty

An old woman named Mary Wiggins got three goose-eggs from a neighbour in order to hatch a clutch of goslings. She put an old clucking hen
over the eggs in a wooden box with a straw bed. The hen proved to be a
bad sitter. She was continually deserting the eggs, possibly because they
were too big. The old woman then kept her shut up in the box. Either
through weariness, want of air or simply pure devilment, the hen died on
the eggs, two days before it was time for the shells to break.

The old woman shed tears of rage, both at the loss of her hen, of which
she was particularly fond, and through fear of losing her goslings. She put
the eggs near the fire in the kitchen, wrapped up in straw and old clothes.
Two days afterwards, one of the eggs broke and a tiny gosling put out its
beak. The other two eggs proved not to be fertile. They were thrown
away.

The little gosling was a scraggy thing, so small and so delicate that the
old woman, out of pity for it, wanted to kill it. But her husband said:
"Kill nothing that is born in your house, woman alive. It's against the
law of God."

"It's a true saying, my honest fellow," said the old woman. "What
comes into the world is sent by God. Praised be He."

For a long time it seemed certain that the gosling was on the point of
death. It spent all the day on the hearth in the kitchen nestling among the
peat ashes, either sleeping or making little tweeky noises. When it was
offered food, it stretched out its beak and pecked without rising off its
stomach. Gradually, however, it became hardier and went out of doors
to sit in the sun, on a flat rock. When it was three months it was still a
yellowish colour with soft down, even though other goslings of that age
in the village were already going to the pond with the flock and able to
flap their wings and join in the cackle at evening time, when the setting
sun was being saluted. The little gosling was not aware of the other geese,
even though it saw them rise on windy days and fly with a great noise
from their houses to the pond. It made no effort to become a goose, and
at four months of age it still could not stand on one leg.

The old woman came to believe that it was a fairy. The village women
agreed with her after some dispute. It was decided to tie pink and red
ribbons around the gosling's neck and to sprinkle holy water on its wing
feathers.

That was done and then the gosling became sacred in the village. No
boy dare throw a stone at it, or pull a feather from its wing, as they were

in the habit of doing with geese, in order to get masts for the pieces of cork they floated in the pond as ships. When it began to move about, every house gave it dainty things. All the human beings in the village paid more respect to it than they did to one another. The little gosling had contracted a great affection for Mary Wiggins and followed her round everywhere, so that Mary Wiggins also came to have the reputation of being a woman of wisdom. Dreams were brought to her for unravelling. She was asked to set the spell of the Big Periwinkle and to tie the Knot of the Snakes on the sides of sick cows. And when children were ill, the gosling was brought secretly at night and led three times around the house on a thin halter of horsehair.

When the gosling was a year old it had not yet become a goose. Its down was still slightly yellowish. It did not cackle, but made curious tweeky noises. Instead of stretching out its neck and hissing at strangers, after the manner of a proper goose, it put its head to one side and made funny noises like a duck. It meditated like a hen, was afraid of water and cleansed itself by rolling on the grass. It fed on bread, fish and potatoes. It drank milk and tea. It amused itself by collecting pieces of cloth, nails, small fish-bones and the limpet-shells that are thrown in a heap beside dung-hills. These pieces of refuse it placed in a pile to the left of Mary Wiggins's door. And when the pile was tall, it made a sort of nest in the middle of it and lay in the nest.

Old Mrs. Wiggins had by now realized that the goose was worth money to her. So she became firmly convinced that the goose was gifted with supernatural powers. She accepted, in return for setting spells, a yard of white frieze cloth for unravelling dreams, a pound of sugar for setting the spell of the Big Periwinkle and half a donkey's load of potatoes for tying the Knot of the Snakes on a sick cow's side. Hitherto a kindly, humorous woman, she took to wearing her shawl in triangular fashion, with the tip of it reaching to her heels. She talked to herself or to her goose as she went along the road. She took long steps like a goose and rolled her eyes occasionally. When she cast a spell she went into an ecstasy, during which she made inarticulate sounds, like "boum, roum, toum, kroum."

Soon it became known all over the countryside that there was a woman of wisdom and a fairy goose in the village, and pilgrims came secretly from afar, at the dead of night, on the first night of the new moon, or when the spring tide had begun to wane.

The men soon began to raise their hats passing old Mary Wiggins's house, for it was understood, owing to the cure of Dara Foddy's cow, that the goose was indeed a good fairy and not a malicious one. Such was the excitement in the village and all over the countryside, that what was kept secret so long at last reached the ears of the parish priest.

The story was brought to him by an old woman from a neighbouring village to that in which the goose lived. Before the arrival of the goose, the other old woman had herself cast spells, not through her own merits but through those of her dead mother, who had a long time ago been the woman of wisdom in the district. The priest mounted his horse as soon as he heard the news and galloped at a break-neck speed towards Mary Wiggins's house, carrying his breviary and his stole. When he arrived in the village he dismounted at a distance from the house, gave his horse to a boy and put his stole around his neck.

A number of the villagers gathered and some tried to warn Mary Wiggins by whistling at a distance, but conscious that they had all taken part in something forbidden by the sacred laws of orthodox religion, they were afraid to run ahead of the priest into the house. Mary Wiggins and her husband were within, making little ropes of brown horsehair which they sold as charms.

Outside the door, perched on her high nest, the little goose was sitting. There were pink and red ribbons around her neck and around her legs there were bands of black tape. She was quite small, a little more than half the size of a normal, healthy goose. But she had an elegant charm of manner, an air of civilization, and a consciousness of great dignity, which had grown out of the love and respect of the villagers.

When she saw the priest approach, she began to cackle gently, making the tweeky noise that was peculiar to her. She descended from her perch and waddled towards him, expecting some dainty gift. But instead of stretching out his hand to offer her something and saying, "Beadai, beadai, come here," as was customary, the priest halted and muttered something in a harsh, frightened voice. He became red in the face and he took off his hat.

Then for the first time in her life the little goose became terrified. She opened her beak, spread her wings and lowered her head. She began to hiss violently. Turning around, she waddled back to her nest, flapping her wings and raising a loud cackle, just like a goose, although she had never been heard to cackle loudly like a goose before. Clambering up on her high nest, she lay there, quite flat, trembling violently.

The bird, never having known fear of human beings, never having been treated with discourtesy, was so violently moved by the extraordinary phenomenon of a man wearing black clothes, scowling at her and muttering, that her animal nature was roused and showed itself with disgusting violence.

The people watching this scene were astounded. Some took off their caps and crossed themselves. For some reason it was made manifest to them that the goose was an evil spirit and not the good fairy which they had supposed her to be. Terrified of the priest's stole and of his breviary and of his scowling countenance, they were only too eager to attribute the goose's strange hissing and her still stranger cackle to supernatural forces of an evil nature. Some present even caught a faint rumble of thunder in the east, and although it was not noticed at the time, an old woman later asserted that she heard a great cackle of geese afar off, raised in answer to the fairy goose's cackle.

"It was," said the old woman, "certainly the whole army of devils offering her help to kill the holy priest."

The priest turned to the people and cried, raising his right hand in a threatening manner:

"I wonder the ground doesn't open up and swallow you all. Idolaters!"

"O father, blessed by the hand of God," cried an old woman, the one who later asserted she had heard the devilish cackle afar off. She threw herself on her knees in the road, crying: "Spare us, father."

Old Mrs. Wiggins, having heard the strange noises, rushed out into the yard with her triangular shawl trailing and her black hair loose. She began to make vague, mystic movements with her hands, as had recently become a habit with her. Lost in some sort of ecstasy, she did not see the priest at first. She began to chant something.

"You hag," cried the priest, rushing up the yard towards her menacingly.

The old woman caught sight of him and screamed. But she faced him boldly.

"Come no farther," she cried, still in an ecstasy, either affected, or the result of a firm belief in her own mystic powers.

Indeed, it is difficult to believe that she was not in earnest, for she used to be a kind, gentle woman.

Her husband rushed out, crying aloud. Seeing the priest, he dropped a piece of rope he had in his hand and fled around the corner of the house.

"Leave my way, you hag," cried the priest, raising his hand to strike her.

"Stand back," she cried. "Don't lay a hand on my goose."

"Leave my way," yelled the priest, "or I'll curse you."

"Curse, then," cried the unfortunate woman. "Curse!"

Instead, the priest gave her a blow under the ear, which felled her smartly. Then he strode up to the goose's nest and seized the goose. The goose, paralyzed with terror, was just able to open her beak and hiss at him. He stripped the ribbons off her neck and tore the tape off her feet. Then he threw her out of the nest. Seizing a spade that stood by the wall, he began to scatter the refuse of which the nest was composed.

The old woman, lying prostrate in the yard, raised her head and began to chant in the traditional fashion, used by the women of wisdom.

"I'll call on the winds of the east and of the west, I'll raise the winds of the sea. The lightning will flash in the sky and there'll be great sounds of giants warring in the heavens. Blight will fall on the earth and calves with fishes' tails will be born of cows . . ."

The little goose, making tweeky noises, waddled over to the old woman and tried to hide herself under the long shawl. The people murmured at this, seeing in it fresh signs of devilry.

Then the priest threw down the spade and hauled the old woman to her feet, kicking aside the goose. The old woman, exhausted by her ecstasy and possibly seeking to gain popular support, either went into a faint or feigned one. Her hands and her feet hung limply. Again the people murmured. The priest, becoming embarrassed, put her sitting against the wall. Then he didn't know what to do, for his anger had exhausted his reason. He either became ashamed of having beaten an old woman, or he felt the situation was altogether ridiculous. So he raised his hand and addressed the people in a sorrowful voice.

"Let this be a warning," he said sadly. "This poor woman and . . . all of you, led astray by . . . foolish and . . . Avarice is at the back of this," he cried suddenly in an angry voice, shaking his fist. "This woman has been preying on your credulity, in order to extort money from you by her pretended sorcery. That's all it is. Money is at the back of it. But I give you warning. If I hear another word about this, I'll . . ."

He paused uncertainly, wondering what to threaten the poor people with. Then he added:

"I'll report it to the Archbishop of the diocese."

The people raised a loud murmur, asking forgiveness.

"Fear God," he added finally, "and love your neighbours."

Then, throwing a stone angrily at the goose, he strode out of the yard and left the village.

It was then the people began to curse violently and threaten to burn the old woman's house. The responsible people among them, however, chiefly those who had hitherto paid no respect to the superstition concerning the goose, restrained their violence. Finally the people went home and Mary Wiggins's husband, who had been hiding in a barn, came and brought his wife indoors. The little goose, uttering cries of amazement, began to collect the rubbish once more, piling it in a heap in order to rebuild her nest. That night, just after the moon had risen, a band of young men collected, approached Mary Wiggins's house and enticed the goose from her nest, by calling, "Beadai, beadai, come here, come here."

The little goose, delighted that people were again kind and respectful to her, waddled down to the gate, making happy noises.

The youths stoned her to death.

And the little goose never uttered a sound, so terrified and amazed was she at this treatment from people who had formerly loved her and whom she had never injured.

Next morning, when Mary Wiggins discovered the dead carcass of the goose, she went into a fit, during which she cursed the village, the priest, and all mankind.

And indeed it appeared that her blasphemous prayer took some effect at least. Although giants did not war in the heavens and though cows did not give birth to fishes, it is certain that from that day the natives of that village are quarrelsome drunkards, who fear God but do not love one another. And the old woman is again collecting followers from among the wives of the drunkards. These women maintain that the only time in the history of their generation that there was peace and harmony in the village was during the time when the fairy goose was loved by the people.

Madame Tellier's Excursion

Guy de Maupassant

Men went there every evening at about eleven o'clock, just as they went to the *café*. Six or eight of them used to meet there; always the same set, not fast men, but respectable tradesmen, and young men in government or some other employ; and they used to drink their Chartreuse, and tease the girls, or else they would talk seriously with Madame, whom everybody respected, and then would go home at twelve o'clock! The younger men would sometimes stay the night.

It was a small, comfortable house, at the corner of a street behind Saint Etienne's church. From the windows one could see the docks, full of ships which were being unloaded, and on the hill the old, gray chapel, dedicated to the Virgin.

Madame, who came of a respectable family of peasant proprietors in the department of the Eure, had taken up her profession, just as she would have become a milliner or dressmaker. The prejudice against prostitution, which is so violent and deeply rooted in large towns, does not exist in the country places in Normandy. The peasant simply says: "It is a paying business," and sends his daughter to keep a harem of fast girls, just as he would send her to keep a girls' school.

She had inherited the house from an old uncle, to whom it had belonged. Monsieur and Madame, who had formerly been innkeepers near Yvetot, had immediately sold their house, as they thought that the business at Fécamp was more profitable. They arrived one fine morning to assume the direction of the enterprise, which was declining on account of the absence of a head. They were good people enough in their way, and soon made themselves liked by their staff and their neighbors.

Monsieur died of apoplexy two years later, for as his new profession kept him in idleness and without exercise, he had grown excessively stout, and his health had suffered. Since Madame had been a widow, all the frequenters of the establishment had wanted her; but people said that personally she was quite virtuous, and even the girls in the house could not discover anything against her. She was tall, stout, and affable, and her complexion, which had become pale in the dimness of her house, the shutters of which were scarcely ever opened, shone as if it had been varnished. She had a fringe of curly, false hair, which gave her a juvenile look, which in turn contrasted strongly with her matronly figure. She was always smiling and cheerful, and was fond of a joke, but there was a shade of reserve about her which her new occupation had not quite made her lose. Coarse words always shocked her, and when any young fellow who

From Selected Tales of Guy de Maupassant, *published by Random House, Inc., New York.*

had been badly brought up called her establishment by its right name, she was angry and disgusted.

In a word, she had a refined mind, and although she treated her women as friends, yet she very frequently used to say that she and they were not made of the same stuff.

Sometimes during the week she would hire a carriage and take some of her girls into the country, where they used to enjoy themselves on the grass by the side of the little river. They behaved like a lot of girls let out from a school, and used to run races, and play childish games. They would have a cold dinner on the grass, and drink cider, and go home at night with a delicious feeling of fatigue, and in the carriage kiss Madame as a kind mother who was full of goodness and complaisance.

The house had two entrances. At the corner there was a sort of low *café*, which sailors and the lower orders frequented at night, and she had two girls whose special duty it was to attend to that part of the business. With the assistance of the waiter, whose name was Frederic, and who was a short, light-haired, beardless fellow, as strong as a horse, they set the half bottles of wine and the jugs of beer on the shaky marble tables and then, sitting astride on the customers' knees, would urge them to drink.

The three other girls (there were only five in all) formed a kind of aristocracy, and were reserved for the company on the first floor, unless they were wanted downstairs, and there was nobody on the first floor. The salon of Jupiter, where the tradesmen used to meet, was prepared in blue, and embellished with a large drawing representing Leda stretched out under the swan. That room was reached by a winding staircase, which ended at a narrow door opening on to the street, and above it, all night long a little lamp burned, behind wire bars, such as one still sees in some towns, at the foot of the shrine of some saint.

The house, which was old and damp, rather smelled of mildew. At times there was an odor of eau de Cologne in the passages, or a half-open door downstairs allowed the noise of the common men sitting and drinking downstairs to reach the first floor, much to the disgust of the gentlemen who were there. Madame, who was quite familiar with those of her customers with whom she was on friendly terms, did not leave the salon. She took much interest in what was going on in the town, and they regularly told her all the news. Her serious conversation was a change from the ceaseless chatter of the three women; it was a rest from the doubtful jokes of those stout individuals who every evening indulged in the commonplace amusement of drinking a glass of liquor in company with girls of easy virtue.

The names of the girls on the first floor were Fernande, Raphaelle, and Rosa "the Jade." As the staff was limited, Madame had endeavored that each member of it should be a pattern, an epitome of each feminine type, so that every customer might find, as nearly as possible, the realization of his ideal. Fernande represented the handsome blonde; she was very tall, rather fat, and lazy; a country girl, who could not get rid of her freckles, and whose short, light, almost colorless, tow-like hair, which was like combed-out flax, barely covered her head.

Raphaelle, who came from Marseilles, played the indispensable part of the handsome Jewess. She was thin, with high cheek-bones covered with rouge, and her black hair, which was always covered with pomatum, curled on to her forehead. Her eyes would have been handsome, if the right one had not had a speck in it. Her Roman nose came down over a square jaw, where two false upper teeth contrasted strangely with the bad color of the rest.

Rosa the Jade was a little roll of fat, nearly all stomach, with very short legs. From morning till night she sang songs, which were alternately indecent or sentimental, in a harsh voice, told silly, interminable tales, and only stopped talking in order to eat, or left off eating in order to talk. She was never still, was as active as a squirrel, in spite of her fat and her short legs; and her laugh, which was a torrent of shrill cries, resounded here and there, ceaselessly, in a bedroom, in the loft, in the *café*, everywhere, and always about nothing.

The two women on the ground floor were Louise, who was nicknamed "la Cocotte," and Flora, whom they called "Balançière," because she limped a little. The former always dressed as Liberty, with a tri-colored sash, and the other as a Spanish woman, with a string of copper coins, which jingled at every step she took, in her carroty hair. Both looked like cooks dressed up for the carnival, and were like all other women of the lower orders, neither uglier nor better looking than they usually are. In fact they looked just like servants at an inn, and were generally called "the Two Pumps."

A jealous peace, very rarely disturbed, reigned among these five women, thanks to Madame's conciliatory wisdom and to her constant good humor; and the establishment, which was the only one of the kind in the little town, was very much frequented. Madame had succeeded in giving it such a respectable appearance; she was so amiable and obliging to everybody, her good heart was so well known, that she was treated with a certain amount of consideration. The regular customers spent money on her, and were delighted when she was especially friendly toward them. When they met during the day, they would say: "This evening, you know where," just as men say: "At the *café*, after dinner." In a word Madame Tellier's house was somewhere to go to, and her customers very rarely missed their daily meetings there.

One evening, toward the end of May, the first arrival, Monsieur Poulin, who was a timber merchant, and had been mayor, found the door shut. The little lantern behind the grating was not alight; there was not a sound in the house; everything seemed dead. He knocked, gently at first, and then more loudly, but nobody answered the door. Then he went slowly up the street, and when he got to the market place, he met Monsieur Duvert, the gun-maker, who was going to the same place, so they went back together, but did not meet with any better success. But suddenly they heard a loud noise close to them, and on going round the corner of the house, they saw a number of English and French sailors, who were hammering at the closed shutters of the *café* with their fists.

The two tradesmen immediately made their escape, for fear of being compromised, but a low *Pst* stopped them; it was Monsieur Tournevau, the fish-curer, who had recognized them, and was trying to attract their attention. They told him what had happened, and he was all the more vexed at it, as he, a married man, and father of a family, only went there on Saturdays—*securitatis causa,* as he said, alluding to a measure of sanitary policy, which his friend Doctor Borde had advised him to observe. That was his regular evening, and now he would be deprived of it for the whole week.

The three men went as far as the quay together, and on the way they met young Monsieur Philippe, the banker's son, who frequented the place regularly, and Monsieur Pinipesse, the collector. They all returned to the Rue aux Juifs together, to make a last attempt. But the exasperated sailors were besieging the house, throwing stones at the shutters, and shouting, and the five first-floor customers went away as quickly as possible, and walked aimlessly about the streets.

Presently they met Monsieur Dupuis, the insurance agent, and then Monsieur Vassi, the Judge of the Tribunal of Commerce, and they all took a long walk, going to the pier first of all. There they sat down in a row on the granite parapet, and watched the rising tide, and when the promenaders had sat there for some time, Monsieur Tournevau said: "This is not very amusing!"

"Decidedly not," Monsieur Pinipesse replied, and they started off to walk again.

After going through the street on the top of the hill, they returned over the wooden bridge which crosses the Retenue, passed close to the railway, and came out again on to the market place, when suddenly a quarrel arose between Monsieur Pinipesse and Monsieur Tournevau, about an edible fungus which one of them declared he had found in the neighborhood.

As they were out of temper already from annoyance, they would very probably have come to blows, if the others had not interfered. Monsieur Pinipesse went off furious, and soon another altercation arose between the ex-mayor, Monsieur Poulin, and Monsieur Dupuis, the insurance agent, on the subject of the tax-collector's salary, and the profits which he might make. Insulting remarks were freely passing between them, when a torrent of formidable cries were heard, and the body of sailors, who were tired of waiting so long outside a closed house, came into the square. They were walking arm-in-arm, two and two, and formed a long procession, and were shouting furiously. The landsmen went and hid themselves under a gateway, and the yelling crew disappeared in the direction of the abbey. For a long time they still heard the noise, which diminished like a storm in the distance, and then silence was restored. Monsieur Poulin and Monsieur Dupuis, who were enraged at each other, went in different directions, without wishing each other good-bye.

The other four set aff again, and instinctively went in the direction of Madame Tellier's establishment, which was still closed, silent, impenetrable. A quiet, but obstinate, drunken man was knocking at the door of the *café;* then he stopped and called Frederic, the waiter, in a low voice, but finding that he got no answer, he sat down on the doorstep, and awaited the course of events.

The others were just going to retire, when the noisy band of sailors reappeared at the end of the street. The French sailors were shouting the "Marseillaise," and the Englishmen, "Rule Britannia." There was a general lurching against the wall, and then the drunken brutes went on their way toward the quay, where a fight broke out between the two nations, in the course of which an Englishman had his arm broken, and a Frenchman his nose split.

The drunken man, who had stopped outside the door, was crying by this time, as drunken men and children cry when they are vexed, and the others went away. By degrees, calm was restored in the noisy town; here and there at moments, the distant sound of voices could be heard, only to die away in the distance.

One man was still wandering about, Monsieur Tournevau, the fish-curer, who was vexed at having to wait until the next Saturday. He hoped for something to turn up, he did not know what; but he was exasperated at the police for thus allowing an establishment of such public utility, which they had under their control, to be thus closed.

He went back to it, examined the walls, and tried to find out the reason. On the shutter he saw a notice stuck up, so he struck a wax vesta, and read the following, in large, uneven hand: "Closed on Account of the Confirmation."

Then he went away, as he saw it was useless to remain, and left the drunken man lying on the pavement fast asleep, outside the inhospitable door.

The next day, all the regular customers, one after the other, found some reason for going through the Rue aux Juifs with a bundle of papers under their arm, to keep them in countenance, and with a furtive glance they all read that mysterious notice:

Closed on Account of the Confirmation.

II

Madame had a brother, who was a carpenter in their native place, Virville, in the department of Eure. When Madame had still kept the inn at Yvetot, she had stood godmother to that brother's daughter, who had received the name of Constance, Constance Rivet; she herself being a Rivet on her father's side. The carpenter, who knew that his sister was in a good position, did not lose sight of her, although they did not meet often, as they were both kept at home by their occupations, and lived a long way from each other. But when the girl was twelve years old, and about to be confirmed, he seized the opportunity to write to his sister, and ask her to come and be present at the ceremony. Their old parents were dead, and as Madame could not well refuse, she accepted the invitation. Her brother, whose name was Joseph, hoped that by dint of showing his sister attentions, she might be induced to make her will in the girl's favor, as she had no children of her own.

His sister's occupation did not trouble his scruples in the least, and, besides, nobody knew anything about it at Virville. When they spoke of her, they only said: "Madame Tellier is living at Fécamp," which might mean that she was living on her own private income. It was quite twenty leagues from Fécamp to Virville, and for a peasant, twenty leagues on land are more than is crossing the ocean to an educated person. The people at Virville had never been further than Rouen, and nothing attracted the people from Fécamp to a village of five hundred houses, in the middle of a plain, and situated in another department. At any rate, nothing was known about her business.

But the confirmation was coming on and Madame was in great embarrassment. She had no under-mistress, and did not at all dare to leave her house, even for a day. She feared the rivalries between the girls upstairs and those downstairs would certainly break out; that Frederic would get drunk, for when he was in that state, he would knock anybody down for a mere word. At last, however, she made up her mind to take them all with her, with the exception of the man, to whom she gave a holiday, until the next day but one.

When she asked her brother, he made no objection, but undertook to put them all up for a night. So on Saturday morning the eight o'clock express carried off Madame and her companions in a second-class carriage. As far as Beuzeille they were alone, and chattered like magpies, but at that station a couple got in. The man, an aged peasant dressed in a blue blouse with a folding collar, wide sleeves tight at the wrist, and ornamented with white embroidery, wore an old high hat with long nap. He held an enormous green umbrella in one hand, and a large basket in the other, from which the heads of three frightened ducks protruded. The woman, who sat stiffly in her rustic finery, had a face like a fowl, and with a nose that was as pointed as a bill. She sat down opposite her husband and did not stir, as she was startled at finding herself in such smart company.

There was certainly an array of striking colors in the carriage. Madame was dressed in blue silk from head to foot, and had over her dress a dazzling red shawl of imitation French cashmere. Fernande was panting in a Scottish plaid dress, whose bodice, which her companions had laced as tight as they could, had forced up her falling bosom into a double dome, that was continually heaving up and down, and which seemed liquid beneath the material. Raphaelle, with a bonnet covered with feathers, so that it looked like a nest full of birds, had on a lilac dress with gold spots on it; there was something Oriental about it that suited her Jewish face. Rosa the Jade had on a pink petticoat with large flounces, and looked like a very fat child, an obese dwarf; while the two Pumps looked as if they had cut their dresses out of old, flowered curtains, dating from the Restoration.

Perceiving that they were no longer alone in the compartment, the ladies put on staid looks, and began to talk of subjects which might give the others a high opinion of them. But at Bolbec a gentleman with light whiskers, with a gold chain, and wearing two or three rings, got in, and put several parcels wrapped in oil cloth into the net over his head. He looked inclined for a joke, and a good-natured fellow.

"Are you ladies changing your quarters?" he asked. The question embarrassed them all considerably. Madame, however, quickly recovered her composure, and said sharply, to avenge the honor of her corps:

"I think you might try to be polite!"

He excused himself, and said: "I beg your pardon, I ought to have said your nunnery."

As Madame could not think of a retort, or perhaps as she thought herself justified sufficiently, she gave him a dignified bow, and pinched in her lips.

Then the gentleman, who was sitting between Rosa the Jade and the old peasant, began to wink knowingly at the ducks, whose heads were sticking out of the basket. When he felt that he had fixed the attention of his public, he began to tickle them under their bills, and spoke funnily to them, to make the company smile.

"We have left our little pond, qu-ack! qu-ack! to make an acquaintance of the little spit, qu-ack! qu-ack!"

The unfortunate creatures turned their necks away to avoid his caresses, and made desperate efforts to get out of their wicker prison, and then, suddenly, all at once, uttered the most lamentable quacks of distress. The women exploded with laughter. They leaned forward and pushed each other, so as to see better; they were very much interested in the ducks, and the gentleman redoubled his airs, his wit, and his teasing.

Rosa joined in, and leaning over her neighbor's legs, she kissed the three animals on the head. Immediately all the girls wanted to kiss them in turn, and the gentleman took them on to his knees, made them jump up and down and pinched them. The two peasants, who were even in greater consternation than their poultry, rolled their eyes as if they were possessed, without venturing to move, and their old wrinkled faces had not a smile nor a movement.

Then the gentleman, who was a commercial traveler, offered the ladies braces by way of a joke and taking up one of his packages, he opened it. It was a trick, for the parcel contained garters. There were blue silk, pink silk, red silk, violet silk, mauve silk garters, and the buckles were made of two gilt metal Cupids, embracing each other. The girls uttered exclamations of delight, and looked at them with that gravity which is natural to a woman when she is hankering after a bargain. They consulted one another, by their looks or in a whisper, and replied in the same manner, and Madame was longingly handling a pair of orange garters that were broader and more imposing than the rest; really fit for the mistress of such an establishment.

"Come, my kittens," he said, "you must try them on."

There was a torrent of exclamations, and they squeezed their petticoats between their legs, as if they thought he was going to ravish them, but he quietly waited his time, and said: "Well, if you will not, I shall pack them up again."

And he added cunningly: "I offer any pair they like, to those who will try them on."

But they would not, and sat up very straight, and looked dignified.

But the Two Pumps looked so distressed that he renewed the offer to them. Flora especially hesitated, and he pressed her.

"Come, my dear, a little courage! Just look at that lilac pair; it will suit your dress admirably."

That decided her, and pulling up her dress she showed a thick leg fit for a milk-maid, in a badly-fitting, coarse stocking. The commercial traveler stooped down and fastened the garter below the knee first of all and then above it; and he tickled the girl gently, which made her scream and jump. When he had done, he gave her the lilac pair, and asked: "Who next?"

"I! I!" they all shouted at once, and he began on Rosa the Jade, who uncovered a shapeless, round thing without any ankle, a regular "sausage of a leg," as Raphaelle used to say.

The commercial traveler complimented Fernande, and grew quite enthusiastic over her powerful columns.

The thin tibias of the handsome Jewess met with less flattery, and Louise Cocotte, by way of a joke, put her petticoats over the man's head, so that Madame was obliged to interfere to check such unseemly behavior.

Lastly, Madame herself put out her leg, a handsome, muscular, Norman leg, and in his surprise and pleasure the commercial traveler gallantly took off his hat to salute that master calf, like a true French cavalier.

The two peasants, who were speechless from surprise, looked askance, out of the corners of their eyes. They looked so exactly like fowls, that the man with the light whiskers, when he sat up, said; "Co—co—ri—co," under their very noses, and that gave rise to another storm of amusement.

The old people got out at Motteville, with their basket, their ducks, and their umbrella, and they heard the woman say to her husband, as they went away:

"They are sluts, who are off to that cursed place, Paris."

The funny commercial traveler himself got out at Rouen, after behaving so coarsely that Madame was obliged sharply to put him into his right place. She added, as a moral: "This will teach us not to talk to the first comer."

At Oissel they changed trains, and at a little station further on Monsieur Joseph Rivet was waiting for them with a large cart with a number of chairs in it, which was drawn by a white horse.

The carpenter politely kissed all the ladies, and then helped them into his conveyance.

Three of them sat on three chairs at the back, Raphaelle, Madame, and her brother on the three chairs in front, and Rosa, who had no seat, settled herself as comfortably as she could on tall Fernande's knees, and then they set off.

But the horse's jerky trot shook the cart so terribly, that the chairs began to dance, throwing the travelers into the air, to the right and to the left, as if they had been dancing puppets. This made them make horrible grimaces and screams, which, however, were cut short by another jolt of the cart.

They clung to the sides of the vehicle, their bonnets fell on to their backs, their noses on their shoulders, and the white horse trotted on, stretching out his head and holding out his tail quite straight, a little hairless rat's tail, with which he whisked his buttocks from time to time.

Joseph Rivet, with one leg on the shafts and the other bent under him, held the reins with elbows high and kept uttering a kind of chuckling sound, which made the horse prick up its ears and go faster.

The green country extended on either side of the road, and here and there the colza in flower presented a waving expanse of yellow, from which there arose a strong, wholesome, sweet and penetrating smell, which the wind carried to some distance.

The cornflowers showed their little blue heads among the rye, and the women wanted to pick them, but Monsieur Rivet refused to stop.

Then sometimes a whole field appeared to be covered with blood, so thickly were the poppies growing, and the cart, which looked as if it were filled with flowers of more brilliant hue, drove on through the fields colored with wild flowers, to disappear behind the trees of a farm, then to reappear and go on again through the yellow or green standing crops studded with red or blue.

One o'clock struck as they drove up to the carpenter's door. They were tired out, and very hungry, as they had eaten nothing since they left home. Madame Rivet ran out, and made them alight, one after another, kissing them as soon as they were on the ground. She seemed as if she would never tire of kissing her sister-in-law, whom she apparently wanted to monopolize. They had lunch in the workshop, which had been cleared out for the next day's dinner.

A capital omelette, followed by boiled chitterlings, and washed down by good, sharp cider, made them all feel comfortable.

Rivet had taken a glass so that he might hob-nob with them, and his wife cooked, waited on them, brought in the dishes, took them out, and asked all of them in a whisper whether they had everything they wanted. A number of boards standing against the walls, and heaps of shavings that had been swept into the corners, gave out the smell of planed wood, of carpentering, that resinous odor which penetrates the lungs.

They wanted to see the little girl, but she had gone to church, and would not be back until evening, so they all went out for a stroll in the country.

It was a small village, through which the high road passed. Ten or a dozen houses on either side of the single street had for tenants the butcher, the grocer, the carpenter, the innkeeper, the shoemaker, and the baker, and others.

The church was at the end of the street. It was surrounded by a small churchyard, and four enormous lime-trees, which stood just outside the porch, shaded it completely. It was built of flint, in no particular style, and had a slated steeple. When you got past it, you were in the open country again, which was broken here and there by clumps of trees which hid some homestead.

Rivet had given his arm to his sister, out of politeness, although he was in his working clothes, and was walking with her majestically. His wife, who was overwhelmed by Raphaelle's gold-striped dress, was walking between her and Fernande, and rotund Rosa was trotting behind with Louise Cocotte and Flora, the Seesaw, who was limping along, quite tired out.

The inhabitants came to their doors, the children left off playing, and a window curtain would be raised, so as to show a muslin cap, while an old woman with a crutch, who was almost blind, crossed herself as if it were a religious procession. They all looked for a long time after those handsome ladies from the town, who had come so far to be present at the confirmation of Joseph Rivet's little girl, and the carpenter rose very much in the public estimation.

As they passed the church, they heard some children singing; little shrill voices were singing a hymn, but Madame would not let them go in, for fear of disturbing the little cherubs.

After a walk, during which Joseph Rivet enumerated the principal landed proprietors, spoke about the yield of the land, and the productiveness of the cows and sheep, he took his flock of women home and installed them in his house, and as it was very small, he had to put them into the rooms, two and two.

Just for once, Rivet would sleep in the workshop on the shavings; his wife was going to share her bed with her sister-in-law, and Fernande and Raphaelle were to sleep together in the next room. Louise and Flora were put into the kitchen, where they had a mattress on the floor, and Rosa had a little dark cupboard at the top of the stairs to herself, close to the loft, where the candidate for confirmation was to sleep.

When the girl came in, she was overwhelmed with kisses; all the women wished to caress her, with that need of tender expression, that habit of professional wheedling, which had made them kiss the ducks in the railway carriage.

They took her on to their laps, stroked her soft, light hair, and pressed her in their arms with vehement and spontaneous outbursts of affection, and the child, who was very good-natured and docile, bore it all patiently.

As the day had been a fatiguing one for everybody, they all went to bed soon after dinner. The whole village was wrapped in that perfect stillness of the country, which is almost like a religious silence, and the girls, who were accustomed to the noisy evenings of their establishment, felt rather impressed by the perfect repose of the sleeping village. They shivered, not with cold, but with those little shivers of solitude which come over uneasy and troubled hearts.

As soon as they were in bed, two and two together, they clasped each other in their arms, as if to protect themselves against this feeling of the calm and profound slumber of the earth. But Rosa the Jade, who was alone in her little dark cupboard, felt a vague and painful emotion come over her.

She was tossing about in bed, unable to get to sleep, when she heard the faint sobs of a crying child close to her head, through the partition. She was frightened, and called out, and was answered by a weak voice, broken by sobs. It was the little girl who, being used to sleeping in her mother's room, was frightened in her small attic.

Rosa was delighted, got up softly so as not to awaken anyone, and went and fetched the child. She took her into her warm bed, kissed her and pressed her to her bosom, caressed her, lavished exaggerated manifestations of tenderness on her, and at last grew calmer herself and went to sleep. And till morning, the candidate for confirmation slept with her head on Rosa's naked bosom.

At five o'clock, the little church bell ringing the "Angelus" woke these women up, who as a rule slept the whole morning long.

The peasants were up already, and the women went busily from house to house, carefully bringing short, starched, muslin dresses in bandboxes, or very long wax tapers, with a bow of silk fringed with gold in the middle, and with dents in the wax for the fingers.

The sun was already high in the blue sky, which still had a rosy tint toward the horizon, like a faint trace of dawn, remaining. Families of fowls were walking about the henhouses, and here and there a black cock, with a glistening breast, raised his head, crowned by his red comb, flapped his wings, and uttered his shrill crow, which the other cocks repeated.

Vehicles of all sorts came from neighboring parishes, and discharged tall, Norman women, in dark dresses, with neck-handkerchiefs crossed over the bosom, and fastened with silver brooches, a hundred years old.

The men had put on blouses over their new frock coats, or over their old dress coats of green cloth, the tails of which hung down below their blouses. When the horses were in the stable, there was a double line of rustic conveyances along the road; carts, cabriolets, tilburies, char-à-bancs, traps of every shape and age, resting on their shafts, or pointing them in the air.

The carpenter's house was as busy as a beehive. The ladies, in dressing jackets and petticoats, with their long, thin, light hair, which looked as if it were faded and worn by dyeing, were busy dressing the child, who was standing motionless on a table, while Madame Tellier was directing the movements of her battalion. They washed her, did her hair, dressed her, and with the help of a number of pins, they arranged the folds of her dress, and took in the waist, which was too large.

Then, when she was ready, she was told to sit down and not to move, and the women hurried off to get ready themselves.

The church bell began to ring again, and its tinkle was lost in the air, like a feeble voice which is soon drowned in space. The candidates came out of the houses, and went toward the parochial building which contained the school and the mansion house. This stood quite at one end of the village, while the church was situated at the other.

The parents, in their very best clothes, followed their children with awkward looks, and with the clumsy movements of bodies that are always bent at work.

The little girls disappeared in a cloud of muslin, which looked like whipped cream, while the lads, who looked like embryo waiters in a *café,* and whose heads shone with pomatum, walked with their legs apart, so as not to get any dust or dirt on to their black trousers.

It was something for the family to be proud of; a large number of relatives from distant parts surrounded the child, and, consequently, the carpenter's triumph was complete.

Madame Tellier's regiment, with its mistress at its head, followed Constance; her father gave his arm to his sister, her mother walked by the side of Raphaelle, Fernande with Rosa, and the Two Pumps together. Thus they walked majestically through the village, like a general's staff in full uniform, while the effect on the village was startling.

At the school, the girls arranged themselves under the Sister of Mercy, and the boys under the schoolmaster, and they started off, singing a hymn as they went. The boys led the way, in two files, between the two rows of vehicles, from which the horses had been taken out, and the girls followed in the same order. As all the people in the village had given the town ladies the precedence out of politeness, they came immediately behind the girls, and lengthened the double line of the procession still more, three on the right and three on the left, while their dresses were as striking as a bouquet of fireworks.

When they went into the church, the congregation grew quite excited. They pressed against each other, they turned round, they jostled one another in order to see. Some of the devout ones almost spoke aloud, so astonished were they at the sight of these ladies, whose dresses were trimmed more elaborately than the priest's chasuble.

The Mayor offered them his pew, the first one on the right, close to the choir, and Madame Tellier sat there with her sister-in-law; Fernande and Raphaelle, Rosa the Jade, and the Two Pumps occupied the second seat, in company with the carpenter.

The choir was full of kneeling children, the girls on one side, and the boys on the other, and the long wax tapers which they held looked like lances, pointing in all directions. Three men were standing in front of the lectern, singing as loud as they could.

They prolonged the syllables of the sonorous Latin indefinitely, holding on to the Amens with interminable *a—a's,* which the serpent of the organ kept up in the monotonous, long-drawn-out notes, emitted by the deep-throated pipes.

A child's shrill voice took up the reply, and from time to time a priest sitting in a stall and wearing a biretta got up, muttered something, and sat down again. The three singers continued, with their eyes fixed on the big book of plainsong lying open before them on the outstretched wings of an eagle, mounted on a pivot.

Then silence ensued. The service went on, and toward the end of it, Rosa, with her head in both her hands, suddenly thought of her mother, and her village church on a similar occasion. She almost fancied that that day had returned, when she was so small, and almost hidden in her white dress, and she began to cry.

First of all she wept silently, the tears dropped slowly from her eyes, but her emotion increased with her recollections, and she began to sob. She took out her pocket-handkerchief, wiped her eyes, and held it to her mouth, so as not to scream, but it was useless.

A sort of rattle escaped her throat, and she was answered by two other profound, heart-breaking sobs; for her two neighbors, Louise and Flora, who were kneeling near her, overcome by similar recollections, were sobbing by her side. There was a flood of tears, and as weeping is contagious, Madame soon found that her eyes were wet, and on turning to her sister-in-law, she saw that all the occupants of the pew were crying.

Soon, throughout the church, here and there, a wife, a mother, a sister, seized by the strange sympathy of poignant emotion, and agitated by the grief of those handsome ladies on their knees, who were shaken by their sobs, was moistening her cambric pocket-handkerchief, and pressing her beating heart with her left hand.

Just as the sparks from an engine will set fire to dry grass, so the tears of Rosa and of her companions infected the whole congregation in a moment. Men, women, old men, and lads in new blouses were soon sobbing; something superhuman seemed to be hovering over their heads—a spirit, the powerful breath of an invisible and all-powerful being.

Suddenly a species of madness seemed to pervade the church, the noise of a crowd in a state of frenzy, a tempest of sobs and of stifled cries. It passed over the people like gusts of wind which bow the trees in a forest, and the priest, overcome by emotion, stammered out incoherent prayers, those inarticulate prayers of the soul, when it soars toward heaven.

The people behind him gradually grew calmer. The cantors, in all the dignity of their white surplices, went on in somewhat uncertain voices, and the organ itself seemed hoarse, as if the instrument had been weeping. The priest, however, raised his hand, as a sign for them to be still, and went to the chancel steps. All were silent, immediately.

After a few remarks on what had just taken place, which he attributed to a miracle, he continued, turning to the seats where the carpenter's guests were sitting:

"I especially thank you, my dear sisters, who have come from such a distance, and whose presence among us, whose evident faith and ardent piety have set such a salutary example to all. You have edified my parish; your emotion has warmed all hearts; without you, this day would not, perhaps, have had this really divine character. It is sufficient, at times, that there should be one chosen to keep in the flock, to make the whole flock blessed."

His voice failed him again, from emotion, and he said no more, but concluded the service.

They all left the church as quickly as possible; the children themselves were restless, tired with such a prolonged tension of the mind. Besides, the elders were hungry, and one after another left the churchyard, to see about dinner.

There was a crowd outside, a noisy crowd, a babel of loud voices, in which the shrill Norman accent was discernible. The villagers formed two ranks, and when the children appeared, each family seized their own.

The whole houseful of women caught hold of Constance, surrounded her and kissed her, and Rosa was especially demonstrative. At last she took hold of one hand, while Madame Tellier held the other, and Raphaelle and Fernande held up her long muslin petticoat, so that it might not drag in the dust. Louise and Flora brought up the rear with Madame Rivet, and the child, who was very silent and thoughtful, set off home, in the midst of this guard of honor.

The dinner was served in the workshop, on long boards supported by trestles, and through the open door they could see all the enjoyment that was going on. Everywhere people were feasting; through every window could be seen tables surrounded by people in their Sunday clothes. There was merriment, in every house—men sitting in their shirt sleeves, drinking cider, glass after glass.

In the carpenter's house the gaiety took on somewhat of an air of reserve, the consequence of the emotion of the girls in the morning. Rivet was the only one who was in good cue, and he was drinking to excess. Madame Tellier was looking at the clock every moment, for, in order not to lose two days following, they ought to take the 3:55 train, which would bring them to Fécamp by dark.

The carpenter tried very hard to distract her attention, so as to keep his guests until the next day. But he did not succeed, for she never joked when there was business to be done, and as soon as they had had their coffee she ordered her girls to make haste and get ready. Then, turning to her brother, she said:

"You must have the horse put in immediately," and she herself went to complete her preparations.

When she came down again, her sister-in-law was waiting to speak to her about the child, and a long conversation took place, in which, however, nothing was settled. The carpenter's wife finessed, and pretended to be very much moved, and Madame Tellier, who was holding the girl on her knees, would not pledge herself to anything definite, but merely gave vague promises: she would not forget her, there was plenty of time, and then, they were sure to meet again.

But the conveyance did not come to the door, and the women did not come downstairs. Upstairs, they even heard loud laughter, falls, little screams, and much clapping of hands, and so, while the carpenter's wife went to the stable to see whether the cart was ready, Madame went upstairs.

Rivet, who was very drunk and half undressed, was vainly trying to kiss Rosa, who was choking with laughter. The Two Pumps were holding him by the arms and trying to calm him, as they were shocked at such a scene after that morning's ceremony; but Raphaelle and Fernande were urging him on, writhing and holding their sides with laughter, and they uttered shrill cries at every useless attempt that the drunken fellow made.

The man was furious, his face was red, his dress disordered, and he was trying to shake off the two women who were clinging to him, while he was pulling Rosa's bodice, with all his might, and ejaculating: "Won't you, you slut?"

But Madame, who was very indignant, went up to her brother, seized him by the shoulders, and threw him out of the room with such violence that he fell against a wall in the passage, and a minute afterward, they heard him pumping water on to his head in the yard. When he came back with the cart, he was already quite calmed down.

They seated themselves in the same way as they had done the day before, and the little white horse started off with his quick, dancing trot. Under the hot sun, their fun, which had been checked during dinner, broke out again. The girls now were amused at the jolts which the wagon gave, pushed their neighbors' chairs, and burst out laughing every moment, for they were in the vein for it, after Rivet's vain attempt.

There was a haze over the country, the roads were glaring, and dazzled their eyes. The wheels raised up two trails of dust, which followed the cart for a long time along the highroad, and presently Fernande, who was fond of music, asked Rosa to sing something. She boldly struck up the "Gros Curé de Meudon," but Madame made her stop immediately as she thought it a song which was very unsuitable for such a day, and added:

"Sing us something of Béranger's."

After a moment's hesitation, Rosa began Béranger's song, "The Grandmother," in her worn-out voice, and all the girls, and even Madame herself, joined in the chorus:

> How I regret
> My dimpled arms,
> My well-made legs,
> And my vanished charms!

"That is first-rate," Rivet declared, carried away by the rhythm. They shouted the refrain to every verse, while Rivet beat time on the shafts with his foot, and on the horse's back with the reins. The animal, himself, carried away by the rhythm, broke into a wild gallop, and threw all the women in a heap, one on top of the other, in the bottom of the conveyance.

They got up, laughing as if they were crazy, and the song went on, shouted at the top of their voices, beneath the burning sky and among the ripening grain, to the rapid gallop of the little horse, who set off every time the refrain was sung, and galloped a hundred yards, to their great delight. Occasionally a stone breaker by the roadside sat up, and looked at the wild and shouting female load, through his wire spectacles.

When they got out at the station, the carpenter said:

"I am sorry you are going; we might have had some fun together."

But Madame replied very sensibly: "Everything has its right time, and we cannot always be enjoying ourselves."

And then he had a sudden inspiration: "Look here, I will come and see you at Fécamp next month." And he gave a knowing look, with his bright and roguish eyes.

"Come," Madame said, "you must be sensible; you may come if you like, but you are not to be up to any of your tricks."

He did not reply, and as they heard the whistle of the train he immediately began to kiss them all. When it came to Rosa's turn, he tried to get to her mouth, which she, however, smiling with her lips closed, turned away from him each time by a rapid movement of her head to one side. He held her in his arms, but he could not attain his object, as his large whip, which he was holding in his hand and waving behind the girl's back in desperation, interfered with his efforts.

"Passengers for Rouen, take your seats, please!" a guard cried, and they got in. There was a slight whistle followed by a loud one from the engine, which noisily puffed out its first jet of steam, while the wheels began to turn a little, with visible effort. Rivet left the station and went to the gate by the side of the line to get another look at Rosa, and as the carriage full of human merchandise passed him, he began to crack his whip and to jump, singing at the top of his voice:

> How I regret
> My dimpled arms,
> My well-made legs,
> And my vanished charms!

And then he watched a white pocket-handkerchief, which somebody was waving, as it disappeared in the distance.

III

They slept the peaceful sleep of quiet consciences, until they got to Rouen. When they returned to the house, refreshed and rested, Madame could not help saying:

"It was all very well, but I was already longing to get home."

They hurried over their supper, and then, when they had put on their usual light evening costumes, waited for their usual customers. The little colored lamp outside the door told the passers-by that the flock had returned to the fold, and in a moment the news spread, nobody knew how, or by whom.

Monsieur Philippe, the banker's son, even carried his audacity so far as to send a special messenger to Monsieur Tournevau who was in the bosom of his family.

The fish-curer used every Sunday to have several cousins to dinner, and they were having coffee, when a man came in with a letter in his hand. Monsieur Tournevau was much excited; he opened the envelope and grew pale; it only contained these words in pencil:

> The cargo of fish has been found; the ship has come into port; good business for you. Come immediately.

He felt in his pockets, gave the messenger two sous, and suddenly blushing to his ears, he said: "I must go out." He handed his wife the laconic and mysterious note, rang the bell, and when the servant came in, he asked her to bring him his hat and overcoat immediately. As soon as he was in the street, he began to run, and the way seemed to him to be twice as long as usual, in consequence of his impatience.

Madame Tellier's establishment had put on quite a holiday look. On the ground floor, a number of sailors were making a deafening noise, and Louise and Flora drank with one and the other, so as to merit their name of the Two Pumps more than ever. They were being called for everywhere at once; already they were not quite sober enough for their business, and the night bid fair to be a very jolly one.

The upstairs room was full by nine o'clock. Monsieur Vassi, the Judge of the Tribunal of Commerce, Madame's usual Platonic wooer, was talking to her in a corner, in a low voice, and they were both smiling, as if they were about to come to an understanding.

Monsieur Poulin, the ex-mayor, was holding Rosa on his knees; and she, with her nose close to his, was running her hands through the old gentleman's white whiskers.

Tall Fernande, who was lying on the sofa, had both her feet on Monsieur Pinipesse the tax-collector's stomach, and her back on young Monsieur Philippe's waistcoat; her right arm was round his neck, and she held a cigarette in her left.

Raphaelle appeared to be discussing matters with Monsieur Dupuis, the insurance agent, and she finished by saying: "Yes, my dear, I will."

Just then, the door opened suddenly, and Monsieur Tournevau came in. He was greeted with enthusiastic cries of: "Long live Tournevau!" and Raphaelle, who was twirling round, went and threw herself into his arms. He seized her in a vigorous embrace, and without saying a word, lifting her up as if she had been a feather, he carried her through the room.

Rosa was chatting to the ex-mayor, kissing him every moment, and pulling both his whiskers at the same time in order to keep his head straight.

Fernande and Madame remained with the four men, and Monsieur Philippe exclaimed: "I will pay for some champagne; get three bottles, Madame Tellier." And Fernande gave him a hug, and whispered to him: "Play us a waltz, will you?" So he rose and sat down at the old piano in the corner, and managed to get a hoarse waltz out of the entrails of the instrument.

The tall girl put her arms round the tax-collector, Madame asked Monsieur Vassi to take her in his arms, and the two couples turned round, kissing as they danced. Monsieur Vassi, who had formerly danced in good society, waltzed with such elegance that Madame was quite captivated.

Frederic brought the champagne; the first cork popped, and Monsieur Philippe played the introduction to a quadrille, through which the four dancers walked in society fashion, decorously, with propriety of deportment, with bows, and curtsies, and then they began to drink.

Monsieur Philippe next struck up a lively polka, and Monsieur Tournevau started off with the handsome Jewess, whom he held up in the air, without letting her feet touch the ground. Monsieur Pinipesse and Monsieur Vassi had started off with renewed vigor and from time to time one or another couple would stop to toss off a long glass of sparkling wine. The dance was threatening to become never-ending, when Rosa opened the door.

"I want to dance," she exclaimed. And she caught hold of Monsieur Dupuis, who was sitting idle on the couch, and the dance began again.

But the bottles were empty. "I will pay for one," Monsieur Tournevau said.

"So will I," Monsieur Vassi declared.

"And I will do the same," Monsieur Dupuis remarked.

They all began to clap their hands, and it soon became a regular ball. From time to time, Louise and Flora ran upstairs quickly, had a few turns while their customers downstairs grew impatient, and then they returned regretfully to the *café*. At midnight they were still dancing.

Madame shut her eyes to what was going on, and she had long private talks in corners with Monsieur Vassi, as if to settle the last details of something that had already been agreed upon.

At last, at one o'clock, the two married men, Monsieur Tournevau and Monsieur Pinipesse, declared that they were going home, and wanted to pay. Nothing was charged for except the champagne, and that only cost six francs a bottle, instead of ten, which was the usual price, and when they expressed their surprise at such generosity, Madame, who was beaming, said to them:

"We don't have a holiday every day."

CRITICAL COMMENTS

Emile Zola:

His [Maupassant's] is certainly one of the sanest and healthiest temperaments of the younger generation. . . . People will ask, "Why choose such subjects? Can't writers write about respectable people?" Of course. But I think Maupassant chose this subject because he felt that it struck a very human note. . . .

H. Taine:

. . . I can only beg you [Maupassant] to increase the range of your observation. You portray peasants, the lower middle class, workers, students and prostitutes. Some day you will doubtless portray the cultivated classes, the upper bourgeoisie, engineers, physicians, professors, big industrialists and men of business. In my opinion, civilization is an asset; a man born into comfortable surroundings, the product of three or four honest, industrious and respectable generations, has a greater chance of being upright, refined and educated. Honor and intelligence are always more or less hothouse plants. This theory is certainly aristocratic, but it is based on experience, and I shall be happy when you devote your talent to men and women who, thanks to their culture and fine feelings, are the honor and the strength of their country.

Leo Tolstoy:

From the first story in *La Maison Tellier,* despite the unseemliness and the vacuousness of the subject-matter, I could not deny that the author possessed what is called talent. But the little volume was unhappily lacking the chief of three conditions which, in addition to talent, are indispensable to any work of art. These are: 1, a normal relationship, that is, a moral relationship, between the author and his subject; 2, clarity of exposition or beauty of form, which are one and the same; and 3, sincerity, that is, a real feeling of love or hatred for what the artist depicts. Of these three conditions, Maupassant possessed only the last two. He was completely devoid of the first.[1]

Henry James:

Not less powerful is his visual sense, the quick, direct discrimination of his eyes, which explains the singularly vivid concision of his descriptions. These are never prolonged nor analytic, have nothing

[1] From *Maupassant: A Lion in the Path,* by Francis Steegmuller (New York: Random House, 1949), pp. 155, 287–288, and 404, quotations from Zola, Taine, and Tolstoy reprinted by permission of the publisher.

of enumeration, of the quality of the observer, who counts the items to be sure he has made up the sum. His eye *selects* unerringly, unscrupulously, almost impudently—catches the particular thing in which the character of the object or the scene resides, and, by expressing it with the artful brevity of a master, leaves a convincing, original picture. If he is inveterately synthetic, he is never more so than in the way he brings this hard, short, intelligent gaze to bear. His vision of the world is for the most part a vision of ugliness, and even when it is not, there is in his easy power to generalize a certain absence of love, a sort of bird's-eye-view contempt. . . . He regards the analytic fashion of telling a story . . . as very much less profitable than the simple epic manner which "avoids with care all complicated explanations, all dissertations upon motives, and confines itself to making persons and events pass before our eyes." M. de Maupassant adds that in his view "psychology should be hidden in a book, as it is hidden in reality under the facts of existence. The novel conceived in this manner gains interest, movement, colour, the bustle of life." [2]

H. E. Bates:

. . . To him [Maupassant] words and humanity were a kind of aphrodisiac, stimulating rapid cycles of creative passion. This tendency of his, working unchecked by others, might have resulted in a tenth-rate sex-romanticist. Fortunately it was checked by others. It was checked by the two things which combine perhaps more than any others to prevent a writer from attaining the junk status of two-penny-library popularity: remorseless clarity of vision and equally remorseless integrity of mind. Whatever else stimulated Maupassant, these forces governed him. They struck out of his finest work any possibility of fake, but equally they removed from it any possibility of moral attitude. Maupassant, of course, has been stigmatized by successive generations of the straitlaced as highly immoral. But in fact he was amoral, and that fact alone kept him from entering the most palatial spaces of popular approval and acceptance. [3]

[2] From *Partial Portraits,* by Henry James (London: Macmillan Company, 1888), pp. 251–254, reprinted by permission of John Farquharson, Ltd., on behalf of the Estate of the late Henry James.

[3] From *The Modern Short Story: A Critical Survey,* by H. E. Bates (Edinburgh: Thomas Nelson & Sons, Ltd., 1941), p. 94, reprinted by permission of the publisher.

Young Goodman Brown

Nathaniel Hawthorne 🎕

Young Goodman Brown came forth at sunset into the street at Salem village; but put his head back, after crossing the threshold, to exchange a parting kiss with his young wife. And Faith, as the wife was aptly named, thrust her own pretty head into the street, letting the wind play with the pink ribbons of her cap while she called to Goodman Brown.

"Dearest heart," whispered she, softly and rather sadly, when her lips were close to his ear, "prithee put off your journey until sunrise and sleep in your own bed tonight. A lone woman is troubled with such dreams and such thoughts that she's afeared of herself sometimes. Pray tarry with me this night, dear husband, of all nights in the year."

"My love and my Faith," replied young Goodman Brown, "of all nights in the year, this one night must I tarry away from thee. My journey, as thou callest it, forth and back again, must needs be done 'twixt now and sunrise. What, my sweet, pretty wife, dost thou doubt me already, and we but three months married?"

"Then God bless you!" said Faith, with the pink ribbons; "and may you find all well when you come back."

"Amen!" cried Goodman Brown. "Say thy prayers, dear Faith, and go to bed at dusk, and no harm will come to thee."

So they parted; and the young man pursued his way until, being about to turn the corner by the meeting-house, he looked back and saw the head of Faith still peeping after him with a melancholy air, in spite of her pink ribbons.

"Poor little Faith!" thought he, for his heart smote him. "What a wretch am I to leave her on such an errand! She talks of dreams, too. Methought as she spoke there was trouble in her face, as if a dream had warned her what work is to be done tonight. But no, no; 't would kill her to think it. Well, she's a blessed angel on earth; and after this one night I'll cling to her skirts and follow her to heaven."

With this excellent resolve for the future, Goodman Brown felt himself justified in making more haste on his present evil purpose. He had taken a dreary road, darkened by all the gloomiest trees of the forest, which barely stood aside to let the narrow path creep through, and closed immediately behind. It was all as lonely as could be; and there is this peculiarity in such a solitude, that the traveller knows not who may be concealed by the innumerable trunks and the thick boughs overhead; so that with lonely footsteps he may yet be passing through an unseen multitude.

"There may be a devilish Indian behind every tree," said Goodman

Brown to himself; and he glanced fearfully behind him as he added, "What if the devil himself should be at my very elbow!"

His head being turned back, he passed a crook of the road, and, looking forward again, beheld the figure of a man, in grave and decent attire, seated at the foot of an old tree. He arose at Goodman Brown's approach and walked onward side by side with him.

"You are late, Goodman Brown," said he. "The clock of the Old South was striking as I came through Boston, and that is full fifteen minutes agone."

"Faith kept me back a while," replied the young man, with a tremor in his voice, caused by the sudden appearance of his companion, though not wholly unexpected.

It was now deep dusk in the forest, and deepest in that part of it where these two were journeying. As nearly as could be discerned, the second traveller was about fifty years old, apparently in the same rank of life as Goodman Brown, and bearing a considerable resemblance to him, though perhaps more in expression than features. Still they might have been taken for father and son. And yet, though the elder person was as simply clad as the younger, and as simple in manner too, he had an indescribable air of one who knew the world, and who would not have felt abashed at the governor's dinner table or in King William's court, were it possible that his affairs should call him thither. But the only thing about him that could be fixed upon as remarkable was his staff, which bore the likeness of a great black snake, so curiously wrought that it might almost be seen to twist and wriggle itself like a living serpent. This, of course, must have been an ocular deception, assisted by the uncertain light.

"Come, Goodman Brown," cried his fellow-traveller, "this is a dull pace for the beginning of a journey. Take my staff, if you are so soon weary."

"Friend," said the other, exchanging his slow pace for a full stop, "having kept covenant by meeting thee here, it is my purpose now to return whence I came. I have scruples touching the matter thou wot'st of."

"Sayest thou so?" replied he of the serpent, smiling apart. "Let us walk on, nevertheless, reasoning as we go; and if I convince thee not thou shalt turn back. We are but a little way in the forest yet."

"Too far! too far!" exclaimed the goodman, unconsciously resuming his walk. "My father never went into the woods on such an errand, nor his father before him. We have been a race of honest men and good Christians since the days of the martyrs; and shall I be the first of the name of Brown that ever took this path and kept—"

"Such company, thou wouldst say," observed the elder person, interpreting his pause. "Well said, Goodman Brown! I have been as well acquainted with your family as with ever a one among the Puritans; and that's no trifle to say. I helped your grandfather, the constable, when he lashed the Quaker woman so smartly through the streets of Salem; and it was I that brought your father a pitch-pine knot, kindled at my own hearth, to set fire to an Indian village, in King Philip's war. They were my good friends, both; and many a pleasant walk have we had along this path, and returned merrily after midnight. I would fain be friends with you for their sake."

"If it be as thou sayest," replied Goodman Brown, "I marvel they never spoke of these matters; or, verily, I marvel not, seeing that the least rumor of the sort would have driven them from New England. We are a people of prayer, and good works to boot, and abide no such wickedness."

"Wickedness or not," said the traveller with the twisted staff, "I have a very general acquaintance here in New England. The deacons of many a church have drunk the communion wine with me; the selectmen of divers towns make me their chairman; and a majority of the Great and General Court are firm supporters of my interest. The governor and I, too—But these are state secrets."

"Can this be so?" cried Goodman Brown, with a stare of amazement at his undisturbed companion. "Howbeit, I have nothing to do with the governor and council; they have their own ways, and are no rule for a simple husbandman like me. But, were I to go on with thee, how should I meet the eye of that good old man, our minister, at Salem village? Oh, his voice would make me tremble both Sabbath day and lecture day."

Thus far the elder traveller had listened with due gravity; but now burst into a fit of irrepressible mirth, shaking himself so violently that his snake-like staff actually seemed to wriggle in sympathy.

"Ha! ha! ha!" shouted he again and again; then composing himself, "Well, go on, Goodman Brown, go on; but, prithee, don't kill me with laughing."

"Well, then, to end the matter at once," said Goodman Brown, considerably nettled, "there is my wife, Faith. It would break her dear little heart; and I'd rather break my own."

"Nay, if that be the case," answered the other, "e'en go thy ways, Goodman Brown. I would not for twenty old women like the one hobbling before us that Faith should come to any harm."

As he spoke he pointed his staff at a female figure on the path, in whom Goodman Brown recognized a very pious and exemplary dame, who had taught him his catechism in youth, and was still his moral and spiritual adviser, jointly with the minister and Deacon Gookin.

"A marvel, truly, that Goody Cloyse should be so far in the wilderness at nightfall," said he. "But with your leave, friend, I shall take a cut through the woods until we have left this Christian woman behind. Being a stranger to you, she might ask whom I was consorting with and whither I was going."

"Be it so," said his fellow-traveller. "Betake you to the woods, and let me keep the path."

Accordingly the young man turned aside, but took care to watch his companion, who advanced softly along the road until he had come within a staff's length of the old dame. She, meanwhile, was making the best of her way, with singular speed for so aged a woman, and mumbling some indistinct words—a prayer, doubtless—as she went. The traveller put forth his staff and touched her withered neck with what seemed the serpent's tail.

"The devil!" screamed the pious old lady.

"Then Goody Cloyse knows her old friend?" observed the traveller, confronting her and leaning on his writhing stick.

"Ah, forsooth, and is it your worship indeed?" cried the good dame. "Yea, truly is it, and in the very image of my old gossip, Goodman Brown, the grandfather of the silly fellow that now is. But—would your worship believe it?—my broomstick hath strangely disappeared, stolen, as I suspect, by that unhanged witch, Goody Cory, and that, too, when I was all anointed with the juice of smallage, and cinquefoil, and wolf's bane—"

"Mingled with fine wheat and the fat of a new-born babe," said the shape of old Goodman Brown.

"Ah, your worship knows the recipe," cried the old lady, cackling aloud. "So, as I was saying, being all ready for the meeting, and no horse to ride on, I made up my mind to foot it; for they tell me there is a nice young man to be taken into communion to-night. But now your good worship will lend me your arm, and we shall be there in a twinkling."

"That can hardly be," answered her friend. "I may not spare you my arm, Goody Cloyse; but here is my staff, if you will."

So saying, he threw it down at her feet, where, perhaps, it assumed life, being one of the rods which its owner had formerly lent to the Egyptian magi. Of this fact, however, Goodman Brown could not take cognizance. He had cast up his eyes in astonishment, and, looking down again, beheld neither Goody Cloyse nor the serpentine staff, but his fellow-traveller alone, who waited for him as calmly as if nothing had happened.

"That old woman taught me my catechism," said the young man; and there was a world of meaning in this simple comment.

They continued to walk onward, while the elder traveller exhorted his companion to make good speed and persevere in the path, discoursing so aptly that his arguments seemed rather to spring up in the bosom of his auditor than to be suggested by himself. As they went, he plucked a branch of maple to serve for a walking stick, and began to strip it of the twigs and little boughs, which were wet with evening dew. The moment his fingers touched them they became strangely withered and dried up as with a week's sunshine. Thus the pair proceeded, at a good free pace, until suddenly, in a gloomy hollow of the road, Goodman Brown sat himself down on the stump of a tree and refused to go any farther.

"Friend," said he, stubbornly, "my mind is made up. Not another step will I budge on this errand. What if a wretched old woman do choose to go to the devil when I thought she was going to heaven: is that any reason why I should quit my dear Faith and go after her?"

"You will think better of this by and by," said his acquaintance, composedly. "Sit here and rest yourself a while; and when you feel like moving again, there is my staff to help you along."

Without more words, he threw his companion the maple stick, and was as speedily out of sight as if he had vanished into the deepening gloom. The young man sat a few moments by the roadside, applauding himself greatly, and thinking with how clear a conscience he should meet the minister in his morning walk, nor shrink from the eye of good old Deacon Gookin. And what calm sleep would be his that very night, which was to have been spent so wickedly, but so purely and sweetly now, in the arms of Faith! Amidst these pleasant and praiseworthy meditations, Goodman Brown heard the tramp of horses along the road, and deemed it advisable to conceal himself within the verge of the forest, conscious of the guilty purpose that had brought him thither, though now so happily turned from it.

On came the hoof tramps and the voices of the riders, two grave old voices, conversing soberly as they drew near. These mingled sounds appeared to pass along the road, within a few yards of the young man's hiding-place; but, owing doubtless to the depth of the gloom at that particular spot, neither the travellers nor their steeds were visible. Though their figures brushed the small boughs by the wayside, it could not be seen that they intercepted, even for a moment, the faint gleam from the strip of bright sky athwart which they must have passed. Goodman Brown alternately crouched and stood on tiptoe, pulling aside the branches and thrusting forth his head as far as he durst without discerning so much as a shadow. It vexed him the more, because he could have sworn, were such a thing possible, that he recognized the voices of the minister and Deacon Gookin, jogging along quietly, as they were wont to do, when bound to some ordination or ecclesiastical council. While yet within hearing, one of the riders stopped to pluck a switch.

"Of the two, reverend sir," said the voice like the deacon's, "I had rather miss an ordination dinner than to-night's meeting. They tell me that some of our community are to be here from Falmouth and beyond, and others from Connecticut and Rhode Island, besides several of the Indian powwows, who, after their fashion, know almost as much deviltry as the best of us. Moreover, there is a goodly young woman to be taken into communion."

"Mighty well, Deacon Gookin!" replied the solemn old tones of the minister. "Spur up, or we shall be late. Nothing can be done, you know, until I get on the ground."

The hoofs clattered again; and the voices, talking so strangely in the empty air, passed on through the forest, where no church had ever been gathered or solitary Christian prayed. Whither, then, could these holy men be journeying so deep into the heathen wilderness? Young Goodman Brown caught hold of a tree for support, being ready to sink down on the ground, faint and overburdened with the heavy sickness of his heart. He looked up to the sky, doubting whether there really was a heaven above him. Yet there was the blue arch, and the stars brightening in it.

"With heaven above and Faith below, I will yet stand firm against the devil!" cried Goodman Brown.

While he still gazed upward into the deep arch of the firmament and had lifted his hands to pray, a cloud, though no wind was stirring, hurried across the zenith and hid the brightening stars. The blue sky was still visible, except directly overhead, where this black mass of cloud was sweeping swiftly northward. Aloft in the air, as if from the depths of the cloud, came a confused and doubtful sound of voices. Once the listener fancied that he could distinguish the accents of towns-people of his own, men and women, both pious and ungodly, many of whom he had met at the communion table, and had seen others rioting at the tavern. The next moment, so indistinct were the sounds, he doubted whether he had heard aught but the murmur of the old forest, whispering without a wind. Then came a stronger swell of those familiar tones, heard daily in the sunshine at Salem village, but never until now from a cloud of night. There was one voice of a young woman, uttering lamentations, yet with an uncertain sorrow, and entreating for some favor, which, perhaps, it would grieve her to obtain; and all the unseen multitude, both saints and sinners, seemed to encourage her onward.

"Faith!" shouted Goodman Brown, in a voice of agony and desperation; and the echoes of the forest mocked him, crying, "Faith! Faith!" as if bewildered wretches were seeking her all through the wilderness.

The cry of grief, rage, and terror was yet piercing the night, when the unhappy husband held his breath for a response. There was a scream, drowned immediately in a louder murmur of voices, fading into far-off laughter, as the dark cloud swept away, leaving the clear and silent sky above Goodman Brown. But something fluttered lightly down through the air and caught on the branch of a tree. The young man seized it, and beheld a pink ribbon.

"My Faith is gone!" cried he, after one stupefied moment. "There is no good on earth; and sin is but a name. Come, devil; for to thee is this world given."

And, maddened with despair, so that he laughed loud and long, did Goodman Brown grasp his staff and set forth again, at such a rate that he seemed to fly along the forest path rather than to walk or run. The road grew wilder and drearier and more faintly traced, and vanished at length, leaving him in the heart of the dark wilderness, still rushing onward with the instinct that guides mortal men to evil. The whole forest was peopled with frightful sounds—the creaking of the trees, the howling of wild beasts, and the yell of Indians; while sometimes the wind tolled like a distant church bell, and sometimes gave a broad roar around the traveller, as if all Nature were laughing him to scorn. But he was himself the chief horror of the scene, and shrank not from its other horrors.

"Ha! ha! ha!" roared Goodman Brown when the wind laughed at him. "Let us hear which will laugh loudest. Think not to frighten me with your deviltry. Come witch, come wizard, come Indian powwow, come devil himself, and here comes Goodman Brown. You may as well fear him as he fear you."

In truth, all through the haunted forest there could be nothing more frightful than the figure of Goodman Brown. On he flew among the black pines, brandishing his staff with frenzied gestures, now giving vent to an inspiration of horrid blasphemy, and now shouting forth such laughter as set all the echoes of the forest laughing like demons around him. The fiend in his own shape is less hideous than when he rages in the breast of man. Thus sped the demoniac on his course, until, quivering among the trees, he saw a red light before him, as when the felled trunks and branches of a clearing have been set on fire, and throw up their lurid blaze against the sky, at the hour of midnight. He paused, in a lull of the tempest that had driven him onward, and heard the swell of what seemed a hymn, rolling solemnly from a distance with the weight of many voices. He knew the tune; it was a familiar one in the choir of the village meeting-house. The verse died heavily away, and was lengthened by a chorus, not of human voices, but of all the sounds of the benighted wilderness pealing in awful harmony together. Goodman Brown cried out, and his cry was lost to his own ear by its unison with the cry of the desert.

In the interval of silence he stole forward until the light glared full upon his eyes. At one extremity of an open space, hemmed in by the dark wall of the forest, arose a rock, bearing some rude, natural resemblance either to an altar or a pulpit, and surrounded by four blazing pines, their tops aflame, their stems untouched, like candles at an evening meeting. The mass of foliage that had overgrown the summit of the rock was all on fire, blazing high into the night and fitfully illuminating the whole field. Each pendent twig and leafy festoon was in a blaze. As the red light arose and fell, a numerous congregation alternately shone forth, then disappeared in shadow, and again grew, as it were, out of the darkness, peopling the heart of the solitary woods at once.

"A grave and dark-clad company," quoth Goodman Brown.

In truth they were such. Among them, quivering to and fro between gloom and splendor, appeared faces that would be seen next day at the council board of the province, and others which, Sabbath after Sabbath, looked devoutly heavenward, and benignantly over the crowded pews, from the holiest pulpits in the land. Some affirm that the lady of the governor was there. At least there were high dames well known to her, and wives of honored husbands, and widows, a great multitude, and ancient maidens, all of excellent repute, and fair young girls, who trembled lest their mothers should espy them. Either the sudden gleams of light flashing over the obscure field bedazzled Goodman Brown, or he recognized a score of the church members of Salem village famous for their especial sanctity. Good old Deacon Gookin had arrived, and waited at the skirts of that venerable saint, his revered pastor. But, irreverently consorting with these grave, reputable, and pious people, these elders of the church, these chaste dames and dewy virgins, there were men of dissolute lives and women of spotted fame, wretches given over to all mean and filthy vice, and suspected even of horrid crimes. It was strange to see that the good shrank not from the wicked, nor were the sinners abashed by the saints. Scattered also among their pale-faced enemies were the Indian priests, or powwows, who had often scared their native forest with more hideous incantations than any known to English witchcraft.

"But where is Faith?" thought Goodman Brown; and, as hope came into his heart, he trembled.

Another verse of the hymn arose, a slow and mournful strain, such as the pious love, but joined to words which expressed all that our nature can conceive of sin, and darkly hinted at far more. Unfathomable to mere mortals is the lore of fiends. Verse after verse was sung; and still the chorus of the desert swelled between like the deepest tone of a mighty organ; and with the final peal of that dreadful anthem there came a sound, as if the roaring wind, the rushing streams, the howling beasts, and every other voice of the unconcerted wilderness were mingling and according with the voice of guilty man in homage to the prince of all. The four blazing pines threw up a loftier flame, and obscurely discovered shapes and visages of horror on the smoke wreaths above the impious assembly. At the same moment the fire on the rock shot redly forth and formed a glowing arch above its base, where now appeared a figure. With reverence be it spoken, the figure bore no slight similitude, both in garb and manner, to some grave divine of the New England churches.

"Bring forth the converts!" cried a voice that echoed through the field and rolled into the forest.

At the word, Goodman Brown stepped forth from the shadow of the trees and approached the congregation, with whom he felt a loathful brotherhood by the sympathy of all that was wicked in his heart. He could have well-nigh sworn that the shape of his own dead father beckoned him to advance, looking downward from a smoke wreath, while a woman, with dim features of despair, threw out her hand to warn him back. Was it his mother? But he had no power to retreat one step, nor to resist, even in thought, when the minister and good old Deacon Gookin seized his arms and led him to the blazing rock. Thither came also the slender form of a veiled female, led between Goody Cloyse, that pious teacher of the catechism, and Martha Carrier, who had received the devil's promise to be queen of hell. A rampant hag was she. And there stood the proselytes beneath the canopy of fire.

"Welcome, my children," said the dark figure, "to the communion of your race. Ye have found thus young your nature and your destiny. My children, look behind you!"

They turned; and flashing forth, as it were, in a sheet of flame, the fiend worshippers were seen; the smile of welcome gleamed darkly on every visage.

"There," resumed the sable form, "are all whom ye have reverenced from youth. Ye deemed them holier than yourselves, and shrank from your own sin, contrasting it with their lives of righteousness and prayerful aspirations heavenward. Yet here are they all in my worshipping assembly. This night it shall be granted you to know their secret deeds: how hoary-bearded elders of the church have whispered wanton words to the young maids of their households; how many a woman, eager for widows' weeds, has given her husband a drink at bedtime and let him sleep his last sleep in her bosom; how beardless youths have made haste to inherit their fathers' wealth; and how fair damsels—blush not, sweet ones—have dug little graves in the garden, and bidden me, the sole guest, to an infant's funeral. By the sympathy of your human hearts for sin ye shall scent out all the places—whether in church, bedchamber, street, field, or forest—where crime has been committed, and shall exult to behold the whole earth one stain of guilt, one mighty blood spot. Far more than this. It shall be yours to penetrate, in every bosom, the deep mystery of sin, the fountain of all wicked arts, and which inexhaustibly supplies more evil impulses than human power—than my power at its utmost—can make manifest in deeds. And now, my children, look upon each other."

They did so; and, by the blaze of the hell-kindled torches, the wretched man beheld his Faith, and the wife her husband, trembling before that unhallowed altar.

"Lo, there ye stand, my children," said the figure, in a deep and solemn tone, almost sad with its despairing awfulness, as if his once angelic nature could yet mourn for our miserable race. "Depending upon one another's hearts, ye had still hoped that virtue were not all a dream. Now are ye undeceived. Evil is the nature of mankind. Evil must be your only happiness. Welcome again, my children, to the communion of your race."

"Welcome," repeated the fiend worshippers, in one cry of despair and triumph.

And there they stood, the only pair, as it seemed, who were yet hesitating on the verge of wickedness in this dark world. A basin was hollowed, naturally, in the rock. Did it contain water, reddened by the lurid light? or was it blood? or, perchance, a liquid flame? Herein did the shape of evil dip his hand and prepare to lay the mark of baptism upon their foreheads, that they might be partakers of the mystery of sin, more conscious of the secret guilt of others, both in deed and thought, than they could now be of their own. The husband cast one look at his pale wife, and Faith at him. What polluted wretches would the next glance show them to each other, shuddering alike at what they disclosed and what they saw!

"Faith! Faith!" cried the husband, "look up to heaven, and resist the wicked one."

Whether Faith obeyed he knew not. Hardly had he spoken when he found himself amid calm night and solitude, listening to a roar of the wind which died heavily away through the forest. He staggered against the rock, and felt it chill and damp; while a hanging twig, that had been all on fire, besprinkled his cheek with the coldest dew.

The next morning young Goodman Brown came slowly into the street of Salem village, staring around him like a bewildered man. The good old minister was taking a walk along the graveyard to get an appetite for breakfast and meditate his sermon, and bestowed a blessing, as he passed, on Goodman Brown. He shrank from the venerable saint as if to avoid an anathema. Old Deacon Gookin was at domestic worship, and the holy words of his prayer were heard through the open window. "What God doth the wizard pray to?" quoth Goodman Brown. Goody Cloyse, that excellent old Christian, stood in the early sunshine at her own lattice, catechizing a little girl who had brought her a pint of morning's milk. Goodman Brown snatched away the child as from the grasp of the fiend himself. Turning the corner by the meeting-house, he spied the head of Faith, with the pink ribbons, gazing anxiously forth, and bursting into such joy at sight of him that she skipped along the street and almost kissed her husband before the whole village. But Goodman Brown looked sternly and sadly into her face, and passed on without a greeting.

Had Goodman Brown fallen asleep in the forest and only dreamed a wild dream of a witch-meeting?

Be it so if you will; but, alas! it was a dream of evil omen for young Goodman Brown. A stern, a sad, a darkly meditative, a distrustful, if not a desperate man did he become from the night of that fearful dream. On the Sabbath day, when the congregation were singing a holy psalm, he could not listen because an anthem of sin rushed loudly upon his ear and drowned all the blessed strain. When the minister spoke from the pulpit with power and fervid eloquence, and, with his hand on the open Bible, of the sacred truths of our religion, and of saint-like lives and triumphant deaths, and of future bliss or misery unutterable, then did Goodman Brown turn pale, dreading lest the roof should thunder down upon the gray blasphemer and his hearers. Often, waking suddenly at midnight, he shrank from the bosom of Faith; and at morning or eventide, when the family knelt down at prayer, he scowled and muttered to himself, and gazed sternly at his wife, and turned away. And when he had lived long, and was borne to his grave a hoary corpse, followed by Faith, an aged woman, and children and grandchildren, a goodly procession, besides neighbors not a few, they carved no hopeful verse upon his tombstone, for his dying hour was gloom.

CRITICAL COMMENTS

Malcolm Cowley:

"Young Goodman Brown" is the greatest of Hawthorne's stories. It is a parable into which one can read several meanings, but the chief of them is that a young man conscious of his own guilt may suddenly find himself in a vast confraternity of the damned. "Evil is the nature of mankind," Satan tells the good man and his wife as they stand before an unholy altar. "Welcome again, my children, to the communion of your race." [1]

[1] From *The Portable Hawthorne*, edited by Malcolm Cowley (New York: The Viking Press, 1948), p. 28, reprinted by permission of the publisher.

Henry James:

When he [Hawthorne] was lightest at heart, he was most creative, and when he was most creative, the moral picturesqueness of the old secret of mankind in general and of the Puritans in particular most appealed to him—the secret that we are really not by any means so good as a well-regulated society requires us to appear. It is not too much to say, even, that the very condition of production of some of these unamiable tales would be that they should be superficial, and, as it were, insincere. The magnificent little romance of "Young Goodman Brown," for instance, evidently means nothing as regards Hawthorne's own state of mind, his conviction of human depravity and his constant melancholy; for the simple reason that if it meant anything, it would mean too much. Mr. Lathrop speaks of it as a "terrible and lurid parable"; but this, it seems to me, is just what it is not. It is not a parable, but a picture, which is a very different thing.[2]

Mark Van Doren:

Nothing that Hawthorne wrote came from a deeper source—not even *The Scarlet Letter,* in whose pages it lives again. It is one of the world's great tales, and for a more serious reason than Henry James supposed. James, who thought it a "magnificent little romance," hastened to deny its depth; for he was committed to the theory that Hawthorne had only an aesthetic interest in evil, so that "Young Goodman Brown," for instance, must be "not a parable but a picture." It is a perfect picture, and hence needs to have no more meaning than one wishes to think it has. If it is a parable it is perfect too, for no statement of its meaning could be as short as it is, or as interesting. It "evidently means nothing," James insists, "as regards Hawthorne's own state of mind, his conviction of human depravity and his consequent melancholy; for the simple reason that, if it meant anything, it would mean too much." Too much, that is, for Henry James. . . . "Young Goodman Brown" means exactly what it says, namely that its hero left his pretty wife one evening—left her with the wind playing among the pink ribbons at her head—to walk by himself in the primitive New England woods, the Devil's territory where black anthems made nightly music; and either to dream or actually to experience (Hawthorne will not say) the discovery that evil exists in every human heart. The older man whom he soon meets, and who looks something like his father, has "an indescribable air of one who knew the world." He is the Devil, walking there with Goodman Brown—or is it but a dream?—to waken in his soul the consciousness of sin, his own and

[2] From *Hawthorne,* by Henry James (New York: Harper and Brothers, 1879), p. 99, reprinted by permission of John Farquharson, Ltd., on behalf of the Estate of the late Henry James.

every other person's. The shadow of sin falls upon his ancestors who persecuted Quakers and murdered Indians in mass; upon saintly elders who still live; and finally upon Faith. . . .

Few things in fiction are more startling, or more important, than this pink ribbon. Is it there, or is it only dreamed? If it is there, what explanation can there be save the one young Brown accepts? The Devil exists, and Faith has become one of his converts. All three answers come at once, in a texture of fact and implication which Hawthorne has woven as closely as life is woven. The ribbon may not be there, but in that case this is no ordinary dream, no nightmare . . . which will be gone tomorrow. For Brown is changed. He thinks there is no good on earth, "and sin is but a name." . . . He has stumbled upon the "mystery of sin" which, rightly understood, provides the only sane and cheerful view of life there is. Understood in Brown's fashion, it darkens and sours the world, withering hope and charity, and perverting whatever is truly good until it looks like evil at its worst: like blasphemy and hypocrisy. . . . "Young Goodman Brown" is not a statement, it is a story. It is so good a story that readers of it must rarely be tempted to decide what it means. But it means so much because it is so good a story; because the pink ribbon, mentioned several times near the beginning, is not mentioned again until it falls out of the sky; because the sounds of this special world are so brilliantly, so heart-breakingly orchestrated; because the hum of a supernatural energy is authentic from beginning to end; because, in short, Hawthorne neglected no triumph of his art in the service of whatever idea it was that possessed him.[3]

F. O. Matthiessen:

Hawthorne's main concern with this material is to use it to develop the theme that mere doubt of the existence of good, the thought that all other men are evil, can become such a corrosive force as to eat out the life of the heart. In handling the question of what the young man really saw during his night in the forest, Hawthorne's imagination is at its most delicately masterful. . . . As long as what Brown saw is left wholly in the realm of hallucination, Hawthorne's created illusion is compelling. For the symbolical truth of what the young man had conjured up in his bewildered vision is heightened by the fact that when he staggered against one of the burning trees, its twigs were cold with dew. The dramatization of his spiritual loss in the form of the agonized struggle and disappearance of his wife allows the description of the inner experience to become concrete, and also doubles its application. Only the literal insistence on that damaging pink ribbon obtrudes the labels of a confining allegory, and short-circuits the range of association.[4]

Thomas E. Connolly:

Young Goodman Brown did not lose his faith (we are even told that his Faith survived him); he learned its full and terrible significance. This story is Hawthorne's criticism of the teachings of Puritanic Calvinism. His implication is that the doctrine of the elect and damned is not a faith which carries man heavenward on its skirts, as Brown once believed, but, instead, condemns him to hell —bad and good alike indiscriminately—and for all intents and purposes so few escape as to make man's chance of salvation almost disappear. It is this awakening to the full meaning of his faith which causes Young Goodman Brown to look upon his minister as a blasphemer . . . for he has learned that according to the truths of his faith there is probably nothing but "misery unutterable" in store for him and all his congregation; it is this awakening which causes him to turn away from prayer; it is this awakening which makes appropriate the fact that "they carved no hopeful verse upon his tombstone." [5]

Caroline Gordon and Allen Tate:

In "Young Goodman Brown," one of his best stories, Hawthorne is dealing with his favorite theme: the unhappiness which the human heart suffers as the result of its innate depravity. . . . The dramatic impact would have been stronger if Hawthorne had let the incidents tell their own story: Goodman Brown's behavior to his neighbors and finally to his wife *show* us that he is a changed man . . . But Hawthorne's weakness for moralizing and his insufficient technical equipment betray him into the anticlimax of the last paragraph.

. . . Brown was willing to lend his own soul to the Devil for a night, but he cannot face the discovery that every other soul has a similar desire and, having lost his faith to the Devil, comes to hate his fellow man.[6]

[4] From *American Renaissance,* by F. O. Matthiessen (New York: Oxford University Press, 1941), pp. 283–284, reprinted by permission of the publisher.

[5] From "Hawthorne's 'Young Goodman Brown': An Attack on Puritanic Calvinism," by Thomas E. Connolly, *American Literature,* XXVIII, No. 3 (November, 1956), p. 375, reprinted by permission of the publisher.

[6] From *The House of Fiction,* by Caroline Gordon and Allen Tate (New York: Charles Scribner's Sons, 1950), pp. 38–39, reprinted by permission of the publisher.

Wounds

~ *Edward Loomis*

A rifle-bullet striking bone hits with a fine hardness, followed instantly by a numbing shock; and then down you go.

When it happened to me, I felt my left leg for blood, thinking to gauge the wound, but could not do it, for the blood was running imperceptibly in my heavy trousers already soaked with the rain. I moved the knee, where the bullet had hit, and said to the man ahead of me: "I think maybe I'm hit, by God! Now what do you think of that?"

It was a November night in the south of Holland, with low gray clouds billowing voluminously close to earth. In the flash of a shell bursting you could see the pale misty bottoms of the clouds, and the rains came stirring out of them against your face with a feeling of impalpable moist depths. Up ahead of me were woods, from which the rifle shot had come; behind me a ditch, its waters flowing black like sooty Acheron itself; and all around me was the war—my war, one of the old ones now—littering the earth, making an ominous dark.

I lay with my face to the ground, padded where my cheek touched it by leaf mold and withered grasses; we were in a pasture, surely, and there was a soft wind. In a little while it was time to go on, and so I rose, finding that I was not badly hurt, but continued marching through the night. Now and then I wondered that a bullet could knock me down and still bounce away, but I was growing used to perplexity and did not mind it. I had no thought of taking my sulfa tablets, for I wanted to save them for a major wound.

Toward morning we dug holes that started water seeping from the earth like wells, and when the dawn came we discovered ourselves in a cultivated field, plowed now and harrowed down, that was bordered on two sides by a dike lined with poplars, and on the third by a clump of houses. These were gray houses, blurred by a faintly falling rain; there were narrow windows and doors, and tile roofs the color of dirty copper. Each house had its trees, black and unidentifiable, glistening with the perpetual damp. The people were gone, I was sure, from those houses five hundred yards away, who have now long since returned to make the fields ripen again in heavy crops of sugar beets and grain.

There was no sign of life, though we had been told that Germans held the houses, and so that morning I thought about the farmers, hiding with their families. It was possible they hid in haystacks, or in the little pine forests of that country, and I could guess how it might be for them, for each chilly family huddled beneath a dripping tree. But of course they were far away; they did not exist, and at nine o'clock that morning came something which did, a British plane, strafing the houses for us. In an instant I had eyes for nothing else.

The plane was a Spitfire, of slim body and wide wings curved at the tips, and its course was to swoop low, fire the machine guns, and rise again. I crouched in my hole, legs folded into the water at the hole's bottom, and stared upward with joy. On the plane's second pass there was an answer from behind the houses, the steady, jarring hammer of 20-millimeter anti-aircraft guns firing synchronously; there would be a flak wagon behind the houses, that was it, a tracked vehicle with four guns in a turret, and so I grew frightened for the plane and its pilot.

But for two more passes the plane came low and then roared away in safety. I rejoiced, and forgot the icy chill gripping my feet and lower legs. The sound of the motor was loud and sweet on the downswing, and I could almost feel the delicate sheen of oil masking each working part in that slick harmony; I could sense the pistons firing in a row, and the electric messages of control vibrating along the wires. And of course I had a notion of the pilot, who would be a thin-faced Englishman like some of the British infantry officers I had seen; he would have a soft voice, and a deprecating way of moving his hands, and be from Kent perhaps, or Lancashire, places I knew from training days.

And then the plane was hit, on the fourth pass, as it was pulling out: one moment there was the screaming sound from the motor as the pilot started his climb, and then there was a silence, hoarse with meaning. The plane climbed ever more steeply, until it became apparent that the arc of its climb would fall back into a circle leading to a crash. Quite distinctly I made out the markings on the upper surfaces of the wings: there were the emblematic rings of white and royal blue and red, and numbers in heavy block forms. For an instant there was a soft glitter on the hood over the cockpit, an aerial shadow of death.

Who was that pilot? I could never know. At the beauty of his fall I sighed. Down he came, and there was a crash at which any man might blink.

Deeply I flung myself into my hole, bringing my forehead close to the earthy smell of water. After the crash there was an explosion, and then the familiar sound of splintered metal going by, a rough *whirroo* that leaves a hard quiet in the wake of its passing. Cautiously I looked out of my hole and saw, not a hundred yards away, the wreckage with smoke clumped upon it and slowly rising. There was nothing to do or say; the man was dead. In the shallow pool of water nearest my hole I observed a few patches of oil film, spattered there by the explosion. They widened; they grew floating there, unchanged by damp, in subtle colors I could not really see. There was a smoky blue perhaps, and a touch of orange or red; the colors had a perfect polish and no reflection in the gray morning.

Later that day another company attacked the houses, and we moved on to the dike with the poplars, where we stayed for a time in shallow holes. Toward nightfall a barrage of 120-millimeter mortars fell on the dike, killing the two men in the hole next to me, and thus stirring the officers to move again. We climbed out of our holes, and I looked at the bodies laid out under somebody's shelter-half; the feet projected from under the canvas, toes up, and the feet looked alive; one left foot was naked and bloody, the shoe blown clean off, exposing the horny toenails of the infantryman. We marched a long time that night, and finally arrived at the still-burning ruins of a barn, near which we dug holes again, for the third time that day.

There was an orchard all around the barn; little trees with sleek black trunks stood there in crooked rows, and our holes went down into a heavy earth that had a pleasant fragrance of rotted apples. The resiny smell of burning timbers carried to me a memory of campfires, and so it was not long before I had the feeling of holiday. My knee was stiffening, and I was wet and cold, but I became cheerful, and with a friend named Curry I decided to go closer to the tumbled fires of the barn. Our idea was to warm ourselves, and we were happy with that idea.

"If there's any shelling, we can duck back to our holes," Curry said. "But I'll bet the Germans are just as tired as we are."

"It's a fool thing to do," I said. "But let's do it. Damn it, I want to do it!"

Cautiously we made our way, staying clear of the German side of the fire so that we would not make silhouettes; and we were stopped only once in our progress, when a horse came charging through the position. There was a commotion behind us; the horse came looming into the light of the fire, clumsily galloping, swaying from side to side. He was high and dark, and somehow marred, moving like a creature stiff-jointed and old, and he stumbled against one of the little trees; then he screamed in terror, and we could see that he was badly burned. He had no mane or tail, and carried a sweet smell of burnt flesh into our holiday air. Again he crashed into a tree, and screamed, and then we knew he was blind. His eyes were singed wounds in his bony head, and he tossed his head as he galloped, as if to shake away the terrible darkness.

He galloped through the position from one end to the other, and disappeared into the night. I was a little shaken, but Curry restored my confidence. "Somebody'll shoot the old thing before morning," he said, "and put him out of his misery. Sure they will."

In a few moments we were back on our quest, and very quickly found what we wanted, an orderly fire, burning in a little stack of the poles used in that country to prop hayricks. It was warm there, and you could stand close without discomfort; and there was shelter from German eyes in a still-untumbled corner of the old barn itself.

"This is the place," Curry said. "By God, I'm going to take off my shoes and pants and get 'em dry."

We set about it, and in fact we stripped off all our clothes, in a gesture of high spirits, and set them out to dry. We drove stakes and placed our shoes and socks on them; I improvised a coat-rack for the shirts and jackets, and Curry arranged a way of stretching trousers between pairs of stakes. We had a game of co-operation, and so in a little while it was possible to enjoy feelings of harmony and peace.

Curry was not my best friend in the squad, but he was a good friend, and we had an understanding. He came from the same sort of family I had come from, and from the same sort of town. He had two brothers and a sister; his father was a purchasing agent, his mother had been to a small college in Michigan; and he lived in a suburb of Detroit. He had been drafted from the University of Michigan three months before his nineteenth birthday, and now he was awaiting his twentieth birthday. We were two of a kind; we understood that we were fortunate in everything except being in the war, and we were getting used to that; and of course we were pleased to be together, to be able to exchange identical sentiments about the unhappy incidents of our life.

Soon we had canned rations bubbling on the embers at the edge of the fire, and all about us were clouds of steam rising from our clothes. Naked we could stand the cold air of night, and even enjoy it; the wind raised gooseflesh on skin grown oily and bitterly resistant. We sparred a little, and in doing this I got several twinges in the knee that only made me happier. I looked at my wound, which was two small holes, each well covered by a crisp black scab, and a moderate swelling to the left of the kneecap. The wound was genuine, clearly, and yet no hindrance to lightheartedness and running.

Ah, that was a time! We leaped in and out of the firelight in that cold soft Holland air, and ate our rations as children eat at picnics, voraciously, so as to gain a quick release to the games of the woods. We were fierce, like children, and felt scorn for our friends crouching in holes, their bodies clotted in damp cloth. Indeed, we were happy, and I will never forget the feeling.

An end came, as it had to, but at first it seemed not serious. A light shelling of 120-millimeter mortars began to fall on the edges of the orchard, and as we headed for the holes we had dug, it was plain that the pattern was moving toward the fire. We left our clothes, naturally, and ran naked, crouching close to earth, and there was no danger, for we had time. The holes were close to us, not twenty yards away, and we were all but safe until Curry fell. Perhaps his bare foot caught on something a heavy shoe would have brushed aside; perhaps he stepped on a hot ember and by flinching from it lost his balance; but he fell, and the pattern of the barrage abruptly included him.

It was a light barrage. Moments after I reached my hole, where one of my other friends was waiting for me with arms braced to catch some of the shock of my diving fall, the barrage was over, and I rose quickly to see what had happened behind me. I was breathing sharply, feeling excited and happy, and so I needed a few moments before I could see clearly. Meanwhile I heard Curry's voice speaking rapidly in a normal tone, though I could not distinguish words. I was perplexed; I looked around, and called the word "Curry" several times into the hush which follows a barrage.

Then I saw him. Like a white flower in the night was the whiteness of his body, and very clearly I saw a spout of blood rising from the base of his throat, And heard him: "Lordy, Lordy," he said, "somebody, the blood's going out of me like water out of a hose. For God's sake, somebody, come help me. Do you want me to die here like a stuck pig?" The tone was almost humorous, and showed the control of the considerate patient who wants not to be a bother.

"I'm coming!" I shouted. "Curry, Curry, I'm coming, hold on!"

I scrambled out of the hole and started for him, charging low as if to knock something down with my shoulders; and I had made perhaps eight or nine yards of the distance when I heard the whispering fall of a mortar shell as the barrage began again. Down I went, as I had been taught, to hide myself against the stained old earth; flat on my belly, hands over my head, and listening to the explosions and whistling flights of shrapnel. The barrage was a little heavier this time, but shorter, and I scarcely had time to think about it before it was over.

I got to my feet a little slowly, with belly and chest darkly washed by a fine, silt-like mud, and began to trot toward Curry, but even before I reached him I saw that there would be no reason for haste. He had been hit again, and was dead now. He lay on his back, arms outspread against the rainy Holland earth. His hands and face were dark, with the weathering that comes to the devoted infantryman.

I could not see the wound that had first caught him; there was no spout of blood to define it now, and a wrinkled sheet of blood was settling all along his throat and collarbone and down his right shoulder. The wounds of the second barrage I could scarcely miss, for they were a great slash across his right thigh and a rip all across his belly, out of which now tumbled bowels and intestines.

Quickly I saw it all, and will not forget it, the death, the great wounds, the white body and scarcely used sex of this boy who had so great a part of his life ahead of him when he died.

In a little while other soldiers came, and a blanket was stretched over the body. I went back to the fire in the hayrick poles and slowly dressed myself, not brushing away the mud from my chest and belly. I was feeling sad, and empty, as I have since felt a few times after rising from women.

Before I went to my hole for sleep, I dressed the body of my friend in the clothes which had dried while he was dying. I wanted whatever was left of him not to be cold, and so I did what had to be done with his spilled guts, and bundled the slippery coils back into the still-warm cage of muscle and tough hide. I got him together, and got him dressed, and thus had what I wanted, the feeling that I had done the few things left me to do.

And then I went back to my hole and started to be cold in a way I had not known before. That night I shivered with cold for the first time in my life, and it seemed to me that I could feel the moist night air seeping into my bones, corrupting the sweet, secret marrow. It was a fancy, but the next morning I was stiff and ailing, and had trouble making the day's march.

I had a recovery to make from Curry's death, however, and so I worked away at it, and was beginning to succeed by four o'clock, when my knee started an action very like the throbbing of blood, except that it was pain moving there. I was glad to have the pain, for it seemed a way of getting along with Curry's death, a way of settling accounts with whatever powers might be.

Also it was true that the pain persuaded me that my wound might soon be serious enough to take me out of the war for a while, and that was a thought which must cheer any soldier of the infantry. Toward dark we stopped near a big farm and were told that we might expect the company cooks that night with hot food and newspapers, and so we knew that our war was about to cease for a little while. We had seen no firing all that day; we were growing cheerful; we dug great holes, and found pleasure in the labor.

I dug with my friend Olney Arnett, a Tennesseean, and we constructed a masterpiece of comfort in the field. We were on a little hill, and so we could go deep without getting water; we went down four and a half feet, in a hole seven feet long and almost five feet wide. We thatched the bottom to a depth of a foot and a half with fragrant hay taken from the barn at the top of the hill, and covered everything against the rain with our two shelter-halves draped across a pole stolen from the same barn.

We had a rough equivalent of a cabin with roof and ridgepole; we fastened the sides of the shelter-halves with well-packed heaps of dirt, and were ready to weather out a gale. "It's the best hole we've had for a week or more," Arnett said. "Just think how it's going to be to sleep in it tonight!"

A furry little mist was in the air, to moisten the face and the backs of hands, but we were sure there would be heavy rain that night, for there was always heavy rain in those nights. We would need our cave. In constructing it, we had achieved something good, and so we could have the pleasure of shared accomplishment. Arnett had for some time been my best friend in the squad, and therefore in the world, though we were not at all like each other; and so my pleasure in the task was augmented by the pleasure of having Arnett take part in it. He was a farm boy who had subtle arts of whittling with a pocket knife sharp as a razor; he knew bird cries, and the Tennessee names for all the trees and grasses of ancient Europe; he came from an old people long rooted in a single country, and he knew strange songs that puzzled me. He was a sturdy boy, not the kind to give in to his circumstances; braver than I, and more calm, so that he could regard the details of our life in the war with a reluctant good humor, where I was given to furious rages.

We were at odds in everything except the necessary arts of living together, but in these we could be at peace. Having finished our hole, we walked like loving brothers to the farmhouse where I had been told to come for treatment of my knee. There we found an agreeable officer who made arrangements for hot water and cloths; he was the platoon leader of the second rifle platoon of our company, and thus it was an act of special condescension for him to forsake his responsibilities to think about easing my pain.

It was a trick to get my trousers down past the huge swelling that had come into my knee, but we managed it, and then Arnett moistened pads of clean white cloth into compresses, which he laid delicately over the sore places. I sat in a chair, with my left leg propped on another, and might have been a little king of that high, narrow room.

Close to my hand was a fire burning in a little porcelain stove. On top of the stove was a canteen cup of coffee, prepared especially for me, with a little of the lieutenant's whisky in it for flavor and comfort, and a big pot of water for the compresses. There had been no destruction in the room; the woodwork in windows and wall moldings was highly polished and dark; the chairs which ringed the old table were plain and hard, but not uncomfortable, and there were two steel engravings on the walls, each showing a skater dashing brilliantly down the winter ice of a canal. It was a Dutch interior, immaculately polished and rich, and not much altered by the litter of soldiers. Rifles leaning against the walls did not really change the look of it, but they were sufficiently present so that I could have a momentary sense of belonging to the room. I was at ease, and could have been happy greeting guests.

When the cooks arrived outside in their two-and-a-half-ton truck, Arnett went to them and got a noble supper for me. I had tomatoes, bread, and two kinds of meat, with a sweet stimulant composed of one part canned milk and sugar, and one part black coffee. The tears almost came to my eyes as I sat in the hot room holding the heavy cup. My skin was alive with the pleasure of warmth; my whole system was growing soft and joyous in the pleasure of being tended to. Two hours I spent in this way before I had to go outside again, and when I left I felt fortified and strong. The cold air, blown against my face by the night wind in such a way as to suggest the rain which was coming, only served to remind me that I had a fine shelter to take myself to, and so I joked with Arnett and even made fun of his country ways as we walked slowly along. When we got to the hole, Arnett offered to take part of my guard that night, and I accepted; I would keep watch for the first three hours, until midnight, and then he would be responsible for the rest of the night. I was grateful, and thanked him.

At the open end of the hole I propped myself up and set my rifle on its sling, sights up, the barrel pointing north. Beside it I placed my three grenades and Arnett's two. For a while I listened to Arnett burrowing in the hay on his side of the hole, and then, when there were no more noises from him, I occupied myself in watching the sky. At ten-thirty I was dismayed to see the sky grow clear, exposing a crystalline darkness and a few stars. I was angry, thinking there might be no rain to test the cave and give me the sounds of rain addressing a roof above my weary head. For half an hour I had this distress, and suffered bitterly, until the sky closed again and I could prepare myself for enjoyment.

At midnight I woke Arnett, and he rose cheerfully. He arranged his hay so that he could sit wrapped in it to the waist while he was keeping guard, and then said good night to me and began softly to hum an old tune.

I was ready for sleep as I crawled slowly into my hay. Deep in it was the musty fragrance of summer; I distinguished three kinds of flower smells, and even found, with darkened fingers, a dry little bur soft to the touch that might have been a clover blossom. As I settled myself, I could feel a pollenous dust crossing the skin of my face and tickling the back of my neck under the shirt collar. I became dry in feeling, as if I too had lain curing through the wet autumn, in the high old barn on the hill.

In a little while I became warm also, and therefore ready for bliss, but for a while no bliss came. My left leg was stiff and sore from the ankle far up into the thigh, and there was an untouchable coldness in the toes of my left foot. There was a steady pain. I could not sleep, and in my wakefulness I remembered the tragic stories of my soldier's life.

I grew angry; there was no rain, and so I softly cursed the weather, for a long time, until at last the rain began. It came hard and beating, just what I wanted, and yet it did not bring me sleep. I heard the drumming on the canvas, and in the not-quite-thorough darkness of a night in the midst of war I could just make out the canvas sagging with the accruing weight of water. I had what I wanted, and yet it did not suffice, and so my spirit for a while approached despair.

Disappointments were severe in those troubled days. I was having an unpleasant time in that sweet hay, and then a thing happened that changed everything in an instant. The heavy rain at last grew too much for the moorings of the shelter-half on Arnett's side of the hole; he had stretched the canvas too near the horizontal, and left no way for the water to run off, and so there were surely ten gallons of water gathered above his head. I did not see what happened, of course, for my eyes were closed, but I knew what it was. Arnett, sitting motionless, his face composed under his helmet, eyes watching out into the night, was allowing himself to remember his mother's face, perhaps, or the look of her kitchen; and then the shelter-half pulled free and loosed those gallons of Holland rain on his head like a flood sent from on high.

"Gre't God A-mighty!" Arnett said, spluttering like one drowning. I opened my eyes and saw instantly what had happened: Arnett was floundering, shaking his dripping head and shoulders like old Neptune himself rising out of troubled waters. He tried standing up, and said: "My God, I'm drownded, the goddamned roof. . . ." And then he sat down again, his haunches splashing. "Oh, no," he groaned. "Oh, goddamned no!" Weakly he raised his right arm and then let it fall. "I'm all wet," he said. "And on a night like this I'll never get dry!"

I half sat up, but then my leg hurt sharply, making me fall back. I shivered, and raised my shoulders, awaiting the shock of icy waters from Arnett's disaster, and for a moment I felt a savage fury that he had been so clumsy in building his side of the roof. "God damn it, Arnett," I called, and then stopped out of regard for our friendship. "Arnett?" I said again. It came to me that I was not yet dampened, and this was an enormous surprise. Cautiously I felt around in my hay, looking for signs of water; but there were none.

"Arnett," I said. "My God, I'm dry! It all fell on you, you poor bastard!"

"Son of a bitch!" Arnett shouted. He was standing now, thrashing his arms about wildly. "Son of a bitch! Son of a bitch! You goddamned water, you rain, may you fairly die, you goddamn, cold, mis'able water!"

His hands fell to his sides, and he shook his head. "Oh, no," he said. "And I done so many *good* deeds today." Slumped over, he stood without moving, and suddenly I began to laugh.

He had helped me, he was the best friend I had in all the world, but I laughed at his misfortune as I have rarely laughed in my life. Tired and dejected, he stood without answering while I laughed with fury. After a long time he threw his wet hay out of the hole and sat down again, on the bare ground, to resume his guard, and I laughed even then. His silence was nothing to me; I could not care; and long after the night had grown quiet again I was still chuckling, deep in my warm hay smelling dryly of wild flowers and clover.

I went to sleep without our speaking to each other again, and I slept a flowing, tide-like sleep that carried me with perfect ease into the wakening chill of the next morning. It was joyous sleep, and I was presiding over it as it happened, with some part of me that will be forever wakeful. I had enjoyment, and knew I was having it, and knew further that no man could ask for more from the earth and the curious things which grow upon it.

I woke in the morning cheerful, with the full expectation that my life would soon improve in all its conditions. I was certain that good luck was coming; and so it did. Arnett had got over his disaster, and held nothing against me, so that we were friends as before. He helped me out of the hole, and caught me when I fell; he was sympathetic when it became apparent that I would not be able to walk all the way to breakfast at the cooks' truck.

I was a cripple now; there was nothing left me but to say good-by to my friends and go to the hospitals. I went with the cooks, sitting in the cab of the truck with the driver and the mess sergeant. I was sorrowful at leaving all my old friends, but anxious to see what the hospitals had to offer, and so I traveled in great serenity of spirit; and of course it happened that the hospitals offered a great deal, enough to please any rational man, any soldier of the infantry.

At the first hospital there was a warm room filled with long narrow tables, at which doctors were working over other wounded men. On one of these tables I had my knee opened and dressed. I was warm once more, looking upward into bright unfocused light, and, being really not badly hurt, I could enjoy the sharpness of the doctor's scalpel. I could feel the edge with a shock of pleasure, knowing that the edge was exposing corruption and cutting it out. Without looking, I could feel the small flow of blood which followed the course of the knife, and enjoy that too, for I was only losing a tainted blood that any man would be happy to have out of him.

Then there was a ride in an ambulance to yet another hospital, where I stayed for a few hours in the late afternoon while a train was making up to carry a load of wounded to Paris. I was in Belgium now, far from the fighting. Over my supper I began to dream about the great luminous city to the south, and I could not quite believe in my good fortune when I was taken to the train at eight o'clock that night.

Events were passing me by, they happened so swiftly. I was borne from one fine place to another like a little boy on a roller-coaster, wild with joy, unable either to get off the car or make it stop. All the faces were friendly, all the machines aided my comfort. I was technically a walking wounded, and so I traveled in one of the standard carriages, and there the seats were fine, for the carriage was of the first class.

Suddenly from walls broken and crumbling I was transported to walls beautifully finished in polished wood. With two other wounded men I established myself in luxury, with my left leg propped up on a little bench the nurse had brought in for me. I was astonished by the dark and glossy walls, and charmed by the patterns of flowers and trees inlaid under the final shellac; the images might have been reflected there, such was the effect, as if the walls had been the shut windows of an old house that mirror the rich, decaying gardens outside. The benches we sat on were covered with a heavy tapestry, on which were a parade of silver bushes and marble fountains, with little golden deer delicately walking by.

I was dazzled, and then, of course, sleepy, but sleepy in a pleasant way; I only wanted to be fresh for the wonderful things the next day might bring. The train rolled southward, whistle screaming as in a dream of fast night trains, and we reached Paris before dawn. Then there was a ride in an ambulance, and disappointment that I would not see Paris that day, but the disappointment did not last.

There was a faint daylight at the hospital doors, and I knew I was entering a fine old building redolent with peace and charity. Above the doors, in a frieze, were sculptured naked angels and cherubic infants; they were gray figures almost lifelike in the hesitant light. Pigeons fluttered near, and as I entered the building I understood that the pigeons had the right to enjoy the mottled purity of the carved stone. Who would worry? The stone would last.

Inside, there was a rhythm of care to draw me in, and I knew I had reached an end. Here I could rest, and be comforted. I was put to bed between sheets of English linen, under blankets of English wool, and the skin of a noble woman could not be finer to my touch than those humble fabrics were. I was fed on a pink ham, surely from the best of Virginia smokehouses, on yams, and asparagus smelling astonishingly of spring; and I was given fine coffee, in a white crockery cup. I talked to a nurse, who smiled at me; she was busy, and she was plainly a dutiful type, but I was her duty, and so in a way she belonged to me.

There was so much to be grateful for that I began to feel guilty, as if no single man could merit such care. Men were dying within those walls, I knew, for I had seen rooms closed behind placards which said that no visitors were allowed, and I had sensed, on my passage upstairs to my ward, several ominous movements of nurses and doctors; they would be walking softly, as if on tiptoe, and solemnly like priests, and they could not fool me. Death was all about me, and might even have left its stench in some of the darker corridors and more distant rooms. And of course I was curious, remembering stories I had heard of other military hospitals; I wondered whether I would have duties in this strange, delightful place, and so I asked the doctor who came to see me, as soon as he had finished his examination.

"Will I have duties here, sir? Like making the bed and scrubbing the floor, say?"

"Of course not," he answered. "Don't even think about it." He was a short, dark man wearing gold-rimmed spectacles; a major, a middle-aged man. He looked shrewd and good-humored, and it came to me, as a summation of all my pieces of wonderful luck, that he was a man I could trust; and so I spoke quite frankly.

"What will I have to do here, then?" I asked. "What *should* I do?"

"Why, just get well, son," he said. "That's all. And enjoy yourself. Don't you like it here? Well, then, enjoy it, there's your duty. Maybe later on you'll be able to go out and see if Paris suits you. It's easy. You'll see. Don't you know how to be happy any more?"

"Happy?" I said, and took thought. "My God, in all my life I've never been so happy!"

Indeed, will I ever be so happy again?

Dawn

J. F. Powers

Father Udovic placed the envelope before the Bishop and stepped back. He gave the Bishop more than enough time to read what was written on the envelope, time to digest *The Pope* and, down in the corner, the *Personal,* and then he stepped forward. "It was in the collection yesterday," he said. "At Cathedral."

"Peter's Pence, Father?"

Father Udovic nodded. He'd checked that. It had been in with the special Peter's Pence envelopes, and not with the regular Sunday ones.

"Well, then . . ." The Bishop's right hand opened over the envelope, then stopped, and came to roost again, uneasily, on the edge of the desk.

Father Udovic shifted a foot, popped a knuckle in his big toe. The envelope was a bad thing all right. They'd never received anything like it. The Bishop was doing what Father Udovic had done when confronted by the envelope, thinking twice, which was what Monsignor Renton at Cathedral had done, and his curates before him, and his housekeeper who counted the collection. In the end, each had seen the envelope as a hot potato and passed it on. But the Bishop couldn't do that. He didn't know *what* might be inside. Even Father Udovic, who had held it up to a strong light, didn't know. That was the hell of it.

The Bishop continued to stare at the envelope. He still hadn't touched it.

"It beats me," said Father Udovic, moving backwards. He sank down on the leather sofa.

"Was there something else, Father?"

Father Udovic got up quickly and went out of the office—wondering how the Bishop would handle the problem, disappointed that he evidently meant to handle it by himself. In a way, Father Udovic felt responsible. It had been his idea to popularize the age-old collection—"to personalize Peter's Pence"—by moving the day for it ahead a month so that the Bishop, who was going to Rome, would be able to present the proceeds to the Holy Father personally. There had been opposition from the very first. Monsignor Renton, the rector at Cathedral, and one of those at table when Father Udovic proposed his plan, was ill-disposed to it (as he was to Father Udovic himself) and had almost killed it with his comment, "Smart promotion, Bruno." (Monsignor Renton's superior attitude was understandable. He'd had Father Udovic's job, that of chancellor of the diocese, years ago, under an earlier bishop.) But Father Udovic had won out. The Bishop had written a letter incorporating

Father Udovic's idea. The plan had been poorly received in some rectories, which was to be expected since it disturbed the routine schedule of special collections. Father Udovic, however, had been confident that the people, properly appealed to, could do better than in the past with Peter's Pence. And the first returns, which had reached him that afternoon, were reassuring—whatever the envelope might be.

It was still on the Bishop's desk the next day, off to one side, and it was there on the day after. On the following day, Thursday, it was in the "In" section of his file basket. On Friday it was still there, buried. Obviously the Bishop was stumped.

On Saturday morning, however, it was back on the desk. Father Udovic, called in for consultation, had a feeling, a really satisfying feeling, that the Bishop might have need of him. If so, he would be ready. He had a plan. He sat down on the sofa.

"It's about this," the Bishop said, glancing down at the envelope before him. "I wonder if you can locate the sender."

"I'll do my best," said Father Udovic. He paused to consider whether it would be better just to go and do his best, or to present his plan of operation to the Bishop for approval. But the Bishop, not turning to him at all, was outlining what he wanted done. And it was Father Udovic's own plan! The Cathedral priests at their Sunday Masses should request the sender of the envelope to report to the sacristy afterwards. The sender should be assured that the contents would be turned over to the Holy Father, if possible.

"Providing, of course," said Father Udovic, standing and trying to get into the act, "it's not something . . ."

"Providing it's possible to do so."

Father Udovic tried not to look sad. The Bishop might express himself better, but he was saying nothing that hadn't occurred to Father Udovic first, days before. It was pretty discouraging.

He retreated to the outer office and went to work on a memo of their conversation. Drafting letters and announcements was the hardest part of his job for him. He tended to go astray without a memo, to take up with the tempting clichés that came to him in the act of composition and sometimes perverted the Bishop's true meaning. Later that morning he called Monsignor Renton and read him the product of many revisions, the two sentences.

"Okay," said Monsignor Renton. "I'll stick it in the bulletin. Thanks a lot."

As soon as Father Udovic hung up, he doubted that that was what the Bishop wanted. He consulted the memo. The Bishop was very anxious that "not too much be made of this matter." Naturally, Monsignor Renton wanted the item for his parish bulletin. He was hard up. At one time he had produced the best bulletin in the diocese, but now he was written out, quoting more and more from the magazines and even from the papal encyclicals. Father Udovic called Monsignor Renton back and asked that the announcement be kept out of print. It would be enough to read it once over lightly from the pulpit, using Father Udovic's version because it said enough without saying too much and was, he implied, authorized by the Bishop. Whoever the announcement concerned would comprehend it. If published, the announcement would be subject to study and private interpretation. "Announcements from the pulpit are soon forgotten," Father Udovic said. "I mean—by the people they don't concern."

"You were right the first time, Bruno," said Monsignor Renton. He sounded sore.

The next day—Sunday—Father Udovic stayed home, expecting a call from Monsignor Renton, or possibly even a visit. There was nothing. That evening he called the Cathedral rectory and got one of the curates. Monsignor Renton wasn't expected in until very late. The curate had made the announcement at his two Masses, but no one had come to him about it. "Yes, Father, as you say, it's quite possible someone came to Monsignor about it. Probably he didn't consider it important enough to call you about."

"Not important!"

"Not important enough to call *you* about, Father. On *Sunday.*"

"I see," said Father Udovic mildly. It was good to know that the curate, after almost a year of listening to Monsignor Renton, was still respectful. Some of the men out in parishes said Father Udovic's job was a snap and maintained that he'd landed it only because he employed the touch system of typing. Before hanging up, Father Udovic stressed the importance of resolving the question of the envelope, but somehow (words played tricks on him) he sounded as though he were accusing the curate of indifference. What a change! The curate didn't take criticism very well, as became all too clear from his sullen silence, and he wasn't very loyal. When Father Udovic suggested that Monsignor Renton might have neglected to make the announcement at his Masses, the curate readily agreed. "Could've slipped his mind all right. I guess you know what that's like."

Early the next morning Father Udovic was in touch with Monsignor Renton, beginning significantly with a glowing report on the Peter's Pence collection, but the conversation languished, and finally he had to ask about the announcement.

"Nobody showed," Monsignor Renton said in an annoyed voice. "What d'ya want to do about it?"

"Nothing right now," said Father Udovic, and hung up. If there had been a failure in the line of communication, he thought he knew where it was.

The envelope had reposed on the Bishop's desk over the weekend and through most of Monday. But that afternoon Father Udovic, on one of his appearances in the Bishop's office, noticed that it was gone. As soon as the Bishop left for the day, Father Udovic rushed in, looking first in the wastebasket, then among the sealed outgoing letters, for a moment actually expecting to see a fat one addressed in the Bishop's hand to the Apostolic Delegate. When he uncovered the envelope in the "Out" section of the file basket, he wondered at himself for looking in the other places first. The envelope had to be filed somewhere—a separate folder would be best—but Father Udovic didn't file it. He carried it to his desk. There, sitting down to it in the gloom of the outer office, weighing, feeling, smelling the envelope, he succumbed entirely to his first fears. He remembered the parable of the cockle. "An enemy hath done this." An enemy was plotting to disturb the peace of the diocese, to employ the Bishop as an agent against himself, or against some other innocent person, some unsuspecting priest or nun—yes, against Father Udovic. Why him? Why not? Only a diseased mind would contemplate such a scheme, Father Udovic thought, but that didn't make it less likely. And the sender, whoever he was, doubtless anonymous and judging others by himself, would assume that the envelope had already been opened and that the announcement was calculated to catch him. Such a person would never come forward.

Father Udovic's fingers tightened on the envelope. He could rip it open, but he wouldn't. That evening, enjoying instant coffee in his room, he could steam it open. But he wouldn't. In the beginning, the envelope might have been opened. It would have been so easy, pardonable then. Monsignor Renton's housekeeper might have done it. With the Bishop honoring the name on the envelope and the intentions of whoever wrote it, up to a point anyway, there was now a principle operating that just couldn't be bucked. Monsignor Renton could have it his way.

That evening Father Udovic called him and asked that the announcement appear in the bulletin.

"Okay. I'll stick it in. It wouldn't surprise me if we got some action now."

"I hope so," said Father Udovic, utterly convinced that Monsignor Renton had failed him before. "Do you mind taking it down verbatim this time?"

"Not at all."

In the next bulletin, an advance copy of which came to Father Udovic through the courtesy of Monsignor Renton, the announcement appeared in an expanded, unauthorized version.

The result on Sunday was no different.

During the following week, Father Udovic considered the possibility that the sender was a floater and thought of having the announcement broadcast from every pulpit in the diocese. He would need the Bishop's permission for that, though, and he didn't dare to ask for something he probably wouldn't get. The Bishop had instructed him not to make too much of the matter. The sender would have to be found at Cathedral, or not at all. If not at all, Father Udovic, having done his best, would understand that he wasn't supposed to know any more about the envelope than he did. He would file it away, and some other chancellor, some other bishop, perhaps, would inherit it. The envelope was most likely harmless anyway, but Father Udovic wasn't so much relieved as bored by the probability that some poor soul was trusting the Bishop to put the envelope into the hands of the Holy Father, hoping for rosary beads blessed by him, or for his autographed picture, and enclosing a small offering, perhaps a spiritual bouquet. Toward the end of the week, Father Udovic told the Bishop that he liked to think that the envelope contained a spiritual bouquet from a little child, and that its contents had already been delivered, so to speak, its prayers and communions already credited to the Holy Father's account in heaven.

"I must say I hadn't thought of that," said the Bishop.

Unfortunately for his peace of mind Father Udovic wasn't always able to believe that the sender was a little child.

The most persistent of those coming to him in reverie was a middle-aged woman saying she hadn't received a special Peter's Pence envelope, had been out of town a few weeks, and so hadn't heard or read the announcement. When Father Udovic tried her on the meaning of the *Personal* on the envelope, however, the woman just went away, and so did all the other suspects under questioning—except one. This was a rich old man suffering from scrupulosity. He wanted his alms to be in secret, as it said in Scripture, lest he be deprived of his eternal reward, but not *entirely* in secret. That was as far as Father Udovic could figure the old man. Who was he? An audacious old Protestant who hated communism, or could some future Knight of St. Gregory be taking his first awkward step? The old man was pretty hard to believe in, and the handwriting on the envelope sometimes struck Father Udovic as that of a woman. This wasn't necessarily bad. Women controlled the nation's wealth. He'd seen the figures on it. The explanation was simple: widows. Perhaps they hadn't taken the right tone in the announcement. Father Udovic's version had been safe and cold, Monsignor Renton's like a summons. It might have been emphasized that the Bishop, under certain circumstances, would *gladly* undertake to deliver the envelope. That might have made a difference. The sender would not only have to appreciate the difficulty of the Bishop's position, but abandon his own. That wouldn't be easy for the sort of person Father Udovic had in mind. He had a feeling that it wasn't going to happen. The Bishop would leave for Rome on the following Tuesday. So time was running out. The envelope could contain a check—quite the cruelest thought—on which payment would be stopped after a limited time by the donor, whom Father Udovic persistently saw as an old person not to be dictated to, or it could be nullified even sooner by untimely death. God, what a shame! In Rome, where the needs of the world, temporal as well as spiritual, were so well known, the Bishop would've been welcome as the flowers in May.

And then, having come full circle, Father Udovic would be hard on himself for dreaming and see the envelope as a whited sepulcher concealing all manner of filth, spelled out in letters snipped from newsprint and calculated to shake Rome's faith in him. It was then that he particularly liked to think of the sender as a little child. But soon the middle-aged woman would be back, and all the others, among whom the hottest suspect was a feeble-minded nun—devils all to pester him, and the last was always worse than the first. For he always ended up with the old man —and what if there was such an old man?

On Saturday, Father Udovic called Monsignor Renton and asked him to run the announcement again. It was all they could do, he said, and admitted that he had little hope of success.

"Don't let it throw you, Bruno. It's always darkest before dawn."

Father Udovic said he no longer cared. He said he liked to think that the envelope contained a spiritual bouquet from a little child, that its contents had already been delivered, its prayers and communions already . . .

"You should've been a nun, Bruno."

"Not sure I know what you mean," Father Udovic said, and hung up. He wished it were in his power to do something about Monsignor Renton. Some of the old ones got funny when they stayed too long in one place.

On Sunday, after the eight o'clock Mass, Father Udovic received a call from Monsignor Renton. "I told 'em if somebody didn't own up to the envelope, we'd open it. I guess I got carried away." But it had worked. Monsignor Renton had just talked with the party responsible for the envelope—a Mrs. Anton—and she was on the way over to see Father Udovic.

"A woman, huh?"

"A widow. That's about all I know about her."

"A widow, huh? Did she say what was in it?"

"I'm afraid it's not what you thought, Bruno. It's money."

Father Udovic returned to the front parlor, where he had left Mrs. Anton. "The Bishop'll see you," he said, and sat down. She wasn't making a good impression on him. She could've used a shave. When she'd asked for the Bishop, Father Udovic had replied instinctively, "He's busy," but it hadn't convinced her. She had appeared quite capable of walking out on him. He invoked the Bishop's name again. "Now one of the things the Bishop'll want to know is why you didn't show up before this."

Mrs. Anton gazed at him, then past him, as she had when he'd tried to question her. He saw her starting to get up, and thought he was about to lose her. He hadn't heard the Bishop enter the room.

The Bishop waved Mrs. Anton down, seated himself near the doorway at some distance from them, and motioned to Father Udovic to continue.

To the Bishop it might sound like browbeating, but Father Udovic meant to go on being firm with Mrs. Anton. He hadn't forgotten that she'd responded to Monsignor Renton's threats. "Why'd you wait so long? You listen to the Sunday announcements, don't you?" If she persisted in ignoring him, she could make him look bad, of course, but he didn't look for her to do that, with the Bishop present.

Calmly Mrs. Anton spoke, but not to Father Udovic. "Call off your trip?"

The Bishop shook his head.

In Father Udovic's opinion, it was one of his functions to protect the Bishop from directness of that sort. "How do we know what's in here?" he demanded. Here, unfortunately, he reached up the wrong sleeve of his cassock for the envelope. Then he had it. "What's in here? Money?" He knew from Monsignor Renton that the envelope contained money, but he hadn't told the Bishop, and so it probably sounded rash to him. Father Udovic could feel the Bishop disapproving of him, and Mrs. Anton still hadn't answered the question.

"Maybe you should return the envelope to Mrs. Anton, Father," said the Bishop.

That did it for Mrs. Anton. "It's got a dollar in it," she said.

Father Udovic glanced at the Bishop. The Bishop was adjusting his cuffs. This was something he did at funerals and public gatherings. It meant that things had gone on too long. Father Udovic's fingers were sticking to the envelope. He still couldn't believe it. "Feels like there's more than that," he said.

"I wrapped it up good in paper."

"You didn't write a letter or anything?"

"Was I supposed to?"

Father Udovic came down on her. "You were supposed to do what everybody else did. You were supposed to use the envelopes we had printed up for the purpose." He went back a few steps in his mind. "You told Monsignor Renton what was in the envelope?"

"Yes."

"Did you tell him how much?"

"No."

"Why not?"

"*He* didn't ask me."

And *he* didn't have to, thought Father Udovic. One look at Mrs. Anton and Monsignor Renton would know. Parish priests got to know such things. They were like weight-guessers, for whom it was only a question of ounces. Monsignor Renton shouldn't have passed Mrs. Anton on. He had opposed the plan to personalize Peter's Pence, but who would have thought he'd go to such lengths to get even with Father Udovic? It was sabotage. Father Udovic held out the envelope and pointed to the *Personal* on it. "What do you mean by that?" Here was where the creatures of his dreams had always gone away. He leaned forward for the answer.

Mrs. Anton leaned forward to give it. "I mean I don't want somebody else takin' all the credit with the Holy Father!"

Father Udovic sank back. It had been bad before, when she'd ignored him, but now it was worse. She was attacking the Bishop. If there were only a way to *prove* she was out of her mind, if only she'd say something that would make all her remarks acceptable in retrospect . . . "How's the Holy Father gonna know who this dollar came from if you didn't write anything?"

"I wrote my name and address on it. In ink."

"All right, Father," said the Bishop. He stood up and almost went out of the room before he stopped and looked back at Mrs. Anton. "Why don't you send it by regular mail?"

"He'd never see it! That's why! Some flunky'd get hold of it! Same as here! Oh, don't I know!"

The Bishop walked out, leaving them together—with the envelope.

In the next few moments, although Father Udovic knew he had an obligation to instruct Mrs. Anton, and had the text for it—"When thou dost an alms-deed, sound not a trumpet before thee"—he despaired. He realized that they had needed each other to arrive at their sorry state. It seemed to him, sitting saying nothing, that they saw each other as two people who'd sinned together on earth might see each other in hell, unchastened even then, only blaming each other for what had happened.

Margins

Donald Barthelme ❦

Edward was explaining to Carl about margins. "The *width* of the margin shows culture, aestheticism and a sense of values or the lack of them," he said. "A very wide left margin shows an impractical person of culture and refinement with a deep appreciation for the best in art and music. Whereas," Edward said, quoting his handwriting analysis book, "whereas, narrow left margins show the opposite. No left margin at all shows a practical nature, a wholesome economy and a general lack of good taste in the arts. A very wide *right* margin shows a person afraid to face reality, oversensitive to the future and generally a poor mixer."

"I don't believe in it," Carl said.

"Now," Edward continued, "with reference to your sign there, you have an *all-around wide margin* which shows a person of extremely delicate sensibilities with love of color and form, one who holds aloof from the multitude and lives in his own dream world of beauty and good taste."

"Are you sure you got that right?"

"I'm communicating with you," Edward said, "across a vast gulf of ignorance and darkness."

"*I* brought the darkness, is that the idea?" Carl asked.

"You brought the darkness, you black mother," Edward said. "Funky, man."

"Edward," Carl said, "for God's sake."

"Why did you write all that jazz on your sign, Carl? Why? It's not true, is it? Is it?"

"It's kind of true," Carl said. He looked down at his brown sandwich boards, which said: *I Was Put In Jail in Selby County Alabama For Five Years For Stealing A Dollar and A Half Which I Did Not Do. While I Was In Jail My Brother Was Killed & My Mother Ran Away When I Was Little. In Jail I Began Preaching & I Preach to People Wherever I Can Bearing the Witness of Eschatological Love. I Have Filled Out Papers for Jobs But Nobody Will Give Me a Job Because I Have Been In Jail & The Whole Scene Is Very Dreary, Pepsi Cola. I Need Your Offerings to Get Food. Patent Applied For & Deliver Us From Evil.* "It's true," Carl said, "with a kind of *merde*-y inner truth which shines forth as the objective correlative of what actually did happen, back home."

"Now, look at the way you made that 'm' and that 'n' there," Edward said. "The tops are pointed rather than rounded. That indicates aggressiveness and energy. The fact that they're also pointed rather than rounded at the bottom indicates a sarcastic, stubborn and irritable nature. See what I mean?"

"If you say so," Carl said.

"Your capitals are very small," Edward said, "indicating humility."

"My mother would be pleased," Carl said, "if she knew."

"On the other hand, the excessive size of the loops in your 'y' and your 'g' displays exaggeration and egoism."

"That's always been one of my problems," Carl answered.

"What's your whole name?" Edward asked, leaning against a building. They were on Fourteenth Street, near Broadway.

"Carl Maria von Weber," Carl said.

"Are you a drug addict?"

"Edward," Carl said, "you *are* a swinger."

"Are you a Muslim?"

Carl felt his long hair. "Have you read *The Mystery of Being*, by Gabriel Marcel? I really liked that one. I thought that one was fine."

"No, c'mon Carl, answer the question," Edward insisted. "There's got to be frankness and honesty between the races. Are you one?"

"I think an accommodation can be reached and the government is doing all it can at the moment," Carl said. "I think there's something to be said on all sides of the question. This is not such a good place to hustle, you know that? I haven't got but two offerings all morning."

"People like people who look neat," Edward said. "You look kind of crummy, if you don't mind my saying so."

"You really think it's too long?" Carl asked, feeling his hair again.

"Do you think I'm a pretty color?" Edward asked. "Are you envious?"

"No," Carl said. "Not envious."

"See? Exaggeration and egoism. Just like I said."

"You're kind of boring, Edward. To tell the truth."

Edward thought about this for a moment. Then he said: "But I'm white."

"It's the color of choice," Carl said. "I'm tired of talking about color, though. Let's talk about values or something."

"Carl, I'm a fool," Edward said suddenly.

"Yes," Carl said.

"But I'm a *white* fool," Edward said. "That's what's so lovely about me."

"You *are* lovely, Edward," Carl said. "It's true. You have a nice look. Your aspect is good."

"Oh, hell," Edward said despondently. "You're very well-spoken," he said. "I noticed that."

"The reason for that is," Carl said, "I read. Did you read *The Cannibal* by John Hawkes? I thought that was a hell of a book."

"Get a haircut, Carl," Edward said. "Get a new suit. Maybe one of those new Italian suits with the tight coats. You could be upwardly mobile, you know, if you just put your back into it."

"Why are you worried, Edward? Why does my situation distress you? Why don't you just walk away and talk to somebody else?"

"You bother me," Edward confessed. "I keep trying to penetrate your inner reality, to find out what it is. Isn't that curious?"

"John Hawkes also wrote *The Beetle Leg* and a couple of other books whose titles escape me at the moment," Carl said. "I think he's one of the best of our younger American writers."

"Carl," Edward said, *"what is* your inner reality? Blurt it out, baby."

"It's mine," Carl said quietly. He gazed down at his shoes, which resembled a pair of large dead brownish birds.

"Are you sure you didn't steal that dollar and a half mentioned on your sign?"

"Edward, I *told* you I didn't steal that dollar and a half." Carl stamped up and down in his sandwich boards. "It sure is *cold* here on Fourteenth Street."

"That's your imagination, Carl," Edward said. "This street isn't any colder than Fifth, or Lex. Your feeling that it's colder here probably just arises from your marginal status as a despised person in our society."

"Probably," Carl said. There was a look on his face. "You know I went to the government, and asked them to give me a job in the Marine Band, and they wouldn't do it?"

"Do you blow good, man? Where's your axe?"

"They wouldn't *give* me that cotton-pickin' job," Carl said. "What do you think of that?"

"This eschatological love," Edward said, "what kind of love is that?"

"That is later love," Carl said. "That's what I call it, anyhow. That's love on the other side of the Jordan. The term refers to a set of conditions which . . . It's kind of a story we black people tell to ourselves to make ourselves happy."

"Oh me," Edward said. "Ignorance and darkness."

"Edward," Carl said, "you don't *like* me."

"I do too like you, Carl," Edward said. "Where do you steal your books, mostly?"

"Mostly in drugstores," Carl said. "I find them good because mostly they're long and narrow and the clerks tend to stay near the prescription counters at the back of the store, whereas the books are usually in those little revolving racks near the front of the store. It's normally pretty easy to slip a couple in your overcoat pocket, if you're wearing an overcoat."

"But . . ."

"Yes," Carl said, "I know what you're thinking. If I'll steal books I'll steal other things. But stealing books is metaphysically different from stealing like money. Villon has something pretty good to say on the subject I believe."

"Is that in 'If I Were King'?"

"Besides," Carl added, "haven't *you* ever stolen anything? At some point in your life?"

"My life," Edward said. "Why do you remind me of it?"

"Edward, you're not satisfied with your life! I thought white lives were *nice!*" Carl said, surprised. "I love that word 'nice.' It makes me so happy."

"Listen Carl," Edward said, "why don't you just concentrate on improving your handwriting."

"My character, you mean."

"No," Edward said, "don't bother improving your character. Just improve your handwriting. Make larger capitals. Make smaller loops in your 'y' and your 'g.' Watch your word-spacing so as not to display disorientation. Watch your margins."

"It's an idea. But isn't that kind of a superficial approach to the problem?"

"Be careful about the spaces between the lines," Edward went on. "Spacing of lines shows clearness of thought. Pay attention to your finals. There are twenty-two different kinds of finals and each one tells a lot about a person. I'll lend you the book. Good handwriting is the key to advancement, or if not *the* key, at least *a* key. You could be the first man of your race to be Vice-President."

"That's something to shoot for, all right."

"Would you like me to go get the book?"

"I don't think so," Carl said, "no thanks. It's not that I don't have any faith in your solution. What I *would* like is to take a leak. Would you mind holding my sandwich boards for a minute?"

"Not at all," Edward said, and in a moment had slipped Carl's sandwich boards over his own slight shoulders. "Boy, they're kind of heavy, aren't they?"

"They cut you a bit," Carl said with a malicious smile. "I'll just go into this men's store here."

When Carl returned the two men slapped each other sharply in the face with the back of the hand, that beautiful part of the hand where the knuckles grow.

Eternal Triangle

Frank O'Connor

Revolutions? I never had any interest in them. A man in my position have to mind his job and not bother about what other people are doing. Besides, I never could see what good they did anybody, and I see more of that kind of thing than most people. A watchman have to be out at all hours in all kinds of weather. He have to keep his eyes open. All I ever seen out of things like that was the damage. And who pays for the damage? You and me and people like us, so that one set of jackeens can get in instead of another set of jackeens. What is it to me who's in or out? All I know is that I have to pay for the damage they do.

I remember well the first one I saw. It was a holiday, and when I turned up to the depot, I was told there was a tram after breaking down in town, and I was to go in and keep an eye on it. A lot of the staff was at the races, and it might be a couple of hours before they could get a breakdown gang. So I took my lunch and away with me into town. It was a nice spring day and I thought I might as well walk.

Mind you, I noticed nothing strange, only that the streets were a bit empty, but it struck me that a lot of people were away for the day. Then all at once, just as I got to town, I noticed a handful of them Volunteer boys in the street. Some of them had green uniforms with slouch hats; more of them had nothing only belts and bandoliers. All of them had guns of one sort or another. I paid no attention. Seeing that it was a holiday, I thought they might be on some sort of manoeuvre. They were a crowd I never had anything to do with. As I say, I'm a man that minds his own business.

Suddenly, one of them raises his gun and halts me.

"Halt!" says he. "Where are you bound for, mate?"

"Just down here, to keep an eye on a tram," I said, taking it in good parts.

"A tram?" says he. "That's the very thing we want for a barricade. Could you drive it?"

"Ah, is it to have the union after me?" says I.

"Ah, to hell with the union," says a second fellow. "If you'll drive it we'll rig it up as an armoured train."

Now, I did not like the tone them fellows took. They were making too free altogether, and it struck me as peculiar that there wouldn't be a bobby there to send them about their business. I went on a couple of hundred yards, and what did I see only a second party. These fellows were wearing khaki, and I recognized them as cadets from the college. They were standing on the steps of the big hotel overlooking the tram, and the young fellow that was supposed to be their officer was very excited.

"That tram is in the direct line of fire," he says. "It's not a safe place."

"Ah, well," I said, "in my job there's a lot of things aren't safe. I hope if anything happens me you'll put in a good word for me with the tramway company."

Mind you, I was still not taking them seriously. I didn't know what I was after walking into. And the first thing I did was to go over the tram to see was there anything missing. The world is full of light-fingered people, and a thing like that, if you only left it for five minutes, you wouldn't know what would be gone. I was shocked when I seen the upstairs. The glass was all broken and the upholstery ripped.

Then the shooting began, and I had to lie on the floor, but after a while it eased off, and I sat up and ate my lunch and read the daily paper. There was no one around, because whenever anyone showed himself at the end of the road, there was a bang and he ran for his life. Coming on to dusk, I began to worry a bit about whether I was going to be relieved at all that day. I knew Danny Delea, the foreman, was a conscientious sort of man, and if he couldn't get a relief, he'd send me word what to do, but no one came, and I was beginning to get a bit hungry. I don't mind admitting that a couple of times I got up to go home. I didn't like sitting there with the darkness coming on, not knowing was I going to be relieved that night or the next week. But each time I sat down again. That is the sort I am. I knew the light-fingered gentry, and I knew that, firing or no firing, they were on the lookout and I wouldn't be out of that tram before one of them would be along to see what could he pick up. I would not give it to say to the rest of the men that I would leave a valuable thing like a tram.

Then, all at once, the firing got hot again, and when I looked out, what did I see in the dusk only a girl coming from behind the railings in the park and running this way and that in an aimless sort of way. She looked as if she was out of her mind with fright, and I could see the fright was more a danger to her than anything else. Mind, I had no wish for her company! I saw what she was, and they are a sort of woman I would never have much to do with. They are always trying to make friends with watchmen, because we are out at all hours. At the same time, I saw if I didn't do something quick, she'd be killed under my eyes, so I stood on the platform and shouted to her to come in. She was a woman I didn't know by sight; a woman of about thirty-five. Cummins her name was. The family was from Waterford. She was a good-looking piece too, considering. I made her lie on the floor to get out of the shooting, but she was nearly hysterical, lifting her head to look at me and lowering it not to see what was going on.

"But who in hell is it, mister?" she says. "God Almighty, I only came out for a bit of sugar for me tea, and look at the capers I'm after walking into! . . . Sacred Heart of Jesus, they're off again. . . . You'd think I was something at a fair, the way they were banging their bloody bullets all around me. Who is it at all?"

"It's the cadets in the hotel here, shooting at the other fellows beyond the park," I said.

"But why don't someone send for the police? Damn soon them fellows would be along if it was only me talking to a fellow!"

" 'Twould take a lot of police to stop this," says I.

"But what are they shooting for, mister?" says she. "Is it for Ireland?"

"Ireland?" says I. "A fat lot Ireland have to hope for from little whipper-snappers like them."

"Still and all," says she, "if 'twas for Ireland, you wouldn't mind so much."

And I declare to God but she had a tear in her eye. That is the kind of women they are. They'll steal the false teeth from a corpse, but let them lay eyes on a green flag or a child in his First Communion suit, and you'd think patriotism and religion were the only two things ever in their minds.

"That sort of blackguarding isn't going to do any good to Ireland or anyone else," says I. "What I want to know is who is going to pay for the damage? Not them. They never did an honest day's work in their lives, most of them. We're going to pay for it, the way we always do."

"I'd pay them every bloody penny I have in the world this minute if only they'd shut up and go away," she says. "For God's sake, will you listen to them!"

Things were getting hotter again. What was after happening was that some of the Volunteer fellows were after crossing the park behind the shrubbery and were firing up at the hotel. They might as well be firing at the moon. The cadets were after knocking out every pane of glass and barricading the windows. One of the Volunteers jumped from a branch of a tree over the railings and ran across the road to the tram. He was an insignificant little article with a saucy air. You could tell by his accent he wasn't from Dublin. I took him to be from somewhere in the North. I didn't like him much. I never did like them Northerners anyway.

"What are ye doing here?" he says in surprise when he seen us lying on the floor.

"I'm the watchman," says I, cutting him short.

"Begor, a watchman ought to be able to watch himself better than that," he says, and without as much as "By your leave" he up with the rifle butt and knocked out every pane of glass in the side of the tram. It went to my heart to see it go. Any other time I'd have taken him and wrung his neck, but, you see, I was lying on the floor and couldn't get up to him with the firing. I pretended not to mind, but I looked at the glass and then I looked at him.

"And who," I said, "is going to pay for that?"

"Och, Mick MacQuaid to be sure," says he.

"Ah, the gentleman is right," says the woman. "Only for him we might all be kilt."

The way she about-faced and started to soft-solder that fellow got on my nerves. It is always the same with that sort of woman. They are people you can't trust.

"And what the hell is it to anyone whether you're killed or not?" I said. "No one asked you to stop. This is the tramway company's property, and if you don't like it you can leave it. You have no claim."

"We'll see whose property this is when it's all over," says the man, and he began shooting up at the windows of the hotel.

"Hey, mister," says the woman, "is that the English you're shooting at?"

"Who else do you think 'twould be?" says he.

"Ah, I was only saying when you came in that I'd never mind if 'twas against the English. I suppose 'twill be in the history books, mister, like Robert Emmet?"

"Robert Emmet!" I said. "I'd like to know where you and the likes of you would be only for the English."

"Well, do you know," she says, as innocent as you please, " 'tis a funny thing about me, but I never cared much for the English soldiers. Of course, mind you, you'd meet nice fellows everywhere, but you'd never know where you were with the English. They haven't the same nature as our own somehow."

Then someone blew a whistle in the park, and your man dropped his rifle and looked out to see how he was going to get back.

"You're going to get your nose shot off if you go out in that, mister," says the woman. "If you'll take my advice, you'll wait till 'tis dark."

"I'm after getting into a tight corner all right," says he.

"Oh, you'll never cross the street alive, mister," she says as if she was delighted with it. "The best thing you could do now would be to wait till after dark and come round to my little place for a cup of tea. You'd be safe there anyway."

"Och, to hell with it," says he. "I have only to take a chance," and he crept down the steps and made for the railings. They spotted him, because they all began to blaze together. The woman got on her hands and knees to look after him.

"Aha, he's away!" says she, clapping her hands like a child. "Good man you are, me bold fellow. . . . I wouldn't wish for a pound that anything would happen that young man," says she to me.

"The shooting on both sides is remarkably wide," says I. "That fellow should have more sense."

"Ah, we won't know till we're dead who have the sense and who haven't," says she. "Some people might get a proper suck-in. God, wouldn't I laugh."

"Some people are going to get a suck-in long before that," says I. "The impudence of that fellow, talking about the tramway company. He thinks they're going to hand it over to him. Whoever is in, he's not going to see much of it."

"Ah, what matter?" she said. " 'Tis only youth. Youth is lovely, I always think. And 'tis awful to think of young fellows being kilt, whoever they are. Like in France. God, 'twould go to your heart. And what is it all for? Ireland! Holy Moses, what did Ireland ever do for us? Bread and dripping and a kick in the ass is all we ever got out of it. You're right about the English, though. You'd meet some very genuine English chaps. Very sincere, in their own way."

"Oh, they have their good points," says I. "I never saw much to criticize in them, only they're given too much liberty."

"Ah, what harm did a bit of liberty ever do anyone, though?" says she.

"Now, it does do harm," says I. "Too much liberty is bad. People ought to mind themselves. Look at me; I'm on this job the best part of my life, and I have more opportunities than most, but thanks to God, I can say I never took twopenceworth belonging to my employers nor never had anything to do with a woman outside my own door."

"And a hell of a lot of thanks you'll get for it in the heel of the hunt," says she. "Five bob a week pension and the old woman stealing it out of your pocket while you're asleep. Don't I know all about it? Oh, God, I wish I was back in me own little room. I'd give all the countries that ever was this minute for a cup of tea with sugar in it. I'd never mind the rations only for the bit of sugar. Hi, mister, would you ever see me home to the doss? I wouldn't be afraid if I had you with me."

"But I have to mind this tram," says I.

"You have what?" says she, cocking her head. "Who do you think is going to run away with it?"

"Now, you'd be surprised," says I.

"Surprised?" says she. "I'd be enchanted."

"Well," I said, "the way I look at it, I'm paid to look after it, and this is my place till I'm relieved."

"But how the hell could you be relieved with this merry-go-round?"

"This is a matter for my employers to decide," says I.

"God," says she, "I may be bad but you're looney," and then she looked at me and she giggled. She started giggling, and she went on giggling, just as if she couldn't stop. That is what I say about them women. There is a sort of childishness in them all, just as if they couldn't be serious about anything. That is what has them the way they are.

So the night came on, and the stars came out, and the shooting only got louder. We were sitting there in the tram, saying nothing, when all at once I looked out and saw the red light over the houses.

"That's a fire," says I.

"If it is, 'tis a mighty big fire," says she.

And then we saw another one to the left of it, and another and another till the whole sky seemed to be lit up, and the smoke pouring away out to sea as if it was the whole sky was moving.

"That's the whole city on fire," says I.

"And 'tis getting mighty close to us," says she. "God send they don't burn this place as well. 'Tis bad enough to be starved and frozen without being roasted alive as well."

I was too mesmerized to speak. I knew what 'twas worth. Millions of pounds' worth of property burning, and no one to pour a drop of water on it. That is what revolutions are like. People talk about poverty, and then it all goes up in smoke—enough to keep thousands comfortable.

Then, all at once, the shooting got nearer, and when I looked out I saw a man coming up the road. The first impression I got of him was that he was badly wounded, for he was staggering from one side of the road to the other with his hands in the air. "I surrender, I surrender," he was shouting, and the more he shouted, the harder they fired. He staggered out into the middle of the road again, stood there for a minute, and then went down like a sack of meal.

"Oh, the poor misfortunate man!" says the woman, putting her hands to her face. "Did you ever see such barbarity? Killing him like that in cold blood!"

But he wasn't killed yet, for he began to bawl all over again, and when he got tired of holding up his hands, he stuck his feet in the air instead.

"Cruel, bloody, barbarous brutes!" says the woman. "They ought to be ashamed of themselves. He told them he surrendered, and they won't let him." And without another word, away with her off down the street to him, bawling: "Here, mister, come on in here and you'll be safe."

A wonder we weren't all killed with her. He got up and started running towards the tram with his hands still in the air. When she grabbed him and pushed him up on the platform, he still had them there. I seen then by his appearance that he wasn't wounded but drunk. He was a thin-looking scrawny man with a cloth cap.

"I surrender," he bawls. *"Kamerad."*

"Hi, mister," says the woman, "would you for the love of the suffering God stop surrendering and lie down."

"But they won't let me lie down," says he. "That's all I want is to lie down, but every time I do they make a cockshot of me. What in hell is it?"

"Oh, this is the Rising, mister," she says.

"The what?" says he.

"The Rising," says she. "Like they said in the papers there would be."

"Who's rising?" says he, grabbing his head. "What paper said that? I want to know is this the D.T.'s I have or isn't it?"

"Oh, 'tisn't the D.T.'s at all, mister," she says, delighted to be able to spread the good news. "This is all real, what you see. 'Tis the Irish rising. Our own boys, don't you know? Like in Robert Emmet's time. The Irish are on that side and the English are on this. 'Twas the English was firing at you, the low scuts!"

"Bugger them!" he says. "They're after giving me a splitting head. There's no justice in this bloody world." Then he sat on the inside step of the tram and put his head between his knees. "Like an engine," he says. "Have you e'er a drop of water?"

"Ah, where would we get it, man?" says the woman, brightening up when she seen him take the half pint of whisky out of his hip pocket. 'Tis a mystery to me still it wasn't broken. "Is that whisky you have, mister?"

"No water?" says he, and then he began to shudder all over and put his hand over his face. "Where am I?" says he.

"Where should you be?" says she.

"How the hell do I know and the trams not running?" says he. "Tell me, am I alive or dead?"

"Well, you're alive for the time being," says the woman. "How long we're all going to be that way is another matter entirely."

"Well, are you alive, ma'am?" says he. "You'll excuse me being personal?"

"Oh, no offence, mister," says she. "I'm still in the queue."

"And do you see what I see?" says he.

"What's that, mister?"

"All them fires."

"Oh," says she, "don't let a little thing like that worry you, mister. That's not hell, if that's what you're afraid of. That's only the city burning."

"The what burning?" says he.

"The city burning," says she. "That's it, there."

"There's more than the bloody city burning," says he. "Haven't you e'er a drop of water at all?"

"Ah, we can spare it," she says. "I think it must be the Almighty God sent you, mister. I declare to you, with all the goings-on, I hadn't a mouthful to eat the whole day, not as much as a cup of tea."

So she took a swig of the bottle and passed it to me. It is stuff I would never much care for, the whisky, but having nothing to eat, I was feeling in the want of something.

"Who's that fellow in there?" says he, noticing me for the first time.

"That's only the watchman," says she.

"Is he Irish or English?" says the drunk.

"Ah, what the hell would he be only Irish?"

"Because if he's English, he's getting none of my whisky," says the drunk, beginning to throw his arms about. "I'd cut the throat of any bloody Englishman."

Oh, pure, unadulterated patriotism! Leave it to a boozer.

"Now, don't be attracting attention, like a good man," she says. "We all have our principles but we don't want to be overheard. We're in trouble enough, God knows."

"I'm not afraid of anyone," says he, staggering to his feet. "I'm not afraid to tell the truth. A bloody Englishman that would shoot a misfortunate man and he on the ground, I despise him. I despise the English."

Then there was a couple of bangs, and he threw up his hands and down with him like a scarecrow in a high wind.

"I declare to me God," says the woman with an ugly glance at the hotel, "them fellows in there are wound up. Are you hit, mister?" says she, giving him a shake. "Oh, begod, I'm afraid his number's up."

"Open his collar and give us a look at him," says I. By this time I was sick of the pair of them.

"God help us, and not a priest nor doctor to be had," says she. "Could you say the prayers for the dying?"

"How would I know the prayers for the dying?" says I.

"Say an act of contrition so," says she.

Well, I began, but I was so upset that I started the Creed instead.

"That's not the act of contrition," says she.

"Say it yourself as you're so smart," says I, and she began, but before she was finished, the drunk shook his fist in the air and said: "I'll cut the living lights out of any Englishman," and then he began to snore.

"Some people have the gift," says she.

Gift was no word for it. We sat there the whole night, shivering and not able to get more than a snooze, and that fellow never stirred, only for the roar of the snoring. He never woke at all until it was coming on to dawn, and then he put his head in his hands again and began complaining of the headache.

"Bad whisky is the ruination of the world," says he.

"Everyone's trouble is their own," says the woman.

And at that moment a lot of cadets came out of the hotel and over to the tram.

"Will you look at them?" says the woman. "Didn't I tell you they were wound up?"

"You'll have to get out of this now," says the officer, swinging his gun.

"And where are we going to go?" says she.

"The city is all yours," says he.

"And so is the Bank of Ireland," says she. "If I was only in my own little room this minute, you could have the rest of the city—with my compliments. Where are you off to?" she asked the drunk.

"I'll have to get the Phibsboro tram," says he.

"You could order two while you're about it," she says. "The best thing the pair of ye can do is come along to my little place and wait till this jigmareel is over."

"I have to stop here," says I.

"You can't," says the officer.

"But I must stop till I'm relieved, man," says I, getting angry with him.

"You're relieved," he says, "I'm relieving you."

And, of course, I had to do what he said. All the same, before I went, I gave him a piece of my mind.

"There's no need for this sort of thing at all," I says. "There's nothing to be gained by destroying valuable property. If people would only do what they were told and mind their own business, there would be no need for any of this blackguarding."

The woman wanted me to come into her room for a cup of tea, but I wouldn't. I was too disgusted. Away with me across the bridge, and the fellows that were guarding it never halted me or anything, and I never stopped till I got home to my own place. Then I went to bed, and I didn't get up for a week, till the whole thing was over. They had prisoners going in by droves, and I never as much as looked out at them. I was never so disgusted with anything in my life.

Strange Comfort
Afforded by the Profession

Malcolm Lowry

Sigbjørn Wilderness, an American writer in Rome on a Guggenheim fellowship, paused on the steps above the flower stall and wrote, glancing from time to time at the house before him, in a black notebook:

> Il poeta inglese Giovanni Keats mente maravigliosa quanto precoce mori in questa casa il 24 Febraio 1821 nel ventiseesimo anno dell' eta sua.

Here, in a sudden access of nervousness, glancing now not only at the house, but behind him at the church of Trinità dei Monti, at the woman in the flower stall, the Romans drifting up and down the steps, or passing in the Piazza di Spagna below (for though it was several years after the war he was afraid of being taken for a spy), he drew, as well as he was able, the lyre, similar to the one on the poet's tomb, that appeared on the house between the Italian and its translation:

Then he added swiftly the words below the lyre:

> The young English poet, John Keats, died in this house on the 24th of February 1821, aged 26.*

This accomplished, he put the notebook and pencil back in his pocket, glanced round him again with a heavier, more penetrating look—that in fact was informed by such a malaise he saw nothing at all but which was intended to say "I have a perfect right to do this," or "If you saw me do that, very well then, I *am* some sort of detective, perhaps even some kind of a painter"—descended the remaining steps, looked wildly once more, and entered, with a sigh of relief like a man going to bed, the comforting darkness of Keats's house.

Here, having climbed the narrow staircase, he was almost instantly confronted by a legend in a glass case which said:

> Remnants of aromatic gums used by Trelawny when cremating the body of Shelley.

And these words, for his notebook with which he was already rearmed felt ratified in this place, he also copied down, though he failed to com-

* Keats died on February 23, 1821.

ment on the gums themselves, which largely escaped his notice, as indeed did the house itself—there had been those stairs, there was a balcony, it was dark, there were many pictures, and these glass cases, it was a bit like a library—in which he saw no books of his—these made about the sum of Sigbjørn's unrecorded perceptions. From the aromatic gums he moved to the enshrined marriage license of the same poet, and Sigbjørn transcribed this document too, writing rapidly as his eyes became more used to the dim light:

> Percy Bysshe Shelley of the Parish *of* Saint Mildred, Bread Street, London, Widower, *and* Mary Wollstonecraft Godwin *of* the City of Bath, Spinster, a minor, *were married in this* Church *by* Licence *with Consent of* William Godwin her father *this* Thirtieth *Day of December in the year one thousand eight hundred and sixteen.* By me Mr. Heydon, Curate. This marriage was solemnized between us.
>
> > Percy Bysshe Shelley
> > Mary Wollstonecraft Godwin
>
> In the presence of:
>
> > William Godwin
> > M. J. Godwin.

Beneath this Sigbjørn added mysteriously:

> Nemesis. Marriage of drowned Phoenician sailor. A bit odd here at all. Sad—feel swine to look at such things.

Then he passed on quickly—not so quickly he hadn't time to wonder with a remote twinge why, if, there was no reason for any of his own books to be there on the shelves above him, the presence was justified of *In Memoriam, All Quiet on the Western Front, Green Light,* and the *Field Book of Western Birds*—to another glass case in which appeared a framed and unfinished letter, evidently from Severn, Keats's friend, which Sigbjørn copied down as before:

> My dear Sir:
> Keats has changed somewhat for the worse—at least his mind has much—very much—yet the blood has ceased to come, his digestion is better and but for a cough he must be improving, that is as respects his body—but the fatal prospect of consumption hangs before his mind yet—and turns everything to despair and wretchedness—he will not hear a word about living—nay, I seem to lose his confidence by trying to give him this hope [the following lines had been crossed out by Severn but Sigbjørn ruthlessly wrote them down just the same: *for his knowledge of internal anatomy enables him to judge of any change accurately and largely adds to his torture*], he will not think his future prospect favorable—he says the continued stretch of his imagination has already killed him and were he to recover he would not write another line—he will not hear of his good friends in England except for what they have done—and this is another load—but of their high hopes of him—his certain success—his experience—he will not hear a word—then the want of some kind of hope to feed his vivacious imagination—

The letter having broken off here, Sigbjørn, notebook in hand, tiptoed lingeringly to another glass case where, another letter from Severn appearing, he wrote:

> My dear Brown—He is gone—he died with the most perfect ease—
> he seemed to go to sleep. On the 23rd at half past four the approaches
> of death came on. "Severn—lift me up for I am dying—I shall die
> easy—don't be frightened, I thank God it has come." I lifted him
> upon my arms and the phlegm seemed boiling in his throat. This in-
> creased until 11 at night when he gradually sank into death so quiet
> I still thought he slept—But I cannot say more now. I am broken
> down beyond my strength. I cannot be left alone. I have not slept for
> nine days—the days since. On Saturday a gentleman came to cast his
> hand and foot. On Thursday the body was opened. The lungs were
> completely gone. The doctors would not—

Much moved, Sigbjørn reread this as it now appeared in his notebook, then added beneath it:

> *On Saturday a gentleman came to cast his hand and foot*—that is
> the most sinister line to me. Who is this gentleman?

Once outside Keats's house Wilderness did not pause nor look to left or right, not even at the American Express, until he had reached a bar which he entered, however, without stopping to copy down its name. He felt he had progressed in one movement, in one stride, from Keats's house to this bar, partly just because he had wished to avoid signing his own name in the visitor's book. Sigbjørn Wilderness! The very sound of his name was like a bell-buoy—or more euphoniously a light-ship—broken adrift, and washing in from the Atlantic on a reef. Yet how he hated to write it down (loved to see it in print?)—though like so much else with him it had little reality unless he did. Without hesitating to ask himself why, if he was so disturbed by it, he did not choose another name under which to write, such as his second name which was Henry, or his mother's, which was Sanderson-Smith, he selected the most isolated booth he could find in the bar, that was itself an underground grotto, and drank two grappas in quick succession. Over his third he began to experience some of the emotions one might have expected him to undergo in Keats's house. He felt fully the surprise which had barely affected him that some of Shelley's relics were to be found there, if a fact no more astonishing than that Shelley—whose skull moreover had narrowly escaped appropriation by Byron as a drinking goblet, and whose heart, snatched out of the flames by Trelawny, he seemed to recollect from Proust, was interred in England —should have been buried in Rome at all (where the bit of Ariel's song inscribed on his gravestone might have anyway prepared one for the rich and strange), and he was touched by the chivalry of those Italians who, during the war, it was said, had preserved, at considerable risk to themselves, the contents of that house from the Germans. Moreover he now thought he began to see the house itself more clearly, though no doubt not as it was, and he produced his notebook again with the object of adding to the notes already taken these impressions that came to him in retrospect.

"Mamertine Prison," he read . . . He'd opened it at the wrong place, at some observations made yesterday upon a visit to the historic dungeon, but being gloomily entertained by what he saw, he read, on as he did so feeling the clammy confined horror of that underground cell, or other underground cell, not, he suspected, really sensed at the time, rise heavily about him.

> MAMERTINE PRISON [ran the heading]
> *The lower is the true prison*
> of Mamertine, the state prison of ancient Rome.
> The lower cell called Tullianus is probably the most ancient build-ing in Rome. The prison was used to imprison malefactors and enemies of the State. In the lower cell is seen the well where accord-ing to tradition St. Peter miraculously made a spring to baptise the gaolers Processus and Martinianus. Victims: politicians. Pontius, King of the Sanniti. Died 290 B.C. Giurgurath (Jugurtha) Aristotulus, Vercingetorix.—The Holy Martyrs, Peter and Paul. Apostles impris-oned in the reign of Nero.—Processus, Abondius, *and many others unknown* were:
> > decapitato
> > suppliziato (suffocated)
> > strangolato
> > morto per fame.

Vercingetorix, the King of the Gauls, was certainly strangolato 49 B.C. and Jugurtha, King of Numidia, dead by starvation 104 B.C.

The lower is the true prison—why had he underlined that? Sigbjørn wondered. He ordered another grappa and, while awaiting it, turned back to his notebook where, beneath his remarks on the Mamertine prison, and added as he now recalled in the dungeon itself, this memo-randum met his eyes:

> Find Gogol's house—where wrote part of Dead Souls—1838. Where died Vielgorsky? "They do not heed me, nor see me, nor listen to me," wrote Gogol. "What have I done to them? Why do they torture me? What do they want of poor me? What can I give them? I have nothing. My strength is gone. I cannot endure all this." Suppliziato. Strangolato. In wonderful-horrible book of Nabokov's when Gogol was dying—he says—"you could feel his spine through his stomach." Leeches dangling from nose: "Lift them up, keep them away . . ." Henrik Ibsen, Thomas Mann, ditto brother: Buddenbrooks and Pippo Spano. A—where lived? became sunburned? Perhaps happy here. Prosper Mérimée and Schiller. Suppliziato. Fitzgerald in Forum. Eliot in Colosseum?

And underneath this was written enigmatically:

> *And many others.*

And beneath this:

> Perhaps Maxim Gorky too. This is funny. Encounter between Volga Boatman and saintly Fisherman.

What was funny? While Sigbjørn, turning over his pages toward Keats's house again was wondering what he had meant, beyond the fact that Gorky, like most of those other distinguished individuals, had at one time lived in Rome, if not in the Mamertine prison—though with another part of his mind he knew perfectly well—he realized that the peculiar stichometry of his observations, jotted down as if he imagined he were writing a species of poem, had caused him prematurely to finish the notebook:

> *On Saturday a gentleman came to cast his hand and foot*—that is the most sinister line to me—who is this gentleman?

With these words his notebook concluded.

That didn't mean there was no more space, for his notebooks, he reflected avuncularly, just like his candles, tended to consume themselves at both ends; yes, as he thought, there was some writing at the beginning. Reversing this, for it was upside down, he smiled and forgot about looking for space, since he immediately recognized these notes as having been taken in America two years ago upon a visit to Richmond, Virginia, a pleasant time for him. So, amused, he composed himself to read, delighted also, in an Italian bar, to be thus transported back to the South. He had made nothing of these notes, hadn't even known they were there, and it was not always easy accurately to visualize the scenes they conjured up:

> The wonderful slanting square in Richmond and the tragic silhouette of interlaced leafless trees.
> On a wall: *dirty stinking Degenerate Bobs was here from Boston. North End, Mass. Warp son of a bitch.*

Sigbjørn chuckled. Now he clearly remembered the biting winter day in Richmond, the dramatic courthouse in the precipitous park, the long climb up to it, and the caustic attestation to solidarity with the North in the (white) men's wash room. Smiling he read on:

> In Poe's shrine, strange preserved news clipping: CAPACITY CROWD HEARS TRIBUTE TO POE'S WORKS. *University student, who ended life, buried at Wytherville.*

Yes, yes, and this he remembered too, in Poe's house, or one of Poe's houses, the one with the great dark wing of shadow on it at sunset, where the dear old lady who kept it, who'd showed him the news clipping, had said to him in a whisper: "So you see, *we* think these stories of his drinking can't *all* be true." He continued:

> Opposite Craig house, where Poe's Helen lived, these words, upon façade, windows, stoop of the place from which E.A.P.—if I am right —must have watched the lady with the agate lamp: Headache—A.B.C.

—Neuralgia: LIC-OFF-PREM—enjoy Pepsi—Drink Royal Crown Cola
—Dr. Swell's Root Beer—"Furnish room for rent": did Poe really live
here? Must have, could only have spotted Psyche from the regions
which are Lic-Off-Prem.—Better than no Lic at all though. Bet Poe
does not still live in Lic-Off-Prem. Else might account for "Furnish
room for rent"?
    Mem: Consult Talking Horse Friday.
    —Give me Liberty or give me death (Sigbjørn now read). In church-
yard, with Patrick Henry's grave; a notice: No smoking within ten
feet of the church; then:
    Outside Robert E. Lee's house:
    Please pull the bell
    To make it ring.
    —Inside Valentine Museum, with Poe's relics—

Sigbjørn paused. Now he remembered that winter day still more clearly.
Robert E. Lee's house was of course far below the courthouse, remote
from Patrick Henry and the Craig house and the other Poe shrine, and it
would have been a good step hence to the Valentine Museum, even had
not Richmond, a city whose Hellenic character was not confined to its
architecture, but would have been recognized in its gradients by a Greek
mountain goat, been grouped about streets so steep it was painful to
think of Poe toiling up them. Sigbjørn's notes were in the wrong order,
and it must have been morning then, and not sunset as it was in the other
house with the old lady, when he went to the Valentine Museum. He saw
Lee's house again, and a faint feeling of the beauty of the whole frost-
bound city outside came to his mind, then a picture of a Confederate
white house, near a gigantic red-brick factory chimney, with far below a
glimpse of an old cobbled street, and a lone figure crossing a waste, as
between three centuries, from the house toward the railway tracks and
this chimney, which belonged to the Bone Dry Fertilizer Company. But
in the sequence of his notes "Please pull the bell, to make it ring," on Lee's
house, had seemed to provide a certain musical effect of solemnity, yet
ushering him instead into the Poe museum which Sigbjørn now in
memory re-entered.

    Inside Valentine Museum, with Poe's relics (he read once more)
    Please
    Do not smoke
    Do not run
    Do not touch walls or exhibits
    Observation of these rules will insure your own and other's en-
joyment of the museum.
    —Blue silk coat and waistcoat, gift of the Misses Boykin, that be-
longed to one of George Washington's dentists.

Sigbjørn closed his eyes, in his mind Shelley's crematory gums and the
gift of the Misses Boykin struggling for a moment helplessly, then he
returned to the words that followed. They were Poe's own, and formed
part of some letters once presumably written in anguished and private

desperation, but which were now to be perused at leisure by anyone whose enjoyment of them would be "insured" so long as they neither smoked nor ran nor touched the glass case in which, like the gums (on the other side of the world), they were preserved. He read:

> Excerpt from a letter by Poe—after having been dismissed from West Point—to his foster father. Feb. 21, 1831.
> "It will however be the last time I ever trouble any human being —I feel I am on a sick bed from which I shall never get up."

Sigbjørn calculated with a pang that Poe must have written these words almost seven years * to the day after Keats's death, then, that far from never having got up from his sick bed, he had risen from it to change, thanks to Baudelaire, the whole course of European literature, yes, and not merely to trouble, but to frighten the wits out of several generations of human beings with such choice pieces as "King Pest," "The Pit and the Pendulum," and "A Descent into the Maelstrom," not to speak of the effect produced by the compendious and prophetic *Eureka*.

> My *ear* has been too shocking for any description—I am wearing away every day, even if my last sickness had not completed it.

Sigbjørn finished his grappa and ordered another. The sensation produced by reading these notes was really very curious. First, he was conscious of himself reading them here in this Roman bar, then of himself in the Valentine Museum in Richmond, Virginia, reading the letters through the glass case and copying fragments from these down, then of poor Poe sitting blackly somewhere writing them. Beyond this was the vision of Poe's foster father likewise reading some of these letters, for all he knew unheedingly, yet solemnly putting them away for what turned out to be posterity, these letters which, whatever they might not be, were certainly—he thought again—intended to be private. But were they indeed? Even here at this extremity Poe must have felt that he was transcribing the story that was E. A. Poe, at this very moment of what he conceived to be his greatest need, his final—however consciously engineered—disgrace, felt a certain reluctance, perhaps, to send what he wrote, as if he were thinking: Damn it, I could use some of that, it may not be so hot, but it is at least too good to waste on my foster father. Some of Keats's own published letters were not different. And yet it was almost bizarre how, among these glass cases, in these museums, to what extent one revolved about, was hemmed in by, this cinereous evidence of anguish. Where was Poe's astrolabe, Keats's tankard of claret, Shelley's "Useful Knots for the Yachtsman"? It was true that Shelley himself might not have been aware of the aromatic gums, but even that beautiful and irrelevant circumstantiality that was the gift of the Misses Boykin

---

* Actually ten years, since Keats died on February 23, 1821.

seemed not without its suggestion of suffering, at least for George Washington.

> Baltimore, April 12, 1833.
> I am perishing—absolutely perishing for want of aid. And yet I am not idle—nor have I committed any offence against society which would render me deserving of so hard a fate. For God's sake pity me and save me from destruction.
>
> E. A. Poe

Oh, God, thought Sigbjørn. But Poe had held out another sixteen years. He had died in Baltimore at the age of forty. Sigbjørn himself was nine behind on that game so far, and—with luck—should win easily. Perhaps if Poe had held out a little longer—perhaps if Keats—he turned over the pages of his notebook rapidly, only to be confronted by the letter from Severn:

> My dear Sir:
> Keats has changed somewhat for the worse—at least his mind has much—very much—yet the blood has ceased to come . . . but the fatal prospect hangs . . . *for his knowledge of internal anatomy . . . largely adds to his torture.*

Suppliziato, strangolato, he thought . . . *The lower is the true prison. And many others.* Nor have I committed any offense against society. Not much you hadn't, brother. Society might pay you the highest honors, even to putting your relics in the company of the waistcoat belonging to George Washington's dentist, but in its heart it cried:—*dirty stinking Degenerate Bobs was here from Boston, North End, Mass. Warp son of a bitch!* . . . "On Saturday a gentleman came to cast his hand and foot . . ." Had anybody done that, Sigbjørn wondered, tasting his new grappa, and suddenly cognizant of his diminishing Guggenheim, compared, that was, Keats and Poe?—But compare in what sense, Keats, with what, in what sense, with Poe? What was it he wanted to compare? Not the aesthetic of the two poets, nor the breakdown of *Hyperion,* in relation to Poe's conception of the short poem, nor yet the philosophic ambition of the one, with the philosophic achievement of the other. Or could that more properly be discerned as negative capability, as opposed to negative achievement? Or did he merely wish to relate their melancholias? potations? hangovers? Their sheer guts—which commentators so obligingly forgot!—character, in a high sense of that word, the sense in which Conrad sometimes understood it, for were they not in their souls like hapless shipmasters, determined to drive their leaky commands full of valuable treasure at all costs, somehow, into port, and always against time, yet through all but interminable tempest, typhoons that so rarely abated? Or merely what seemed funereally analogous within the mutuality of their shrines? Or he could even speculate, starting with Baudelaire again, upon what the French movie director Epstein who had made *La Chute de la Maison Usher* in a way that would have delighted Poe himself, might have done with *The Eve of St. Agnes: And they are gone!* . . . "For God's sake pity me and save me from destruction!"

Ah ha, now he thought he had it: did not the preservation of such relics betoken—beyond the filing cabinet of the malicious foster father who wanted to catch one out—less an obscure revenge for the poet's non-conformity, than for his magical monopoly, his possession of words? On the one hand he could write his translunar "Ulalume," his enchanted "To a Nightingale" (which might account for the *Field Book of Western Birds*), on the other was capable of saying, simply, "I am perishing . . . For God's sake pity me . . ." You see, after all, he's just like folks . . . What's this? . . . Conversely there might appear almost a tragic condescension in remarks such as Flaubert's often quoted "Ils sont dans le vrai" perpetuated by Kafka—Kaf—and others, and addressed to child-bearing rosy-cheeked and jolly humanity at large. Condescension, nay, inverse self-approval, something downright unnecessary. And Flaub— Why should they be dans le vrai any more than the artist was dans le vrai? All people and poets are much the same but some poets are more the same than others, as George Orwell might have said. George Or— And yet, what modern poet would be caught dead (though they'd do their best to catch him all right) with his "For Christ's sake send aid," un-repossessed, unincinerated, to be put in a glass case? It was a truism to say that poets not only were, but looked like folks these days. Far from ostensible nonconformists, as the daily papers, the very writers them-selves—more shame to them—took every opportunity triumphantly to point out, they dressed like, and as often as not, were bank clerks, or, marvelous paradox, engaged in advertising. It was true. He, Sigbjørn, dressed like a bank clerk himself—how else should he have courage to go into a bank? It was questionable whether poets especially, in utter-most private, any longer allowed themselves to say things like "For God's sake pity me!" Yes, they had become more like folks even than folks. And the despair in the glass case, all private correspondence carefully destroyed, yet destined to become ten thousand times more public than ever, viewed through the great glass case of art, was now transmuted into hieroglyphics, masterly compressions, obscurities to be deciphered by experts—yes, and poets—like Sigbjørn Wilderness. Wil—

And many others. Probably there was a good idea somewhere, lurking among these arrant self-contradictions; pity could not keep him from using it, nor a certain sense of horror that he felt all over again that these mummified and naked cries of agony should lie thus exposed to human view in permanent incorruption, as if embalmed evermore in their separate eternal funeral parlors: separate, yet not separate, for was it not as if Poe's cry from Baltimore, in a mysterious manner, in the manner that the octet of a sonnet, say, is answered by its sestet, had already been answered, seven years before, by Keats's cry from Rome; so that according to the special reality of Sigbjørn's notebook at least, Poe's own death appeared like something extraformal, almost extraprofes-sional, an afterthought. Yet inerrably it was part of the same poem, the same story. "And yet the fatal prospect hangs . . ." "Severn, lift me up, for I am dying." "Lift them up, keep them away." Dr. Swell's Root Beer.

Good idea or not, there was no more room to implement his thoughts within this notebook (the notes on Poe and Richmond ran, through Fredericksburg, into his remarks upon Rome, the Mamertine Prison, and Keats's house, and vice versa), so Sigbjørn brought out another one from his trousers pocket.

This was a bigger notebook altogether, its paper stiffer and stronger, showing it dated from before the war, and he had brought it from America at the last minute, fearing that such might be hard to come by abroad.

In those days he had almost given up taking notes: every new notebook bought represented an impulse, soon to be overlaid, to write afresh; as a consequence he had accumulated a number of notebooks like this one at home, yet which were almost empty, which he had never taken with him on his more recent travels since the war, else a given trip would have seemed to start off with a destructive stoop, from the past, in its soul: this one had looked an exception so he'd packed it.

Just the same, he saw, it was not innocent of writing: several pages at the beginning were covered with his handwriting, so shaky and hysterical of appearance, that Sigbjørn had to put on his spectacles to read it. Seattle, he made out. July? 1939. Seattle! Sigbjørn swallowed some grappa hastily. Lo, death hath reared himself a throne in a strange city lying alone far down within the dim west, where the good and the bad and the best and the rest, have gone to their eternal worst! The lower is the true Seattle . . . Sigbjørn felt he could be excused for not fully appreciating Seattle, its mountain graces, in those days. For these were not notes he had found but the draft of a letter, written in the notebook because it was that type of letter possible for him to write only in a bar. A bar? Well, one might have called it a bar. For in those days, in Seattle, in the State of Washington, they still did not sell hard liquor in bars—as, for that matter to this day they did not, in Richmond, in the State of Virginia—which was half the gruesome and pointless point of his having been in the State of Washington. LIC-OFF-PREM, he thought. No, no, go not to Virginia Dare . . . Neither twist Pepsi—tight-rooted!—for its poisonous bane. The letter dated—no question of his recognition of it, though whether he'd made another version and posted it he had forgotten—from absolutely the lowest ebb of those low tides of his life, a time marked by the baleful circumstance that the small legacy on which he then lived had been suddenly put in charge of a Los Angeles lawyer, to whom this letter indeed was written, his family, who considered him incompetent, having refused to have anything further to do with him, as, in effect, did the lawyer, who had sent him to a religious-minded family of Buchmanite tendencies in Seattle on the understanding he be entrusted with not more than 25c a day.

> Dear Mr. Van Bosch:
> It is, psychologically, apart from anything else, of extreme urgency that I leave Seattle and come to Los Angeles to see you. I fear a complete mental collapse else. I have cooperated far beyond what I

thought was the best of my ability here in the matter of liquor and
I have also tried to work hard, so far, alas, without selling anything.
I cannot say either that my ways have been as circumscribed exactly
as I thought they would be by the Mackorkindales, who at least have
seen my point of view on some matters, and if they pray for guidance
on the very few occasions when they do see fit to exceed the stipu-
lated 25c a day, they are at least sympathetic with my wishes to return. This may be because the elder Mackorkindale is literally and
physically worn out following me through Seattle, or because you
have failed to supply sufficient means for my board, but this is certainly as far as the sympathy goes. In short, they sympathize, but
cannot honestly agree; nor will they advise you I should return. And
in anything that applies to my writing—and this I find almost the
hardest to bear—I am met with the opinion that I "should put all
that behind me." If they merely claimed to be abetting yourself or
my parents in this it would be understandable, but this judgment is
presented to me independently, somewhat blasphemously in my view
—though without question they believe it—as coming directly from
God, who stoops daily from on high to inform the Mackorkindales,
if not in so many words, that as a serious writer I am lousy. Scenting
some hidden truth about this, things being what they are, I would
find it discouraging enough if it stopped there, and were not beyond
that the hope held out, miraculously congruent also with that of my
parents and yourself, that I could instead turn myself into a successful writer of advertisements. Since I cannot but feel, I repeat, and
feel respectfully, that they are sincere in their beliefs, all I can say is
that in this daily rapprochement with their Almighty in Seattle I
hope some prayer that has slipped in by mistake to let the dreadful
man for heaven's sake return to Los Angeles may eventually be answered. For I find it impossible to describe my spiritual isolation in
this place, nor the gloom into which I have sunk. I enjoyed of course
the seaside—the Mackorkindales doubtless reported to you that the
Group were having a small rally in Bellingham (I wish you could go
to Bellingham one day) but I have completely exhausted any therapeutic value in my stay. God knows I ought to know, I shall never
recover in this place, isolated as I am from Nancy who, whatever you
may say, I want with all my heart to make my wife. It was with the
greatest of anguish that I discovered that her letters to me were being
opened, finally, even having to hear lectures on her moral character
by those who had read these letters, which I had thus been prevented
from replying to, causing such pain to her as I cannot think of. This
separation from her would be an unendurable agony, without anything else, but as things stand I can only say I would be better off
in a prison, in the worst dungeon that could be imagined, than to
be incarcerated in this damnable place with the highest suicide rate
in the Union. Literally I am dying in this macabre hole and I appeal to you to send me, out of the money that is after all mine,
enough that I may return. Surely I am not the only writer, there
have been others in history whose ways have been misconstrued and
who have failed . . . who have won through . . . success . . . pub-
licans and sinners . . . I have no intention—

Sigbjørn broke off reading, and resisting an impulse to tear the letter out of the notebook, for that would loosen the pages, began meticulously to cross it out, line by line.

And now this was half done he began to be sorry. For now, damn it, he wouldn't be able to use it. Even when he'd written it he must have thought it a bit too good for poor old Van Bosch, though one admitted that wasn't saying much. Wherever or however he could have used it. And yet, what if they had found this letter—whoever "they" were—and put it, glass-encased, in a museum among *his* relics? Not much— Still, you never knew!—Well, they wouldn't do it now. Anyhow, perhaps he would remember enough of it . . . "I am dying, absolutely perishing." "What have I done to them?" "My dear Sir." "The worst dungeon." And many others: and *dirty stinking Degenerate Bobs was here from Boston, North End, Mass. Warp son—!*

Sigbjørn finished his fifth unregenerate grappa and suddenly gave a loud laugh, a laugh which, as if it had realized itself it should become something more respectable, turned immediately into a prolonged— though on the whole relatively pleasurable—fit of coughing. . . .

Twilight
and Nocturnal Storm

Hugo von Hofmannsthal

The sparrow-hawk which the boys had nailed to the barn door twisted itself dreadfully towards the breaking night. Euseb, the eldest of those who had done it, stood in the dusk and stared at the bird, from whose shining eyes fury shot forth while it jerked itself to death on the iron nails that pierced its wings. Then its mate dived down from the darkening air; with a shrill cry she flew as though bereft of her senses in giddy little circles, then hung rigid in the air with outspread wings and glimmering eyes, flung herself upwards, backwards, towards the mountain wall, vanishing, then reappearing in wild flights of frenzy. It seemed as though her screams were intended to attract the night-black storm that lay there, its own body afire with suppressed lightning, and with magic circles pull it down on the village. The boy Euseb could hardly stand on his legs; terror gripped him by the neck so that he dared not move his eyeballs. But when, under a silent flash of lightning, the whole barn blazed out in an ashen light, and when to his right a bearded goat-owl, disturbed by a gust of wind, shot out of a hole in the wall to spear a beetle and to his left a bat tumbled down, then horror seized him and drove him with chattering teeth down into the village. And now right in front of him a fresh flash revealed the cemetery wall with all its crevices wherein wood-lice lived; under the sudden glare the crosses seemed to stretch, and on the one fresh child's grave a bush, its blossoms of bleeding hearts hanging by threads, began to shake. But as the lightning flickered out and darkness settled down with the weight of a blanket, a gleam of light fell slantingly from the rear window of a small house on to the cemetery wall. In this chamber slept the butcher's daughter, the most beautiful girl in the village; and it was common knowledge that here one evening, while she was undressing and until she blew out the light, one of the older boys had been able to see the shadows of her breasts upon the curtains.

So Euseb pressed himself under a projecting roof where shingles lay piled up high; and his heart beat differently from hitherto. Facing him, its head dangling, hung the calf he had seen being led past in the afternoon; warm breath still seemed to be coming from its soft mouth. To the boy Euseb the time he spent lying here in wait passed like nothing;

Translated from the German by Tanya and James Stern, from Selected Prose *of* Hugo von Hofmannsthal, *Bollingen Series XXXIII, copyright 1952 by Bollingen Foundation, New York, distributed by Princeton University Press, reprinted by permission of the Bollingen Foundation.*

the quarter-hours striking almost over his head and booming on the fearful air he failed to hear. Nor did he heed the lightning that laid bare in dazzling brightness the bells in their belfry; he was absorbed only with the calf, absorbed only with the girl who there in the house would soon be preparing for bed in her chamber. Now she was busying herself in the parlour, wherein sat two or three men, for the butcher was pouring out some year-old wine.

Presently two dark figures approached the house; they were menservants of townsfolk who owned country estates round about the village and on the slopes of the mountains; one was in livery and knee-breeches, the other clad as a gamekeeper. While the first remained behind, the other strode ahead and entered the parlour. Whereupon, from a dark spot close to a gushing well, a wench stepped forth in the direction of the man who had remained behind, raised her hands towards him, and tried to take his arm. The lower half of her figure was shapelessly broad and Euseb knew immediately that she was the maidservant to the keeper of the "Crown," a young stranger to the place at whom he and the other boys would steal glances when, with heavy body, she knelt down beside the dammed-up mill-stream to rinse the washing, for all were aware that she was with child. Now the servant shook the pleading woman with such force that she had to support herself with one hand on the edge of the well, while with the other she convulsively grasped her belly, and the sound of her sobbing drowned out the gushing of the water. Soon there appeared on the threshold the other servant with the butcher's beautiful daughter, and the one in livery lent to his speech, while half turning towards the maid standing in the dark, a loud and strangely superior tone. "That was last year," he shouted back. "Now we are in another year. Amen." And when, with a "Joseph, Joseph!" from a mouth stretched wide in fear, she tried once more to come near him, he reproached her with knife-sharp words that actually had the power to strike her dumb—to the effect that a person in her condition should be ashamed of loitering in the streets and outside inns, that he regretted the time he had wasted with her during the bygone year and even now would regret every additional minute, since he had better things to do than hang about here with her.

These knife-sharp words penetrated the boy Euseb in his hiding-place with a kind of cruel delight; the skill wherewith the servant had uttered his words and then, whistling three bars and without turning round, disappeared into the inn, gave him much the same sensation he frequently felt when the dresses of women and girls from the town brushed against him: they cast off a subtle, benumbing fragrance which, as he inhaled it, filled him with a divided feeling of sinking down, gently surrendering, while at the same time something within him violently revolted. The twofold sensation now seized him again; it seemed as if, like a door in the dark, the secret splendour of the life of the townsfolk and their servants opened up to him and he was driven to prowl after the maid who stumbled away before him, moaning to herself, hand in mouth, face distorted, to continue following her unobserved and to play a cruel game with the unsuspecting girl. As she walked in heavy despair down the middle of the road, he slipped sideways between the hedges hunched in the storm, under the trees shaken by the storm, past barns that groaned in their beams. Though the nocturnal storm flung dust and chaff into his wide-stretched eyes, he paid no heed; he had lost consciousness of his body, for minutes on end he felt no bigger than the weasels, the toads, or any of the other things that lay in wait and rustled on the trembling earth; an instant later he was of gigantic stature, he stretched up between the trees and it was he who seized their crests and bent them, groaning, down; he was the Terrible who lies in wait in the dark and leaps forth at the cross-roads, yet in him was the timidity of a frightened deer, and all the dread that emanated from him he felt rippling down his spine. She who stumbled along before him had become his prey; he was a gentleman from town and had several of her kind; the new ones he had locked into his house and this one he was now driving to join them; he was the butcher who sneaked up on a runaway animal to lead it to its death, but the animal was an animal bewitched; it was this woman here before him. He ducked when the wind ceased and sprang forth again when it roared; between the breath of the wind and his wild secret chase lay an intimate harmony; the wind was his ally and the brilliant lightning illuminated the road with its cart-tracks, cast its light on the chalk walls of the houses and between the hedges, shone into the forest and revealed the roots of the trees—all that he might keep his victim in sight should she try to slip away from him in the dark.*

.   .   .   .

---

* This "complete" fragment was to be the first part of Euseb's night of destiny and of his way into life. It was published posthumously.

In My Indolence

ॐ Italo Svevo

The present may be sought in neither calendar nor clock; calendars and clocks are consulted merely to establish one's relationship with the past or in order to move with some semblance of consciousness into the future. I and the things and people surrounding me constitute the true present.

What is more, my present also consists of various stages. Thus there is this very lengthy and very significant present stage: the abandonment of business. Touching inertia! It has lasted for eight years. Then there are some important events that break it up, like my daughter's marriage, an event long past and one that is becoming a part of another protracted present, interrupted—or perhaps renewed or, better, rectified—by her husband's death. The birth of my little grandson is now distant too, because the real present as far as Umberto is concerned is my affection for him and his winning of it. He is not aware of this since he believes it a birthright—or, generally speaking, is that wee soul able to believe anything at all? His present, and mine in relation to him, are actually his short, steady steps interrupted by painful moments of fear and relieved by the company of dolls when he cannot win help from his mother or me, his grandfather. My present is also Augusta (the poor woman!), reduced now to her animals—dogs, cats, birds—and her eternal petty ailments, to which she is not devoting energy enough to recover. She does the little bit prescribed by Dr. Raulli, but refuses to listen to me, who by superhuman effort was able to overcome a similar tendency toward heart strain; nor does she see fit to listen to Carlo, our nephew (Guido's son), who is just out of the university and is therefore acquainted with the most up-to-date medicines.

Unquestionably a great part of my present has its origins in the pharmacy. I cannot recall exactly when this present began, but every now and then it was intersected by medicines and new theories. Where now is the time when once I believed I was fulfilling all my organic needs by gulping down every evening a hearty dose of some compound of powdered licorice or those simple bromides that you take powdered or dissolved in broth. Now, however, with Carlo's help, I have at my disposal much better means for the struggle against disease. Carlo is imparting all he knows; I, however, am not telling all I surmise, because I am afraid that he does not agree with me and may with his objections demolish the castle which I put such effort into seeking and which gave me a measure of tranquillity, a security which people at my age do not normally have. A real castle it is! Carlo believes that it is out of confidence in him that I accept all his suggestions so readily. Nonsense. I am quite aware that he knows a great deal; I am trying to pick it up, to put it to use—but with discretion. My arteries are not what they ought to be, and about this there is no doubt. Last summer my blood pressure went up to 240 mm. I cannot say whether it was due to that or something else, at any rate I was very depressed at the time. The depression ended as soon as generous doses of iodide and another chemical, the name of which I never remember, brought my pressure down to 160, where it has remained till now. . . . (I have just now interrupted my writing in order to measure it at the machine I keep ever ready on my writing table. It is exactly 160!) In the past, I always used to feel threatened by an apoplectic stroke which I honestly felt was coming on. In the presence of death, I did not really become any kinder, since I was unable to abide all those people who weren't threatened by a stroke, and had the disgusting look of safe people who pity, commiserate, and amuse themselves.

But guided by Carlo, I even treated some organs which had in no way required help. But it has to be understood that every one of my organs cannot help feeling fagged out after so many years of work, and that they profited from being assisted. I sent them unasked-for aid. When disease strikes, the doctor is very apt to sigh: "I've been called too late!" For that reason it is better to look ahead.

I cannot initiate cures for the liver when it shows no sign of malfunction; but all the same I must not lay myself open to a death like that of a son of a friend of mine, who one fine day, at the age of thirty-two, and in full health, turned yellow as a melon with a violent attack of jaundice and then expired within forty-eight hours.

"He had never been sick," his poor father told me. "He was a giant, yet he had to die."

Many giants finish badly. I have noticed this, and am quite happy not being one.

But prudence is a fine thing. So every Monday I donate a pill to my liver, and this protects it from violent and sudden maladies, at least until the following Monday. I watch over my kidneys with periodic analyses, and until now they have shown no sign of malfunction. But I know that they can stand some help. My exclusively milk diet on Tuesdays affords me a certain security for the rest of the week. But wouldn't it be fine while others, who never give a thought to their kidneys, keep them running merrily along, for me, sacrificing myself to them every week, suddenly to be rewarded by a surprise like that which befell poor Copler!

About five years ago I was disturbed by chronic bronchitis. It interfered with my sleep, and from time to time had me jumping out of bed to spend several hours nightly sitting in an easy chair. The doctor did not see fit to tell me so, but doubtless a cardiac weakness was involved. Raulli proceeded to prescribe that I give up smoking, that I lose weight,

and that I eat very little meat. Inasmuch as giving up smoking was difficult, I sought to fulfill the prescription by renouncing all meat. But not
even losing weight was easy. At the time I had a net weight of ninety-four
kilos. In three years I succeeded in losing two, but at that rate, to reach
the weight Raulli wanted, another eighteen years would have been
called for. It was rather difficult to eat moderately when I was abstain-
ing from meat.

And here I must confess that I really owe my loss of weight to Carlo.
It was one of his first curative successes. He proposed that I forgo one
of my three daily meals; and I resolved to sacrifice supper, which we
Triestines take at eight in the evening, as distinguished from other
Italians, who have lunch at noon and dinner at seven. Every day I fast
uninterruptedly for eighteen hours.

First of all, I slept better. I felt at once that my heart, no longer assist-
ing in digestive work, could devote every beat to filling the veins, to
carrying waste matter from the organism, and, above all, to nourishing
the lungs. I who had once suffered from terrible periods of insomnia—
the great unsettlement of one who longs for peace and who, for that
very reason, loses it—would lie there motionless, calmly awaiting the
approach of warmth and sleep: a genuine parenthesis in an exhausting
life. Sleep after a sumptuous dinner is something else again: then the
heart is occupied with digestion alone, and its other duties are dismissed.

In the first place, it was proved that I was better suited for abstinence
than for moderation. It was easier not to eat supper at all than to limit
the amount of food at lunch and breakfast. At these times there were
no limitations. Twice a day I could gorge myself. And there was no
harm in it, because eighteen hours of autophagy followed. In the beginning, the midday meal of *pasta asciutta* and vegetables was topped off
with some eggs. Then I gave up even these, not because Raulli or Carlo
asked me to, but in accordance with the judicious advice of a philosopher, Herbert Spencer, who discovered some law or other to the effect
that organs which developed too fast—through overnourishment—are less
strong than those taking a longer time to grow. The law, naturally, per-
tained to children, but I am convinced that going back to it is a step
forward, that even a seventy-year-old child would do well to starve his
organs rather than overnourish them. Carlo, moreover, agreed with my
theory, and sometimes would like others to believe that he had formulated it himself.

In this effort to renounce dinner, smoking was a tremendous boon; by
smoking, for the first time in my life I was adjusted even in theory. The
smoker can fast better than others. A good smoke numbs whatever appetite there is. It is precisely to smoking that I believe I owe having been
able to reduce my net weight to eighty kilos. It was a great relief to
smoke for hygienic reasons. I smoked a little more with a perfectly clear
conscience.

Basically, health is a truly miraculous condition. Since it is brought about by the interworking of various organs whose functions we can never fully know (even Carlo, who has grasped the entire science, even the areas of our ignorance, admits that), it derives from the belief that perfect health never exists. If it did exist, its termination would be still more miraculous. Moving things ought to be able to move forever. Why not? Isn't this the law in heaven, which is the same as that in force on earth? But I know that from birth onward diseases are predestined and prepared. From the very beginning, some organs start out weaker than others, overexerting themselves and driving related organs to greater effort; and wherever there is exertion, fatigue results, and from it, ultimately, death.

For that reason, and only for that reason, a malady followed by death does not reveal any disorders in our constitutions. I am too ignorant to know whether at the end, up there in heaven, as down here on earth, the possibilities of death and reproduction exist. All I know is that some stars, and even some planets, have less complete movements than others. It must be that a planet which does not rotate on itself is either lame, blind, or humpbacked.

But among our organs there is one that is the center, almost the sun in a solar system. Up until a few years ago this organ was thought to be the heart. At the moment everybody knows that our entire life turns on the genital organs. Carlo turns up his nose at rejuvenation operations, but still, he doffs his cap when the genitals are mentioned. He says: If the sexual organs could be rejuvenated, they would naturally rejuvenate the whole organism. This was nothing new to me. I would have known that without his telling me. But it will never come to pass. It's impossible. God only knows what the effects of monkey glands are. Perhaps a rejuvenated man will be driven to climb the nearest tree when he sees a beautiful woman. Even so, this is a pretty juvenile act.

This I understand: Mother Nature is a maniac. That is to say, she has a mania for reproduction. She maintains life within an organism so long as there is hope of its reproducing itself. Then she kills it off, and does so in the most diverse ways because of her other mania of remaining mysterious. She does not wish to give herself away by always finding recourse in the same malady to do away with old folks—like a malady that might shed light on our deaths, a little tumor always in the same place, say.

I have always been quite enterprising. And without resorting to an operation I wanted to hoodwink Mother Nature into believing that I was still fit for reproduction, so I took a mistress. This was the least disturbing affair I have ever had in my life: first of all, I considered it neither a lapse in character nor a betrayal of Augusta. I should have felt a trifle ill at ease, but I regarded taking a mistress as a decision equivalent to entering a pharmacy.

Then, of course, matters complicated themselves a little. It ended with my awareness that a whole person cannot be used as a medicine: besides, it is a complex medicine containing a goodly amount of poison. I was still not really old. It was an episode that occurred three years ago, when I was sixty-seven. I was not yet a very old man. Therefore, my heart, which was an organ of secondary importance in the adventure and should not have had to figure in it, ended by taking part. And it so happened that at one point even Augusta profited from my adventure, and was caressed, fondled, and rewarded, as she had been during the time I had had Carla. The curious thing was that it did not surprise her and that she was not even aware of the novelty. Augusta inhabits her great calm and finds it only natural that I should occupy myself with her less than in the past; still, our present inertia does not weaken the bond between us, which is knotted with caresses and affectionate words. These caresses and affectionate words do not have to be repeated in order to endure, to exist anywhere, to remain always live and always equally intimate.

When, one day, in order to salve my conscience, I placed two fingers underneath her chin and gazed long into her faithful eyes, she abandoned herself to me, offering up her lips: "You have always been loving."

At the moment I was a little taken aback. Then, examining the past, I saw, in fact, that I have never been so wanting in affection as to deny her my old love. I had even hugged her (a little distractedly) every evening before closing my eyes in sleep.

It was somewhat difficult to find the woman I sought. There was no one in the house who was suited for such a role; no more was I eager to sully my home. But I would have done so, since I had to hoodwink Mother Nature in order to prevent her thinking that the moment for my final illness had now arrived, and since there was the grand, the enormous task of finding one who would serve the purposes of an old man interested in political science. But, really, that was not the approach. The handsomest woman in the house was Augusta herself. Then there was a little fourteen-year-old girl Augusta made use of for certain household chores. But I knew that if I were to accost this child, Mother Nature, not believing me, would have at once struck me down with one of those thunderbolts she always keeps at her disposal.

It is pointless to relate how I came to find Felicita. Out of sheer devotion to hygiene, I used to go every day to supply myself with cigarettes some distance beyond Piazza Unità, and this called for a walk of more than a half-hour. The clerk was an old woman, but the actual owner of the tobacco shop, who spent occasional hours there supervising, was Felicita, a girl about twenty-four years old. At first I was under the impression that she had inherited the shop; much later I learned that she had bought it with her own money. It was there that I made her acquaintance.

We struck it off well at once. I liked her. She was a blonde who dressed in a variety of colors, in material that did not seem to me expensive, but was always new and gaudy. She took pride in that beauty of hers: the small head puffed out on the sides with close-cropped very curly hair, and the very erect and lovely little body which appeared to contain a staff within it arching backward a little. It was not long before I came to learn something of her liking for varied colors. At her house, this taste was revealed all over the place. From time to time the house was not well heated, and once I took note of the colors she was wearing: she had a red kerchief bound around her head in the style of a peasant woman, a yellow brocaded shawl about her shoulders, a quilted apron in red, yellow, and green over her blue skirt, and a pair of particolored quilted slippers on her feet. She was a perfect oriental figurine; but her pale face was actually one of our region, with eyes that scrutinized things and people to draw from them as much as possible.

A monthly allotment was established at the outset, and, frankly, it was so high that I could not help comparing it with regret with the much lower allowances given before the war. And as early as the twentieth of the month Felicita (the dear girl) began to talk about the stipend that was falling due, thereby disturbing a good part of the month. She was sincere, transparent. Less so was I, and she never learned that I had come to her after having studied medical texts.

But I soon lost sight of that fact. I must say that at the moment I long for that house, so completely rural in aspect except for one room alone appointed in good taste and luxury corresponding with what I was paying, very soberly colored and dimly lighted, where Felicita stood out like a multicolored blossom.

She had a brother who was living in the same house: a good, hardworking electrician whose daily wages were more than enough for him. He was extremely skinny, but it was not because of that, that he was not married; rather, as one easily saw, it was due to his tight-fistedness. I spoke with him at such times as Felicita called him in to check the fuses in our room. I discovered that brother and sister were partners, and were about to make themselves some money. Felicita carried on a very serious life between the tobacconist's shop and the house, and Gastone between his repair shop and the house. Felicita must have been making more than Gastone but that hardly mattered, since—as I later learned —she apparently needed her brother's help. It was he who had organized the tobacco-shop business, which was proving itself such a sound investment. And he was so convinced that he was leading the life of an upright man as to speak contemptuously of the many workers who frittered their earnings away with never a thought for the morrow.

All in all, we three got along rather well together. The room, so soberly and meticulously kept, smacked of a doctor's consultation room. But only because Felicita was a slightly tart medicine that had to be gulped down without the palate's savoring it at its leisure.

At the very beginning—rather, before drawing up terms, and to encourage me to do it—she threw her arms around me and said, "I assure you, I don't find you repulsive."

It was said nicely enough, because said so sweetly; but it gave me pause. I had never really thought of myself as repulsive. On the contrary, I had believed that I was returning to love, from which I had so long abstained through a misinterpretation of hygienic laws, in order to surrender, to offer myself up, to whoever wanted me. This would have been real hygienic practice, which was my aim, and which in any other form would have been incomplete and ineffectual. But notwithstanding the money the treatment was costing me, I did not dare explain to Felicita how I wanted her to be. And she, very often throwing herself at me, would spoil the cure with her complete naïveté:

"Isn't it curious! I don't find you repulsive."

One day, with the crudeness I can sink to on certain occasions, I murmured gently in her ear, "Isn't it curious! I don't find you repulsive, either."

This made her giggle so much that the cure was interrupted.

And off and on, in my mind, I even dare to boast—to give myself a lift, to feel more confident of myself, more worthy, loftier, to forget that I dedicated a part of my life to the task of making myself unrepulsive—I boast that Felicita, during brief moments of our long relationship, was actually in love with me. But seeking a genuine expression of her affection, I find it neither in the never changing sweetness with which she invariably greeted me nor in the maternal care with which she protected me from drafts, nor in her solicitude once when she covered me with one of her brother's overcoats and lent me an umbrella, because while we were together a storm had blown up; but I remember this honest prattle of hers:

"Oh, how I loathe you! How I *loathe* you!"

One day when, as usual, I was talking with Carlo about medicine, he remarked: "What you need is an affectionate girl given to gerontophilia."

Who knows? I did not confess to Carlo, but perhaps once I had already found and then lost such a girl. Except that I do not believe Felicita was a gerontophile through and through. She took me for too much money for me to think that she loved me as I was.

She was certainly the most costly woman I have known in my life. She quietly studied me with those cool, tender eyes of hers, often squinting the better to determine the extent to which I would allow myself to be plundered. In the beginning, and for a long time thereafter, she was completely satisfied with her allowance, because I, not yet enslaved by habit, intimated that I would refuse to spend more on her. On several occasions she tried to reach for my money, but withdrew her hand from my pocket so as not to expose herself to the risk of losing me. Once, though, she did bring it off. She got money out of me to buy a rather expensive fur piece, which I never laid eyes on. Another time, she got me to pay for an entire Parisian ensemble and then let me see it: but even for one as blind as I, her multicolored clothes were unforgettable, and I found that I had seen her in that suit before. She was an economy-minded woman who pretended caprice only because she thought that a man understood caprice in a woman more easily than avarice.

And now this is how, against my wishes, the liaison was broken off.

I had visited her at set hours twice a week. Then, one Tuesday after

I had started for her house, it occurred to me midway there that I would be better off by myself. I returned to my study and quietly devoted myself to Beethoven's *Ninth Symphony* on records.

On Wednesday I should not have felt so strong a craving for Felicita, but it was avarice, really, that drove me to her. I was giving her a substantial allowance, and somehow, if I didn't get what was due me, I would be paying too much. One must bear in mind that when undergoing treatment I am very conscientious in its application, resorting to the greatest and most scientific exactitude. At the end, only in this way may it be determined whether the treatment was good or bad.

As fast as my legs could carry me, I was in that room which I believed to be ours. For the moment it belonged to another. Fat old Misceli, a man about my age, was sitting in an easy chair in a corner while Felicita lounged comfortably on the couch, concentrating on the flavor of a long and very choice cigarette—of a brand which was not to be had in her shop. Essentially, it was the very same position in which Felicita and I found ourselves when we were left together, the only difference being that whereas Misceli was not smoking, I joined Felicita in it.

"What can I do for you?" Felicita asked icily, studying her nails on the hand holding the cigarette aloft.

Words failed me. Presently I found it easier to speak because, to tell the truth, I did not feel the least resentment toward Misceli. This fat man, who was as old as I, looked considerably older because of his tremendous weight. He eyed me warily over the rim of the shiny spectacles he wore perched on the tip of his nose. I always feel other old men to be older than I am.

"Oh, Misceli," I said forthrightly, fully resolved not to make a scene, "it's a long time since we've seen each other." And I extended my hand. He laid his ham of a hand in mine without returning the clasp. Still he said nothing. He was indeed showing himself to be older than I.

At the moment, with the objectivity precisely that of a wise man, I understood perfectly that my position and Misceli's were identical. I felt that, this being the case, we were in no position to resent each other. After all, our meeting here amounted to no more than an ordinary sidewalk collision. However painful it may be, one continues on one's way, mumbling a word of pardon.

With this thought, the gentleman I always was reformed within me. I even felt called on to make Felicita's situation more tolerable. And I said to her, "Signorina, listen: I've got to have a hundred packets of well-selected Sport cigarettes, because I have to make a gift. Would you see that they're soft, please? The tobacco shop is a little too far, and I've dropped up here for a moment."

Felicita stopped staring at her nails and her attitude softened. She even rose and walked with me to the door. In a low voice, with intense accents of reproach, she managed to say: "Why didn't you come yesterday?" And then, quickly: "And what have you come today for?"

I was offended. It was disgusting to see myself limited to fixed days at the price I was paying. I allowed myself immediate relief by giving vent to my annoyance.

"I've only come here today to let you know that I don't want to see you any more! We're not going to see each other again!"

She looked at me astonished, and the better to see me stepped away, leaning far back for a moment. Quite frankly, she had struck an odd pose, but it was one that lent her a certain grace, that of a self-assured person capable of maintaining the most difficult equilibrium.

"As you like," she said, shrugging her shoulders. Then, to be sure she had understood me perfectly, just as she opened the door, she asked me: "Then we're not going to see any more of each other?" And she searched my face.

"Of course we're not," said I a little querulously.

I was just starting down the stairs when fat old Misceli came bumbling to the door, calling: "Wait! wait! I'm coming with you too. I've already told the Signorina how many Sport cigarettes I need. One hundred. Just like you."

We descended the stair together as Felicita, after a long pause, closed the door; it was a pause that gave me a certain amount of delight.

We went down the long slope that leads into Piazza Unità, slowly, careful where we placed our feet. Lumbering along on the slope, he certainly appeared older than I. There was even a moment when he stumbled and nearly fell. I helped him immediately. He did not thank me. He was panting a little, and the effort on the slope was still not over. Because of that, and only because of that, he did not speak. This is borne out by the fact that when we reached the level area behind the town hall, he loosened up and started talking.

"I never smoke Sports. But they're preferred as a cigarette. I have to make a present to my carpenter. And then, I want to buy those good ones Signorina Felicita can get." Now that he was talking he had to walk very slowly. He stopped dead to rummage about in a trouser pocket. He pulled out a gold cigarette case, pressed a little button, and the case flew open. "Would you like one?" he asked. "They're denicotinized."

I accepted one, and also stopped, in order to light it. He remained stock-still merely to put the case back in his pocket. And I thought, At least she could have given me a manlier rival. In fact, I handled myself better than he both on the slope and on the flat area. Compared with him, I was really a youngster. He even smoked denicotinized cigarettes, which are devoid of all flavor. I was more a man because, though I had always tried not to smoke, I had never thought of stooping to the cowardice of denicotinized cigarettes.

Somehow we arrived at the gate of the Tergesteo, where we had to part. Misceli was now talking about other things: affairs in the Exchange, at which he was very adept. He seemed a trifle excited to me, even a little distraught. Briefly, he acted as though he were speaking without listening to himself. He was like me, who was not listening to him at all;

rather, I was studying him, trying to determine exactly what he was *not* saying.

I did not want to break away from him without having tried to acquaint myself better with what he was thinking. And to this end I began by giving myself away completely. That is to say, I burst out with: "Felicita is nothing but a whore!"

Misceli showed himself in a new light: that of his embarrassment. His fat lower jaw began to move like a ruminant's. Did he do this when he was uncertain what to say?

Presently he said, "She doesn't seem so to me. She's the best one for Sports." He wanted to prolong this stupid comedy forever.

I became angry. "Then, in other words, you intend to continue seeing Signorina Felicita?"

Another pause. His jaw jutted out, swung to the left, returned to the right before fixing itself. Then, for the first time betraying an impulse to laugh, he said, "I'll be going back as soon as I need some Sports again."

I laughed myself. But I wanted further explanation. "Well, why did you leave her today?"

He hesitated, and I detected, in his darkened eyes focused on the far end of the street, great sadness.

"I'm a little superstitious. When I'm interrupted in something, I believe in immediately recognizing the hand of Providence, and I drop everything I'm doing. Once I was called to Berlin on important business and I stopped in Sesanna, where the train was held up several hours for I don't know what reason. I don't believe in forcing worldly things—especially at our age."

For me that was enough, and I asked, "You didn't mind when you saw me going to Signorina Felicita for Sports too, did you?"

He shot back with such decisiveness that his jaw did not have time to swivel: "What difference should it make to me? Me jealous? Absolutely not! We two are old. We're old! There's no harm in our making love occasionally; but we mustn't become jealous, because we easily come to look ludicrous. We ought never to get jealous. Listen to me and don't ever let yourself seem jealous, because it would only make you look foolish."

His words sounded friendly enough—just as they are written here on paper—but their tone was rather heavily saturated with anger and scorn. His fat face aflame, he approached me; being smaller than I, he looked up at me as though trying to find the weakest point in my body to strike. Why had he become angry while declaring that we should not be jealous? What could I have done to him? Maybe he was angry with me because I had held his train up at Sesanna when he should have been arriving in Berlin.

But I was not jealous. I should, however, have liked to know how much he paid Felicita monthly. I felt that if I had known that he paid more than I—as seemed fitting to me—I would be satisfied.

But I did not have time to investigate. All of a sudden Misceli became gentler and addressed himself to my discretion. His gentleness was converted into a threat when he recalled that we were in each other's hands. I reassured him: I too was married, and was aware of the importance of an imprudent word by either of us.

"Oh," he said with an offhand gesture, "it's not because of my wife that I ask discretion. There are certain things that have not interested her for years. But I know that you're under Dr. Raulli's care too. He threatened to leave me if I didn't follow his prescriptions, if I drank just one glass of wine, if I smoked more than ten, even denicotinized, cigarettes a day, if I didn't give up . . . well, all the rest. He says that at our age a man's body is one that maintains its equilibrium only because it can't decide what part must collapse. For that reason you shouldn't hint at the part, because then the decision would be easy." He went on in a self-pitying frame of mind: "When you come right down to it, it's simple to prescribe things for another person: Don't do this, that or the other. He might just as well say that one had better resign oneself to living a few months less than to live like that."

He lingered a moment, using the time to extract some information about my own health. I told him that I had once reached a blood pressure of 240 millimeters, which pleased him enormously, because he had reached only 220.

With one foot on the step that leads into the Tergesteo, he departed with a friendly wave, adding: "Now, please, don't breathe a word about this."

I was obsessed for some days by Raulli's fine rhetorical figure of an old man's body that continues to run because it does not know what part should collapse first. Of course, when the old doctor spoke of a "part" he meant *organ.* And "equilibrium" also had its meaning for him. Raulli must have known what he was talking about. With us oldsters, health can only mean a gradual and simultaneous weakening of all the organs. Woe if one of them should lag behind; that is, remain too young! I suspect that their interdependence is capable of changing into a struggle, and that the weak organs are beaten up—with magnificent results on the general economy, one can imagine. Misceli's intervention must, therefore, have been desired by Providence, who guards over my life, and who had even sent word as to how I should behave by way of that mouth with the wandering jaw.

And I returned, pensive, to my phonograph. In the *Ninth Symphony,* I again found my organs working in concert and struggling. Working together during the first movements, and especially in the scherzo, when with two notes, the tympani are allowed to synthesize what all the instruments are murmuring around them. The joy of the last movement seemed rebellion to me. Crude, with a strength which is violence, with light, brief moments of regret and hesitation. Not for nothing does the human voice, this least sensible of all sounds in nature, enter into the last movement. I admit that on other occasions I had interpreted this

symphony differently—as the most intense representation of accord between the most divergent of forces, into which, finally, even the human
voice is received and fused. But that day, the symphony, played by the
same records, appeared as I say.

"Farewell, Felicita," I whispered when the music had faded away. "I
need not think of you any longer."

She was not worth risking a sudden collapse. There are so many
medical theories in the world that it is hard to be governed by them.
Those rascally doctors' only contribution is toward making life more
difficult. The simplest things are too complicated. To abstain from drinking alcohol is a prescription made from an evident truth, but all the
same, it is known that alcohol at times has curative properties. Then why
must I await the intervention of the doctor to offer me the solace of this
potent medicine? There is no doubt that death sometimes results from
an organ's occasionally brief and sudden caprice, or is the incidental and
coincidental product of a variety of weaknesses. I mean, it would be
momentary if it were not followed by death. Things must be so managed as to make the coincidence only momentary. So aid has to be at
hand, ready even before the onset of cramps from overactivity or a collapse due to inertia. Why should one wait for the doctor, who comes running merely to scribble out his bill? Only I am able to tell in time when
I need something, by a feeling of discomfort. Doctors, unfortunately,
have not made a study of what can help in a case like that. For that reason, then, I take various things: a physic and a sip of wine; and then I
study myself. I might need something else: a glass of milk—but also a
drop of digitalis. And all taken in the most minute quantities, as recom-
mended by the great Hannemann. The mere presence of these minute
quantities is enough to produce reactions necessary for the activation of
life, just as though an organ, more than being nourished or stimulated,
had to be reminded. Seeing a drop of calcium, it exclaims: "Oh, look!
I'd forgotten. I've got to work!"

This was what I had against Felicita. It is impossible to take her in
doses.

That evening Felicita's brother came to call on me. On seeing him I
was shaken with fear because Augusta herself showed him to my study.
Fearing what he had to say to me, I was very happy when Augusta
promptly withdrew.

He unknotted a bandanna from which he pulled a package: one hundred boxes of Sport cigarettes. He broke them down into five stacks,
each of twenty boxes, and it was therefore easy to verify the quantity.
Then he had me feel how soft each box was. They had been selected one
by one from a large stock. He was sure I would be pleased.

Actually, I was tremendously pleased, because after having been so
frightened I felt completely at ease. I at once paid the hundred and
sixty lire I owed him and cheerfully thanked him. Cheerfully, because I
really wanted to laugh. A curious women, Felicita; even though jilted,
she was not neglecting her interest in the tobacco shop.

But the pale, lean man, after jamming the lire he had received into his pocket, still made no move to leave. He did not seem Felicita's brother. I had seen him before, on other occasions, but better dressed. Now he was without a collar, and his clothes, though neat, were utterly threadbare. Strange that he felt he had to have a special hat for work-days: and the one he had was positively filthy and misshapen from long use.

He looked at me intently, hesitating to speak. It struck me that his look was a little dark, and the light that glowed in his eyes, inviting me to guess what was on his mind, seemed off-center. When at last he spoke, his look became even more imploring—so imploring that it seemed finally to be threatening me. Intense supplications border on threats. I can understand perfectly how it is that there are peasants who punish the images of saints they have prayed to by throwing them down beneath their beds.

Finally, in a steady voice, he said to me: "Felicita says we have reached the tenth of the month."

I looked at the calendar from which I tore a sheet every day and said: "She's quite right. We *have* reached the tenth of the month. There's no doubt about it."

"But then," he said hesitantly, "you owe her for all the month."

A second before he spoke I understood why he had led me to look at the calendar. I believe I blushed the moment I discovered that between brother and sister everything was clear and honest where money was concerned. The only thing that surprised me was the out-and-out request to pay for the whole month. I even doubted whether I had to pay anything. In my relations with Felicita I had failed to keep very accurate accounts. But hadn't I always paid in advance? And because of that, didn't the last payment overlap this fraction of the month? And I sat there, with my mouth somewhat agape, having to look into those strange eyes, trying to determine whether they were imploring or threatening me. It is precisely the man of vast and long experience like myself who does not know how to behave, because he is aware that by a single word of his, by a single deed, the most unforeseen events are liable to happen. One has only to peruse world history to learn that causes and effects can work themselves into the most peculiar relationships. During my hesitation I took out my wallet and also counted and sorted out my money so as not to mistake a hundred-lira note for a five hundred. And when I had the bills counted out, I handed them over. Everything was done with the thought of gaining time through action. I was thinking: I'll pay now and I'll think about it later.

Felicita's brother himself had ceased to think about it, and his eye, no longer fixed on me, had lost all its intensity. He put the money in a different pocket from the one in which he had deposited the hundred and sixty lire. He kept accounts and money separate.

He bowed to me. "Good evening, Signor," he said, leaving.

But presently he returned, because he had forgotten another package similar to the one he had given me. By way of excusing himself for having come back, he said to me: "This is another hundred boxes of Sports I have to deliver to another gentleman."

They were, of course, for poor Misceli, who couldn't stand them, either. However, I smoked all of mine, except for some boxes I gave to Fortunato, my chauffeur. When I have paid for something, sooner or later I finish by using it up. This is proof of my sense of thrift. And every time I had that taste of straw in my mouth I remembered Felicita and her brother more vividly. By thinking about it over and over, I was able to remember with absolute certainty that I had, in fact, not paid the allowance in advance. After thinking that I had been cheated by so much, I was relieved to find that they had been paid for only twenty days extra.

I think that I must have returned to see Felicita once again, before the twenty days I had paid for elapsed, only because of my above-mentioned sense of economy: my sense of thrift which had even got me into accepting the Sports. I said to myself: Now that I have paid, I'd like to risk once more—for the last time—the danger of tipping off my organism to the part it ought to have collapse. Just once! It'll never know the difference.

The door of her apartment opened just as I was about to ring. Startled in the darkness, I saw her pale, lovely little face as though in a vise, clamped in a hat that covered her head and ears, down to the nape of her neck. A solitary blond curl stole from the cloche down her forehead. I knew that at about this hour she was accustomed to go to the tobacco shop to supervise the more complicated part of her money-making enterprises. But I hoped to induce her to wait for that short while I wanted to have with her.

In the dark, she did not immediately recognize me. In a questioning tone she uttered a name, neither mine nor Misceli's, but which I could not make out. When she recognized me, she extended her hand without a trace of unkind feeling, and a little inquisitively. I clasped her cold hand in both of mine and grew bold. She let her hand lie still, but drew back her head. Never had that staff within her arched back so far; so far that I felt like releasing her hand and seizing her by the waist, if only to steady her.

And that faraway face, adorned with the single curl, regarded me. Or was it actually looking at me? Wasn't it really looking at a problem which she had brought on herself and which demanded a ready solution, then and there on those steps?

"It's impossible now," she said after a long pause.

She was still looking at me. Then every shadow of hesitancy vanished. She stood there, that lovely body of hers holding its extremely perilous position, immobile, her little face wan and serious below the yellow ringlet; but slowly, just as if she were acting on some serious resolution, she withdrew her hand.

"Yes! It's impossible," she said again.

It was repeated to convince me that she was still considering the mat-

ter to see if there might be some way to content me, but apart from this
repetition, there was no other evidence that she was really looking into
and thinking about it. She had already made her final decision.

And then she said to me: "You might return on the first of the month,
if you wish. . . . I'll see . . . I'll think about it."

It is only recently, only since I have set to paper this account of my
liaison with Felicita, that I have become objective enough to judge her
and myself with sufficient justice. I found myself there asserting my rights
to those few days due my subscription. She let me know, instead, that by
my renunciation I had lost those rights. I believe that if she had proposed that I immediately enter a new subscription I would have suffered
less. I am sure that I would not have run away. At the moment I was
bent on love, and, to tell the truth, at my age it very much resembles the
crocodile on land, where, they say, he needs a great deal of time to
change direction. I would have paid for the whole month, even though
resolved to make it the last time.

Instead, this way, she was making me angry. I could not find words; I
hardly found air enough to breathe. I said: "Ouf!" with the maximum of
indignation. I was of the impression that I had said something, and even
remained still for an instant as if I thought that at my "Ouf," a cry that
must have wounded her and given evidence of my deep-seated unhappiness, she would reply. But neither she nor I had anything more to say. I
started down the stairs. A few steps down, I turned to look at her again.
Perhaps on her colorless face now there was some sign to belie such hard-
hearted selfishness, so cold and calculated. I did not see her face. She was
completely absorbed in locking up the apartment, which must have remained unvisited for some hours. Once again I said: "Ouf," but not so
loudly as to be heard by her. I said it to all the world, to society, to our
institutions, and to Mother Nature—all that were responsible for me
finding myself on that staircase, in that position.

She was my last love. Now that the whole adventure has straightened
itself out in the past, I no longer consider it so worthless, because Felicita
—with that blond hair of hers, her pallid face, her slender nose and inscrutable eyes, her disinclination to talk, only seldom revealing the ici-
ness of her heart—Felicita is not unworthy of being regretted. But after
her there was no room for another mistress. She had educated me. Up till
then, whenever I happened to be in a woman's company for more than
ten minutes, I used to feel hope and desire surging in my heart. Naturally, I hoped to conceal both, but still, my strongest desire was to let
them grow so that I might feel more alive and enjoy a sense of participation in life. In order to let hope and desire grow, I had to convert emotions into words and let them out. Who knows how many times I was
laughed at? To the career of old man to which I am now condemned, it
was Felicita who educated me. I can scarcely bring myself to realize that
now, in the field of love, I am worth no more than I pay.

My ugliness is ever before my eyes. This morning, upon awakening, I
studied the position in which I found my mouth the moment I opened

my eyes. My lower jaw lolled on the side I was lying on; also, my tongue was dead and swollen and felt out of place.

I thought of Felicita, whom I very often think of with desire and hatred. At that moment I murmured: "She's right."

"Who's right?" asked Augusta, who was dressing.

And I promptly replied: "A man named Misceli, whom I ran into yesterday, who told me that he doesn't understand why one is born to live and grow old.—He's right."

Thus I actually told her everything without compromising myself in the least.

And up to now no one has ever taken Felicita's place. Nevertheless, I seek to deceive Mother Nature, who is keeping an eye on me to liquidate me as soon as it becomes apparent that I can no longer reproduce. With wise dosages in Hannemann's prescribed quantities, I take a little of that medicine every day. I watch women passing by; I follow them with my eyes, seeking to discover in their legs something other than motor apparatus, so that I may again feel a craving to stop and fondle them. In this respect, the dosages are becoming more measured than Hannemann or I should like. That is, I have to control my eyes lest they betray what they are looking for, and so it must be understood how rarely the medicine is of service. One may do without the caresses of others in order to attain a complete feeling, but it is impossible to feign indifference without running the risk of chilling one's heart.

And having written this, I can better understand my adventure with Signorina Dondi, whom I greeted to do right by her and make her aware of her beauty. The fate of old men is gallantry.

It is not to be believed that such ephemeral relations, which are entered upon with the intention merely of rescuing oneself from death, do not leave their mark, do not contribute to the adornment and troubling of one's life, like my affairs with Carla and Felicita. On rare occasions, because of the strong impression received, they reach the point of leaving an indelible memory.

I recall a girl who was seated opposite me in a streetcar. She left me a memory. We reached a certain intimacy because I gave her a name: Amphora. She did not have a very striking face, but her eyes, luminous and rather round, stared at everything with great curiosity and something of a little girl's inquisitiveness. She might have been over twenty, but I would not have been surprised if she had playfully jerked the rope-like pigtail of the baby girl sitting next to her. I do not know whether it was because of her uncommon figure, or because her dress made her appear to have one, but from the waist up, her slender body resembled an exquisite amphora placed upon her hips. And I was greatly taken by her breasts. The better to deceive Mother Nature, who had her eyes on me, I thought: Naturally, I can't die yet, because if this girl wants me to, I've got to stand ready to reproduce.

My face must have taken on a curious look as I gazed at that amphora. But I dismiss its having been that of a lecher, since I was thinking of death. Still, it was interpreted as suppressed lust. As I later noticed, the girl, who must have been of a well-to-do family, was accompanied by a rather old maidservant who got off the tram with her.

And it was this old woman who, when she passed me, looked down and whispered: "Old lecher."

She called me old. She was summoning death.

I said to her: "You old fool."

But she left without replying.

The Silence of the Valley

Sean O'Faolain

Only in the one or two farmhouses about the lake, or in the fishing hotel at its edge—preoccupations of work and pleasure—does one ever forget the silence of the valley. Even in the winter, when the great cataracts slide down the mountain-face, the echoes of falling water are fitful: the winds fetch and carry them. In the summer a fisherman will hear the tinkle of the ghost of one of those falls only if he steals among the mirrored reeds under the pent of the cliffs, and withholds the plash of his oars. These tiny muted sounds will awe and delight him by the vacancy out of which they creep, intermittently.

One May evening a relaxed group of early visitors were helping themselves to drink in the hotel-bar, throwing the coins into a pint glass. There were five of them all looking out the door at the lake, the rhododendrons on the hermit's island, the mountain towering beyond it, and the wall of the blue air above the mountain line. Behind the counter was an American soldier, blonde, blankly handsome, his wide-vision glasses convexing the sky against his face. Leaning against the counter was a priest; jovial, fat, ruddy, his Roman collar off and his trousers stuck into his socks—he had been up the mountain all day rough-shooting. Leaning against the pink-washed wall was a dark young man with pince-nez; he had the smouldering ill-disposed eyes of the incorrigible Celt—"always eager to take offence" as the fourth of the party had privately cracked. She was a sturdy, red-mopped young woman in blue slacks now sitting on the counter drinking whisky. She sometimes seemed not at all beautiful, and sometimes her heavy features seemed to have a strong beauty of their own, for she was on a hair-trigger between a glowering Beethoven and The Laughing Cavalier. Sometimes her mouth was broody; suddenly it would expand into a half-batty gaiety. Her deep-set eyes ran from gloom to irony, to challenge, to wild humour. She had severe eyebrows that floated as gently as a veil in the wind. She was a Scot. The fifth of the group was a sack of a man, a big fat school-inspector, also with his collar off. He had cute ingratiating eyes. He leaned against the opposite pink-washed wall.

In the middle of the tiled floor was a very small man, a tramp with a fluent black beard, long black curls, a billycock hat, a mackintosh to his toes, and a gnarled stick with a hairy paw. The tramp (a whisper from the priest had informed them all that he had once been a waiter on the Holyhead-Euston Express) held a pint of porter in his free hand and was singing to them in a fine tenor voice a ballad called *Lonely I Wandered from the Scenes of My Childhood.* They heard him in quizzical boredom. He had been singing ballads to them on and off for nearly two hours now.

Outside, the sun was seeping away behind the far end of the valley. From the bar they could see it touching the tips of the tallest rowans on the island. Across the lake the tip of a green cornfield on a hillock blazed and went out. Then vast beams, cutting through lesser defiles, flowed like a yellow searchlight for miles to the open land to the east, picking out great escarpments and odd projections on the mountains. The wavelets were by now blowing in sullenly on the shore, edging it with froth.

The tramp ended. They applauded perfunctorily. He knew they were sated and when the red-headed young woman cried, "Tommy, give us *The Inchigeela Puck Goat,*" he demurred politely.

"I think, miss, ye have enough of me now, and sure I'm as dry as a lime-kiln."

"More porter for the singer," cried the priest with lazy authority, and the lieutenant willingly poured out another bottle of stout and rattled a coin into the pint-glass.

"I suppose," asked the Celtic-looking young man, in a slightly critical voice, "you have no songs in Irish?"

"Now," soothed the school-inspector, "haven't you the Irish the whole bloody year round? Leave us take a holiday from it while we can."

"I had been under the impression," yielded the Celt, with a—for him— amicable smile, "that we came out here to learn the language of our forefathers? Far be it from me to insist pedantically on the point." And he smiled again like a stage curate.

"Tell me, brother," asked the American, as he filled up the tramp's glass, "do you remain on the road the whole year round?"

"Summer and winter, for fifteen years come next September, and no roof over my head but the field of stars. And would you believe it, sur, never wance did I get as much as a shiver of a cold in my head."

"That is certainly a remarkable record."

The proprietor of the hotel entered the bar from the kitchen behind it and planked a saucepan full of fowls' guts on the counter. He was accompanied by a small boy, long-lashed, almost pretty, obviously a city-child, who kept dodging excitedly about him.

"Have any of ye a match?" he asked. He was a powerful man, with the shoulders of a horse. He wore neither coat nor vest. His cap was on his poll. His face round and weather-beaten as a mangold. He had a mouthful of false-teeth.

"What do you want a match for, Dinny?" asked the priest with a wink at the others.

The American produced a match. Dinny deftly pinched a fold of his trousers between the eye of his suspenders and inserted the match through the fold: there it effectively did the work of a button. The priest twisted him around familiarly. A nail had performed the same service behind. They all laughed, but Dinny was too preoccupied to heed.

"What's this mess for?" The American pointed to the stinking saucepan.

Dinny paid no attention. He stretched up over the top of the shelves and after much fumbling brought down a fishing-rod.

"Give it to me, Dinny, give it to me," shouted the child.

Dinny ignored him also as he fiddled with the line. He glanced out the door, turned to the kitchen and roared:

"Kitty cows coming home tell Patsy James have ye the buckets scalded blosht it boys the day is gone."

Or he said something like that, for he mouthed all his words in his gullet and his teeth clacked and he spoke too fast. They all turned back to watch the frieze of small black cows passing slowly before the scalloped water, the fawny froth, the wall of mountain.

"The cobbler won't lasht the night," said Dinny, pulling with his teeth at the tangled pike-line. The priest whirled.

"Is he bad? Did you see him? Should I go down?"

"Still unconscious, Father. No use for you. Timeen was up. He was buying the drink."

"Drink?" asked the Scots girl grinning hopefully.

"For the wake," explained the Celt.

"Well, do you know what it is, by Harry?" cried the inspector earnestly to them all. "He's making a great fight for it."

"He may as well go now and be done with it," said Dinny. "Gimme the rod, Dinny, gimme the rod," screamed the child and taking it he dashed off like a lancer, shouting with joy. Dinny lumbered after him with the saucepan.

"I reckon these people are pretty heartless?" suggested the soldier.

"We Irish," explained the Celt, "are indifferent to the affairs of the body. We are a spiritual people."

"What enchanting nonsense," laughed the young woman and threw back her whisky delightedly.

"It is none the less true," reprimanded the Celt.

"You make me feel so old," sighed the young woman, "so old and so wise."

"Are you a Catholic?" asked the Celt suspiciously.

"Yes, but what on earth has that to do with anything?"

"Well, I reckon I don't know much about the spirit, but you may be right about the body. Did you see those hens' guts?"

The priest intervened diplomatically.

"Did you ever see them fishing for eels? It's great fun. Come and watch them."

All but the tramp walked idly to the edge of the lake. The waves were beating in among the stones, pushing a little wrack of straw and broken reeds before them. Dinny had stuck a long string of windpipe to the hook and the boy had slung it out about twelve feet from the shore. To lure the eels a few random bits of guts had been thrown into the brown shallows at their feet and there swayed like seaweed. The group peered. Nothing happened. Suddenly Dinny shouted as fast as a machine-gun's burst.

"Look at 'em look at 'em look at the devils blosht it look at 'em look at 'em."

A string of intestines was streaking away out into the lake. Dark serpentine shapes whirled snakily in and out of the brown water. The eels had smelled the rank bait and were converging on it.

"By golly," cried the American, "they must smell that bait a mile away."

The reel whirred, the line flew, the rod bent, they all began to shout, the child trembled with excitement.

"You have him pull him you divil," roared Dinny and seized the rod and whirled a long white belly in over their dodging heads. The girl gave a cry of disgust as the five men leaped on the eel, now lashing in the dust, and hammered savagely at it with heels, stones, a stick, screaming, laughing, shoving. The eel seemed immortal. Though filthy and bleeding it squirmed galvanically. The child circled dancing around the struggling group, half-delighted, half-terrified.

"Well, Jo," said the young woman as she looked disdainfully at the last wriggles of the corpse, "it seems that boys will be boys. Dinny, do you really eat eels?"

"Christ, gurl I wouldn't touch one of 'em for a hundred pounds."

"Then why catch them?"

"For fun."

Her face gathered, ceased to be The Laughing Cavalier and became Beethoven in Labour. She saw that the men had now become absorbed entirely in the sport. The American had thrown out the line again and they were all peering excitedly into the water. The sun left the last tips of the mountains. The lake grew sullen. Its waves still hissed. They did not weary of the game until eight eels lay writhing in the dust.

Just as they were becoming bored they observed a silent countryman at the edge of the ring looking down at the eels. The priest spoke to him, saying, "Well, Timeen, how is he?" He was a lithe, lean, hollow-cheeked young man with his cap pulled low over his eyes. He lifted his face and they saw that he was weeping.

"He's gone, Father," he said in a low voice.

"The Lord have mercy on him," said the priest and his own eyes filled and the others murmured the prayer after him. "The poor old cobbler. I must go and see herself."

He hastened away and presently, tidy and brushed and in his Roman collar, they saw him cycle down the road. The child called after him, "Will you roast the eels for me tonight?" and over his shoulder the priest called, "I will, Jo, after supper," and disappeared wobblingly over the first hill.

"By Harry," cried the inspector, "there'll be a powerful gathering of the clans to-night."

"How's that?" from the American.

"For the wake," explained the Celt.

"I'd certainly like to see a wake."

"You'll be very welcome, sur," said Timeen.

"Did he go easy?" asked the inspector.

Dinny threw the guts into the lake, and took Timeen by the arm.

"He went out like a candle," said Timeen, and let Dinny lead him away gently to some private part of the house.

The group dissolved.

"I do wish," said the American, "they wouldn't throw guts into the lake. After all we swim in it."

"It's very unsanitary all right," the inspector agreed.

"What are we all," said the Celt philosophically, "but a perambulating parcel of guts."

The girl sighed heavily and said, "The lamp is lighting."

In the hotel window the round globe of the lamp was like a full moon. A blue haze had gathered over everything. They strolled back to the bar for a last drink, the child staggering after them with the heavy saucepan of dead eels.

The cobbler's cottage was on the brow of a hill about a mile down the road. It was naked, slated, whitewashed, two-storied. It had a sunken haggard in front and a few fuchsias and hollies behind it, blown almost horizontally by the storms. On three sides lay an expanse of moor, now softened by the haze of evening. From his front door the dead cobbler used to look across this barren moor at the jagged mountain-range, but he could also see where the valley opened out and faded into the tentative and varying horizons of forty miles away.

When the priest entered the kitchen the wife was alone—the news had not yet travelled. She was a tiny, aged woman who looked as if her whole body from scalp to soles was wrinkled and yellow; her face, her bare arms, her bare chest were as golden as a dried apple; even her eyeballs seemed wrinkled. But her white hair flowed upward all about her like a Fury in magnificent wild snakes from under an old fisherman's tweed hat, and her mobile mouth and her loud—too loud—voice gave out a tremendous vitality. When she was a young girl she must have been as lively as a minnow in a mountain-stream. The priest had known her for most of his adult life as a woman whose ribald tongue had made the neighbours delight in her and fear her: he was stirred to tears to find her looking up at him now like a child who has been beaten. She was seated on the long settle underneath the red lamp before the picture of the Sacred Heart.

He sat beside her and took her hand.

"Can I go up and pray for him?"

"Katey Dan is readying him," she whispered, and the priest became aware of footsteps moving in the room over their heads.

She lumbered up the ladder-like stairs to see if everything was ready. While he waited he looked at the cobbler's tools by the window—the last, and the worn hammer, and the old butter-box by the fire where the cobbler used to sit. Everything in the kitchen had the same worn look of time and use, and everything was dusted with the gray dust of turf—the kettle over the peat fire, the varied pot-hooks on the crane, the bright metal of the tongs, the dresser with its pieces of delft, a scalded churn-lid leaning in the window to dry. There was nothing there that was not necessary; unless, perhaps, the red lamp and the oleograph of the Sacred Heart, and even that had the stiff and frozen prescription of an ikon. The only unusual thing was two plates on the table under the window, one of snuff and one of shredded tobacco for the visitors who would soon be coming down from every corner of the glens. The only light in the cottage came from the turf-fire.

As he sat and looked at the blue smoke curling up against the brown soot of the chimney's maw he became aware, for the first time in his life, of the silence of this moor. He heard the hollow feet above the rafters. A cricket chirruped somewhere behind the fire. Always up to now he had thought of this cottage as a place full of the cobbler's satirical talk, his wife's echoes and contradictions. Somebody had once told the old man that he was not only the valley's storyteller but its "gossip-columnist": the old chap had cocked a suspicious eye, too vain to admit that he did not know the phrase, and skated off into one of his yarns about the days when he had cobbled for the Irish workers laying rails out of Glasgow along the Clyde. The priest smiled at the incident. Then he frowned as he looked at the fire, a quiet disintegration: a turf-fire never emits even the slightest whisper. He realized that this cottage would be completely silent from now on. Although it was May he had a sudden poignant sensation of autumn, why he could not tell.

The old woman called him up. After the dusk of the kitchen this upper room was brilliant. She had lighted five wax-candles about her husband's head. Snowy sheets made a canopy about this face. The neighbour-woman had just finished the last delicately fluted fold on the lacey counterpane that lay ridged over the stomach and toes. Silently the three knelt and prayed.

When they rose the old woman said looking down at the calm countenance on the pillow:

"He's a fine corse and a heavy corse."

"He was a great man. I loved him."

"He had a fierce veneration for you, Father."

They lumbered down the steep stairs. She was as quiet as if the business in hand was something that had happened outside the course of nature. She thanked God for the fine weather. She asked him were there many staying at the hotel. When he told her, she muttered, "We must be satisfied," as if she were talking about the hotel and not about her man. When two more neighbour women came and stood looking at them from the doorway, he took leave of her saying that he would return later in the night.

The hollies at the door were rubbing squeakingly against each other. The moon was rising serenely over the Pass to the East. He felt the cold wind as he rode back to the lake.

They were at supper when he entered the hotel. He joined them about the round table in the bay window through which he could barely discern the stars above the mountains. The rest of the long room, beyond the globe of the lamp, was in shadow. He mentioned that he had seen the cobbler, that they must go down later to the wake, and then set about his food. He paid small heed to the conversation although he gathered that they were loud in discussion over the delay in serving supper.

"Just the same," the American was saying, "I cannot see why it would not be perfectly simple to hang up a card on the wall announcing mealtimes. Breakfast, eight to ten. Luncheon, one to three. And so on. It's quite simple."

"Just as they do," suggested the young Scotswoman, "in the Regent Palace Hotel?"

"Exactly," he agreed, and then looked in puzzlement at her because she was giggling happily to herself.

"You must admit," the inspector assured her, following his usual role of trying to agree with everybody, "that they have a wonderful opportunity here if they only availed of it. Why don't they cater more for the wealthy clientéle? I mean, now, suppose they advertised Special Duck Dinners, think of the crowds that would come motoring out of Cork for them on summer afternoons. It's only about forty miles, a nice run."

"Gee, how often have I driven forty miles and more for a barbecue supper down the coast? I can see those lobster suppers at Cohasset, now, two dollars fifty, and the rows and rows of automobiles lined outside on the concrete."

"What does our Celt say to this perfectly hideous picture?" asked the redmop.

"I can see no objection—provided the language spoken is Gaelic."

She broke into peals of laughter.

"We," the Celt went on, dark with anger, "envisage an Ireland both modern and progressive. Christianity," he went on, proud both of the rightness and intellectual tolerance of his argument, "is not opposed to modernity, or to comfort, or to culture. I should not mind," his voice was savage, for she was chuckling like a zany, "if seaplanes landed on that lake outside. Why should I? All this admiration for backwardness and inefficiency is merely so much romantic nonsense. Ireland has had enough of it."

She groaned comically.

"Fascist type. Definitely schizoid. Slight sadistic tendency. Would probably be Socialist in Britain, if not—" she wagged her flaming head warningly and made eyes of mock horror— "dare I say it, C.P.?"

"You," cried the Celt scornfully, "merely like the primitive so long as it is not in your own country. Let's go to Nigeria and love the simple ways of the niggers. Let's holiday in Ireland among the beautiful peasants. Imperialist!"

"I beg your pardon," she cried, quite offended. "I am just as happy in the Shetlands or the Hebrides as I am here. Britain's pockets of primitiveness are her salvation. If she ever loses them she's doomed. I very much fear she's doomed already with all these moth-eaten church-wardens in Parliament trying to tidy us up!"

And she drew out her cigar-case and, pulling her coffee towards her, lit a long Panatella. As she puffed she was sullen and unbeautiful again as if his hate had quenched her loveliness as well as her humour.

"Well, now, now, after all," soothed the inspector, "it's all very well for you. Your country is a great country with all the most modern conveniences . . ."

"Heaven help it!"

". . . whereas we have a long leeway to make up. Now, to take even a small thing. Those guts in the lake."

"O God!" she groaned. "What a fuss you make over one poor little chicken's guts! Damn it, it's all phosphates. The Chinese use human phosphates for manure."

The priest shook in his fat with laughter—it was a joke exactly to his liking—but the other three took the discussion from her and she smoked in dudgeon until the priest too was pulling his pipe and telling her about the dead cobbler, and how every night in winter his cottage used to be full of men coming to hear his views on Hitler and Mussolini and the Prophecies of Saint Columcille which foretold that the last battle of the last world-war would be fought at Ballylickey Bridge. The others began to listen as he retold some of the cobbler's more earthy stories that were as innocent and sweaty as any Norse or Celtic yarn of the Golden Age: such as the dilemma of the sow eating the eel which slipped out of her as fast as it went into her until, at last, the sow shouted in a fury: "I'll settle you, you slippery divil!" and at one and the same moment snapped up the eel and clapped her backside to the wall.

Laughing they rose and wandered, as usual into the kitchen for the night. They expected to find it empty, thinking that everybody would be going down to the wakehouse; instead it was more crowded than ever, it had become a sort of clearing-house where the people called on their way to and from the cobbler's cottage, either too shy to go there directly or unwilling to go home after visiting their old friend.

The small boy was eagerly awaiting them with the sauce-pan of eels. The priest set to. He took off his clerical jacket and put on a green windjammer, whose brevity put an equator around his enormous paunch, so that when he stooped over the fire he looked like one of those global toys that one cannot knock over. When the resinous fir-stumps on the great flat hearth flamed up—the only light in the kitchen—he swelled up, shadows and all, like a necromancer. He put an eel down on the stone floor and with his penknife slit it to its tail and gutted it. The offal glistened oilily. While he was cutting the eel its tail had slowly wound about his wrist, and when he tied its nose to a pothook and dangled it over a leaning flame and its oil began to drip and sizzle in the blaze the eel again slowly curved as if in agony. The visitors amused themselves by making sarcastic comments on the priest as cook, but four countrymen who lined the settle in the darkness with their caps on and their hands in their pockets watched him, perfectly immobile, not speaking, apparently not interested.

"Aha, you divil, you," taunted the priest, "now will you squirm? If the cobbler's sow was here now she would make short work of you!"

That was the only time any of the countrymen spoke: from the darkness of a far corner an old man said:

"I wondher is the cobbler telling that story to Hitler now?"

"I sincerely hope," said the Scots girl, "that they're not in the same place."

The old man said:

"God is good. I heard a priesht say wan time that even Judas might be saved."

"Jo," said the inspector, steering as usual into pleasant channels, "do you think that eel is alive?"

The small boy was too absorbed to heed, lost in his own delight.

Now and again a handsome, dark serving-girl came to the fire to tend the pots or renew the sods, for meals were eaten in this house at all hours: she seemed fascinated by the eel and every time she came she made disgusted noises. The men loved these expressions of disgust and tried in various ways to provoke more of them, offering her a bite or holding up the entangled saucepan to her nose. Once the American chased her laughingly with an eel in his fist and from the dark back-kitchen they could hear them scuffling playfully. By this time many more neighbours had come into the kitchen and into the bar and into the second back-kitchen, and two more serving-girls became busy as drinks and teas and dishes of ham passed to and fro, so that the shadows of the men about the fire, the scurrying girls, the wandering neighbours fluttered continually on the white walls and the babble of voices clucked through the house like ducks clacking at a nightpond.

Above this murmuring and clattering they heard the tramp singing in the bar a merry dancing tune, partly in Gaelic and partly in English:

> So, little soldier of my heart
> Will you marry, marry me now,
> With a heigh and a ho
> And a sound of drum now?

"So the little bastard does know Irish," cried the Celt much affronted as the song broke into Gaelic:

> A chailin og mo chroidhe
> Conus a phosfainn-se thu
> Agus gan pioc de'n bhrog do chur orm . . .

"Perhaps he suits his language to his company?" the red-haired girl suggested.

> I went to the cobbler
> The besht in the town
> For a fine pair of shoes
> For my soldiereen brown,
>   So-o-o . . .
> Little soldier of my heart,
> Will you marry, marry me now . . .

The girl peered around the jamb of the door into the bar and then scurried back dismayed. The tramp had spotted her and at once came dancing fantastically into the kitchen on her heels. His long mackintosh tails leaped, and their shadows with them. His black beard flowed left and right as his head swayed to the tune and his black locks swung with it. His hands expressively flicked left and right as he capered about the girl. His billycock hat hopped.

> But O girl of my heart
> How could I marry you
> And I without a shirt
> Either white or blue?

"Would you ate an eel?" asked the greenjacketed porpoise by the fire holding up the shrivelled carcase to the dancer, who at once gaily doffed his hat (into which the priest dropped the eel) and went on his way back to the bar dancing and singing, followed in delight by the boy:

> So chuadhas dti an tailliúr
> The besht to be found
> And I bought a silken shirt
> For my saighdiúrin donn

"Come, lad," cried the priest, suddenly serious, "it's time for us to visit the cobbler."

It was full moonlight. The lake crawled livingly under it. The mountains were like the mouth of hell. It seemed to the priest as if the dark would come down and claw at them. He said so to the Celt who had become wildly excited at the sight of the dark and the light and the creeping lake and strode down to the beach and threw up his arms crying,

"O Love! O Terror! O Death!"—and he broke into Balfe's song to the moon from *The Lily of Killarney:*

> The Moon hath raised her lamp above.

"If you don't stop that emotional ass," growled the girl as she wheeled out her bicycle, "he'll start singing The Barcarolle," and showed her own emotion by cycling madly away by herself.

"Grim! Grim!" said the American and the inspector agreed with, "In the winter! Ah! In the winter!"

They were cycling now in single file switchbacking up and down over the little hills until the glow of the cobbler's window eyed them from the dark. Near the cottage dark shapes of men and boys huddled under the hedges and near the walls and as they alighted drew aside to let them pass, fingers to caps for the priest. The causeway to the kitchen door was crowded, unexpectedly noisy with talk, smelling of turf-smoke and pipe-smoke and bogwater and sweat and hens.

In her corner by the enormous peat-fire, the little old woman seemed almost to be holding pleasant court, her spirits roused by the friendliness and excitement of the crowds of neighbours.

The babble fell as the strangers entered. It rose again as they disappeared up the ladder-stairs to pay their respects to the cobbler. It sank again when they clambered down. Then gradually it rose and steadied as they settled into the company. They were handed whisky or stout or tea by Timeen and the priest began to chat pleasantly and unconcernedly with the nearest men to him. To the three Irishmen all this was so familiar that they made no wonder of it, and they left the American and the girl to the cobbler's wife who at once talked to them about America and Scotland with such a fantastic mixture of ignorance and personal knowledge—gleaned from years upon years of visitors—that all their embarrassment vanished in their pleasure at her wise and foolish talk.

Only twice did her thoughts stray upstairs. A neighbour lifted a red coal in the tongs to kindle his pipe: she glanced sharply and drew a sharp breath.

"Light away, Dan Frank," she encouraged then. "Lasht week my ould divil used to be ever reddening his pipe, God rest him, although I used to be scolding him for burning his poor ould belly with all the shmoking."

Once when the babble suddenly fell into a trough of silence they heard a dog across the moor baying at the moon. She said,

"Times now I do be thinking that with the cobbler gone from me I'll be afraid to be by meself in the house with all the idle shtallions going the road."

It was her commonest word for men, shtalls or shtallions, and all the neighbours who heard her must have pictured a lone tramp or a tinker walking the mountain road, and she inside listening through the barred door to the passing feet.

Elsewhere she talked of things like hens and of prices and several times seemed to forget the nature of the occasion entirely. Then, in her most ribald vein she became scabrous in her comments on her visitors, to the delight of everybody except the victims, who could only scuttle red-faced out the door without, in respect for her, as much as the satisfaction of a curse. It was after one of these sallies that the priest decided to close his visit with a laughing command to them all to kneel for the Rosary. With a lot of scuffling they huddled over chairs or sank on one knee, hiding their faces reverently in their caps.

Only the soldier did not join them. He went out and found more men, all along the causeway and under the hedges, kneeling likewise, so that the mumbling litany of prayer mingled with the tireless baying of the dog. All about them the encircling jags of mountains were bright and jet, brilliant craters, quarries of blackness, gleaming rocks, grey undergrowth.

The journey back was even more eerie than the journey out, the moon now behind them, their shadows before, and as they climbed the hills the mountains climbed before them as if to bar their way and when they rushed downward to the leaden bowl that was the lake, and into the closed gully of the coom, it was as if they were cycling not through space but through a maw of Time that would never move.

The kitchen was empty. The eels lay in the pot. Two old boots lay on their sides drying before the fading fire. The crickets whistled loudly in the crannies. They took their candles and went in their stockinged feet up the stairs to bed, whispering.

The morning was a blaze of heat. The island was a floating red flower. The rhododendrons around the edges of the island were replicated in the smooth lee-water which they barely touched. As the American, the girl, and the Celt set off for their pre-breakfast swim from the island they heard the sounds of spades striking against gravel. The saw the tall thin figure of an aged man, with grey side-chops, in a roundy black hat and a swallow-tailed coat, standing against the sky. He held a piece of twig in his hand like a water-diviner. He was measuring, taking bearings, solicitously encouraging the gravediggers below him to be accurate in their lines. He greeted the strangers politely, but they could see that they were distracting him and that he was weighed down by the importance of his task.

"For do you see, gentlemen, the cobbler was most particular about where he would be buried. I had a long talk with him about it lasht week and the one thing he laid down was for him to be buried in the one line with all the Cronins from Baurlinn."

"But," demurred the American, "would a foot or two make all that difference?"

"It is an old graveyard," the old man admonished him solemnly, "and there are many laid here before him, and there will be many another after him."

They left him to his task. The water was icy and they could only bear to dive in and clamber out. To get warm again they had to race up and down the brief sward before they dressed, hooting with pleasure in the comfort of the sun, the blue sky, the smells of the island and the prospect of trout and bacon-and-eggs for breakfast. As they stepped back on the mainland they met a mountainy lad coming from the depths of the coom, carrying a weighted sack. His grey tweed trousers were as dark with wetness to the hips as if he had jumped into a bog-hole. He walked with them to the hotel and explained that he was wet from the dew on the mountain-heather and the young plantations. He had just crossed from the next valley, about two hours away. He halted and opened the mouth of the sack to show them, with a grin of satisfaction, the curved silver and blue of a salmon. He said he would be content to sell it to the hotel for five shillings and they agreed heartily with him when he said, "Sure what is it only a night's sport and a walk over the mountain?" Over breakfast they upbraided one another for their lie-abed laziness on such a glorious day.

The day continued summer-hot burning itself away past high noon. The inspector got his car and drove away to visit some distant school. The American took his rod and rowed out of sight to the head of the lake. The girl walked away alone. The Celt went fishing from the far shore. The priest sat on the garden-seat before the hotel and read his Office and put a handkerchief over his head and dozed, and when the postman came took the morning paper from him. Once a farm-cart made a crockety-crock down the eastern road and he wondered if it was bringing the coffin. In the farmyard behind the hotel the milk-separator whirred. For most of the time everything was still—the sparkling lake, the idle shore, the tiny fields, the sleeping hermit's island, the towering mountains, the flawless sky. "It is as still," thought the priest, "as the world before life began." All the hours that the priest sat there, or walked slowly up and down reading his breviary, or opened a lazy eye under his handkerchief, he saw only one sign of life—a woman came on top of a hillock across the lake, looked about her for man or animal and went back to her chores.

Towards two o'clock the red-headed girl returned from her walk and sat near him. She was too tired or lazy to talk; but she did ask after a time,

"Do you think they really believe that the cobbler is talking to Hitler?"

"They know no more about Hitler than they do about Cromwell. But I'm sure they believe that the cobbler is having nice little chats with his old pals Jerry Coakley and Shamus Cronin—that's Dinny's father that he will be lying next to—up there in the graveyard—in a half an hour's time."

She smiled happily.

"I wish I had their faith."

"If you were born here you would."

"I'd also have ten children," she laughed. "Will you join me in a drink?"

He could not because he must await the funeral and the local curate at the chapel on the island, and, rising, he went off there. She went alone into the bar and helped herself to a whisky, and leaned over the morning paper. She was joined presently by the Celt, radiant at having caught nothing. To pass the time she started a discussion about large families and the ethics of birth-control. He said that he believed that everybody "practised it in secret," a remark which put her into such good humour that, in gratitude, she made him happy by assuring him that in ten years' time the birth-rate in England would be the lowest in the world; and for the innocent joy he showed at this she glowed with so much good-feeling towards him that she told him also how hateful birth-control is to the poor in the East End of London.

"I always knew it," he cried joyfully. "Religion has nothing to do with these things. All that counts is the Natural Law. For, as I hope you do realize, there is a Law of Nature!"

And he filled out two more whiskies and settled down to the un-burthening of his soul.

"You see, I'm not really an orthodox Catholic at all. To me Religion is valid only because and in so far as it is based on Nature. That is why Ireland has a great message for the world. Everywhere else but here civilization has taken the wrong turning. Here Nature still rules Man, and Man still obeys Nature. . . ."

"As in the East End?" she said.

He hurried on, frowning crossly.

"I worship these mountains and these lakes and these simple Gaelic people because they alone still possess . . ."

"But you were angry last night when I defended primitive life. You wanted sea-planes on the lake and tourists from Manchester in Austin Sevens parked in front of . . ."

"I have already explained to you," he reproved her, "that to be natural doesn't mean that we must be primitive! That's the romantic illusion. What I mean to say is—that is in very simple words of course . . ."

And his dark face buttoned up and he became ill disposed again as he laboured to resolve his own contradictions.

She was about to fly from him when, through the wide-open door, she saw a dark group top the hillock to the east. As the sky stirred between their limbs she saw that they were a silhouette of six men lumbering under a coffin. Its brass plate caught the sun. They were followed by a darker huddle of women. After these came more men, and then a double file of horsemen descended out of the blue sky. On the hermit's island some watcher began to toll a bell.

"I'm going to the island," she said. He followed her, nattering about Darwin and Lamarck.

The priest stood under the barrel-arch of the little Romanesque chapel, distent in his white surplice, impressive, a magician. The two went shyly among the trees and watched the procession dissolving by the lakeside. The priest went out to meet the local curate.

Presently the coffin lumbered forward towards the chapel on the six shoulders and was laid rockingly on four chairs. The crowd seeped in among the trees. The widow sat in the centre of the chapel steps, flanked on each side by three women. She was the only one who spoke and it was plain from the way her attendants covered their faces with their hands that she was being ribald about each new arrival; the men knew it too, for as each one came forward on the sward, to meet the judgment of her dancing, wicked eyes, he skipped hastily into the undergrowth, with a wink or a grin at his neighbours. There was now a prolonged delay. The men looked around at the weather, or across the lake at the crops. Some turned their heads where, far up the lake, the American in his boat was rhythmically casting his invisible line. Then the two priests returned and entered the chapel. Their voices mumbling the *De Profundis* was like the buzzing of bees. The men bowed their heads, as usual holding their caps before their faces. Silence fell again as the procession reformed.

In the graveyard the familiar voices of the men lowering the dead into the earth outraged the silence. Nobody else made a sound until the first shovel of earth struck the brass plate on the lid and then the widow, defeated at last, cried out without restraint. As the earth began to fall more softly her wailing became more quiet. The last act of the burial was when the tall man, the cobbler's friend, smoothened the last dust of earth with his palms as if he were smoothening a blanket over a child. The priest said three Aves. They all responded hollowly.

They dispersed slowly, as if loath to admit that something final had happened to them all. As each one went down to the path he could see the fisherman far away, steadily flogging the water. But they did not go home. They hung around the hotel all the afternoon, the men in the crowded bar, drinking; the women clucking in the back-kitchens. Outside the hotel the heads of the patient horses, growing fewer as the hours went by, drooped lower and lower with the going down of the sun, until only one cart was left and that, at last, ambled slowly away.

It was twilight before the visitors, tired and not in a good temper—they had only been given tea and boiled eggs for lunch—could take possession of the littered bar. They helped themselves to drinks and threw the coins into the pint-glass. Drinking they looked out at the amber light touching the mountain line.

"It's queer," murmured the priest. "Why is it, all to-day and yesterday, I keep on thinking it's the autumn?"

" 'Tis a bit like it all right," the inspector agreed pleasantly.

"Nonsense," said the red-haired girl. "It's a beautiful May day."

"Thanks be to God," agreed the inspector.

A frieze of small black cows passed, one by one, along the beach. They watched them go. Then Dinny put his head in from the kitchen.

"Supper, gentlemen."

"I hope we'll have that salmon that came over the mountains," smiled the Celt.

Nobody stirred.

"In America, you know, we call it the Fall."

"The Fall?" said the priest.

"The fall of the leaves," explained the soldier, thinking he did not understand.

The priest looked out over the dark lake—a stranger would hardly have known there was a lake if it had not been for the dun edge of froth —and, jutting out his lower lip, nodded to himself, very slowly, three times.

"Yes, indeed," the inspector sighed, watching his face sympathetically.

"Aye," murmured the priest, and looked at him, and nodded again, knowing that this was a man who understood.

Then he whirled, gave the Celt a mighty slap on the back, and cried, "Come on and we'll polish off that salmon. Quick march!"

They finished their drinks and strolled into the lamplit dining-room. As they sat around the table and shook out their napkins the soldier said, "I reckon tomorrow will be another fine day."

The red-haired girl leaned to the window and shaded her eyes against the pane. She could see how the moon touched the trees on the island with a ghostly tenderness. One clear star above the mountain wall gleamed. Seeing it her eyebrows floated upward softly for sheer joy.

"Yes," she said quietly. "It will be another grand day—tomorrow."

And her eyebrows sank, very slowly, like a falling curtain.

The Legend of St. Julian the Hospitaller

Gustave Flaubert 🐝

Julian's father and mother lived in a castle on a hillside in the deep woods. At the four corners were pointed towers roofed with lead; the walls sprang from shafts of living rock which sloped steeply to the moat's bottom. The flagstones in the courtyard were tidy as a church floor; long spouts, representing dragons with their jaws wide, spat rainwater into cisterns; and at every window on every floor bloomed basil or heliotrope in painted pots.

Outside the castle was a second enclosure fenced in with stakes and containing first an orchard, then a flower garden of intricately patterned beds, then an arbor with many bowers where you sat to take the air, finally a playing field for the sport-loving pages. At the far side of the castle were kennels, stables and barns, a bakehouse and a winepress. Beyond lay green-turfed pastures, enclosed in turn by a stout hedge of thorn.

The castle had long been at peace with the world and the portcullis was never lowered now, grass grew in the moat, and swallows nested in the rotting battlements. If there was too much sun the bowman who paced the rampart all day long would retire into his sentry-house and sleep like a monk.

There was a gleam of polished metals in the great rooms; walls were hung with tapestries against the cold; cupboards bulged with linen, cellars with wine casks, coffers with bags of gold and silver coin. In the armory, among captive banners and the heads of hunted beasts, were weapons of every age and nation, from slings of the Amalekites and javelins of the Garamantes, to Saracen swords and Norman coats of mail. The great spit in the kitchen could roast an ox whole, the chapel was as splendid as a king's oratory. In a secluded corner there was even a Roman bath, although the old lord thought it a heathen device and abstained from putting it to use.

Wrapped always in a foxskin cape, he wandered about the castle, administering justice to his vassals and settling disputes among his neighbors. In winter he studied the flying snowflakes or had stories read to him. With the first fine days he rode out on his mule along country roads through fields of greening wheat, stopping every now and then to chat with the serfs and give them advice. He had many light loves, then at last took to wife a woman of the highest birth.

Translated from the French by F. W. Dupee, copyright 1952 by F. W. Dupee, reprinted from Great French Short Novels *(New York: Dial Press, 1952) by permission of F. W. Dupee.*

Pale, serious, a little proud, she wore headdresses which brushed the tops of doors and her train trailed three paces behind her. She ran her household as if it were a convent. Every morning she set the servants to their tasks, supervised the making of unguents and preserves, then turned to spinning or to embroidering altar cloths. She prayed God for a son and a son was born to her.

There was great rejoicing then. There was a feast that went on for three days and four nights while torches flared and harps sounded and the strewn greens wilted underfoot. Rare spices were eaten and fowls the size of sheep, and a dwarf entertained by emerging unexpectedly from a pie. The crowd swelled so from hour to hour that the supply of wine cups gave out at last and men took to swilling from helmets and hunting horns.

The young mother shunned the festivities, keeping quietly to her bed. One night she came suddenly awake and made out a sort of shadow in vague motion beneath her moon-streaked window. It was an old man in monk's cloth; he had a rosary at his side and a sack on his shoulder and the look and bearing of a hermit. He came toward her where she lay, and while his lips did not move, a voice spoke distinctly through them. "Be glad," it said, "be glad, O mother, for this son of yours will be a saint."

She would have cried out, but the old man rose softly into the air and glided off and out of sight along a streak of moonlight. Now the banqueters' voices grew loud in song. She heard angels' voices; and her head fell back upon the pillow, above which hung some great martyr's bone in a jeweled frame.

Next morning she questioned the servants, who denied having seen any hermit. What she herself had seen and heard then was surely a message from heaven whether it had happened in reality or in a dream. But she was careful not to speak of it for fear she should be accused of presumption.

The guests went off at daybreak and Julian's father had just seen the last of them out and was standing by the gate alone when someone emerged suddenly from the morning mist—a man with the braided beard and silver finery and intense dark stare of a gypsy. He began to speak, to stammer crazily, as if he were possessed. "Your son, your son!" he cried, and went on to speak of someone "winning a lot of glory and shedding a lot of blood," and he ended by hailing Julian's parents as "the blest family of an emperor." The excited lord tossed him a purse full of coins. The man stooped to retrieve it, the high grass covered him, and he was gone. Looking this way and that the old lord called and called again. No answer! The wind was loud, the mists of morning blew away.

He blamed the vision on his exhausted state: he had been too long without sleep. "I shall be laughed at if I speak of it," he thought but the glory promised to his son continued to excite him even though he was unsure that he had heard the prophecy aright or that he had heard anything at all.

Husband and wife kept their secrets from each other but loved their son equally and made much of him and were intensely careful of his person because they believed him to be chosen by God. He lay in his down-stuffed cradle, a dove-shaped lamp burning always just above; three nurses kept the cradle in motion; and with his blue eyes and rosy cheeks, his heavy swaddling, his embroidered gown and pearl-sewn cap, he did really resemble an infant Jesus. He cut all his teeth without crying.

When he was seven his mother taught him to sing and his father put him astride a huge battle horse to make him brave. The boy smiled with pleasure and soon was expert in the lore of battle horses. Meanwhile a learned old monk taught him Holy Writ, the Arabic numerals, the Latin alphabet and how to make dainty pictures on vellum. They worked together in a tower room high above the uproar of the castle; and when the lesson was over they came down into the garden to stroll and pause, studying the flowers.

Sometimes a train of pack animals was seen advancing through the valley below, driven by a man dressed like an Oriental. The lord, knowing the driver for a merchant, would send a servant after him; and the driver, confident of not being robbed, would consent to turn out of his road and be conducted into the great hall where he would throw open his trunks and hand around the many treasures within: the silks and velvets and perfumes and jewels, the various curios and inventions whose use was unknown in those parts. Finally he would be off, greatly enriched and quite unharmed. Or some pilgrim band would come knocking at the gate and when they had been fed and their wet clothes hung steamingly by the fire they would recount the story of their travels: the errant rocking voyages by sea, the long marches over hot sands, the fury of the paynims, the Syrian caves, the Manger and the Sepulcher. Before leaving they would present the young lord with seashells such as they wore sewed to their coats in token of their travels.

There were days when the lord feasted his old companions-at-arms. They drank and talked, recalling old engagements: the fortresses stormed, the rams and catapults making their din, the terrible wounds. Julian shouted as he listened and his father was now convinced that some day he would be a conquerer. But then evening came, and seeing the noble modesty with which, after prayers, he went among the kneeling poor to distribute alms, his mother decided that he was a future archbishop.

His place in chapel was next to his parents and even when the services were very protracted he stayed quietly on his knees with hands clasped firmly and his cap beside him on the floor. One day during Mass he looked up and saw a small white mouse creep from a hole in the wall, travel the length of the first altar step, explore about uncertainly, then trot back to its hole. Thinking to see the mouse again next Sunday, he felt strangely anxious. He did see it: the mouse reappeared; and each Sunday thereafter he watched for it, more and more anxious, hating the creature, intent on destroying it. So one Sunday after Mass he closed the door and strewed crumbs along the altar steps and stood waiting by the hole, armed with a stick. Long minutes passed, a small pink snout appeared, at last the entire mouse. He struck lightly, then stood amazed when the small body no longer moved. On the floor was a single drop of blood. Hastily Julian wiped it up with his sleeve, and tossed the dead mouse outside, saying nothing to anyone.

So many small birds pecked at the seeds in the garden that he thought of making a weapon out of a hollow reed filled with dried peas. When he came upon some tree that was noisy with birds, he approached it quietly, leveled his shooter, and blew out his cheeks. Birds came raining down in such abundance that he laughed aloud, pleased with his cleverness. As he was returning one morning along the rampart he spied a fat pigeon taking the sun there. He stopped to look at it; and as the wall was breached at this point and loose stones lay at hand, he grabbed one and swung and the bird dropped heavily into the moat.

He raced down after it, tearing his flesh on the brambles, searching wildly, as keen on the hunt as a young dog. The pigeon hung quivering in a bush with its wings broken. Its obstinate life filled him with rage. He took its throat in his hands and squeezed; the bird's struggles made his heart pound and his loins crawl with a strange lust and when it finally stiffened he was close to fainting.

At supper that night his father announced that the boy was old enough to learn to hunt. He got out an ancient book treating of the art of venery, written in the form of questions and answers exchanged between some master hunter and a pupil. It told how to train dogs and falcons, set traps, know a stag by its droppings, a fox by its tracks, a wolf by its lair, how best to start and track animals, where they are apt to take cover, which winds are most favorable, what cries to employ in the chase and what rules govern the division of the quarry. When Julian was able to repeat all this by heart his father made him a present of a magnificent pack of hunting dogs. There were twenty-four Barbary greyhounds, faster than gazelles but terribly wild and apt to get out of hand. There were seventeen pairs of loud-baying deep-chested white-and-russet Breton dogs, which looked wild but were easily controlled. For hunting wild boar with their ugly tactic of doubling back on the hunter, there were forty great shaggy boarhounds; and for bison hunting there were Tartary mastiffs which stood almost as tall as a jackass. Spaniels' black coats shone like satin; beagles sang out and setters yapped in chorus. In a yard by themselves were eight growling, eye-rolling, chain-rattling bulldogs—terrible beasts that leap at men's throats and are quite unafraid of lions.

Every dog in the pack ate white bread, drank from troughs of hewn stone, and answered to some high-sounding name.

At that the dogs were probably inferior to the falcons. Spending money freely, the old lord acquired tiercelets from the Caucasus, sakers from Babylonia, gerfalcons from Germany; he had the kind of pilgrim-hawks which are only captured along the high shores of cold seas in far parts of the world. A special shed housed all the birds; there they were chained along a perch according to size, and led out every so often to stretch and play on their own strip of turf. In the shops of the castle men were busy making purse-nets, hooks, traps and snares of all kinds.

Julian's family sometimes got up large parties to go quail hunting in the fields. There the bird dogs soon began to point, then crouched motionless while the runners-in advanced with care and spread an immense net over and around them. A word from the huntsmen and the dogs barked; the quail took wing, and the ladies of the neighborhood with their husbands, children and maidservants, dashed for the net and captured the birds with ease. Or hares were started by beating on drums or foxes tumbled into pits or wolves thrust unsuspecting paws into cruel traps.

But Julian scorned these easy contrivances, preferring to hunt alone with horse and hawk. The hawk was usually a great white Scythian tararet, which perched firmly on his master's arm while they covered the plain at a gallop, a plume nodding on its leather hood and golden bells tinkling around its blue claws. When Julian loosed the jesses, letting him go, the wonderful bird shot arrow-like into the sky. Julian saw two dark specks circle and meet and vanish into the blue altitudes; then the falcon would drop dizzily from the skies, tearing at some bird in his claws, and resume his perch on the gauntlet with shaking wings. So Julian hunted heron, kites, crows and vultures.

He loved also to sound his horn and follow the dogs as they raced down the hills and jumped the streams and climbed to the next woods; and when a stag fell among them, moaning as they attacked it with their teeth, he skillfully dispatched it, then looked on with pleasure while they tore and devoured the bloody carcass.

On foggy days he hid out in the marshes to watch for geese, otter or wild duck. Three of his squires would have been waiting for him on the steps since daybreak; and even though the old monk his teacher made admonitory signs at him from his high window, Julian refused to look back. He went out in rain or storm or broiling sun, drank with his cupped hand from springs, ate wild apples as he went, snatched brief naps under trees; and reached home at midnight with burrs in his hair, mud and gore on his clothes, and the smell of game all over him. Gradually he came to resemble the wild things he hunted. He was indifferent to his mother's entreaties, cold to her kisses, and seemed to be caught in the dark toils of a dream.

He killed bears with a knife, bulls with a hatchet and wild boars with a spear. And once, with nothing but a stick, he kept off a lot of wolves which were feeding on the corpses around a gallows.

There came a winter morning when he set out before daybreak, thoroughly equipped, with his bow astride his shoulder and his quiver slung to his pommel. A couple of terriers trailed his Danish hunter, all three of them keeping step and pounding the ground in unison while the wind blew and frost collected on his coat. Toward the east the sky began to clear and in the pallid light he saw a multitude of rabbits leaping and running among their burrows. Immediately the dogs were among them, upon them, cracking their frail spines. Next he was in a stretch of woods and, spying a woodcock that perched as if frozen to a branch, with head under wing, he made at it with a backstroke of his sword and severed its two feet from its body and was off without stopping to retrieve it.

Three hours more and he was cresting a mountain so immensely high that the heavens hung blue-black around him; and there in front of him was an expanse of flat rock with a precipice beyond and a couple of wild goats standing far out on it gazing idly into the gulf. Having no arrows— he had left his horse behind—he decided to fall directly upon them; and so, barefoot, bent double, dagger in hand, he advanced painfully towards them and brought the near one down with a sudden thrust in the ribs. The other, in a panic, leaped towards the void and Julian was after it to strike it down in turn when he stumbled and fell headlong across the body of the dead goat and there he lay, arms flung wide, staring down into space.

Then he was on the flats once more, following a willow-bordered stream, and a great number of cranes were in low shuttling flight above his head. Julian cut them all down, one by one, with his whip.

Meanwhile the day grew warmer, the frost melted and the sun broke through the haze. He now saw far off, lead-gray and gleaming, a small lake, and breasting its bright still surface was some unknown beaver-like animal. Across the distance he let fly an arrow and saw the creature sink and was sorry because he could not bring home the skin.

Now he was in an avenue of great trees, and passing under them as under some triumphal arch he entered a forest that lay beyond. A deer suddenly broke cover there, a buck showed in a side road, a badger came out of a hole, a peacock spread his tail along the grass; and when he had slain them all, there suddenly was another deer, more bucks and badgers sprang up around him, more peacocks and jays and blackbirds and foxes and porcupines and polecats and lynxes—an infinity of beasts, increasing as he advanced.

They crowded round him, trembling, with eyes of mild entreaty. But Julian attacked them tirelessly, having no thought except to be upon them with arrow or sword or knife. There was only the brute fact of his existence to remind him that he had been hunting for incalculable hours in some vague country where things happened with the same ease as in our dreams.

Then he saw an astonishing thing that made him pause at last. There opened before him a steep-sided sandy-bottomed valley, a sort of natural coliseum; and it was full of stags, an army of them, which huddled close and breathed warmth on one another, the steamy cloud from a hundred nostrils rising to mingle with the morning haze. For a moment, the prospect of so much slaughter made Julian go faint with excitement; then, springing from his horse, he thrust back his sleeves and began to take aim. With the twang of the first arrow all the stags looked up as one, a diffused moan broke from them, fissures opened in their solid ranks and panic shook the whole herd. As Julian's arrows fell upon them, hemmed in as they were by the valley walls, the herd stampeded. Stags reared, pawed, locked antlers, climbed heavily on each other. And all the while they fell, bodies and antlers piling up into one vast inextricable ever-growing ever-shifting mound. So one by one, with heaving lungs and bursting bowels, they died along the sands and soon everything was still and night came down and the tree-screened sky was the color of blood.

Julian leaned against a tree and stared on the enormous massacre, trying to remember how it had been done. Then across the valley at the wood's edge he saw another stag with its hind and fawn. Dark, enormous, the stag had a white beard and an intricate many-pointed growth of horn; the hind, pale as a dead leaf, grazed idly by while her spotted fawn trotted alongside, pulling at her dugs. Again Julian's bow sang out. The fawn dropped. The mother, looking up, uttered a single shattering all but human cry. Julian, tense, exasperated, brought her down as well, with a shot full in the breast. Seeing her fall the great stag leaped and received Julian's arrow, his last one, between the eyes. There it stuck fast but the stag, indifferent, came striding over the bodies of his dead, came on and on, while Julian retreated in horror, seeing himself charged and laid flat and disemboweled. Then the great stag halted and with burning eyes, solemn, accusing, like some patriarch or judge, he spoke, while off in the distance a bell tolled.

"Accurst! accurst! accurst! one day, O savage heart, you will destroy your father and mother."

The stag dropped quietly to earth and closed his eyes and died.

Julian stood as if stunned; then a weariness swept over him, followed by great waves of disgust and sadness. His horse was lost, his dogs had taken to their heels, the solitude around him seemed full of vague alarms. He fled, striking across country, following a trail at random. And there, suddenly, was the castle gate.

That night he did not sleep but lay staring into the uneven light of the hanging lamp and saw always the great black, bearded wide-antlered stag. The stag's words obsessed him; repeatedly he denied them. "It cannot be that I should kill them. No, no! I have no wish to kill them." Then in a moment he thought, "But suppose I *should* wish—" And he lay and trembled for fear the Devil should implant that unspeakable wish in him.

Three months his mother prayed in anguish by his bed while his father, groaning, paced the corridors. Specialists were brought in, famous doctors and apothecaries; they said he was sick with a miasma or with carnal desire; they prescribed drugs and more drugs. When they questioned him, however, Julian merely shook his head.

Growing stronger, he walked briefly in the courtyard, leaning on his father and the old monk. When he had quite recovered he obstinately refused to hunt again. His father, hoping to bring him around, made him a present of a fine stout Saracen sword. It hung aloft on a pillar among other arms and trophies, and Julian had to mount a ladder to bring it down. It was very heavy and slipped from his hands and, clattering down, grazed the old lord's shoulder and slashed his mantle. Julian fainted, thinking he had killed his father.

From then on he felt a horror of weapons and went white at the sight of a bare blade. This weakness grieved his family and at last the old monk, in the name of God, honor, and the ancestral dead, bade him take up again the exercises of a gentleman.

The squires amused themselves by practicing daily with javelins. Julian soon excelled at this sport and could drive his javelin into a bottle's mouth or strike the tail-feathers from a weathercock or pick out doornails at a hundred paces.

One summer evening he loitered in the arbor, now dim in the failing light; and spying beyond the arbor, against a wall, what he thought to be two white fluttering wings, surely a stork, he hurled his javelin. There was a terrible cry; it was the voice of his mother, whose bonnet with its long white fluttering ribbons stayed pinned to the wall.

Julian fled the castle and was seen there no more.

II

He fell in with a passing troop of adventuring soldiers and came to know thirst, hunger, fever, and vermin, the noise of battle, the sight of dying men. His skin browned in the wind; his arms and legs grew hard under the weight of his armor; and being strong, fearless, just and shrewd, he was soon in command of a company.

With sword aloft he waved his men into battle; he scaled fortress walls by night, hanging to knotted ropes, tugged at by the wind, while sparks of Greek fire clung to his cuirass and boiling tar and molten lead poured hissing down from the battlements. Stones crashed on his buckler, shivering it; bridges overloaded with men gave way beneath him. On one occasion he felled fourteen men with a single swing of his battle-ax; in the lists he overcame all challengers; many times he was left on the field for dead.

Yet he always walked away, thanks to the divine favor which he enjoyed now, because he had become the protector of churchmen, orphans, widows and aged men. Of aged men most of all, and seeing some old stranger on the road ahead he would call out to him to show his face, as if afraid he might kill him in error.

Desperate men flocked to his banner, runaway slaves, serfs in revolt, bastards without fortune; and soon he had an army of his own, its fame increasing with its numbers, until the world sought him out and he was able to give aid by turns to the French Dauphin, the English king, the Templars of Jerusalem, the Surena of the Parthians, the Negus of Abyssinia, the Emperor of Calcutta. He did battle with Scandinavians in fish-scale armor, with Negroes astride red asses and brandishing shields of hippopotamus hide, with East Indians the color of pale gold who waved shining swords and wore their crowns into battle. He subdued the Troglodytes and the Anthropophages. He journeyed through hot countries where men's hair took fire from the sun and they flared up like torches, through cold countries where men's arms snapped freezing from their sockets and fell heavily to earth, through fog-bound countries where they marched among phantoms.

He was consulted by republics in distress, he conferred with ambassadors and obtained unexpected terms, he rebuked tyrants, delivered captive queens and set whole peoples free. It was Julian and no other who slew the Milanese serpent and the dragon of Oberbirbach.

Now the Emperor of Occitania was victorious over the Spanish Moslems and took the Caliph of Cordova's sister as his concubine and by her had a daughter whom he brought up in the Christian faith. But the Caliph, feigning a desire to be converted, arrived with a numerous escort as if on a visit to the Emperor, put his entire garrison to the sword and threw him into a dungeon where he used him cruelly to extort his treasure.

Julian hastened to his aid, destroyed the infidel army, laid siege to the town, slew the Caliph, chopped off his head and tossed it over the ramparts like a ball. Then he released the Emperor and set him on his throne again in the presence of his entire court. By way of reward the Emperor offered him money, whole basketfuls; Julian would have none of it. Did he want more?—the Emperor offered him three-quarters of his wealth and was refused again; then half his kingdom; Julian thanked him and declined. The Emperor was in tears, he saw no way of showing his gratitude. At last he slapped his brow and turned whispering to one of his attendants; a curtain was drawn and there stood a young girl.

Her great dark eyes were like two soft lights and she had a charming smile. Her curls tangled with the jewels on her half-open bodice; through her transparent tunic shone the young lines of her body, which was plump, small, finely made.

Julian was dazzled, all the more because he had been chaste till now. So he took the Emperor's daughter in marriage, with a castle which she held from her mother and, the wedding over, quitted his host after an exchange of many courtesies.

Their palace was built of white marble in the Moorish style and stood on a promontory among orange groves. There was an expanse of bright bay below, a fanlike spread of forest behind, and terraces of flowers descending to a rosy beach where small shells crackled underfoot. The sky was an unchanging blue. Trees stirred in light winds that blew, now from off the sea, now down from the steep all-enveloping mountains.

The rooms were full of shadow yet drew soft light from encrusted walls. Tall reedlike columns supported domed vaults sculptured to represent stalactites in a cave. In the great halls were fountains, in the courts mosaics, on the walls festoons; delicate instances of architectural fancy abounded; and such was the silence everywhere that you could hear plainly the rustle of a scarf, the echo of a sigh.

Julian made war no longer but lived at ease among a tranquil people, contingents of them arriving daily to kneel before him and kiss his hand and do him homage like people of the East, while he lounged in purple dress in some deep-set window and called to mind the old hunting days. He longed to hunt again, to scour the desert after gazelle and ostrich, stalk leopards among the bamboos, strike into forests full of rhinoceros, scale impossible mountains where the eagle screamed, and wrestle with bears on icebergs in the polar sea. Sometimes, in dreams, he saw himself like our father Adam sitting in the middle of Paradise with the entire race of animals around him. He stretched forth an arm and they died. Or else they paraded before him two by two in order of size, from elephants and lions to ermines and ducks, as on the day when they entered Noah's ark. Standing in a cave's mouth, hidden, he rained darts on them, darts that never missed. More animals appeared, endless animals, until, wild-eyed, he woke at last.

There were princes among his acquaintance who invited him to hunt. He refused, thinking by such penance to turn aside the curse. He believed that the fate of his father and mother was linked in some way with the slaughtering of animals. Yet he grieved because he could not see his parents; and his other great desire, the secret one, became more and more unbearable.

His wife hoped to divert him and so engaged jugglers and dancers to perform in the castle, or traveled with him into the country in an open litter, or lay beside him in a boat while they watched the play of wandering fish in sky-clear water. She pelted him with flowers; she sat at his feet and plucked charmingly at the three strings of an old mandolin; and then, in despair, "My dear good lord, what ails you?" she asked mildly, laying a hand on his shoulder.

For a long time he refused to answer though sometimes he wept. Then one day he told her what was horribly on his mind. She fought against it, she argued well. Very probably his father and mother were dead already; and if by chance they were alive still and he should see them again, whatever could make him commit so abominable an act, what weird circumstance or impossible motive? His fears were all groundless, she said, and he should go back to hunting. Julian listened smiling but could not bring himself to yield.

One August night as they were preparing for sleep and she was already in bed and Julian was at his prayers, he heard a fox barking at a distance and, nearer by, directly under the window, soft, stealthy, padding footfalls. Now he was at the window and looking down in the gloom on some vague prowling forms, the shadows, as it were, of animals. He was too strongly tempted. From its hook on the wall, he seized his old quiver; and when his wife looked at him, astonished, he said, "You see! I obey you. I shall be back at sunrise." Suddenly she was afraid and began to speak of accidents and injuries but Julian comforted her and left, surprised to see her so changed.

Soon afterwards a page informed her that two strangers had come inquiring for the lord; in his absence they begged to see his lady at once. They came in to her, an aged couple, each of them leaning heavily on a stick, the dust of the road on their ragged clothes. They made bold to say that they brought news of Julian's father and mother and she leaned from her bed to listen. But first they exchanged a glance and asked if he ever spoke of his parents, still loved them.

"Ah, yes!" she said.

"Well, we are his parents!" they cried, and sat themselves down because they were very tired.

She hesitated. Could it be so? They guessed her doubt and went on to offer proof by describing a curious birthmark on Julian's body. She leaped from bed crying to the page to bring them food. But hungry as they looked, they ate little and she saw how their bony fingers shook when they raised their cups. She answered their many questions about their son but took pains to conceal his terrible obsession. They told her that they had left their castle when Julian failed to return, and wandered for years in search of him, following vague clues, never losing hope. So much of their money had gone into meeting river tolls and inn charges, princes' exactions and those of highwaymen, that they were now quite penniless and had to beg their way. But what of that, when they would soon be able to take Julian in their arms! How happy he must be to have so pretty a wife, they said; and they gazed long at her and kissed and kissed her. The fine room made them stare; and the old man inquired why the walls bore the Emperor of Occitania's coat-of-arms.

"He is my father," she said.

He started, remembering what the gypsy had prophesied, while his wife called to mind the prophecy of the hermit. No doubt their son's present happiness promised some even greater, some eternal, glory to come; and the old couple sat wide-eyed in the blaze of the great candelabra on the table.

They must have been very handsome in their youth. The mother, her fine abundant hair intact, wore it in lengthy white braids along her cheek; while the father, with his great height and great beard, resembled some statue in a church. Julian's wife persuaded them not to wait up for him. She made them sleep in her own bed, tucked them away like children and drew the curtains. They were asleep soon, and outside, in the first gleams of dawn, small birds were singing.

Julian had crossed the park and come into the forest, his step eager, his senses alert to the soft grass and mild moonlit air. Shadows were deep on the moss banks under trees. At intervals there were moon-drenched clearings where he abruptly halted, thinking he was about to plunge into a woodland pond; and there were real ponds, which he mistook for clearings. Everywhere the silence was intense; there was no trace of the animals which only a moment ago had been prowling around the castle. He was now in a dense stand of trees where the gloom was especially thick. He felt the play of warm scented airs on his flesh. His feet sank among dead leaves and he stopped, leaning breathless against an oak.

Then a dark, still darker, something leaped suddenly from behind him, a wild boar, which was off before he had time to seize his bow and which he mourned the loss of as if that was a great misfortune. Leaving the woods he spied a wolf stealing along a hedge and let fly an arrow. The wolf stopped, looked briefly around at him, and went on. It trotted evenly along, keeping the same distance from him, halting at intervals; but when Julian started to take aim, it fled. Thus he covered a wide plain, then a tract of sand hills, and came out on high ground overlooking miles of country below.

He was among great flat jumbled stones, the scatterings of some old graveyard long abandoned to the weather. He stumbled over moldy crosses leaning sadly askew among the stones, and he trod on the bones of the dead. There was a stirring of vague shapes in the dark of the tombs, hyenas in wild-eyed panting flight. Their hooves came clattering over the stones and they closed in on Julian, sniffing, yawning, showing their gums. He drew his sword and they fled, severally, at a headlong limping gallop, kicking up a dust which finally hid them from sight.

Later, in a ravine, there was a wild bull pawing the sand and menacing him with lowered horns. Julian thrust at it with his lance but the lance sang out and fell in splinters as if it had come against some bull cast in bronze and he closed his eyes, expecting to be charged and killed. When he opened them the bull was gone.

His heart sank with shame, his strength gave way before some higher power, and striking back into the forest, he headed for home. He was in a tangle of creepers, cutting a passage with his sword, when a weasel shot between his legs; a panther, leaping, cleared his shoulder; around the trunk of an ash a snake coiled upward; from out the leaves above, a huge jackdaw eyed him; and it was as if the sky had rained down all its stars upon the forest, for everywhere around him, sparking the darkness, were the innumerable eyes of beasts—owls, squirrels, monkeys, parrots, bobcats.

Julian attacked them with arrows but the feathered shafts only showered like white butterflies among the leaves. He threw stones, but they dropped harmlessly to earth. He raged, cursed himself, made the forest loud with imprecations. Then the various animals he had just been hunting showed themselves and came round him in a narrow circle, keeping erect or going down on their haunches. There he stood in the midst of them, terrified and quite unable to move. By making a great effort he succeeded in taking a step forward. As soon as he moved, wings began to flutter in the trees, paws stirred on the ground, and the whole assemblage moved with him. He went on, the hyenas striding ahead, the wolf and the boar behind; the bull, swinging its enormous head, on his left; the snake coiling along through the grass on his right; the panther advancing at a distance with arched back and long soft-footed strides. He walked very slowly to avoid exciting them and as he went he saw porcupines, foxes, jackals, vipers and bears breaking cover around him. He began to run and they ran too. The snake hissed, the dirtier creatures slavered; he felt the boar's tusks prodding at his heels, the wolf's hairy snout nuzzling his hand. Monkeys pinched him and made faces; a weasel somersaulted over his feet; a bear knocked his cap from his head with a backswing of its paw; and the panther, after chewing placidly on an arrow, let it drop with disdain.

There was irony in their sly motions. Watching him from the corners of their eyes, they seemed to be planning some revenge; and Julian, dazed by buzzing insects and the slapping of birds' tails and the breath from many nostrils, walked like a blind man with eyes closed and arms flung out, not daring even to cry, "Have mercy!"

A cock crowed, others replied, day was breaking; and Julian made out the lines of the castle roof riding above the orange trees. Then he discovered some partridges fluttering in a stubblefield close by. He flung off his cloak and threw it over them like a net. On lifting it, however, he found only the decaying body of a bird long dead. This was the worst irony yet; he raged anew; the thirst to kill came over him and, failing beasts, he would gladly have killed men. Quickly he mounted the three terraces and with a blow of his fist swung the door wide. But on the stairs within he remembered his darling wife and his heart softened. She was no doubt asleep and he would have the pleasure of surprising her. Quietly, his sandals in his hand, he turned the knob and entered their bedroom.

The early light came dimly through leaded windows, Julian stumbled over some clothes lying on the floor; a little farther, and he knocked against a table loaded with dishes. "She must have eaten," he thought and advanced with caution towards the alcove where, in total darkness, the bed stood. He stooped to kiss his wife, bending over the two who lay there side by side in sleep. His lips touched a man's beard and he fell back, thinking he was out of his mind. He stooped over the bed again and this time his searching fingers discovered a woman's long hair. To assure himself that he had been mistaken, he felt for the beard again—and found it! found a man there, a man lying with his wife.

He was upon them in a fury, striking with his dagger, foaming, stamping, howling like a wild beast. At last he stopped. Pierced through the heart they had not so much as stirred, they were dead. He heard the rattle of death in their throats, rhythmic, prolonged, growing feebler at last, mingling then with another sound, now vague and far off, now coming steadily closer, swelling, ringing out cruelly; and he recognized in terror the belling of the great black stag.

He turned and saw in the door, candle in hand, ghostlike, the pale figure of his wife. Drawn there by the sounds of violence, she took it all in with one wide glance and fled in horror, dropping the candle. Julian picked it up.

His father and mother lay face up before him with great wounds in their breasts. In their superb gentle eyes was the look of people intent on keeping a secret forever. There was blood on their white hands, the bedclothes, the floor, the ivory crucifix on the alcove wall. The glare of the newly risen sun made the whole room red as if with blood. Julian looked at the dead. He said to himself, endeavored to believe, that this thing could not be, that he must be entangled in some fearful error. To make sure of their identity he stooped close over the old man's face and saw beneath open lids two eyes, now glazed, which scorched him like fire. He then circled the bed to where, in the dark recesses of the alcove, the other body lay, the face half hidden by white hair. He lifted the head with one hand and with the other held the candle close to it while drop by drop the bed discharged its load of blood upon the floor.

At evening he came in where his wife was and speaking with a stranger's voice bade her first of all not to answer him or come near him or even look at him; then to obey, under penalty of damnation, his various commands, every one of which she must consider irrevocable.

In the death-chamber she would find written instructions for the funeral. These she must carry out to the letter. To her he made over everything he owned: castle, serfs, goods—even the clothes on his back and the sandals on his feet, which she would find presently at the stair head.

The dead were splendidly interred in an abbey church at three days' journey from the castle. A monk, his face concealed by his hood, followed the procession at a distance and to him no one dared speak. All during the Mass he lay flat on the porch floor, his arms crossed, his face in the dust.

After the burial he was seen to take the road leading to the mountains. He looked back at intervals and finally was gone.

III

He went about the world begging his way. He reached up a hand to horsemen on the roads, bent a knee to reapers in the fields, stood patiently at castle gates, and looked so grief-stricken that he was not refused. Humbly, again and again, he told his story and people fled crossing themselves. When he passed through a village where he had been before, they abused and stoned him and shut their doors in his face, although a few charitable souls put plates of food on their windowsills before banging the shutters on the unholy sight of him.

Shunned by all, he began to shun mankind himself, feeding on roots, plants and windfalls, and shellfish gathered along the beaches of the world. Sometimes, on coming over a hill, he would find himself in sight of some multitudinous jumble of roofs and spires below; from the dark maze of streets came the steady hum of human life and he would be drawn downward by a need to be with other people. No sooner was he in the streets, however, than the brutal look on people's faces, the bustle in the stores, the uproar of shops and foundries, the callous idle talk, would begin to freeze his heart. On feast days when bells began tolling at daybreak and people responded with excitement, he watched them pouring from their houses, the dancers in the public squares, the beer fountains at the crossroads, the rich bright hangings on the princely houses; and then after dark he spied through windows on the long family tables where old people sat with children in their laps. He would turn away in tears and strike back into the country.

He gazed with yearning at colts in their pastures, birds in their nests, insects among flowers; all fled at his approach. He sought out deserted places but there was the rattle of death in the blowing of wind, tears in the dewdrops, blood in the sun at evening, and parricide by night in his dreams. He undertook acts of mortification, ascended on his knees to high and holy places. But the horror in his mind corrupted the splendor of tabernacles and nullified the rigor of his penances. He did not curse God for having caused him to murder, but having murdered he despaired of

God. The horror he felt of his own person made him risk it eagerly in dangerous enterprises. He rescued children from pits in the earth and helpless men and women from their burning houses. But the earth rejected him, the flames spared him. With the passing of time he suffered not less but more and finally he resolved to die.

One day, however, while he was staring into a spring of water to judge of its depth, he saw appear on the far side an old man with so much misery on his lean white-bearded face that Julian suddenly wept. The old man fell to weeping too; and Julian, looking him in the face, knew him and did not know him. "My father!" he cried and thought no more of destroying himself.

So, weighed down with memories, he traversed many lands and came at last to a river which tore along swiftly between marshy shores and had long defied anyone to cross it. Mud-bound and half concealed in the reeds lay an old boat, and on looking around Julian also discovered a pair of oars. It came over him that he might devote his life to the service of others.

He began by constructing a sort of ramp across the marsh, connecting the river's channel with solid ground. He broke his nails on enormous stones, carried them pressed against his heaving stomach, sprawled in the mud, sank into it, was nearly drowned several times. Then he set to patching up the boat from the debris of other vessels and he made himself a hut of logs and clay.

Travelers soon heard of Julian's ferry and began to flock to it. On the far side a flag was raised to summon him and Julian would leap aboard and row across for the waiting passengers. The boat was heavy to begin with and when it was loaded with men and their belongings including domestic animals that kicked and reared in alarm, it could only be managed with difficulty. He asked nothing for his trouble though some of the passengers gave him wornout clothes or leftovers from their store of food. The ugly ones cursed him out and he reproved them gently. If they went on cursing, he was satisfied to bless them.

A small table, a stool, a bed made of dry leaves, and three earthen bowls were all the furnishings he had while a couple of holes in the wall served as windows. In front the great river rolled its turgid green flood; at the rear stretched a vast colorless barrens strewn with shallow ponds. In spring the damp soil reeked of decay; then came powerful winds driving dust before them till it roiled the water and gritted between his teeth; then came mosquitoes in endless humming biting clouds; then appalling frosts which turned the earth to stone and gave him in his chilled and exhausted state a tremendous appetite for meat. Months passed when Julian, seeing no one, sat with his eyes shut trying to revive in memory the days of his youth. A castle courtyard would rise before him with greyhounds at rest on the terraces, grooms busy in the armory, and a yellow-haired boy sitting in a bower of vines between an old man wrapped in furs and a lady in a tall bonnet. Suddenly an image of two dead bodies would intervene and he would fling himself on his bed and sob, "Ah, poor father!

Poor mother, poor mother!" and, dozing off, he would continue to see them in dreams.

There came a night when he thought he heard someone calling him in his sleep. He strained to listen but made out nothing except the river's roar. Then "Julian!" the same voice cried again, "Julian!" It reached him, amazingly, from the far shore of the broad and noisy river. "Julian!" he heard again, the voice loud, vibrant, like a church bell. With lantern alight, he stepped from the hut into a night wild with wind and rain, the river foaming white in the intense darkness.

He hesitated briefly then leapt into the boat and cast off. Instantly the waves subsided and the boat sped easily to the far shore. There a man stood waiting in a ragged coat, his face white as a plaster mask, his eyes redder than coals. Holding up his lantern Julian saw that the stranger was covered with hideous sores. He was a leper but he had the majesty of a king. The boat gave alarmingly under his weight, then rose again, and Julian began to work the oars.

At every stroke the bow slapped against a wave and was flung aloft, while dark water streamed alongside. Masses of water gathered beneath, thrusting the boat skyward, then fell away, leaving it to skitter down into some deep trough where it spun helplessly. Julian could only keep it under control by leaning far forward and then, feet powerfully braced, hands riveted to the oar handles, flinging his torso backward with a convulsive pull at the oars. Hail cut his hands, rain poured down his back, and suddenly breathless in the terrible wind, he paused, letting the boat drift with the waves. But feeling that something very great was at stake, a mission that he must not fail, he once more seized the oars and made them rattle on their pins in the loud wind. At the bow the lantern burned, its rays intercepted at intervals by the fluttering passages of storm-blown birds. But always he saw the eyes of the Leper who stood immobile at the stern. And they were a long, long time in crossing.

Arrived in the hut Julian closed the door behind them. The Leper took the stool and sat. His shroudlike dress fell to his loins; his chest, his shoulders, his lean arms were plastered with sores. There were great pained wrinkles on his forehead. Skeleton-like, he had a hole instead of a nose; his lips were blue, a steamy and malodorous exhalation pouring from them.

"I am hungry!" he, said.

Julian gave him what he had, a black loaf and rind of bacon. When he had devoured them, the table, bowl and knife handle bore the same sores that he had on his body. Then he said,

"I am thirsty!"

Julian went to get the water jug and found it full of some exciting sweet-smelling liquid. It was wine—a wonderful find. The Leper reached for it and drank the jug dry at a draught.

Then he said, "I am cold."

Julian put his candle to a heap of dried fern in the middle of the floor. The Leper, on his knees, crouched by the fire, body shaking, sores running, eyes growing dim. He was weakening visibly, and in a faint voice murmured,

"Your bed!"

Julian helped him to it gently and covered him with everything he had, even the tarpaulin for his boat. The Leper groaned through his teeth, the rattle of death came faster in his chest, and with every breath he took his belly sank into his spine. At last his eyes went closed.

"My bones are like ice! Come close to me!"

And Julian, raising the tarpaulin, lay down at his side on the dry leaves. The Leper turned his head. "Take off your clothes," he commanded, "that I may have the warmth of your body." Julian flung off his clothes and lay down once more as naked as on the day he was born. Against his thigh he felt the Leper's skin, colder than a snake and rough as a file. He tried to cheer him but the other merely said in a low whisper, "I am dying. Come closer, get me warm! No! not with your hands, with your whole body."

Julian laid himself at full length upon him, mouth to mouth, breast to breast. The Leper clasped him hard and suddenly his eyes shone like stars, the hair on his head was like the rays of the sun, his breath was like the breath of the rose, there was incense in the smoke of the fern-fire, music on the water. To Julian, fainting, came a great bliss, a joy more than human; and the one who held him grew tall, grew taller, till his head and feet touched the two walls of the hut. The roof gaped, the wide firmament looked down—and Julian rose into blue altitudes face to face with Our Lord Jesus who carried him up to heaven.

And that is the story of Saint Julian the Hospitaller more or less as you will find it on a church window in my part of the country.

Following is the life of the saint as gathered by Jacques de Voragine in the *Légende Dorée,* the fundamental text from which Flaubert borrowed his narrative outline. The reader should find it interesting to compare the original with Flaubert's artistic reworking of the material.*

The Story of St. Julian
From The Golden Legend

There was yet another Saint Julian. This one, who was of noble family, was hunting one day, while still a youth, and set out in pursuit of a stag. Suddenly the stag turned upon the young man, and said to him: "Why dost thou pursue me, thou who are destined to be

* From *The Golden Legend of Jacobus de Voragine, Part One,* translated from the Latin and adapted by Granger Ryan and Helmut Ripperger (London: Longmans, Green & Co. Ltd., 1941), pp. 130–131, reprinted by permission of Granger Ryan and Helmut Ripperger.

the murderer of thy father and mother?" The youth was so affrighted at these words that, in order to escape the fulfillment of the stag's presage, he went away secretly, travelled over boundless distances, and finally reached a kingdom where he took service with the king. He bore himself so manfully in war and in peace that the king dubbed him a knight, and gave him, as his wife, the widow of a very rich lord. Meanwhile Julian's parents, bereaved at his disappearance, wandered about the earth in search of their son; and one day they chanced to halt at the castle which was now Julian's home. But he happened to be away from home, and his wife received the two wayfarers. And when they had told her their story, she saw that they were her husband's parents; for he had doubtless often told her of them. So she tendered them a heartfelt welcome, and bade them take their rest in her own bed. The next morning, while she was at church, Julian returned home. He approached the bed to awaken his wife; and seeing two figures asleep beneath the coverings, he thought that his wife was lying with a lover. Without a word he drew his sword, and slew the two who lay asleep. Then, going out of the house, he came upon his wife returning from the church, and, aghast, asked her who the two persons were who slept in her bed. And his wife answered: "They are thy parents, who have been long in quest of thee! And I gave them our bed for their rest." Hearing this, Julian would have died of grief. He burst into tears, and said: "What will become of me, wretch that I am? Now I have done my dear parents to death, and fulfilled what the stag foretold, all in trying to avoid it! Farewell, then, sweet my sister, for I shall not rest until I have received assurance of the forgiveness of God!" But she replied: "Think not, beloved brother, that thou must set out without me! I have shared thy joys; it is mine to share thy sorrows!" Hence they took flight together, and went to live on the bank of a great river, where the crossing was fraught with danger; and there, while they did penance, they carried those who wished to cross from one shore to the other. They likewise received travellers in a hospice which they had built with their own hands. Long after this, in the middle of a freezing night, Julian, who had lain down overcome with weariness, heard the plaintive voice of a wayfarer asking to be set across the stream. Straightway he arose and ran to the stranger, who was half dead with cold, and carried him into his house, where he lighted a great fire to warm him. Then, seeing that he was still nearly frozen, he laid him in his own bed and covered him with care. But on a sudden this stranger, who was eaten with leprosy and horrible to look upon, changed into a shining angel. And as he rose into the air he said to his host: "Julian, the Lord has sent me to say to thee that thy repentance has been accepted, and that soon, with thy wife, thou shalt have rest in God." And the angel disappeared: and shortly thereafter, Julian and his wife, full of charity and good works, fell asleep in the Lord.

Nina of Ashkelon

Yehuda Amichai 🦌

Once I had a summer girl who left me at summer's end. At first I
thought when she left and autumn came that if she hadn't gone there
would have been no autumn, that her leaving had caused the coming of
autumn. Since then I have learned that there was no connection between
the two events. There are many such parallel cycles: the cycle of seasons,
the cycle of my life, the cycle of my loves, and that of my loneliness. Because of her and others too, and because of all of these, I was late going
on my vacation to Ashkelon.

I came to the place like the Roman merchant who was buried there
upon his return from a visit to Southern Italy, his birthplace; he returned to the East and died. Artists were brought to decorate the interior
of his grave. This same Roman merchant inspired various reflections
and dreams in me. Not far from the hotel was his grave, in a hollow
between two sand dunes.

People sitting on the grass in the hotel garden said: "One has to see
the antiquities." Why are people in our country so excited about antiquities? Perhaps because the present is not certain, and the future less
so. In ancient times they used to forecast the future. Now we program
the past.

In the evening, the proprietor of the hotel strolled among his guests,
delighted to see that they ate with gusto. He was red all over, like
sausages boiled in water. Sometimes he put his hands on the table as if
he wanted to serve himself up, so eager was he to please his guests. Aside
from myself, the guests included a young couple who had been married
the day before, and a muscular German woman with a strong, aggressive
voice, and many others.

The next day we went to the historic excavations near the hotel. In
the grave of the Roman merchant were some mosaics and broken pillars
and marking places for the archaeologists—little notations like price tags
in a shop window. Also there were chalk lines and wires strung about to
aid the digging. We clustered around our guide. Once upon a time I
hated to go to such places in an organized group. Now I loved the crowd,
the closeness of bodies, the voices. Watch your step, behold, see the bas
relief. Marvelous!

Sometimes I return alone to a place like this after having toured it with
a group. And so it happened that in the evening I returned to the dead
Roman's grave and sat in the soft, loose sand among the slips of paper
and wires. On the road a car was passing slowly, like a police car, cruis-

*Translated from the Hebrew by Ada Hameirit-Sarell, copyright © 1967 by the
American Jewish Committee, reprinted from* Commentary, *July 1967, by permission.*

ing, looking for something. Young men and women were sitting in the car, discussing whether they should stop and get out. Finally they drove on toward the tall tower in town. I studied the excavations. As in an architect's plans, you could see the foundations. This was house construction in reverse. The site had been turned into a plan, the plan flew into the builder's head, and from his head to the wide world.

I walked down to the sea and took off my shoes. The small crabs fled from me and disappeared into their holes, as did the sun, which was speeding toward the hole in the West where it would vanish. I watched the sun set while tying my sandals. We have learned to perform many actions simultaneously: I could sit tying on my sandals, sit and kneel and look toward the setting sun. If we are trained well, we can do three or four things together at the same time: ride in a car, cry, and look through a window; eat, love, think. And all the time consciousness passes like an elevator among the floors.

Later in the evening, a movie was shown in the garden. Everyone took a chair and sat down. Dogs and children ran about, draining off the attention of the audience; then they ran away and our attention returned to the preparations for the movie, the memory of supper, and gossip. The movie projectionists arrived late. A chair was placed on top of another chair to raise the projector to the proper height. The movie was about dancing, stabbing, and loving, all three of which seemed to be going on at the same time.

A girl passed between the screen and the projector. All the adventures mounted her back. I was jealous of her; she smiled. Her body moved in her dress as in a sea. Tomorrow she would go down once more to the soft beach. She did not have to labor much; life came her way, as readily as the movie that was now being shown on her white back. Two dogs jumped on each other. In a distant wing of the hotel a light went on. Someone left the audience. Someone didn't feel well. From the kitchen we heard the voice of a girl, singing.

The hotel owner said, "Later we shall go down to the beach and fry sausages." Those were his exact words. The movie ended and the chairs were left for the waiters to replace. We all descended to the beach. On the way we passed Shemuel's coffee-house, where there were many pillars and a paved floor for dancing. That was Shemuel's coffee-house. Shemuel had tried many things before he opened his coffee-house near the sea that was black by night and green by day. That evening he had strung colored bulbs in happy chains in the sky of his coffee-house, along the tops of the pillars which surrounded the dance floor. He governed his skies with the help of electric wires at night, and by day with canvas awnings that fenced out the noonday sun. That evening, soldiers from a nearby camp sat under his skies near the whispery sand. They had come to celebrate a victory, or to be comforted after defeat. At any rate, they had come to rest from the training-grounds, the outposts, and the army offices. Silken girls put fumbling hands on their shoulders. Girls with rosy ice-cream thighs and eyes of chocolate cake. Whispering sand-girls who kept their warmth at night. Some of the soldiers had come with their heavy boots on, and danced like bears, swayed like drunkards. Shemuel looked upon all of them with pleasure and satisfaction; every once in a while he took a tray and passed among the dancers to attend to their wishes. We decided to postpone the sausage business until the following night. Some of the older women wanted to stay and watch the young soldiers dance. We sat with the local doctor. He nudged my shoulder and said: "Look, there is Shemuel's beautiful wife."

She was standing near the exit, in front of a sign which said: "Discount for soldiers. Today—shashlik and liver." She had green eyes and a week ago she had returned to her husband. Once, a rich American had come to Ashkelon and she had run after him—literally. They had exchanged a few words while she served him in her husband's restaurant, then, simple as it sounds, she ran to the kitchen, threw off her apron, and ran after him across the sands through the thin bushes. That is to say, sitting in his hotel room in the town of Ashkelon, he did not yet know that she was pursuing him. Her shoes had filled with sand and she threw them away, she almost did the same with her skirt and lace panties. All these things—shoes, clothes, strange thoughts, the outgrowths of culture—disturbed her in her flight and her green eyes were those of a wildcat in an ancient forest. It was early morning when she arrived at the American's room. The next day she married him and they left together. After three months she returned. It is not to be supposed that she crossed the sea on her own power, although she was an able swimmer and fully capable of leaving her clothes in a heap near the shore in Naples and swimming to the shores of Israel. How and why they parted was not known.

Anyway, she came back through the sands, without a suitcase and clad in the same dress she had been wearing when she left; she was tired and barefoot. A week ago the exact same thing happened; she came back, disheveled, from a similar adventure, and refused to utter a word. She had to be taught to speak all over again.

That evening, as I have said, she stood near the exit, framed by the large sign, green-eyed, nose tossing, her mouth large and quiet in her white, traveler's face. The fat doctor looked her over and said: "She is ready for new sands and new dances. That one will never be cured. She's like a Siamese twin to the whole world. A new American will come, or even a Greek or a Roman, as they used to come here in ancient days, and she will run after him." The doctor pointed to the Roman's tomb and fell silent.

One of the officers on the dance floor went out, picked some narcissus flowers, and handed them to her. She said to him: "I know their scent." He answered: "I do not yet know yours." She said: "For you it is not worthwhile." Her husband was not jealous, and he permitted the officer to hand her the flowers. Shemuel had learned not to be jealous. Every day he wrote out the menu on the board in front of which his wife was now standing. He knew what was to be served at the noon meal, and he knew whether there would be a dance for the soldiers in the evening. But he didn't know if his wife would stay with him.

A dog ran after a moth but failed to trap it. A soldier caught his girl while dancing and lifted her up, swung her about like a young palm branch so that she would bring him a blessing. Shemuel's wife stood still, as if she were examining cloth in a shop. Her eyes were open. The moth tried to fly into her eyes; she shut her lids. The elderly guests returned to the hotel. The doctor stayed with us. The soldiers returned to camp. No one blew the bugle.

At breakfast, conversation was lively. Plans for the day were spread out on the tables. Most of the women came down in shorts; the older the women, the shorter the shorts. After the meal I strolled out toward the bushes, to the site of ancient Ashkelon. I had seen the area by night, surrounded and protected from the three winds by a rampart on which could be seen the remains of walls and towers, and in the West the sea. At night it had looked foreboding and somber, like a snarled entanglement with no exit. So I had decided to explore the area by morning light.

Still, the moment I entered the tangled bushes, my mood became blunt and heavy; I felt threatened. After walking a few hundred yards down the blue road, I reached the edge of the ancient townsite. My feet sank into the flour-like sand. Instantly I found myself in a deserted orange grove. In our country we are used to deserted places, to seeing houses without roofs, windows without houses, bodies without life, blackened plantations, and the remains of cracked roads. But nothing ever nauseated me as much as that orange grove. The dead branches were covered with white snails, the whole grove seemed stricken with leprosy. I stared at the broken aqueducts, partly filled by sand from the sea. Thorns at once beautiful and terrible twined their way to the tops of the branches. There were dark corners among the trees that were too large, too large for their own good: ruined corners that guarded the sterility of their shadows. Green flies buzzed around the sweat on my forehead. I continued walking. Fat fruits dropped from sycamore trees and burst on the ground. Everywhere there was the depressing sensation of sand over dead bodies, of dead bodies over the earth. Sand flies burst in a cloud. The road turned, pathways opened, leading into thickets of tamarisks, pathways at the end of which anything at all might happen. A lair of dark curses in various Mediterranean tongues, the vomit of cultures torn from their homeland and transported here. Now this unholy thicket had all those layers beneath it. Such Mediterranean trickery! Phoenician merchants, Greek merchants, Jewish merchants—striking bargains with heaven and with the dead, bringing the smell of perfume and expensive cloth to the detriment of the native population. It is like this: a skeleton, but not yet a clean skeleton; the odor of a rotting cadaver. I do not mean the odor of the coyotes and wildcats that die night after night in this thicket among the salted branches covered with snails. Such an odor would not nauseate me as did the sweet smell of this skeleton, but not yet a skeleton, of the ancient cultures rotting here in this thicket.

Here, for example, is a sycamore tree, leaning sideways in an un-natural fashion. I know there are trees near the sea and on the slopes that have been bent by the wind, but these sycamores had been per-manently twisted by some intrinsic, predetermined corruptness. This landscape had been prostituted, pampered, spoiled. It destroyed its stomach on sweets. It should not pretend now to have a face of white marble, a girl's face, the tanned face of a soldier. All that is conjuring.

But I, at least, knew what lay underneath, what nourished the syca-mores and the groves, what had really caused the marble pillars to be built. Even those narcissus flowers, so innocent in their whiteness—where did they get that exaggerated scent? It did not come from the sand. Indeed, it is best not to inquire what is in their roots. And those flies of Beelzebub that prey on live bodies and sculptures alike? I speak here of things which have refused to die, that continue an underground existence, beneath the sand and beneath the water, like submerged and incoherent whispers. A landscape that tosses in its bed with wild dreams. And what about that figure of Pan in the Roman's grave? By what metamorphosis did it arrive on this shore? And Shemuel's wife—where was she from? How did she escape, running through the sands, through the sea? And her green eyes?

I went on until I reached the small amphitheater where statues and broken mosaic tiles and Greek ledges lay about in disorder. Every his-torical period had collected in this hole, as in a textbook. The wind rose from the sea and the trees leaned toward the East.

From the amphitheater I took a side trail and walked down past one of the terrible sycamores that bent almost to the earth—that is to say, it was still standing, but in repose. The sycamore was not dead, because the ends of its branches sprouted leaves and sickening, fat fruits. An old, crumbling well-house stood there, with an apparatus made of a double chain and small rectangular scoops for drawing water. I did what every man does when he passes a well: I threw a stone into it, but I heard nothing, neither the sound of water nor the smack of stone on stone. I threw a second stone, but nothing happened. I tried to pull the draw chain. I bent over and suddenly I felt myself covered with a cold sweat. I turned around.

Shemuel's wife was sitting on the trunk of the sycamore, swinging. She bared her teeth:

"Such a one as you are then, a snooper."

"Where do you know me from?"

"You—don't you live in the hotel?"

"Yes . . . but you . . ."

"Yesterday you were sitting with the fat doctor. He is also my doctor. How funny he is. When he examined me after I came back he wanted to kiss me. He's the same size as the Roman merchant buried in the sands."

"What do you know about the merchant?"

"And what are you looking for underneath this town?"

"I'm not looking for anything."

All that time she was sitting swinging on that evil tree. Then she asked me:

"Have you been to the ancient harbor already?"

Again she bared her teeth, then jumped off the tree in a bound and disappeared down one of the trails, parting the bushes with her hands to work her way through. The bushes sprang back after she passed. I was still standing near the old well. Nothing had changed here, I saw. This landscape was no more strange and terrible today than it was a week ago, years ago, millennia ago. Shemuel's wife could as easily have sat in the private amphitheater watching two wrestlers as she stood last night on the dance floor, watching the soldiers. I can imagine one of the wrestlers felling his opponent, then kneeling over him, gripping him with tong-like thighs while looking up at her for further instructions. She sticks to character: "Continue to the death!" The results are known. One of the two, the one lying upon the ground, grapples the other's chest with such force that a jet of blood breaks from his nostrils. The results are well known, known to this landscape, to the sycamore, to the marble, and to the wife of Shemuel, who pretends.

I went on to the harbor and stood on the hill where the pillars faced the sea and there were no ships. In the distance I saw the beach. A whitened skeleton of a cat lay in the deep grass. Near it was a yellow paper and empty cans. I saw that I was standing above some Arab houses. Suddenly I heard a voice calling me; it was the masculine woman from the hotel. All this time I had tried to avoid her, but now I was happy to see her waving to me from the trail. At once the spell vanished. Together we climbed the sand ramparts above which stood the remnants of an ancient wall. She said: "I saw Shemuel's wife, the one from last night. She's a whore. Do you like her?" As she said this she poked me in the chest with her fist and laughed in a coarse, masculine manner. "When I was young, the men looked for sporty girls. I was good at winter sports. I caught my husband on a steep slope in the Alps. What do young men look for today? Fluttering, spoiled, green-eyed, elastic-limbed females like Shemuel's wife."

In the midst of this onesided conversation we reached the orange groves at the entrance to the ancient town. I discovered that many of the trees bore green fruit. It was the end of summer and yet the fruit had not ripened. On a single, broken branch, two oranges were yellowing in sterile, premature ripeness.

Before arriving at the hotel I took leave of my sportive companion, and was again rewarded with a punch that shook me to my bones. I went down to the sea. This time the beach was empty. I had not realized that I had spent almost a whole day on the site of ancient Ashkelon. A blackbird perched on a pillar that had once been consecrated to the gods. Two girls rolled in the sand and shouted. The sea left lines in the sand, but it was impossible to read the future in the palm of this shore. I ran after a crab that was sparkling with a strange silver color, but the silver—a tiny fish, the crab's prey—disappeared. The tamarisks finished their preparations for the night. The sun began to descend into the sea. When I returned to the hotel I was once more surprised by the amount of time that had passed.

After supper, the red-faced hotel keeper donned a white hat and apron. With a huge fork in his hand, he entered the reading room: "Be ready to go down to the sea." Two cooks were kept busy transporting a large stove to the beach; one of the young hotel maids adorned her neck with chains of red sausages, the way daughters of the Hawaiian Islands decorate themselves with flower chains. A merry procession then made its way to the sands. The young married couple preferred not to join us, but remained seated in the reading room. They had not yet acquired an apartment, and they wanted to make believe they owned the hotel.

The landlord and the masculine woman did most of the talking. It did their hearts good to be on the beach, so they began singing, first a Hebrew song, then German hiking songs. The landlord's white hat served to illuminate the way for us. The sea was lazy that night and the moon had not yet come up. The cooks placed the stove on the sand and began stoking it with charcoal. Everyone was enchanted with the blaze, especially those who were close to the stove. Behind us dozed the somber mass of ancient Ashkelon. I did not sit close to the fire. We finished eating the sausages. Then came watermelon, and after the watermelon there were party games. One or two people would leave the group, the rest sat around in a circle, whispering. Then the people who left were called back; they were supposed to guess the plans of those who were sitting in the circle. Later, someone brought out a drum and a harmonica and everyone became sad. Still later they started dancing.

"Let's dance barefoot!" The hotel owner began to worry about the good name of his hotel, and about the welfare of the stove. He told the cooks to take the stove back to the hotel. Some people came from Shemuel's cafe—a few officers, some girl soldiers, the doctor and his quiet wife, and also Shemuel and his wife. At first they participated in the dancing and singing, then they split into separate groups. Suddenly, Shemuel's wife got up and ran in the direction of the waves. She left her shoes near me. The doctor said: "It is nothing. That is always her custom. It is a sort of courtesy visit she pays to the sea."

After a few minutes she came back, all wild and untidy and strange, the hems of her dress wet like lips after drinking. She caught up the hem of her dress and squeezed water out of it and bared her teeth in my face like a terrible biting animal. I saw that her watch had gotten wet. She took off her watch and held it between her teeth.

I told her: "Your watch got wet."

She took her watch out of her mouth and put it next to my ear. Then she walked away. From walking she switched to jumping and from jumping to high, wonderful dance steps near the sea. When she returned, she said to me, "This is a *mitzvah* dance."

I said: "What's possessed you, Penina?"

She laughed and said: "My name is not Penina. They call me Nina."

"A nice name that is."

"That isn't the entire name. They call me Nina the Seagull."

Her voice was hoarse, as if lined with salt and seaweed. Shemuel approached and said:

"Here is a crate brought here by the sea. Once the sea brought a crate full of sardines. Once it brought a young dead whale. The sea brings many strange things. It brings things to my wife too. Sometimes in the morning I see strange objects lying near her sleeping body, like branches, like snails, like objects from an ancient ship that foundered on the rocks. Maybe you could tell me what to do about her?"

"Get her pregnant."

Shemuel laughed, and sighed, and then became silent. Later, one of the officers suggested playing tag near the sea. I remained sitting with Shemuel, who was slow. The doctor took part in the game, then he joined us. Because of his fat belly he couldn't keep running very long. Shemuel stopped talking when the doctor approached. Suddenly we heard screams and laughter and before I knew what had happened Nina jumped up and hid behind me. A young officer passed by us, running in great strides; he didn't realize that she was hiding. Nina's heart was beating hard.

The moon began to rise. Everybody put on bathing suits and went into the sea. Nina's voice was hoarse. All that she had left behind in the world was her little bundle of clothes on the wide sands. The doctor said: "After all, God himself is like that. He is far away from us, and all He left behind is a little pack of clothes on the vast sand, and to us that seems God." Nina screamed from the sea. I rose in alarm, but the doctor calmed me: "That is her custom. Don't be alarmed." I left the doctor and Shemuel and God and Nina's parcel of clothes and joined another group. The masculine woman was among them, demonstrating such heroic feats as running fast, lifting rocks, and other manly deeds. The soldiers stood around her. Some tried to race with her, but she always won. When I approached she shouted: "Come, come!"

Afterward they brought drinks and we drank and the night never became cold. They made a fire in the sand out of old crates. I heard a whisper, a moan: "Get me out! Get me out!" Nobody heard it but me. I went in the direction of the voice. Nina was buried up to her hips in the sand, like a statue found on the beach, laughing. I uncovered her.

"Why don't you ask me? Sometimes intelligent people and artists come from the city and they are glad to find an interesting type like me."

"If I asked, you would lie to me anyway."

"But that, too, is a truth."

"I was convinced you had a fish-tail like the daughters of the sea."

"Come with me to the hotel bar," Nina said.

I agreed; we went up to the hotel in our bathing suits. In came the suntanned Roman merchant and sat with us at the bar. There was no bartender because the hour was late. I went behind the bar and served them. The Roman looked in my direction and said: "Who is he?"

Nina said: "He's mine. I caught him in the sea."

The merchant looked at me from under his short, curly hair and said: "He is good for the big games in the arena." They both laughed until I fell asleep.

I woke up as the first morning chill penetrated the room. I heard a car stop; a man jumped out and called for the cafe owner. I came out wearing pajamas. The man seemed to have come from afar; he asked me: "Are you the cafe owner?" I explained that I was not the cafe owner and that this was a hotel. I could not see clearly in the early dawn.

He said: "Never mind. Come quick!"

I climbed into his car and we drove the length of the shore road in the direction of the dunes. He stopped the car in the high grass, jumped out and ran toward the sea. A woman was lying under a rough army blanket. I was alarmed.

"Don't be afraid," my companion said. Angrily, he pulled the blanket from the figure. The woman was nude. She woke up instantly. It was Nina.

"What are you doing here?" I asked.

"Are you a worrier too? Enough people worry about me."

I told her: "Come back with me to your home."

She laughed: "I have no clothes. He took my clothes as a pawn."

I advised her to cover herself with the blanket. The man who drove me out said: "The blanket is mine, I was passing by and saw a woman lying nude on the sand by the first light of dawn, and I covered her." Finally he agreed to drive us home. On the way she cried on my shoulder.

Shemuel was waiting at the gate of his house. All that day Nina didn't show up at the beach. I sat in the sand by myself and felt the first winds of autumn. Many of the awnings that had been spread against the summer sun were now torn. Papers were flying about or lay on the beach, covered with sand. A group of soldiers, boys and girls, arranged themselves to be photographed, then rearranged themselves after each snapshot. The ones who were standing lay down, a boy put his hand on a girl's shoulder, they posed in profile, then in groups of two and five, and then they all lay down as if dead. The two girls I had seen earlier rolling in the sand came over. They were still laughing and rolling. One of them wore a red bathing suit and her face was loud with pleasure. Everyone cleared a passage for them and they rolled on by us. The place where we had sat the night before was already covered with new sand. The old people sat in red lounge chairs and looked at the sea and waited in silence for death—hoping that death, too, would come to them in silence. Where do they derive their certainty that death will come from the West?

Near the lifeguard's tower a crowd had gathered. Two women undressed underneath a towel, twisting like snakes so as not to reveal their bodies. The lifeguard's skin was covered with tattoos and drawings of daughters of the sea, flowers, and an anchor in deep grass. People dragged up lounge chairs. A woman came out dressed in a white apron embroidered with the Star of David. She turned to me: "Do you see that blanket? The gray one?"

"Yes, I see it."

"Yesterday it was used to cover a dead man who had drowned."

A girl walked by, arm-in-arm with a young man. The camera hanging on his bare chest was like a third eye. They chatted together, then the girl began to leap in happy dancing steps. She ran up to a sandstone boulder, leaned against it with her hands folded behind her back, her face to the sea. There she stood like Andromeda in the Greek legend, waiting for her savior. She wore a helpless smile. The lifeguard, big and husky, walked toward her with a camera in his hands. She stood against the rock; there was no place for her to hide. He came closer, raised a hand as if to hold up a sword, counted aloud, one, two, three, and the girl, saved, jumped against him. But he was too busy turning knobs keeping the pictures in order.

Later, the afternoon games began. Mothers called their children. All the gods in heaven and on earth called their prophets, who began to prophesy without pity, near the terrible woods and the sea. Toward nightfall, everything awoke, and the foreign sea gurgled in small waves toward the beach. People shook the sand from their bodies as if preparing for the resurrection. Some of them walked over to the concrete breakwater where they sat emptying the sand from their sandals and stockings and hair. They were all in a hurry to forget the sea. The shoreline, too, was in a hurry, and raced to join the sea and the sandstone wall at the horizon. I know it was a false joining, a play of perspective. Everything was an illusion of the eyes. The children's cries, too, joined the great silence on the horizon. And everything covered itself with the somber soft grass of night. The sea's thoughts were dry and empty like darkening ears of corn thrown onto the sand. Everything was burnt.

I lay for a short while longer in the sand, watching the feet of those returning home. Then I too returned to the hotel, where I saw Nina sitting on the terrace. Her limbs were elastic and brown from a surfeit of sun. She was wearing red shorts that were so tight I could see the crease of her buttocks. I sat next to her, behind a bush that had provided a screen for us. She rested her feet on the railing, lifting her legs until they looked like a gate, like wings. Then she laughed: "This morning you were quite alarmed—this morning when he awakened you and you found me lying among the weeds at dawn."

We watched a procession of black ants traverse the terrace floor. Nina put on her glasses and took a letter out of her purse. I asked if it was from an admirer. She said she had no admirer because one did not admire her but became crazy about her. Did it please her to have men become crazed at the sight of her face? Why not? Why, then, did she, too, become crazed when she lay out on the sands covered by a strange blanket? She was infected by the craziness of the crazed. There was nothing left for me to say to her. Nina took out her hairpins, letting her hair fall. Her hair flowed down to her waist, to her hips. And my thoughts at that instant were unknit and wild.

In the evening I took leave from Shemuel, her good husband. The next day I was to return to my town. Shemuel received me by himself. We talked about all the subjects in the world but Nina. Each time we felt the conversation coming around to Nina I led him around the subject without fail. Later, I got up to say goodbye. The bedroom door was open and I saw Nina lying in bed. One of her eyes was hidden by the pillow. The second was awake and open. For me, it will never close.

The next day I returned home and right away started work and forgot everything. My profession is to forget; my destination is to remember. One evening I forgot to shut off the radio after the news broadcast. I went to shut it off when they began to announce that the Israeli police were asking for the public's help to locate a certain Nina. They mentioned her family name. Last seen wearing a striped white skirt and a white blouse with rolled sleeves. I returned to my guests and remained silent. How had I seen her last? Dressed in short red pants and with her hair loose. We sat up until midnight and talked about the announcements that are made to the public concerning missing persons. One of my guests said that it was all exaggerated. No sooner does someone go to visit his friends than everybody gets alarmed and announces on the radio that he is lost. Many people get lost in the world. Some of them are announced, some not. I told my guests that in Nina's case it was very serious and that I knew her. At midnight I suddenly heard voices coming from one of the houses nearby. A woman was screaming through her tears: "Go away! Leave me alone, you bastard!" I stood near the window. I saw nothing and then the voices stopped. A train whistled as it passed through the valley. It seemed to me that I had heard Nina's voice. Maybe she needed help. Maybe she was hiding in one of the houses in the neighborhood. The suntanned Roman, who once sat with us at the bar, must have kidnapped her. Maybe they were still hiding around Ashkelon, in the white sands, among the statues.

The following day there was another call for help on the radio. But in this broadcast Nina was described as wearing red pants and with her hair wild. They also announced the languages she knew, and some of the special habits she had, like pulling up her knees, and such personal characteristics as the smile in her eyes. I remembered her with one eye hidden in the pillow and one eye awake and staring. Poor Nina—she must certainly be very tired, wandering through the world with a Roman who wore the uniform of a UN officer. I was sure that he would treat her rudely whenever she became tired or asked for a few minutes' rest by the side of the blue road.

And so the two of them wandered about, hiding from time to time in various places. Once they hid at the house of her girlfriend, who was an expert manicurist. In the same building there was a movie theater, and her friend's apartment adjoined the projection booth and loudspeakers. The soundtrack could be heard on the staircase. I came in haste but Nina was not there. Her friend asked me if I wanted a manicure.

Then they hid in the Caves of the Judges in Sanhedria. Nina sat, her head leaning on his chest; she was pulling and tearing at the hair on his bare chest. Near them was a radio in a small suitcase. To the police description of Nina the Roman added his own: her breasts are brown and small, her thighs are fast and never rest.

On the next news bulletin they again detailed the languages Nina knew. All the Mediterranean tongues: a little bit of Greek and a little Italian and Spanish and Hebrew and a bit of Arabic.

One night, walking along the street, I saw a display window that was still lit. It belonged to a dress shop. One of the big mannequins in the window moved and I saw that it was Nina. Quickly she came out to me and said, "Be quiet, be quiet, don't say a thing." Also, she said that it had become impossible for her to imagine his hands without his voice, nor his eyes without his blood, and at last she said: "I am happy in my wanderings. Don't reveal anything to anyone, otherwise I will die."

I told her: "All this will end in a terrible fall, like the fall of the sycamore fruits."

They began to change their clothing from time to time to avoid being recognized. The radio description no longer corresponded to the real Nina. Yet, if they had known her true description and had searched with true love they would have found them easily. After a while the broadcasts stopped and the police began looking for other people: lunatics who had escaped from asylums, children who had run away from home. One evening, as I was on my way home, I was reminded of a letter that had been lying in my inside pocket. In the street the children were throwing stones at the metal telephone poles, and the poles rang out with each hit. Sometimes a little piece of paper in your pocket becomes more important than all the stones and metal and houses in the outside world. I opened the letter and knew where they were. They had reached the ruined crusader's castle that is near Jerusalem and is called Aqua Bella.

I went there alone. Near the road lay the charred trunk of an olive tree, and near the tree grew five red poppies. I reached the fountains near the ruin. The two of them were sitting under a tall oak tree. Their sandals lay nearby and their belts were loose—a sign that they intended to remain here for a while. I looked into their eyes with an inquisitorial gaze. First I spoke to him alone near one of the thick roots, but he didn't listen to me. His hair was smooth and had been greased with shiny oil. My words did not stay with him. Nina's hair was loose; dry oak leaves and flying thorn seeds clung to it. Her hair was open, and my words clung to her heart. I sat opposite her in the arch of the ruined window over the fountain. Nina didn't look too happy. Vagabonding was not good for her. Her eyes were too wide. She had not slept. Questions and replies played about her eyes and mouth and ears and in her anxious sleep; there were few answers in her mouth. The night came and devoured us like the wolf in the fairy tale.

The next day Nina returned to her husband Shemuel. Shemuel wrote me that she had returned, that one morning she was standing in front of his door, that he had bathed her and put her to bed and that she slept fourteen full hours. I wanted to write him that he must leave Ashkelon because it was a bad place for both of them. Once, as I rode in a darkened bus, I thought I heard Nina's voice. I turned around and no one was there, but it seemed to me that I caught a glimpse of her bright dress and of a white strap shining over her collarbone. Maybe her dress had fallen down over her shoulder, revealing the straps of her brassiere.

Autumn arrived soon after and the clock had to be turned back an hour. All my friends looked forward to the night when they would win a free hour of anarchy, an extra hour of life. For some reason I was afraid of that hour as of an unhealthy growth on the body—a terrible hour of luxury, of Ashkelon. I awoke a bit before the moment when the clock was to be set back. I stood next to the window. Cries for help filled the vacuum of the night, like distress signals from ships at sea. I rolled up my thoughts as if to put them in an empty bottle and set them loose on the wide sea.

At that hour there came a knock on Nina's window. The Roman stood outside, white, smooth, and wonderful like the statue of a god. She followed him to that terrible thicket. There they sat on the trunk of that bent sycamore. Then he drew her with his kisses toward the deserted well house, where the draw chain hung deep into the abyss. She guessed his intention and began to struggle. But he, who had been trained to wrestle from his youth and was nude and greased with wrestler's oil, only laughed. He lifted her and her arms flew upward, as in the ancient sculptures depicting the rape of helpless women. Then he dropped her into the abyss.

The extra hour passed and I closed the window. Next day the radio again began to request help in finding Nina. She had last been seen wearing a white nightgown in the manner of a Greek goddess. After a few days these broadcasts stopped too.

I forgot Nina. But sometimes, I remember her well. First I see her head, then her whole body, her elastic, brown Mediterranean body. They say that sailors first discovered the world was round when they noticed that only the top of a mountain was visible from afar at sea, but that as they approached land, the entire mountain loomed into view. So does Nina rise in the horizon of my memory. First her head, then her entire body. Then I know, like those sailors, that my life too never rests, but revolves and revolves without end.

The Library of Babel

℘ *Jorge Luis Borges*

> By this art you may contemplate
> the variation of the 23 letters . . .
>
> *The Anatomy of Melancholy*,
> part 2, sect. II, mem. IV

The universe (which others call the Library) is composed of an indefinite and perhaps infinite number of hexagonal galleries, with vast air shafts between, surrounded by very low railings. From any of the hexagons one can see, interminably, the upper and lower floors. The distribution of the galleries is invariable. Twenty shelves, five long shelves per side, cover all the sides except two; their height, which is the distance from floor to ceiling, scarcely exceeds that of a normal bookcase. One of the free sides leads to a narrow hallway which opens onto another gallery, identical to the first and to all the rest. To the left and right of the hallway there are two very small closets. In the first, one may sleep standing up; in the other, satisfy one's fecal necessities. Also through here passes a spiral stairway, which sinks abysmally and soars upwards to remote distances. In the hallway there is a mirror which faithfully duplicates all appearances. Men usually infer from this mirror that the Library is not infinite (if it really were, why this illusory duplication?); I prefer to dream that its polished surfaces represent and promise the infinite . . . Light is provided by some spherical fruit which bear the name of lamps. There are two, transversally placed, in each hexagon. The light they emit is insufficient, incessant.

Like all men of the Library, I have traveled in my youth; I have wandered in search of a book, perhaps the catalogue of catalogues; now that my eyes can hardly decipher what I write, I am preparing to die just a few leagues from the hexagon in which I was born. Once I am dead, there will be no lack of pious hands to throw me over the railing; my grave will be the fathomless air; my body will sink endlessly and decay and dissolve in the wind generated by the fall, which is infinite. I say that the Library is unending. The idealists argue that the hexagonal rooms are a necessary form of absolute space or, at least, of our intuition of space. They reason that a triangular or pentagonal room is inconceivable. (The mystics claim that their ecstasy reveals to them a circular chamber containing a great circular book, whose spine is continuous and which follows the complete circle of the walls; but their testimony is suspect;

their words, obscure. This cyclical book is God.) Let it suffice now for me to repeat the classic dictum: *The Library is a sphere whose exact center is any one of its hexagons and whose circumference is inaccessible.*

There are five shelves for each of the hexagon's walls; each shelf contains thirty-five books of uniform format; each book is of four hundred and ten pages; each page, of forty lines, each line, of some eighty letters which are black in color. There are also letters on the spine of each book; these letters do not indicate or prefigure what the pages will say. I know that this incoherence at one time seemed mysterious. Before summarizing the solution (whose discovery, in spite of its tragic projections, is perhaps the capital fact in history) I wish to recall a few axioms.

First: The Library exists *ab aeterno.* This truth, whose immediate corollary is the future eternity of the world, cannot be placed in doubt by any reasonable mind. Man, the imperfect librarian, may be the product of chance or of malevolent demiurgi; the universe, with its elegant endowment of shelves, of enigmatical volumes, of inexhaustible stairways for the traveler and latrines for the seated librarian, can only be the work of a god. To perceive the distance between the divine and the human, it is enough to compare these crude wavering symbols which my fallible hand scrawls on the cover of a book, with the organic letters inside: punctual, delicate, perfectly black, inimitably symmetrical.

Second: *The orthographical symbols are twenty-five in number.*[1] This finding made it possible, three hundred years ago, to formulate a general theory of the Library and solve satisfactorily the problem which no conjecture had deciphered: the formless and chaotic nature of almost all the books. One which my father saw in a hexagon on circuit fifteen ninety-four was made up of the letters MCV, perversely repeated from the first line to the last. Another (very much consulted in this area) is a mere labyrinth of letters, but the next-to-last page says *Oh time thy pyramids.* This much is already known: for every sensible line of straightforward statement, there are leagues of senseless cacophonies, verbal jumbles and incoherences. (I know of an uncouth region whose librarians repudiate the vain and superstitious custom of finding a meaning in books and equate it with that of finding a meaning in dreams or in the chaotic lines of one's palm . . . They admit that the inventors of this writing imitated the twenty-five natural symbols, but maintain that this application is accidental and that the books signify nothing in themselves. This dictum, we shall see, is not entirely fallacious.)

For a long time it was believed that these impenetrable books corresponded to past or remote languages. It is true that the most ancient men, the first librarians, used a language quite different from the one we now speak; it is true that a few miles to the right the tongue is dialectal and that ninety floors farther up, it is incomprehensible. All this, I re-

[1] The original manuscript does not contain digits or capital letters. The punctuation has been limited to the comma and the period. These two signs, the space and the twenty-two letters of the alphabet are the twenty-five symbols considered sufficient by this unknown author. (*Editor's note.*)

peat, is true, but four hundred and ten pages of inalterable MCV's cannot correspond to any language, no matter how dialectal or rudimentary it may be. Some insinuated that each letter could influence the following one and that the value of MCV in the third line of page 71 was not the one the same series may have in another position on another page, but this vague thesis did not prevail. Others thought of cryptographs; generally, this conjecture has been accepted, though not in the sense in which it was formulated by its originators.

Five hundred years ago, the chief of an upper hexagon [1] came upon a book as confusing as the others, but which had nearly two pages of homogeneous lines. He showed his find to a wandering decoder who told him the lines were written in Portuguese; others said they were Yiddish. Within a century, the language was established: a Samoyedic Lithuanian dialect of Guarani, with classical Arabian inflections. The content was also deciphered: some notions of combinative analysis, illustrated with examples of variation with unlimited repetition. These examples made it possible for a librarian of genius to discover the fundamental law of the Library. This thinker observed that all the books, no matter how diverse they might be, are made up of the same elements: the space, the period, the comma, the twenty-two letters of the alphabet. He also alleged a fact which travelers have confirmed: *In the vast Library there are no two identical books.* From these two incontrovertible premises he deduced that the Library is total and that its shelves register all the possible combinations of the twenty-odd orthographical symbols (a number which, though extremely vast, is not infinite): in other words, all that it is given to express, in all languages. Everything: the minutely detailed history of the future, the archangels' autobiographies, the faithful catalogue of the Library, thousands and thousands of false catalogues, the demonstration of the fallacy of those catalogues, the demonstration of the fallacy of the true catalogue, the Gnostic gospel of Basilides, the commentary on that gospel, the commentary on the commentary on that gospel, the true story of your death, the translation of every book in all languages, the interpolations of every book in all books.

When it was proclaimed that the Library contained all books, the first impression was one of extravagant happiness. All men felt themselves to be the masters of an intact and secret treasure. There was no personal or world problem whose eloquent solution did not exist in some hexagon. The universe was justified, the universe suddenly usurped the unlimited dimensions of hope. At that time a great deal was said about the Vindications: books of apology and prophecy which vindicated for all time the acts of every man in the universe and retained prodigious arcana for his future. Thousands of the greedy abandoned their sweet native hexagons and rushed up the stairways, urged on by the vain inten-

---

[1] Before, there was a man for every three hexagons. Suicide and pulmonary diseases have destroyed that proportion. A memory of unspeakable melancholy: at times I have traveled for many nights through corridors and along polished stairways without finding a single librarian.

tion of finding their Vindication. These pilgrims disputed in the narrow corridors, proffered dark curses, strangled each other on the divine stairways, flung the deceptive books into the air shafts, met their death cast down in a similar fashion by the inhabitants of remote regions. Others went mad . . . The Vindications exist (I have seen two which refer to persons of the future, to persons who perhaps are not imaginary) but the searchers did not remember that the possibility of a man's finding his Vindication, or some treacherous variation thereof, can be computed as zero.

At that time it was also hoped that a clarification of humanity's basic mysteries—the origin of the Library and of time—might be found. It is verisimilar that these grave mysteries could be explained in words: if the language of philosophers is not sufficient, the multiform Library will have produced the unprecedented language required, with its vocabularies and grammars. For four centuries now men have exhausted the hexagons . . . There are official searchers, *inquisitors*. I have seen them in the performance of their function: they always arrive extremely tired from their journeys; they speak of a broken stairway which almost killed them; they talk with the librarian of galleries and stairs; sometimes they pick up the nearest volume and leaf through it, looking for infamous words. Obviously, no one expects to discover anything.

As was natural, this inordinate hope was followed by an excessive depression. The certitude that some shelf in some hexagon held precious books and that these precious books were inaccessible, seemed almost intolerable. A blasphemous sect suggested that the searches should cease and that all men should juggle letters and symbols until they constructed, by an improbable gift of chance, these canonical books. The authorities were obliged to issue severe orders. The sect disappeared, but in my childhood I have seen old men who, for long periods of time, would hide in the latrines with some metal disks in a forbidden dice cup and feebly mimic the divine disorder.

Others, inversely, believed that it was fundamental to eliminate useless works. They invaded the hexagons, showed credentials which were not always false, leafed through a volume with displeasure and condemned whole shelves: their hygienic, ascetic furor caused the senseless perdition of millions of books. Their name is execrated, but those who deplore the "treasures" destroyed by this frenzy neglect two notable facts. One: the Library is so enormous that any reduction of human origin is infinitesimal. The other: every copy is unique, irreplaceable, but (since the Library is total) there are always several hundred thousand imperfect facsimiles: works which differ only in a letter or a comma. Counter to general opinion, I venture to suppose that the consequences of the Purifiers' depredations have been exaggerated by the horror these fanatics produced. They were urged on by the delirium of trying to reach the books in the Crimson Hexagon: books whose format is smaller than usual, all-powerful, illustrated and magical.

We also know of another superstition of that time: that of the Man of the Book. On some shelf in some hexagon (men reasoned) there must exist a book which is the formula and perfect compendium *of all the rest:* some librarian has gone though it and he is analogous to a god. In the language of this zone vestiges of this remote functionary's cult still persist. Many wandered in search of Him. For a century they exhausted in vain the most varied areas. How could one locate the venerated and secret hexagon which housed Him? Someone proposed a regressive method: To locate book A, consult first a book B which indicates A's position; to locate book B, consult first a book C, and so on to infinity . . . In adventures such as these, I have squandered and wasted my years. It does not seem unlikely to me that there is a total book on some shelf of the universe; [1] I pray to the unknown gods that a man—just one, even though it were thousands of years ago!—may have examined and read it. If honor and wisdom and happiness are not for me, let them be for others. Let heaven exist, though my place be in hell. Let me be outraged and annihilated, but for one instant, in one being, let Your enormous Library be justified. The impious maintain that nonsense is normal in the Library and that the reasonable (and even humble and pure coherence) is an almost miraculous exception. They speak (I know) of the "feverish Library whose chance volumes are constantly in danger of changing into others and affirm, negate and confuse everything like a delirious divinity." These words, which not only denounce the disorder but exemplify it as well, notoriously prove their authors' abominable taste and desperate ignorance. In truth, the Library includes all verbal structures, all variations permitted by the twenty-five orthographical symbols, but not a single example of absolute nonsense. It is useless to observe that the best volume of the many hexagons under my administration is entitled *The Combed Thunderclap* and another *The Plaster Cramp* and another *Axaxaxas mlö.* These phrases, at first glance incoherent, can no doubt be justified in a cryptographical or allegorical manner; such a justification is verbal and, *ex hypothesi,* already figures in the Library. I cannot combine some characters

dhcmrlchtdj

which the divine Library has not foreseen and which in one of its secret tongues do not contain a terrible meaning. No one can articulate a syllable which is not filled with tenderness and fear, which is not, in one of these languages, the powerful name of a god. To speak is to fall into tautology. This wordy and useless epistle already exists in one of the thirty volumes of the five shelves of one of the innumerable hexagons—and its refutation as well. (An *n* number of possible languages use the same vocabulary; in some of them, the symbol *library* allows the correct definition *a ubiquitous and lasting system of hexagonal galleries,* but *library* is *bread*

---

[1] I repeat: it suffices that a book be possible for it to exist. Only the impossible is excluded. For example: no book can be a ladder, although no doubt there are books which discuss and negate and demonstrate this possibility and others whose structure corresponds to that of a ladder.

or *pyramid* or anything else, and these seven words which define it have another value. You who read me, are You sure of understanding my language?)

The methodical task of writing distracts me from the present state of men. The certitude that everything has been written negates us or turns us into phantoms. I know of districts in which the young men prostrate themselves before books and kiss their pages in a barbarous manner, but they do not know how to decipher a single letter. Epidemics, heretical conflicts, peregrinations which inevitably degenerate into banditry, have decimated the population. I believe I have mentioned the suicides, more and more frequent with the years. Perhaps my old age and fearfulness deceive me, but I suspect that the human species—the unique species —is about to be extinguished, but the Library will endure: illuminated, solitary, infinite, perfectly motionless, equipped with precious volumes, useless, incorruptible, secret.

I have just written the word "infinite." I have not interpolated this adjective out of rhetorical habit; I say that it is not illogical to think that the world is infinite. Those who judge it to be limited postulate that in remote places the corridors and stairways and hexagons can conceivably come to an end—which is absurd. Those who imagine it to be without limit forget that the possible number of books does have such a limit. I venture to suggest this solution to the ancient problem: *The Library is unlimited and cyclical.* If an eternal traveler were to cross it in any direction, after centuries he would see that the same volumes were repeated in the same disorder (which, thus repeated, would be an order: the Order). My solitude is gladdened by this elegant hope.[1]

---

[1] Letizia Álvarez de Toledo has observed that this vast Library is useless: rigorously speaking, *a single volume* would be sufficient, a volume of ordinary format, printed in nine or ten point type, containing an infinite number of infinitely thin leaves. (In the early seventeenth century, Cavalieri said that all solid bodies are the superimposition of an infinite number of planes.) The handling of this silky vade mecum would not be convenient: each apparent page would unfold into other analogous ones; the inconceivable middle page would have no reverse.

Grace

ꙮ   James Joyce

Two gentlemen who were in the lavatory at the time tried to lift him up: but he was quite helpless. He lay curled up at the foot of the stairs down which he had fallen. They succeeded in turning him over. His hat had rolled a few yards away and his clothes were smeared with the filth and ooze on the floor on which he had lain, face downwards. His eyes were closed and he breathed with a grunting noise. A thin stream of blood trickled from the corner of his mouth.

These two gentlemen and one of the curates carried him up the stairs and laid him down again on the floor of the bar. In two minutes he was surrounded by a ring of men. The manager of the bar asked everyone who he was and who was with him. No one knew who he was but one of the curates said he had served the gentleman with a small rum.

"Was he by himself?" asked the manager.

"No, sir. There was two gentlemen with him."

"And where are they?"

No one knew; a voice said:

"Give him air. He's fainted."

The ring of onlookers distended and closed again elastically. A dark medal of blood had formed itself near the man's head on the tessellated floor. The manager, alarmed by the grey pallor of the man's face, sent for a policeman.

His collar was unfastened and his necktie undone. He opened his eyes for an instant, sighed and closed them again. One of the gentlemen who had carried him upstairs held a dinged silk hat in his hand. The manager asked repeatedly did no one know who the injured man was or where had his friends gone. The door of the bar opened and an immense constable entered. A crowd which had followed him down the laneway collected outside the door, struggling to look in through the glass panels.

The manager at once began to narrate what he knew. The constable, a young man with thick immobile features, listened. He moved his head slowly to right and left and from the manager to the person on the floor, as if he feared to be the victim of some delusion. Then he drew off his glove, produced a small book from his waist, licked the lead of his pencil and made ready to indite. He asked in a suspicious provincial accent:

"Who is the man? What's his name and address?"

A young man in a cycling-suit cleared his way through the ring of bystanders. He knelt down promptly beside the injured man and called for water. The constable knelt down also to help. The young man washed the blood from the injured man's mouth and then called for some brandy. The constable repeated the order in an authoritative voice until a curate came running with the glass. The brandy was forced down the man's throat. In a few seconds he opened his eyes and looked about him. He looked at the circle of faces and then, understanding, strove to rise to his feet.

"You're all right now?" asked the young man in the cycling-suit.

"Sha, 's nothing," said the injured man, trying to stand up.

He was helped to his feet. The manager said something about a hospital and some of the bystanders gave advice. The battered silk hat was placed on the man's head. The constable asked:

"Where do you live?"

The man, without answering, began to twirl the ends of his moustache. He made light of his accident. It was nothing, he said: only a little accident. He spoke very thickly.

"Where do you live?" repeated the constable.

The man said they were to get a cab for him. While the point was being debated a tall agile gentleman of fair complexion, wearing a long yellow ulster, came from the far end of the bar. Seeing the spectacle, he called out:

"Hallo, Tom, old man! What's the trouble?"

"Sha, 's nothing," said the man.

The new-comer surveyed the deplorable figure before him and then turned to the constable, saying:

"It's all right, constable. I'll see him home."

The constable touched his helmet and answered:

"All right, Mr. Power!"

"Come now, Tom," said Mr. Power, taking his friend by the arm. "No bones broken. What? Can you walk?"

The young man in the cycling-suit took the man by the other arm and the crowd divided.

"How did you get yourself into this mess?" asked Mr. Power.

"The gentleman fell down the stairs," said the young man.

"I' 'ery 'uch o'liged to you, sir," said the injured man.

"Not at all."

" 'ant' we have a little . . . ?"

"Not now. Not now."

The three men left the bar and the crowd sifted through the doors in to the laneway. The manager brought the constable to the stairs to inspect the scene of the accident. They agreed that the gentleman must have missed his footing. The customers returned to the counter and a curate set about removing the traces of blood from the floor.

When they came out into Grafton Street, Mr. Power whistled for an outsider. The injured man said again as well as he could:

"I' 'ery 'uch o'liged to you, sir. I hope we'll 'eet again. 'y na'e is Kernan."

The shock and the incipient pain had partly sobered him.

"Don't mention it," said the young man.

They shook hands. Mr. Kernan was hoisted on to the car and, while Mr. Power was giving directions to the carman, he expressed his gratitude to the young man and regretted that they could not have a little drink together.

"Another time," said the young man.

The car drove off towards Westmoreland Street. As it passed the Ballast Office the clock showed half-past nine. A keen east wind hit them, blowing from the mouth of the river. Mr. Kernan was huddled together with cold. His friend asked him to tell how the accident had happened.

"I 'ain't 'an," he answered, " 'y 'ongue is hurt."

"Show." .

The other leaned over the well of the car and peered into Mr. Kernan's mouth but he could not see. He struck a match and, sheltering it in the shell of his hands, peered again into the mouth which Mr. Kernan opened obediently. The swaying movement of the car brought the match to and from the opened mouth. The lower teeth and gums were covered with clotted blood and a minute piece of the tongue seemed to have been bitten off. The match was blown out.

"That's ugly," said Mr. Power.

"Sha, 's nothing," said Mr. Kernan, closing his mouth and pulling the collar of his filthy coat across his neck.

Mr. Kernan was a commercial traveller of the old school which believed in the dignity of its calling. He had never been seen in the city without a silk hat of some decency and a pair of gaiters. By grace of these two articles of clothing, he said, a man could always pass muster. He carried on the tradition of his Napoleon, the great Blackwhite, whose memory he evoked at times by legend and mimicry. Modern business methods had spared him only so far as to allow him a little office in Crowe Street, on the window blind of which was written the name of his firm with the address—London, E. C. On the mantelpiece of this little office a little leaden battalion of canisters was drawn up and on the table before the window stood four or five china bowls which were usually half full of a black liquid. From these bowls Mr. Kernan tasted tea. He took a mouthful, drew it up, saturated his palate with it and then spat it forth into the grate. Then he paused to judge.

Mr. Power, a much younger man, was employed in the Royal Irish Constabulary Office in Dublin Castle. The arc of his social rise intersected the arc of his friend's decline, but Mr. Kernan's decline was mitigated by the fact that certain of those friends who had known him at his highest point of success still esteemed him as a character. Mr. Power was one of these friends. His inexplicable debts were a byword in his circle; he was a debonair young man.

The car halted before a small house on the Glasnevin road and Mr. Kernan was helped into the house. His wife put him to bed, while Mr. Power sat downstairs in the kitchen asking the children where they went to school and what book they were in. The children—two girls and a boy, conscious of their father's helplessness and of their mother's absence—began some horseplay with him. He was surprised at their manners and at their accents, and his brow grew thoughtful. After a while Mrs. Kernan entered the kitchen, exclaiming:

"Such a sight! O, he'll do for himself one day and that's the holy alls of it. He's been drinking since Friday."

Mr. Power was careful to explain to her that he was not responsible, that he had come on the scene by the merest accident. Mrs. Kernan, remembering Mr. Power's good offices during domestic quarrels, as well as many small, but opportune loans, said:

"O, you needn't tell me that, Mr. Power. I know you're a friend of his, not like some of the others he does be with. They're all right so long as he has money in his pocket to keep him out from his wife and family. Nice friends! Who was he with to-night, I'd like to know?"

Mr. Power shook his head but said nothing.

"I'm so sorry," she continued, "that I've nothing in the house to offer you. But if you wait a minute I'll send round to Fogarty's, at the corner."

Mr. Power stood up.

"We were waiting for him to come home with the money. He never seems to think he has a home at all."

"O, now, Mrs. Kernan," said Mr. Power, "we'll make him turn over a new leaf. I'll talk to Martin. He's the man. We'll come here one of these nights and talk it over."

She saw him to the door. The carman was stamping up and down the footpath, and swinging his arms to warm himself.

"It's very kind of you to bring him home," she said.

"Not at all," said Mr. Power.

He got up on the car. As it drove off he raised his hat to her gaily.

"We'll make a new man of him," he said. "Good-night, Mrs. Kernan."

Mrs. Kernan's puzzled eyes watched the car till it was out of sight. Then she withdrew them, went into the house and emptied her husband's pockets.

She was an active, practical woman of middle age. Not long before she had celebrated her silver wedding and renewed her intimacy with her husband by waltzing with him to Mr. Power's accompaniment. In her days of courtship, Mr. Kernan had seemed to her a not ungallant figure: and she still hurried to the chapel door whenever a wedding was reported and, seeing the bridal pair, recalled with vivid pleasure how she had passed out of the Star of the Sea Church in Sandymount, leaning on the arm of a jovial well-fed man, who was dressed smartly in a frock-coat and lavender trousers and carried a silk hat gracefully balanced upon his other arm. After three weeks she had found a wife's life irksome and, later on, when she was beginning to find it unbearable, she had become a mother. The part of mother presented to her no insuperable difficulties and for twenty-five years she had kept house shrewdly for her husband.

Her two eldest sons were launched. One was in a draper's shop in Glasgow and the other was clerk to a tea merchant in Belfast. They were good sons, wrote regularly and sometimes sent home money. The other children were still at school.

Mr. Kernan sent a letter to his office next day and remained in bed. She made beef-tea for him and scolded him roundly. She accepted his frequent intemperance as part of the climate, healed him dutifully whenever he was sick and always tried to make him eat a breakfast. There were worse husbands. He had never been violent since the boys had grown up, and she knew that he would walk to the end of Thomas Street and back again to book even a small order.

Two nights after, his friends came to see him. She brought them up to his bedroom, the air of which was impregnated with a personal odour, and gave them chairs at the fire. Mr. Kernan's tongue, the occasional stinging pain of which had made him somewhat irritable during the day, became more polite. He sat propped up in the bed by pillows and the little colour in his puffy cheeks made them resemble warm cinders. He apologised to his guests for the disorder of the room, but at the same time looked at them a little proudly, with a veteran's pride.

He was quite unconscious that he was the victim of a plot which his friends, Mr. Cunningham, Mr. M'Coy and Mr. Power had disclosed to Mrs. Kernan in the parlour. The idea had been Mr. Power's, but its development was entrusted to Mr. Cunningham. Mr. Kernan came of Protestant stock and, though he had been converted to the Catholic faith at the time of his marriage, he had not been in the pale of the Church for twenty years. He was fond, moreover, of giving side-thrusts at Catholicism.

Mr. Cunningham was the very man for such a case. He was an elder colleague of Mr. Power. His own domestic life was not very happy. People had great sympathy with him, for it was known that he had married an unpresentable woman who was an incurable drunkard. He had set up house for her six times; and each time she had pawned the furniture on him.

Everyone had respect for poor Martin Cunningham. He was a thoroughly sensible man, influential and intelligent. His blade of human knowledge, natural astuteness particularised by long association with cases in the police courts, had been tempered by brief immersions in the waters of general philosophy. He was well informed. His friends bowed to his opinions and considered that his face was like Shakespeare's.

When the plot had been disclosed to her, Mrs. Kernan had said:

"I leave it all in your hands, Mr. Cunningham."

After a quarter of a century of married life, she had very few illusions left. Religion for her was a habit, and she suspected that a man of her husband's age would not change greatly before death. She was tempted to see a curious appropriateness in his accident and, but that she did not wish to seem bloody-minded, she would have told the gentlemen that Mr. Kernan's tongue would not suffer by being shortened. However, Mr. Cunningham was a capable man; and religion was religion. The scheme might do good and, at least, it could do no harm. Her beliefs were not extravagant. She believed steadily in the Sacred Heart as the most generally useful of all Catholic devotions and approved of the sacraments. Her faith was bounded by her kitchen, but, if she was put to it, she could believe also in the banshee and in the Holy Ghost.

The gentlemen began to talk of the accident. Mr. Cunningham said that he had once known a similar case. A man of seventy had bitten off a piece of his tongue during an epileptic fit and the tongue had filled in again, so that no one could see a trace of the bite.

"Well, I'm not seventy," said the invalid.

"God forbid," said Mr. Cunningham.

"It doesn't pain you now?" asked Mr. M'Coy.

Mr. M'Coy had been at one time a tenor of some reputation. His wife, who had been a soprano, still taught young children to play the piano at low terms. His line of life had not been the shortest distance between two points and for short periods he had been driven to live by his wits. He had been a clerk in the Midland Railway, a canvasser for advertisements for *The Irish Times* and for *The Freeman's Journal,* a town traveller for a coal firm on commission, a private inquiry agent, a clerk in the office of the Sub-Sheriff, and he had recently become secretary to the City Coroner. His new office made him professionally interested in Mr. Kernan's case.

"Pain? Not much," answered Mr. Kernan. "But it's so sickening. I feel as if I wanted to retch off."

"That's the boose," said Mr. Cunningham firmly.

"No," said Mr. Kernan. "I think I caught cold on the car. There's something keeps coming into my throat, phlegm or—"

"Mucus," said Mr. M'Coy.

"It keeps coming like from down in my throat; sickening thing."

"Yes, yes," said Mr. M'Coy, "that's the thorax."

He looked at Mr. Cunningham and Mr. Power at the same time with an air of challenge. Mr. Cunningham nodded his head rapidly and Mr. Power said:

"Ah, well, all's well that ends well."

"I'm very much obliged to you, old man," said the invalid.

Mr. Power waved his hand.

"Those other two fellows I was with—"

"Who were you with?" asked Mr. Cunningham.

"A chap. I don't know his name. Damn it now, what's his name? Little chap with sandy hair. . . ."

"And who else?"

"Harford."

"Hm," said Mr. Cunningham.

When Mr. Cunningham made that remark, people were silent. It was known that the speaker had secret sources of information. In this case the monosyllable had a moral intention. Mr. Harford sometimes formed one of a little detachment which left the city shortly after noon on Sunday with the purpose of arriving as soon as possible at some public-house on the outskirts of the city where its members duly qualified themselves as *bona-fide* travellers. But his fellow-travellers had never consented to overlook his origin. He had begun life as an obscure financier by lending small sums of money to workmen at usurious interest. Later on he had become the partner of a very fat, short gentleman, Mr. Goldberg, in the Liffey Loan Bank. Though he had never embraced more than the Jewish ethical code, his fellow-Catholics, whenever they had smarted in person or by proxy under his exactions, spoke of him bitterly as an Irish Jew and an illiterate, and saw divine disapproval of usury made manifest through the person of his idiot son. At other times they remembered his good points.

"I wonder where did he go to," said Mr. Kernan.

He wished the details of the incident to remain vague. He wished his friends to think there had been some mistake, that Mr. Harford and he had missed each other. His friends, who knew quite well Mr. Harford's manners in drinking, were silent. Mr. Power said again:

"All's well that ends well."

Mr. Kernan changed the subject at once.

"That was a decent young chap, that medical fellow," he said. "Only for him—"

"O, only for him," said Mr. Power, "it might have been a case of seven days, without the option of a fine."

"Yes, yes," said Mr. Kernan, trying to remember. "I remember now there was a policeman. Decent young fellow, he seemed. How did it happen at all?"

"It happened that you were peloothered, Tom," said Mr. Cunningham gravely.

"True bill," said Mr. Kernan, equally gravely.

"I suppose you squared the constable, Jack," said Mr. M'Coy.

Mr. Power did not relish the use of his Christian name. He was not strait-laced, but he could not forget that Mr. M'Coy had recently made a crusade in search of valises and portmanteaus to enable Mrs. M'Coy to fulfill imaginary engagements in the country. More than he resented the fact that he had been victimised he resented such low playing of the game. He answered the question, therefore, as if Mr. Kernan had asked it.

The narrative made Mr. Kernan indignant. He was keenly conscious of his citizenship, wished to live with his city on terms mutually honourable and resented any affront put upon him by those whom he called country bumpkins.

"Is this what we pay rates for?" he asked. "To feed and clothe these ignorant bostooms . . . and they're nothing else."

Mr. Cunningham laughed. He was a Castle official only during office hours.

"How could they be anything else, Tom?" he said.

He assumed a thick, provincial accent and said in a tone of command: "65, catch your cabbage!"

Everyone laughed. Mr. M'Coy, who wanted to enter the conversation by any door, pretended that he had never heard the story. Mr. Cunningham said:

"It is supposed—they say, you know—to take place in the depot where they get these thundering big country fellows, omadhauns, you know, to drill. The sergeant makes them stand in a row against the wall and hold up their plates."

He illustrated the story by grotesque gestures.

"At dinner, you know. Then he has a bloody big bowl of cabbage before him on the table and a bloody big spoon like a shovel. He takes up a wad of cabbage on the spoon and pegs it across the room and the poor devils have to try and catch it on their plates: *65, catch your cabbage.*"

Everyone laughed again: but Mr. Kernan was somewhat indignant still. He talked of writing a letter to the papers.

"These yahoos coming up here," he said, "think they can boss the people. I needn't tell you, Martin, what kind of men they are."

Mr. Cunningham gave a qualified assent.

"It's like everything else in this world," he said. "You get some bad ones and you get some good ones."

"O yes, you get some good ones, I admit," said Mr. Kernan, satisfied.

"It's better to have nothing to say to them," said Mr. M'Coy. "That's my opinion!"

Mrs. Kernan entered the room and, placing a tray on the table, said: "Help yourselves, gentlemen."

Mr. Power stood up to officiate, offering her his chair. She declined it, saying she was ironing downstairs, and, after having exchanged a nod with Mr. Cunningham behind Mr. Power's back, prepared to leave the room. Her husband called out to her:

"And have you nothing for me, duckie?"

"O, you! The back of my hand to you!" said Mrs. Kernan tartly.

Her husband called after her:

"Nothing for poor little hubby!"

He assumed such a comical face and voice that the distribution of the bottles of stout took place amid general merriment.

The gentlemen drank from their glasses, set the glasses again on the table and paused. Then Mr. Cunningham turned towards Mr. Power and said casually:

"On Thursday night, you said, Jack?"

"Thursday, yes," said Mr. Power.

"Righto!" said Mr. Cunningham promptly.

"We can meet in M'Auley's," said Mr. M'Coy. "That'll be the most convenient place."

"But we mustn't be late," said Mr. Power earnestly, "because it is sure to be crammed to the doors."

"We can meet at half-seven," said Mr. M'Coy.

"Righto!" said Mr. Cunningham.

"Half-seven at M'Auley's be it!"

There was a short silence. Mr. Kernan waited to see whether he would be taken into his friends' confidence. Then he asked:

"What's in the wind?"

"O, it's nothing," said Mr. Cunningham. "It's only a little matter that we're arranging about for Thursday."

"The opera, is it?" said Mr. Kernan.

"No, no," said Mr. Cunningham in an evasive tone, "it's just a little . . . spiritual matter."

"O," said Mr. Kernan.

There was silence again. Then Mr. Power said, point blank:

"To tell you the truth, Tom, we're going to make a retreat."

"Yes, that's it," said Mr. Cunningham, "Jack and I and M'Coy here— we're all going to wash the pot."

He uttered the metaphor with a certain homely energy and, encouraged by his own voice, proceeded:

"You see, we may as well all admit we're a nice collection of scoundrels, one and all. I say, one and all," he added with gruff charity and turning to Mr. Power. "Own up now!"

"I own up," said Mr. Power.

"And I own up," said Mr. M'Coy.

"So we're going to wash the pot together," said Mr. Cunningham.

A thought seemed to strike him. He turned suddenly to the invalid and said:

"D'ye know what, Tom, has just occurred to me? You might join in and we'd have a four-handed reel."

"Good idea," said Mr. Power. "The four of us together."

Mr. Kernan was silent. The proposal conveyed very little meaning to his mind, but, understanding that some spiritual agencies were about to concern themselves on his behalf, he thought he owed it to his dignity to show a stiff neck. He took no part in the conversation for a long while, but listened, with an air of calm enmity, while his friends discussed the Jesuits.

"I haven't such a bad opinion of the Jesuits," he said, intervening at length. "They're an educated order. I believe they mean well, too."

"They're the grandest order in the Church, Tom," said Mr. Cunningham, with enthusiasm. "The General of the Jesuits stands next to the Pope."

"There's no mistake about it," said Mr. M'Coy, "if you want a thing well done and no flies about, you go to a Jesuit. They're the boyos have influence. I'll tell you a case in point. . . ."

"The Jesuits are a fine body of men," said Mr. Power.

"It's a curious thing," said Mr. Cunningham, "about the Jesuit Order. Every other order of the Church had to be reformed at some time or other but the Jesuit Order was never once reformed. It never fell away."

"Is that so?" asked Mr. M'Coy.

"That's a fact," said Mr. Cunningham. "That's history."

"Look at their church, too," said Mr. Power. "Look at the congregation they have."

"The Jesuits cater for the upper classes," said Mr. M'Coy.

"Of course," said Mr. Power.

"Yes," said Mr. Kernan. "That's why I have a feeling for them. It's some of those secular priests, ignorant, bumptious—"

"They're all good men," said Mr. Cunningham, "each in his own way. The Irish priesthood is honoured all the world over."

"O yes," said Mr. Power.

"Not like some of the other priesthoods on the continent," said Mr. M'Coy, "unworthy of the name."

"Perhaps you're right," said Mr. Kernan, relenting.

"Of course I'm right," said Mr. Cunningham. "I haven't been in the world all this time and seen most sides of it without being a judge of character."

The gentlemen drank again, one following another's example. Mr. Kernan seemed to be weighing something in his mind. He was impressed. He had a high opinion of Mr. Cunningham as a judge of character and as a reader of faces. He asked for particulars.

"O, it's just a retreat, you know," said Mr. Cunningham. "Father Purdon is giving it. It's for business men, you know."

"He won't be too hard on us, Tom," said Mr. Power persuasively.

"Father Purdon? Father Purdon?" said the invalid.

"O, you must know him, Tom," said Mr. Cunningham stoutly. "Fine, jolly fellow! He's a man of the world like ourselves."

"Ah, . . . yes. I think I know him. Rather red face; tall."

"That's the man."

"And tell me, Martin. . . . Is he a good preacher?"

"Munno. . . . It's not exactly a sermon, you know. It's just a kind of a friendly talk, you know, in a common-sense way."

Mr. Kernan deliberated. Mr. M'Coy said:

"Father Tom Burke, that was the boy!"

"O, Father Tom Burke," said Mr. Cunningham, "that was a born orator. Did you ever hear him, Tom?"

"Did I ever hear him!" said the invalid, nettled. "Rather! I heard him. . . ."

"And yet they say he wasn't much of a theologian," said Mr. Cunningham.

"Is that so?" said Mr. M'Coy.

"O, of course, nothing wrong, you know. Only sometimes, they say, he didn't preach what was quite orthodox."

"Ah! . . . he was a splendid man," said Mr. M'Coy.

"I heard him once," Mr. Kernan continued. "I forget the subject of his discourse now. Crofton and I were in the back of the . . . pit, you know . . . the—"

"The body," said Mr. Cunningham.

"Yes, in the back near the door. I forget now what. . . . O yes, it was on the Pope, the late Pope. I remember it well. Upon my word it was magnificent, the style of the oratory. And his voice! God! hadn't he a voice! *The Prisoner of the Vatican,* he called him. I remember Crofton saying to me when we came out—"

"But he's an Orangeman, Crofton, isn't he?" said Mr. Power.

" 'Course he is," said Mr. Kernan, "and a damned decent Orangeman, too. We went into Butler's in Moore Street—faith, I was genuinely moved, tell you the God's truth—and I remember well his very words. *Kernan,* he said, *we worship at different altars,* he said, *but our belief is the same.* Struck me as very well put."

"There's a good deal in that," said Mr. Power. "There used always be crowds of Protestant in the chapel when Father Tom was preaching."

"There's not much difference between us," said Mr. M'Coy. "We both believe in—"

He hesitated for a moment.

". . . in the Redeemer. Only they don't believe in the Pope and in the mother of God."

"But, of course," said Mr. Cunningham quietly and effectively, "our religion is *the* religion, the old, original faith."

"Not a doubt of it," said Mr. Kernan warmly.

Mrs. Kernan came to the door of the bedroom and announced:

"Here's a visitor for you!"

"Who is it?"

"Mr. Fogarty."

"O, come in! come in!"

A pale, oval face came forward into the light. The arch of its fair trailing moustache was repeated in the fair eyebrows looped above pleasantly astonished eyes. Mr. Fogarty was a modest grocer. He had failed in business in a licensed house in the city because his financial condition had constrained him to tie himself to second-class distillers and brewers. He had opened a small shop on Glasnevin Road where, he flattered himself, his manners would ingratiate him with the housewives of the district. He bore himself with a certain grace, complimented little children and spoke with a neat enunciation. He was not without culture.

Mr. Fogarty brought a gift with him, a half-pint of special whisky. He inquired politely for Mr. Kernan, placed his gift on the table and sat down with the company on equal terms. Mr. Kernan appreciated the gift all the more since he was aware that there was a small account for groceries unsettled between him and Mr. Fogarty. He said:

"I wouldn't doubt you, old man. Open that, Jack, will you?"

Mr. Power again officiated. Glasses were rinsed and five small measures of whisky were poured out. This new influence enlivened the conversation. Mr. Fogarty, sitting on a small area of the chair, was specially interested.

"Pope Leo XIII," said Mr. Cunningham, "was one of the lights of the age. His great idea, you know, was the union of the Latin and Greek Churches. That was the aim of his life."

"I often heard he was one of the most intellectual men in Europe," said Mr. Power. "I mean, apart from his being Pope."

"So he was," said Mr. Cunningham, "if not *the* most so. His motto, you know, as Pope, was *Lux upon Lux—Light upon Light*."

"No, no," said Mr. Fogarty eagerly. "I think you're wrong there. It was *Lux in Tenebris*, I think—*Light in Darkness*."

"O yes," said Mr. M'Coy, "*Tenebrae*."

"Allow me," said Mr. Cunningham positively, "it was *Lux upon Lux*. And Pius IX his predecessor's motto was *Crux upon Crux*—that is, *Cross upon Cross*—to show the difference between their two pontificates."

The inference was allowed. Mr. Cunningham continued.

"Pope Leo, you know, was a great scholar and a poet."

"He had a strong face," said Mr. Kernan.

"Yes," said Mr. Cunningham. "He wrote Latin poetry."

"Is that so?" said Mr. Fogarty.

Mr. M'Coy tasted his whisky contentedly and shook his head with a double intention, saying:

"That's no joke, I can tell you."

"We didn't learn that, Tom," said Mr. Power, following Mr. M'Coy's example, "when we went to the penny-a-week school."

"There was many a good man went to the penny-a-week school with a sod of turf under his oxter," said Mr. Kernan sententiously. "The old system was the best: plain honest education. None of your modern trumpery. . . ."

"Quite right," said Mr. Power.

"No superfluities," said Mr. Fogarty.

He enunciated the word and then drank gravely.

"I remember reading," said Mr. Cunningham, "that one of Pope Leo's poems was on the invention of the photograph—in Latin, of course."

"On the photograph!" exclaimed Mr. Kernan.

"Yes," said Mr. Cunningham.

He also drank from his glass.

"Well, you know," said Mr. M'Coy, "isn't the photograph wonderful when you come to think of it?"

"O, of course," said Mr. Power, "great minds can see things."

"As the poet says: *Great minds are very near to madness*," said Mr. Fogarty.

Mr. Kernan seemed to be troubled in mind. He made an effort to recall the Protestant theology on some thorny points and in the end addressed Mr. Cunningham.

"Tell me, Martin," he said. "Weren't some of the popes—of course, not our present man, or his predecessor, but some of the old popes—not exactly . . . you know . . . up to the knocker?"

There was a silence. Mr. Cunningham said:

"O, of course, there were some bad lots . . . But the astonishing thing is this. Not one of them, not the biggest drunkard, not the most . . . out-and-out ruffian, not one of them ever preached *ex cathedra* a word of false doctrine. Now isn't that an astonishing thing?"

"That is," said Mr. Kernan.

"Yes, because when the Pope speaks *ex cathedra*," Mr. Fogarty explained, "he is infallible."

"Yes," said Mr. Cunningham.

"O, I know about the infallibility of the Pope. I remember I was younger then. . . . Or was it that—?"

Mr. Fogarty interrupted. He took up the bottle and helped the others to a little more. Mr. M'Coy, seeing that there was not enough to go round, pleaded that he had not finished his first measure. The others accepted under protest. The light music of whisky falling into glasses made an agreeable interlude.

"What's that you were saying, Tom?" asked Mr. M'Coy.

"Papal infallibility," said Mr. Cunningham, "that was the greatest scene in the whole history of the Church."

"How was that, Martin?" asked Mr. Power.

Mr. Cunningham held up two thick fingers.

"In the sacred college, you know, of cardinals and archbishops and bishops there were two men who held out against it while the others were all for it. The whole conclave except these two was unanimous. No! They wouldn't have it!"

"Ha!" said Mr. M'Coy.

"And they were a German cardinal by the name of Dolling . . . or Dowling . . . or—"

"Dowling was no German, and that's a sure five," said Mr. Power, laughing.

"Well, this great German cardinal, whatever his name was, was one; and the other was John MacHale."

"What?" cried Mr. Kernan. "Is it John of Tuam?"

"Are you sure of that now?" asked Mr. Fogarty dubiously. "I thought it was some Italian or American."

"John of Tuam," repeated Mr. Cunningham, "was the man."

He drank and the other gentlemen followed his lead. Then he resumed:

"There they were at it, all the cardinals and bishops and archbishops from all the ends of the earth and these two fighting dog and devil until at last the Pope himself stood up and declared infallibility a dogma of the Church *ex cathedra*. On the very moment John MacHale, who had been arguing and arguing against it, stood up and shouted out with the voice of a lion: 'Credo!'"

"*I believe!*" said Mr. Fogarty.

"*Credo!*" said Mr. Cunningham. "That showed the faith he had. He submitted the moment the Pope spoke."

"And what about Dowling?" asked Mr. M'Coy.

"The German cardinal wouldn't submit. He left the church."

Mr. Cunningham's words had built up the vast image of the church in the minds of his hearers. His deep, raucous voice had thrilled them as it uttered the word of belief and submission. When Mrs. Kernan came into the room, drying her hands, she came into a solemn company. She did not disturb the silence, but leaned over the rail at the foot of the bed.

"I once saw John MacHale," said Mr. Kernan, "and I'll never forget it as long as I live."

He turned towards his wife to be confirmed.

"I often told you that?"

Mrs. Kernan nodded.

"It was at the unveiling of Sir John Gray's statue. Edmund Dwyer Gray was speaking, blathering away, and here was this old fellow, crabbed-looking old chap, looking at him from under his bushy eyebrows."

Mr. Kernan knitted his brows and, lowering his head like an angry bull, glared at his wife.

"God!" he exclaimed, resuming his natural face, "I never saw such an eye in a man's head. It was as much as to say: *I have you properly taped, my lad.* He had an eye like a hawk."

"None of the Grays was any good," said Mr. Power.

There was a pause again. Mr. Power turned to Mrs. Kernan and said with abrupt joviality:

"Well, Mrs. Kernan, we're going to make your man here a good holy pious and God-fearing Roman Catholic."

He swept his arm round the company inclusively.

"We're all going to make a retreat together and confess our sins—and God knows we want it badly."

"I don't mind," said Mr. Kernan, smiling a little nervously.

Mrs. Kernan thought it would be wiser to conceal her satisfaction. So she said:

"I pity the poor priest that has to listen to your tale."

Mr. Kernan's expression changed.

"If he doesn't like it," he said bluntly, "he can . . . do the other thing. I'll just tell him my little tale of woe. I'm not such a bad fellow—"

Mr. Cunningham intervened promptly.

"We'll all renounce the devil," he said, "together, not forgetting his works and pomps."

"Get behind me, Satan!" said Mr. Fogarty, laughing and looking at the others.

Mr. Power said nothing. He felt completely out-generalled. But a pleased expression flickered across his face.

"All we have to do," said Mr. Cunningham, "is to stand up with lighted candles in our hands and renew our baptismal vows."

"O, don't forget the candle, Tom," said Mr. M'Coy, "whatever you do."

"What?" said Mr. Kernan. "Must I have a candle?"

"O yes," said Mr. Cunningham.

"No, damn it all," said Mr. Kernan sensibly, "I draw the line there. I'll do the job right enough. I'll do the retreat business and confession, and . . . all that business. But . . . no candles! No, damn it all, I bar the candles!"

He shook his head with farcical gravity.

"Listen to that!" said his wife.

"I bar the candles," said Mr. Kernan, conscious of having created an effect on his audience and continuing to shake his head to and fro. "I bar the magic-lantern business."

Everyone laughed heartily.

"There's a nice Catholic for you!" said his wife.

"No candles!" repeated Mr. Kernan obdurately. "That's off!"

The transept of the Jesuit Church in Gardiner Street was almost full; and still at every moment gentlemen entered from the side door and, directed by the lay-brother, walked on tiptoe along the aisles until they found seating accommodation. The gentlemen were all well dressed and orderly. The light of the lamps of the church fell upon an assembly of black clothes and white collars, relieved here and there by tweeds, on dark mottled pillars of green marble and on lugubrious canvases. The gentlemen sat in the benches, having hitched their trousers slightly above their knees and laid their hats in security. They sat well back and gazed formally at the distant speck of red light which was suspended before the high altar.

In one of the benches near the pulpit sat Mr. Cunningham and Mr. Kernan. In the bench behind sat Mr. M'Coy alone: and in the bench behind him sat Mr. Power and Mr. Fogarty. Mr. M'Coy had tried unsuccessfully to find a place in the bench with the others, and, when the party had settled down in the form of a quincunx, he had tried unsuccessfully to make comic remarks. As these had not been well received, he had desisted. Even he was sensible of the decorous atmosphere and even he began to respond to the religious stimulus. In a whisper, Mr. Cunningham drew Mr. Kernan's attention to Mr. Harford, the moneylender, who sat some distance off, and to Mr. Fanning, the registration agent and mayor maker of the city, who was sitting immediately under the pulpit beside one of the newly elected councillors of the ward. To the right sat old Michael Grimes, the owner of three pawnbroker's shops, and Dan Hogan's nephew, who was up for the job in the Town Clerk's office. Farther in front sat Mr. Hendrick, the chief reporter of *The Freeman's Journal,* and poor O'Carroll, an old friend of Mr. Kernan's, who had been at one time a considerable commercial figure. Gradually, as he recognised familiar faces, Mr. Kernan began to feel more at home. His hat, which had been rehabilitated by his wife, rested upon his knees. Once or twice he pulled down his cuffs with one hand while he held the brim of his hat lightly, but firmly, with the other hand.

A powerful-looking figure, the upper part of which was draped with a white surplice, was observed to be struggling up into the pulpit. Simultaneously the congregation unsettled, produced handkerchiefs and knelt upon them with care. Mr. Kernan followed the general example. The priest's figure now stood upright in the pulpit, two-thirds of its bulk, crowned by a massive red face, appearing above the balustrade.

Father Purdon knelt down, turned towards the red speck of light and, covering his face with his hands, prayed. After an interval, he uncovered his face and rose. The congregation rose also and settled again on its benches. Mr. Kernan restored his hat to its original position on his knee and presented an attentive face to the preacher. The preacher turned back each wide sleeve of his surplice with an elaborate large gesture and slowly surveyed the array of faces. Then he said:

> *"For the children of this world are wiser in their generation than the children of light. Wherefore make unto yourselves friends out of the mammon of iniquity so that when you die they may receive you into everlasting dwellings."*

Father Purdon developed the text with resonant assurance. It was one of the most difficult texts in all the Scriptures, he said, to interpret properly. It was a text which might seem to the casual observer at variance with the lofty morality elsewhere preached by Jesus Christ. But, he told his hearers, the text had seemed to him specially adapted for the guidance of those whose lot it was to lead the life of the world and who yet wished to lead that life not in the manner of worldlings. It was a text for business men and professional men. Jesus Christ, with His divine understanding of every cranny of our human nature, understood that all men were not called to the religious life, that by far the vast majority were forced to live in the world, and, to a certain extent, for the world: and in this sentence He designed to give them a word of counsel, setting before them as exemplars in the religious life those very worshippers of Mammon who were of all men the least solicitous in matters religious.

He told his hearers that he was there that evening for no terrifying, no extravagant purpose; but as a man of the world speaking to his fellowmen. He came to speak to business men and he would speak to them in a businesslike way. If he might use the metaphor, he said, he was their spiritual accountant; and he wished each and every one of his hearers to open his books, the books of his spiritual life, and see if they tallied accurately with conscience.

Jesus Christ was not a hard taskmaster. He understood our little failings, understood the weaknesses of our poor fallen nature, understood the temptations of this life. We might have had, we all had from time to time, our temptations: we might have, we all had, our failings. But one thing only, he said, he would ask of his hearers. And that was: to be straight and manly with God. If their accounts tallied in every point to say:

"Well, I have verified my accounts. I find all well."

But if, as might happen, there were some discrepancies, to admit the truth, to be frank and say like a man:
"Well, I have looked into my accounts. I find this wrong and this wrong. But, with God's grace, I will rectify this and this. I will set right my accounts."

CRITICAL COMMENTS

Letter from James Joyce to Grant Richards:

5 May 1906

. . . My intention was to write a chapter of the moral history of my country and I chose Dublin for the scene because that city seemed to me the centre of paralysis. . . . I have written it for the most part in a style of scrupulous meanness and with the conviction that he is a very bold man who dares to alter in the presentment, still more to deform, whatever he has seen and heard. . . . I have come to the conclusion that I cannot write without offending people. . . .[1]

Stanislaus Joyce:

Before my brother left Paris an absurd incident at home supplied him, through my letters and diaries, with the materials for another story, "Grace," which some years later he wrote at Trieste. A retreat for businessmen was to be conducted by a Jesuit father in Gardiner Street Church, and one of my father's friends ("Mr. Cunningham" in the story) persuaded his broogy cronies, including my father, to attend it, "all together, my boys." . . .

Out of sarcastic curiosity I followed them to the church on the last evening of the retreat to listen to the sermon and watch my father fumbling shamefacedly with his lighted candle. The sermon was a man-to-man talk in a chatty tone. I came out into the fresh air before the end. . . .

My brother has used this thin material, transforming it in his own way. The accident with which the story begins happened to my father, but as model for the recalcitrant convert my brother substituted an acquaintance of my father's, a plump, rubicund commercial traveler and tea-taster. . . .

The strange doctrine of actual and sanctifying grace and its relation to original sin . . . had puzzled and fascinated my brother, as

---

[1] From *Letters of James Joyce,* Vol. II, edited by Richard Ellmann (New York: The Viking Press, 1966; London: Faber and Faber, Ltd., 1966), p. 134, reprinted by permission of the publishers.

he found it in the teaching of the Church, and in his reading of St. Augustine. . . . In "Grace," . . . he has used as model for the preacher of the sermon, "Father Purdon," the figure of Father Bernard Vaughan, a very popular evangelist in those days. . . . My brother's contempt for him is evident in the choice of the name with which he has adorned him, Father Purdon. The old name for the street of the brothels in Dublin was Purdon Street.

. . . "Grace" is, so far as I am aware, the first instance of the use of a pattern in my brother's work. It is a simple pattern not new and not requiring any great hermeneutical acumen to discover—inferno, purgatorio, paradiso. Mr. Kernan's fall down the steps of the lavatory is his descent into hell, the sickroom is purgatory, and the Church in which he and his friends listen to the sermon is paradise at last. In "Grace" the pattern is ironical with a touch of suppressed anger. . . .[2]

F. X. Newman:

[T]he universal acceptance of Stanislaus Joyce's statement has obscured the presence of a much more precise and detailed mock-heroic pattern in the story. While Joyce may have conceived a parallel between his story and the *Comedy,* an examination of "Grace" shows that the actual source of its structure and much of its narrative detail is the *Book of Job.* . . . The *Book of Job* is similarly arranged [in a series of three scenes]. It begins with the depiction of Job's calamitous fall from prosperity, its central section is devoted to the dialogue between Job and his three (subsequently four) "comforters," and it concludes with the great tirade of the voice of the Lord out of the whirlwind. The structure of fall, "comforting" dialogue, and divine epiphany in *Job* is clearly analogous to the arrangement of "Grace." . . . As a modern retelling of *Job,* "Grace" is parody, a deliberate mimicking whose effect is a *reductio ad absurdum* of its original. . . . [I]n Dublin greatness can appear only in parody form. Rebellion is a "side-thrust," dogmatic certainty is clumsy assertiveness, power is flattery. Job in Dublin's land of ooze is a drunk in a dinged silk hat whose most violent gesture of refusal is to "bar the candles."[3]

Julian B. Kaye:

In my opinion, Joyce is hostile towards the Irish Church and towards the Jesuits because he believes them to be tainted by the

[2] From *My Brother's Keeper: James Joyce's Early Years,* by Stanislaus Joyce, edited by Richard Ellmann, pp. 225–228, copyright © 1958 by Nelly Joyce, reprinted by permission of The Viking Press, Inc., New York, and Faber and Faber, Ltd., London.

[3] From "The Land of Ooze: Joyce's 'Grace' and The Book of Job," by F. X. Newman, *Studies in Short Fiction,* Vol. IV (Fall 1966), pp. 70–71, 77, 79, reprinted by permission of *Studies in Short Fiction.*

sin of simony—a sin held in great abhorrence by Catholic theologians and moralists. . . . In Joyce's fiction the Catholic conception of simony is the principal moral criterion of value. . . .

The most striking example . . . of the simony of Joyce's Dublin is found in "Grace." Martin Cunningham's well-intentioned plan of having Mr. Kernan make a retreat as a cure for drinking reveals the religion of most middle-class Dubliners and of the Jesuit Order, which they admire and which regards itself as their spiritual guide, as thoroughly corrupted by simony. The scene in which Mr. Kernan's friends play upon all his vanities and snobberies in order to persuade him to make a retreat is amusing rather than painful because of its brilliant social comedy and trenchant satire upon ignorance and stupidity, but the crudity of the simoniacal inducements held out to Mr. Kernan is at times overwhelming. The retreat is presented as a theatrical entertainment—that is, the church is described as a theatre and the priests as actors. . . .

. . . the reader is shocked to learn that Father Purdon confirms what has been said about his order. . . . Completely misinterpreting the text [Luke xvi. 8–9], he takes Jesus's bitter irony for sound advice. . . . The rest of his address only confirms what is to Joyce the simoniacal exchange of religious approval of sharp business practices for formal adherence to religious doctrine and formal participation in religious ritual.[4]

Marvin Magalaner:

In "Grace" (1905) Joyce first experiments seriously with gentle juxtaposition of a public and universal mythical structure, on the one hand, and, on the other, a sordid contemporary narrative. . . . "Grace" allowed Joyce to test his skill at simultaneous presentation of two cultures, two ways of thought, two views of, say, grace, religious ecstasy, and the fullness of human life. . . . Appeal must be made to social prestige, self-interest, personal vanity, before the religious ritual will be embraced. . . . For the Philistines of Dublin, salesmen and constabulary officials like Kernan and Power, religion has become not a matter of heart and spirit but of practical considerations, good business, a sop to conscience, and a prop of respectability—in much the same way that Kernan's silk hat is all these things. Practicality is the keynote of the story. . . . Speaking to them as a "man of the world," Purdon uses the diction of the businessman, the metaphor of the "spiritual accountant," which so sickens Joyce that he will not even deign to comment

4 From "Simony, the Three Simons, and Joycean Myth," by Julian B. Kaye, in *A James Joyce Miscellany*, edited by Marvin Magalaner (New York: The James Joyce Society, 1957), pp. 20–21, 23–24, reprinted by permission of the author and the publisher.

upon it. He simply allows the sermon to condemn the one who delivers it.[5]

Marvin Magalaner and Richard Kain:

When a writer depicts life in realistic detail, he must be careful not to suggest artificiality by arranging his plot so that the details are too pat, too obvious and artful, for that is not how events seem to happen in life. Maupassant, with his structural hardness, his fixed opening and trick closing, disregarded that modern dictum. Chekhov made it his trademark. He felt that "a story should have neither beginning nor end." Like Joyce, he preferred to seem "inconclusive." . . . Joyce's characters and situations extend themselves far beyond the pages on which they actually appear and take on an independent life of their own. What happened to them before they walked across the stage and what will happen after the curtain descends are important to the reader. . . . "Grace" closes in the middle of a sermon.[6]

[5] From *Time of Apprenticeship: The Fiction of Young James Joyce,* by Marvin Magalaner, pp. 129–130, 132–133, 135, copyright 1959 by Abelard-Schuman, Ltd., reprinted by permission of Abelard-Schuman, Ltd., New York.

[6] From *Joyce: The Man, the Work, the Reputation,* by Marvin Magalaner and Richard Kain, p. 73, © 1956 by New York University, reprinted by permission of the New York University Press, New York, and Calder & Boyars, Ltd., London.

Powerhouse

ಀ *Eudora Welty*

Powerhouse is playing!

He's here on tour from the city—"Powerhouse and His Keyboard"—
"Powerhouse and His Tasmanians"—think of the things he calls himself!
There's no one in the world like him. You can't tell what he is: "Nigger
man"?—he looks more Asiatic, monkey, Jewish, Babylonian, Peruvian,
fanatic, devil. He has pale gray eyes, heavy lids, maybe horny like a
lizard's, but big glowing eyes when they're open. He has African feet of
the greatest size, stomping, both together, on each side of the pedals.
He's not coal black—beverage colored—looks like a preacher when his
mouth is shut, but then it opens—vast and obscene. And his mouth is
going every minute: like a monkey's when it looks for something. Impro-
vising, coming on a light and childish melody—*smooch*—he loves it with
his mouth.

Is it possible that he could be this! When you have him there performing for you, that's what you feel. You know people on a stage—and
people of a darker race—so likely to be marvelous, frightening.

This is a white dance. Powerhouse is not a show-off like the Harlem
boys, not drunk, not crazy—he's in a trance; he's a person of joy, a fanatic.
He listens as much as he performs, a look of hideous, powerful rapture on
his face. Big arched eyebrows that never stop traveling, like a Jew's—
wandering-Jew eyebrows. When he plays he beats down piano and seat
and wears them away. He is in motion every moment—what could be
more obscene? There he is with his great head, fat stomach, and little
round piston legs, and long yellow-sectioned strong big fingers, at rest
about the size of bananas. Of course you know how he sounds—you've
heard him on records—but still you need to see him. He's going all the
time, like skating around the skating rink or rowing a boat. It makes
everybody crowd around, here in this shadowless steel-trussed hall with
the rose-like posters of Nelson Eddy and the testimonial for the mind-
reading horse in handwriting magnified five hundred times. Then all
quietly he lays his finger on a key with the promise and serenity of a
sibyl touching the book.

Powerhouse is so monstrous he sends everybody into oblivion. When
any group, any performers, come to town, don't people always come out
and hover near, leaning inward about them, to learn what it is? What is
it? Listen. Remember how it was with the acrobats. Watch them carefully, hear the least word, especially what they say to one another, in

another language—don't let them escape you; it's the only time for hallucination, the last time. They can't stay. They'll be somewhere else this time tomorrow.

Powerhouse has as much as possible done by signals. Everybody, laughing as if to hide a weakness, will sooner or later hand him up a written request. Powerhouse reads each one, studying with a secret face: that is the face which looks like a mask—anybody's; there is a moment when he makes a decision. Then a light slides under his eyelids, and he says, "92!" or some combination of figures—never a name. Before a number the band is all frantic, misbehaving, pushing, like children in a schoolroom, and he is the teacher getting silence. His hands over the keys, he says sternly, "You-all ready? You-all ready to do some serious walking?"—waits— then, STAMP. Quiet. STAMP, for the second time. This is absolute. Then a set of rhythmic kicks against the floor to communicate the tempo. Then, O Lord! say the distended eyes from beyond the boundary of the trumpets, Hello and good-bye, and they are all down the first note like a waterfall.

This note marks the end of any known discipline. Powerhouse seems to abandon them all—he himself seems lost—down in the song, yelling up like somebody in a whirlpool—not guiding them—hailing them only. But he knows, really. He cries out, but he must know exactly. "Mercy! . . . What I say! . . . Yeah!" And then drifting, listening—"Where that skin beater?"—wanting drums, and starting up and pouring it out in the greatest delight and brutality. On the sweet pieces such a leer for everybody! He looks down so benevolently upon all our faces and whispers the lyrics to us. And if you could hear him at this moment on "Marie, the Dawn is Breaking"! He's going up the keyboard with a few fingers in some very derogatory triplet-routine, he gets higher and higher, and then he looks over the end of the piano, as if over a cliff. But not in a show-off way—the song makes him do it.

He loves the way they all play, too—all those next to him. The far section of the band is all studious, wearing glasses, every one—they don't count. Only those playing around Powerhouse are the real ones. He has a bass fiddler from Vicksburg, black as pitch, named Valentine, who plays with his eyes shut and talking to himself, very young: Powerhouse has to keep encouraging him. "Go on, go on, give it up, bring it on out there!" When you heard him like that on records, did you know he was really pleading?

He calls Valentine out to take a solo.

"What you going to play?" Powerhouse looks out kindly from behind the piano; he opens his mouth and shows his tongue, listening.

Valentine looks down, drawing against his instrument, and says without a lip movement, " 'Honeysuckle Rose.' "

He has a clarinet player named Little Brother, and loves to listen to anything he does. He'll smile and say, "Beautiful!" Little Brother takes a step forward when he plays and stands at the very front, with the whites of his eyes like fishes swimming. Once when he played a low note, Power-house muttered a dirty praise, "He went clear downstairs to get that one!"

After a long time, he holds up the number of fingers to tell the band how many choruses still to go—usually five. He keeps his directions down to signals.

It's a bad night outside. It's a white dance, and nobody dances, except a few straggling jitterbugs and two elderly couples. Everybody just stands around the band and watches Powerhouse. Sometimes they steal glances at one another, as if to say, Of course, you know how it is with *them*—Negroes—band leaders—they would play the same way, giving all they've got, for an audience of one. . . . When somebody, no matter who, gives everything, it makes people feel ashamed for him.

Late at night they play the one waltz they will ever consent to play—by request, "Pagan Love Song." Powerhouse's head rolls and sinks like a weight between his waving shoulders. He groans, and his fingers drag into the keys heavily, holding on to the notes, retrieving. It is a sad song.

"You know what happened to me?" says Powerhouse.

Valentine hums a response, dreaming at the bass.

"I got a telegram my wife is dead," says Powerhouse, with wandering fingers.

"Uh-huh?"

His mouth gathers and forms a barbarous O while his fingers walk up straight, unwillingly, three octaves.

"Gypsy? Why how come her to die, didn't you just phone her up in the night last night long distance?"

"Telegram say—here the words: Your wife is dead." He puts 4/4 over the 3/4.

"Not but four words?" This is the drummer, an unpopular boy named Scoot, a disbelieving maniac.

Powerhouse is shaking his vast cheeks. "What the hell was she trying to do? What was she up to?"

"What name has it got signed, if you got a telegram?" Scoot is spitting away with those wire brushes.

Little Brother, the clarinet player, who cannot now speak, glares and tilts back.

"Uranus Knockwood is the name signed." Powerhouse lifts his eyes open. "Ever heard of him?" A bubble shoots out on his lip like a plate on a counter.

Valentine is beating slowly on with his palm and scratching the strings with his long blue nails. He is fond of a waltz. Powerhouse interrupts him.

"I don't know him. Don't know who he is." Valentine shakes his head with the closed eyes.

"Say it again."

"Uranus Knockwood."

"That ain't Lenox Avenue."

"It ain't Broadway."

"Ain't ever seen it wrote out in any print, even for horse racing."

"Hell, that's on a star, boy, ain't it?" Crash of the cymbals.

"What the hell was she up to?" Powerhouse shudders. "Tell me, tell me, tell me." He makes triplets, and begins a new chorus. He holds three fingers up.

"You say you got a telegram." This is Valentine, patient and sleepy, beginning again.

Powerhouse is elaborate. "Yas, the time I go out, go way downstairs along a long cor-ri-dor to where they puts us: coming back along the cor-ri-dor: steps out and hands me a telegram: Your wife is dead."

"Gypsy?" The drummer like a spider over his drums.

"Aaaaaaaaa!" shouts Powerhouse, flinging out both powerful arms for three whole beats to flex his muscles, then kneading a dough of bass notes. His eyes glitter. He plays the piano like a drum sometimes—why not?

"Gypsy? Such a dancer?"

"Why you don't hear it straight from your agent? Why it ain't come from headquarters? What you been doing, getting telegrams in the *cor-ridor,* signed nobody?"

They all laugh. End of that chorus.

"What time is it?" Powerhouse calls. "What the hell place is this? Where is my watch and chain?"

"I hang it on you," whimpers Valentine. "It still there."

There it rides on Powerhouse's great stomach, down where he can never see it.

"Sure did hear some clock striking twelve while ago. Must be *midnight.*"

"It going to be intermission," Powerhouse declares, lifting up his finger with the signet ring.

He draws the chorus to an end. He pulls a big Northern hotel towel out of the deep pocket in his vast, special-cut tux pants and pushes his forehead into it.

"If she went and killed herself!" he says with a hidden face. "If she up and jumped out that window!" He gets to his feet, turning vaguely, wearing the towel on his head.

"Ha, ha!"

"Sheik, sheik!"

"She wouldn't do that." Little Brother sets down his clarinet like a precious vase, and speaks. He still looks like an East Indian queen, implacable, divine, and full of snakes. "You ain't going to expect people doing what they says over long distance."

"Come on!" roars Powerhouse. He is already at the back door, he has pulled it wide open, and with a wild, gathered-up face is smelling the terrible night.

Powerhouse, Valentine, Scoot and Little Brother step outside into the drenching rain.

"Well, they emptying buckets," says Powerhouse in a mollified voice.

On the street he holds his hands out and turns up the blanched palms like sieves.

A hundred dark, ragged, silent, delighted Negroes have come around from under the eaves of the hall, and follow wherever they go.

"Watch out Little Brother don't shrink," says Powerhouse. "You just the right size now, clarinet don't suck you in. You got a dry throat, Little Brother, you in the desert?" He reaches into the pocket and pulls out a paper of mints. "Now hold 'em in your mouth—don't chew 'em. I don't carry around nothing without limit."

"Go in that joint and have beer," says Scoot, who walks ahead.

"Beer? Beer? You know what beer is? What do they say is beer? What's beer? Where I been?"

"Down yonder where it say World Café—that do." They are in Negro-town now.

Valentine patters over and holds open a screen door warped like a sea shell, bitter in the wet, and they walk in, stained darker with the rain and leaving footprints. Inside, sheltered dry smells stand like screens around a table covered with a red-checkered cloth, in the center of which flies hang onto an obelisk-shaped ketchup bottle. The midnight walls are checkered again with admonishing "Not Responsible" signs and black-figured, smoky calendars. It is a waiting, silent, limp room. There is a burned-out-looking nickelodeon and right beside it a long-necked wall instrument labeled "Business Phone, Don't Keep Talking." Circled phone numbers are written up everywhere. There is a worn-out peacock feather hanging by a thread to an old, thin, pink, exposed light bulb, where it slowly turns around and around, whoever breathes.

A waitress watches.

'Come here, living statue, and get all this big order of beer we fixing to give."

"Never seen you before anywhere." The waitress moves and comes forward and slowly shows little gold leaves and tendrils over her teeth. She shoves up her shoulders and breasts. "How I going to know who you might be? Robbers? Coming in out of the black of night right at midnight, setting down so big at my table?"

"Boogers," says Powerhouse, his eyes opening lazily as in a cave.

The girl screams delicately with pleasure. O Lord, she likes talk and scares.

"Where you going to find enough beer to put out on this here table?"

She runs to the kitchen with bent elbows and sliding steps.

"Here's a million nickels," says Powerhouse, pulling his hand out of his pocket and sprinkling coins out, all but the last one, which he makes vanish like a magician.

Valentine and Scoot take the money over to the nickelodeon, which looks as battered as a slot machine, and read all the names of the records out loud.

"Whose 'Tuxedo Junction'?" asks Powerhouse.

"You know whose."

"Nickelodeon, I request you please to play 'Empty Bed Blues' and let Bessie Smith sing."

Silence: they hold it like a measure.

"Bring me all those nickels on back here," says Powerhouse. "Look at that! What you tell me the name of this place?"

"White dance, week night, raining, Alligator, Mississippi, long ways from home."

"Uh-huh."

"Sent for You Yesterday and Here You Come Today" plays.

The waitress, setting the tray of beer down on a back table, comes up taut and apprehensive as a hen. "Says in the kitchen, back there putting their eyes to little hole peeping out, that you is Mr. Powerhouse. . . . They knows from a picture they seen."

"They seeing right tonight, that is him," says Little Brother.

"You him?"

"That is him in the flesh," says Scoot.

"Does you wish to touch him?" asks Valentine. "Because he don't bite."

"You passing through?"

"Now you got everything right."

She waits like a drop, hands languishing together in front.

"Little-Bit, ain't you going to bring the beer?"

She brings it, and goes behind the cash register and smiles, turning different ways. The little fillet of gold in her mouth is gleaming.

"The Mississippi River's here," she says once.

Now all the watching Negroes press in gently and bright-eyed through the door, as many as can get in. One is a little boy in a straw sombrero which has been coated with aluminum paint all over.

Powerhouse, Valentine, Scoot and Little Brother drink beer, and their eyelids come together like curtains. The wall and the rain and the humble beautiful waitress waiting on them and the other Negroes watching enclose them.

"Listen!" whispers Powerhouse, looking into the kechup bottle and slowly spreading his performer's hand over the damp, wrinkling cloth with the red squares. "Listen how it is. My wife gets missing me. Gypsy. She goes to the window. She looks out and sees you know what. Street. Sign saying Hotel. People walking. Somebody looks up. Old man. She looks down, out the window. Well? . . . *Ssssst! Plooey!* What she do? Jump out and bust her brains all over the world."

He opens his eyes.

"That's it," agrees Valentine. "You gets a telegram."

"Sure she misses you," Little Brother adds.

"No, it's night time." How softly he tells them! "Sure. It's the night time. She say, What do I hear? Footsteps walking up the hall? That him? Footsteps go on off. It's not me. I'm in Alligator, Mississippi, she's crazy. Shaking all over. Listens till her ears and all grow out like old music-box horns but still she can't hear a thing. She says, All right! I'll jump out the window then. Got on her nightgown. I know that nightgown, and her thinking there. Says, Ho hum, all right, and jumps out the window. Is she mad at me? Is she crazy? She don't leave *nothing* behind her!"

"Ya! Ha!"

"Brains and insides everywhere, Lord, Lord."

All the watching Negroes stir in their delight, and to their higher delight he says affectionately, "Listen! Rats in here."

"That must be the way, boss."

"Only, naw, Powerhouse, that ain't true. That sound too *bad*."

"Does? I even know who finds her," cries Powerhouse. "That no-good pussyfooted crooning creeper, that creeper that follow around after me, coming up like weeds behind me, following around after me everything I do and messing around on the trail I leave. Bets my numbers, sings my songs, gets close to my agent like a Betsybug; when I going out he just coming in. I got him now! I got my eye on him."

"Know who he is?"

"Why, it's that old Uranus Knockwood!"

"Ya! Ha!"

"Yeah, and he coming now, he going to find Gypsy. There he is, coming around that corner, and Gypsy kadoodling down, oh-oh, watch out! *Sssssst! Plooey!* See, there she is in her little old nightgown, and her insides and brains all scattered round."

A sigh fills the room.

"Hush about her brains. Hush about her insides."

"Ya! Ha! You talking about her brains and insides—old Uranus Knockwood," says Powerhouse, "look down and say Jesus! He say, Look here what I'm walking round in!"

They all burst into halloos of laughter. Powerhouse's face looks like a big hot iron stove.

"Why, he picks her up and carries her off!" he says.

"Ya! Ha!"

"Carries her *back* around the corner. . . ."

"Oh, Powerhouse!"

"You know him."

"Uranus Knockwood!"

"Yeahhh!"

"He take our wives when we gone!"

"He come in when we goes out!"

"Uh-huh!"

"He go out when we comes in!"

"Yeahhh!"

"He standing behind the door!"

"Old Uranus Knockwood."

"You know him."

"Middle-size man."

"Wears a hat."

"That's him."

Everybody in the room moans with pleasure. The little boy in the fine silver hat opens a paper and divides out a jelly roll among his followers.

And out of the breathless ring somebody moves forward like a slave, leading a great logy Negro with bursting eyes, and says, "This here is Sugar-Stick Thompson, that dove down to the bottom of July Creek and pulled up all those drownded white people fall out of a boat. Last summer, pulled up fourteen."

"Hello," says Powerhouse, turning and looking around at them all with his great daring face until they nearly suffocate.

Sugar-Stick, their instrument, cannot speak; he can only look back at the others.

"Can't even swim. Done it by holding his breath," says the fellow with the hero.

Powerhouse looks at him seekingly.

"I his half brother," the fellow puts in.

They step back.

"Gypsy say," Powerhouse rumbles gently again, looking at *them,* " 'What is the use? I'm gonna jump out so far—so far. . . .' *Sssssst—!*"

"Don't, boss, don't do it again," says Little Brother.

"It's awful," says the waitress. "I hates that Mr. Knockwoods. All that the truth?"

"Want to see the telegram I got from him?" Powerhouse's hand goes to the vast pocket.

"Now wait, now wait, boss." They all watch him.

"It must be the real truth," says the waitress, sucking in her lower lip, her luminous eyes turning sadly, seeking the windows.

"No, babe, it ain't the truth." His eyebrows fly up, and he begins to whisper to her out of his vast oven mouth. His hand stays in his pocket. "Truth is something worse, I ain't said what, yet. It's something hasn't come to me, but I ain't saying it won't. And when it does, then want me to tell you?" He sniffs all at once, his eyes come open and turn up, almost too far. He is dreamily smiling.

"Don't, boss, don't, Powerhouse!"

"Oh!" the waitress screams.

"Go on git out of here!" bellows Powerhouse, taking his hand out of his pocket and clapping after her red dress.

The ring of watchers breaks and falls away.

"*Look* at that! Intermission is up," says Powerhouse.

He folds money under a glass, and after they go out, Valentine leans back in and drops a nickel in the nickelodeon behind them, and it lights up and begins to play "The Goona Goo." The feather dangles still.

"Take a telegram!" Powerhouse shouts suddenly up into the rain over the street. "Take a answer. Now what was that name?"

They get a little tired.

"Uranus Knockwood."

"You ought to know."

"Yas? Spell it to me."

They spell it all the ways it could be spelled. It puts them in a wonderful humor.

"Here's the answer. I got it right here. 'What in the hell you talking about? Don't make any difference: I gotcha.' Name signed: Powerhouse."

"That going to reach him, Powerhouse?" Valentine speaks in a maternal voice.

"Yas, yas."

All hushing, following him up the dark street at a distance, like old rained-on black ghosts, the Negroes are afraid they will die laughing.

Powerhouse throws back his vast head into the steaming rain, and a look of hopeful desire seems to blow somehow like a vapor from his own dilated nostrils over his face and bring a mist to his eyes.

"Reach him and come out the other side."

"That's it, Powerhouse, that's it. You got him now."

Powerhouse lets out a long sigh.

"But ain't you going back there to call up Gypsy long distance, the way you did last night in that other place? I seen a telephone. . . . Just to see if she there at home?"

There is a measure of silence. That is one crazy drummer that's going to get his neck broken some day.

"No," growls Powerhouse. "No! How many thousand times tonight I got to say No?"

He holds up his arm in the rain.

"You sure-enough unroll your voice some night, it about reach up yonder to her," says Little Brother, dismayed.

They go on up the street, shaking the rain off and on them like birds.

Back in the dance hall, they play "San" (99). The jitterbugs start up like windmills stationed over the floor, and in their orbits—one circle, another, a long stretch and a zigzag—dance the elderly couples with old smoothness, undisturbed and stately.

When Powerhouse first came back from intermission, no doubt full of beer, they said, he got the band tuned up again in his own way. He didn't strike the piano keys for pitch—he simply opened his mouth and gave falsetto howls—in A, D and so on—they tuned by him. Then he took hold of the piano, as if he saw it for the first time in his life, and tested it for strength, hit it down in the bass, played an octave with his elbow, lifted the top, looked inside, and leaned against it with all his might. He sat down and played it for a few minutes with outrageous force and got it under his power—a bass deep and coarse as a sea net—then produced something glimmering and fragile, and smiled. And who could ever remember any of the things he says? They are just inspired remarks that roll out of his mouth like smoke.

They've requested "Somebody Loves Me," and he's already done twelve or fourteen choruses, piling them up nobody knows how, and it will be a wonder if he ever gets through. Now and then he calls and shouts, " 'Somebody loves me! Somebody loves me, I wonder who!' " His mouth gets to be nothing but a volcano. "I wonder who!"

"Maybe . . ." He uses all his right hand on a trill.

"Maybe . . ." He pulls back his spread fingers, and looks out upon the place where he is. A vast, impersonal and yet furious grimace transfigures his wet face.

". . . Maybe it's you!"

A Clean, Well-Lighted Place

❧ *Ernest Hemingway*

It was late and every one had left the café except an old man who sat in the shadow the leaves of the tree made against the electric light. In the day time the street was dusty, but at night the dew settled the dust and the old man liked to sit late because he was deaf and now at night it was quiet and he felt the difference. The two waiters inside the café knew that the old man was a little drunk, and while he was a good client they knew that if he became too drunk he would leave without paying, so they kept watch on him.

"Last week he tried to commit suicide," one waiter said.

"Why?"

"He was in despair."

"What about?"

"Nothing."

"How do you know it was nothing?"

"He has plenty of money."

They sat together at a table that was close against the wall near the door of the café and looked at the terrace where the tables were all empty except where the old man sat in the shadow of the leaves of the tree that moved slightly in the wind. A girl and a soldier went by in the street. The street light shone on the brass number on his collar. The girl wore no head covering and hurried beside him.

"The guard will pick him up," one waiter said.

"What does it matter if he gets what he's after?"

"He had better get off the street now. The guard will get him. They went by five minutes ago."

The old man sitting in the shadow rapped on his saucer with his glass. The younger waiter went over to him.

"What do you want?"

The old man looked at him. "Another brandy," he said.

"You'll be drunk," the waiter said. The old man looked at him. The waiter went away.

"He'll stay all night," he said to his colleague. "I'm sleepy now. I never get into bed before three o'clock. He should have killed himself last week."

The waiter took the brandy bottle and another saucer from the counter inside the café and marched out to the old man's table. He put down the saucer and poured the glass full of brandy.

"You should have killed yourself last week," he said to the deaf man. The old man motioned with his finger. "A little more," he said. The waiter poured on into the glass so that the brandy slopped over and ran down the stem into the top saucer of the pile. "Thank you," the old man said. The waiter took the bottle back inside the café. He sat down at the table with his colleague again.

"He's drunk now," he said.

"He's drunk every night."

"What did he want to kill himself for?"

"How should I know."

"How did he do it?"

"He hung himself with a rope."

"Who cut him down?"

"His niece."

"Why did they do it?"

"Fear for his soul."

"How much money has he got?"

"He's got plenty."

"He must be eighty years old."

"Anyway I should say he was eighty."

"I wish he would go home. I never get to bed before three o'clock. What kind of hour is that to go to bed?"

"He stays up because he likes it."

"He's lonely. I'm not lonely. I have a wife waiting in bed for me."

"He had a wife once too."

"A wife would be no good to him now."

"You can't tell. He might be better with a wife."

"His niece looks after him."

"I know. You said she cut him down."

"I wouldn't want to be that old. An old man is a nasty thing."

"Not always. This old man is clean. He drinks without spilling. Even now, drunk. Look at him."

"I don't want to look at him. I wish he would go home. He has no regard for those who must work."

The old man looked from his glass across the square, then over at the waiters.

"Another brandy," he said, pointing to his glass. The waiter who was in a hurry came over.

"Finished," he said, speaking with that omission of syntax stupid people employ when talking to drunken people or foreigners. "No more tonight. Close now."

"Another," said the old man.

"No. Finished." The waiter wiped the edge of the table with a towel and shook his head.

The old man stood up, slowly counted the saucers, took a leather coin purse from his pocket and paid for the drinks, leaving half a peseta tip.

The waiter watched him go down the street, a very old man walking unsteadily but with dignity.

"Why didn't you let him stay and drink?" the unhurried waiter asked. They were putting up the shutters. "It is not half-past two."

"I want to go home to bed."

"What is an hour?"

"More to me than to him."

"An hour is the same."

"You talk like an old man yourself. He can buy a bottle and drink at home."

"It's not the same."

"No, it is not," agreed the waiter with a wife. He did not wish to be unjust. He was only in a hurry.

"And you? You have no fear of going home before your usual hour?"

"Are you trying to insult me?"

"No, hombre, only to make a joke."

"No," the waiter who was in a hurry said, rising from pulling down the metal shutters. "I have confidence. I am all confidence."

"You have youth, confidence, and a job," the older waiter said. "You have everything."

"And what do you lack?"

"Everything but work."

"You have everything I have."

"No. I have never had confidence and I am not young."

"Come on. Stop talking nonsense and lock up."

"I am of those who like to stay late at the café," the older waiter said. "With all those who do not want to go to bed. With all those who need a light for the night."

"I want to go home and into bed."

"We are of two different kinds," the older waiter said. He was now dressed to go home. "It is not only a question of youth and confidence although those things are very beautiful. Each night I am reluctant to close up because there may be some one who needs the café."

"Hombre, there are bodegas open all night long."

"You do not understand. This is a clean and pleasant café. It is well lighted. The light is very good and also, now, there are shadows of the leaves."

"Good night," said the younger waiter.

"Good night," the other said. Turning off the electric light he continued the conversation with himself. It is the light of course but it is necessary that the place be clean and pleasant. You do not want music. Certainly you do not want music. Nor can you stand before a bar with dignity although that is all that is provided for these hours. What did he fear? It was not fear or dread. It was a nothing that he knew too well. It was all a nothing and a man was nothing too. It was only that and light was all it needed and a certain cleanness and order. Some lived in it and never felt it but he knew it all was nada y pues nada y pues nada. Our nada who art in nada, nada be thy name thy kingdom nada thy will be nada in nada as it is in nada. Give us this nada our daily nada and nada us our nada as we nada our nadas and nada us not into nada but deliver us from nada; pues nada. Hail nothing full of nothing, nothing is with thee. He smiled and stood before a bar with a shining steam pressure coffee machine.

"What's yours?" asked the barman.

"Nada."

"Otro loco mas," said the barman and turned away.

"A little cup," said the waiter.

The barman poured it for him.

"The light is very bright and pleasant but the bar is unpolished," the waiter said.

The barman looked at him but did not answer. It was too late at night for conversation.

"You want another copita?" the barman asked.

"No, thank you," said the waiter and went out. He disliked bars and bodegas. A clean, well-lighted café was a very different thing. Now, without thinking further, he would go home to his room. He would lie in the bed and finally, with daylight, he would go to sleep. After all, he said to himself, it is probably only insomnia. Many must have it.

The Judgment

🍃 *Franz Kafka*

It was a Sunday morning in the very height of spring. Georg Bendemann, a young merchant, was sitting in his own room on the first floor
of one of a long row of small, ramshackle houses stretching beside the river
which were scarcely distinguishable from each other except in height and
coloring. He had just finished a letter to an old friend of his who was now
living abroad, had put it into its envelope in a slow and dreamy fashion,
and with his elbows propped on the writing table was gazing out of the
window at the river, the bridge and the hills on the farther bank with
their tender green.

He was thinking about his friend, who had actually run away to Russia
some years before, being dissatisfied with his prospects at home. Now he
was carrying on a business in St. Petersburg, which had flourished to
begin with but had long been going downhill, as he always complained
on his increasingly rare visits. So he was wearing himself out to no purpose in a foreign country; the unfamiliar full beard he wore did not quite
conceal the face Georg had known so well since childhood, and his skin
was growing so yellow as to indicate some latent disease. By his own
account he had no regular connection with the colony of his fellow countrymen out there and almost no social intercourse with Russian families,
so that he was resigning himself to becoming a permanent bachelor.

What could one write to such a man, who had obviously run off the
rails, a man one could be sorry for but could not help? Should one advise
him to come home, to transplant himself and take up his old friendships
again—there was nothing to hinder him—and in general to rely on the
help of his friends? But that was as good as telling him, and the more
kindly the more offensively, that all his efforts hitherto had miscarried,
that he should finally give up, come back home, and be gaped at by everyone as a returned prodigal, that only his friends knew what was what and
that he himself was just a big child who should do what his successful and
home-keeping friends prescribed. And was it certain, besides, that all
the pain one would have to inflict on him would achieve its object? Perhaps it would not even be possible to get him to come home at all—he said
himself that he was now out of touch with commerce in his native country
—and then he would still be left an alien in a foreign land embittered by
his friends' advice and more than ever estranged from them. But if he did
follow their advice and then didn't fit in at home—not out of malice, of
course, but through force of circumstances—couldn't get on with his

friends or without them, felt humiliated, couldn't be said to have either friends or a country of his own any longer, wouldn't it have been better for him to stay abroad just as he was? Taking all this into account, how could one be sure that he would make a success of life at home?

For such reasons, supposing one wanted to keep up correspondence with him, one could not send him any real news such as could frankly be told to the most distant acquaintance. It was more than three years since his last visit, and for this he offered the lame excuse that the political situation in Russia was too uncertain, which apparently would not permit even the briefest absence of a small business man while it allowed hundreds of thousands of Russians to travel peacefully abroad. But during these three years Georg's own position in life had changed a lot. Two years ago his mother had died, since when he and his father had shared the household together, and his friend had of course been informed of that and had expressed his sympathy in a letter phrased so dryly that the grief caused by such an event, one had to conclude, could not be realized in a distant country. Since that time, however, Georg had applied himself with greater determination to the business, as well as to everything else.

Perhaps during his mother's lifetime his father's insistence on having everything his own way in the business had hindered him from developing any real activity of his own, perhaps since her death his father had become less aggressive, although he was still active in the business, perhaps it was mostly due to an accidental run of good fortune—which was very probable indeed—but at any rate during those two years the business had developed in a most unexpected way, the staff had had to be doubled, the turnover was five times as great, no doubt about it, further progress lay just ahead.

But Georg's friend had no inkling of this improvement. In earlier years, perhaps for the last time in that letter of condolence, he had tried to persuade Georg to emigrate to Russia and had enlarged upon the prospects of success for precisely Georg's branch of trade. The figures quoted were microscopic by comparison with the range of Georg's present operations. Yet he shrank from letting his friend know about his business success, and if he were to do it now retrospectively that certainly would look peculiar.

So Georg confined himself to giving his friend unimportant items of gossip such as rise at random in the memory when one is idly thinking things over on a quiet Sunday. All he desired was to leave undisturbed the idea of the home town which his friend must have built up to his own content during the long interval. And so it happened to Georg that three times in three fairly widely separated letters he had told his friend about the engagement of an unimportant man to an equally unimportant girl, until indeed, quite contrary to his intentions, his friend began to show some interest in this notable event.

Yet Georg preferred to write about things like these rather than to confess that he himself had got engaged a month ago to a Fräulein Frieda Brandenfeld, a girl from a well-to-do family. He often discussed this friend of his with his fiancée and the peculiar relationship that had developed between them in their correspondence. "So he won't be coming to our wedding," said she, "and yet I have a right to get to know all your friends." "I don't want to trouble him," answered Georg. "Don't misunderstand me, he would probably come, at least I think so, but he would feel that his hand had been forced and he would be hurt, perhaps he would envy me and certainly he'd be discontented and without being able to do anything about his discontent he'd have to go away again alone. Alone—do you know what that means?" "Yes, but may he not hear about our wedding in some other fashion?" "I can't prevent that, of course, but it's unlikely, considering the way he lives." "Since your friends are like that, Georg, you shouldn't ever have got engaged at all." "Well, we're both to blame for that; but I wouldn't have it any other way now." And when, breathing quickly under his kisses, she still brought out: "All the same, I do feel upset," he thought it could not really involve him in trouble were he to send the news to his friend. "That's the kind of man I am and he'll just have to take me as I am," he said to himself, "I can't cut myself to another pattern that might make a more suitable friend for him."

And in fact he did inform his friend, in the long letter he had been writing that Sunday morning, about his engagement, with these words: "I have saved my best news to the end. I have got engaged to a Fräulein Frieda Brandenfeld, a girl from a well-to-do family, who only came to live here a long time after you went away, so that you're hardly likely to know her. There will be time to tell you more about her later, for today let me just say that I am very happy and as between you and me the only difference in our relationship is that instead of a quite ordinary kind of friend you will now have in me a happy friend. Besides that, you will acquire in my fiancée, who sends her warm greetings and will soon write you herself, a genuine friend of the opposite sex, which is not without importance to a bachelor. I know that there are many reasons why you can't come to see us, but would not my wedding be precisely the right occasion for giving all obstacles the go-by? Still, however that may be, do just as seems good to you without regarding any interests but your own."

With this letter in his hand Georg had been sitting a long time at the writing table, his face turned towards the window. He had barely acknowledged, with an absent smile, a greeting waved to him from the street by a passing acquaintance.

At last he put the letter in his pocket and went out of his room across a small lobby into his father's room, which he had not entered for months. There was in fact no need for him to enter it, since he saw his father daily at business and they took their midday meal together at an eating house; in the evening, it was true, each did as he pleased, yet even then, unless Georg—as mostly happened—went out with friends or, more recently, visited his fiancée, they always sat for a while, each with his newspaper, in their common sitting room.

It surprised Georg how dark his father's room was even on this sunny morning. So it was overshadowed as much as that by the high wall on the other side of the narrow courtyard. His father was sitting by the window in a corner hung with various mementoes of Georg's dead mother, reading a newspaper which he held to one side before his eyes in an attempt to overcome a defect of vision. On the table stood the remains of his breakfast, not much of which seemed to have been eaten.

"Ah, Georg," said his father, rising at once to meet him. His heavy dressing gown swung open as he walked and the skirts of it fluttered round him.—"My father is still a giant of a man," said Georg to himself.

"It's unbearably dark here," he said aloud.

"Yes, it's dark enough," answered his father.

"And you've shut the window, too?"

"I prefer it like that."

"Well, it's quite warm outside," said Georg, as if continuing his previous remark, and sat down.

His father cleared away the breakfast dishes and set them on a chest.

"I really only wanted to tell you," went on Georg, who had been vacantly following the old man's movements, "that I am now sending the news of my engagement to St. Petersburg." He drew the letter a little way from his pocket and let it drop back again.

"To St. Petersburg?" asked his father.

"To my friend there," said Georg, trying to meet his father's eye.—In business hours he's quite different, he was thinking. How solidly he sits here with his arms crossed.

"Oh, yes. To your friend," said his father, with peculiar emphasis.

"Well, you know, Father, that I wanted not to tell him about my engagement at first. Out of consideration for him, that was the only reason. You know yourself he's a difficult man. I said to myself that someone else might tell him about my engagement, although he's such a solitary creature that that was hardly likely—I couldn't prevent that—but I wasn't ever going to tell him myself."

"And now you've changed your mind?" asker his father, laying his enormous newspaper on the window sill and on top of it his spectacles, which he covered with one hand.

"Yes, I've been thinking it over. If he's a good friend of mine, I said to myself, my being happily engaged should make him happy too. And so I wouldn't put off telling him any longer. But before I posted the letter I wanted to let you know."

"Georg," said his father, lengthening his toothless mouth, "listen to me! You've come to me about this business, to talk it over with me. No doubt that does you honor. But it's nothing, it's worse than nothing, if you don't tell me the whole truth. I don't want to stir up matters that shouldn't be mentioned here. Since the death of our dear mother certain things have been done that aren't right. Maybe the time will come for mentioning them, and maybe sooner than we think. There's many a thing in the business I'm not aware of, maybe it's not done behind my back—I'm not going to say that it's done behind my back—I'm not equal to things any longer, my memory's failing, I haven't an eye for so many things any longer. That's the course of nature in the first place, and in the second place the death of our dear mother hit me harder than it did you.—But since we're talking about it, about this letter, I beg you, Georg, don't deceive me. It's a trivial affair, it's hardly worth mentioning, so don't deceive me. Do you really have this friend in St. Petersburg?"

Georg rose in embarrassment. "Never mind my friends. A thousand friends wouldn't make up to me for my father. Do you know what I think? You're not taking enough care of yourself. But old age must be taken care of. I can't do without you in the business, you know that very well, but if the business is going to undermine your health, I'm ready to close it down tomorrow forever. And that won't do. We'll have to make a change in your way of living. But a radical change. You sit here in the dark, and in the sitting room you would have plenty of light. You just take a bite of breakfast instead of properly keeping up your strength. You sit by a closed window, and the air would be so good for you. No, Father! I'll get the doctor to come, and we'll follow his orders. We'll change your room, you can move into the front room and I'll move in here. You won't notice the change, all your things will be moved with you. But there's time for all that later. I'll put you to bed now for a little; I'm sure you need to rest. Come, I'll help you to take off your things, you'll see I can do it. Or if you would rather go into the front room at once, you can lie down in my bed for the present. That would be the most sensible thing."

Georg stood close beside his father, who had let his head with its unkempt white hair sink on his chest.

"Georg," said his father in a low voice, without moving.

Georg knelt down at once beside his father. In the old man's weary face he saw the pupils, over-large, fixedly looking at him from the corners of the eyes.

"You have a friend in St. Petersburg. You've always been a leg-puller and you haven't even shrunk from pulling my leg. How could you have a friend out there! I can't believe it."

"Just think back a bit, Father," said Georg, lifting his father from the chair and slipping off his dressing gown as he stood feebly enough, "it'll soon be three years since my friend came to see us last. I remember that you used not to like him very much. At least twice I kept you from seeing him, although he was actually sitting with me in my room. I could quite well understand your dislike of him, my friend has his peculiarities. But then, later, you got on with him very well. I was proud because you listened to him and nodded and asked him questions. If you think back you're bound to remember. He used to tell us the most incredible stories of the Russian Revolution. For instance, when he was on a business trip to Kiev and ran into a riot, and saw a priest on a balcony who cut a broad cross in blood on the palm of his hand and held the hand up and appealed to the mob. You've told that story yourself once or twice since."

Meanwhile Georg had succeeded in lowering his father down again and carefully taking off the woollen drawers he wore over his linen underpants and his socks. The not particularly clean appearance of this underwear made him reproach himself for having been neglectful. It should have certainly been his duty to see that his father had clean changes of underwear. He had not yet explicitly discussed with his bride-to-be what arrangements should be made for his father in the future, for they had both of them silently taken it for granted that the old man would go on living alone in the old house. But now he made a quick, firm decision to take him into his own future establishment. It almost looked, on closer inspection, as if the care he meant to lavish on his father might come too late.

He carried his father to bed in his arms. It gave him a dreadful feeling to notice that while he took the few steps toward the bed the old man on his breast was playing with his watch chain. He could not lay him down on the bed for a moment, so firmly did he hang on to the watch chain.

But as soon as he was laid in bed, all seemed well. He covered himself up and even drew the blankets farther than usual over his shoulders. He looked up at Georg with a not unfriendly eye.

"You begin to remember my friend, don't you?" asked Georg, giving him an encouraging nod.

"Am I well covered up now?" asked his father, as if he were not able to see whether his feet were properly tucked in or not.

"So you find it snug in bed already," said Georg, and tucked the blankets more closely around him.

"Am I well covered up?" asked the father once more, seeming to be strangely intent upon the answer.

"Don't worry, you're well covered up."

"No!" cried his father, cutting short the answer, threw the blankets off with a strength that sent them all flying in a moment and sprang erect in bed. Only one hand lightly touched the ceiling to steady him.

"You wanted to cover me up, I know, my young sprig, but I'm far from being covered up yet. And even if this is the last strength I have, it's enough for you, too much for you. Of course I know your friend. He would have been a son after my own heart. That's why you've been playing him false all these years. Why else? Do you think I haven't been sorry for him? And that's why you had to lock yourself up in your office—the Chief is busy, mustn't be disturbed—just so that you could write your lying little letters to Russia. But thank goodness a father doesn't need to be taught how to see through his son. And now that you thought you'd got him down, so far down that you could set your bottom on him and sit on him and he wouldn't move, then my fine son makes up his mind to get married!"

Georg stared at the bogey conjured up by his father. His friend in St. Petersburg, whom his father suddenly knew too well, touched his imagination as never before. Lost in the vastness of Russia he saw him. At the door of an empty, plundered warehouse he saw him. Among the wreckage of his showcases, the slashed remnants of his wares, the falling gas brackets, he was just standing up. Why did he have to go so far away!

"But attend to me!" cried his father, and Georg almost distracted, ran towards the bed to take everything in, yet came to a stop halfway.

"Because she lifted up her skirts," his father began to flute, "because she lifted her skirts like this, the nasty creature," and mimicking her he lifted his shirt so high that one could see the scar on his thigh from his war wound, "because she lifted her skirts like this and this you made up to her, and in order to make free with her undisturbed you have disgraced your mother's memory, betrayed your friend and stuck your father into bed so that he can't move. But he can move, or can't he?"

And he stood up quite unsupported and kicked his legs out. His insight made him radiant.

Georg shrank into a corner, as far away from his father as possible. A long time ago he had firmly made up his mind to watch closely every least movement so that he should not be surprised by any indirect attack, a pounce from behind or above. At this moment he recalled this long-forgotten resolve and forgot it again, like a man drawing a short thread through the eye of a needle.

"But your friend hasn't been betrayed after all!" cried his father, emphasizing the point with stabs of his forefinger. "I've been representing him here on the spot."

"You comedian!" Georg could not resist the retort, realized at once the harm done and, his eyes starting in his head, bit his tongue back, only too late, till the pain made his knees give.

"Yes, of course I've been playing a comedy! A comedy! That's a good expression! What other comfort was left to a poor old widower? Tell me—and while you're answering me be you still my living son—what else was left to me, in my back room, plagued by a disloyal staff, old to the marrow of my bones? And my son strutting through the world, finishing off deals that I had prepared for him, bursting with triumphant glee and stalking away from his father with the closed face of a respectable business man! Do you think I didn't love you, I, from whom you are sprung?"

Now he'll lean forward, thought Georg. What if he topples and smashes himself! These words went hissing through his mind.

His father leaned forward but did not topple. Since Georg did not come any nearer, as he had expected, he straightened himself again.

"Stay where you are, I don't need you! You think you have strength enough to come over here and that you're only hanging back of your own accord. Don't be too sure! I am still much the stronger of us two. All by myself I might have had to give way, but your mother has given me so much of her strength that I've established a fine connection with your friend and I have your customers here in my pocket!"

"He has pockets even in his shirt!" said Georg to himself, and believed that with this remark he could make him an impossible figure for all the world. Only for a moment did he think so, since he kept on forgetting everything.

"Just take your bride on your arm and try getting in my way! I'll sweep her from your very side, you don't know how!"

Georg made a grimace of disbelief. His father only nodded, confirming the truth of his words, towards Georg's corner.

"How you amuse me today, coming to ask me if you should tell your friend about your engagement. He knows it already, you stupid boy, he knows it all! I've been writing to him, for you forgot to take my writing things away from me. That's why he hasn't been here for years, he knows everything a hundred times better than you do yourself, in his left hand he crumples your letters unopened while in his right hand he holds up my letters to read through!"

In his enthusiasm he waved his arm over his head. "He knows everything a thousand times better!" he cried.

"Ten thousand times!" said Georg, to make fun of his father, but in his very mouth the words turned into deadly earnest.

"For years I've been waiting for you to come with some such question! Do you think I concern myself with anything else? Do you think I read my newspapers? Look!" and he threw Georg a newspaper sheet which he had somehow taken to bed with him. An old newspaper, with a name entirely unknown to Georg.

"How long a time you've taken to grow up! Your mother had to die, she couldn't see the happy day, your friend is going to pieces in Russia, even three years ago he was yellow enough to be thrown away, and as for me, you see what condition I'm in. You have eyes in your head for that!"

"So you've been lying in wait for me!" cried Georg.

His father said pityingly, in an offhand manner: "I suppose you wanted to say that sooner. But now it doesn't matter." And in a louder voice: "So now you know what else there was in the world besides yourself, till now you've known only about yourself! An innocent child, yes, that you were, truly, but still more truly have you been a devilish human being!— And therefore take note: I sentence you now to death by drowning!"

Georg felt himself urged from the room. The crash with which his father fell on the bed behind him was still in his ears as he fled. On the staircase, which he rushed down as if its steps were an inclined plane, he ran into his charwoman on her way up to do the morning cleaning of the room. "Jesus!" she cried, and covered her face with her apron, but he was already gone. Out of the front door he rushed, across the roadway, driven towards the water. Already he was grasping at the railings as a starving man clutches food. He swung himself over, like the distinguished gymnast he had once been in his youth, to his parents' pride. With weakening grip he was still holding on when he spied between the railings a motor-bus coming which would easily cover the noise of his fall, called in a low voice: "Dear parents, I have always loved you, all the same," and let himself drop.

At this moment an unending stream of traffic was just going over the bridge.

CRITICAL COMMENTS

Philip Rahv:

The quarrel between the religious and the psychoanalytic interpreters of Kafka is of no great moment, as his work is sufficiently meaningful to support some of the "truths" of both schools. Thus the father who condemns his son to death by drowning (in *The Judgment*) can be understood as the tyrannical father of Freudian lore and at the same time as the God of Judgment rising in His wrath to destroy man's illusion of self-sufficiency in the world. At bottom there is no conflict between the two interpretations. For one thing, they are not really mutually exclusive; for another, the reading we give the story depends as much on our own outlook—within certain limits, of course—as on that of the author. There was in Kafka's character an element of radical humility not permitting him to set out to "prove" any given attitude toward life or idea about it. This he plainly tells us in some of the aphorisms that he wrote about himself in the third person: "He proves nothing but himself, his sole proof is himself, all his opponents overcome him at once, not by refuting him (he is irrefutable) but by proving themselves." [1]

Herbert Tauber:

The assumptions and the plot of the story are not guilt and atonement, but fatuity and destruction. As a punishment for an established guilt, the judgment is absurd. But as a "judgment," it is something more comprehensive: it qualifies the whole of Georg's self-confident existence as nothingness, and that on no other grounds than that of this empty self-confidence. In his relations with his distant friend no kind of malice is expressed, nothing but this self-confidence that even knows what is good for everyone. . . . Georg lives in falsehood; but it is only in the uneasiness of his reflections about his friend that he feels a slight consciousness of this. His first step toward truth destroys him. The father rises as the friend's advocate. " 'For years I have been waiting for you to come with some such question! Do you think I concern myself with anything else?

[1] From the Introduction, by Philip Rahv, to *Selected Stories of Franz Kafka* (New York: The Modern Library—Random House, Inc., 1952), pp. xiii–xiv, reprinted by permission of Schocken Books, Inc., New York.

Do you think I read the papers? Look!' And he threw Georg a paper that had somehow found its way into the bed. An old newspaper, with a name entirely unknown to Georg." The outward, historical events which newspapers record, and in which Georg's existence also moves, mean nothing to the father. He belongs to a different sphere, from whose existence Georg is entirely withdrawn, and of which he is aware only in suppressed stirrings. The struggle between father and son develops into a struggle between two worlds: that of the vital existence, in which probability and reservation rule, and conscience is relegated to the position of watchdog of a drugged smugness, and that other world in which each step has an incalculable importance, because it is taken under the horizon of an absolute summons to the right road. The father is the authoritative bearer of this summons—an aspect of God.

For God, beyond question, plays in our existence the role of a man once powerful, but now come down in life and neglected, to whom a certain measure of reverence and attention is paid, but who has nothing more to say in our "affairs"—particularly since the death of "mother"—the decay of the church, the Synagogue, religion in general. Man is autonomous in his decisions, and takes the world on self-confidently—just as Georg does his fiancée. From the point of view of this human autonomy, the sudden coming to life of God as a complete annulment of the might of man is absurd. But the man who just lives a life without principles cannot evade this madness of God when it suddenly becomes actual. He has to listen to his worldliness being presented as randiness—"Because she raised her skirts. . . ."—and finally in his unmasked carnalism he has to destroy himself.[2]

Franz Kafka:

February 11 [1913]. While I read the proofs of *The Judgment,* I'll write down all the relationships which have become clear to me in the story as far as I now remember them. This is necessary because the story came out of me like a real birth, covered with filth and slime, and only I have the hand that can reach to the body itself and the strength of desire to do so:

The friend is the link between father and son, he is their strongest common bond. Sitting alone at his window, Georg rummages voluptuously in this consciousness of what they have in common, believes he has his father within him, and would be at peace with everything if it were not for a fleeting, sad thoughtfulness. In the course of the story the father, with the strengthened position that the other, lesser things they share in common give him—love, devotion to the mother, loyalty to her memory, the clientele that he (the father) had been

2 From *Franz Kafka,* by Herbert Tauber (New Haven: Yale University Press, 1948), pp. 15–17, reprinted by permission of the publisher.

the first to acquire for the business—uses the common bond of the friend to set himself up as Georg's antagonist. Georg is left with nothing; the bride, who lives in the story only in relation to the friend, that is, to what father and son have in common, is easily driven away by the father since no marriage has yet taken place, and so she cannot penetrate the circle of blood relationship that is drawn around father and son. What they have in common is built up entirely around the father, Georg can feel it only as something foreign, something that has become independent, that he has never given enough protection, that is exposed to Russian revolutions, and only because he himself has lost everything except his awareness of the father does the judgment, which closes off his father from him completely, have so strong an effect on him.

Georg has the same number of letters as Franz. In Bendemann, "mann" is a strengthening of "Bende" to provide for all the as yet unforeseen possibilities in the story. But Bende has exactly the same number of letters as Kafka, and the vowel *e* occurs in the same place as does the vowel *a* in Kafka.

Frieda has as many letters as F. and the same initial, Brandenfeld has the same initial as B., and in the word "Feld" a certain connection in meaning, as well. Perhaps even the thought of Berlin was not without influence and the recollection of the Mark Branden-burg perhaps had some influence.

February 12. . . . After I read the story at Weltsch's yesterday, old Mr. Weltsch went out and, when he returned after a short time, praised especially the graphic descriptions in the story. With his arm extended he said, "I see this father before me," all the time looking directly at the empty chair in which he had been sitting while I was reading.

My sister said, "It is our house." I was astonished at how mistaken she was in the setting and said, "In that case, then, Father would have to be living in the toilet." [3]

Heinz Politzer:

"The Judgment" moves constantly in two spheres, the realistic and the superrealistic, the psychological and the metaphysical; but these two spheres have not been satisfactorily integrated. In old Bendemann, Kafka seized a likeness of his father and treated it as an Oedipal tyrant very much the way the expressionists used to treat their father images; he strove to elevate it to a godlike figure endowed with omniscience, omnipotence, and the authority of absolute jurisdiction. Being a child of the twentieth century, the writer could not muster the strength to accomplish this design. Thus he left old Bendemann suspended between earth and heaven, a

[3] From *The Diaries of Franz Kafka 1910–1913* (New York: Schocken Books, 1948), pp. 278–280, reprinted by permission of the publisher.

figment of his imagination, a fearful wish dream, an expression of his psychological insecurity as well as of his never-fulfilled desire for a genuine metaphysical orientation.[4]

[4] From *Franz Kafka: Parable and Paradox*, by Heinz Politzer, pp. 60–61, copyright © 1962 by Cornell University, reprinted by permission of Cornell University Press, Ithaca, New York.

Death in Venice

꼍 *Thomas Mann*

Gustave Aschenbach—or von Aschenbach, as he had been known officially since his fiftieth birthday—had set out alone from his house in
Prince Regent Street, Munich, for an extended walk. It was a spring afternoon in that year of grace 19—, when Europe sat upon the anxious seat
beneath a menace that hung over its head for months. Aschenbach had
sought the open soon after tea. He was overwrought by a morning of
hard, nerve-taxing work, work which had not ceased to exact his utter-
most in the way of sustained concentration, conscientiousness, and tact;
and after the noon meal found himself powerless to check the onward
sweep of the productive mechanism within him, that *motus animi con-
tinuus* in which, according to Cicero, eloquence resides. He had sought
but not found relaxation in sleep—though the wear and tear upon his
system had come to make a daily nap more and more imperative—and
now undertook a walk, in the hope that air and exercise might send him
back refreshed to a good evening's work.

May had begun, and after weeks of cold and wet a mock summer had
set in. The English Gardens, though in tenderest leaf, felt as sultry as
in August and were full of vehicles and pedestrians near the city. But
towards Aumeister the paths were solitary and still, and Aschenbach
strolled thither, stopping awhile to watch the lively crowds in the restaurant garden with its fringe of carriages and cabs. Thence he took his
homeward way outside the park and across the sunset fields. By the time
he reached the North Cemetery, however, he felt tired, and a storm was
brewing above Föhring; so he waited at the stopping-place for a tram to
carry him back to the city.

He found the neighbourhood quite empty. Not a wagon in sight, either
on the paved Ungererstrasse, with its gleaming tram-lines stretching off
towards Schwabing, nor on the Föhring highway. Nothing stirred behind
the hedge in the stone-mason's yard, where crosses, monuments, and
commemorative tablets made a supernumerary and untenanted graveyard
opposite the real one. The mortuary chapel, a structure in Byzantine style,
stood facing it, silent in the gleam of the ebbing day. Its façade was
adorned with Greek crosses and tinted hieratic designs, and displayed a
symmetrically arranged selection of scriptural texts in gilded letters, all
of them with a bearing upon the future life, such as: "They are entering
into the House of the Lord" and "May the Light Everlasting shine upon
them." Aschenbach beguiled some minutes of his waiting with reading

Translated from the German by H. T. Lowe-Porter, from Stories of Three Decades,
*by Thomas Mann, copyright 1930, 1936 by Alfred A. Knopf, Inc., reprinted by permis-
sion of Alfred A. Knopf, Inc., New York.*

these formulas and letting his mind's eye lose itself in their mystical mean-ing. He was brought back to reality by the sight of a man standing in the portico, above the two apocalyptic beasts that guarded the staircase, and something not quite usual in this man's appearance gave his thoughts a fresh turn.

Whether he had come out of the hall through the bronze doors or mounted unnoticed from outside, it was impossible to tell. Aschenbach casually inclined to the first idea. He was of medium height, thin, beard-less, and strikingly snub-nosed; he belonged to the red-haired type and possessed its milky, freckled skin. He was obviously not Bavarian; and the broad, straight-brimmed straw hat he had on even made him look distinctly exotic. True, he had the indigenous rucksack buckled on his back, wore a belted suit of yellowish woollen stuff, apparently frieze, and carried a grey mackintosh cape across his left forearm, which was propped against his waist. In his right hand, slantwise to the ground, he held an iron-shod stick, and braced himself against its crook, with his legs crossed. His chin was up, so that the Adam's apple looked very bald in the lean neck rising from the loose shirt; and he stood there sharply peering up into space out of colourless, red-lashed eyes, while two pronounced per-pendicular furrows showed on his forehead in curious contrast to his little turned-up nose. Perhaps his heightened and heightening position helped out the impression Aschenbach received. At any rate, standing there as though at survey, the man had a bold and domineering, even a ruthless, air, and his lips completed the picture by seeming to curl back, either by reason of some deformity or else because he grimaced, being blinded by the sun in his face; they laid bare the long, white, glistening teeth to the gums.

Aschenbach's gaze, though unawares, had very likely been inquisitive and tactless; for he became suddenly conscious that the stranger was returning it, and indeed so directly, with such hostility, such plain intent to force the withdrawal of the other's eyes, that Aschenbach felt an un-pleasant twinge and, turning his back, began to walk along the hedge, hastily resolving to give the man no further heed. He had forgotten him the next minute. Yet whether the pilgrim air the stranger wore kindled his fantasy or whether some other physical or psychical influence came in play, he could not tell; but he felt the most surprising consciousness of a widening of inward barriers, a kind of vaulting unrest, a youthfully ardent thirst for distant scenes—a feeling so lively and so new, or at least so long ago outgrown and forgot, that he stood there rooted to the spot, his eyes on the ground and his hands clasped behind him, exploring these sentiments of his, their bearing and scope.

True, what he felt was no more than a longing to travel; yet coming upon him with such suddenness and passion as to resemble a seizure, almost a hallucination. Desire projected itself visually: his fancy, not quite yet lulled since morning, imaged the marvels and terrors of the manifold earth. He saw. He beheld a landscape, a tropical marshland, beneath a reeking sky, steaming, monstrous, rank—a kind of primeval wilderness-world of islands, morasses, and alluvial channels. Hairy palm-trunks rose near and far out of lush brakes of fern, out of bottoms of crass vegetation, fat, swollen, thick with incredible bloom. There were trees, misshapen as a dream, that dropped their naked roots straight through the air into the ground or into water that was stagnant and shadowy and glassy-green, where mammoth milk-white blossoms floated, and strange high-shouldered birds with curious bills stood gazing side-wise without sound or stir. Among the knotted joints of a bamboo thicket the eyes of a crouching tiger gleamed—and he felt his heart throb with terror, yet with a longing inexplicable. Then the vision vanished. Aschen-bach, shaking his head, took up his march once more along the hedge of the stone-mason's yard.

He had, at least ever since he commanded means to get about the world at will, regarded travel as a necessary evil, to be endured now and again willy-nilly for the sake of one's health. Too busy with the tasks imposed upon him by his own ego and the European soul, too laden with the care and duty to create, too preoccupied to be an amateur of the gay outer world, he had been content to know as much of the earth's surface as he could without stirring far outside his own sphere—had, indeed, never even been tempted to leave Europe. Now more than ever, since his life was on the wane, since he could no longer brush aside as fanciful his artist fear of not having done, of not being finished before the works ran down, he had confined himself to close range, had hardly stepped outside the charming city which he had made his home and the rude country house he had built in the mountains, whither he went to spend the rainy summers.

And so the new impulse which thus late and suddenly swept over him was speedily made to conform to the pattern of self-discipline he had followed from his youth up. He had meant to bring his work, for which he lived, to a certain point before leaving for the country, and the thought of a leisurely ramble across the globe, which should take him away from his desk for months, was too fantastic and upsetting to be seriously en-tertained. Yet the source of the unexpected contagion was known to him only too well. This yearning for new and distant scenes, this craving for freedom, release, forgetfulness—they were, he admitted to himself, an impulse toward flight, flight from the spot which was the daily theatre of a rigid, cold, and passionate service. That service he loved, had even almost come to love the enervating daily struggle between a proud, tena-cious, well-tried will and this growing fatigue, which no one must suspect, nor the finished product betray by any faintest sign that his inspiration could ever flag or miss fire. On the other hand, it seemed the part of common sense not to span the bow too far, not to suppress summarily a need that so unequivocally asserted itself. He thought of his work, and the place where yesterday and again today he had been forced to lay it down, since it would not yield either to patient effort or a swift *coup de main*. Again and again he had tried to break or untie the knot—only to retire at last from the attack with a shiver of repugnance. Yet the difficulty was actually not a great one; what sapped his strength was distaste for the task, betrayed by a fastidiousness he could no longer satisfy. In his youth, indeed, the nature and inmost essence of the literary gift had been, to him, this very scrupulosity; for it had bridled and tempered his sensibilities, knowing full well that feeling is prone to be content with easy gains and blithe half-perfection. So now, perhaps, feeling, thus tyrannized, avenged itself by leaving him, refusing from now on to carry and wing his art and taking away with it all the ecstasy he had known in form and expression. Not that he was doing bad work. So much, at least, the years had brought him, that at any moment he might feel tranquilly assured of mastery. But he got no joy of it—not though a nation paid it homage. To him it seemed his work had ceased to be marked by that fiery play of fancy which is the product of joy, and more, and more potently, than any intrinsic content, forms in turn the joy of the receiving world. He dreaded the summer in the country, alone with the maid who prepared his food and the man who served him; dreaded to see the familiar mountain peaks and walls that would shut him up again with his heavy discontent. What he needed was a break, an interim existence, a means of passing time, other air and a new stock of blood, to make the summer tolerable and productive. Good, then, he would go a journey. Not far—not all the way to the tigers. A night in a *wagon-lit,* three or four weeks of lotus-eating at some one of the gay world's playgrounds in the lovely south. . . .

So ran his thoughts, while the clang of the electric tram drew nearer down the Ungererstrasse; and as he mounted the platform he decided to devote the evening to a study of maps and railway guides. Once in, he bethought him to look back after the man in the straw hat, the companion of this brief interval which had after all been so fruitful. But he was not in his former place, nor in the tram itself, nor yet at the next stop; in short, his whereabouts remained a mystery.

Gustave Aschenbach was born at L_____, a country town in the province of Silesia. He was the son of an upper official in the judicature, and his forebears had all been officers, judges, departmental functionaries—men who lived their strict, decent, sparing lives in the service of king and state. Only once before had a livelier mentality—in the quality of a clergyman—turned up among them; but swifter, more perceptive blood had in the generation before the poet's flowed into the stock from the mother's side, she being the daughter of a Bohemian musical conductor. It was from her he had the foreign traits that betrayed themselves in his appearance. The union of dry, conscientious officialdom and ardent, obscure impulse, produced an artist—and this particular artist: author of the lucid and vigorous prose epic on the life of Frederick the Great; careful, tireless weaver of the richly patterned tapestry entitled *Maia,* a novel that gathers up the threads of many human destinies in the warp of a single idea; creator of that powerful narrative *The Abject,* which taught a whole grateful generation that a man can still be capable of moral resolution even after he has plumbed the depths of knowledge; and lastly—

to complete the tale of works of his mature period—the writer of that impassioned discourse on the theme of Mind and Art whose ordered force and antithetic eloquence led serious critics to rank it with Schiller's *Simple and Sentimental Poetry*.

Aschenbach's whole soul, from the very beginning, was bent on fame —and thus, while not precisely precocious, yet thanks to the unmistakable trenchancy of his personal accent he was early ripe and ready for a career. Almost before he was out of high school he had a name. Ten years later he had learned to sit at his desk and sustain and live up to his growing reputation, to write gracious and pregnant phrases in letters that must needs be brief, for many claims press upon the solid and successful man. At forty, worn down by the strains and stresses of his actual task, he had to deal with a daily post heavy with tributes from his own and foreign countries.

Remote on one hand from the banal, on the other from the eccentric, his genius was calculated to win at once the adhesion of the general public and the admiration, both sympathetic and stimulating, of the connoisseur. From childhood up he was pushed on every side to achievement, and achievement of no ordinary kind; and so his young days never knew the sweet idleness and blithe *laissez aller* that belong to youth. A nice observer once said of him in company—it was at the time when he fell ill in Vienna in his thirty-fifth year: "You see, Aschenbach has always lived like this"— here the speaker closed the fingers of his left hand to a fist—"never like this"—and he let his open hand hang relaxed from the back of his chair. It was apt. And this attitude was the more morally valiant in that Aschenbach was not by nature robust—he was only called to the constant tension of his career, not actually born to it.

By medical advice he had been kept from school and educated at home. He had grown up solitary, without comradeship; yet had early been driven to see that he belonged to those whose talent is not so much out of the common as is the physical basis on which talent relies for its fulfilment. It is a seed that gives early of its fruit, whose powers seldom reach a ripe old age. But his favourite motto was "Hold fast"; indeed, in his novel on the life of Frederick the Great he envisaged nothing else than the apotheosis of the old hero's word of command, *"Durchhalten,"* which seemed to him the epitome of fortitude under suffering. Besides, he deeply desired to live to a good old age, for it was his conviction that only the artist to whom it has been granted to be fruitful on all stages of our human scene can be truly great, or universal, or worthy of honour.

Bearing the burden of his genius, then, upon such slender shoulders and resolved to go so far, he had the more need of discipline—and discipline, fortunately, was his native inheritance from the father's side. At forty, at fifty, he was still living as he had commenced to live in the years when others are prone to waste and revel, dream high thoughts and postpone fulfilment. He began his day with a cold shower over chest and back; then, setting a pair of tall wax candles in silver holders at the head of his manuscript, he sacrificed to art, in two or three hours of almost religious fervour, the powers he had assembled in sleep. Outsiders might be pardoned for believing that his *Maia* world and the epic amplitude revealed by the life of Frederick were a manifestation of great power working under high pressure, that they came forth, as it were, all in one breath. It was the more triumph for his morale; for the truth was that they were heaped up to greatness in layer after layer, in long days of work, out of hundreds and hundreds of single inspirations; they owed their excellence, both of mass and detail, to one thing and one alone: that their creator could hold out for years under the strain of the same piece of work; with an endurance and a tenacity of purpose like that which had conquered his native province of Silesia, devoting to actual composition none but his best and freshest hours.

For an intellectual product of any value to exert an immediate influence which shall also be deep and lasting, it must rest on an inner harmony, yes, an affinity, between the personal destiny of its author and that of his contemporaries in general. Men do not know why they award fame to one work of art rather than another. Without being in the faintest connoisseurs, they think to justify the warmth of their commendations by discovering in it a hundred virtues, whereas the real ground of their applause is inexplicable—it is sympathy. Aschenbach had once given direct expression—though in an unobtrusive place—to the idea that almost everything conspicuously great is great in despite: has come into being in defiance of affliction and pain, poverty, destitution, bodily weakness, vice, passion, and a thousand other obstructions. And that was more than observation—it was the fruit of experience, it was precisely the formula of his life and fame, it was the key to his work. What wonder, then, if it was also the fixed character, the outward gesture, of his most individual figures?

The new type of hero favoured by Aschenbach, and recurring many times in his works, had early been analysed by a shrewd critic: "The conception of an intellectual and virginal manliness, which clenches its teeth and stands in modest defiance of the swords and spears that pierce its side." That was beautiful, it was *spirituel,* it was exact, despite the suggestion of too great passivity it held. Forbearance in the face of fate, beauty constant under torture, are not merely passive. They are a positive achievement, an explicit triumph; and the figure of Sebastian is the most beautiful symbol, if not of art as a whole, yet certainly of the art we speak of here. Within that world of Aschenbach's creation were exhibited many phases of this theme: there was the aristocratic self-command that is eaten out within and for as long as it can conceals its biologic decline from the eyes of the world; the sere and ugly outside, hiding the embers of smouldering fire—and having power to fan them to so pure a flame as to challenge supremacy in the domain of beauty itself; the pallid languors of the flesh, contrasted with the fiery ardours of the spirit within, which can fling a whole proud people down at the foot of the Cross, at the feet of its own sheer self-abnegation; the gracious bearing preserved in the stern, stark service of form; the unreal, precarious existence of the born intrigant with its swiftly enervating alternation of schemes and desires—all these human fates and many more of their like one read in Aschenbach's pages, and reading them might doubt the existence of any other kind of heroism than the heroism born of weakness. And, after all, what kind could be truer to the spirit of the times? Gustave Aschenbach was the poet-spokesman of all those who labour at the edge of exhaustion; of the overburdened, of those who are already worn out but still hold themselves upright; of all our modern moralizers of accomplishment, with stunted growth and scanty resources, who yet contrive by skilful husbanding and prodigious spasms of will to produce, at least for a while, the effect of greatness. There are many such, they are the heroes of the age. And in Aschenbach's pages they saw themselves; he justified, he exalted them, he sang their praise—and they, they were grateful, they heralded his fame.

He had been young and crude with the times and by them badly counselled. He had taken false steps, blundered, exposed himself, offended in speech and writing against tact and good sense. But he had attained to honour, and honour, he used to say, is the natural goal towards which every considerable talent presses with whip and spur. Yes, one might put it that his whole career had been one conscious and overweening ascent to honour, which left in the rear all the misgivings or self-derogation which might have hampered him.

What pleases the public is lively and vivid delineation which makes no demands on the intellect; but passionate and absolutist youth can only be enthralled by a problem. And Aschenbach was as absolute, as problematist, as any youth of them all. He had done homage to intellect, had overworked the soil of knowledge and ground up her seed-corn; had turned his back on the "mysteries," called genius itself in question, held up art to scorn—yes, even while his faithful following revelled in the characters he created, he, the young artist, was taking away the breath of the twenty-year-olds with his cynic utterances on the nature of art and the artist life.

But it seems that a noble and active mind blunts itself against nothing so quickly as the sharp and bitter irritant of knowledge. And certain it is that the youth's constancy of purpose, no matter how painfully conscientious, was shallow beside the mature resolution of the master of his craft, who made a right-about-face, turned his back on the realm of knowledge, and passed it by with averted face, lest it lame his will or power of action, paralyse his feelings or his passions, deprive any of these of their conviction or utility. How else interpret the oft-cited story of *The Abject* than as a rebuke to the excesses of a psychology-ridden age, embodied in the delineation of the weak and silly fool who manages to lead fate by the nose; driving his wife, out of sheer innate pusillanimity, into the arms of a beardless youth, and making this disaster an excuse for trifling away the rest of his life?

With rage the author here rejects the rejected, casts out the outcast —and the measure of his fury is the measure of his condemnation of

to pass over the landing-stage and on to the wet decks of a ship lying there with steam up for the passage to Venice.

It was an ancient hulk belonging to an Italian line, obsolete, dingy, grimed with soot. A dirty hunchbacked sailor, smirkingly polite, conducted him at once belowships to a cavernous, lamplit cabin. There behind a table sat a man with a beard like a goat's; he had his hat on the back of his head, a cigar-stump in the corner of his mouth; he reminded Aschenbach of an old-fashioned circus-director. This person put the usual questions and wrote out a ticket to Venice, which he issued to the traveller with many commercial flourishes.

"A ticket for Venice," repeated he, stretching out his arm to dip the pen into the thick ink in a tilted ink-stand. "One first-class to Venice! Here you are, *signore mio.*" He made some scrawls on the paper, strewed bluish sand on it out of a box, thereafter letting the sand run off into an earthen vessel, folded the paper with bony yellow fingers, and wrote on the outside. "An excellent choice," he rattled on. "Ah, Venice! What a glorious city! Irresistibly attractive to the cultured man for her past history as well as her present charm." His copious gesturings and empty phrases gave the odd impression that he feared the traveller might alter his mind. He changed Aschenbach's note, laying the money on the spotted table-cover with the glibness of a croupier. "A pleasant visit to you, signore," he said, with a melodramatic bow. "Delighted to serve you." Then he beckoned and called out: "Next" as though a stream of passengers stood waiting to be served, though in point of fact there was not one. Aschenbach returned to the upper deck.

He leaned an arm on the railing and looked at the idlers lounging along the quay to watch the boat go out. Then he turned his attention to his fellow-passengers. Those of the second class, both men and women, were squatted on their bundles of luggage on the forward deck. The first cabin consisted of a group of lively youths, clerks from Pola, evidently, who had made up a pleasure excursion to Italy and were not a little thrilled at the prospect, bustling about and laughing with satisfaction at the stir they made. They leaned over the railings and shouted, with a glib command of epithet, derisory remarks at such of their fellow-clerks as they saw going to business along the quay; and these in turn shook their sticks and shouted as good back again. One of the party, in a dandified buff suit, a rakish panama with a coloured scarf, and a red cravat, was loudest of the loud: he outcrowed all the rest. Aschenbach's eyes dwelt on him, and he was shocked to see that the apparent youth was no youth at all. He was an old man, beyond a doubt, with wrinkles and crow's-feet round eyes and mouth; the dull carmine of the cheeks was rouge, the brown hair a wig. His neck was shrunken and sinewy, his turned-up moustaches and small imperial were dyed, and the unbroken double row of yellow teeth he showed when he laughed were but too obviously a cheapish false set. He wore a seal ring on each forefinger, but his hands were those of an old man. Aschenbach was moved

to shudder as he watched the creature and his association with the rest
of the group. Could they not see he was old, that he had no right to wear
the clothes they wore or pretend to be one of them? But they were used
to him, it seemed; they suffered him among them, they paid back his
jokes in kind and the playful pokes in the ribs he gave them. How could
they? Aschenbach put his hand to his brow, he covered his eyes, for he
had slept little, and they smarted. He felt not quite canny, as though
the world were suffering a dreamlike distortion of perspective which
he might arrest by shutting it all out for a few minutes and then looking at it afresh. But instead he felt a floating sensation, and opened his
eyes with unreasoning alarm to find that the ship's dark sluggish bulk
was slowly leaving the jetty. Inch by inch, with the to-and-fro motion
of her machinery, the strip of iridescent dirty water widened, the boat
manœuvred clumsily and turned her bow to the open sea. Aschenbach
moved over to the starboard side, where the hunchbacked sailor had set
up a deck-chair for him, and a steward in a greasy dress-coat asked for
orders.

The sky was grey, the wind humid. Harbour and island dropped behind, all sight of land soon vanished in mist. Flakes of sodden, clammy
soot fell upon the still undried deck. Before the boat was an hour out a
canvas had to be spread as a shelter from the rain.

Wrapped in his cloak, a book in his lap, our traveller rested; the hours
slipped by unawares. It stopped raining, the canvas was taken down. The
horizon was visible right round: beneath the sombre dome of the sky
stretched the vast plain of empty sea. But immeasurable unarticulated
space weakens our power to measure time as well: the time-sense falters
and grows dim. Strange, shadowy figures passed and repassed—the elderly
coxcomb, the goat-bearded man from the bowels of the ship—with vague
gesturing and mutterings through the traveller's mind as he lay. He fell
asleep.

At midday he was summoned to luncheon in a corridor-like saloon
with the sleeping-cabins giving off it. He ate at the head of the long
table; the party of clerks, including the old man, sat with the jolly captain at the other end, where they had been carousing since ten o'clock.
The meal was wretched, and soon done. Aschenbach was driven to seek
the open and look at the sky—perhaps it would lighten presently above
Venice.

He had not dreamed it could be otherwise, for the city had ever given
him a brilliant welcome. But sky and sea remained leaden, with spurts
of fine, mistlike rain; he reconciled himself to the idea of seeing a different Venice from that he had always approached on the landward
side. He stood by the foremast, his gaze on the distance, alert for the
first glimpse of the coast. And he thought of the melancholy and susceptible poet who had once seen the towers and turrets of his dreams rise
out of these waves; repeated the rhythms born of his awe, his mingled
emotions of joy and suffering—and easily susceptible to a prescience
already shaped within him, he asked his own sober, weary heart if a new

enthusiasm, a new preoccupation, some late adventure of the feelings could still be in store for the idle traveller.

The flat coast showed on the right, the sea was soon populous with fishing-boats. The Lido appeared and was left behind as the ship glided at half speed through the narrow harbour of the same name, coming to a full stop on the lagoon in sight of garish, badly built houses. Here it waited for the boat bringing the sanitary inspector.

An hour passed. One had arrived—and yet not. There was no conceivable haste—yet one felt harried. The youths from Pola were on deck, drawn hither by the martial sound of horns coming across the water from the direction of the Public Gardens. They had drunk a good deal of Asti and were moved to shout and hurrah at the drilling *bersaglieri*. But the young-old man was a truly repulsive sight in the condition to which his company with youth had brought him. He could not carry his wine like them: he was pitiably drunk. He swayed as he stood— watery-eyed, a cigarette between his shaking fingers, keeping upright with difficulty. He could not have taken a step without falling and knew better than to stir, but his spirits were deplorably high. He buttonholed anyone who came within reach, he stuttered, he giggled, he leered, he fatuously shook his beringed old forefinger; his tongue kept seeking the corner of his mouth in a suggestive motion ugly to behold. Aschenbach's brow darkened as he looked, and there came over him once more a dazed sense, as though things about him were just slightly losing their ordinary perspective, beginning to show a distortion that might merge into the grotesque. He was prevented from dwelling on the feeling, for now the machinery began to thud again, and the ship took up its passage through the Canale di San Marco which had been interrupted so near the goal.

He saw it once more, that landing-place that takes the breath away, that amazing group of incredible structures the Republic set up to meet the awe-struck eye of the approaching seafarer: the airy splendour of the palace and Bridge of Sighs, the columns of lion and saint on the shore, the glory of the projecting flank of the fairy temple, the vista of gateway and clock. Looking, he thought that to come to Venice by the station is like entering a palace by the back door. No one should approach, save by the high seas as he was doing now, this most improbable of cities.

The engines stopped. Gondolas pressed alongside, the landing-stairs were let down, customs officials came on board and did their office, people began to go ashore. Aschenbach ordered a gondola. He meant to take up his abode by the sea and needed to be conveyed with his luggage to the landing-stage of the little steamers that ply between the city and the Lido. They called down his order to the surface of the water where the gondoliers were quarreling in dialect. Then came another delay while his trunk was worried down the ladder-like stairs. Thus he was forced to endure the importunities of the ghastly young-old man, whose drunken state obscurely urged him to pay the stranger the honour of a formal farewell. "We wish you a very pleasant sojourn," he babbled, bowing and scraping. "Pray keep us in mind. *Au revoir, excusez et bon jour, votre Excellence.*" He drooled, he blinked, he licked the corner of his mouth, the little imperial bristled on his elderly chin. He put the tips of two fingers to his mouth and said thickly: "Give her our love, will you, the p-pretty little dear"—here his upper plate came away and fell down on the lower one. . . . Aschenbach escaped. "Little sweety-sweety-sweetheart!" he heard behind him, gurgled and stuttered, as he climbed down the rope stair into the boat.

Is there anyone but must repress a secret thrill, on arriving in Venice for the first time—or returning thither after long absence—and stepping into a Venetian gondola? That singular conveyance, come down unchanged from ballad times, black as nothing else on earth except a coffin—what pictures it calls up of lawless, silent adventures in the plashing night; or even more, what visions of death itself, the bier and solemn rites and last soundless voyage! And has anyone remarked that the seat in such a bark, the armchair lacquered in coffin-black and dully black-upholstered, is the softest, most luxurious, most relaxing seat in the world? Aschenbach realized it when he had let himself down at the gondolier's feet, opposite his luggage, which lay neatly composed on the vessel's beak. The rowers still gestured fiercely; he heard their harsh, incoherent tones. But the strange stillness of the water-city seemed to take up their voices gently, to disembody and scatter them over the sea. It was warm here in the harbour. The lukewarm air of the sirocco breathed upon him, he leaned back among his cushions and gave himself to the yielding element, closing his eyes for very pleasure in an indolence as unaccustomed as sweet. "The trip will be short," he thought, and wished it might last forever. They gently swayed away from the boat with its bustle and clamour of voices.

It grew still and stiller all about. No sound but the splash of the oars, the hollow slap of the wave against the steep, black, halbert-shaped beak of the vessel, and one sound more—a muttering by fits and starts, expressed as it were by the motion of his arms, from the lips of the gondolier. He was talking to himself, between his teeth. Aschenbach glanced up and saw with surprise that the lagoon was widening, his vessel was headed for the open sea. Evidently it would not do to give himself up to sweet *far niente;* he must see his wishes carried out.

"You are to take me to the steamboat landing, you know," he said, half turning round towards it. The muttering stopped. There was no reply.

"Take me to the steamboat landing," he repeated, and this time turned quite round and looked up into the face of the gondolier as he stood there on his little elevated deck, high against the pale grey sky. The man had an unpleasing, even brutish face, and wore blue clothes like a sailor's, with a yellow sash; a shapeless straw hat with the braid torn at the brim perched rakishly on his head. His facial structure, as well as the curling blond moustache under the short snub nose, showed him to be of non-Italian stock. Physically rather undersized, so that one would not have expected him to be very muscular, he pulled vigorously at the oar, putting all his body-weight behind each stroke. Now and then the effort he made curled back his lips and bared his white teeth to the gums. He spoke in a decided, almost curt voice, looking out to sea over his fare's head: "The signore is going to the Lido."

Aschenbach answered: "Yes, I am. But I only took the gondola to cross over to San Marco. I am using the *vaporetto* from there."

"But the signore cannot use the *vaporetto*."

"And why not?"

"Because the *vaporetto* does not take luggage."

It was true. Aschenbach remembered it. He made no answer. But the man's gruff, overbearing manner, so unlike the usual courtesy of his countrymen towards the stranger, was intolerable. Aschenbach spoke again: "That is my own affair. I may want to give my luggage in deposit. You will turn round."

No answer. The oar splashed, the wave struck dull against the prow. And the muttering began anew, the gondolier talked to himself, between his teeth.

What should the traveller do? Alone on the water with this tongue-tied, obstinate, uncanny man, he saw no way of enforcing his will. And if only he did not excite himself, how pleasantly he might rest! Had he not wished the voyage might last forever? The wisest thing—and how much the pleasantest!—was to let matters take their own course. A spell of indolence was upon him; it came from the chair he sat in—this low, black-upholstered arm-chair, so gently rocked at the hands of the despotic boatman in his rear. The thought passed dreamily through Aschenbach's brain that perhaps he had fallen into the clutches of a criminal; it had not power to rouse him to action. More annoying was the simpler explanation: that the man was only trying to extort money. A sense of duty, a recollection, as it were, that this ought to be prevented, made him collect himself to say:

"How much do you ask for the trip?"

And the gondolier, gazing out over his head, replied: "The signore will pay."

There was an established reply to this; Aschenbach made it, mechanically:

"I will pay nothing whatever if you do not take me where I want to go."

"The signore wants to go to the Lido."

"But not with you."

"I am a good rower, signore. I will row you well."

"So much is true," thought Aschenbach, and again he relaxed. "That is true, you row me well. Even if you mean to rob me, even if you hit me in the back with your oar and send me down to the kingdom of Hades, even then you will have rowed me well."

But nothing of the sort happened. Instead, they fell in with company: a boat came alongside and waylaid them, full of men and women singing to guitar and mandolin. They rowed persistently bow for bow with the gondola and filled the silence that had rested on the waters with their lyric love of gain. Aschenbach tossed money into the hat they held out. The music stopped at once, they rowed away. And once more the gondolier's mutter became audible as he talked to himself in fits and snatches.

Thus they rowed on, rocked by the wash of a steamer returning city-wards. At the landing two municipal officials were walking up and down with their hands behind their backs and their faces turned towards the lagoon. Aschenbach was helped on shore by the old man with a boat-hook who is the permanent feature of every landing-stage in Venice; and having no small change to pay the boatman, crossed over into the hotel opposite. His wants were supplied in the lobby; but when he came back his possessions were already on a hand-car on the quay, and gondola and gondolier were gone.

"He ran away, signore," said the old boatman. "A bad lot, a man without a license. He is the only gondolier without one. The others tele-phoned over, and he knew we were on the look-out, so he made off."

Aschenbach shrugged.

"The signore has had a ride for nothing," said the old man, and held out his hat. Aschenbach dropped some coins. He directed that his lug-gage be taken to the Hôtel des Bains and followed the hand-car through the avenue, that white-blossoming avenue with taverns, booths, and pensions on either side it, which runs across the island diagonally to the beach.

He entered the hotel from the garden terrace at the back and passed through the vestibule and hall into the office. His arrival was expected, and he was served with courtesy and dispatch. The manager, a small, soft, dapper man with a black moustache and a caressing way with him, wearing a French frock-coat, himself took him up in the lift and showed him his room. It was a pleasant chamber, furnished in cherry-wood, with lofty windows looking out to sea. It was decorated with strong-scented flowers. Aschenbach, as soon as he was alone, and while they brought in his trunk and bags and disposed them in the room, went up to one of the windows and stood looking out upon the beach in its afternoon emptiness, and at the sunless sea, now full and sending long, low waves with rhythmic beat upon the sand.

A solitary, unused to speaking of what he sees and feels, has mental experiences which are at once more intense and less articulate than those of a gregarious man. They are sluggish, yet more wayward, and never without a melancholy tinge. Sights and impressions which others brush aside with a glance, a light comment, a smile, occupy him more than their due; they sink silently in, they take on meaning, they become ex-perience, emotion, adventure. Solitude gives birth to the original in us, to beauty unfamiliar and perilous—to poetry. But also, it gives birth to the opposite: to the perverse, the illicit, the absurd. Thus the traveller's mind still dwelt with disquiet on the episodes of his journey hither: on

the horrible old fop with his drivel about a mistress, on the outlaw boatman and his lost tip. They did not offend his reason, they hardly afforded food for thought; yet they seemed by their very nature fundamentally strange, and thereby vaguely disquieting. Yet here was the sea;
even in the midst of such thoughts he saluted it with his eyes, exulting
that Venice was near and accessible. At length he turned round, disposed
his personal belongings and made certain arrangements with the cham-
bermaid for his comfort, washed up, and was conveyed to the ground
floor by the green-uniformed Swiss who ran the lift.

He took tea on the terrace facing the sea and afterwards went down
and walked some distance along the shore promenade in the direction
of Hôtel Excelsior. When he came back it seemed to be time to change
for dinner. He did so, slowly and methodically as his way was, for he
was accustomed to work while he dressed; but even so found himself a
little early when he entered the hall, where a large number of guests had
collected—strangers to each other and affecting mutual indifference, yet
united in expectancy of the meal. He picked up a paper, sat down in a
leather arm-chair, and took stock of the company, which compared most
favourably with that he had just left.

This was a broad and tolerant atmosphere, of wide horizons. Subdued
voices were speaking most of the principal European tongues. That uniform of civilization, the conventional evening dress, gave outward con-
formity to the varied types. There were long, dry Americans, large-
familied Russians, English ladies, German children with French *bonnes*.
The Slavic element predominated, it seemed. In Aschenbach's neighbourhood Polish was being spoken.

Round a wicker table next him was gathered a group of young folk
in charge of a governess or companion—three young girls, perhaps fifteen
to seventeen years old, and a long-haired boy of about fourteen. Aschenbach noticed with astonishment the lad's perfect beauty. His face recalled
the noblest moment of Greek sculpture—pale, with a sweet reserve, with
clustering honey-coloured ringlets, the brow and nose descending in one
line, the winning mouth, the expression of pure and godlike serenity.
Yet with all this chaste perfection of form it was of such unique personal
charm that the observer thought he had never seen, either in nature or
art, anything so utterly happy and consummate. What struck him further
was the strange contrast the group afforded, a difference in educational
method, so to speak, shown in the way the brother and sisters were
clothed and treated. The girls, the eldest of whom was practically grown
up, were dressed with an almost disfiguring austerity. All three wore
half-length slate-coloured frocks of cloister-like plainness, arbitrarily unbecoming in cut, with white turn-over collars as their only adornment.
Every grace of outline was wilfully suppressed; their hair lay smoothly
plastered to their heads, giving them a vacant expression, like a nun's.
All this could only be by the mother's orders; but there was no trace of
the same pedagogic severity in the case of the boy. Tenderness and softness, it was plain, conditioned his existence. No scissors had been put to

the lovely hair that (like the Spinnario's) curled about his brows, above his ears, longer still in the neck. He wore an English sailor suit, with quilted sleeves that narrowed round the delicate wrists of his long and slender though still childish hands. And this suit, with its breast-knot, lacings, and embroideries, lent the slight figure something "rich and strange," a spoilt, exquisite air. The observer saw him in half profile, with one foot in its black patent leather advanced, one elbow resting on the arm of his basket-chair, the cheek nestled into the closed hand in a pose of easy grace, quite unlike the stiff subservient mien which was evidently habitual to his sisters. Was he delicate? His facial tint was ivory-white against the golden darkness of his clustering locks. Or was he simply a pampered darling, the object of a self-willed and partial love? Aschenbach inclined to think the latter. For in almost every artist nature is inborn a wanton and treacherous proneness to side with the beauty that breaks hearts, to single out aristocratic pretensions and pay them homage.

A waiter announced, in English, that dinner was served. Gradually the company dispersed through the glass doors into the dining-room. Latecomers entered from the vestibule or the lifts. Inside, dinner was being served; but the young Poles still sat and waited about their wicker table. Aschenbach felt comfortable in his deep arm-chair, he enjoyed the beauty before his eyes, he waited with them.

The governess, a short, stout, red-faced person, at length gave the signal. With lifted brows she pushed back her chair and made a bow to the tall woman, dressed in palest grey, who now entered the hall. This lady's abundant jewels were pearls, her manner was cool and measured; the fashion of her gown and the arrangement of her lightly powdered hair had the simplicity prescribed in certain circles whose piety and aristocracy are equally marked. She might have been, in Germany, the wife of some high official. But there was something faintly fabulous, after all, in her appearance, though lent it solely by the pearls she wore: they were well-nigh priceless, and consisted of ear-rings and a three-stranded necklace, very long, with gems the size of cherries.

The brother and sisters had risen briskly. They bowed over their mother's hand to kiss it, she turning away from them, with a slight smile on her face, which was carefully preserved but rather sharp-nosed and worn. She addressed a few words in French to the governess, then moved towards the glass door. The children followed, the girls in order of age, then the governess, and last the boy. He chanced to turn before he crossed the threshold, and as there was no one else in the room, his strange, twilit grey eyes met Aschenbach's, as our traveller sat there with the paper on his knee, absorbed in looking after the group.

There was nothing singular, of course, in what he had seen. They had not gone in to dinner before their mother, they had waited, given her a respectful salute, and but observed the right and proper forms on entering the room. Yet they had done all this so expressly, with such self-respecting dignity, discipline, and sense of duty that Aschenbach was impressed. He lingered still a few minutes, then he, too, went into the dining-room, where he was shown a table far off the Polish family, as he noted at once, with a stirring of regret.

Tired, yet mentally alert, he beguiled the long, tedious meal with abstract, even with transcendent matters: pondered the mysterious harmony that must come to subsist between the individual human being and the universal law, in order that human beauty may result; passed on to general problems of form and art, and came at length to the conclusion that what seemed to him fresh and happy thoughts were like the flattering inventions of a dream, which the waking sense proves worthless and insubstantial. He spent the evening in the park, that was sweet with odours of evening—sitting, smoking, wandering about; went to bed betimes, and passed the night in deep, unbroken sleep, visited, however, by varied and lively dreams.

The weather next day was no more promising. A land breeze blew. Beneath a colourless, overcast sky the sea lay sluggish, and as it were shrunken, so far withdrawn as to leave bare several rows of long sandbanks. The horizon looked close and prosaic. When Aschenbach opened his window he thought he smelt the stagnant odour of the lagoons.

He felt suddenly out of sorts and already began to think of leaving. Once, years before, after weeks of bright spring weather, this wind had found him out; it had been so bad as to force him to flee from the city like a fugitive. And now it seemed beginning again—the same feverish distaste, the pressure on his temples, the heavy eyelids. It would be a nuisance to change again; but if the wind did not turn, this was no place for him. To be on the safe side, he did not entirely unpack. At nine o'clock he went down to the buffet, which lay between the hall and the dining-room and served as breakfast-room.

A solemn stillness reigned here, such as it is the ambition of all large hotels to achieve. The waiters moved on noiseless feet. A rattling of tea-things, a whispered word—no other sounds. In a corner diagonally to the door, two tables off his own, Aschenbach saw the Polish girls with their governess. They sat there very straight, in their stiff blue linen frocks with little turn-over collars and cuffs, their ash-blond hair newly brushed flat, their eyelids red from sleep; and handed each other the marmalade. They had nearly finished their meal. The boy was not there.

Aschenbach smiled. "Aha, little Phæax," he thought. "It seems you are privileged to sleep yourself out." With sudden gaiety he quoted:

"Oft veränderten Schmuck und warme Bäder und Ruhe."

He took a leisurely breakfast. The porter came up with his braided cap in his hand, to deliver some letters that had been sent on. Aschenbach lighted a cigarette and opened a few letters and thus was still seated to witness the arrival of the sluggard.

He entered through the glass doors and passed diagonally across the room to his sisters at their table. He walked with extraordinary grace —the carriage of the body, the action of the knee, the way he set down his foot in its white shoe—it was all so light, it was at once dainty and proud, it wore an added charm in the childish shyness which made him twice turn his head as he crossed the room, made him give a quick glance and then drop his eyes. He took his seat, with a smile and a murmured word in his soft and blurry tongue; and Aschenbach, sitting so that he could see him in profile, was astonished anew, yes, startled, at the godlike beauty of the human being. The lad had on a light sailor suit of blue and white striped cotton, with a red silk breast-knot and a simple white standing collar round the neck—a not very elegant effect—yet above this collar the head was poised like a flower, in incomparable loveliness. It was the head of Eros, with the yellowish bloom of Parian marble, with fine serious brows, and dusky clustering ringlets standing out in soft plenteousness over temples and ears.

"Good, oh, very good indeed!" thought Aschenbach, assuming the patronizing air of the connoisseur to hide, as artists will, their ravishment over a masterpiece. "Yes," he went on to himself, "if it were not that sea and beach were waiting for me, I should sit here as long as you do." But he went out on that, passing through the hall, beneath the watchful eye of the functionaries, down the steps and directly across the board walk to the section of the beach reserved for the guests of the hotel. The bathing-master, a barefoot old man in linen trousers and sailor blouse, with a straw hat, showed him the cabin that had been rented for him, and Aschenbach had him set up table and chair on the sandy platform before it. Then he dragged the reclining-chair through the pale yellow sand, closer to the sea, sat down, and composed himself.

He delighted, as always, in the scene on the beach, the sight of sophisticated society giving itself over to a simple life at the edge of the element. The shallow grey sea was already gay with children wading, with swimmers, with figures in bright colours lying on the sand-banks with arms behind their heads. Some were rowing in little keelless boats painted red and blue, and laughing when they capsized. A long row of *capanne* ran down the beach, with platforms, where people sat as on verandas, and there was social life, with bustle and with indolent repose; visits were paid, amid much chatter, punctilious morning toilettes hob-nobbed with comfortable and privileged dishabille. On the hard wet sand close to the sea figures in white bath-robes or loose wrappings in garish colours strolled up and down. A mammoth sandhill had been built up on Aschenbach's right, the work of children, who had stuck it full of tiny flags. Vendors of sea-shells, fruit, and cakes knelt beside their wares spread out on the sand. A row of cabins on the left stood obliquely to the others and to the sea, thus forming the boundary of the enclosure on this side; and on the little veranda in front of one of these a Russian family was encamped; bearded men with strong white teeth, ripe, indolent women, a Fräulein from the Baltic provinces, who sat at an easel painting the sea and tearing her hair in despair; two ugly but good-natured children and an old maidservant in a head-cloth, with the caressing, servile manner of the born dependent. There they sat to-

gether in grateful enjoyment of their blessings: constantly shouting at
their romping children, who paid not the slightest heed; making jokes
in broken Italian to the funny old man who sold them sweetmeats, kissing each other on the cheeks—no jot concerned that their domesticity
was overlooked.

"I'll stop," thought Aschenbach. "Where could it be better than here?"
With his hands clasped in his lap he let his eyes swim in the wideness
of the sea, his gaze lose focus, blur, and grow vague in the misty immensity of space. His love of the ocean had profound sources: the hard-
worked artist's longing for rest, his yearning to seek refuge from the
thronging manifold shapes of his fancy in the bosom of the simple and
vast; and another yearning, opposed to his art and perhaps for that very
reason a lure, for the unorganized, the immeasurable, the eternal—in
short, for nothingness. He whose preoccupation is with excellence longs
fervently to find rest in perfection; and is not nothingness a form of
perfection? As he sat there dreaming thus, deep, deep into the void, suddenly the margin line of the shore was cut by a human form. He gathered
up his gaze and withdrew it from the illimitable, and lo, it was the lovely
boy who crossed his vision coming from the left along the sand. He was
barefoot, ready for wading, the slender legs uncovered above the knee,
and moved slowly, yet with such a proud, light tread as to make it seem
he had never worn shoes. He looked towards the diagonal row of cabins;
and the sight of the Russian family, leading their lives there in joyous
simplicity, distorted his features in a spasm of angry disgust. His brow
darkened, his lips curled, one corner of the mouth was drawn down in a
harsh line that marred the curve of the cheek, his frown was so heavy
that the eyes seemed to sink in as they uttered beneath the black and
vicious language of hate. He looked down, looked threateningly back
once more; then giving it up with a violent and contemptuous shoulder-
shrug, he left his enemies in the rear.

A feeling of delicacy, a qualm, almost like a sense of shame, made
Aschenbach turn away as though he had not seen; he felt unwilling to
take advantage of having been, by chance, privy to this passionate reaction. But he was in truth both moved and exhilarated—that is to say,
he was delighted. This childish exhibition of fanaticism, directed against
the good-naturedest simplicity in the world—it gave to the godlike and
inexpressive the final human touch. The figure of the half-grown lad, a
masterpiece from nature's own hand, had been significant enough when
it gratified the eye alone; and now it evoked sympathy as well—the little
episode had set it off, lent it a dignity in the onlooker's eyes that was
beyond its years.

Aschenbach listened with still averted head to the boy's voice announcing his coming to his companions at the sand-heap. The voice
was clear, though a little weak, but they answered, shouting his name—
or his nickname—again and again. Aschenbach was not without curiosity
to learn it, but could make out nothing more exact than two musical
syllables, something like Adgio—or, oftener still, Adjiu, with a long-drawn-

out *u* at the end. He liked the melodious sound, and found it fitting; said it over to himself a few times and turned back with satisfaction to his papers.

Holding his travelling-pad on his knees, he took his fountain-pen and began to answer various items of his correspondence. But presently he felt it too great a pity to turn his back, and the eyes of his mind, for the sake of mere commonplace correspondence, to this scene which was, after all, the most rewarding one he knew. He put aside his papers and swung round to the sea; in no long time, beguiled by the voices of the children at play, he had turned his head and sat resting it against the chair-back, while he gave himself up to contemplating the activities of the exquisite Adgio.

His eye found him out at once, the red breast-knot was unmistakable. With some nine or ten companions, boys and girls of his own age and younger, he was busy putting in place an old plank to serve as a bridge across the ditches between the sand-piles. He directed the work by shouting and motioning with his head, and they were all chattering in many tongues—French, Polish, and even some of the Balkan languages. But his was the name oftenest on their lips, he was plainly sought after, wooed, admired. One lad in particular, a Pole like himself, with a name that sounded something like Jaschiu, a sturdy lad with brilliantined black hair, in a belted linen suit, was his particular liegeman and friend. Operations at the sand-pile being ended for the time, they two walked away along the beach, with their arms round each other's waists, and once the lad Jaschiu gave Adgio a kiss.

Aschenbach felt like shaking a finger at him. "But you, Critobulus," he thought with a smile, "you I advise to take a year's leave. That long, at least, you will need for complete recovery." A vendor came by with strawberries, and Aschenbach made his second breakfast of the great luscious, dead-ripe fruit. It had grown very warm, although the sun had not availed to pierce the heavy layer of mist. His mind felt relaxed, his senses revelled in this vast and soothing communion with the silence of the sea. The grave and serious man found sufficient occupation in speculating what name it could be that sounded like Adgio. And with the help of a few Polish memories he at length fixed on Tadzio, a shortened form of Thaddeus, which sounded, when called, like Tadziu or Adziu.

Tadzio was bathing. Aschenbach had lost sight of him for a moment, then descried him far out in the water, which was shallow a very long way—saw his head, and his arm striking out like an oar. But his watchful family were already on the alert; the mother and governess called from the veranda in front of their bathing-cabin, until the lad's name, with its softened consonants and long-drawn *u* sound, seemed to possess the beach like a rallying-cry; the cadence had something sweet and wild: "Tadziu! Tadziu!" He turned and ran back against the water, churning the waves to a foam, his head flung high. The sight of this living figure, virginally pure and austere, with dripping locks, beautiful as a tender young god, emerging from the depths of sea and sky, outrunning the element—it conjured up mythologies, it was like a primeval legend, handed down from the beginning of time, of the birth of form, of the origin of the gods. With closed lids Aschenbach listened to this poesy hymning itself silently within him, and anon he thought it was good to be here and that he would stop awhile.

Afterwards Tadzio lay on the sand and rested from his bathe, wrapped in his white sheet, which he wore drawn underneath the right shoulder, so that his head was cradled on his bare right arm. And even when Aschenbach read, without looking up, he was conscious that the lad was there; that it would cost him but the slightest turn of the head to have the rewarding vision once more in his purview. Indeed, it was almost as though he sat there to guard the youth's repose; occupied, of course, with his own affairs, yet alive to the presence of that noble human creature close at hand. And his heart was stirred, it felt a father's kindness: such an emotion as the possessor of beauty can inspire in one who has offered himself up in spirit to create beauty.

At midday he left the beach, returned to the hotel, and was carried up in the lift to his room. There he lingered a little time before the glass and looked at his own grey hair, his keen and weary face. And he thought of his fame, and how people gazed respectfully at him in the streets, on account of his unerring gift of words and their power to charm. He called up all the worldly successes his genius had reaped, all he could remember, even his patent of nobility. Then went to luncheon down in the dining-room, sat at his little table and ate. Afterwards he mounted again in the lift, and a group of young folk, Tadzio among them, pressed with him into the little compartment. It was the first time Aschenbach had seen him close at hand, not merely in perspective, and could see and take account of the details of his humanity. Someone spoke to the lad, and he, answering, with indescribably lovely smile, stepped out again, as they had come to the first floor, backwards, with his eyes cast down. "Beauty makes people self-conscious," Aschenbach thought, and considered within himself imperatively why this should be. He had noted, further, that Tadzio's teeth were imperfect, rather jagged and bluish, without a healthy glaze, and of that peculiar brittle transparency which the teeth of chlorotic people often show. "He is delicate, he is sickly," Aschenbach thought. "He will most likely not live to grow old." He did not try to account for the pleasure the idea gave him.

In the afternoon he spent two hours in his room, then took the *vaporetto* to Venice, across the foul-smelling lagoon. He got out at San Marco, had his tea in the Piazza, and then, as his custom was, took a walk through the streets. But this walk of his brought about nothing less than a revolution in his mood and an entire change in all his plans.

There was a hateful sultriness in the narrow streets. The air was so heavy that all the manifold smells wafted out of houses, shops, and cook-shops—smells of oil, perfumery, and so forth—hung low, like exhalations, not dissipating. Cigarette smoke seemed to stand in the air, it drifted so slowly away. Today the crowd in these narrow lanes oppressed the stroller instead of diverting him. The longer he walked, the more was he in tortures under that state, which is the product of the sea air and the sirocco and which excites and enervates at once. He perspired painfully. His eyes rebelled, his chest was heavy, he felt feverish, the blood throbbed in his temples. He fled from the huddled, narrow streets of the commercial city, crossed many bridges, and came into the poor quarter of Venice. Beggars waylaid him, the canals sickened him with their evil exhalations. He reached a quiet square, one of those that exist at the city's heart, forsaken of God and man; there he rested awhile on the margin of a fountain, wiped his brow, and admitted to himself that he must be gone.

For the second time, and now quite definitely, the city proved that in certain weathers it could be directly inimical to his health. Nothing but sheer unreasoning obstinacy would linger on, hoping for an unprophesiable change in the wind. A quick decision was in place. He could not go home at this stage, neither summer nor winter quarters would be ready. But Venice had not a monopoly of sea and shore: there were other spots where these were to be had without the evil concomitants of lagoon and fever-breeding vapours. He remembered a little bathing-place not far from Trieste of which he had had a good report. Why not go thither? At once, of course, in order that this second change might be worth the making. He resolved, he rose to his feet and sought the nearest gondola-landing, where he took a boat and was conveyed to San Marco through the gloomy windings of many canals, beneath balconies of delicate marble traceries flanked by carven lions; round slippery corners of wall, past melancholy façades with ancient business shields reflected in the rocking water. It was not too easy to arrive at his destination, for his gondolier, being in league with various lace-makers and glass-blowers, did his best to persuade his fare to pause, look, and be tempted to buy. Thus the charm of this bizarre passage through the heart of Venice, even while it played upon his spirit, yet was sensibly cooled by the predatory commercial spirit of the fallen queen of the seas.

Once back in his hotel, he announced at the office, even before dinner, that circumstances unforeseen obliged him to leave early next morning. The management expressed its regret, it changed his money and receipted his bill. He dined, and spent the lukewarm evening in a rocking-chair on the rear terrace, reading the newspapers. Before he went to bed, he made his luggage ready against the morning.

His sleep was not of the best, for the prospect of another journey made him restless. When he opened his window next morning, the sky was still overcast, but the air seemed fresher—and there and then his rue began. Had he not given notice too soon? Had he not let himself be swayed by a slight and momentary indisposition? If he had only been patient, not lost heart so quickly, tried to adapt himself to the climate, or even waited for a change in the weather before deciding! Then, instead of the hurry and flurry of departure, he would have before him now a morning like yesterday's on the beach. Too late! He must go on wanting what he had wanted yesterday. He dressed and at eight o'clock went down to breakfast.

When he entered the breakfast-room it was empty. Guests came in while he sat waiting for his order to be filled. As he sipped his tea he saw the Polish girls enter with their governess, chaste and morning-fresh, with sleep-reddened eyelids. They crossed the room and sat down at their table in the window. Behind them came the porter, cap in hand, to announce that it was time for him to go. The car was waiting to convey him and other travellers to the Hôtel Excelsior, whence they would go by motor-boat through the company's private canal to the station. Time pressed. But Aschenbach found it did nothing of the sort. There still lacked more than an hour of train-time. He felt irritated at the hotel habit of getting the guests out of the house earlier than necessary; and requested the porter to let him breakfast in peace. The man hesitated and withdrew, only to come back again five minutes later. The car could wait no longer. Good, then it might go, and take his trunk with it, Aschenbach answered with some heat. He would use the public convey-ance, in his own time; he begged them to leave the choice of it to him. The functionary bowed. Aschenbach, pleased to be rid of him, made a leisurely meal, and even had a newspaper of the waiter. When at length he rose, the time was grown very short. And it so happened that at that moment Tadzio came through the glass doors into the room.

To reach his own table he crossed the traveller's path, and modestly cast down his eyes before the grey-haired man of the lofty brows—only to lift them again in that sweet way he had and direct his full soft gaze upon Aschenbach's face. Then he was past. "For the last time, Tadzio," thought the elder man. "It was all too brief!" Quite unusually for him, he shaped a farewell with his lips, he actually uttered it, and added: "May God bless you!" Then he went out, distributed tips, exchanged farewells with the mild little manager in the frock-coat, and, followed by the porter with his hand-luggage, left the hotel. On foot as he had come, he passed through the white-blossoming avenue, diagonally across the island to the boat-landing. He went on board at once—but the tale of his journey across the lagoon was a tale of woe, a passage through the very alley of regrets.

It was the well-known route: through the lagoon, past San Marco, up the Grand Canal. Aschenbach sat on the circular bench in the bows, with his elbow on the railing, one hand shading his eyes. They passed the Public Gardens, once more the princely charm of the Piazzetta rose up before him and then dropped behind, next came the great row of palaces, the canal curved, and the splendid marble arches of the Rialto came in sight. The traveller gazed—and his bosom was torn. The atmos-phere of the city, the faintly rotten scent of swamp and sea, which had driven him to leave—in what deep, tender, almost painful draughts he breathed it in! How was it he had not known, had not thought, how much his heart was set upon it all! What this morning had been slight regret, some little doubt of his own wisdom, turned now to grief, to actual wretchedness, a mental agony so sharp that it repeatedly brought tears to his eyes, while he questioned himself how he could have foreseen it. The hardest part, the part that more than once it seemed he could not bear, was the thought that he should never more see Venice again. Since now for the second time the place had made him ill, since for the second time he had had to flee for his life, he must henceforth regard it as a forbidden spot, to be forever shunned; senseless to try it again, after he had proved himself unfit. Yes, if he fled it now, he felt that wounded pride must prevent his return to this spot where twice he had made actual bodily surrender. And this conflict between inclination and capacity all at once assumed, in this middle-aged man's mind, immense weight and importance; the physical defeat seemed a shameful thing, to be avoided at whatever cost; and he stood amazed at the ease with which on the day before he had yielded to it.

Meanwhile the steamer neared the station landing; his anguish of irresolution amounted almost to panic. To leave seemed to the sufferer impossible, to remain not less so. Torn thus between two alternatives, he entered the station. It was very late, he had not a moment to lose. Time pressed, it scourged him onward. He hastened to buy his ticket and looked round in the crowd to find the hotel porter. The man appeared and said that the trunk had already gone off. "Gone already?" "Yes, it has gone to Como." "To Como?" A hasty exchange of words—angry questions from Aschenbach, and puzzled replies from the porter—at length made it clear that the trunk had been put with the wrong luggage even before leaving the hotel, and in company with other trunks was now well on its way in precisely the wrong direction.

Aschenbach found it hard to wear the right expression as he heard this news. A reckless joy, a deep incredible mirthfulness shook him almost as with a spasm. The porter dashed off after the lost trunk, returning very soon, of course, to announce that his efforts were unavailing. Aschenbach said he would not travel without his luggage; that he would go back and wait at the Hôtel des Bains until it turned up. Was the company's motorboat still outside? The man said yes, it was at the door. With his native eloquence he prevailed upon the ticket-agent to take back the ticket already purchased; he swore that he would wire, that no pains should be spared, that the trunk would be restored in the twinkling of an eye. And the unbelievable thing came to pass: the traveller, twenty minutes after he had reached the station, found himself once more on the Grand Canal on his way back to the Lido.

What a strange adventure indeed, this right-about face of destiny—incredible, humiliating, whimsical as any dream! To be passing again, within the hour, these scenes from which in profoundest grief he had but now taken leave forever! The little swift-moving vessel, a furrow of foam at its prow, tacking with droll agility between steamboats and gondolas, went like a shot to its goal; and he, its sole passenger, sat hiding the panic and thrills of a truant schoolboy beneath a mask of forced resignation. His breast still heaved from time to time with a burst of laughter over the contretemps. Things could not, he told himself, have fallen out more luckily. There would be the necessary explanations, a few astonished faces—then all would be well once more, a mischance prevented, a grievous error set right; and all he had thought to have left forever was his own once more, his for as long as he liked. . . . And did the boat's swift motion deceive him, or was the wind now coming from the sea?

The waves struck against the tiled sides of the narrow canal. At Hôtel Excelsior the automobile omnibus awaited the returned traveller and bore him along by the crisping waves back to the Hôtel des Bains. The little mustachioed manager in the frock-coat came down the steps to greet him.

In dulcet tones he deplored the mistake, said how painful it was to the management and himself; applauded Aschenbach's resolve to stop on until the errant trunk came back; his former room, alas, was already taken, but another as good awaited his approval. *"Pas de chance, monsieur,"* said the Swiss lift-porter, with a smile, as he conveyed him upstairs. And the fugitive was soon quartered in another room which in situation and furnishings almost precisely resembled the first.

He laid out the contents of his hand-bag in their wonted places; then, tired out, dazed by the whirl of the extraordinary forenoon, subsided into the arm-chair by the open window. The sea wore a pale-green cast, the air felt thinner and purer, the beach with its cabins and boats had more colour, notwithstanding the sky was still grey. Aschenbach, his hands folded in his lap, looked out. He felt rejoiced to be back, yet displeased with his vacillating moods, his ignorance of his own real desires. Thus for nearly an hour he sat, dreaming, resting, barely thinking. At midday he saw Tadzio, in his striped sailor suit with red breast-knot, coming up from the sea, across the barrier and along the board walk to the hotel. Aschenbach recognized him, even at this height, knew it was he before he actually saw him, had it in mind to say to himself: "Well, Tadzio, so here you are again too!" But the casual greeting died away before it reached his lips, slain by the truth in his heart. He felt the rapture of his blood, the poignant pleasure, and realized that it was for Tadzio's sake the leavetaking had been so hard.

He sat quite still, unseen at his high post, and looked within himself. His features were lively, he lifted his brows; a smile, alert, inquiring, vivid, widened the mouth. Then he raised his head, and with both hands, hanging limp over the chair-arms, he described a slow motion, palms outward, a lifting and turning movement, as though to indicate a wide embrace. It was a gesture of welcome, a calm and deliberate acceptance of what might come.

Now daily the naked god with cheeks aflame drove his four fire-breathing steeds through heaven's spaces; and with him streamed the strong east wind that fluttered his yellow locks. A sheen, like white satin, lay over all the idly rolling sea's expanse. The sand was burning hot. Awnings of rust-coloured canvas were spanned before the bathing-huts, under the ether's quivering silver-blue; one spent the morning hours within the small, sharp square of shadow they purveyed. But evening too was rarely lovely: balsamic with the breath of flowers and shrubs from the near-by park, while overhead the constellations circled in their spheres, and the murmuring of the night-girted sea swelled softly up and whispered to the soul. Such nights as these contained the joyful promise of a sunlit morrow, brim-full of sweetly ordered idleness, studded thick with countless precious possibilities.

The guest detained here by so happy a mischance was far from finding the return of his luggage a ground for setting out anew. For two days he had suffered slight inconvenience and had to dine in the large salon in his travelling-clothes. Then the lost trunk was set down in his room, and he hastened to unpack, filling presses and drawers with his possessions. He meant to stay on—and on; he rejoiced in the prospect of wearing a silk suit for the hot morning hours on the beach and appearing in acceptable evening dress at dinner.

He was quick to fall in with the pleasing monotony of this manner of life, readily enchanted by its mild soft brilliance and ease. And what a spot it is, indeed!—uniting the charms of a luxurious bathing-resort by a southern sea with the immediate nearness of a unique and marvellous city. Aschenbach was not pleasure-loving. Always, wherever and whenever it was the order of the day to be merry, to refrain from labour and make glad the heart, he would soon be conscious of the imperative summons—and especially was this so in his youth—back to the high fatigues, the sacred and fasting service that consumed his days. This spot and this alone had power to beguile him, to relax his resolution, to make him glad. At times—of a forenoon perhaps, as he lay in the shadow of his awning, gazing out dreamily over the blue of the southern sea, or in the mildness of the night, beneath the wide starry sky, ensconced among the cushions of the gondola that bore him Lido-wards after an evening on the Piazza, while the gay lights faded and the melting music of the serenades died away on his ear—he would think of his mountain home, the theatre of his summer labours. There clouds hung low and trailed through the garden, violent storms extinguished the lights of the house at night, and the ravens he fed swung in the tops of the fir trees. And he would feel transported to Elysium, to the ends of the earth, to a spot most carefree for the sons of men, where no snow is, and no winter, no storms or downpours of rain; where Oceanus sends a mild and cooling breath, and days flow on in blissful idleness, without effort or struggle, entirely dedicated to the sun and the feasts of the sun.

Aschenbach saw the boy Tadzio almost constantly. The narrow confines of their world of hotel and beach, the daily round followed by all alike, brought him in close, almost uninterrupted touch with the beautiful lad. He encountered him everywhere—in the salons of the hotel, on the cooling rides to the city and back, among the splendours of the

Piazza, and besides all this in many another going and coming as chance vouchsafed. But it was the regular morning hours on the beach which gave him his happiest opportunity to study and admire the lovely apparition. Yes, this immediate happiness, this daily recurring boon at the hand of circumstance, this it was that filled him with content, with joy in life, enriched his stay, and lingered out the row of sunny days that fell into place so pleasantly one behind the other.

He rose early—as early as though he had a panting press of work—and was among the first on the beach, when the sun lay dazzling white in its morning slumber. He gave the watchman a friendly good-morning and chatted with the barefoot, white-haired old man who prepared his place, spread the awning, trundled out the chair and table onto the little platform. Then he settled down; he had three or four hours before the sun reached its height and the fearful climax of its power; three or four hours while the sea went deeper and deeper blue; three or four hours in which to watch Tadzio.

He would see him come up, on the left, along the margin of the sea; or from behind, between the cabins; or, with a start of joyful surprise, would discover that he himself was late, and Tadzio already down, in the blue and white bathing-suit that was now his only wear on the beach; there and engrossed in his usual activities in the sand, beneath the sun. It was a sweetly idle, trifling, fitful life, of play and rest, of strolling, wading, digging, fishing, swimming, lying on the sand. Often the women sitting on the platform would call out to him in their high voices: "Tadziu! Tadziu!" and he would come running and waving his arms, eager to tell them what he had done, show them what he had found, what caught—shells, seahorses, jelly-fish, and sidewards-running crabs. Aschenbach understood not a word he said; it might be the sheerest commonplace, in his ear it became mingled harmonies. Thus the lad's foreign birth raised his speech to music; a wanton sun showered splendour on him, and the noble distances of the sea formed the background which set off his figure.

Soon the observer knew every line and pose of this form that limned itself so freely against sea and sky; its every loveliness, though conned by heart, yet thrilled him each day afresh; his admiration knew no bounds, the delight of his eye was unending. Once the lad was summoned to speak to a guest who was waiting for his mother at their cabin. He ran up, ran dripping wet out of the sea, tossing his curls, and put out his hand, standing with his weight on one leg, resting the other foot on the toes; as he stood there in a posture of suspense the turn of his body was enchanting, while his features wore a look half shamefaced, half conscious of the duty breeding laid upon him to please. Or he would lie at full length, with his bath-robe around him, one slender young arm resting on the sand, his chin in the hollow of his hand; the lad they called Jaschiu squatting beside him, paying him court. There could be nothing lovelier on earth than the smile and look with which the playmate thus singled out rewarded his humble friend and vassal. Again, he might be at the water's edge, alone, removed from his family, quite close to Aschenbach; standing erect, his hands clasped at the back of his neck, rocking slowly on the balls of his feet, day-dreaming away into blue space, while little waves ran up and bathed his toes. The ringlets of honey-coloured hair clung to his temples and neck, the fine down along the upper vertebrae was yellow in the sunlight; the thin envelope of flesh covering the torso betrayed the delicate outlines of the ribs and the symmetry of the breast-structure. His armpits were still as smooth as a statue's, smooth the glistening hollows behind the knees, where the blue network of veins suggested that the body was formed of some stuff more transparent than mere flesh. What discipline, what precision of thought were expressed by the tense youthful perfection of this form! And yet the pure, strong will which had laboured in darkness and succeeded in bringing this god-like work of art to the light of day—was it not known and familiar to him, the artist? Was not the same force at work in himself when he strove in cold fury to liberate from the marble mass of language the slender forms of his art which he saw with the eye of his mind and would body forth to men as the mirror and image of spiritual beauty?

Mirror and image! His eyes took in the proud bearing of that figure there at the blue water's edge; with an outburst of rapture he told himself that what he saw was beauty's very essence; form as divine thought, the single and pure perfection which resides in the mind, of which an image and likeness, rare and holy, was here raised up for adoration. This was very frenzy—and without a scruple, nay, eagerly, the aging artist bade it come. His mind was in travail, his whole mental background in a state of flux. Memory flung up in him the primitive thoughts which are youth's inheritance, but which with him had remained latent, never leaping up into a blaze. Has it not been written that the sun beguiles our attention from things of the intellect to fix it on things of the sense? The sun, they say, dazzles; so bewitching reason and memory that the soul for very pleasure forgets its actual state, to cling with doting on the loveliest of all the objects she shines on. Yes, and then it is only through the medium of some corporeal being that it can raise itself again to contemplation of higher things. Amor, in sooth, is like the mathematician who in order to give children a knowledge of pure form must do so in the language of pictures; so, too, the god, in order to make visible the spirit, avails himself of the forms and colours of human youth, gilding it with all imaginable beauty that it may serve memory as a tool, the very sight of which then sets us afire with pain and longing.

Such were the devotee's thoughts, such the power of his emotions. And the sea, so bright with glancing sunbeams, wove in his mind a spell and summoned up a lovely picture: there was the ancient plane-tree outside the walls of Athens, a hallowed, shady spot, fragrant with willow-blossom and adorned with images and votive offerings in honour of the nymphs and Achelous. Clear ran the smooth-pebbled stream at the foot of the spreading tree. Crickets were fiddling. But on the gentle grassy slope, where one could lie yet hold the head erect, and shelter from the scorching heat, two men reclined, an elder with a younger, ugliness paired with beauty and wisdom with grace. Here Socrates held forth to youthful Phædrus upon the nature of virtue and desire, wooing him with insinuating wit and charming turns of phrase. He told him of the shuddering and unwonted heat that come upon him whose heart is open, when his eye beholds an image of eternal beauty; spoke of the impious and corrupt, who cannot conceive beauty though they see its image, and are incapable of awe; and of the fear and reverence felt by the noble soul when he beholds a godlike face or a form which is a good image of beauty: how as he gazes he worships the beautiful one and scarcely dares to look upon him, but would offer sacrifice as to an idol or a god, did he not fear to be thought stark mad. "For beauty, my Phædrus, beauty alone, is lovely and visible at once. For, mark you, it is the sole aspect of the spiritual which we can perceive through our senses, or bear so to perceive. Else what should become of us, if the divine, if reason and virtue and truth, were to speak to us through the senses? Should we not perish and be consumed by love, as Semele aforetime was by Zeus? So beauty, then, is the beauty-lover's way to the spirit—but only the way, only the means, my little Phædrus." . . . And then, sly arch-lover that he was, he said the subtlest thing of all: that the lover was nearer the divine than the beloved; for the god was in the one but not in the other —perhaps the tenderest, most mocking thought that ever was thought, and source of all the guile and secret bliss the lover knows.

Thought that can merge wholly into feeling, feeling that can merge wholly into thought—these are the artist's highest joy. And our solitary felt in himself at this moment power to command and wield a thought that thrilled with emotion, an emotion as precise and concentrated as thought: namely, that nature herself shivers with ecstasy when the mind bows down in homage before beauty. He felt a sudden desire to write. Eros, indeed, we are told, loves idleness, and for idle hours alone was he created. But in this crisis the violence of our sufferer's seizure was directed almost wholly towards production, its occasion almost a matter of indifference. News had reached him on his travels that a certain problem had been raised, the intellectual world challenged for its opinion on a great and burning question of art and taste. By nature and experience the theme was his own; and he could not resist the temptation to set it off in the glistering foil of his words. He would write, and moreover he would write in Tadzio's presence. This lad should be in a sense his model, his style should follow the lines of this figure that seemed to him divine; he would snatch up this beauty into the realms of the mind, as once the eagle bore the Trojan shepherd aloft. Never had the pride of the word been so sweet to him, never had he known so well that Eros is in the word, as in those perilous and precious hours when he sat at his rude table, within the shade of his awning, his idol full in his view and the music of his voice in his ears, and fashioned his little essay after the model Tadzio's beauty set: that page and a half of choicest prose, so chaste, so lofty, so poignant with feeling, which would shortly be the wonder and admiration of the multitude. Verily it is well for the world that it sees only the beauty of the completed work and not its origins nor the conditions whence it sprang; since knowledge of the artist's inspiration might often but confuse and alarm and so prevent the full effect of its excellence. Strange hours, indeed, these were, and strangely unnerving the labour that filled them! Strangely fruitful intercourse this, between one body and another mind! When Aschenbach put aside his work and left the beach he felt exhausted, he felt broken—conscience reproached him, as it were after a debauch.

Next morning on leaving the hotel he stood at the top of the stairs leading down from the terrace and saw Tadzio in front of him on his way to the beach. The lad had just reached the gate in the railings, and he was alone. Aschenbach felt, quite simply, a wish to overtake him, to address him and have the pleasure of his reply and answering look; to put upon a blithe and friendly footing his relation with this being who all unconsciously had so greatly heightened and quickened his emotions. The lovely youth moved at a loitering pace—he might easily be overtaken; and Aschenbach hastened his own step. He reached him on the board walk that ran behind the bathing-cabins, and all but put out his hand to lay it on shoulder or head, while his lips parted to utter a friendly salutation in French. But—perhaps from the swift pace of his last few steps—he found his heart throbbing unpleasantly fast, while his breath came in such quick pants that he could only have gasped had he tried to speak. He hesitated, sought after self-control, was suddenly panic-stricken lest the boy notice him hanging there behind him and look round. Then he gave up, abandoned his plan, and passed him with bent head and hurried step.

"Too late! Too late!" he thought as he went by. But was it too late? This step he had delayed to take might so easily have put everything in a lighter key, have led to a sane recovery from his folly. But the truth may have been that the aging man did not want to be cured, that his illusion was far too dear to him. Who shall unriddle the puzzle of the artist nature? Who understands that mingling of discipline and license in which it stands so deeply rooted? For not to be able to want sobriety is licentious folly. Aschenbach was no longer disposed to self-analysis. He had no taste for it; his self-esteem, the attitude of mind proper to his years, his maturity and single-mindedness, disinclined him to look within himself and decide whether it was constraint or puerile sensuality that had prevented him from carrying out his project. He felt confused, he was afraid someone, if only the watchman, might have been observing his behaviour and final surrender—very much he feared being ridiculous. And all the time he was laughing at himself for his serio-comic seizure. "Quite crestfallen," he thought. "I was like the gamecock that lets his wings droop in the battle. That must be the Love-God himself, that makes us hang our heads at sight of beauty and weighs our proud spirits low as the ground." Thus he played with the idea—he embroidered upon it, and was too arrogant to admit fear of an emotion.

The term he had set for his holiday passed by unheeded; he had no thought of going home. Ample funds had been sent him. His sole concern was that the Polish family might leave, and a chance question put to the hotel barber elicited the information that they had come only very shortly before himself. The sun browned his face and hands, the invigorating salty air heightened his emotional energies. Heretofore he had been wont to give out at once, in some new effort, the powers accumulated by sleep or food or outdoor air; but now the strength that flowed in upon him with each day of sun and sea and idleness he let go up in one extravagant gush of emotional intoxication.

His sleep was fitful; the priceless, equable days were divided one from the next by brief nights filled with happy unrest. He went, indeed, early to bed, for at nine o'clock, with the departure of Tadzio from the scene, the day was over for him. But in the faint greyness of the morning a tender pang would go through him as his heart was minded of its adventure; he could no longer bear his pillow and, rising, would wrap himself against the early chill and sit down by the window to await the sunrise. Awe of the miracle filled his soul new-risen from its sleep. Heaven, earth, and its waters yet lay enfolded in the ghostly, glassy pallor of dawn; one paling star still swam in the shadowy vast. But there came a breath, a winged word from far and inaccessible abodes, that Eos was rising from the side of her spouse; and there was that first sweet reddening of the farthest strip of sea and sky that manifests creation to man's sense. She neared, the goddess, ravisher of youth, who stole away Cleitos and Cephalus and, defying all the envious Olympians, tasted beautiful Orion's love. At the world's edge began a strewing of roses, a shining and a blooming ineffably pure; baby cloudlets hung illumined, like attendant amoretti, in the blue and blushful haze; purple effulgence fell upon the sea, that seemed to heave it forward on its welling waves; from horizon to zenith went great quivering thrusts like golden lances, the gleam became a glare; without a sound, with godlike violence, glow and glare and rolling flames streamed upwards, and with flying hoof-beats the steeds of the sun-god mounted the sky. The lonely watcher sat, the splendour of the god shone on him, he closed his eyes and let the glory kiss his lids. Forgotten feelings, precious pangs of his youth, quenched long since by the stern service that had been his life and now returned so strangely metamorphosed—he recognized them with a puzzled, wondering smile. He mused, he dreamed, his lips slowly shaped a name; still smiling, his face turned seawards and his hands lying folded in his lap, he fell asleep once more as he sat.

But that day, which began so fierily and festally, was not like other days; it was transmuted and gilded with mythical significance. For whence could come the breath, so mild and meaningful, like a whisper from higher spheres, that played about temple and ear? Troops of small feathery white clouds ranged over the sky, like grazing herds of the gods. A stronger wind arose, and Poseidon's horses ran up, arching their manes, among them too the steers of him with the purpled locks, who lowered their horns and bellowed as they came on; while like prancing goats the waves on the farther strand leaped among the craggy rocks. It was a world possessed, peopled by Pan, that closed round the spellbound man, and his doting heart conceived the most delicate fancies. When the sun was going down behind Venice, he would sometimes sit on a bench in the park and watch Tadzio, white-clad, with gay-coloured sash, at play there on the rolled gravel with his ball; and at such times it was not Tadzio whom he saw, but Hyacinthus, doomed to die because two gods were rivals for his love. Ah, yes, he tasted the envious pangs that Zephyr knew when his rival, bow and cithara, oracle and all forgot, played with the beauteous youth; he watched the discus, guided by torturing jealousy, strike the beloved head; paled as he received the broken body in his arms, and saw the flower spring up, watered by that sweet blood and signed forevermore with his lament.

There can be no relation more strange, more critical, than that between two beings who know each other only with their eyes, who meet daily, yes, even hourly, eye each other with a fixed regard, and yet by some whim or freak of convention feel constrained to act like strangers. Uneasiness rules between them, unslaked curiosity, a hysterical desire to give rein to their suppressed impulse to recognize and address each other; even, actually, a sort of strained but mutual regard. For one human being instinctively feels respect and love for another human being so long as he does not know him well enough to judge him; and that he does not, the craving he feels is evidence.

Some sort of relation and acquaintanceship was perforce set up between Aschenbach and the youthful Tadzio; it was with a thrill of joy the older man pereived that the lad was not entirely unresponsive to all the tender notice lavished on him. For instance, what should move the lovely youth, nowadays when he descended to the beach, always to avoid the board walk behind the bathing-huts and saunter along the sand, passing Aschenbach's tent in front, sometimes so unnecessarily close as almost to graze his table or chair? Could the power of an emotion so beyond his own so draw, so fascinate its innocent object? Daily Aschenbach would wait for Tadzio. Then sometimes, on his approach, he would pretend to be preoccupied and let the charmer pass unregarded by. But sometimes he looked up, and their glances met; when that happened both were profoundly serious. The elder's dignified and cultured mien let nothing appear of his inward state; but in Tadzio's eyes a question lay—he faltered in his step, gazed on the ground, then up again with that ineffably sweet look he had; and when he was past, something in his bearing seemed to say that only good breeding hindered him from turning round.

But once, one evening, it fell out differently. The Polish brother and sisters, with their governess, had missed the evening meal, and Aschenbach had noted the fact with concern. He was restive over their absence, and after dinner walked up and down in front of the hotel, in evening dress and a straw hat; when suddenly he saw the nunlike sisters with their companion appear in the light of the arc-lamps, and four paces behind them Tadzio. Evidently they came from the steamer-landing, having dined for some reason in Venice. It had been chilly on the lagoon, for Tadzio wore a dark-blue reefer-jacket with gilt buttons, and a cap to match. Sun and sea air could not burn his skin, it was the same creamy hue as at first—though he did look a little pale, either from the cold or in the bluish moonlight of the arc-lamps. The shapely brows were so delicately drawn, the eyes so deeply dark—lovelier he was than words could say, and as often the thought visited Aschenbach, and brought its own pang, that language could but extol, not reproduce, the beauties of the sense.

The sight of that dear form was unexpected, it had appeared un-hoped-for, without giving him time to compose his features. Joy, surprise, and admiration might have painted themselves quite openly upon his face—and just at this second it happened that Tadzio smiled. Smiled at Aschenbach, unabashed and friendly, a speaking, winning, captivating smile, with slowly parting lips. With such a smile it might be that Narcissus bent over the mirroring pool, a smile profound, infatuated, lingering, as he put out his arms to the reflection of his own beauty; the lips just slightly pursed, perhaps half-realizing his own folly in trying to kiss the cold lips of his shadow—with a mingling of coquetry and curiosity and a faint unease, enthralling and enthralled.

Aschenbach received that smile and turned away with it as though entrusted with a fatal gift. So shaken was he that he had to flee from the lighted terrace and front gardens and seek out with hurried steps the darkness of the park at the rear. Reproaches strangely mixed of tenderness and remonstrance burst from him: "How dare you smile like that! No one is allowed to smile like that!" He flung himself on a bench, his composure gone to the winds, and breathed in the nocturnal fragrance of the garden. He leaned back, with hanging arms, quivering from head to foot, and quite unmanned he whispered the hackneyed phrase of love and longing—impossible in these circumstances, absurd, abject, ridiculous enough, yet sacred too, and not unworthy of honour even here: "I love you!"

In the fourth week of his stay on the Lido, Gustave von Aschenbach made certain singular observations touching the world about him. He noticed, in the first place, that though the season was approaching its height, yet the number of guests declined and, in particular, that the German tongue had suffered a rout, being scarcely or never heard in the land. At table and on the beach he caught nothing but foreign words. One day at the barber's—where he was now a frequent visitor—he heard something rather startling. The barber mentioned a German family who had just left the Lido after a brief stay, and rattled on in his obsequious way: "The signore is not leaving—he has no fear of the sickness, has he?" Aschenbach looked at him. "The sickness?" he repeated. Whereat the prattler fell silent, became very busy all at once, affected not to hear.

When Aschenbach persisted he said he really knew nothing at all about it, and tried in a fresh burst of eloquence to drown the embarrassing subject.

That was one afternoon. After luncheon Aschenbach had himself ferried across to Venice, in a dead calm, under a burning sun; driven by his mania, he was following the Polish young folk, whom he had seen with their companion, taking the way to the landing-stage. He did not find his idol on the Piazza. But as he sat there at tea, at a little round table on the shady side, suddenly he noticed a peculiar odour, which, it seemed to him now, had been in the air for days without his being aware: a sweetish, medicinal smell, associated with wounds and disease and suspect cleanliness. He sniffed and pondered and at length recognized it; finished his tea and left the square at the end facing the cathedral. In the narrow space the stench grew stronger. At the street corners placards were stuck up, in which the city authorities warned the population against the danger of certain infections of the gastric system, prevalent during the heated season; advising them not to eat oysters or other shell-fish and not to use the canal waters. The ordinance showed every sign of minimizing an existing situation. Little groups of people stood about silently in the squares and on the bridges; the traveller moved among them, watched and listened and thought.

He spoke to a shopkeeper lounging at his door among dangling coral necklaces and trinkets of artificial amethyst, and asked him about the disagreeable odour. The man looked at him, heavy-eyed, and hastily pulled himself together. "Just a formal precaution, signore," he said, with a gesture. "A police regulation we have to put up with. The air is sultry—the sirocco is not wholesome, as the signore knows. Just a precautionary measure, you understand—probably unnecessary. . . ." Aschenbach thanked him and passed on. And on the boat that bore him back to the Lido he smelt the germicide again.

On reaching his hotel he sought the table in the lobby and buried himself in the newspapers. The foreign-language sheets had nothing. But in the German papers certain rumours were mentioned, statistics given, then officially denied, then the good faith of the denials called in question. The departure of the German and Austrian contingent was thus made plain. As for other nationals, they knew or suspected nothing—they were still undisturbed. Aschenbach tossed the newspapers back on the table. "It ought to be kept quiet," he thought, aroused. "It should not be talked about." And he felt in his heart a curious elation at these events impending in the world about him. Passion is like crime: it does not thrive on the established order and the common round; it welcomes every blow dealt the bourgeois structure, every weakening of the social fabric, because therein it feels a sure hope of its own advantage. These things that were going on in the unclean alleys of Venice, under cover of an official hushing-up policy—they gave Aschenbach a dark satisfaction. The city's evil secret mingled with the one in the depths of his heart—and he would have staked all he possessed to keep it, since in his infatuation he cared for nothing but to keep Tadzio here, and owned to himself, not without horror, that he could not exist were the lad to pass from his sight.

He was no longer satisfied to owe his communion with his charmer to chance and the routine of hotel life; he had begun to follow and waylay him. On Sundays, for example, the Polish family never appeared on the beach. Aschenbach guessed they went to mass at San Marco and pursued them thither. He passed from the glare of the Piazza into the golden twilight of the holy place and found him he sought bowed in worship over a prie-dieu. He kept in the background, standing on the fissured mosaic pavement among the devout populace, that knelt and muttered and made the sign of the cross; and the crowded splendour of the oriental temple weighed voluptuously on his sense. A heavily ornate priest intoned and gesticulated before the altar, where little candle-flames flickered helplessly in the reek of incense-breathing smoke; and with that cloying sacrificial smell another seemed to mingle—the odour of the sickened city. But through all the glamour and glitter Aschenbach saw the exquisite creature there in front turn his head, seek out and meet his lover's eye.

The crowd streamed out through the portals into the brilliant square thick with fluttering doves, and the fond fool stood aside in the vestibule on the watch. He saw the Polish family leave the church. The children took ceremonial leave of their mother, and she turned towards the Piazzetta on her way home, while his charmer and the cloistered sisters, with their governess, passed beneath the clock tower into the Merceria. When they were a few paces on, he followed—he stole behind them on their walk through the city. When they paused, he did so too; when they turned round, he fled into inns and courtyards to let them pass. Once he lost them from view, hunted feverishly over bridges and in filthy *culs-de-sac,* only to confront them suddenly in a narrow passage whence there was no escape, and experience a moment of panic fear. Yet it would be untrue to say he suffered. Mind and heart were drunk with passion, his footsteps guided by the dæmonic power whose pastime it is to trample on human reason and dignity.

Tadzio and his sisters at length took a gondola. Aschenbach hid behind a portico or fountain while they embarked, and directly they pushed off did the same. In a furtive whisper he told the boatman he would tip him well to follow at a little distance the other gondola, just rounding a corner, and fairly sickened at the man's quick, sly grasp and ready acceptance of the go-between's rôle.

Leaning back among soft, black cushions, he swayed gently in the wake of the other black-snouted bark, to which the strength of his passion chained him. Sometimes it passed from his view, and then he was assailed by an anguish of unrest. But his guide appeared to have long practice in affairs like these; always, by dint of short cuts or deft manœuvres, he contrived to overtake the coveted sight. The air was heavy and foul, the sun burnt down through a slate-coloured haze. Water slapped gurgling against wood and stone. The gondolier's cry, half warning, half salute, was answered with singular accord from far within the silence of the labyrinth. They passed little gardens, high up the crumbling wall, hung with clustering white and purple flowers that sent down an odour of almonds. Moorish lattices showed shadowy in the gloom. The marble steps of a church descended into the canal, and on them a beggar squatted, displaying his misery to view, showing the whites of his eyes, holding out his hat for alms. Farther on a dealer in antiquities cringed before his lair, inviting the passer-by to enter and be duped. Yes, this was Venice, this the fair frailty that fawned and that betrayed, half fairy-tale, half snare; the city in whose stagnating air the art of painting once put forth so lusty a growth, and where musicians were moved to accords so weirdly lulling and lascivious. Our adventurer felt his senses wooed by this voluptuousness of sight and sound, tasted his secret knowledge that the city sickened and hid its sickness for love of gain, and bent an ever more unbridled leer on the gondola that glided on before him.

It came at last to this—that his frenzy left him capacity for nothing else but to pursue his flame; to dream of him absent, to lavish, lover-like, endearing terms on his mere shadow. He was alone, he was a foreigner, he was sunk deep in this belated bliss of his—all which enabled him to pass unblushing through experiences well-nigh unbelievable. One night, returning late from Venice, he paused by his beloved's chamber door in the second storey, leaned his head against the panel, and remained there long, in utter drunkenness, powerless to tear himself away, blind to the danger of being caught in so mad an attitude.

And yet there were not wholly lacking moments when he paused and reflected, when in consternation he asked himself what path was this on which he had set his foot. Like most other men of parts and attainments, he had an aristocratic interest in his forebears, and when he achieved a success he liked to think he had gratified them, compelled their admiration and regard. He thought of them now, involved as he was in this illicit adventure, seized of these exotic excesses of feeling; thought of their stern self-command and decent manliness, and gave a melancholy smile. What would they have said? What, indeed, would they have said to his entire life, that varied to the point of degeneracy from theirs? This life in the bonds of art, had not he himself, in the days of his youth and in the very spirit of those bourgeois forefathers, pronounced mocking judgment upon it? And yet, at bottom, it had been so like their own! It had been a service, and he a soldier, like some of them; and art was war—a grilling, exhausting struggle that nowadays wore one out before one could grow old. It had been a life of self-conquest, a life against odds, dour, steadfast, abstinent; he had made it symbolical of the kind of overstrained heroism the time admired, and he was entitled to call it manly, even courageous. He wondered if such a life might not be somehow specially pleasing in the eyes of the god who had him in his power. For Eros had received most countenance among the most valiant nations—yes, were we not told that in their cities prowess made him flourish exceedingly? And many heroes of olden time had willingly borne his yoke, not counting any humiliation such if it happened by the god's decree; vows, prostrations, self-abasements, these were no source of shame to the lover; rather they reaped him praise and honour.

Thus did the fond man's folly condition his thoughts; thus did he seek to hold his dignity upright in his own eyes. And all the while he kept doggedly on the traces of the disreputable secret the city kept hidden at its heart, just as he kept his own—and all that he learned fed his passion with vague, lawless hopes. He turned over newspapers at cafés, bent on finding a report on the progress of the disease; and in the German sheets, which had ceased to appear on the hotel table, he found a series of contradictory statements. The details, it was variously asserted, ran to twenty, to forty, to a hundred or more; yet in the next day's issue the existence of the pestilence was, if not roundly denied, reported as a matter of a few sporadic cases such as might be brought into a seaport town. After that the warnings would break out again, and the protests against the unscrupulous game the authorities were playing. No definite information was to be had.

And yet our solitary felt he had a sort of first claim on a share in the unwholesome secret; he took a fantastic satisfaction in putting leading questions to such persons as were interested to conceal it, and forcing them to explicit untruths by way of denial. One day he attacked the manager, that small, soft-stepping man in the French frock-coat, who was moving about among the guests at luncheon, supervising the service and making himself socially agreeable. He paused at Aschenbach's table to exchange a greeting, and the guest put a question, with a negligent, casual air: "Why in the world are they forever disinfecting the city of Venice?" "A police regulation," the adroit one replied; "a precautionary measure, intended to protect the health of the public during this unseasonably warm and sultry weather." "Very praiseworthy of the police," Aschenbach gravely responded. After a further exchange of meteorological commonplaces the manager passed on.

It happened that a band of street musicians came to perform in the hotel gardens that evening after dinner. They grouped themselves beneath an iron stanchion supporting an arc-light, two women and two men, and turned their faces, that shone white in the glare, up towards the guests who sat on the hotel terrace enjoying this popular entertainment along with their coffee and iced drinks. The hotel lift-boys, waiters, and office staff stood in the doorway and listened; the Russian family displayed the usual Russian absorption in their enjoyment—they had their chairs put down into the garden to be nearer the singers and sat there in a half-circle with gratitude painted on their features, the old serf in her turban erect behind their chairs.

These strolling players were adepts at mandolin, guitar, harmonica, even compassing a reedy violin. Vocal numbers alternated with instrumental, the younger woman, who had a high shrill voice, joining in a love-duet with the sweetly falsettoing tenor. The actual head of the company, however, and incontestably its most gifted member, was the other man, who played the guitar. He was a sort of baritone buffo; with no voice to speak of, but possessed of a pantomimic gift and remarkable burlesque *élan*. Often he stepped out of the group and advanced towards the terrace, guitar in hand, and his audience rewarded his sallies with bursts of laughter. The Russians in their parterre seats were beside themselves with delight over this display of southern vivacity; their shouts and screams of applause encouraged him to bolder and bolder flights.

Aschenbach sat near the balustrade, a glass of pomegranate-juice and soda-water sparkling ruby-red before him, with which he now and then moistened his lips. His nerves drank in thirstily the unlovely sounds, the vulgar and sentimental tunes, for passion paralyses good taste and makes its victim accept with rapture what a man in his senses would either laugh at or turn from with disgust. Idly he sat and watched the antics of the buffoon with his face set in a fixed and painful smile, while inwardly his whole being was rigid with the intensity of the regard he bent on Tadzio, leaning over the railing six paces off.

He lounged there, in the white belted suit he sometimes wore at dinner, in all his innate, inevitable grace, with his left arm on the balustrade, his legs crossed, the right hand on the supporting hip; and looked down on the strolling singers with an expression that was hardly a smile, but rather a distant curiosity and polite toleration. Now and then he straightened himself and with a charming movement of both arms drew down his white blouse through his leather belt, throwing out his chest. And sometimes—Aschenbach saw it with triumph, with horror, and a sense that his reason was tottering—the lad would cast a glance, that might be slow and cautious, or might be sudden and swift, as though to take him by surprise, to the place where his lover sat. Aschenbach did not meet the glance. An ignoble caution made him keep his eyes in leash. For in the rear of the terrace sat Tadzio's mother and governess; and matters had gone so far that he feared to make himself conspicuous. Several times, on the beach, in the hotel lobby, on the Piazza, he had seen, with a stealing numbness, that they called Tadzio away from his neighbourhood. And his pride revolted at the affront, even while conscience told him it was deserved.

The performer below presently began a solo, with guitar accompaniment, a street song in several stanzas, just then the rage all over Italy. He delivered it in a striking and dramatic recitative, and his company joined in the refrain. He was a man of slight build, with a thin, undernourished face; his shabby felt hat rested on the back of his neck, a great mop of red hair sticking out in front; and he stood there on the gravel in advance of his troupe, in an impudent, swaggering posture, twanging the strings of his instrument and flinging a witty and rollicking recitative up to the terrace, while the veins on his forehead swelled with the violence of his effort. He was scarcely a Venetian type, belonging rather to the race of the Neapolitan jesters, half bully, half comedian, brutal, blustering, an unpleasant customer, and entertaining to the last degree. The words of his song were trivial and silly, but on his lips, accompanied with gestures of head, hands, arms, and body, with leers and winks and the loose play of the tongue in the corner of his mouth, they took on meaning; an equivocal meaning, yet vaguely offensive. He wore a white sports shirt with a suit of ordinary clothes, and a strikingly large and naked-looking Adam's apple rose out of the open collar. From that pale, snub-nosed face it was hard to judge of his age; vice sat on it, it was furrowed with grimacing, and two deep wrinkles of defiance and self-will, almost of desperation, stood oddly between the red brows, above the grinning, mobile mouth. But what more than all drew upon him the profound scrutiny of our solitary watcher was that this suspicious figure seemed to carry with it its own suspicious odour. For whenever the refrain occurred and the singer, with waving arms and antic gestures, passed in his grotesque march immediately beneath Aschenbach's seat, a strong smell of carbolic was wafted up to the terrace.

After the song he began to take up money, beginning with the Russian family, who gave liberally, and then mounting the steps to the terrace. But here he became as cringing as he had before been forward. He glided between the tables, bowing and scraping, showing his strong white teeth in a servile smile, though the two deep furrows on the brow were still very marked. His audience looked at the strange creature as he went about collecting his livelihood, and their curiosity was not unmixed with disfavour. They tossed coins with their fingertips into his hat and took care not to touch it. Let the enjoyment be never so great, a sort of embarrassment always comes when the comedian oversteps the physical distance between himself and respectable people. This man felt it and sought to make his peace by fawning. He came along the railing to Aschenbach, and with him came that smell no one else seemed to notice.

"Listen!" said the solitary, in a low voice, almost mechanically; "they are disinfecting Venice—why?" The mountebank answered hoarsely: "Because of the police. Orders, signore. On account of the heat and the sirocco, The sirocco is oppressive. Not good for the health." He spoke as though surprised that anyone could ask, and with the flat of his hand he demonstrated how oppressive the sirocco was. "So there is no plague in Venice?" Aschenbach asked the question between his teeth, very low. The man's expressive face fell, he put on a look of comical innocence. "A plague? What sort of plague? Is the sirocco a plague? Or perhaps our police are a plague! You are making fun of us, signore! A plague! Why should there be? The police make regulations on account of the heat and the weather. . . ." He gestured. "Quite," said Aschenbach, once more, soft and low; and dropping an unduly large coin into the man's hat dismissed him with a sign. He bowed very low and left. But he had not reached the steps when two of the hotel servants flung themselves on him and began to whisper, their faces close to him. He shrugged, seemed to be giving assurances, to be swearing he had said nothing. It was not hard to guess the import of his words. They let him go at last and he went back into the

garden, where he conferred briefly with his troupe and then stepped
forward for a farewell song.

It was one Aschenbach had never to his knowledge heard before, a
rowdy air, with words in impossible dialect. It had a laughing-refrain
in which the other three artists joined at the top of their lungs. The
refrain had neither words nor accompaniment, it was nothing but rhyth-
mical, modulated, natural laughter, which the soloist in particular knew
how to render with most deceptive realism. Now that he was farther off
his audience, his self-assurance had come back, and this laughter of his
rang with a mocking note. He would be overtaken, before he reached
the end of the last line of each stanza; he would catch his breath, lay his
hand over his mouth, his voice would quaver and his shoulders shake,
he would lose power to contain himself longer. Just at the right moment
each time, it came whooping, bawling, crashing out of him, with a veri-
similitude that never failed to set his audience off in profuse and unpre-
meditated mirth that seemed to add gusto to his own. He bent his knees,
he clapped his thigh, he held his sides, he looked ripe for bursting. He
no longer laughed, but yelled, pointing his finger at the company there
above as though there could be in all the world nothing so comic as they;
until at last they laughed in hotel, terrace, and garden, down to the waiters, lift-boys, and servants—laughed as though possessed.

Aschenbach could no longer rest in his chair, he sat poised for flight.
But the combined effect of the laughing, the hospital odour in his nostrils, and the nearness of the beloved was to hold him in a spell; he felt
unable to stir. Under cover of the general commotion he looked across
at Tadzio and saw that the lovely boy returned his gaze with a seriousness
that seemed the copy of his own; the general hilarity, it seemed to say,
had no power over him, he kept aloof. The grey-haired man was over-
powered, disarmed by this docile, childlike deference; with difficulty he
refrained from hiding his face in his hands. Tadzio's habit, too, of drawing himself up and taking a deep sighing breath struck him as being due
to an oppression of the chest. "He is sickly, he will never live to grow up,"
he thought once again, with that dispassionate vision to which his madness of desire sometimes so strangely gave way. And compassion struggled
with the reckless exultation of his heart.

The players, meanwhile, had finished and gone; their leader bowing
and scraping, kissing his hands and adorning his leave-taking with antics
that grew madder with the applause they evoked. After all the others
were outside, he pretended to run backwards full tilt against a lamp-
post and slunk to the gate apparently doubled over with pain. But
there he threw off his buffoon's mask, stood erect, with an elastic straight-
ening of his whole figure, ran out his tongue impudently at the guests on
the terrace, and vanished in the night. The company dispersed. Tadzio
had long since left the balustrade. But he, the lonely man, sat for long, to
the waiters' great annoyance, before the dregs of pomegranate-juice in his
glass. Time passed, the night went on. Long ago, in his parental home,
he had watched the sand filter through an hour-glass—he could still see,

as though it stood before him, the fragile, pregnant little toy. Soundless and fine the rust-red streamlet ran through the narrow neck, and made, as it declined in the upper cavity, an exquisite little vortex.

The very next afternoon the solitary took another step in pursuit of his fixed policy of baiting the outer world. This time he had all possible success. He went, that is, into the English travel bureau in the Piazza, changed some money at the desk, and posing as the suspicious foreigner, put his fateful question. The clerk was a tweed-clad young Britisher, with his eyes set close together, his hair parted in the middle, and radiating that steady reliability which makes his like so strange a phenomenon in the *gamin*, agile-witted south. He began: "No ground for alarm, sir. A mere formality. Quite regular in view of the unhealthy climatic conditions." But then, looking up, he chanced to meet with his own blue eyes the stranger's weary, melancholy gaze, fixed on his face. The Englishman coloured. He continued in a lower voice, rather confused: "At least, that is the official explanation, which they see fit to stick to. I may tell you there's a bit more to it than that." And then, in his good, straightforward way, he told the truth.

For the past several years Asiatic cholera had shown a strong tendency to spread. Its source was the hot, moist swamps of the delta of the Ganges, where it bred in the mephitic air of that primeval island-jungle, among whose bamboo thickets the tiger crouches, where life of every sort flourishes in rankest abundance, and only man avoids the spot. Thence the pestilence had spread throughout Hindustan, raging with great violence; moved eastwards to China, westward to Afghanistan and Persia; following the great caravan routes, it brought terror to Astrakhan, terror to Moscow. Even while Europe trembled lest the spectre be seen striding westward across country, it was carried by sea from Syrian ports and appeared simultaneously at several points on the Mediterranean littoral; raised its head in Toulon and Malaga, Palermo and Naples, and soon got a firm hold in Calabria and Apulia. Northern Italy had been spared—so far. But in May the horrible vibrions were found on the same day in two bodies: the emaciated, blackened corpses of a bargee and a woman who kept a green-grocer's shop. Both cases were hushed up. But in a week there were ten more—twenty, thirty in different quarters of the town. An Austrian provincial, having come to Venice on a few days' pleasure trip, went home and died with all the symptoms of the plague. Thus was explained the fact that the German-language papers were the first to print the news of the Venetian outbreak. The Venetian authorities published in reply a statement to the effect that the state of the city's health had never been better; at the same time instituting the most necessary precautions. But by that time the food supplies—milk, meat, or vegetables—had probably been contaminated, for death unseen and unacknowledged was devouring and laying waste in the narrow streets, while a brooding, unseasonable heat warmed the waters of the canals and encouraged the spread of the pestilence. Yes, the disease seemed to flourish and wax strong, to redouble its generative powers. Recoveries were rare. Eighty out of every hundred died, and horribly, for the onslaught was of the extremest violence, and not infrequently of the "dry" type, the most malignant form of the contagion. In this form the victim's body loses power to expel the water secreted by the blood-vessels, it shrivels up, he passes with hoarse cries from convulsion to convulsion, his blood grows thick like pitch, and he suffocates in a few hours. He is fortunate indeed, if, as sometimes happens, the disease, after a slight *malaise,* takes the form of a profound unconsciousness, from which the sufferer seldom or never rouses. By the beginning of June the quarantine buildings of the *ospedale civico* had quietly filled up, the two orphan asylums were entirely occupied, and there was a hideously brisk traffic between the *Nuovo Fundamento* and the island of San Michele, where the cemetery was. But the city was not swayed by high-minded motives or regard for international agreements. The authorities were more actuated by fear of being out of pocket, by regard for the new exhibition of paintings just opened in the Public Gardens, or by apprehension of the large losses the hotels and the shops that catered to foreigners would suffer in case of panic and blockade. And the fears of the people supported the persistent official policy of silence and denial. The city's first medical officer, an honest and competent man, had indignantly resigned his office and been privily replaced by a more compliant person. The fact was known; and this corruption in high places played its part, together with the suspense as to where the walking terror might strike next, to demoralize the baser elements in the city and encourage those antisocial forces which shun the light of day. There was intemperance, indecency, increase of crime. Evenings one saw many drunken people, which was unusual. Gangs of men in surly mood made the streets unsafe, theft and assault were said to be frequent, even murder; for in two cases persons supposedly victims of the plague were proved to have been poisoned by their own families. And professional vice was rampant, displaying excesses heretofore unknown and only at home much farther south and in the east.

Such was the substance of the Englishman's tale. "You would do well," he concluded, "to leave today instead of tomorrow. The blockade cannot be more than a few days off."

"Thank you," said Aschenbach, and left the office.

The Piazza lay in sweltering sunshine. Innocent foreigners sat before the cafés or stood in front of the cathedral, the centre of clouds of doves that, with fluttering wings, tried to shoulder each other away and pick the kernels of maize from the extended hand. Aschenbach strode up and down the spacious flags, feverishly excited, triumphant in possession of the truth at last, but with a sickening taste in his mouth and a fantastic horror at his heart. One decent, expiatory course lay open to him; he considered it. Tonight, after dinner, he might approach the lady of the pearls and address her in words which he precisely formulated in his mind: "Madame, will you permit an entire stranger to serve you with a word of advice and warning which self-interest prevents others from uttering? Go away. Leave here at once, without delay, with Tadzio and your daughters. Venice is in the grip of pestilence." Then might he lay his hand in farewell upon the head of that instrument of a mocking deity; and thereafter himself flee the accursed morass. But he knew that he was far indeed from any serious desire to take such a step. It would restore him, would give him back himself once more; but he who is beside himself revolts at the idea of self-possession. There crossed his mind the vision of a white building with inscriptions on it, glittering in the sinking sun—he recalled how his mind had dreamed away into their transparent mysticism; recalled the strange pilgrim apparition that had wakened in the aging man a lust for strange countries and fresh sights. And these memories, again, brought in their train the thought of returning home, returning to reason, self-mastery, an ordered existence, to the old life of effort. Alas! the bare thought made him wince with a revulsion that was like physical nausea. "It must be kept quiet," he whispered fiercely. "I will not speak!" The knowledge that he shared the city's secret, the city's guilt —it put him beside himself, intoxicated him as a small quantity of wine will a man suffering from brain-fag. His thoughts dwelt upon the image of the desolate and calamitous city, and he was giddy with fugitive, mad, un-reasoning hopes and visions of monstrous sweetness. That tender senti-ment he had a moment ago evoked, what was it compared with such images as these? His art, his moral sense, what were they in the balance beside the boons that chaos might confer? He kept silence, he stopped on.

That night he had a fearful dream—if dream be the right word for a mental and physical experience which did indeed befall him in deep sleep, as a thing quite apart and real to his senses, yet without his seeing himself as present in it. Rather its theatre seemed to be his own soul, and the events burst in from outside, violently overcoming the profound resistance of his spirit; passed him through and left him, left the whole cultural structure of a lifetime trampled on, ravaged, and destroyed.

The beginning was fear; fear and desire, with a shuddering curiosity. Night reigned, and his senses were on the alert; he heard loud, confused noises from far away, clamour and hubbub. There was a rattling, a crash-ing, a low dull thunder; shrill halloos and a kind of howl with a long-drawn *u*-sound at the end. And with all these, dominating them all, flute-notes of the cruellest sweetness, deep and cooing, keeping shamelessly on until the listener felt his very entrails bewitched. He heard a voice, naming, though darkly, that which was to come: "The stranger god!" A glow lighted up the surrounding mist and by it he recognized a moun-tain scene like that about his country home. From the wooded heights, from among the tree-trunks and crumbling moss-covered rocks, a troop came tumbling and raging down, a whirling rout of men and animals, and overflowed the hillside with flames and human forms, with clamour and the reeling dance. The females stumbled over the long, hairy pelts that dangled from their girdles; with heads flung back they uttered loud hoarse cries and shook their tambourines high in air; brandished naked daggers or torches vomiting trails of sparks. They shrieked, holding their breasts in both hands; coiling snakes with quivering tongues they clutched about their waists. Horned and hairy males, girt about the loins with hides, drooped heads and lifted arms and thighs in unison, as they beat on brazen vessels that gave out droning thunder, or thumped madly on drums. There were troops of beardless youths armed with garlanded staves; these ran after goats and thrust their staves against the creatures' flanks, then clung to the plunging horns and let themselves be borne off with triumphant shouts. And one and all the mad rout yelled that cry, composed of soft consonants with a long-drawn *u*-sound at the end, so sweet and wild it was together, and like nothing ever heard before! It would ring through the air like the bellow of a challenging stag, and be given back many-tongued; or they would use it to goad each other on to dance with wild excess of tossing limbs—they never let it die. But the deep, beguiling notes of the flute wove in and out and over all. Beguiling too it was to him who struggled in the grip of these sights and sounds, shamelessly awaiting the coming feast and the uttermost surrender. He trembled, he shrank, his will was steadfast to preserve and uphold his own god against this stranger who was sworn enemy to dignity and self-control. But the mountain wall took up the noise and howling and gave it back manifold; it rose high, swelled to a madness that carried him away. His senses reeled in the steam of panting bodies, the acrid stench from the goats, the odour as of stagnant waters—and another, too familiar smell—of wounds, uncleanness, and disease. His heart throbbed to the drums, his brain reeled, a blind rage seized him, a whirling lust, he craved with all his soul to join the ring that formed about the obscene symbol of the godhead, which they were unveiling and elevating, monstrous and wooden, while from full throats they yelled their rallying-cry. Foam dripped from their lips, they drove each other on with lewd gesturings and beckoning hands. They laughed, they howled, they thrust their pointed staves into each other's flesh and licked the blood as it ran down. But now the dreamer was in them and of them, the stranger god was his own. Yes, it was he who was flinging himself upon the animals, who bit and tore and swallowed smoking gobbets of flesh—while on the trampled moss there now began the rites in honour of the god, an orgy of promiscuous embraces—and in his very soul he tasted the bestial degradation of his fall.

The unhappy man woke from this dream shattered, unhinged, powerless in the demon's grip. He no longer avoided men's eyes nor cared whether he exposed himself to suspicion. And anyhow, people were leaving; many of the bathing-cabins stood empty, there were many vacant places in the dining-room, scarcely any foreigners were seen in the streets. The truth seemed to have leaked out; despite all efforts to the contrary, panic was in the air. But the lady of the pearls stopped on with her family; whether because the rumours had not reached her or because she was too proud and fearless to heed them. Tadzio remained; and it seemed at times to Aschenbach, in his obsessed state, that death and fear together might clear the island of all other souls and leave him there alone with him he coveted. In the long mornings on the beach his heavy gaze would rest, a fixed and reckless stare, upon the lad; towards nightfall, lost to shame, he would follow him through the city's narrow streets where horrid death stalked too, and at such time it seemed to him as though the moral law were fallen in ruins and only the monstrous and perverse held out a hope.

Like any lover, he desired to please; suffered agonies at the thought of failure, and brightened his dress with smart ties and handkerchiefs and other youthful touches. He added jewellery and perfumes and spent hours each day over his toilette, appearing at dinner elaborately arrayed and tensely excited. The presence of the youthful beauty that had bewitched him filled him with disgust of his own aging body; the sight of his own sharp features and grey hair plunged him in hopeless mortification; he made desperate efforts to recover the appearance and freshness of his youth and began paying frequent visits to the hotel barber. Enveloped in the white sheet, beneath the hands of that garrulous personage, he would lean back in the chair and look at himself in the glass with misgiving.

"Grey," he said, with a grimace.

"Slightly," answered the man. "Entirely due to neglect, to a lack of regard for appearances. Very natural, of course, in men of affairs, but, after all, not very sensible, for it is just such people who ought to be above vulgar prejudice in matters like these. Some folk have very strict ideas about the use of cosmetics; but they never extend them to the teeth, as they logically should. And very disgusted other people would be if they did. No, we are all as old as we feel, but no older, and grey hair can misrepresent a man worse than dyed. You, for instance, signore, have a right to your natural colour. Surely you will permit me to restore what belongs to you?"

"How?" asked Aschenbach.

For answer the oily one washed his client's hair in two waters, one clear and one dark, and lo, it was as black as in the days of his youth. He waved it with the tongs in wide, flat undulations, and stepped back to admire the effect.

"Now if we were just to freshen up the skin a little," he said.

And with that he went on from one thing to another, his enthusiasm waxing with each new idea. Aschenbach sat there comfortably; he was incapable of objecting to the process—rather as it went forward it roused his hopes. He watched it in the mirror and saw his eyebrows grow more even and arching, the eyes gain in size and brilliance, by dint of a little application below the lids. A delicate carmine glowed on his cheeks where the skin had been so brown and leathery. The dry, anæmic lips grew full, they turned the colour of ripe strawberries, the lines round eyes and mouth were treated with a facial cream and gave place to youthful bloom. It was a young man who looked back at him from the glass— Aschenbach's heart leaped at the sight. The artist in cosmetic at last professed himself satisfied; after the manner of such people, he thanked his client profusely for what he had done himself. "The merest trifle, the merest, signore," he said as he added the final touches. "Now the signore can fall in love as soon as he likes." Aschenbach went off as in a dream, dazed between joy and fear, in his red neck-tie and broad straw hat with its gay striped band.

A lukewarm storm-wind had come up. It rained a little now and then, the air was heavy and turbid and smelt of decay. Aschenbach, with fevered cheeks beneath the rouge, seemed to hear rushing and flapping sounds in his ears, as though storm-spirits were abroad—unhallowed ocean harpies who follow those devoted to destruction, snatch away and defile their viands. For the heat took away his appetite and thus he was haunted with the idea that his food was infected.

One afternoon he pursued his charmer deep into the stricken city's huddled heart. The labyrinthine little streets, squares, canals, and bridges, each one so like the next, at length made him lose his bearings. He did not even know the points of the compass; all his care was not to lose sight of the figure after which his eyes thirsted. He slunk under walls, he lurked behind buildings or people's backs; and the sustained tension of his senses and emotions exhausted him more and more, though for a long time he was unconscious of fatigue. Tadzio walked behind the others, he let them pass ahead in the narrow alleys, and as he sauntered slowly after, he would turn his head and assure himself with a glance of his strange, twilit grey eyes that his lover was still following. He saw him—and he did not betray him. The knowledge enraptured Aschenbach. Lured by those eyes, led on the leading-string of his own passion and folly, utterly lovesick, he stole upon the footsteps of his unseemly hope—and at the end found himself cheated. The Polish family crossed a small vaulted bridge, the height of whose archway hid them from his sight, and when he climbed it himself they were nowhere to be seen. He hunted in three directions—straight ahead and on both sides the narrow, dirty quay—in vain. Worn quite out and unnerved, he had to give over the search.

His head burned, his body was wet with clammy sweat, he was plagued by intolerable thirst. He looked about for refreshment, of whatever sort, and found a little fruit-shop where he bought some strawberries. They were overripe and soft; he ate them as he went. The street he was on opened out into a little square, one of those charmed, forsaken spots he liked; he recognized it as the very one where he had sat weeks ago and conceived his abortive plan of flight. He sank down on the steps of the well and leaned his head against its stone rim. It was quiet here. Grass grew between the stones, and rubbish lay about. Tall, weather-beaten houses bordered the square, one of them rather palatial, with vaulted windows, gaping now, and little lion balconies. In the ground floor of another was an apothecary's shop. A waft of carbolic acid was borne on a warm gust of wind.

There he sat, the master: this was he who had found a way to reconcile art and honours; who had written *The Abject*, and in a style of classic purity renounced bohemianism and all its works, all sympathy with the abyss and the troubled depths of the outcast human soul. This was he who had put knowledge underfoot to climb so high; who had outgrown the ironic pose and adjusted himself to the burdens and obligations of fame; whose renown had been officially recognized and his name ennobled, whose style was set for a model in the schools. There he sat. His eyelids were closed, there was only a swift, sidelong glint of the eyeballs now and again, something between a question and a leer; while the rouged and flabby mouth uttered single words of the sentences shaped in his disordered brain by the fantastic logic that governs our dreams.

"For mark you, Phædrus, beauty alone is both divine and visible; and so it is the sense way, the artist's way, little Phædrus, to the spirit. But, now tell me, my dear boy, do you believe that such a man can ever attain wisdom and true manly worth, for whom the path to the spirit must lead through the senses? Or do you rather think—for I leave the point to you—that it is a path of perilous sweetness, a way of transgression, and must surely lead him who walks in it astray? For you know that we poets cannot walk the way of beauty without Eros as our companion and guide. We may be heroic after our fashion, disciplined warriors of our craft, yet are we all like women, for we exult in passion, and love is still our desire—our craving and our shame. And from this you will perceive that we poets can be neither wise nor worthy citizens. We must needs be wanton, must needs rove at large in the realm of feeling. Our magisterial style is all folly and pretence, our honourable repute a farce, the crowd's belief in us is merely laughable. And to teach youth, or the populace, by means of art is a dangerous practice and ought to be forbidden. For what good can an artist be as a teacher, when from his birth up he is headed direct for the pit? We may want to shun it and attain to honour in the world; but however we turn, it draws us still. So, then, since knowledge might destroy us, we will have none of it. For knowledge, Phædrus, does not make him who possesses it dignified or austere. Knowledge is all-knowing, understanding, forgiving; it takes up no position, sets no store by form. It has compassion with the abyss—it *is* the abyss. So we reject it, firmly, and henceforward our concern shall be with beauty alone. And by beauty we mean simplicity, largeness, and renewed severity of discipline; we mean a return to detachment and to form. But detachment, Phædrus, and preoccupation with form lead to intoxication and desire, they may lead the noblest among us to frightful emotional excesses, which his own stern cult of the beautiful would make him the first to condemn. So they too, they too, lead to the bottomless pit. Yes, they lead us thither, I say, us who are poets—who by our natures are prone not to excellence but to excess. And now, Phædrus, I will go. Remain here; and only when you can no longer see me, then do you depart also."

A few days later Gustave Aschenbach left his hotel rather later than usual in the morning. He was not feeling well and had to struggle against spells of giddiness only half physical in their nature, accompanied by a swiftly mounting dread, a sense of futility and hopelessness—but whether this referred to himself or to the outer world he could not tell. In the lobby he saw a quantity of luggage lying strapped and ready; asked the porter whose it was, and received in answer the name he already knew he should hear—that of the Polish family. The expression of his ravaged features did not change; he only gave that quick lift of the head with which we sometimes receive the uninteresting answer to a casual query. But he put another: "When?" "After luncheon," the man replied. He nodded, and went down to the beach.

It was an unfriendly scene. Little crisping shivers ran all across the wide stretch of shallow water between the shore and the first sand-bank. The whole beach, once so full of colour and life, looked now autumnal, out of season; it was nearly deserted and not even very clean. A camera on a tripod stood at the edge of the water, apparently abandoned; its black cloth snapped in the freshening wind.

Tadzio was there, in front of his cabin, with the three or four play-fellows still left him. Aschenbach set up his chair some half-way between the cabins and the water, spread a rug over his knees, and sat looking on. The game this time was unsupervised, the elders being probably busy with their packing, and it looked rather lawless and out-of-hand. Jaschiu, the sturdy lad in the belted suit, with the black, brilliantined hair, became angry at a handful of sand thrown in his eyes; he challenged Tadzio to a fight, which quickly ended in the downfall of the weaker. And perhaps the coarser nature saw here a chance to avenge himself at last, by one cruel act, for his long weeks of subserviency: the victor would not let the vanquished get up, but remained kneeling on Tadzio's back, pressing Tadzio's face into the sand—for so long a time that it seemed the exhausted lad might even suffocate. He made spasmodic efforts to shake the other off, lay still, and then began a feeble twitching. Just as Aschenbach was about to spring indignantly to the rescue, Jaschiu let his victim go. Tadzio, very pale, half sat up, and remained so, leaning on one arm, for several minutes, with darkening eyes and rumpled hair. Then he rose and walked slowly away. The others called him, at first gaily, then imploringly; he would not hear. Jaschiu was evidently overtaken by swift remorse; he followed his friend and tried to make his peace, but Tadzio motioned him back with a jerk of one shoulder and went down to the water's edge. He was barefoot and wore his striped linen suit with the red breast-knot.

There he stayed a little, with bent head, tracing figures in the wet sand with one toe; then stepped into the shallow water, which at its deepest did not wet his knees; waded idly through it and reached the sand-bar. Now he paused again, with his face turned seaward; and next began to move slowly leftwards along the narrow strip of sand the sea left bare. He paced there, divided by an expanse of water from the shore, from his mates by his moody pride; a remote and isolated figure, with floating locks, out there in sea and wind, against the misty inane. Once more he paused to look: with a sudden recollection, or by an impulse, he turned from the waist up, in an exquisite movement, one hand resting on his hip, and looked over his shoulder at the shore. The watcher sat just as he had sat that time in the lobby of the hotel when first the twilit grey eyes had met his own. He rested his head against the chair-back and followed the movements of the figure out there, then lifted it, as it were in answer to Tadzio's gaze. It sank on his breast, the eyes looked out beneath their lids, while his whole face took on the relaxed and brooding expression of deep slumber. It seemed to him the pale and lovely Summoner out there smiled at him and beckoned; as though, with the hand he lifted from his hip, he pointed outward as he hovered on before into an immensity of richest expectation.

Some minutes passed before anyone hastened to the aid of the elderly man sitting there collapsed in his chair. They bore him to his room. And before nightfall a shocked and respectful world received the news of his decease.